THE YEAR'S BEST FANTASY

Second Annual Collection

Other Best of the Year Anthologies from St. Martin's Press

The Year's Best Fantasy: First Annual Collection, edited by Ellen Datlow
and Terri Windling
The Year's Best Science Fiction: Fourth Annual Collection, edited by Gardner Dozois
The Year's Best Science Fiction: Fifth Annual Collection, edited by Gardner Dozois
The Year's Best Science Fiction: Sixth Annual Collection, edited by Gardner Dozois

THE YEAR'S BEST FANTASY

Second Annual Collection

Edited by
Ellen Datlow
and
Terri Windling

ST. MARTIN'S PRESS

New York

ISBN 0-312-03006-1 (hardcover)
ISBN 0-312-03007-X (paperback)

First Edition
10 9 8 7 6 5 4 3 2 1

A Bluejay Books Production

CONTENTS

ACKNOWLEDGMENTS

I'd like to thank the following for their support and help throughout the year on this project:

All the publishers who sent me material and gave me recommendations, Gordon Van Gelder, Merrilee Heifetz, Stuart Moore, the Forbidden Planet employees in London who made recommendations, Ed Bryant, Gardner Dozois, Sheila Williams, Anne D. Jordan, Edward L. Ferman, and Ginjer Buchanan. And special thanks to Jim Frenkel for encouragement, support, and his hard work in helping make this volume happen.

Also, thanks to Charles L. Brown, whose magazine *Locus* (Locus Publications, Inc., P.O. Box 13305, Oakland, CA 94661; $28.00 for a one-year subscription, 12 issues) was used as a reference source throughout the summation, and to Andrew Porter, whose magazine *Science Fiction Chronicle* (*SF Chronicle*, P.O. Box 2730, Brooklyn, NY 11202-0056; $27.00 for a one-year subscription, 12 issues) was also used as a reference source throughout.

—Ellen Datlow

Many thanks to the writers, artists, editors, and readers who sent books and recommendations and shared their thoughts on the year in fantasy publishing with me. Thanks in particular to Craig Shaw Gardner, Ellen Kushner, Beth Meachan and Tappan King, Sylvia Peretz, Valerie Smith, Jane Yolen, and the staff of the Boston Public Library; to Thomas Canty for the art; to Brian O'Donovan of WBGH radio, Boston, and Michael Korolenko for the music recommendations; to Endicott Studio-mates Sheila Berry, Anita Dobbs, and Elisabeth Roberts for their support; to Stuart Moore and Gordon Van Gelder at St. Martin's Press; and especially to Jim Frenkel and Ellen Datlow.

—Terri Windling

INTRODUCTION

Summation 1988: Fantasy

The most fascinating, and daunting, aspect of selecting material for an anthology titled *The Year's Best Fantasy* is that the field of fantasy is as broad and transmutable as the whole field of literature. In American publishing today we have a genre called Adult Fantasy, which evolved after J. R. R. Tolkien's books proved so popular in the late 1960s and early 1970s. These books are often filed away in bookstores with two other genre categories: Horror and Science Fiction. A genre label such as adult fantasy is created for the marketing and selling of books rather than as a literary distinction—thus, under the fantasy label you will find a bewildering variety of books, from excellent to dreadful, from simple adventure tales to complex literary experimentations (just as under the fiction label you will find everything from Harold Robbins to Thomas Pynchon). To further confuse a fantasy lover wandering through a bookstore in search of a "good read," books published as adult fantasy account for only a portion of all fantasy books published. You will also find fantasy books—sometimes indistinguishable from those found on the science fiction shelves—published as "mainstream" fiction, "literary" fiction, classics, foreign works in translations, children's fiction, folklore, fairy tales, myth, poetry, and Jungian psychology.

There is no way a volume such as this can possibly cover *every* fantastical, magical, or surrealistic work published here and abroad, nor can this summation of the year provide you with more than a brief overview of fantasy in the contemporary arts. But I hope my experiences as an editor working with fantasy writers and artists across this country and England will help point the way to some material you might have overlooked, some new works you might enjoy.

Fantasy is flourishing in the contemporary arts, becoming more prevalent and more accepted in all areas of adult popular culture. (Only in this last century has fantasy been deemed fit merely for children, relegated to the nursery, as Professor Tolkien pointed out, like unfashionable furniture that adults no longer wanted.) In addition to fantasy books on the bestseller lists, there are fairy tales on prime-time television, on Broadway, at the movies, in popular music—and they continue to be a staple of opera and ballet as well. A review of Stephen Sondheim's fairy-tale musical *Into the Woods* deplored "this trend toward escaping into the never-never lands of fantasy"; yet fantasy at its best—when created with heart and intelligence—not only enables us to escape from reality, but returns us to the real world again with the ability to see it all the more clearly. I believe fantasy has been so popular in recent years because the fantasy tale speaks with a language capable of touching us deeply and because it comes from the folklore tradition of "the tale well told." Well-told tales are too noticeably absent from much of today's popular culture, and even from much of the literary mainstream.

Nineteen eighty-eight has produced a bumper crop of wonderful fantasy books—so many that I can't condense a list of the best books of the year down to twelve but must give you *twenty* instead (in alphabetical order by author):

Unicorn Mountain by Michael Bishop (Arbor House/Morrow)
The Last Coin by James P. Blaylock (Ace Books)
Krazy Kat by Jay Cantor (Macmillan/Collier)
Red Prophet by Orson Scott Card (Tor Books)
Sleeping in Flame by Jonathan Carroll (Legend, U.K.)
The Nightingale by Kara Dalkey (Ace Books/Adult Fairy Tales)
A Mirror for Princes by Tom de Haan (Knopf)
Lavondyss by Robert Holdstock (Gollancz, U.K.)
The Story of the Stone by Barry Hughart (Bantam/Spectra)
The Lives of Christopher Chant by Diana Wynne Jones (Greenwillow)*
The Changeling Sea by Patricia A. McKillip (Atheneum)*
The Outlaws of Sherwood by Robin McKinley (Greenwillow)*
Mother London by Michael Moorcock (Secker & Warburg, U.K.)
The Satanic Verses by Salman Rushdie (Viking)
The Healer's War by Elizabeth Ann Scarborough (Doubleday/Foundation)
The Hex Witch of Seldem by Nancy Springer (Baen Books)
The Satyr of the Dark Jungle by Amos Tutuola (City Lights Books)
There Are Doors by Gene Wolfe (Tor Books)
The Devil's Arithmetic by Jane Yolen (Viking Kestrel)*
Sister Light, Sister Dark by Jane Yolen (Tor Books)

Can be found in the children's section of your bookstore or library.

There have also been several good books by first novelists and new-comers to fantasy in 1989. My vote for the best of these goes to Matt Ruff for *Fool on the Hill* (Atlantic Monthly Press), with Caroline Stevermer as a runner up for *The Serpent's Egg* (Ace). And the Best Peculiar Book designation this year goes to *Dictionary of the Khazars* by Milorad Pavic (Knopf). Take a look and you'll see why.

In addition to the Blaylock, Dalkey, and Stevermer titles listed above, recommended books from Ace (The Berkley Publishing Group) this year are: *Taltos* by Steven Brust: *Euryale* by Kara Dalkey; *Green Mantle* by Charles deLint; *On the Seas of Destiny* by Ru Emerson; *Remscela* by Gregory Frost; *An Excess of Enchantments* by Craig Shaw Gardner; *The Reindeer People* and *Brother Wolf* (really one book split into two because of its prohibitive length) by Megan Lindholm; and mass market editions of Tim Powers' *On Stranger Tides*; and Steven Brust's *The Sun, the Moon, and the Stars*. First novel debuts were made by: Constance Ash (*The Horse Girl*); artist Stephen Hickman (*The Lemurian Stone*), and M. Lucie Chin (*The Fairy of Ku-She*, a Chinese fantasy.)

Arbor House and William Morrow publish only a handful of fantasy titles, but what they publish is almost always of high quality. Editor David G. Hartwell, who acquires titles for both Arbor House and Tor, has a very good eye for fantasy with a literary bent. In the 1988 list, I particularly enjoyed *Unicorn Mountain* by Michael Bishop, *The Knight and Knave of Swords* by Fritz Leiber, and *The Wine-Dark Sea*, (dark fantasy) by Robert Aickman. Morrow also put a large marketing push behind Diana L. Paxson's mythological romance *The White Raven*, looking for the audience that made Marion Zimmer Bradley's *The Mists of Avalon* a bestseller.

At Baen Books, James Baen's publishing philosophy, as espoused by editor Toni Weiskopf, is that a successful Baen fantasy does not stray too far from genre conventions and delivers what readers want in the way of fantasy adventure (preferably well-written fantasy adventure, Weiskopf hastens to add). They've had particular success with Poul and Karen Anderson's *King of Ys* series, C. J. Cherryh's *The Palladin*, David Drake's *The Sea Hag*, Melissa Scott and Lisa Barnett's Elizabethan fantasy *Armor of Light*, and Elizabeth Moon's *Pakenarrion Trilogy*. In my reading of Baen titles, what I would most highly recommend are two gentle tales of girls and horses—Nancy Springer's *The Hex Witch of Seldem*, a lovely tale of Pennsylvania Dutch magic, and Mary Stanton's *The Heavenly Horse of the Outermost West*; and Manly Wade Wellman's collected *John the Balladeer* stories. Coming up from Baen in '89: *The Complete Compleat Enchanter*— all the now-classic L. Sprague de Camp–Fletcher Pratt stories in one volume for the first time.

Bantam/Spectra and Doubleday/Foundation share an editorial staff and philosophy that encourage exploration into many different types of fantasy fiction—from the standard Tolkienesque "magical quest" fantasy such as Weis and Hickman's 1988 bestseller *Triumph of the Darkworld* (following up the success of numerous books by the same authors published by the fantasy gaming company TSR), to the "magical realism" of authors such as Lisa Goldstein and John Crowley. Books I recommend highly from their 1988 list: *The Healer's War* by Elizabeth Ann Scarborough, *The Story of the Stone*—a Chinese fantasy—by Barry Hughart (sequel to *Bridge of Birds*), *Neon Lotus* by Marc Laidlaw, and *Walkabout Woman* by Michaela Roessner. In 1989 publisher Lou Aronica is launching the Spectra Special Editions, a series that will include magical realism and other innovative works that promise to broaden the definition of adult fantasy. It is hoped that the Spectra Special Editions will avoid the disappointments of the Ace Fantasy Specials, a series that published good, solid first novels but failed as a whole to be innovative or visionary in the manner of the acclaimed Ace Science Fiction Specials after which they were modeled. I hope serious fantasy readers will support such publishing experimentation by seeking out the Spectra Special Editions.

DAW Books publishes the annual collection *Swordswomen and Sorceresses* (edited by Marion Zimmer Bradley) and is itself the leading publisher of the "swordswomen and sorceresses" school of fantasy, with books such as Jennifer Roberson's *Daughter of the Lion*; *A Gathering of Stones* by Jo Clayton; *Dragon Prince* by Melanie Rawn; *Oathbreaker* by Mercedes Lackey; and *Spell-Singers*, a collection of novellas by Bradley, Roberson, Lackey, and Ru Emerson, edited by Alan Bard Newcomer. (Which is not to imply that they don't have their share of male writers as well—most notably the popular Tad Williams.) Of the DAW books I read in 1988, I would particularly recommend Stephanie A. Smith's *The Boy Who Was Thrown Away*, and *The Dragonbone Chair* by Williams (author of *Tail-chaser's Song*.) Since taking over the publisher's seat, Betsy Wollhcim, along with senior editor Sheila Gilbert, is to be commended for increasing DAW's fantasy list and experimenting with the look of DAW covers, coming up with some striking new designs.

Lester Del Rey of Del Rey Books is one of the people who originated the adult fantasy genre. With a lifetime of experience in the writing and publishing of fantasy tales, he has very definite opinions about what makes a good fantasy—opinions that are upheld by the books published under the Del Rey logo. As a result, there are some readers reluctant to pick up a Del Rey fantasy, and others who are reluctant to read anything else—doubtless more of the latter than the former, judging by the number of titles Del Rey puts on the national bestseller lists. Del Rey had its share of bestsellers in 1988: *Being a Green Mother* by Piers Anthony, *The Black Unicorn* by Terry Brooks, *Unfinished Tales* by J. R. R. Tolkien, *King of Murgos* and *Demon Lord of Karanda* by David Eddings, and *A Man Rides Through* by Stephen Donaldson. Editor Veronica Chapman points out that Del Rey Books still has a commitment to developing new writers (noting that Donaldson, Brooks, and Eddings were once Del Rey first novelists) such as Dave Duncan (*The Coming of Wisdom* and *The Reluctant Swordsman*) and Craig Mills (*The Dreamer in Discord*.) The books I enjoyed most from Del Rey this year were both by the versatile Barbara Hambly: *The Silicon Mage* and the excellent dark fantasy *Those Who Hunt the Night*.

Signet/New American Library has revived a flagging fantasy program under the direction of executive editor John Silbersack. Building on such commercially successful staples as Stephen King, Joel Rosenberg, Dennis McKiernan, and Robert Adams, Signet is expanding its list to include a quirky but interesting mix of titles such as Charles de Lint's *Wolf Moon*; Phyllis Eisenstein's sequel (at long last) to *Sorcerer's Son*, titled *The Crystal Palace*; various works of humorous fantasy by Terry Pratchett and Esther M. Friesner; and reprints such as A. A. Milne's *Once on a Time* and Michael G. Coney's *Fang the Gnome*. Under the NAL logo: Ursula K. Le Guin's lovely collection *Buffalo Gals and Other Animal Presences*. And under the Signet Classics logo: new reprints of Rudyard Kipling's *Puck of Pook's Hill*, L. Frank Baum's *The Adventures of Santa Claus*, *The Best of Andrew Lang's Fairy Books*, J. M. Barrie's *Peter Pan* (if you only know the Disney version and haven't read the original—which is arch and strange and wonderful—I highly recommend it), and other children's fantasy classics.

Tor Books has cut back on the number of titles it publishes after several years of rapid expansion, but has reaffirmed its commitment to the fantasy portion of the list with several major acquisitions, the first of which was published at the end of 1988: *Sister Light, Sister Dark* by the acclaimed storyteller Jane Yolen. Publisher Tom Doherty and editor-in-chief Beth Meacham note that Orson Scott Card's "American fantasy" books *The Seventh Son* and *Red Prophet* have been a particular success, as were Gene Wolfe's *There Are Doors*, Louise Cooper's *Mirage*, and Sheri S. Tepper's dark fantasies: *Northshore* and *Southshore*. I strongly recommend the above titles, and would also note Judith Tarr's *A Fall of Princes*, Chelsea Quinn Yarbro's historical dark fantasy *Crusader's Torch*, and (available in paperback this year) Gene Wolfe's *Urth of the New Sun* and Judith Tarr's *The Lady of Han-Gilen*. Books to watch for: *Prentice Alvin* by Orson Scott Card, *White Jenna* by Jane Yolen, *Swordspoint* by Ellen Kushner, and a major new book from Steven Brust. Tor has also taken over publication of the Adult Fairy Tales series from Ace Books; the first of the six new fairy tale retellings is an Elizabethan novel by Patricia C. Wrede: *Snow White and Rose Red*.

Warner Books' Questar science fiction and fantasy line is an interesting place to watch, because editor Brian Thomsen has a weakness for good, very quirky books; his love of the genre shows in his selections. In 1988, he's particularly enthusiastic about William Sanders' alternate history novel *Journey to Fusang*, which Thomsen describes as a pun-filled "picaresque"; *The Quest for the Thirty Six* by Steven Billias, a novel based on the Judeo-Christian end-of-the-world mythos by the author of *The Book of the Dead*; and *Goblin Market* by Richard Bowes, as wonderfully offbeat as last year's *Feral Cell*. Two fantasy debuts to watch for in 1989: Melinda Snodgrass's first historical fantasy novel, and *Laying the Muse to Rest* by *Pulphouse* magazine publisher Dean Wesley Smith.

Other recommended titles published in 1988: *The King of the Fields* by Isaac Bashevis Singer (Farrar, Straus, Giroux), *Simbi* by Amos Tutuola (City Lights), *The Teapot Opera* by Arthur Tress (Abbeville Press), *Unquenchable Fire* by Rachel Pollack (Century, U.K.), and *The Secret Books of Paradys Vol. I & II* by Tanith Lee (Unwin, U.K.) Writers to watch (being a list of writers who have not published fantasy in 1988 and with whom you may not be familiar, worth watching out for in 1989): Terry Bisson, Tom de Haven, Pamela Dean, Tom Dietz, Teresa Edgerton, Greer Gilman, Gwyneth Jones, Ellen Kushner, Margaret Mahy, Cordelia Sherman, and Midori Snyder.

I am often asked whether I see any trends in the adult fantasy field, or notice a particular direction the field is heading. What I've noticed most is a *lack* of a single direction, which I find heartening. The genre is spilling over boundary lines self-imposed a decade ago, when most adult fantasy was consciously derivative of J. R. R. Tolkien or Robert E. Howard. We still have our share of Tolkienesque and Howardian books, and with new generations growing up and discovering them there will probably always be a core market for such stories. But the genre is by no means limited to or even dominated by these books; contemporary fantasy, magic realism, and fantasy derived from nonwestern cultures are also abundant. The direction I find the most exciting is the creation of a truly American form of the literature (as opposed to pseudo-Celtic, pseudo-medieval), as exemplified by magical realist novels such as John Crowley's *Little, Big*, Orson Scott Card's *Seventh Son*, and Megan Lindholm's *The Wizard of the Pigeons*. While a genuinely well-written "imaginary lands" fantasy book shall always be a welcome addition to the field, it is encouraging to see that it will not define the whole length and breadth of it. For it is the very nature of fantasy to take us into hitherto uncharted territories; that is the experience many fantasy readers seek.

In addition to the adult fantasy genre, many good fantasy books could be found published as young adult or children's books in 1988. And since many adult readers' favorite books started out as children's books (from classic writers such as Tolkien or T. H. White to modern favorites such as Patricia A. McKillip or Ursula K. Le Guin), it is well worth taking a look at the children's shelves in the bookstore even if you are not generally a lover of children's fiction.

Titles to look for, published in 1988: *The Changeling Sea* by Patricia A. McKillip (Atheneum); *The Outlaws of Sherwood* by Robin McKinley (Greenwillow); *The Lives of Christopher Chant*, *Eight Days of Luke*, and *Dogsbody* by Diana Wynne Jones (Greenwillow); *Urn Burial* by Robert Westall (Greenwillow); *The Warriors of Taan* by Louise Lawrence (Harper and Row), *The Mermaid Summer* by Molly Hunter (Harper and Row); *The Magicians of Erianne* by James R. Berry (Harper and Row); *Merlin Dreams* by Peter Dickinson (Delacorte); *A Box of Nothing* by Peter Dickinson (Delacorte); *The Monster Garden* by Vivien Alcock (Delacorte), *All the King's Men* by William Mayne (Delacorte), *The Brave Little Toaster Goes to Mars* by Thomas M. Disch (Doubleday); *The Drackenberg Adventure* by Lloyd Alexander (E. P. Dutton); *Where the Wild Geese Go* by Meredith Ann Pierce (E. P. Dutton); *Moon-dark* by Patricia Wrightson (Margaret McElderry Books); *Deep Wizardry* by Diane Duane (Dell); *The Book of Beasts* and *The Town in the Library* by E. Nesbit (1st U.S. publication, Dial); *The Singing Stone* by O.R. Melling (Viking Kestrel); *The Mystery of Drear House* by Virginia Hamilton (Macmillan/Collier); *The Thorn Key* by Louise Cooper (Orchard, U.K.); *Voices* by Joan Aiken (Hippo, U.K.); *Ghost Abbey* by Robert Westall (Hippo, U.K.); *The Devil's Arithmetic* by Jane Yolen (Viking Kestrel).

In 1988 it was announced that Harcourt Brace Jovanovich will start a new hardcover imprint under the direction of World Fantasy Award—winning editor and author Jane Yolen, to be called Jane Yolen Books. The imprint will focus on original science fiction and fantasy for young adult readers—some of it by writers from the young adult fantasy field such as Patricia C. Wrede. The line will begin in the fall of 1989.

Good fantasy short fiction was abundant in 1988, making it particularly difficult to choose the stories for this volume—there were more good stories than we had room to print. Fantasy stories could be found in a wide variety of venues, from slick newsstand magazines to stapled-together small press efforts; from literary journals, tucked away between stories of social realism, to children's book collections.

Notable collections of fantasy published in '88: *The Book of Fantasy*, edited by Jorge Luis Borges, Silvina Ocampa, and Adolfo Bioy Casares (first published in Argentina fifty years ago, updated in 1965, containing classic nineteenth-century stories and lesser known offerings from South America and ancient China, published in '88 by Viking); *Masterpieces of Fantasy and Enchantment*, edited by David G. Hartwell (an attractive and useful survey of the field from classic stories to modern favorites, published by Nelson Doubleday and St. Martin's Press); *Spells of Binding: Liavek #4*, edited by Will Shetterly and Emma Bull (featuring good original fiction from the Minneapolis Fantasy Writers' Group and others, from Ace Books); *The Year's Best Fantasy Stories #14*, edited by Arthur W. Saha (from DAW Books, containing 13 enjoyable reprints from 1987); *Invitation to Camelot*, edited by Parke Godwin (an Arthurian collection from Ace Books); *Arabesques*, edited by Susan Shwartz (Arabian fantasies from Avon Books); *The Unicorn Treasury*, edited by Bruce Coville (an illustrated children's collection from Doubleday); *Werewolves*, edited by Jane Yolen and Martin Harry Greenberg (a children's collection from Harper and Row); and *Tales of the Witch World I and II*, created by Andre Norton (for Andre Norton lovers, from Tor). *Other Edens II*, edited by Christopher Evans and Robert Holdstock (Unwin, U.K.), and *Full Spectrum*, edited by Lou Aronica and Shawna McCarthy (Bantam/Spectra), are both superior collections containing some fantasy stories.

Notable single-author story collections: *The Toynbee Convector* by Ray Bradbury (Knopf): *Angry Candy* by Harlan Ellison (Houghton Mifflin); *Under the Jaguar Sun* by Italo Calvino (Harcourt Brace Jovanovich); *The Selected Stories of Sylvia Townsend Warner* (Viking); *A Book of Spells* by Sara Maitland (Methuen, U.K.); *The Hidden Side of the Moon* by Joanna Russ (St. Martin's Press); *Margaret of the Imperfections* by Lynda Sexton (Persea Books); *Doctor of Silence* by Robert Kelly (McPherson and Co.); and *The Knight and Knave of Swords* by Fritz Leiber (Morrow).

In the magazines: Magazines that regularly included fantasy fiction in 1988, from which several of the stories in the volume are drawn, are: *The Magazine of Fantasy and Science Fiction, Twilight Zone, Isaac Asimov's SF Magazine, Amazing, Omni*, and *American Fantasy*, all of which can usually be found on newstands. Magazines less easy to find: *Pulphouse, Argos, Fantasy Macabre, Dragon, Weird Tales, Ice River, The Magazine of Speculative Poetry, Redlight, New Pathways, EOTU, Fantasy Tales*, and the excellent *Interzone*. One can find the *occasional* story that uses magical realism or surrealism in literary and academic journals—but these journals overall still tend to be shy of such works. I hope we will see a change in this, as magic realism becomes more prevalent in New American Fiction circles. Sadly, New York's *The Little Magazine*, which was more open than most to speculative fiction and poetry, published its last issue in 1988.

There is a great deal of energy and excitement evident in the fantasy small press magazines (as well as beautiful limited edition books published by specialty press publishers such as Donald M. Grant, Underwood-Miller, The Axolotl Press or Mark Ziesing, to name but a few), providing a forum for new writers and works with less mass commercial potential.

A new award has been established in 1988 to honor speculative fiction in the small presses, to be presented at the World SF Convention in 1989. The judges are: Algis Budrys, Samuel R. Delany, David G. Hartwell, Arthur Hlavaty, Joe Shea, Mark Ziesing, and myself.

The 1988 Chesley Awards, presented by the Association of SF and Fantasy Artists, went to: James Gurney (Best Jacket Illustration/hardcover: *On Stranger Tides*); Don Maitz (Best Cover/Paperback; *Wizard's War*); Terry Lee (Best Cover/Magazine: *Amazing*, January 1988); Janet Aulisio (Best Interior Illustration: *Amazing*, May 1987); Don Maitz (Best Unpublished Work in Color: "Conjure Maitz"); Dawn Wilson (Best Unpublished Work in Black & White: "Study for the Queen of the Snows"); and John Longendorfer (Best Three Dimensional Work: "Hawk Mountain").

1988 produced no innovative new directions in adult fantasy illustration/design, but the best artists in the field continue to produce good work. My vote for the best artist of the year goes to English watercolorist Alan Lee, who produced a number of superlative works in 1988, most notably: Houghton Mifflin's new hardcover editions of J. R. R. Tolkien's *The Hobbit* and *Ring* trilogy (which makes up for the dreadful new covers Ballantine has put on the paperbacks); *Lavondyss* (Robert Holdstock, from Gollancz, U.K.); *The Outlaws of Sherwood* (Robin McKinley, from Greenwillow); the lavishly illustrated *Merlin's Dream* with text by Peter Dickinson (Delacorte); and the U.S. edition of the picture book *The Moon's Revenge*, text by Joan Aiken (Knopf).

Other cover illustrations of note: Mel Odom's *Undersea* (Paul Hazel, from Bantam/Spectra) and *Euryale* (Kara Dalkey, Ace); Robert Gould's *Mirage* (Louise Cooper, Tor), *The Blind Knight* (Gail van Asten, Ace) and design/illustration for *The Dancers at the End of Time* (Michael Moorcock, Ace); Thomas Canty's design/illustration for *The White Raven* (Diana L. Paxson, Morrow); Dennis Nolan's *Hart's Hope* (Orson Scott Card, Tor), interior illustration for *Red Prophet* (Orson Scott Card, Tor) and design for *Sister Light, Sister Dark* (Jane Yolen, Tor); James Christensen's *Northshore* and *Southshore* (Sheri S. Tepper, Tor); Martin Springett's design for *On the Seas of Destiny* (Ru Emerson, Ace); Alix Berenzy's cover and interiors for *The Last Slice of Rainbow* (Joan Aiken, Harper and Row); Keith Parkinson's *Isle of Destiny* (Kenneth Flint, Bantam/Spectra); Rowena Morrill's *The Hex Witch of Seldem* (Nancy Springer, Baen); Dean Morrissey's *Kedrigern in Wanderland* (John Morressy, Ace); Jill Karla Schwartz's *Invitation to Camelot* (Ace) and Jody Lee's *Oathbreaker* and *Oathbound* (Mercedes Lackey, DAW).

Several fantasy artists had books published this year: Donning/Starblaze published *A Midsummer Night's Dream* by William Shakespeare, lavishly illustrated by Charles Vess; *Metropolis* by Thea von Harbou, delicately rendered by Michael W. Kaluta; and a collection of David Cherry's work: *Imaginations—The Art and Technique of David Cherry*. Don Maitz also had a compilation of his work published: *First Maitz: A Book of Selected Works*, by Ursus Imprints (5539 Jackson, Dept. O, Kansas City, MO 61430). Janny Wurts published two novels that also bore her cover paintings and interior illustrations: *Shadowfane* and *Keeper of the Keys* (Ace Books); Stephen Hickman also published a novel with his own cover: *The Leumurian Stone* (Ace). James Christensen had prints of his work published by Greenwich Workshop (P.O. Box 393, Trumble, CT 06611); Real Musgrave exhibited in a museum in Louisiana; Janny Wurts was part of an exhibit at the Delaware Art Museum; Rich and Sheila Berry exhibited at a gallery in Boston; and quite a number of artists from both sides of the ocean participated in the exhibit at The World Fantasy Convention in London, England. Most notable were several never-before-seen works from British artist/moviemaker Brian Froud. Terry Booth has begun to feature contemporary fantasy artists along with Brandywine School artists (such as Wyeth and Pyle) at The Brandywine Fantasy Gallery in Illinois. And The Delaware Art Museum is now putting together a show of fantasy and sf works for a major exhibit running in Dec. '89/Jan. '90 (for more information: Rowland Elzea, Curator, The Delaware Art Museum, 2301 Kentmere Parkway, Wilmington, DE 19806.)

1988 saw the publication of a number of excellent picture books, of which I'd recommend you take a look at the following: *Solomon Leviathan's Nine Hundred and Thirty-first Trip Around the World* by Ursula K. Le Guin, illustrated by Alicia Austin (Philomel); *In the Beginning: Creation Stories from Around the World*, told by Virginia Hamilton, designed and illustrated by the amazing Barry Moser of Pennyroyal Press; *Charles Dickens: A Christmas Carol*, illustrated by the superb Viennese watercolorist Lizbeth Zwerger (Picture Book Studio); *Dear Mili*, a newly discovered Wilhelm Grimm tale, illustrated by Maurice Sendak; *Two Bad Ants* by World Fantasy Award winner Chris van Allsburg; *Alfi and the Dark* by Sally Miles, illustrated by Errol Le Cain (Chronicle Books) as well as a gorgeous Le Cain book I missed last year, *The Enchanter's Daughter* by Antonia Barber; *The Rumor of Pavel and Paali*, a Ukranian folktale adapted by Carole Kismaric and illustrated by Charles Mikolaycak; *The Forbidden Door*, written and beautifully illustrated by Marilee Heyer (Viking); *Geoffrey Chaucer's Canterbury Tales*, selected and adapted by Barbara Cohen and illustrated by Trina Schart Hyman (Lothrop, Lee and Shepard Books); *The Wishing Well* and *The Fiddler's Son* by Eugene Bradley Coco, with lovely linoleum block illustrations by Robert Sabuda (Green Tiger Press);

Rootabaga Stories by Carl Sandburg, illustrated by Michael Hague (Henry Holt); *The Adventures of Pinnochio* by Carlo Collodi, illustrated by Roberto Innocenti (Knopf); and *Little Daylight* by George MacDonald, adapted and illustrated by Erick Ingraham (Morrow.)

David R. Godine, Publisher, has issued a beautiful new edition of George MacDonald's fantasy classic *At the Back of the North Wind*, with illustrations by Lauren A. Mills. And Peter Glassman, co-owner of Books of Wonder children's bookshop in New York City, is putting together a series of gorgeously produced children's classics for Morrow; 1988 publications are *A Connecticut Yankee in King Arthur's Court* by Mark Twain, illustrated by Trina Schart Hyman and *Around the World in Eighty Days* by Jules Verne, illustrated by Barry Moser. These are superior editions, lovingly produced.

Other books of interest to fantasy readers: *The Complete Fairy Tales of the Brothers Grimm*, newly translated by Jack Zipes and published in two volumes (Bantam); *The Brothers Grimm* by Jack Zipes, a collection of biographical and scholarly essays about the nineteenth-century folklore collectors (Bantam); *Disenchantments: An Anthology of Modern Fairy Tale Poetry*, edited by Wolfgang Mieder (not an '88 publication, but you shouldn't miss it, from University Press of New England); *Victorian Fairy Tales*, edited by Michael Patrick Hearn (Pantheon); *The Faber Book of Favorite Fairy Tales*, edited by Sara and Stephen Corrin (editors of the nice collection *The Faber Book of Modern Fairy Tales*, Faber & Faber, U.K.); *Lenten Lands: My Childhood with Joy Davidman and C. S. Lewis* by Lewis' stepson Douglas H. Gresham (Macmillan); *The Essential C. S. Lewis* (fiction, autobiographical writings, essays, from Macmillan); *The Selected Poems of Mervyn Peake* (Faber & Faber, U.K.); *The Gormenghast Trilogy* by Mervyn Peake—published in one volume with thirty drawings by Peake and an introduction by Anthony Burgess (The Overlook Press/Viking); *Fantasy: 100 Best Books* by Michael Moorcock and James Cawthorn (Xanadu, U.K.); *Modern Fantasy: The Hundred Best Novels* by David Pringle (Grafton, U.K.); and *Fantasy Literature for Children: An Annotated Bibliography, Third Editon* by Ruth Nadelman Lynn (R. R. Bowker).

Celtic music is an area of interest to many lovers of fantasy, as the old songs—particularly in the British folk music tradition—work with many of the same mythic and fairy tale elements found in many fantasy stories. Recommended this year: *Flight of the Green Linnet*, an anthology album from Green Linnet Records, is a good introduction to this music. Billed as "Celtic Music: The Next Generation," it features a sterling lineup of Irish, Scottish, and Breton bands, including Relativity, Silly Wizard, Capercaillie, The Tannahill Weavers, and others. Sileas (pronounced Sheelis), a harp duo at the forefront of the Scottish music revival, released a new album titled *Beating Harps*. Relativity, a band that successfully integrates rock and traditional music in English and Gaelic, released *Gathering Pace*. Ireland's legendary De Dannan released *Song for Ireland*, featuring instrumental pieces performed with consummate skill as well as the singing of Mary Black. Patrick Street, a powerful band formed by four renowned Irish musicians (Kevin Burke, Jackie Daly, Andy Irvine, and Arty McGlynn), released their second album. Capercaillie, a band that sounds like early Clannad crossed with Silly Wizard, has released *Crosswinds*. Enya (sister to the lead singer of Clannad) produced a new album titled *Watermark*, and released *The Celts*, theme music to the BBC documentary of the same name. Nightnoise, which consists of Bill Oskay and Michael O Dohmnaill, continue to play their eclectic blend of traditional music and jazz on their third album: all three are recommended. Moving Hearts, an Irish band blending rock, jazz, and traditional music (*Sweet Potato* magazine says this band "makes the Pogues sound like a bunch of old farts"), released a live album this year. Tommy Sands has released *Down by Bendy's Lane*, Irish songs and stories for children. And, in the rock section of the store, The Waterboys are worth giving a listen to as they slide further and further back to folk music roots. The biggest Celtic music news of the year, however, is the long-awaited second Silly Sisters album, reuniting singers June Tabor and Steeleye Span's Maddy Prior after their debut album nearly a decade ago. Also of interest: Cats Laughing, a Minneapolis band featuring fantasy novelists Emma Bull and Steven Brust, has released a cassette available from Steeldragon Press containing fantasy songs, among others, by Brust, Bull, and Adam Stemple.

The 1988 World Fantasy Convention was held in October in London, England; Guests of Honor were writers James Herbert and Diana Wynne Jones, and artist Michael Foreman. The 1988 World Fantasy Award winners were: Life Achievement: Everett F. Bleiler; Best Novel: *Replay* by Ken Grimwood (Berkley); Best Novella: "Buffalo Gals Won't You Come Out Tonight" by Ursula K. Le Guin; Best Short Story: "Friend's Best Man" by Jonathan Carroll; Best Anthology: *The Architecture of Fear*, edited by Kathryn Cramer & Peter D. Pautz (Tor) and *The Dark Descent*, edited by David G. Hartwell (Arbor House); *Best Artist*: J. K. Potter; Special Award/Professional: David G. Hartwell; Special Award/Nonprofessional: David B. Silva (*The Horror Show*) and Robert and Nancy Garcia (*American Fantasy Magazine*). The 1988 British Fantasy Award winners were: Best Novel: *The Hungry Moon* by Ramsey Campbell (Tor); Best Short Story: "Leaks" by Steve Rasnic Tem; Best Artist: J. K. Potter;

Best Film: *Hellraiser*; Best Small Press: Carl Ford (Dagon); Icarus Award (Most Promising Newcomer): Carl Ford. Next year's World Fantasy Convention will be held in Seattle, Washington. Judges for the 1989 World Fantasy Award are: Susan Allison, Edward Bryant, Lisa Goldstein, Peter Dennis Pautz, and Jon White.

The Mythopoeic Society Annual Convention was held in Berkeley, California. The Mythopoeic Awards went to Orson Scott Card for his novel *Seventh Son* (Tor), and to Joe R. Christopher for his scholarly work on C. S. Lewis. The International Conference on the Fantastic was held in Ft. Lauderdale, Florida. Guests of Honor were writer Peter Beagle, and scholar Kathryn Hume from the University of Pennsylvania. The conference's Scholarship Award was presented to Kathryn Hume, and the William L. Crawford Award for work by a new writer in the fantasy field went to Elizabeth Marshall Thomas for her book *Reindeer Moon* (Houghton Mifflin). The Fourth Street Fantasy Convention was held, as always, in Minneapolis. The Guests of Honor were author John Crowley and editor David G. Hartwell.

In the following pages, you'll find the best fantasy stories that we could squeeze into this volume, along with a list at the end of the book of many more good stories that we couldn't. These four novellas, excluded only because of their length, should also be deemed among the year's best and are worth seeking out: "An Act of Love" by Steven Brust, Gregory Frost, and Megan Lindholm (*Liavek #4*, edited by Shetterly & Bull); "Dowser" by Orson Scott Card (*Isaac Asimov's SF Magazine*, December '88); "The Falling Man" by David J. Schow (*Twilight Zone Magazine*, August '88); and "The Scalehunter's Beautiful Daughter" by Lucius Shepard (Mark Ziesing).
Enjoy.

—Terri Windling

Summation 1988: Horror

Nineteen eighty-eight heralded few significant changes overall in the horror field, but there were some interesting events that might have long-term effects. Pageant Books, a copublishing venture started by Crown and Waldenbooks, is essentially dead after only six months, a casualty of the acquisition of Crown by Random House. Initially, it was announced that Pageant would not be affected by Crown's sale and that its program was already exceeding previously set goals for income and units sold; however, the last of the line was published in April 1989, the staff was laid off, and acquisitions were halted. Even though the Pageant imprint is ostensibly for sale, Waldenbooks has not actively sought a new partner. Pageant had been a controversial entity from the start; they were publishing eight to ten category fiction books per month, prompting Waldenbooks to cut back on orders for other midlist category books, thereby hurting other publishers.

The Pinnacle imprint has been resurrected by Zebra books. *Feast*, by British horror writer Graham Masterton, will inaugurate the program.

Tudor Books, the paperback house established by the late Ron Busch in 1987, was acquired by Stanley J. Corwin and Gerald Seth Sindell, book packagers and film producers. Editor Kate Duffy is actively looking for horror and occult novels and in May 1988 Tudor published its first horror novel, *Amityville: The Evil Escapes* by John G. Jones.

St. Martin's Press announced that it was cutting back its regular sf line and irregular horror line, primarily because of the competition with Tor. St. Martin's is completely dropping its mass market sf program and cutting back on its sf hardcover program. This didn't come as that much of a surprise to industry experts, who speculated on the wisdom of creating a new line in competition with an established one within the same corporation. Tor, however, is also cutting its mass market list by 25 percent, from four horror titles a month to three.

Beginning with *Sphinx* by David Lindsay last July, Carroll & Graf started publishing a series of books called Supernatural Fictions, selected and featuring introductions by Colin Wilson. The hardcover titles have a unified format, with the covers proclaiming them part of "The Supernatural Library."

In the fall, McGraw-Hill announced that it was selling its trade book division, but as of January 1989 there was still no sale and the unit was still working on its spring and fall 1989 lists. In the last couple of years they've published *Bare Bones: Conversations on Terror with Stephen King*, edited by Tim Underwood and Chuck Miller; *Age of Wonders* by David Hartwell; *The Unlikely Ones* by Mary Brown; and *Eddy Deco's Last Caper: An Illustrated Mystery* by Gahan Wilson.

Most book publishers in 1988 either had horror programs or at least published the occasional horror novel or anthology on their mainstream lists. Tor, Berkley, NAL Onyx, and, on the lower level of both quality and payment, Zebra and Leisure had very visible horror lists. According to Locus, at least 170 supernatural horror novels were published (Locus doesn't count psychological horror novels) in 1988. This is almost double the number published last year. While aficionados of horror fiction could be encouraged by these numbers, I'm not. I'm worried because most of what I see is "generic" horror, horror as the romance novel of the late eighties. There's no way to tell the schlock from the quality. The packaging makes it all look and sound the same. This may not be bad for established horror writers who already have followings, but it could be deadly for writers breaking into the field.

The "controversy" over splatterpunk vs. quiet horror continues to rage—and is about as important to the horror field in actual meaningfulness as was cyberpunk vs. everything in sf a few years ago. It's all just as silly and manufactured; there's enough room in the field for all kinds of horror. And as with the "cyberpunks," the best writers of horror today are those whose fine writing and versatility make labels meaningless. What is more interesting, and to me more disturbing, is the rash of horror novels that take gratuitous potshots at women. There is an underlying hostility in this that I find unsettling. Some of the characterizations are so unbelievable that I wonder if the answer is simpler than misogyny: bad writing by males who are absolutely ignorant as to what women think or talk about.

My horror novel reading was peripatetic this year and admittedly the following opinions are completely biased. Also, some of the books were published before 1988 and I've just found them or gotten to them:

The Scream by John Skipp and Craig Spector (Bantam) is an effective rock and roll horror novel but lacks the discipline evident in their excellent short stories.

The Cormorant by Stephen Gregory (St. Martin's, first U.S.) is a short literary horror novel about a man who inherits an ungainly and unfriendly cormorant from a relative. Won the Somerset Maugham Award in England. So-so.

Bones of the Moon by Jonathan Carroll (Arbor House/Morrow, first U.S.). As always, the writing is wonderful but this one struck me as a bit too insular and precious. Not a favorite Carroll of mine.

Sleeping in Flame by Jonathan Carroll (Century Hutchinson/Doubleday). There's some overlap with *Bones* but this is not a sequel. This is the Carroll novel I've been waiting for since *Land of Laughs*. It's about magic and the darkness just around the corner—as are all his books—and it's the "true" story of Rumpelstiltskin. A brilliant and satisfying build-up leads to a disappointing last page. But this time he almost makes it all work. Highly recommended.

Mascara by Ariel Dorfman (Viking). A "literary" horror novel about a man whom no one notices and his obsession with faces, this book has been embraced by the New York literary establishment as a brilliant political statement, but as horror, I found it virtually unreadable—oblique and no meat. I couldn't get through it but it has gotten some very positive review attention.

Cabal by Clive Barker (Poseidon). A good novella by a writer who is always entertaining, at the very least. The stories in the volume, which made up the sixth *Book of Blood* in England, are excellent. Highly recommended.

The Kill Riff by David J. Schow (Tor). His first novel. It's very well-written, as one would expect from Schow, but I had a problem with the fact that there are no sympathetic characters. The "protagonist" is a psychotic anti-hero with a very nasty little secret who is bent on avenging the death of his teenage daughter at a rock concert.

The Fifth Child by Doris Lessing (Knopf). A very upsetting short novel about a couple who crave the "ideal" family and decide to have as many children as they can until their fifth is born—an inhuman goblin whom no one, not even his mother, can love. The mother's inability to divest herself of this creature leads to the dissolution of the entire family. This odd, powerful fable is borderline horror recommended for those willing to broaden their definitions.

Possession by Peter James (Doubleday). A frightening, effective supernatural thriller that falls apart when you think back on it, a problem novels of the supernatural often have. Is it that writers don't bother to tie up loose ends or that they lose track of what they've previously established, or simply that the supernatural inherently doesn't make sense if you think about it too hard? Recommended with strong reservations.

Sleep: A Horror Story by Lynn Biederstadt (St. Martin's/Richard Marek). This is an excellent novel about a man haunted by an entity within, "sleep," who begins to take over his waking life in addition to generating nightmares. The characters are engaging and this is an incredibly powerful, terrifying, and well-wrought horror tale that maintains its logic throughout and doesn't give the reader a bullshit trick ending. A very satisfying read. First published in 1986 in hardover and reprinted by Paperjacks. This is one I unequivocally recommend. If you can find a copy, buy it.

Koko by Peter Straub (E. P. Dutton). A serial killer is "inspired" by a Vietnam atrocity. Good reading but doesn't really get cooking until about halfway through. Could have cut about 100 pages from its 560-plus page length. Recommended.

Necroscope by Brian Lumley (Tor). Despite a truly disgusting and (I think) misleading, although not completely inaccurate cover, an excellent book about ESP, vampires, Soviet/West rivalries and what death is really like. While the blurb says it's the first volume of a trilogy, the book is satisfyingly independent. Recommended.

Roofworld by Christopher Fowler (Ballantine). A first novel about a society existing above London and the deadly warfare that erupts between two factions, one of which wants to impose a new, dark order on the world below. Science fiction but macabre, with hints of the supernatural. Very readable, although the ending goes on too long. Nice characterizations. Read this and forget his short stories (*City Jitters* and *More City Jitters*).

The Drive-In by Joe R. Lansdale (Bantam/Spectra). A good read. Violent and virulently funny and with a lighter touch than much of Lansdale's recent work. No, it doesn't exactly have a happy ending but it makes you feel pretty good, anyway. Recommended.

Sepulchre by James Herbert (Putnam) is a good horror/thriller with believable characters. Herbert is excellent at building and sustaining suspense. A good read.

The Dark Door by Kate Wilhelm (St. Martin's), while billed on the cover as science fiction, is actually more horror. It's a novel about a malfunctioning alien space probe that causes madness wherever it shows up. Excellent characterizations.

The Silence of the Lambs by Thomas Harris (St. Martin's), while not as dazzling as *Red Dragon*, ain't bad. Harris brings back Hannibal (the Cannibal) Lector, the brilliant, evil serial killer/psychiatrist from the earlier novel, and introduces him to FBI trainee Clarice Starling. She is looking for insight into the mind of a serial killer nicknamed Buffalo Bill. Lector, a monster in human form, is a very believable character. While he loves "playing games" and is a vicious killer, there is something endearing in his relationship with Starling and his "psychoanalysis" of her. Highly recommended. One of the best of the year.

The Arabian Nightmare by Robert Irwin (Penguin). I was first made aware of this remarkable book in London in 1987. Viking published it in 1987 and it's now out in trade paperback. A funny, horrific, byzantine adventure of an innocent in medieval Cairo. Highly recommended for those who like cross-over material.

The Songbirds of Pain by Garry Kilworth (Unwin, pb., U.K.) is finally out in paperback, albeit only in England. This remarkable collection by an underrated British writer was published in 1982 and disgracefully has still not been published in the U.S. A mixture of sf, fantasy, and horror. Beg, steal, or borrow.

The People of the Dark by T. M. Wright (Tor) is a reprint of the 1985 hardcover. Good eerie story, much better than his recent novel *The Island*. Subtle and low-key and very frightening. A confusing prologue that didn't make sense to me even after reading the entire book should be skipped. Go right to the meat. Recommended.

Waking the Dead by Scott Spencer (Ballantine). The paperback was published in 1987 but I just got to it. The author of *Endless Love* writes a beautiful, heartbreaking ghost story about a lawyer offered a chance at public office—something he has worked for his whole life—who begins to see (or thinks he does) the woman he loved, and who was killed twelve years before. It's about ideals, ambition, passion, and love. An exquisite book that's only peripherally a ghost story, but still. . . . Highly recommended.

Queen of the Damned by Anne Rice (Knopf), the third in her vampire chronicles. Goes into more depth about the genesis of the creatures. Mythical, legendary, historical, and of course, talky. But an excellent addition to vampire lore. Recommended.

Black Wind by F. Paul Wilson (Tor) is a *big* book, more suspense novel and thriller than horror but there are occult elements. If only everything weren't so coincidental. All these people just happen to meet over and over again in the period before WWII. Contrived and demands a great suspension of disbelief, but there's some real horror here.

For Fear of the Night by Charles L. Grant (Tor). An excellent ghost story. Subtle, well-written; something you can sink your teeth into. Well-rounded characters and no trick endings. Recommended.

The Fire Worm by Ian Watson (Gollancz, U.K.) is an sf/horror novel that expands Watson's brilliant story from *Interzone* (1986), "Jingling Geordie's Hole." It's about a reincarnation therapist who mesmerizes patients into their past lives during the day and writes horror fiction under a pseudonym by night. It's also about AIDS, reincarnation, and an evil telepathic wormlike creature that corrupts the innocent. A tough but very good read. Recommended if you can find it.

Cities of the Dead by Michael Paine (Charter) is a first novel about Egypt in the early 1900's, about the horrifying yet fascinating clash of cultures and religions. There isn't enough action in it, but the book is unsettling and frightening. Paine's someone to watch. Skip the generic prologue.

Dreamer by Daniel Quinn (Tor). A good, convoluted first novel about a man who is either being fiendishly manipulated or is crazy.

Other noteworthy novels published in 1988 were: *Demon Night* by J. Michael Straczynski (E. P. Dutton), *Faerie Tale* by Raymond E. Feist (Doubleday), *The Island* by T. M. Wright (Tor), *The Suiting* by Kelly Wilde (Tor), *Stinger* by Robert McCammon (Pocket), *Meat* by Ian Watson (Headline, U.K.), *Mirror* by Graham Masterton (Tor), *In Silence Sealed* by Kathryn Ptacek (Tor); *White Chapel Scarlet Tracings* by Iain Sinclair (Goldmark, U.K., 1987—now in trade pb. in U.K.), an unusual novel about Jack the Ripper and other things; *The Secret Books of Paradys II: The Book of the Damned* by Tanith Lee (Unwin, U.K.); *Adversary* by Daniel Rhodes (St. Martin's/Thomas Dunne); *The Lives of Christopher Chant* by Diana Wynne Jones (Greenwillow); *Those Who Hunt the Night* by Barbara Hambly (Del Rey); *Black Ambrosia* by Elizabeth Engstrom (Tor); *Lowland Rider* by Chet Williamson (Tor); *Lightning* by Dean R. Koontz (Putnam); and *In Darkness Waiting* by John Shirley (Onyx/NAL).

The magazine field also saw many changes in the past year. In January 1989, Montcalm Publishing Corporation decided without warning to "suspend publication of *Twilight Zone Magazine* indefinitely." The same language was used in describing the death of *Night Cry*, so one can only assume that this means *Twilight Zone* is, in effect, dead. This decision took the editorial staff by surprise because although circulation had declined over the last two to three years, there seemed to be no precipitating factor to influence the shutdown decision. The last issue (June 1989) will be available in March.

The magazine, named after Rod Serling's famous television show, was started up by Montcalm in April 1981. T. E. D. Klein was the founding editor, with Carol Serling, Rod Serling's widow, acting as consultant. Since it was conceived as an homage to Rod Serling and his vision, the magazine always featured a good deal of television and film coverage and the fiction combined the nostalgia, wonder, and terror inspired by the TV show. After T. E. D. Klein left in 1985, the two subsequent editors, Michael Blaine and Tappan King, both, in different ways, moved the fiction into more experimental territory. In 1988, the magazine moved away from "strong horror" and returned to its earlier nostalgia and media magazine focus.

Twilight Zone Magazine, with its annual short story contest and later through its TZ First policy, provided a forum for new writers. Two of the writers first published in *TZ* this way are Dan Simmons (*Song of Kali, Carrion Comfort*) and Elizabeth Hand (who has sold but not yet published a first novel). There has never been a professional horror magazine market comparable to the science fiction market, and *TZ* was one of the few slick magazines regularly publishing horror. It's a devastating loss to the field.

As far as *Twilight Zone*'s 1988 fiction was concerned, the magazine published less "dangerous" (read "offensive") material, by order of the publishers. So while there was some very good short fiction by John Skipp and Craig Spector, Elizabeth Hand (a very impressive first sale), T. M. Wright, Charles L. Grant, Chet Williamson, Barbara Owens, and Michael Blumlein, in general I think the breadth of fiction suffered.

Several other horror and horror-related magazines published good fiction in 1988. *Fantasy and Science Fiction*, edited by Ed Ferman, published fine horror stories by Brian Lumley, Rory Harper, Brian Stableford, Lucius Shepard, Charles L. Grant, Ian Watson, Brad Strickland, and Jessie Thompson (another impressive debut).

Isaac Asimov's Science Fiction Magazine, edited by Gardner Dozois, published excellent horror by Alexander Jablokov, Pat Cadigan, Thomas Wylde, Martha Soukup, Somtow Sucharitkul, Lisa Mason, Gregory Frost, and Cherry Wilder.

Interzone, until recently Britain's only sf/fantasy magazine, has gone from quarterly to bi-monthly as of its August 1988 issue. It published a surprising number of horror stories in 1988, including some very good ones by Greg Egan, Julio Buck, Brain Stableford, Susan Beetlestone, Ian Watson and Bob Shaw.

OMNI (of which I'm fiction editor) also published more horror than usual, mostly as a result of my having commissioned five horror short-shorts for a special horror theme project in April. There were good stories by Dan Simmons, Pat Cadigan, Edward Bryant, Richard Matheson (his first new one in seventeen years), Harlan Ellison, Garry Kilworth, and Lucius Shepard.

Weird Tales, revived in the winter of 1987–8 by George Scithers, Darrell Schweitzer, and John Gregory Betancourt, published three issues in 1988, the first a special Gene Wolfe issue featuring six stories by Gene Wolfe, all but one reprints from obscure sources, the exception being an original. Summer '88 featured two novelettes by Tanith Lee, and Fall '88 featured three pieces of fiction by Keith Taylor. Very little of the fiction so far impressed me as being particularly horrific, notable exceptions being a couple of the Tanith Lee stories and the Brian Lumley.

There are occasional horror pieces mixed in with the straight suspense and mystery in *Alfred Hitchcock Mystery Magazine* and *Ellery Queen Mystery Magazine*. In *AHMM* there were good borderline horror stories by Bill Crenshaw and David Kaufman. IN *EQMM* there were good stories by E. J. Wagner, Thomas Adcock, Robert Twohy, and Stringfellow Forbes.

Fantasy Tales, edited by Stephen Jones and David Sutton and one of the oldest and most respected of the semi-pro magazines, has just gone to a different format: perfect bound, digest-size with a full color cover. It is now called "A Paperback Magazine of Fantasy and Terror" and is being published by Robinson Publishing twice a year. (Available by subscription at £3.60 for four issues in U.K. and $14 airmail overseas. Subscription Dept., Robinson Publishing, 11 Shepherd House, Shepherd St., London, W1Y 7LD, U.K.). In the first new format issue, which appeared at the World Fantasy convention in London, there were good stories by Charles L. Grant and C. Bruce Hunter.

The Horror Show, edited by David B. Silva, looked very good in 1988.

The covers and inside illustrations were for the most part imaginative, sophisticated looking, and usually appropriate to what they were illustrating. There was a particularly good piece of art by Russ Miller called "Metamorphosis" in the Winter '87 issue (I received the Winter 1987 issue after last year's deadline so didn't cover it in the previous volume). There were excellent stories by Dennis Etchison, Brian Hodge, John Strickland, A. R. Morlan, Susan M. Watkins, Bentley Little, and Benjamin T. Gibson.

New Pathways, edited by Michael G. Adkisson, doesn't often publish horror fiction, but there are occasional reviews of horror material and black humor graphics by Ferret.

Weirdbook, published by Paul Ganley, wasn't very visible in 1988, but this award-winning magazine did bring out a twentieth-year anniversary issue late in the year—unfortunately too late for review in the current anthology; a review will appear in next year's *Year's Best*.

Despite these continuing markets, the death of *Twilight Zone Magazine* leaves a great gap begging to be filled. Several new magazines began publication in 1988. Pulphouse Publishing, a small press in Eugene, Oregon, started a quarterly magazine in hardcover format. The first issue of *Pulphouse: The Hardback Magazine of Dangerous Science Fiction, Fantasy and Horror* was an all-horror issue that came out in Fall 1988. The trade edition is an attractive and well-made volume, although the print is a little small. The fiction was uniformly interesting, with fine stories by William F. Wu, Steve Rasnic Tem, Lori Ann White, Harlan Ellison, Jeannette M. Hopper, Nina Kiriki Hoffman, Edward Bryant, and Randolph Cirilo. The Winter issue was devoted exclusively to speculative fiction; it featured an excellent crossover story by Charles de Lint and a fine horror piece by Spider Robinson. The Spring issue will concentrate on fantasy, and the Summer issue will be sf. The magazine is published by Dean Wesley Smith and edited by Kristine Kathryn Rusch. (Pulphouse Publishing, P.O. Box 1227, Eugene, OR 97440. $15.95 per issue, $25 (2), $45 (4), trade edition limited to 1000; $40 single issue leather bound, limited to 250 numbered and signed.)

Fear, a new slick, professional-looking magazine devoted to horror, fantasy, and sf, appeared in Britain the third week in June 1988. Judging from the first issue, the nonfiction emphasis seems to be on media. There were three pieces of fiction: schlock by king of schlock Shaun Hutson, average Ramsey Campbell, and a pretty good story by newcomer Nicholas Royle. But four writer profiles in one issue is just too much. And so are three "competitions." Still, it's a good-looking, colorfully illustrated magazine and it's scheduled to be bimonthly. The publisher, Newsfield Ltd.—a company best known for its computer magazines—has committed to six issues. John Gilbert is editor (write for subscription information and general inquiries to: Denise Roberts, P.O. Box 20, Ludlow, Shropshire SY8 1DB, U.K. Six issues £15 incl. postage. Outside U.K. and Europe £30 airmail).

Midnight Graffiti is a slick new large-format quarterly focusing on dark fantasy and horror. The first issue, available May 1988, featured interesting fiction by David J. Schow and Harlan Ellison, some good articles and reviews, good interior illustration and a powerful Giger-inspired cover by Martin Cannon. The second issue, published in Fall 1988, had stories by Steven R. Boyett and Joe Lansdale, and the "censored" chapter of Ray Garton's *Crucifax* (originally cut more in the interest of good taste, I think, than because the material was too hot to handle). The issue also included serial killer John Wayne Gacy's art portfolio, a preview of John Skipp and Craig Spector's forthcoming *Book of the Dead* anthology, and another smashing full-color cover by Martin Cannon. So far, it's very promising, although I'd like to see more fiction in it. Highly recommended. The publisher is James Van Hise and he is also editor, along with Jessie Horsting. (13101 Sudan Road, Poway, CA 92064. One year, $24 first-class mailing).

What would you expect of a magazine named *Slaughterhouse?* Blood and gore, right? Well, that's exactly what you get in this new bimonthly, first published in October. Edited by Jim Whiting and Mark Gibson, this four-color horror magazine specializes in spectacular and disgusting photos of special effects: rotting corpses, monstrosities sprouting from human bodies, etc. The first issue, which is kind of amateurish-looking, also contains one so-so piece of fiction, some good capsule movie and book reviews, and interviews with horror stars Linnea Quigley and Vic Noto and director John Carpenter. The second issue looks much better but lacks fiction, although the editors promise more next issue. (HCS Associates, 55 Avenue of the Americas, Suite 309, P.O. Box 24, New York, NY 10013. $16.50 for six issues. $20.00 outside of U.S.A.)

The Starlog Group, which publishes *Starlog* and *Fangoria*, is now also publishing *Gorezone*, a bimonthly. The first issue appeared in May 1988. It's more a media magazine than anything else, but there is one original horror story per issue. (Not seen by me.)

Horrorstruck, Paul Olson's ambitious and much needed news magazine specializing in horror, unfortunately folded after only two issues, which leaves the field with no news source covering horror exclusively and extensively (*Science Fiction Chronicle, Locus, S.F. Eye*, and other magazines only cover it peripatetically).

(*Locus*, Locus Publications, Inc. P.O. Box 13305, Oakland, CA 94661,

$40.00 for a one-year first-class subscription, 12 issues; $28.00 for a second-class subscription; *Science Fiction Chronicle*, P.O. Box 2730, Brooklyn, NY 11202-0056, $27.00 for one year, 12 issues; *Science Fiction Eye*, P.O. Box 43244, Washington, D.C. 20010-9244, $10.00 for three issues (one year); $18.00 for six issues (two years); $15.00 overseas (one year).

There were also noteworthy horror stories by William F. Wu, Buzz Dixon, Kathleen Jurgens, Jeffrey Osier, D. P. Pavlovic, Steve Rasnic Tem, John Shirley, Philip Sidney Jennings, Archie N. Roy, Joe Clifford Faust, Ron Weighell, Roger Johnson, Jeannette M. Hopper, D. W. Taylor, Ronald Burnight, and Stefan Grabinski in *Eldritch Tales*, *2 A.M.*, *South-east Arts Review, The Grabinski Reader, Tales of Lovecraftian Horror, Grue, Dagon, Ghosts and Scholars, Cemetary Dance,* and *Noctulpa*.

And there was some excellent poetry by Bruce Boston, Sue Marra, Leonard Wallace Robinson, and Ree Young, in *The Nightmare Collector* (a chapbook produced by 2 A.M. Publications), *Not One of Us, The Atlantic Monthly,* and *Noctulpa*.

Some comments on small press horror magazines: *Deathrealm*, published by Mark Rainey, has tiny but readable type and excellent illustrations by Jeffrey Osier and Mark Rainey.

2 A.M., published by Gretta Anderson, varied greatly in 1988. In general, the spring issue contained stories that started off well then trailed into sloppiness and/or unoriginal endings and in the summer issue I felt there wasn't enough variety in theme. But there were some standout stories.

Perdition Press issue #0, edited by Wayne Allen Sallee in December. It looks like a one-shot and Sallee writes that the "magazine was initially put together to spotlight the artwork of some of my fellow Chicagoans." It does a nice job of it. The magazine is an attractive-looking and readable digest-size publication. There were stories by up and coming names in the horror field but none of the fiction really stood out.

Not One of Us #3 had an excellent story that actually is mainstream by John Rosenman. The magazine is difficult to read, though, because the type is single-spaced.

Fantasy Macabre #10 had some good work by David Starkey, Carol Reid, and Jules Faye. #11 had consistently good writing but too many familiar ideas, and some excellent collage illustrations.

Nightmares January-March had a good story by Richard King, and a good interview with Joe Lansdale. However, the art was sophomoric and most of the story endings were telegraphed miles away (sometimes in the title or illustration).

Crypt of Cthulhu #56 was good in general, especially the Lin Carter and Thomas Ligotti stories. The magazine is a good one for those interested in the Lovecraft mythos.

The Fishers from Outside (Crypt of Cthulhu Presents) is a special Lin Carter issue (he died February 7, 1988). All the stories are by Carter and were never published before.

Ghosts and Scholars #10 had some good artwork by Nick Blinko.

(Many of the horror magazines listed here are only available by subscription, and very few—particularly of the small press magazines—come out on a regular schedule. Here are some addresses and prices: *The Horror Show*, edited by David Silva, $14 for a year's subscription from Phantasm Press, 14848 Misty Springs Land, Oak Run, CA 96069; *Weirdbook*, published by Paul Ganley, P.O. Box 149, Buffalo, NY 14226-0149, $10.00 for the special anniversary double issue plus $1.50 postage and handling, subscription rate seven issues for $25.00 ($30.00 outside the U.S.A.); *Fantasy Macabre*, edited by Jessica Amanda Salmonson, $9.00 for three issues from RHF, 61 Teecomwas Drive, Uncasville, CT 06382; *Not One of Us*, edited by John Benson, $3.50 per issue plus $.75 postage from 44 Shady Lane, Storrs, CT 06268; *Noctulpa, Journal of Horror*, edited by George Hatch, issues 1 and 2 $4.00 each or two for $7.00 (in 1989 it will be published annually as a trade pb of 160 pages and the first new one is scheduled for fall 1989), from George Hatch, P.O. Box 5175, Long Island City, NY 11105; *Grue*, edited by Peggy Nadramia, three issues for $11.00 from Hell's Kitchen Productions, Inc. P.O. Box 370, Times Square Station, New York, NY 10108; *Crypt of Cthulhu, Tales of Lovecraftian Horror, The Fishers from Outside*, and other related magazines all edited by Robert Price, various prices from Robert Price, Cryptic Publications, 107 East James St., Mount Olive, NC 28365; *Eldritch Tales*, edited by Crispin Burnham, $20 for four issues payable to Crispin Burnham, Eldritch Tales, 1051 Wellington Rd., Lawrence, KS 66044; *Nightmares: Excursions into Darkness*, edited by Scott Becker, $14.00 for four issues from P.O. Box 9156, Helena, MT 59601; *Dagon*, edited by Carl T. Ford, £6 for six issues in the U.K., $20 seamail, $30 airmail for six issues in the U.S.A., payable to Carl Ford, 11 Warwick Rd., Twickenham, Middlesex TW2 6SW, U.K.; *Perdition Press*, edited by Wayne Allen Sallee, $4.00 from 3909 W. 85th St., Chicago, Il 60652-3738; *New Pathways into science fiction and fantasy*, c/o MGA Services, P.O. Box 863994, Plano, TX 75086–3994; $10.00 for a four-issue subscription.

For more information on various small press magazines get *The Scavenger's Newsletter*, which bills itself as a "marketing co-op for sf/fantasy/

horror writers/artists interested in the small press." $9.00 a year (12 issues), $4.50/6 months, $12.50/$6.25 first class. Overseas $16.00/$8.00 airmail. Checks payable to Janet Fox, overseas payable in U.S. funds or U.S. stamps.

Even though there are now a few more slick magazines publishing horror fiction, original anthologies continue to dominate the short horror fiction field. Probably the most hyped anthology of the year was *Prime Evil*, edited by Douglas E. Winter (NAL). On the cover, the publisher boldly announces "new stories by the Masters of Modern Horror" and inside proclaims "this is writing that will shape the way horror is viewed and written well into the next century." Does the anthology live up to these extravagant claims? Well, in general the level of writing is excellent, but there's an abundance of old ideas not freshened up enough to make the anthology as exciting as it could have been. Very few stories are of *Cutting Edge* (edited by Dennis Etchison; St. Martin's Press) quality, challenging the reader or even attempting to stretch the boundaries of the acceptable, the major exception being Peter Straub's novelette "The Juniper Tree," which was one of the best pieces of horror fiction published in 1988. And the inclusion of Paul Hazel and Jack Cady as "masters of horror" is perplexing to me. Neither is known for his horror, and Cady, while a good writer, is barely known at all, even in the mainstream. Also, there is a glaring absence of female writers in the anthology considering it's being touted by the publisher as the "future of horror." This is not a criticism of the editor, who I know has little influence on how a book is advertised, but of the way the book was marketed. Another gripe is that the stories are advertised as "never before published," but Thomas Ligotti's "Alice's Last Adventure" appeared three years ago in a small press collection of his stories, *Song of a Dead Dreamer*. Despite all this, the anthology is a good solid one, with excellent stories by M. John Harrison, Peter Straub, Jack Cady, Clive Barker, and David Morrell.

The most hyped collection of the year was *Blood and Water* by Patrick McGrath (Poseidon), who is touted by his publisher (who also publishes Clive Barker) as the "Poe of the 80's." I found the collection (mostly reprints from literary magazines) disappointing, the prose stilted and self-conscious, the ideas a combination of warmed-over T. Coraghessan Boyle and Angela Carter without the obsession of Boyle or the grace of either. McGrath works too hard at trying to convey atmosphere and his work comes across as precious.

Silver Scream, edited by David J. Schow (Dark Harvest/Tor), is a theme anthology about the medium of film and filmmaking and is made up primarily of original stories. The best are by John M. Ford, Joe R. Lansdale, Edward Bryant, F. Paul Wilson, Robert McCammon (more fantasy than horror), and Richard Christian Matheson.

Ripper! (Tor), published to commemorate the centennial of Jack the Ripper's crimes, edited by Gardner Dozois and Susan Casper, also contains mostly original material. In it are powerful stories by Lewis Shiner, Sarah Clemons (her first), Gene Wolfe (reminiscent of his early mysterious and perplexing stories such as "Three Fingers"), Pat Cadigan, Charles L. Grant, Lucius Shepard, Scott Baker, and Tim Sullivan. Some of the stories would have had more impact if they'd appeared separately in various places rather than all in one theme anthology. My advice is not to read through the anthology all at once, but savor one or two stories at a time.

Tropical Chills (Avon), edited by Tim Sullivan, features eleven original stories and three reprints. On the whole, the anthology is entertaining, with standouts by Steve Rasnic Tem and Pat Cadigan.

14 Vicious Valentines (Avon), an original anthology (with two reprints) edited by Rosalind M. Greenberg, Martin Harry Greenberg, and Charles G. Waugh is uninspired with the exception of stories by Barry N. Malzberg and Jeannette M. Hopper.

Scare Tactics (Tor) is a collection of two new stories and a short novel by John Farris. Farris first became famous for his teenage potboiler of the early sixties. *Harrison High* (it was on par with *Peyton Place* as far as "checking out the dirty parts"), and then wrote a number of energetic and effective horror novels that gave him a different sort of fame and following. The new short novel isn't bad but the two stories are quite predictable. Also, Farris's characterizations are needlessly confusing because he refers to every female as "girl." As a result, readers have no idea how old any of his female characters are.

Women of Darkness (Tor), edited by Kathryn Ptacek, is disappointing. It doesn't do justice to either women horror writers in general or to the variety of horror fiction women write. The book has an overabundance of undistinguished stories—even some of the better known writers included aren't at their best. Also, too many of the stories are stereotypical of what people think women write about: relationships, family, and baby/child stories. This does a disservice to the many women writing horror today who aren't in the anthology, such as Chelsea Quinn Yarbro, Suzy McKee Charnas, Joyce Carol Oates, and Pat Cadigan, all of whom write a variety of types of horror. Despite the anthology's flaws, it contains quite good stories by Tanith Lee, Nancy Varian Berberick, Elizabeth Massie, Melanie Tem, Melissa Mia Hall, and Karen Haber.

City Jitters and *More City Jitters* by Christopher Fowler (Dell). The first collection, *City Jitters*, was originally published in England in 1986; in 1988, Dell published it in the U.S. along with *More City Jitters*. Both books feature some colorful writing and some good imagery, but the basic plots are pretty unoriginal. These stories are a real disappointment after reading his first novel, *Roofworld* (Ballantine, See above).

Tales from the Hidden World by R. Chetwynd-Hayes (William Kimber) is an original collection. Chetwynd-Hayes does a certain kind of British ghost story and haunted/tainted house quite well. In this collection there is a nice inkling of humor but also a low-level anti-female bias in some of the stories.

Gaslight and Ghosts, the 1988 World Fantasy convention program book, was a good-looking hardcover package with excellent, previously unpublished stories by Charles L. Grant, Lisa Tuttle, Robert Holdstock, and others. It also includes lovely color illustrations by Michael Foreman.

Night Visions V (Dark Harvest) featured fiction by Stephen King, Dan Simmons, and George R. R. Martin. The King material was so-so, the Simmons pretty good, but the Martin novella, "The Skin Trade," is a knockout, and alone is worth the price of the book. *Night Visions VI* (Dark Harvest) boasted "Faces," the excellent short fiction piece by F. Paul Wilson, and powerful novellas by Ray Garton and Sheri Tepper.

Lord John Ten, edited by Dennis Etchison (Lord John Press), is a volume created specially for this specialty press's anniversary and includes original material by most of the writers (mainstream and genre) who have contributed to the small press's success in its first ten years. There's excellent horror fiction by Ramsey Campbell and Roberta Lannes.

Charles Beaumont: Selected Stories, edited by Roger Anker, is selected and introduced by writers who knew him. A handsome volume illustrated by Peter Scanlan (Dark Harvest). There are five original stories by Beaumont, none of which are bad and a couple of which are excellent.

Tales from the Darkside Vol. 1, edited by Mitchell Galin and Tom Allen (Berkley), is an anthology of stories from which various episodes of the TV show have been taken. Two of the stories are based on original teleplays by Michael McDowell. The writing is excellent, but perhaps because of the limitations of television, the ideas, while effectively used, just aren't all that new.

Other Edens II, Edited by Christopher Evans and Robert Holdstock (Unwin Hyman, U.K.) had only three stories that could remotely be considered horror—Graham Charnock's beautiful "She Shall Have Music," Ian Watson's "The Resurrection Man" and Colin Greenland's "The Wish."

Wild Cards IV: Aces Abroad edited by George R. R. Martin (Bantam/

Spectra) had some good borderline horror by John Miller and Victor W. Milan, and *Synergy 2*, edited by George Zebrowski (Harcourt Brace Jovanovich) had a good horror story by James Morrow.

There was also horror or borderline horror in the mostly reprint collections *The Consolation of Nature*, by Valerie Martin (Houghton Mifflin), Alan Ryan's *The Bones Wizard* (Doubleday), Dennis Etchison's *The Blood Kiss* (Scream/Press), Rick DeMarinis's *The Coming Triumph of the Free World* (Viking); and Isaac Bashevis Singer's *The Death of Methuselah and other Stories* (Farrar, Straus & Giroux). And there was an interestingly bizarre story by Kurt Tidmore in *Soho Square*, edited by Isobel Fonseca (Bloomsbury Publishers).

Some other notable reprint collections or anthologies published in 1988 were *John the Balladeer*, the only complete set of this series of stories by Manley Wade Wellman (Baen); *The Year's Best Horror*, edited by Karl Edward Wagner (DAW); *A Double Life: Newly Discovered Thrillers of Louisa May Alcott*, edited by Madeleine B. Stern (Little, Brown); *The Signalman and other Ghost Stories* by Charles Dickens (Academy Chicago); *The Best Horror Stories of Arthur Conan Doyle*, edited by Frank McSherry, Martin Harry Greenberg, and Charles Waugh (Academy Chicago); The Best Horror from *The Magazine of Fantasy and Science Fiction*, edited by Edward L. Ferman and Anne Jordan (St. Martin's); *The Best of Shadows*, edited by Charles L. Grant (Doubleday Foundation); *The Best of Masques*, edited by J. N. Williamson (Berkley); *The Horror in the Museum and Other Revisions* by H. P. Lovecraft (Arkham House); *Darkness at Dawn* (some occult) by Cornell Woolrich (Peter Bedrick); *The Mammoth Book of Short Horror Novels*, edited by Mike Ashley (First U.S., Carroll & Graf); *Tales of Mystery and Imagination* by Edgar Allan Poe (Mysterious Press); *White Wolf Calling and Others: The Year's Best Horror Stories IV*, edited by Gerald W. Page (Starmont); *Scars* by Richard Christian Matheson (Tor paperback edition features an additional screenplay); *Haunting Women*, edited by Alan Ryan (Avon); *A Rendezvous in Averoigne* by Clark Ashton Smith, with an introduction by Ray Bradbury and illustrations by J. K. Potter, containing thirty of his best stories (Arkham House); *Ghosts of The Carolinas, Ghosts of the Southern Mountains and Appalachia*, and *This Haunted Southland: Where Ghosts Still Roam*, all edited by Nancy Roberts (U. of South Carolina Press); *The Wine-Dark Sea* by Robert Aickman (Arbor House/Morrow); *The Supernatural Tales of Fitz-James O'Brien*, volumes one and two edited with notes and introduction by Jessica Amanda Salmonson (Doubleday); *The Book of Fantasy*, edited by Jorge Luis Borges, Silvina Ocampo, and Adolfo Bioy Casares (Viking); *Fine Frights: Stories that Scared Me* by Ramsey Campbell (Tor); *Monsters*, edited by Isaac Asimov, Martin Harry Greenberg, and Charles Waugh (Signet); *Hunger for Horror*, edited by Robert Adams, Martin Harry Greenberg, and Pamela Crippen Adams (DAW); and the following edited by McSherry, Greenberg, and Waugh: *Yankee Witches* (Lance Tapley), *Haunted New England: Classic Tales of the Strange and Supernatural* (Yankee Books), *Pirate Ghosts of the American Coast* (August House), and *Red Jack* (DAW).

The small specialty presses were fairly active in 1988, producing attractive high-priced "collectors' " editions of books along with more reasonably priced trade editions. Donald M. Grant published a special signed-by-all-authors edition of the anthology *Prime Evil*, which is already sold out, and also published Robert E. Howard's *The Hour of the Dragon* (illustrated by Ezra Tucker), *My Lady of Hy-Brasil* by Peter Tremayne (illustrated by Duncan Eagleson), and *Madame Two Swords* by Tanith Lee (illustrated by Thomas Canty). Hill House Publishers offered an attractive limited edition of *Faerie Tale*, by Raymond E. Feist, with a jacket by Don Maitz and interiors by Lela Dowling. This year Dark Harvest published, in addition to the *Night Visions* collections, the limited edition of *Silver Scream*, edited by David J. Schow, and Ray Garton's *Crucifax Autumn* (interior illustrations and cover art by Bob Eggleton), as well as *House of Thunder*, a Dean Koontz novel originally published under his pseudonym Leigh Nichols, and *Charles Beaumont: Selected Stories*. Underwood-Miller released *The Selected Stories of Robert Bloch* (three volumes); *Bare Bones: Conversations with Stephen King*, edited by Tim Underwood and Chuck Miller (published to the trade by McGraw-Hill) and *Reign of Fear: Fiction and Film of Stephen King* edited by Don Herron. *Space and Time* published a novel by Jeffrey Ford called *Vanitas*. Paul Ganley published a signed and numbered slipcased edition of Brian Lumley's *The Burrowers Beneath*. Jeff Conner's Scream/Press long awaited special edition of Clive Barker's *Books of Blood IV–VI* finally made an appearance—or at least, number IV did. Scheduled for 1987 but plagued by production delays, the limited edition illustrated by Harry O. Morris finally appeared in 1988. It's a handsome volume and was worth the wait. *The Blood Kiss*, Dennis Etchison's collection, also was published in 1988 by Scream/Press.

There were also several chapbooks published in limited editions. Mark Ziesing published *The Silver Pillow: A Tale of Witchcraft* by Thomas M. Disch, illustrated by Harry O. Morris. 2 A.M. Publications put out *The Nightmare Collector*, mostly reprint poems by Bruce Boston, illustrated by Gregorio Montejo, and also a novella by David Starkey called "Wishes and Fears" (an ambitious ten titles are scheduled for 1989). Bill Munster's Footsteps Press released Richard Christian Matheson's short story, "Holiday." Chris Drumm published the mostly reprint collection *Skin Trades: Ten Tales of Terror and Transformation* by Bruce Boston. Wordcraft (David and Susan Memmott) published Misha's mixed genre pieces in *Prayers of Steel*, illustrated by Ferret.

Some of the more intriguing nonfiction books concerning the horror field were: *Private Demons: The Life of Shirley Jackson* by Judy Oppenheimer (Putnam); *Horror: 100 Best Books*, edited by Stephen Jones and Kim Newman (Carroll & Graf); *Raising Goosebumps for Fun and Profit* by T. E. D. Klein (Footsteps Press); *Bare Bones: Conversations on Terror With Stephen King*, edited by Tim Underwood and Chuck Miller (McGraw-Hill, first trade edition); *Cornell Woolrich: First You Dream, Then You Die* by Francis M. Nevins, Jr. (Mysterious Press); *Dr. Jekyll and Mr. Hyde After 100 Years*, edited by William Veeder and Gordon Hirsch (U. of Chicago Press); *The Gothic World of Stephen King: Landscape of Nightmares*, edited by Gary Hoppenstand and Ray B. Browne (Bowling Green State U. Press); *The Letters of Mary Wollstonecraft Shelley Volume 3*, edited by Betty T. Bennett (John Hopkins U. Press); *Dracula: The Vampire and the Critics* by Margaret L. Carter (UMI); *Lovecraft: A Study in the Fantastic* by Maurice Levy (Wayne State U., first English translation); *Redefining the American Gothic: From Wieland to Day of the Dead* by Louis Gross (UMI); *Mary Shelley: Her Life, Her Fiction, Her Monsters* by Anne K. Mellor (Routledge, Chapman and Hall); *Gothic Fiction: A Master List of 20th Century Criticism and Research* by Frederick S. Frank (Meckler Publishing); *Sudden Fear: The Horror and Dark Suspense Novels of Dean R. Koontz*, edited by Bill Munster (Starmont); *Roald Dahl* by Alan Warren (Starmont); *Dream Lovers and Their Victims in British Fiction* by Toni Reed (U. Press of Kentucky); *Science Fiction, Fantasy and Horror: 1987* by Charles L. Brown and William G. Contento (Locus Press).

Some of the nonfiction movie books published included *Revenge of the Creature Feature Movie Guide* by John Stanley (Creatures at Large Press); *Roger Corman*, a short biography and picture-by-picture description of his films by Mark McGee (McFarland); *The Dead That Walk: Dracula, Frankenstein, The Mummy and Other Favorite Movie Monsters* by Leslie Halliwell (Crossroad/Continuum); *Interviews with "B" SF and Horror Movie Makers; Writers, Producers, Directors, Actors, Moguls and Makeup* by Tom Weaver (McFarland); *Films of Science Fiction and Fantasy* by Baird Searles (Abrams); *Forgotten Horrors: Early Talkie Chillers from Poverty Row* by George Turner and Michael Price (Eclipse); and *The De Palma Cut: the Films of America's Most Controversial Director* by Laurent Bouzerean (Dembner Books).

A couple of sf/fantasy/horror bookstores moved. A Change of Hobbit, the seventeen-year-old Santa Monica, California, sf/fantasy specialty store owned by Sherry Gerson Gottlieb, had to move when its lease expired. It is now in a larger location in downtown Santa Monica. Dark Carnival, the Berkeley, California, specialty bookstore owned by Jack Rems, has moved to a larger location after twelve years in cramped quarters on Telegraph Avenue. The new store is eight times larger than the older one.

The first Horror Writers of America banquet and conference took place in New York City at the Warwick Hotel the weekend of June 24–26. To start things off, Friday evening HWA and Berkley/Putnam publishers co-hosted a cocktail party. The official program started Saturday morning with an HWA business meeting, and panels were held that afternoon on various aspects of the publishing business. In the evening there was another cocktail reception, and then the Bram Stoker Awards Banquet. The actual award, given for Superior Achievement, is an eerily detailed haunted house sculpture with the winner's name inscribed behind a little door that opens. It was designed by Stephen M. Kirk. The recipients were: for Life Achievement: Fritz Leiber, Frank Belknap Long, and Clifford D. Simak; for Novel (tie): *Misery*, Stephen King (Viking) and *Swan Song*, Robert McCammon (Pocket); First Novel: *The Manse*, Lisa Cantrell (Tor); Novelette (tie): "The Pear-Shaped Man," George R. R. Martin (*OMNI*) and "The Boy Who Came Back From the Dead," Alan Rodgers (*Masques II*, Maclay pub.); Short Story: "The Deep End," Robert McCammon (*Night Visions IV*, Dark Harvest); Collection: *The Essential Ellison* (Nemo Press); Nonfiction: *Mary Shelley*, Muriel Spark (E. P. Dutton). The new officers of the Horror Writers of America are Chelsea Quinn Yarbro, president; Joe R. Lansdale, vice president; Lisa Cantrell, secretary; Joseph Citro, treasurer. Last year I mentioned a number of people responsible for making the Horror Writers of America a reality. It has been pointed out to me that I neglected to mention Karen Lansdale, whose participation was crucial in the organization's creation. My apologies.

The Gigamesh Awards, given by the magazine of the same name, are given for work first published in Spanish in 1988. Some of the winners were: in the fantasy category, Novel: *Night's Master* by Tanith Lee; Short Story (tie): "House of Thieves," and "The Bazaar of the Strange," both by Fritz Leiber. In the horror category, Anthology/Collection: *Songs the Dead Men Sing* by George R. R. Martin tied with *Books of Blood #1* by Clive Barker; Short story: "Down Among the Dead Men," by Gardner Dozois and Jack Dann tied with Clive Barker's two stories, "The Midnight Meat Train" and "In the Hills, the Cities." The translator of *Night's Master*, Albert Sole, received a special award.

1988 was the year *Phantom of the Opera* became the biggest hit on Broadway. Yet only after unofficial (and finally legal) protests was the author of the original 1910 novel, Gaston Leroux, credited in the production notes. It was also the year Stephen King's novel *Carrie* made it to the Great White Way and became one of the biggest flops in Broadway history—thanks to its savaging (undeserved) by the critics. I saw the show in preview and it was pretty good, despite some silly moments. The rest of the audience seemed to enjoy it, too.

The following are some odds and ends I've come across in the past year that defy classification but are worthy of attention. They may be mixed genres or mixed media or merely associational.

Graphic novels have become the newest hot artform, thanks in part to Alan Moore's brilliant work in *Watchmen* (Warner) and Frank Miller's *The Dark Knight Returns* (Warner). This year brought a new Batman special by Alan Moore, Brian Bolland, and John Higgins, *The Killing Joke* (DC Comics)—fascinating, horrific, atmospheric, and downbeat.

Then there's *Hard-boiled Defective Stories* by Charles Burns (Pantheon). It's from RAW, producers of Art Spiegelman's *Maus*. The cover sports a gorgeous dame with a gun—and two heads. The demented oversize comic features El Borbah, a big mug of an anti-hero detective in a world of mutants, mad scientists, greedy humans with weird hairdos, and ungrateful children. Bizarre and wonderful. *Violent Cases* by Neil Gaiman and Dave McKean (Escape Magazine) was published in England in 1987 and is worth looking for. An excellent evocation of confused childhood memories and the roaring '20s, it's about a child's encounter with Al Capone's oesteopath. *Phoenix Restaurant* by Ferret (Fandom House) provides dark humor with horrific elements and could be subtitled "Eating Well During the Apocalypse." Quirky and weird. *Taboo*, published by Stephen R. Bissette and Nancy O'Connor, packaged by Bissette and John Totleben (Spiderbaby Graphix), is an anthology of mixed genre work by S. Clay Wilson, Alan Moore, Charles Burns, and others I'm not familiar with. Most of the material is horrific, all of it is disturbing. *Stray Toasters*, created, written, and drawn by Bill Sienkiewicz (*Epic*) is a brilliant dark mini-series that dredges up the unconscious by enveloping the reader in abstract rather than literal impressions in its art and text. The first three of four parts came out in 1988, the fourth is due in early 1989. *Fly in my Eye* (Arcane), an anthology of comics edited by Steve Niles, has an art portfolio by Clive Barker, effective horror comics by Steve Bissette, Ted McKeever, and others, and an excellent, chilling horror story by John Shirley.

Oddkins by Dean Koontz and illustrated by Phil Parks is a charming illustrated novel (Warner). *Uncle Ovid's Exercise Book* by Don Webb (Illinois State University Press) is a selection of 97 "metamorphoses," updating the classic (not seen). *Everybody's Favorite Duck: A Novel of Crime and Adventure* by Gahan Wilson (Mysterious Press) is quirky and should be of interest to anyone who enjoys his work. *The Magic Mirror* by Mickey

Friedman (Viking) is a mystery about murder and the theft of what is purported to be the mirror Nostradamus used for predictions. Not horrific, but dark fantasy. *Apocalypse Culture* is a trade paperback by Adam Parfrey published by Amok Press. It's true-life horror, a collection of essays on such subjects as self-mutilation and necrophilia. Brought to you by the folks at the Amok bookstore in L.A., which carries the paintings of convicted serial killer John Wayne Gacy (killer clown) and photographic books on freaks and oddities, in addition to cutting edge fiction by Ballard, Dick, Gibson, Burroughs, et al.

Bad Behavior, a collection by Mary Gaitskill (Poseidon). From the publisher of Clive Barker and the overhyped Patrick McGrath, these nine stories are horror only by the skin of their teeth—they provide horrifying glimpses of sado-masochistic relationships in modern day N.Y.C. Quirky and fascinating, Gaitskill's writing is unpretentious and direct in contrast to McGrath's purportedly Poe-like baroque pretension. Highly recommended for anyone who wants to see mainstream blended with horror and surrealism.

The Two Deaths of Senora Puccini by Stephen Dobyns (Viking) is most definitely a stretch but very worthwhile. A dark novel about obsession, passion, morality, reminiscent of some Luis Buñuel films, a Don Juan becomes obsessed with the one woman who shows no interest in him. Although written by a North American, the book takes place in an unnamed Latin American country and is magical realist in feel. Brilliant, powerful, depressing.

The Second Black Lizard Anthology of Crime, edited by Ed Gorman (Creative Arts). Cross-genre fertilization. The first one published Harlan Ellison's award-winning story "Soft Monkey." Check it out.

High Weirdness by Mail: A Directory of the Fringe—Mad Prophets, Crackpots, Kooks and True Visionaries by Rev. Ivan Stang (Church of the Subgenius). A subversive, anarchic, absurdist cult which is an elaborate parody of nut-cult religions. *Factsheet Five* is the magazine of "crosscurrents and cross-pollination." Listings for everything and anything weird. (Mike Gunderloy, 6 Arizona Avenue, Rensselaer, NY 12144–4502. $2.00 per issue). Definitely worth a look.

Phantom of the Opera by Gaston Leroux (Mysterious Press). A special edition in honor of the seventy-fifth anniversary of its first publication. Illustrated by Andre Castaigne. *Frankenstein* by Mary Shelley (Peter Bedrick). A new edition illustrated by Charles Keeping. *Dracula* by Bram Stoker (Peter Bedrick). A new edition illustrated by Charles Keeping.

The Monster Garden by Vivian Alcock (Delacorte) is a charming and poignant young adult novel that's more sf than horror—about young Frankie Stein, the motherless daughter of a busy geneticist who decides to "create" her own creature from some leftovers from the lab. Highly recommended.

A special treat for those who like pop-up books is *Classic Tales of Horror: A Fiendish Pull-the-Tab Pop-Up Book* by Terry Oakes (Souvenir Press/ Dutton), containing pop-up scenes from *Frankenstein, Dracula, The Legend of Sleepy Hollow, The Pit and the Pendulum*, and *The Phantom of the Opera*. And *The Phantom of the Opera Pop-Up Book* (Harper and Row).

For Clive Barker fans, a couple of art portfolios: One, called *Nightmares in Blood*, is work by artist Stephen Fabian based on Barker's *Books of Blood*. Included are twelve black-and-white plates in a color wraparound portfolio jacket. (Outland Publishers). The other is artwork by Barker himself, a portfolio of six full-color lithographs of the British cover art for *The Books of Blood*, with one new black-and-white print specially created for this limited edition, signed and numbered by Barker (Arcane).

Nightmares in the Sky, text by Stephen King, photographs by F-stop Fitzgerald (Viking). Photographs of gargoyles from buildings.

Running Wild, by J. G. Ballard (A Hutchinson Novella—new series, U.K.). A wonderful psychological horror about an upscale planned community in England which becomes the site of an inexplicable massacre and apparent kidnapping of the victims' children. Chilling.

Audio rights to books have been an increasingly important part of subsidiary rights. I'm only mentioning two audio cassetttes because they're unabridged readings by the authors themselves, which is unusual. NAL released Stephen Kings's *The Gunslinger* last July and *The Drawing of the Three* in January 1989. S & S Audio Works released *The Hellbound Heart* by Clive Barker in June.

—Ellen Datlow

1988: Horror and Fantasy on the Screen

1988 was not a good year for science fiction on the big screen. It was, however, not too bad for horror, and was even better for outright fantasy. Sf on television was negligible, though fantasy and horror got a big, if low-budget, boost through a rush of syndicated series.

Arguably the best science fiction movie of the year was John Carpenter's

They Live. It didn't have a lot of competition. Based on a short story by Ray Nelson, *They Live* was constructed from start to finish as a deliberately manic B-movie and as such, it worked just fine. Concerning the alien yuppies who manipulate our society and live among us, the film nicely combined broad satire and melodrama, not to mention pro wrestlers as cast members. *They Live* waited until the absolutely final scene to show us what it *could* have accomplished. The stinger wrapped up the content of the movie in one absolutely brilliant image.

The other decent sf film (I told you it wasn't a good year) was George Romero's *Monkey Shines*. Basing his story on the ongoing programs training monkeys to aid paralysis victims, Romero constructed a taut suspense thriller about helplessness and survival.

The level of other sf features sank rapidly. *Lightyears* was an animated import from France in the mode of *Fantastic Planet*. Isaac Asimov's name was co-opted to help sell the picture (he did some work on the translated script). It didn't help. The film was tedious. Asimov fared no better with *Nightfall*, the low-budget adaptation of his classic tale. Filmed in Arizona, using Paolo Soleri's arcologies for locations, *Nightfall* looked beautiful. Unfortunately the script, direction, and cast didn't match it. This independent release, slowly making the rounds of America's theaters, insistently ripped off the Science Fiction Writers of America for a blurb.

Things, however, get worse. The big-budget *My Stepmother is An Alien* tried a comedic approach to first contact. Its somnolence was stupendous. Kim Basinger gamely tried to make her part in the script work. It was a hopeless task. Then there was a Canadian translation of Dean R. Koontz's *Watchers*. Unless Koontz was paid an inordinately large amount of money for the rights, he should sue. Probably he ought to sue anyway. This melodrama of genetic manipulation and government chicanery came across as complete amateur night. The makers couldn't even get simple plot continuity straight. Michael Ironside got to chew the scenery in his patented psycho role, but that, along with a cute dog, couldn't stifle the yawns. **Batteries Not Included* is a comparatively benign product of the Spielberg factory. This warm and sweet story about outcasts, old folks, and do-gooder aliens could only have been helped by a stiff jolt of insulin.

Alien Nation, a cop-bonding story about the extraterrestrial equivalent of Boat People living in L.A., was neither terrific nor all that bad. It was a fairly untaxing adventure that unfortunately fell short of realizing its melodramatic potential.

A Danish film called *Rami and Julie* was set in an extrapolated Euro-future in which Scandinavia is crowded with expatriate Arabs. Using *Romeo and Juliet* as a template, the movie slogged to a surprising—or at least surprisingly maladroit—variation on Shakespeare's tragic finale.

Rami and Julie was to be found more at film festivals than in regular theatrical engagements. The same goes for *Split*, Chris Shaw's disappointing attempt to create the first hardcore cyberpunk film. *Split* looked pretty good for its minuscule budget, but finally foundered in pretension.

The flood of sequels and remakes continued to evoke the image of an elephant laboring mightily to produce a batch of gimp-legged mice. About the only one of the lot to justify the raw film stock it used up was *Hellraiser II: Hellbound*. Clive Barker neither wrote nor directed this direct sequel, but his hand and sensibilities were in ample evidence. Clearly interstitial in a trilogy, *Hellbound*'s strength was in its (usually) nasty images. The sequences set in hell worked beautifully. Much less successful than its predecessor, *Hellbound* still did not deserve even a tenth of the scorn heaped upon it by the critics. Whatever else it was, it succeeded in being fascinating.

Less interesting, but still not as useless as bad press would have you believe, was *Critters II*. This continuation of shape-changing alien bounty hunters vs. toothy Tribble-oids had its clever and amusing moments. *Cocoon II* and *Short Circuit II* had their narcoleptic qualities. Surprisingly, so did the remake of *The Blob*. There was a lot of slime, and a major increase in budget over the '50s original, but the cheesy result was not terribly involving, or even exciting.

That classic supernatural sociopath Michael Myers returned in *Halloween IV*, but to little avail. He simply hasn't had a worthy opponent since Jamie Lee Curtis. Donald Pleasance, as the long-suffereing shrink, seems to be getting tired of the whole mess. The seventh chapter in the *Friday the 13th* Spam-in-a-cabin saga had nothing new to offer, not even novel techniques of offing lubricious teenagers. Even the continuing family suffering of *Poltergeist III* ran out of oomph without such actors as Will Sampson and Julian Beck. It was clever to set the plot in the Hancock Tower, but then the script utterly ran out of logic. In the meantime, Freddy Krueger continued his steady employment in *Nightmare on Elm Street 4*, but all the movie really did was to serve as a sterile and carefully calculated example of how to construct a paranoid horror film that would fulfill the low expectations of indiscriminate teen viewers.

Non-series horror fared considerably better. There were three genuinely impressive horror pictures. The first, David Cronenberg's *Dead Ringers*, is in a class by itself. Based on the novel *Twins*, by Bari Wood and Jack Geasland, this was a case where the film adaptation was vastly superior to the original work. Even more impressive, director Cronenberg was clearly in firm control all the way through this viscerally effective drama of twin wacko gynecologists played by Jeremy Irons in both roles. Cronenberg yielded to his old extravagant impulses only once (in a dream sequence involving the separation of Siamese twins). It is a cryogenically chilly examination of madness and identity that has most of the audience—especially women—squirming uncomfortably in their seats before the final frame. The squirming is not from boredom. Believe me.

Ken Russell, another fitfully brilliant director not known for his sense of strict control, came up a winner with *Lair of the White Worm*, based on the novella by Bram Stoker. This slyly exuberant melodrama of pre-Roman snake gods, serpent transformation, and human sacrifice in the wilds of rural England, is one of the most entertaining movies of the year. The film has wit, charm, and a great Pogues-ish tune under the credit roll. Every once in a while when you think Russell has finally and totally lost it, he proves he can rein in his over-the-top impulses to precisely the right degree. Neither a parody nor a straight horror flick, *Lair of the White Worm* comes across as an affectionate gesture toward the British tradition of Dennis Wheatley.

The third first-rate horror film of 1988 is Stan Winston's *Pumpkinhead*, a somewhat orphaned low-budget tale of supernatural vengeance that is slowly winding its way across the U.S. in regional release. Set in a vaguely Ozarkian location that looks all too much like summertime California, *Pumpkinhead* starts off good and only gets better. The creature of the title is a demon summoned by an old hoodoo woman at the request of locals who have been wronged and require revenge. The price, as Lance Henriksen discovers after setting Pumpkinhead on the trail of teen tourists who accidentally killed his little boy, is high indeed. The script and plot are first-rate. The effects work fine. It you've ever wished for a truly good Manly Wade Wellman type of southern film fantasy (aside from the cheap *Legend of Hillbilly John*), *Pumpkinhead* is it.

Also recommended is Tom Holland's *Child's Play*. I don't usually like horror flicks about animate malign dolls, but this one's an exception. Once Brad Dourif's psycho gangster character dies after using voodoo to transfer his soul into a particularly ugly doll called Chuckie, the tension of the plot rises precipitously. The logic isn't always impeccable, but the commendably taut direction and plot carry the viewer through.

Go down a level and you find what was *supposed* to be the big horror comedy of the year, *Beetlejuice*. The picture has its moments—particularly a formal dinner set-piece in which the possessed characters do a wonderful version of the "Banana Boat Song"—but Michael Keaton's grating performance as the eponymous bio-exorcist is only half as successful as Kevin Kline's similar personality portrayal in *A Fish Called Wanda*.

Spellbinder, The Lady in White, and *Phantasm II* were all partial successes. The first concerned African myth and possession, and didn't completely make sense. The second was a commendable attempt at a contemporary ghost story, but it hinged on a plot that, at a key moment, didn't make sense. The third was Don Coscarelli's attempt to create a true EC Comics–style horror flick; the movie was enthusiastic, but it, too, didn't always make sense. I think I see a pattern with a lot of horror movies . . . .

Wes Craven contributed *The Serpent and the Rainbow*, a fictional version of Wade Davis's nonfiction exploration of voodoo customs and techniques. There were a lot of great images and fine moments, but the plot—you guessed it—didn't make sense.

Producer Gale Anne Hurd did a good thing in putting up the cash so that novices could create *Bad Dreams*. Indeed, Richard Lynch did his usual wonderful job as the villain. The sound track music was absolutely sensational, and beautifully appropriate. But the plot . . . Lame. Oh, and yeah, it didn't always make sense.

The Unholy and *The 7th Sign* were two tales of Catholic horror that were ghastly in their ineptness, the sorts of wretched plots that give the Anti-Christ a bad name. *High Spirits* tried for a different tone altogether. It tried for rollicking comedy and achieved perhaps thirty seconds of humor in its entire running time. A good cast that included Daryl Hannah and Peter O'Toole was entirely wasted. A strange and ambitious low-budgeter called *Anguish* sneaked into and then quickly out of theaters. It attempted to keep shifting realities for the viewer. While it concentrated on the normal human fear of eyeball-mutilation it did fine. When it departed from that sure bet, it fell completely apart.

Dead Heat (not to be confused with *Red Heat* or *Outer Heat*) was your basic zombie cop-buddy male-bonding movie, combined with *D.O.A.* After a promising start, it died of silliness.

By way of celebrating an entire century for Jack the Ripper, *Jack's Back* started promisingly enough. Rowdy Herrington directed the always watchable James Spader in the role of twins. It's not that the plot didn't make sense. It was just dumb.

Fantasy was well represented in 1988 with both the superior and the mediocre. Two of the most successful and popular films of the year were *Who Framed Roger Rabbit* and *Big*. The former was an amazing quantum jump in film technology with its virtually seamless fusing of animation and live action. Bob Hoskins, as a world-weary private eye, did his best to lend an earthy and grounded contrast to the hyperactive animated maniacs of Toon Town. It was still an exhausting movie.

Big, directed by Penny Marshall and starring Tom Hanks, was a surprisingly good realization of an unpromising idea. Hanks did a superlative job as the adult version of a frustrated kid who successfully wishes that he could be "big." In spite of the movie's message being—as described by poet and critic Linda Hogan—that "if you kick and scream, you'll get your way," the tale came across as funny, affecting, and sweet in a noncloying way.

There were other "body-switching" movies such as *18 Again* and *Vice Versa*, but none measured up to the standard of *Big*.

An absolutely stunning fantasy that didn't attain the attention of *Big* or *Roger Rabbit* was *Alice*, a combination animated and live action version of the Lewis Carroll classic. Created by the Czech master of animation Jan Svankmajer and filmed in Switzerland, *Alice* combined eerie imagery with the most ominous and astonishing Wonderland figures since Jim Henson's distinctive animation in *Dreamchild*.

Robert Redford's translation of the John Nichols novel *The Milagro Beanfield War* ought to count as a superb contemporary fantasy, or as magical realism or Latin American fabulation or whatever other category sounds comfortable. In any case, it was a first-rate depiction of how the supernatural can be subtly interwoven with what is presumably rational everyday life.

Ditto with Manuel Gutierrez Aragon's *Half of Heaven*, a wonderful contemporary fantasy in which the paranormal is simply taken for granted by the characters. No zombies, no low-rent possessions, just the tale of a young Spanish girl's rise through Madrid society with the help of her psychic fairy godmother–type granny who happens to be, well, *dead*.

The year saw George Lucas's *Willow*, a pleasant enough fantasy that borrowed kitchen-sink-style from a variety of sources including Tolkien and *The Bible*. Directed by Ron Howard, *Willow* was okay but not great, and did not, for all its huge budget, turn out to be the definitive fantasy epic most hoped Lucas could create. There were moments, but *only* moments.

The holiday season saw *Ernest Saves Christmas*. Uh huh. This jolly time also saw Bill Murray starring in *Scrooged*. This skewed version of *A Christmas Carol* wasn't terribly good, but it did boast a fabulous first quarter hour or so with some spectacularly funny parodies of TV network promotions.

On the more intellectual side, Wim Wenders' *Wings of Desire* showed us a drama of angelic intervention in Berlin. While Peter Falk was a wonderful guest star, this two-hour film felt like six. The pacing of the first half seemed designed to recreate the leaden feel of the angels' eternal life.

The translation of Hugh Leonard's play *Da* starred Martin Sheen as a playwright returning to Ireland, only to encounter Barnard Hughes as his ghostly father. It was decently bittersweet, but was sadly slow and stagey. On the other hand, Mary Lambert's *Siesta* spanked right along, for all its deliberate obscurity. Ellen Barkin starred in this peculiar left-handed remake of *Carnival of Souls*.

Julie and Julie was an odd parallel-worlds fantasy about a woman coming apart. And as for *Hot to Trot*, the revisionist revival of the old *Mr. Ed* show, it was neither entertaining nor intellectual. In fact, it wasn't much of anything at all.

Aside from *Roger Rabbit*, there were two major animation releases. One was Don Bluth's *Land Before Time*, a sort of *Bambi* with dinosaurs. The quality of sophisticated animation didn't seem to be up to Bluth's usual standard, and the script appeared to have been written with an advisory panel of child psychologists standing over the writer's shoulder. The film was perfectly fine, but still disappointing considering the height of expectation I'd invested in Bluth's new project. The Disney Studios released *Oliver and Company* for Christmas. The technical side was more than adequate. The plot was the very Dickens. Most of the adult audience seemed to go to catch Cheech (of Cheech and Chong) as a speed-freak chihuahua.

The year also saw at least three compilations of animated short subjects: *The 21st International Tournée of Animation*, *Futuropolis*, and *Outrageous Animation*. As usual with projects of this sort, some of the material was new, some old, with the quality equally as varied. *Futuropolis* did boast some great footage of Phil Tippett—animated dinosaurs wandering the remote vastness of Alberta.

I have a category known as guilty pleasures. These are films that I can't necessarily recommend as terribly good or successful, yet they afforded me hours of genuine entertainment. My favorite for 1988 was *The Nest*, a cheerily gruesome SF/horror movie about a little island where an amoral multinational's experiments with cockroaches have unleashed a horde of people-eaters on the unsuspecting populace. Produced by Julie Corman for Concorde, the picture boasts a sublimely tasteless advertising poster of a beautiful woman being ravished by a giant roach. *The Nest* is another of my nominations for being a nearly perfect B-movie. I found it wittily written, decently acted, and carefully produced.

Then there was *Elvira: Mistress of the Dark*. It's the puppy of the year. The sheer innocence of this silly examination of bigotry is so pervasive, it is impossible to kick the movie. *Burning Love* (also known as *Love at Stake*) had a similar theme, dealing as it did with anti-witchcraft prejudice. Starring Barbara Carrera, *Burning Love* was a dumb comedy with *moments* such as sixteenth-century New Englanders linking hands and swaying in a circle around a burning witch while singing "Kumbaya."

Eat the Rich and *Consuming Passions* are both British comedies about cannibalism. Well, there's lots of social commentary too, but it's hard to overlook the anthropophagy. Finally I'd like to mention *The Howling III*. It's a completely over-the-top movie about lycanthropy that depends on fast tap dancing so the viewer doesn't realize just how impossible the whole film is. Director Philippe Mora combines such unlikely elements as defecting Soviet werewolves, marsupial werewolves dwelling in the Australian Outback, and film-within-film parodies of *Howling*-type movies. There's also a truly strange love scene between an innocent human filmmaker and a nubile young lycanthrope who genuinely objects to baring her belly while making love. This ain't a classic, but it gets points for novelty.

Television has become an interesting hunting ground for aficionados of the fantastic who own VCRs with timers. As *The Charmings* perish, *ALF* staggers, and *Beauty and the Beast* starts to lurch, there's a lot of interesting stuff appearing at odd, usually late, hours on independent stations that carry syndicated series. On cable there's still HBO's *The Hitchhiker*. But on broadcast channels, you can find *Friday the 13th, Freddy's Nightmares, Monsters*, reruns of *Tales from the Darkside*, and the new, new, *Twilight Zone*. There's also *War of the Worlds*, which somehow manages to be both incredibly inept and deliberately funny.

The professed ideal of the low-budget series concept is to make up for limited effects and production costs with good writing. That only seems to happen sometimes.

So what's up for 1989? Horror under water. Note *Deep Star Six, Leviathan,* and *The Abyss*. Await *Baron Munchausen*. Holy budgets, expect *Batman*. One of these months, *Aliens III* and *Total Recall* will meander along. Ditto *Pet Sematary, New Rose Hotel*, and *Ghostbusters II*. Hope for the best, but—just in case—expect the worst.

—Edward Bryant

Obituaries

No part of the community that creates fantasy was spared the grim reaper's mark in 1988. Major figures in writing, art, film, music, and publishing died, leaving the field the poorer. Our consolation lies in the enduring contributions left by those who will no longer create. Their legacy will be with us as long as there is a record of their work, or a living memory of their presence.

Charles Addams, seventy-six, was famous for his delightfully macabre and dry wit. His cartoons were a staple for over forty years at *The New*

Yorker, and a television series, *The Addams Family*, had a successful run for several years, featuring a cast of characters he created in hundreds of cartoons. Addams was an original whose style extended into his life as well as his art. When he married, the bride wore black. One would like to think that Addams is still chuckling at the strangeness of life.

Lin Carter, fifty-seven, was a major figure in the development of the adult fantasy movement in the United States in the late 1960s and early 1970s. Author of more than one hundred fantasy novels, his most important contributions lay in his roles as editor and anthologist. He was the editor of Ballantine Books' Sign of the Unicorn Adult Fantasy series, which was the first concerted effort by a mass-market publisher to sell fantasy as a genre not considered either juvenile literature or something other than fantasy. He reprinted numerous classic works and published many new talents for the first time in paperback, and while the Adult Fantasy imprint didn't last, his work for Ian and Betty Ballantine was groundbreaking, and was an essential step in the eventual development of the market for written fantasy that flourishes today. He also edited both reprint and original anthologies, including series such as *Flashing Swords!*, in which he commissioned some fine work from most of the major fantasy authors writing sword-and-sorcery fantasy in the mid-1970s. Carter was also involved in the revival of interest in *Conan* and other heroic series by Robert E. Howard. Along with L. Sprague de Camp, Carter took an active part in completing many unfinished stories and writing from Howard's outlines. His and de Camp's work became Lancer Books' series of Howard paperbacks, which in the 1960s was the first heroic fantasy series to break out in the mass-market format. Carter had personal problems and was seriously ill in the last few years of his life, factors which considerably reduced his literary output and made those final years difficult ones. One hopes that his contributions to the genre will be fully recognized, for he truly was a pivotal figure in the American fantasy renaissance.

Another important editorial figure who died in 1988 was **Ursula Nordstrom**, seventy-eight, who as an editor and then Publisher of Harper and Row's juvenile division was responsible for publishing many fine juvenile books in hardcover, including fantasy, at a time when fantasy could only be published as juvenile books. Under her aegis such works as *Charlotte's Web* and *Where the Wild Things Are* saw the light of day, changing the face of children's publishing.

E. Hoffman Price, eighty-nine, was an author whose career spanned the pulp days of *Weird Tales* and the 1980s, when such novels as his *The Devil Wives of Li Fong* were published for the first time in paperback. Price's work included all sorts of pulp fiction but was best represented by his oriental fantasies. **Randall Garrett,** a very popular science fiction and fantasy writer in the fifties and sixties, was probably best known for his Lord Darcy stories. A man of great charm and wit, Garrett was a figure of renown not only for his writing, but also for his personal qualities, which endeared him to the creative community of science fiction and fantasy writers and fans, of which he is a cherished member. A stroke suffered several years before his death made it impossible for him to be the warm, charming man he had been.

John Myers Myers, eighty-two, was best known for his novel *Silverlock*, which was filled with literary allusions and became a cult classic. He wrote other fantasies, but none attained the cachet of his most famous work. **Mark Saxton,** seventy-three, was an author and editor. As the editor of Austin Tappan Wright's classic, *Islandia,* he played a major role in bringing that book to print. Subsequently, he wrote several books of his own based on Wright's creation. He was a book editor for over forty years.

Two major science fiction writers died in 1988, **Robert A. Heinlein,** eighty, and **Clifford D. Simak,** eighty-three. Both were Grand Masters of Science Fiction, awarded that status by their peers in the Science Fiction Writers of America and acknowledged by numerous awards to their works. Heinlein was arguably the most influential science fiction writer since the beginning of the field. His work, in more than forty novels and dozens of short stories, was published in all the major science fiction and fantasy magazines from 1939 until he concentrated solely on novels in the 1960s. While his science fiction was noted for its rigorous engineering bias in solid structure and well-crafted prose, he also wrote a number of fine and sometimes wildly imaginative fantasy tales, including such classics as "The Unpleasant Profession of Jonathan Hoag," and "Magic, Inc.," among others. He wrote for *Unknown* magazine, and others, and some of his science fiction, such as *Waldo,* had more than a little fantasy to it. Heinlein was the first science fiction writer to reach bestselling status, with his novel *Stranger in a Strange Land* (1961). He also influenced innumerable writers who entered the field after him.

Clifford D. Simak, while not the giant Heinlein was in the field, nonetheless was a major figure in science fiction and fantasy from the early 1930s until his death. A newspaperman for most of his adult life, Simak brought a strong humanistic touch to all of his work, and the grace and subtlety of his prose were fresh in a field that was just learning the elements of style when he started out. Best known for his novel *Way Station* and a number of fine stories, Simak's work was not as adventurous as some in a literal way, but it sparked the sense of wonder that is the hallmark of the best-loved science fiction, and Simak's strong sense of the dignity of all life was a gift that has fueled the creative fires of some of the finest authors in the genre.

Other writers who died in 1988 include **Peggy Parish,** sixty-one, the author of some very fine children's books, including *The Ghosts of Cougar Island* and *Dinosaur Time.* **Marguerite Yourcenar,** eighty-four, a well-known French novelist, was, at the time of her death, the only woman to be named a member of the Academie Française. She wrote a fantasy novel, *The Abyss.* **Charles Keeping,** sixty-three, was a noted British fantasy artist and author.

Harold Matson, eighty-nine, started and for many years ran the agency bearing his name, representing such major fantasy figures as Charles Beaumont, Ray Bradbury, C. L. Moore and Henry Kuttner, C. M. Kornbluth, Richard Matheson, and others. **Lurton Blassingame,** eighty-four, was one of the most influential agents in the field for over forty years, representing such authors as Robert A. Heinlein, Frank Herbert, Jerry Pournelle, Piers Anthony, and others. In the late 1970s he took as partners Kirby McCauley and Eleanor Wood to form a powerful partnership in which he was active until illness slowed him down several years ago.

A number of people involved in fantasy film and theater died last year. **Frederik Lowe,** eighty-six, was best known as a composer of the music for many Broadway musicals, including *Camelot,* which he also scored for film. He had a famously successful partnership with Alan Jay Lerner for many years as well. **John Houseman,** seventy-one, was a versatile and creative force in theater, radio, and film. He was the producer of Mercury Theater on the Air, which produced Orson Welles's famous *War of the Worlds* Halloween broadcast in 1938, and caused a nationwide sensation and panic. Houseman was also an actor and director, and was known as well for his television work late in his career. **Joshua Logan,** seventy-nine, was the director of *Camelot* and *Mr. Roberts,* as well as being a prolific and successful director of many other Broadway plays and films.

John Carradine, eighty-two, was for decades a mainstay of American horror films. His tall, lantern-jawed presence lent credibility to many films that otherwise would have had a much tougher time making an impression. He acted in over four hundred films, including many Westerns and horror productions. Also missed will be **Trevor Howard,** seventy-one, who was featured in the film *Around the World in 80 Days,* as well as dozens of other films in his long career.

Other people in show business who worked in the fantasy genre included **Melvin Frank,** seventy-five, who collaborated with Norman Panama on a number of projects including *L'il Abner* (on stage and screen) and Danny Kaye's *The Court Jester,* among others. **Roy Kinnear,** fifty-four, was an actor in many British and American films and plays, including the Beatles' film, *Help!* **DeWitt Bodeen,** seventy-nine, was a screenwriter whose credits included *The Cat People.* **Jack Cutty,** eighty, was a member of Walt Disney's original group of animators when he started out in 1929. He was with Disney for forty years. **Howard Jeffrey,** fifty-three, was a choreographer and producer whose work included *On a Clear Day You Can See Forever* and *The Seven-Percent Solution.* **Tom Allen,** fifty, was a creative consultant/story editor on *Tales of the Darkside* and *Monsters.* In addition to his television work, he was a Christian Brother in the teaching order of The Sacred Heart.

Milton Caniff, eighty-one, was the creator of the *Terry and the Pirates* comic strip, and also did good work on *Steve Canyon.*

Alan Napier, eighty-five, was a well-known British actor who, among other films, played in *Cat People*, and was featured on the *Batman* television series. **Duane L. Jones,** fifty-one, was a star of George Romero's *Night of the Living Dead.* **Milton Krasner,** seventy-five, was a cinematographer of various fantasy films. **Lester Lewis,** seventy-five, was a radio and television producer of fantasy and other types of productions. **Michael Fessier,** eighty-two, was a fantasy writer and screenwriter. He wrote the film *Fully Dressed and in His Right Mind* (1935). **Ted Tiller,** seventy-five, was an actor, director, and playwright. His most outstanding credit was the play *Count Dracula* (1971).

John D. Clark, eighty, was a writer and a friend of L. Sprague de Camp and Fletcher Pratt. Clark introduced the two collaborators, and was a lifelong friend of de Camp's. **Oswald Train,** seventy-two, was the publisher of Prime Press, a small fantasy and sf press in the late forties and early fifties, and then started his own small press, Oswald Train: Publisher in the late 1960s. He published some very fine books, and was an avid collector of fantasy material. **Roy Squires,** sixty-eight, was also a specialty publisher and fan for many years. **Henry E. "Hank" Jankus, Jr.,** fifty-nine, was an illustrator of sf and fantasy magazines and books, as well as being an active fan of the genre.

—J. F.

LISA GOLDSTEIN

Death Is Different

Lisa Goldstein is one of the most prominent authors in a new generation of American writers whose work challenges the boundary lines between fantasy and realism, between "genre" and "mainstream" publishing. Her first novel, *The Red Magician*, won the American Book Award. Her second novel, *The Dream Years*, re-created the fantastical world of the Surrealists' Paris in the 1920s. Her most recent novel is *Tourists*. She is also the author of several works of short fiction. The following story, "Death Is Different," is a typical Goldstein mix of the real and the fantastic, seamlessly interwoven.

Goldstein currently makes her home in northern California.

—T. W.

DEATH IS DIFFERENT

Lisa Goldstein

She had her passport stamped and went down the narrow corridor to collect her suitcase. It was almost as if they'd been waiting for her, dozens of them, the women dressed in embroidered shawls and long skirts in primary colors, the men in clothes that had been popular in the United States fifty or sixty years ago.

"Taxi? Taxi to hotel?"

"Change money? Yes? Change money?"

"Jewels, silver, jewels—"

"Special for you—"

"Cards, very holy—"

Monica brushed past them. One very young man, shorter even than she was, grabbed hold of the jacket she had folded over her arm. "Anything, *mem*," he said. She turned to look at him. His eyes were wide and earnest. "Anything, I will do anything for you. You do not even have to pay me."

She laughed. He drew back, looking hurt, but his hand still held her jacket. "All right," she said. They were nearly to the wide glass doors leading out into the street. The airport was hot and dry, but the heat coming from the open glass doors was worse. It was almost evening. "Find me a newspaper," she said.

He stood a moment. The others had dropped back, as if the young man had staked a claim on her. "A—a newspaper?" he said. He was wearing a gold earring, a five-pointed star, in one ear.

"Yeah," she said. Had she ever known the Lurqazi word for newspaper? She looked in her purse for her dictionary and realized she must have packed it in her luggage. She could only stand there and repeat helplessly, "A newspaper. You know."

"Yes. A newspaper." His eyes lit up, and he pulled her by her jacket outside into the street.

"Wait—" she said. "My luggage—"

"A newspaper," the young man said. "Yes." He led her to an old man

2

squatting by the road, a pile of newspapers in front of him. At least she supposed they were newspapers. They were written in Lurqazi, a language which used the Roman alphabet but which, she had been told, had no connection with any Indo-European tongue.

"I meant—is there an English newspaper?" she asked.

"English," he said. He looked defeated.

"All right," she said. "How much?" she asked the old man.

The old man seemed to come alive. "Just one, *mem*," he said. "Just one." His teeth were stained red.

She gave him a one (she had changed some money at the San Francisco airport), and, as an afterthought, gave the young man a one too. She picked up a paper and turned to the young man. "Could you come back in there with me while I pick up my suitcase?" she said. "I think the horde will descend if you don't."

He looked at her as if he didn't understand what she'd said, but he followed her inside anyway and waited until she got her suitcase. Then he went back outside with her. She stood a long time watching the cabs—every make and year of car was standing out at the curb, it seemed, including a car she recognized from Czechoslovakia and a horse-drawn carriage—until he guided her toward a late model Volkswagen Rabbit. She had a moment of panic when she thought he was going to get in the car with her, but he just said something to the driver and waved good-bye. The driver, she noticed, was wearing the same five-pointed star earring.

As they drove to the hotel she felt the familiar travel euphoria, a loosening of the fear of new places she had felt on the plane. She had done it. She was in another place, a place she had never been, ready for new sights and adventures. Nothing untoward had happened to her yet. She was a seasoned traveler.

She looked out of the car and was startled for a moment to see auto lights flying halfway into the air, buildings standing on nothing. Then she realized she was looking at a reflection in the car's window. She bent closer to the window, put her hands around her eyes, but she could see nothing real outside, only the flying lights, the phantom buildings.

At the air-conditioned hotel she kicked off her shoes, took out her dictionary and opened the newspaper. She had studied a little Lurqazi before she'd left the States, but most of the words in the paper were unfamiliar, literary words like "burnished' and "celestial." She took out a pen and started writing above the lines. After a long time she was pretty sure that the right margins of the columns in the paper were ragged not because of some flaw in the printing process but because she was reading poetry. The old man had sold her poetry.

She laughed and began to unpack, turning on the radio. For a wonder someone was speaking English. She stopped and listened as the announcer said, ". . . fighting continues in the hills with victory claimed by both sides. In the United States the president pledged support today against what he called Russian-backed guerrillas. The Soviet Union had no comment.

"The weather continues hot—"

Something flat and white stuck out from under the shoes in her suitcase, a piece of paper. She pulled it out. "Dear Monica," she read, "I know this is part of your job but don't forget your husband who's waiting for you at home. I know you want to have adventures, but please *be careful*. See you in two weeks. I love you. I miss you already, and you haven't even gone yet. Love, Jeremy."

The dinner where she'd met Jeremy had been for six couples. On Jeremy's other side was a small blond woman. On her other side was a conspicuously empty chair. She must have looked unhappy, because Jeremy introduced himself and asked, in a voice that sounded genuinely worried, if she was all right.

"I'm fine," she said brightly. She looked at the empty chair on the other side of her as if it were a person and then turned back to Jeremy. "He said he might be a little late. He does deep sea salvaging." And then she burst into tears.

That had been embarrassing enough, but somehow, after he had offered her his napkin and she'd refused it and used hers instead, she found herself telling him the long sad chronology of her love life. The man she was dating had promised to come, she said, but you could never count on him to be anywhere. And the one before that had smuggled drugs, and the one before that had taken her to some kind of religious commune where you weren't allowed to use electricity and could only bathe once a week, and the one before that had said he was a revolutionary. . . . His open face was friendly, his green eyes looked concerned. She thought the blond woman on his other side was very lucky. But she could never go out with him, even if the blond woman wasn't there. He was too . . . safe.

"It sounds to me," he said when she was done (and she realized guiltily that she had talked for nearly half an hour; he must have been bored out of his mind), "that you like going out with men who have adventures."

"You mean," she said slowly, watching the thought surface as she said it, "that I don't think women can have adventures too?"

The next day she applied to journalism school.

She didn't see him until nearly a year later, at the house of the couple who had invited them both to dinner. This time only the two of them were invited. The set-up was a little too obvious to ignore, but she decided she didn't mind. "What have you been doing?" he asked between courses.

"Going to journalism school," she said.

He seemed delighted. "Have you been thinking of the conversation we had last year?" he asked. "I've thought about it a lot."

"What conversation?"

"Don't you remember?" he asked. "At dinner last year. About women having adventures. You didn't seem to think they could."

"No," she said. "I'm sorry. I don't remember."

He didn't press it, but she became annoyed with him anyway. Imagine him thinking that a conversation with him was responsible for her going to journalism school. And now that she was looking at him she realized that he was going bald, that his bald spot had widened quite a bit since she'd seen him last. Still, when he asked for her phone number at the end of the evening she gave it to him. What the hell.

It was months later that he confessed he had asked their mutual friends to invite them both to dinner. But it was only after they were married she admitted that he might have been right, that she might have enrolled in school because of him.

For a while, since he didn't seem to mind, since he neither praised nor blamed, she told him about her old lovers. The stories became a kind of exorcism for her. The men had all been poor (except, for a brief time, the drug smuggler, until his habit exceeded his supply), they had all been interesting, they had all been crazy or nearly so. Once he mixed up the revolutionary who had stolen her stereo with the would-be writer who had also stolen her stereo, and they'd laughed about it for days. After that the chorus line of old lovers had faded, grown less insistent, and had finally disappeared altogether. And that was when she knew something she had not been certain of before. She had been right to marry Jeremy.

The radio was playing what sounded like an old English folk song. She turned it off, read and reread the short letter until she memorized it, and went to sleep.

The young man was on the sidewalk when she stepped out of the hotel the next morning. "What can I do for you today, *mem?*" he asked. "Anything."

She laughed, but she wondered what he wanted, why he had followed her. She felt uneasy. "I don't—I don't really need anything right now," she said. "Thanks."

"Anything," he said. He was earnest but not pleading. "What would you desire most if you could have anything at all? Sincerely."

"Anything," she said. You mean, besides wanting Jeremy here with me right now, she thought. Should she confide in him? It would get rid of him, anyway. "I want," she said slowly, "to talk to the head of the Communist party."

"It will be done," he said. She almost laughed, but could not bear to damage his fragile dignity. "I will see you tomorrow with your appointment," he said, and walked away.

She watched him go, then opened her guidebook and began to look through it. A travel magazine had commissioned her to do a piece on the largest city in Amaz, the ruins, the beaches, the marketplace, the famous park designed by Antonio Gaudí. How was the country holding up under the attack by the guerrillas, under the loss of the income from tourists which was its major source of revenue? "Don't go out of the city," the magazine editor had said. "Be careful. I don't want you to get killed doing this." Five hours later, when she'd told him about the assignment, Jeremy had repeated the editor's warning almost word for word.

But she had other ideas. As long as the magazine was paying her travel expenses she might as well look around a bit. And if she could find out if the Russians were arming the guerrillas or not, well, that would be a major scoop, wouldn't it? No one had seen the head of the Communist party for months. There were rumors that he was dead, that he was with the guerrillas in the hills, that the party itself was about to be outlawed and that he had fled to Moscow. She laughed. Wouldn't it be funny if the young man could get her an interview?

She began to walk, stopping every so often to take notes or snap a picture. The morning was humid, a portent of the heat to come. Her blouse clung to her back. She passed fish stalls, beggars, a building of white marble big as a city block she supposed was a church, a used car lot, a section of the city gutted by fire. On the street, traffic had come to a standstill, and the smells of exhaust and asphalt mingled with that of fish and cinnamon. Cars honked furiously, as though that would get them moving again. The sidewalk had filled with people moving with a leisured grace. Silver bracelets and rings flashed in the sunlight. Once she came face to face with a man carrying a monkey on his shoulder, but he was gone before she could take his picture.

She took a wrong turn somewhere and asked a few people in Lurqazi where the Gaudí Park was. No one, it seemed, had ever heard of it, but everyone wanted to talk to her, a long stream of Lurqazi she could not understand. She smiled and moved on, and looked at the map in the guidebook. Most of the streets, she read, were unnamed, so the guidebook had rather unimaginatively called them Street 1, Street 2, and so on. After a long time of walking she found the park and sat gratefully on a bench.

The benches were wavy instead of straight, made of a mosaic of broken tile and topped with grotesque and fanciful figures. The park looked a little like Gaudí's Guell Park in Barcelona, but with harsher colors, more adapted, she thought, to this country. She was trying to turn the thought into a caption for a photograph, and at the same time wondering about the structure on the other side of the park—was it a house? a sculpture of flame made of orange tile and brass?—when a small dirty boy sat on the bench next to her.

"Cards?" he asked. "Buy a pack of cards?" He took a few torn and bent cards from his pocket and spread them out in the space between the two of them.

"No thanks," she said absently.

"Very good buy," he said, tapping one of the cards. It showed a man with a square, neatly trimmed beard framing a dark face. His eyes, large with beautiful lashes, seemed to stare at her from the card. He looked a little like Cumaq, the head of the Communist party. No, she thought. You have Cumaq on the brain. "Very good," the boy said insistently.

"No," she said. "Thanks."

"I can tell time by the sun," the boy said suddenly. He bent his head way back, further than necessary, she thought, to see the sun, and said gravely, "It is one o'clock."

She laughed and looked at her watch. It was 11:30. "Well, if it's that late," she said, "I have to go." She got up and started over to the other side of the park.

"I can get more cards!" the boy said, calling after her. "Newer. Better!"

She got back to the hotel late in the evening. The overseas operator was busy and she went down to the hotel restaurant for dinner. Back in her room she began to write. "Why Antonio Gaudí accepted the old silver baron's commission in 1910 no one really knows, but the result—"

The phone rang. It was Jeremy. "I love you," they told each other, raising their voices above the wailing of a bad connection. "I miss you."

"Be careful," Jeremy said. The phone howled.

"I am," she said.

The young man was waiting for her outside the hotel the next morning. "I did it," he said. "All arranged." He pronounced "arranged' with three syllables.

"You did what?" she asked.

"The interview," he said. "It is all arranged. For tomorrow."

"Interview?"

"The one you asked for," he said gravely. "With Cumaq. The head of the Communist party."

"You arranged it?" she said. "An interview?"

"Yes," he said. Was he starting to sound impatient? "You asked me to and I did it. Here." He held out a piece of paper with something written on it. "For tomorrow. Ten o'clock."

She took the paper and read the ten or twelve lines of directions on it, what they had in this crazy place instead of addresses, she supposed. She didn't know whether to laugh or to throw her arms around him and hug him. Could this slight young man really have gotten her an interview with the man everyone had been trying to find for the past six months? Or was it a hoax? Some kind of trap? She knew one thing: nothing was going to keep her from following the directions the next morning. "Thank you," she said finally.

He stood as if waiting for more. She opened her purse and gave him a five. He nodded and walked away.

But that night, listening to the English news in her hotel room, she realized that there would be no interview, the next day or ever. "Government troops killed Communist party head Cumaq and fifteen other people, alleged to be Communist party members, in fighting in the Old Quarter yesterday," the announcer said. "Acting on an anonymous tip the troops surrounded a building in the Old Quarter late last night. Everyone inside the building was killed, according to a government spokesman."

She threw her pen across the room in frustration. So that was it. No doubt the young man had heard about Cumaq's death this morning on the Lurqazi broadcasts (But were there Lurqazi broadcasts? She had never heard one.) and had seen the opportunity to make some money off her. She thought of his earnest young face and began to get angry. So far he had sold her a sheet of poetry she couldn't read and some completely useless information. If she saw him again tomorrow she would tell him to get lost.

But he wasn't in front of the hotel the next day. She went off to the Colonial House, built in layers of Spanish, English, and Dutch architecture, one layer for each foreign occupation. The place had been given four stars by the guidebook, but now it was nearly empty. As she walked through the cool white stucco rooms, her feet clattering on the polished wooden floors, as she snapped pictures and took notes, she thought about the piece of paper, still in her purse, that he had given her. Should she follow the directions anyway and see where they led her? Probably they were as useless as everything else the young man had given her, they would lead her into a maze that would take her to the fish stalls or back to her hotel. But time was running out. Just ten more days, ten days until she had to go back, and she was no closer to the secret of the rebels. Maybe she should follow the directions after all.

She got back to the hotel late in the afternoon, hot and tired and hungry. The young man was standing in the marble portico. She tried to brush past him but he stopped her. "Why were you not at the interview this morning?" he asked.

She looked at him in disbelief. "The interview?" she said. "The man's dead. How the hell could I have interviewed him? I mean, I know you don't read the papers—hell, you probably don't even have newspapers, just that poetry crap—but don't you at least listen to the radio? They got him last night."

He drew himself up. He looked offended, mortally wounded, and at the same time faintly comic. She saw for the first time that he was trying to grow a mustache. "We," he said, gesturing grandly, "are a nation of poets. That is why we read poetry instead of newspapers. For news we—"

"You read poetry?" she said. All her anger was spilling out now; the slightest word from him could infuriate her. How dare he make a fool of her? "I'd like to see that. There's ninety percent illiteracy in this country, did you know that?"

"Those who can read read the poems to us," he said. "And then we make up new poems. In our villages, late at night, after the planting has been done. We have no television. Television makes you lazy and stupid. I would have invited you to my village, to hear the poems. But no longer. You have not followed my directions."

"I didn't follow your directions because the man was dead," she said. "Can't you understand that? Can't you get that through your head? Dead. There wouldn't have been much of an interview."

He was looking offended again. "Death is different in this country," he said.

"Oh, I see," she said. "You don't have television and you don't have death. That's very clever. Someday you should tell me just how you—"

"He will be there again tomorrow," the young man said, and walked away.

She felt faintly ridiculous, but she followed the directions he had given her the next day. She turned left at the statue, right at the building gutted by fire, left again at the large intersection. Maybe what the young man had been trying to tell her was that Cumaq was still alive, that he had somehow survived the shooting in the Old Quarter. But every major radio station, including those with Communist leanings, had reported Cumaq's death. Well, maybe the Communists wanted everyone to think he was dead. But then why were they giving her this interview?

The directions brought her to an old, sagging three-story building. The map in the guidebook had lost her three turns back: according to the guidebook the street she was standing on didn't exist. But as near as she could tell she was nowhere near the Old Quarter. She shrugged and started up the wooden steps to the building. A board creaked ominously beneath her.

She knocked on the door, knocked again when no one came. The door opened. She was not at all surprised to see the young man from the airport. Here's where he beats me up and takes my traveler's checks, she thought, but he motioned her in with broad gestures, grinning widely.

"Ah, come in, come in," he said. "It is important to be in the right place, no? Not in the wrong place."

She couldn't think of any answer to this and shrugged instead. "Where is he?" she asked, stepping inside and trying to adjust her eyes to the dim light.

"He is here," he said. "Right in front of you."

Now she could see another man in a chair, and two men standing close behind him. She took a few steps forward. The man in the chair looked like all the pictures of Cumaq she had ever seen, the neat beard, the long eyelashes. Her heart started to beat faster and she ignored the peeling paint and spiderwebs on the walls, the boarded-over windows, the plaster missing from the ceiling. She would get her scoop after all, and it was better than she ever thought it would be.

The young man introduced her to Cumaq in Lurqazi. "How did you survive the shooting in the Old Quarter?" she asked the man in the chair.

Cumaq turned his head toward her. He was wearing the same earring as the young man and the taxi driver at the airport, a gold five-pointed star. "He does not speak English," the young man said. "I will translate." He said something to Cumaq and Cumaq answered him.

"He says," the young man said, "that he did not survive. That he came back from the dead to be with us."

"But how?" she asked. Her frustration returned. The young man could be making up anything, anything at all. The man in the chair had no wounds that she could see. Could he be an impostor, not Cumaq after all? "What do you mean by coming back from the dead? I thought you people were Marxists. I thought you didn't believe in life after death, things like that."

"We are mystical Marxists," the young man translated.

This was ridiculous. Suddenly she remembered her first travel assignment, covering the centenary of Karl Marx's death. She had gone to Marx's grave in Highgate Cemetery in London and taken pictures of the solemn group of Chinese standing around the grave. A week later she had gone back, and the Chinese group—the same people? different people? the same uniforms, anyway—was still there. Now she imagined the group standing back, horrified, as a sound came from the tomb, the sound of Marx turning in his grave. "What on earth is a mystical Marxist?"

The man in the chair said two words. "Magicians," the young man said. "Wizards."

She was not getting anywhere following this line of questioning. "Are the Russians giving you arms?" she asked. "Can you at least tell me that?"

"What is necessary comes to us," the young man said after Cumaq had finished.

That sounded so much like something the young man would have said on his own that she couldn't believe he was translating Cumaq faithfully. "But what is necessary comes . . . from the Russians?" she asked. She waited for the young man to translate.

Cumaq shrugged.

She sighed. "Can I take a picture?" she asked. "Show the world you're still alive?"

"No," the young man said. "No pictures."

An hour later she was still not sure if she had a story. Cumaq—if it really was Cumaq—spoke for most of that time, mixing Marxist rhetoric about the poor downtrodden masses with a vague, almost fatalistic belief that the world was working on his side. "You see," he said, "it is as Marx said. Our victory is inevitable. And our astrologers say the same thing." She wondered what they made of him in Moscow, if he had ever been to Moscow.

"You must go now," the young man said. "He has been on a long journey. He must rest now."

"How about some proof?" she asked. "Some proof that he isn't dead?"

"He spoke to you," the young man said. "That is proof enough, surely."

"No one will believe me," she said. "I can't sell this story anywhere without proof. A picture, or—"

"No," the young man said. "You must leave now."

She sighed and left.

The next day she rented a car and drove to the beaches, took pictures of the white sand, the tropical blue water, the palm trees. The huge air-conditioned hotels facing the water were nearly empty, standing like monuments to a forgotten dynasty. In one the elevators didn't run. In another the large plate-glass window in the lobby had been broken and never replaced.

She stayed at one of the hotels and took the car the next day to the ruins of Marmaz. Even here the tourists had stayed away. Only a few were walking through the echoing marble halls, sticking close together like the stunned survivors of a disaster. A man who spoke excellent English was leading a disheartened-looking group of Americans on a tour.

She and the tour finished at the same place, the central chamber with its cracked and empty pool made of white marble. "Tour, miss?" the guide asked her. "The next one starts in half an hour."

"No, thank you," she said. They stood together looking at the pool. "Your English is very good," she said finally.

He laughed. "That's because I'm American," he said. "My name's Charles."

She turned to him in surprise. "How on earth did you end up here?" she asked.

"It's a long story," he said.

"Well, can you tell me—?" she asked.

"Probably not," he said. They both laughed. Ghosts of their laughter came back to them from the marble pool.

"How do people get news around here?" she said. "I mean, the only broadcasts I can find on the radio are foreign, the United States and China, mostly, and what I thought was a newspaper turns out to be poetry, I think. . . ."

He nodded. "Yeah, they're big on poetry here," he said. "They get their news from the cards."

"The—cards?"

"Sure," he said. "Haven't you had half a dozen people try to sell you a deck of cards since you got here? Used to sell them myself for a while. That's their newspaper. And—other things."

She was silent a moment, thinking about the boy who had tried to sell her the deck of cards, the card with Cumaq's picture, the boy shouting after her that he could get newer cards. "So that's it," she said. "It doesn't seem very, well, accurate."

"Not a lot out here is accurate," Charles said. "Sometimes I think accuracy is something invented by the Americans."

"Well, what about—" She hesitated. How much could she tell him without him thinking she was crazy? "Well, someone, a native, told me that death is different in this country. What do you think he meant?"

"Just what he said, I guess," he said. "Lots of things are different here. It's hard to—to pin things down. You have to learn to stop looking for rational explanations."

"I guess I'll never make it here, then," she said. "I'm a journalist. We're always looking for rational explanations."

"Yeah, I know," he said. "It's a hard habit to break."

She did a short interview with him— "How has the shortage of tourists affected your job as a guide to the ruins?"—and then she drove back to the city.

In the next few days she tried to find the shabby three-story building again. It seemed to her that the city was shifting, moving landmarks, growing statues and fountains, swallowing parks and churches. The building had vanished. She showed a taxi driver her directions, and they ended up lost in the city's maze for over two hours.

She went back to the airport, but the young man was gone and no one seemed to remember who he was. The old man who had sold poetry was gone too.

And finally her time in the city was up. She packed her suitcase, read the note from Jeremy one more time, and took her plane back to San Francisco. She tried to read on the plane but thoughts of Jeremy kept intruding. She would see him in three hours, two hours, one hour. . . .

He wasn't at the airport to meet her. For an instant she was worried, and then she laughed. He was always so concerned about her safety, so protective. Now that it was her turn to be worried she would show him. She would take a taxi home and wait calmly for him to get back. No doubt there was a logical explanation.

The apartment was dark when she let herself in, and she could see the red light blinking on their answering machine. Six blinks, six calls. For the first time she felt fear catch at her. Where was he?

"Hello, Mrs. Schwartz," the first caller said, an unfamiliar voice. She felt annoyance start to overlay her fear. She had never taken Jeremy's name. Who was this guy that he didn't know that? "This is Dr. Escobar, at the county hospital. Please give me a call. I'm afraid it's urgent."

The doctor again, asking her to call back. Then Jeremy's brother— "Hey, Jer, where the hell are you? You're late for the game." Then a familiar-sounding voice that she realized with horror was hers. But she had tried to call Jeremy *last night*. Hadn't he been home since then? Then the would-be writer—she fast-forwarded over him—and another strange voice. "Mrs. Schwartz? This is Sergeant Pierce. Your next-door neighbor tells me you're away for two weeks. Please call me at the police station when you get back."

With shaking fingers she pressed the buttons on the phone for the police station. Sergeant Pierce wasn't in, and after a long wait they told her. Jeremy had died in a car accident.

She felt nothing. She had known the moment she found herself calling the police and not the hospital.

She called a taxi. She picked up her suitcase and went outside. The minutes passed like glaciers, but finally she saw the lights of a car swing in toward the curb. She ran to the taxi and got in. "To the airport, please," she said.

At the airport she ran to the Cathay Pacific counter. "One ticket to—" Damn. She had forgotten the name of the country. She fumbled through her purse, looking for her passport. "To Amaz, please."

"To where?" the woman behind the counter said.

"Amaz. Here." She showed her the stamp in the book.

"I never heard of it," the woman said.

"I just got back this evening," Monica said. "On Cathay Pacific. Amaz. In the Far East. Do you want to see my ticket?"

The woman had backed away a little and Monica realized she had been shouting. "I'm sorry," the woman said. "Here's a list of the places we fly. See? Amaz is not one of them. Are you sure it's in the Far East?"

"Of course I'm sure," Monica said. "I just got back this evening. I told you—"

"I'm sorry," the woman said again. She turned to the next person in line. "Can I help you?"

Monica moved away. She sat on a wooden bench in the center of the echoing terminal and watched people get in line, check their gate number, run for their planes. She was too late. The magic didn't work this far away. It had been stupid, anyway, an idea born out of desperation and something the crazy American had said at the ruins. She would have to face reality, have to face the fact that Jeremy—

A woman walked past her. She was wearing a gold five-pointed earring in one ear. Monica stood up quickly and followed her. The woman turned a corner and walked past a few ticket windows, her heels clicking unnaturally loudly on the marble floor, and got in line at Mexican Airlines. Monica stood behind her. The glass windows behind them were dark, and the lights of the cars and buses shone through the windows like strange pearls. "One ticket for Amaz, please," the woman said, and Monica watched with renewed hope as the clerk issued her a ticket. Amaz had apparently moved to Latin America. Monica could not bring herself to see anything very strange in that. "One ticket to Amaz, please," she said to the clerk, her voice shaking.

The plane left almost immediately. She was very tired. She leaned back in her seat and tried to sleep. Two sentences looped through her mind, like fragments of a forgotten song. "Death is different in this country." And, "You have to learn to stop looking for rational explanations." She tried not to hope too much.

She must have slept, because the next thing she knew the stewardess was shaking her awake. "We've landed," she said.

Monica picked up her suitcase and followed the others out of the plane. The landing field was almost pitch dark, but the heat of the day persisted. She went inside the terminal and had her passport stamped, and then followed the crowd down the narrow corridor.

Jeremy came up to her out of the crowd. She dropped her suitcase and ran to him, put her arms around him, held on to him as if her life depended on it.

GENE WOLFE

The Tale of the Rose and the Nightingale (and What Came of It)

Gene Wolfe is one of the most highly respected writers of fantasy fiction, having written such masterful works as *The Book of the New Sun, Soldier of the Mist, The Devil in a Forest,* and *The Island of Doctor Death and Other Stories, and Other Stories.* He has received The World Fantasy Award, the Campbell Award, and the Nebula Award for his work. Wolfe and his wife make their home near Chicago.

"The Story of the Rose and the Nightingale (and What Came of It)" shows a more lighthearted side of Wolfe's writing, a poetic tale of adventure reminiscent of Burton's translation of *The Book of the Thousand and One Nights.* It comes from the pages of the anthology *Arabesques* (edited by Susan Shwartz), which eschews the well-trodden paths of Western myth and folk tradition for the sun-soaked roads that lead to the Far East.

—T. W.

THE TALE OF THE ROSE AND THE NIGHTINGALE (AND WHAT CAME OF IT)

Gene Wolfe

"Tum, tum, tump!" sang the new storyteller's drum. *"TUMPTY, tum, tum, tup!"*

And Ali ben Hassan, the beggar boy, who sometimes claimed his true name was Ali Baksheesh, the boy Ali who was—it was sometimes reported—more thief than beggar, turned to look. The new recounter of old tales was young and handsome, his beard as brown as a chestnut; there was a pistol of Fez (which is where they make the best ones) in his sash and a smile on his lips.

Ali ceased to pester a camel driver and dashed past the potter's stall to squat beside the storyteller and extend cupped hands. "Baksheesh!" Ali whined. "Most noble lord, sultan of story! Ailaho A'alam! I have nothing—nothing!"

"What!" exclaimed the storyteller, continuing to tap his little drum with his fingers. "You say you have nothing, but first beg the indulgence of Allah for telling lies? You won't get fat like that."

"But, prince of parable, I desire to see those gardens of lasting delight which Allah—the Creator! the Ever Beneficent!—reserves for the faithful. How am I to do so if I tell lies?"

"By lying to Allah, I suppose."

"Master of mystery!" protested Ali. "Master of history! Far be it from you to say such a thing. I did not hear it."

"Nor did I hear your importunate demand for baksheesh," the storyteller replied calmly, still tapping his drum.

"Do not all good Moslems give alms?" Ali raised his voice. "Ailaho A'alam! I have nothing!"

"It is truly written that none shall starve," replied the storyteller. "Tell me what it is you have, and possibly I may give you something— though it will not be money."

"I have three things," Ali answered eagerly. "Harken, O raja of romance, and I shall enumerate them—no, four! By the Beard! Four! For I have this clout, which conceals my private parts—"

"Which may remain so."

"My turban, my lice, and you! It is not written that food mete to each shall be appointed to him? You—"

"No," interrupted the storyteller. "It is not."

"—have surely been appointed by the Most Compassionate to feed me. Are you a scholar? And so young?"

"I'd a good master," the storyteller said. "Mullah Ibrahim the Wise, that holy man."

"To teach you to tell stories in the bazaar? What are you going to give me?"

"A story, of course. I've one to give, and you've ears in which to receive it. And perhaps if I tell you a story, others will come to listen as well."

The Tale of the Rose and the Nightingale

Long, long ago (so the storyteller began) there bloomed in the pasha's garden a lovely white rose, the most beautiful flower ever seen. Her waist was a date palm in the wind, her breasts twin white doves, her hips the saddle of a milk-white dromedary without flaw, her face the moon; the perfume of her limbs filled the whole garden, and her flesh shone like silver.

Ali nodded, knowing that in a story a flower might readily be a woman.

A little brown nightingale wandered into the garden (so the storyteller continued) in search of a mate. He beheld the white rose and fell hopelessly in love with her. He began to build a palace for her in the mulberry tree, and each night he serenaded her from its lowest limb, songs filled with passion and parting, songs sorrowful, and songs that wept with so much joy that the stars bent to listen. *"I love you—you—you!"* he sang. *"Only you! Oh, be my bride!"*

And the rose nodded on her stem, and smiled, and at last sent a message by a moth. *"Come closer, O my dearest love,"* it ran. *"But come not too near."*

The little nightingale was mad with delight. So beat his heart in his tiny bosom that it seemed it must soon burst. She loves me! he thought; and he sang, *"You love me! You love me! You love me!"* Fools may believe it was but the soft wind that caressed the garden, but the nightingale knew better, and so do I. The rose nodded on her stem, and he fluttered for joy.

A stranger had come into the bazaar, an old man whose eyes were always shut, who felt out his path with a long white stick. The boy, Ali, had been too intent on the story to notice him at first; but he caught sight of him as the storyteller said *joy*, for this old man was feeling his way past the potter's stall, tapping each pot with his stick.

"Here, venerable one," quickly cried the potter, fearful his wares might be broken. "Permit a wretched man of clay to guide you." He took the old man by the elbow. "Where do you desire to go, venerable one?"

"I heard a story told," answered the old man. "Or rather, I heard the speech of a storyteller, for now I hear it no more. Once, O my brother, it was my only pleasure to read that which is sacred, heeding nought else, but I did so till I had learned every verse as no man since. Observing that I had no more need for them, the All Seeing One put out my eyes. Now I mumble his verses in the dark—but hear storytellers, sometimes."

"What wisdom!" cried the potter. "Hear him, O you sons of the Moslems! Here's the storyteller, venerable one. Please to be seated."

"Thank you, my brother," replied the old man. "Thump your clay gently."

The nightingale flew to a honeysuckle bush near the rose and sang again, and when he had finished his song, a crystal drop of dew fell from the rose.

"Why do you weep, lovely one?" inquired the nightingale. "Was my song so sad?"

"Because I am to be uprooted tomorrow," answered the rose. "Because I am not red. Today, O my lover, while you slept, I heard the pasha instructing our gardener. A red rose of Isfahan is to take my place, for the pasha does not like white roses."

At this the little nightingale wept too, and for the rest of the night his songs were the saddest he knew, filled with love unrequited and lovers sundered by death.

As dawn came he said to the rose, "I would save you if I could; but I no more than you can prevail against the might of the pasha. May I have one kiss? I shall count it most sacred for the remainder of my time upon earth."

The rose shook her dew-weighed head as she stared at the ground. "You are certain to tear yourself on my thorns," she said.

But the nightingale cared not a copper for that. At once he flew to the rose's stem and pressed his lips to hers; and as he drew away, his bright eyes noticed a single fleck of scarlet on one of the rose's outermost petals.

"Oh, look!" he cried. "See this! My kiss has left a red spot there. If we were to kiss a thousand times, dearest Rose, you would be a red rose, and so might live."

"That dot of scarlet is your own heart's blood," the rose told him. "It is there because you tore your wing on my thorns, just as I feared."

"One drop is nothing," cried the little nightingale, for he knew then what he must do. Taking wing and flying to a dizzying height, he plunged into the rosebush, where he was torn like one who suffers the Death of a Thousand Cuts.

Bleeding everywhere, he fluttered above the rose.

"That's a very sad story," said Ali, who was approaching that age at which young men desire women and so come to ruin. "But a beautiful one too. I'll remember it for a long time."

"There's more," the old man whispered. "I've heard this tale before —we must discover what became of them both."

In the hour that follows the morning prayer (continued the storyteller) the gardener came into the garden with his spade; he set its blade to the root of the rosebush, paying no heed at all to the dead bird lying there. But before he had dug deep, he noticed that one single white rose was splattered and dotted everywhere with scarlet.

"How odd!" he said to himself. And then, "But how lovely! By the Jannat al-Na'im! For the honor of all gardeners, such a bush must not be destroyed. What am I to do?" And so when he had thought upon the matter for a time, he dug up the rosebush indeed, and planted a red rose of Isfahan in its place as his master had ordered him. But he carried the bush that bore the rose the little nightingale had loved to a part of the garden where few ever came, and dug a goodly hole for its roots there. Into this hole, he cast the body of the dead bird he had found in his garden, and he replanted the rosebush on top of it.

Since that day, most of its blossoms have been crimson—the hue of old blood. But once in each year, always at the full of the last moon of summer, the bush bears a white rose spotted and dotted everywhere with scarlet; and it is said that he who picks that rose may choose any love he wished for so long as the rose remains unwithered, and hold her forever.

After this, the storyteller recounted many another strange tale, such as that of Yunus the Scribe and Walid bin Sahl, that of Gharib and his brother Ajib, that of the City of Brass, and that of the Four Accused. Listeners came and went, idlers and porters, sherbet vendors, shopkeepers, soldiers, and the boatmen of the Nile. But always Ali and the old man remained where they were, and though they put nothing in the storyteller's bowl, he did not complain of them.

At length the hour drew near when the gates are shut, and there was no one left to listen but Ali and the old man. Then Ali said, "O master of myth, you have given me far more than I expected. What gold is like your words! I shall ask no more—but if I were to ask more, I would ask that you tell your tale of the Rose and the Nightingale again before we go to our beds."

The storyteller feigned to make a salaam. "I will indeed tell it yet again," he said, "though upon some other day. And I am happy to hear you liked it so well, for to my own mind it possesses every merit a tale requires, of which fantasy, color, and pathos are the chief."

The old man combed his white beard with his fingers. "It has another," said he, "one you have not touched upon: that of truth. For it is indeed written that such a bush grows in the pasha's garden."

"What!" exclaimed the boy Ali. "Why, I'd give my life to see it!"

The blind old man nodded. "And so would I, boy. So would I. It does indeed."

"I wouldn't," said the storyteller. "For I have found that I'm able to net loves enough without magic. And as for holding them forever, who but a madman would wish it? Yet I too would like to see a magic rose if I could."

Ali shook his head. "I'm afraid you can't, O lord of long words. They say there's a high wall around the pasha's garden, so his wives and the other ladies of his harem can walk there."

The old man laid a dry hand upon Ali's thigh. "Nor can I, ever. Yet you might, boy—for I know a means by which one such as yourself may be admitted to that garden."

Then the boy Ali's mouth opened wide, for he could scarcely believe his good fortune. And at last he said, "Might it be, O monarch of muezzins, that the rose blooms tonight?"

And the old man answered, "That rose opened today, for last night saw the final full moon of summer."

"Then tell me how I can get into the pasha's garden!"

The old man shook his head. "That I may not do, boy, for it is a secret that may never be spoken; but if you will guide me there, I will instruct you in the method."

"This very night, my master, if you can walk so far."

"I cannot," the old man told him. "But a donkey can trot any distance one wishes."

Then the storyteller exclaimed, "By the Prophet! I must go with you.

I'll see the pasha's garden myself, if it be the will of Allah, and I'll hire a donkey too."

"O my masters," said the boy Ali, for he knew that though they might ride he must walk, "if you're both going there's no need. Let's hire a boat instead. I know a rais—a captain, my masters—who has a good one, small, fleet, and cheap. A boat does not jolt, and it will be cool tonight upon the river."

"Wisely spoken, boy," said the old man, preparing to rise. "If this storyteller and I combine our purses, it should not be too much. But you must guide me to this boat."

"And I," said the storyteller. "For I'm newly come from Baghdad."

"Then come," said Ali, "and I'll show you everything on the way." And he took the sleeve of the old man's robe and led them down one crooked street after another.

"Here's the water buffalo that turns the well-pump for the whole quarter. His name's Kubbar. See, he lets me put my hand on his horn. Now go through yonder door, my masters, and we'll save ourselves much walking."

They did as he bid, entering a high-walled building through a narrow hall that soon opened into a wide court.

"This is our slave market. The auction's over for today. Never fear, my masters, there's another door on the other side just like the one we came in through. Over there are the sick slaves—you can get one for next to nothing if you want to feed the crows. Here are the well ones. The dark ones are Nubians—they're the best. The yellow-skins are Abyssinians. People say they're too smart to make good slaves. The women are in those booths."

A light-skinned Abyssinian girl with a great deal of brass jewelry thrust her head through the curtains of one to smile at the storyteller, then put out her tongue.

"She wants to show you that she's not sick," Ali explained. "She thinks you're rich because you're dressed so well. She'd like a rich handsome young master. Most storytellers dress in rags."

"As did I. But while I was in Baghdad, I told my tale of the Rose and the Nightingale to the Caliph, who filled my mouth with gold."

"Ah," said Ali. "I wondered about that. Then you could buy her, for she could be had for silver. There's Circassians too, and Galla girls— they have cool flesh for the hot nights—and some Franks, I think, but you have to beat the Franks every day, or they'll murder their masters."

"What's that?" inquired the storyteller as they came out the second door.

"That shaft of stone? The idol of an infidel queen. It ought to be pulled down, only it's so tall it would take the houses of believers with it."

"Ah!" The old man nodded, smiling to himself. "That's an obelisk, boy. Cleopatra erected that to the honor of her son by Julius Caesar."

"And right over there's the Woman's Bath, my masters," Ali announced. "Our eunuchs used to wash there too, but some young men learned to draw their stones up into their bodies and pass for eunuchs, so now they won't let them."

Another street, wider but as contorted as the rest, led to the docks, where lounging sailors were jostled by the impatient travelers of half a dozen nations: Bedouins, Greeks, Armenians, and Jews, a proud Turk with a small black boy to carry his pipe, an angry janissary with a cocked fusil in one hand and a letter in the other.

"Way!" shrilled Ali. "Way for the holy one! Way, make way for the Caliph's favorite!"

No one paid him the least attention, and they had to push through the crowd as best they could. At the very end of a long wharf three nearly naked Arabs lounged in a small canjiah. "Up the river to the palace at once!" Ali called to them. "And with all speed!"

The rais, whose turban was a trifle larger than the others, yawned and rose. "You wish us to wait for you sir?" he asked the storyteller. "You will return to the city with us? Fifty piasters."

After some reasoned discussion in which the storyteller and the old man frequently swore they would prefer to walk, and the rais declared that it had been his intention to sink his vessel at once and so escape the tax collectors, thirty-one was agreed upon, fifteen to be paid on the spot, and the remaining sixteen on their return; the storyteller counted out the money, the rais shouted to his crew, the crew climbed the stubby masts and freed the enormous rust-colored sails from the long, slanting lateen yards, and as quickly as a man lights his chibouque, the little canjiah was cracking up the river with white water boiling at her bow.

"Our Nile is the most wonderful river in the whole world," Ali explained happily. "It runs—behold, my masters—to the Great Sea in the north. The wind blows toward the cataracts of the south—"

"Except when it doesn't," the rais put in softly.

"And so a man may sail up and come down with the current all his life and never wet an oar."

The old man grunted as he made himself comfortable in the stern. "It's a long time since I've been on this river. I had my eyes then. You'll have to tell me what we're passing, boy, so I know where we are."

"Then hear, most holy one," said Ali, who was even more respectful in the presence of the rais and the crew, "that on my right hand stand the mighty tombs of the infidel kings, black as pitch against the setting of the sun and peaked like so many tents, though each is loftier than many a mountain. Opposite are mountains indeed, carved by Allah and not by infidels, the Mountains of Moqattam, my master, where your servant has never set his foot. Behind our craft, the great, the beautiful city lights the lamps no man can count, which fade with distance, my master, even as the host of heaven brightens. Before us rise the famous cliffs." Ali looked about for something with which to cover himself, for the night air was indeed chill upon the Nile.

"You grope for your robe, boy," said the old man. "But you're sitting on it."

At that, the storyteller laughed.

It was so, though the boy Ali had never in his life owned a robe. When he stretched his hand toward the wooden seat, it was not wood his fingers encountered but cotton cloth. He stood and held it up, and it was indeed just such a robe as someone of his size might wear, of white striped with a darker color.

"Ten thousand blessings, my master!" exclaimed Ali. Then he muttered to himself, "I wish I had a light."

The old man said, "The stripes are brown, boy. Now put it on."

When the robe was settled in place, so that Ali was covered from his shoulders to his ankles, he said, "O my master, holiest wazir of all wisdom, I had thought you blind."

And the old man answered, "Now that night has come, I see more clearly."

The storyteller touched Ali's arm and pointed. "What are those dark openings in the cliffs?"

"Tombs, my master. The tombs of infidels of long ago."

"Some are lit from within. Their lights are faint, but I see them. Look there."

"Those are ghûl lights, my master," Ali told him. "Ghûls dwell in the tombs."

The old man said, "Tell him of them."

"It is unlucky to speak of them, my master," Ali said, and he looked to one side.

"Speak nevertheless," said the storyteller, "and may your ill luck fall upon me."

"Have they no ghûls in Baghdad?"

The storyteller nodded. "Evil things that claw at graves by night and sometimes kill the watchmen."

"So are they here," said Ali. "They devour the sere bodies of infidels long dead, and eat the funeral meats left with them. They don their jewels too, and hold an evil carouse, dancing to a music that would drive a true believer mad. When day comes, they hide the jewels, so that honest men cannot find them."

The storyteller thought upon this for a time, and at last he said, "What of the kings' tombs we saw? Are there greater ghûls in those?"

The boy Ali shook his head. "There's a guardian set there by the kings, with a man's face and a lion's feet. Should any ghûl approach those tombs, he would rise and tear it to pieces. If its face were a lion's, my master, it would flee, for all beasts fear them greatly. If its hands were a man's, it could do nothing, for the hands of men are weak against ghûls. Thus it is as it is, and they fear it and do not come. Now let us speak no more of these evil things."

"Boy," said the old man, "take up my stick."

Ali picked it up—a long slender rod of heavy wood, topped with a knob of bone.

"I can't see which tombs show a light," the old man said. "But you can. Stand up, boy! Are you standing up?"

Ali rose again. "Yes, my master. I stand."

"Then point my stick at a tomb that shows a light, boy. At the nearest."

They were abreast such a tomb as he spoke. A faint blue ghûl-light played about its mouth, at times weakly, at others more strongly. "I have done so, my master," whispered Ali.

Slowly, though not feebly, the old man's hand reached for his staff, a dark serpent that tested the distance between one branch and the next. After what seemed to Ali a very long time indeed, the strong brown fingers touched the white wood.

And the radiance at the tomb's entrance brightened, as if a balefire had been kindled within, and a great voice boomed forth from the narrow stone doorway. All the horrors of death were in it: the stench of corpses, and the dust and the dirt that follow that stench. As the hyena gives tongue though its mouth chokes on putrescence, it howled, "*Hail to thee, Mullah Ibrahim! Peace be, between thee and me!*"

Ali returned the old man's stick to the place at his side where it had lain. And thereafter he sat with his head in his hands, and said nothing of cliff or mountain, ruined temple or mosque of faith, or of anything else that the boat passed. For he recalled that the storyteller had told him that his teacher had been the Mullah Ibrahim; and he knew that the two, although they might feign to have met first that day in the bazaar, were in reality pupil and master, and that they had snared him for a purpose he could not guess.

At last the storyteller took him by the shoulder and said, "Come!"

Ali raised his head and saw they were at the landing of the pasha's palace. He saw too that dawn had come, or nearly, for it was almost the hour at which a man can distinguish between a fine white thread and a black one, which in Ramadan signals the beginning of the fast.

He rose as he was bid and mounted the slippery stone steps, the storyteller following him with his hand still gripping Ali's shoulder, and the old man walking before them, tapping each step with his stick.

Sandalwood gates studded with iron stood at the top of the stair. A janissary dozed before them, his back to a pillar, his hand folded across the muzzle of his long, ivory-inlaid musket.

"Hush," commanded the old man. "He will not wake, but should we make too much noise, he may lift his head and speak." He brushed the gray stones of the wall with one hand and held his stick before him with the other.

Ali nodded, though he wanted to shout.

For a thousand steps and more they crept in the shadow of those gray stones, until the wall curved away from the river. The storyteller said, "Now we must make haste. Night is nearly flown."

"Not for me," the old man told him.

Before them stood a cracked ashlar from which the unholy glyphs of infidel times were almost weathered away, the refuse of the pasha's garden on the other side of the wall. Here the old man seated himself, saying, "Take off your robe, boy, and cast it at my feet."

Ali did not wish to do so, but the storyteller cuffed him until he thought it better to obey.

But while they scuffled and Ali wept, the old man paid them no heed. His blind eyes were upturned to the dimming stars, his crooked legs crossed under him, the palms of his hands flattened upon the glyphs. He neither moved nor spoke.

"O my master, what is he doing?" Ali ventured when he had tossed his robe at the base of the rose-hued ashlar.

Fingering his beard, the storyteller said, "He sends his soul to Jinnistan, the Land of Sorcery."

"Is it near?" Ali inquired.

"As close as the ground under our feet," the storyteller told him. "And as distant as Mount Kaf."

Then Ali opened his mouth to frame another question; and though he did not speak, it remained thus open for some time after, for he saw his robe stir as though there were a serpent beneath it.

"Now," said the storyteller, speaking softly and quickly. "Hear me. I'll instruct you only once, and if you should fail it's your life. In the garden, find the great fountain. From it lead half a dozen paths. Follow the narrowest, the path of pink stones. A woman waits at the end, beside the bush I told you of. She'll indicate the correct rose to you. Bring it to me, and you'll be restored to your proper shape. You'll be well rewarded, and all will be well for you."

Poor Ali did not nod, nor did he express his understanding in any other way; and although he heard the storyteller's words, he scarcely knew they had been spoken. For the robe the old man had given him danced like a pot on the fire, waved its arms, and lifted into the air, filled out in a fashion that showed plainly that another wore it, though that other was not to be seen.

The storyteller pinned Ali's arms to his sides. "Cease your squirming," he hissed. "Move or cry out, and I'll break both your legs and throw you into the river."

And the robe settled over poor Ali's head, blinding him.

Then he could see once more, though the world appeared to his eyes a larger and a far stranger place than he would ever have believed it could. The storyteller had released him; but the robe held both his arms to his sides still, for they were not in its sleeves. Rather, the empty sleeves now flapped and fluttered as if a gale blew for them alone, though the body of the robe was quiet.

The wall of the pasha's rose higher than the sky, and though the gray light of dawn was all the light there was, everything Ali saw seemed brighter and newer than he had ever seen anything before. The stars were amethysts and jacinths, sapphires and hyacinths; the Nile a rich moca sea, a crocodile on a distant mudbank a living emerald. He wished both to sing and to fly, and very much to his own astonishment he did both at once, rising on wings that seemed to fan the air without effort, and trilling like such a music box as ears have never heard.

The pasha's wall, which had appeared an impassible barrier, was no more than a rope of stones trailed over the ground. He had crossed it before he could decide whether to cross or not, and a country of silver fish ponds and gay flower beds stretched beneath him, like the most gorgeous of carpets in the far-away palace of the sultan. In a wink he saw the great fountain and the path of pink stones, which soon vanished, however, beneath stately palms and lush fruit trees.

I'm a bird, he thought; and if I wish to be a boy again I must follow that path. But do I really wish it? What is this thing they call the soul, that flies to Jinnistan or Paradise, but a bird that sleeps in the body until it is time to quit the nest? Thus I have died, very likely, already. Why should I die twice?

Besides, when I was a boy I had to beg my bread. As a bird I can eat bugs—there are more than enough to feed all the birds that Allah's hatched since the beginning of the world. As a boy I had lice, which could not be checked without coppers for the bath. As a bird I have mites, which can be checked with a bath of dust. As a boy I played with my fellow boys. But as a bird, shall I not sing all day with my fellow birds? There passes one now, my comrade in the air.

At this thought, the bird Ali glanced to his right, where a wild duck winged its way toward the marshes of the Faiyum. Just as he looked, a falcon stooped for it like a thunderbolt; the unfortunate duck gave an eerie, despairing cry and plummeted to earth.

As did the bird Ali, diving under the shelter of a friendly orange tree and whizzing down the path of pink stones like an arrow.

Through a grotto it wound, past lesser fountains and over a bridge not much larger than a table. At last it ended in a cul-de-sac closed by a large rosebush. A young woman waited there, unveiled, her dainty feet upon a slab of pink stone; but though any man would have called her lovely, she seemed a giantess to the terrified Ali, with hands that could break his bones as a squirrel cracks nuts. And though she whistled most plaintively to him, he was careful to perch well out of her reach.

"Are you the bird?" she inquired of him.

Her voice was gunfire and thunder to poor Ali, and yet he understood her words. He struggled to speak, but his lips were stiff, and he sang instead.

"Then there's no reason to delay," said the young woman, "for that fat Omar will soon discover I'm absent from my bed." With that, she drew scissors from the waist of her embroidered trousers and cut a dappled rose from the bush.

Ali the bird fluttered to the rosebush and clamped his beak on the rose, but no sooner had it shut than the face of the sun peeped over the garden wall. Its first rays struck the little nightingale in the rosebush; at once his feathers were the brown stripes of a cotton robe, and Ali the boy who wore that robe.

And as he staggered from the rosebush, his robe torn and his arms and cheeks scratched and bleeding, still too dazed to speak, the young woman caught him in such an embrace as he had never felt since the day his mother died.

"I love you!" cried the young woman. "I love you, I love you, I love no one but you! You and you only are the pearl of the firmament to me, and shall be forever!"

Ali took the rose from his mouth and discovered that the young woman was scarcely taller than he; and now that he was a boy once more (and nearly a man) he learned too how lovely she was, her flesh silver and her face the moon.

"Will you tell me your name?" she asked, suddenly shy.

"I'm Ali," he told her. "And you are . . . ?"

"Zandra," she said, and they kissed. As their lips met, the dappled rose she had cut for him withered and dropped from his fingers to the ground.

And though he was a trifle the smaller, Ali knew that he was taller than the sky. What had Rustam, what had Akbar-Khan, that he had not? A horse? A sword? A banner and a thousand ragged rascals to follow it? They were trivialities and would be his as soon as he wanted them.

"You're unlucky, Zandra," he whispered. "The spell of the rose has made you love a beggar boy; but though he will not be a boy always, nor a beggar always, he will be your slave always."

"I am unluckier than you know, O my heart," she replied. "For this is the pasha's garden, and I am the pasha's. Should Omar the Chief Eunuch, or any of the others, find us here, he will slay you and hew my quivering body into four quarters."

"Then they must not find us. Tell me quickly—why did the storyteller send me for the rose?"

"A storyteller?" inquired Zandra. "Describe him to me!"

"He's tall and straight, and very fine looking," said Ali, recalling the man to his mind's eye. "He has a beautiful brown beard, and a masterful gaze. His turban is silk, his vest is green kid, and he wears a pistol from Fez in a red sash. With him is a blind old man, a little taller even than he but stooped, Mullah Ibrahim the Wise."

"I know nothing of such an old man" Zandra told him. "But the young one is no storyteller but Prince Abdullah al Hazik. A month past, he was my master's guest in this palace. He met me in this garden, where no stranger is to be."

"And are you the pasha's most favored wife?"

Sadly, Zandra shook her head. "Only his concubine. There are more than a hundred of us."

"How did you come to meet my storyteller here? Was it by chance?"

"No," she said. She drew away from him by half a step, and her eyes found the pink stone at her feet.

"Tell me!" demanded Ali. "It might save our lives. Do you think it really matters to me that another has seen my beloved's face? I, who love you, and have worn others' rags all my life?"

"We danced for him," confessed poor Zandra. "I and all the youngest of the pasha's concubines. Our elders played for us on their lutes and zithers, and on the flute and the little woman's drum. I had cymbals for my fingers, and gold bells on my wrists and ankles, and I played my tambourine. We had danced like that before, but never for a guest so young and handsome. O my heart, you should have heard the music, as fierce and sweet as the wind from the sea!"

She whirled, hands above her head and fingers snapping; and her hips were the tossing billows of the wild Aegean from which she came, and her little feet thumped the path of pink stones in the rhythm of her dance.

And though every fool in the bazaar would have said that there was no music, yet Ali heard it plainly, the shrilling of the shabbäbi and the thudding of the darabukka.

Abruptly, she stopped. "And he looked at me, beloved, and I at him, and I knew he would meet me in the garden, beneath the moon. We went there to cool ourselves when we had danced, and I hid till all the rest had gone. Since that time old Rashsha has carried many messages for us." Her eyes filled with tears.

"I understand," said Ali, who had once or twice assisted in the transmission of such messages himself. "But why did he want the rose?"

Zandra wiped her eyes. "Because of the inscription on a certain stone that lies beyond our wall. I've never seen it, and I couldn't read it anyway. But he says it says, 'Here is the treasure of Osiris.' That was a king of the infidels, I think. 'I open to love alone.' Prince Abdullah said it would open to the bearer of the rose. Where is it?"

"I dropped it," Ali confessed.

"Here it is—on the stone. But how fast it faded!"

Zandra bent to pick it up, and Ali was seized with shame to think that he had made this lovely child weep, and that she, the pasha's concubine, should wait upon him, a pauper and a beggar. "No, no!" he protested. "Let me get it for you, my lady!"

Their hands met upon the pink stone. It lifted at once as if hinged, and the rose slid from it to die at the foot of the bush where it lies still. Before them opened a murky and narrow shaft which a flight of steep stone steps descended, as it seemed, forever.

"*Caught!*" exclaimed a reedy voice behind them.

They turned as one, and Zandra cried, "Omar! Omar, please we—"

"*Silence, I say!*" Twice Ali's height, the eunuch lumbered toward them, penning them in the cul-de-sac; his belly preceded his advance as a battering ram leads a storming party, and he held a heavy scimitar at the ready. "I fear that you must die, my children. I . . . what is this?"

"The secret road to a great treasure, sir," said Ali, whose wits had been honed on many a dinnerless day. "Jewels and gold beyond counting. Look here." Quickly he pointed to the glyphs carved on the underside of the stone: a bent object that might be a whip, a human leg and foot, a shallow cup, and a crocodile.

"It's plain enough, surely," continued Ali, who had heard that eunuchs hunger after money and respect as whole men lust for power and women, though he could not read even plain Arabic. "The lash and the foot mean that anyone who walks here without permission will be beaten. The cup shows that this is where the drinking vessels are, and the crocodile that they belong to the king of the river."

Zandra whispered, "Oh, what a pity you must kill us, Omar! My screams and our blood, still more the hacked limbs of our dismembered bodies, will attract a great deal of attention to this spot. You'll be lucky to get so much as a single goblet before the janissaries take charge of everything."

"But if you were to spare us," Ali added quickly, "we could assist you. And since it would be our lives to reveal a word of this, we would reveal nothing, ever."

"Never!" confirmed Zandra.

"Hmm," said the eunuch. With his left hand he stroked his chin, which was smoother than Ali's. He looked from one to the other with the clever little eyes of a pig. "I could take you elsewhere, however. Indeed it seems a capital idea. You, of course, will flee, young man—" Sudden as a cobra's strike, his left hand seized Ali's arm and clamped it like a vise. "And I should have the greatest difficulty catching you. I suppose you might even scale the wall—no doubt that's how you got in. It would be best if you did not. Our Zandra may fly if she likes. She won't get over the wall so easily, I think, and I shall hunt her down. Come, my children."

He swung Ali about, and Zandra followed weeping.

With a crash like a thunderclap, the stone slammed closed behind them. The eunuch spun around to stare at it. "How did you get that open?"

"We just touched it," Zandra told him.

Ali cleared his throat. "There's another pink stone on the other side of the wall, sir. It's all rather complicated—"

The eunuch set his foot upon the stone; nothing happened. "Why, I've touched this myself a score of times," he muttered. "What's this about another stone outside?"

"And into that stone," Ali continued in his most impressive voice, "are carved the following words: '*I reveal the treasure to true love only.*' There's also a man—a most evil man, sir—a certain Prince Abdullah of Baghdad—"

"I know him well," put in the eunuch. "A true son of the prophet and a most generous, nobly-spirited gentleman."

"Who's hot on the trail of this very treasure, sir, aided by his old tutor, Mullah Ibrahim. Prince Abdullah, however—"

"Still your chatter," ordered the eunuch. "You two touched it, you say, and it opened?"

Ali and Zandra nodded.

"Then touch it again, at once!"

Zandra said softly, "Our hands were together, Omar. We touched it together."

"Then do so again. The boy may use his free hand."

Ali and Zandra joined hands and looked at each other for a moment before they touched the pink stone, which sprang up as it thrown wide by the djinn.

The eunuch nodded to himself. "You are quite correct, I must spare you. Serve me well, and by my honor you both shall live. His excellency will hear nothing of this."

"We will!" cried Ali, and "Oh, we will!" Zandra.

"And that scoundrel Prince Abdullah wishes to seize my treasure, you say?"

Ali nodded. "But he thinks it's underneath the pink stone outside. So did I, until we opened this a moment ago. Mullah Ibrahim must have read the writing on the stone for him, but the mullah's blind. Either he read it by feeling the carvings, or Abdullah described them to him. He couldn't see the stone; if he had, he probably would have guessed it wasn't where it had been in the days of the infidels. I suppose the masons wanted it to build the wall—but it cracked, and they threw it away."

"And this unworthy prince is still seeking to discover how it may be opened?"

"Yes, sir."

"Then I'm far ahead of the rogue. And now, children, we must see what I have found. You will go ahead of me, I think. I wouldn't want that stone to shut with myself inside."

Ali went first, biting his lips, for the darkness and the dank smell of the place frightened him. Zandra followed close behind him, trembling and gulping down sobs. The eunuch brought up the rear with his big scimitar in his hand and a little smile of complacency on his face.

When the three had descended a hundred steps and were far beneath the ground, the stair ended in mud. Had it been night in the pasha's garden above, or even afternoon, the cavern in which they found themselves would have been as black as the pit. As it was, the morning sun shot its rays down the long straight stair after them, tracing a rectangle of tarnished gold at the bottom that seemed to their eyes almost blinding and lent some faint illumination to the whole.

It was not a very prepossessing whole, and scarcely looked like a treasure house—a wide, low cave in which mud mixed with rock and gravel sloped toward an underground pool of dark water. In places, slabs had fallen from the ceiling and lay level with the mud, forming paths of stepping stones that led nowhere. In others, long stalactites nearly touched the floor, or touched it to form pillars; and in still others, delicate white curtains of stone had been drawn before small and secret chambers. Poor Ali shivered, feeling he breathed the chill air of a bygone time, of the age that had ended on the day the Nile turned to blood. Its unclean idols gathered invisibly about him, half-human figures having the heads and horns and tusks of beasts.

The eunuch hurried into the cavern to search for treasure, forgetful of his captives. Ali would have fled up the stair if it could have been done without abandoning Zandra, who clung to his arm.

"No cups here," the eunuch grumbled. "Mere emptiness—dark—dampness—and nothing more. This tomb was rifled long ago, and the miserable grave robbers took everything."

Zandra whispered. "I'm not sure it's a tomb at all, or that it ever was."

"All the worse for us, then," said the eunuch, returning to them. "I ought to slay you both on the spot. It's my duty, in fact—one I've neglected too long already."

"I think the treasure might be under the water, Omar. I saw a gleam of gold there, I think."

"So did I," said Ali.

And as he spoke the still water was roiled, boiling and rippling with the movements of something beneath the surface.

"Did you?" muttered the eunuch. "Well, I'll have a look."

And the snout of a huge crocodile appeared, but the eunuch seemed not to see it.

"Watch out, Omar!" Zandra called. "The bubbles!"

He glanced at her over his shoulder. "Look out? For what?"

Only the eyes and nostrils of the crocodile appeared above the water, but they raced toward him, trailing a sharp wake like a small, swift boat's upon the river.

"Omar!"

"What?" the eunuch asked testily.

Then it was too late. More quickly than any man could run, thrown forward by a tremendous stroke of its tail as it left the water and carrying with it a wave half again as large as itself, the crocodile mounted the bank. It was as long as a tree trunk, broader than two camels; gold rings set with rubies pierced its armored head below the ear vents, and bands of pure gold studded with amethysts had been riveted around its forelegs. Its jaws seized the eunuch, who fell with a thud that seemed to shake the entire cavern. Once he groaned; an arm moved, and fell back.

He lay still.

Yet there was no blood, and when the crocodile had dragged the eunuch's swollen body beneath the water, that body lay near the water's edge as before.

"Come!" Ali said, and took Zandra's hand.

Already the time for flight had passed. Again the enormous crocodile rushed from the pool, and before they could mount the first step, its jaws closed about them.

It seemed to Ali then that the darkness grew darker still—darker than he had ever known, darker than he had ever believed darkness and night could ever be; it was a long while, sad hours it seemed, before he understood what had happened, what the dark was and why it had come.

There was no more Allah, not then or ever. He had seldom been in a mosque, scarcely ever recited the prescribed prayers at dawn, midday, and evening; yet he had known Allah was there, always present in his life, like air. Now Allah was gone, and nothing remained of life but the savage fight—a fight that he, small and weak, could never win.

The darkness opened. He saw Zandra's face and knew he had been wrong.

"O my heart!" Zandra cried. "What is the matter?"

"Nothing's the matter," Ali said, and meant it. He sat up.

"First Omar, then you! There's something evil in this terrible place."

He was weak, but with her help he was able to get to his feet. "Did you see the crocodile?" he asked.

"A crocodile? No. A crocodile couldn't live down here, could it?"

"But you saw gold, under the water."

"I thought I did. Something that gleamed like gold, yes. And the water bubbled. I thought that was strange, and I tried to warn Omar, but he didn't pay any attention."

Ali nodded.

"It was as if something you couldn't see were coming out of the water—coming for Omar. Do you think he's dead?"

"I don't know," Ali told her, and they went over to look at the fat eunuch.

He lay upon his back and seemed not to breathe. Ali touched his chest; the skin was as cold as the mud where he lay, but his eyes opened at Ali's touch, and he groaned.

"Omar!" Zandra cried. "Are you all right?"

"No," the eunuch groaned. "Oh, decidedly not, my child." He put his fingers to his temples. "My head—it throbs most abominably and I've had a horrible dream."

Ali said, "Maybe you'd better lie where you are until you feel better. One of us can go for help."

"Master!" The eunuch's eyes flew wide open. "Your slave must not rest while you stand!" He struggled to sit up, fell backward, rolled on his side and managed, with Ali and Zandra's help, to rise.

"O my master," the eunuch said when he stood upon his feet at last. "It is you alone who must be our pasha, and not that brute up there. I see it now. I beg—I most humbly beg—your pardon for not having done so previously."

He bowed, and for a moment Ali feared he might fall on his face.

"Where is my sword? I shall hew him to kabobs, master, in the bedchamber. It is yet early, I believe, and he'll be still abed. I can manage the other servants for you, never fear. The janissaries must wait your arrival, master, but I doubt you'll have much difficulty with them. And where the janissaries go the army will surely follow. A few gifts to the Porte should then secure your postion."

The eunuch had been looking about distractedly as he spoke. By using both her hands, Zandra was able to lift the somewhat muddy scimitar and return it to him.

"I dreamed I was a whole man, my child," the eunuch told her, smiling at little at himself. "Isn't that odd? I've never been one, to be sure—I was only ten. Yet I dreamed I was a whole man, and standing before the gates of paradise. An angel told me—" He shook his head. "Excuse my wandering, I beg, my master, my lady. I'm still not quite myself. And so terribly cold. I shall return to the surface and do as you have bid at once. No doubt the exercise will warm me."

Ali raised his hand to stop the eunuch, but Zandra pulled it down again. When he was gone, Ali asked her, "Do you think he'll really do that? Kill the pasha?"

Zandra shrugged. "As Allah wills it, O my lover."

Together they climbed the stair. They climbed slowly, with Ali's hand reaching back to grasp Zandra's, and the eunuch had reached the top and vanished before Ali had mounted the twelfth step. When they stepped out into the sunshine, the sun was only a bit higher than it had been when its first rays had struck the little nightingale. The dew of heaven still lay heavy on grass and bush, and a lark was singing as it flew.

The pink stone shut behind them; and although they have spoken of it now and then, they have never tried to open it again.

"All will be well now, my lover," Zandra said. "I feel it. And yet it might be wise for you to climb over this wall before someone who doesn't know it finds you here."

Ali nodded, and at that very instant Prince Abdullah al Hazik of Baghdad seized him from behind.

"So here you are, guttersnipe! Here you are at last. And you, you little slut."

He struck Zandra across the face, and Ali, with his free hand, jerked the pistol of Fez from the Prince's sash and shot him through the heart.

Next day, smoking his pipe upon the divan, Pasha Ali ben Hassan ordered that Mullah Ibrahim the Wise be brought before him. The captain of the janissaries did as he was bid, and when the old man stood in the audience chamber in his chains, cast his broken staff at his feet.

"O mullah," said Ali, "I am informed that there is known to you a certain stone, known also to me, inscribed, 'Here is the magic of Osiris.' "

The old man nodded without speaking.

"And who was this Osiris?"

"The first king of this country, Great Pasha," the old man mumbled.

"In the infidel times?"

"In any times, Great Pasha." Calling thus upon his wisdom seemed to strengthen the old man. He stood straighter and spoke with something of his earlier, proud manner. "The first of the pharaohs, learned and good, beloved of all his people and loving them. Or so it was written long ago."

"I take it then that he is dead," remarked Ali, and all his courtiers laughed.

"Long since," the old man told him.

"I have myself discovered a stone bearing certain infidel signs," Ali murmured. He described them. "Tell me—and if you wish to keep your life you had better tell me truly—what they read."

"They form the name of the god Sobek."

"And nothing more?" Ali asked.

"And nothing more, boy," the old man said.

The captain of the janissaries raised his whip, but Ali shook his head. "Tell me his legend."

"After a lifetime of study, I know but little," the old man confessed. "Sobek was pictured as a man having the head of a crocodile. He was the patron of the throne, and the protector and councilor of the pharaohs. His sacred crocodile was kept in a lake not far from here, where one who sees may see the ruins of Sobek's temple. I know no more."

"If this Sobek was the protector of the pharaohs," hazarded Ali, "he must have been the protector of Osiris."

"That is so, boy."

"And what befell Osiris?"

"He had an enemy," the old man said slowly. "Sutekh. It was well known in those times that crocodiles could steal magic, seizing the magician's power and dragging it into the river. Sutekh took the shape of such a crocodile—some say of Sobek's own sacred beast—and stole the powers of Osiris. Thus were his human foes enabled to take his life."

Ali stroked his chin, feeling the beard beginning to sprout there. "If this Sobek was an infidel god, surely he would take Sutekh's life for such a crime."

"Sutekh also was a god," the old man said. "None but Allah himself could encompass Sutekh's destruction."

"Yet he might be imprisoned?"

"As you say, boy."

From behind the screen behind the divan, Zandra whispered, "Ask him whether our love might destroy Sutekh, Ali."

"O mullah," said Ali, "if Allah *were* to desire the death of this Sutekh, might he not act through love?"

The old man nodded. "It is by that means and no other that Allah acts. Yet what is that, but to say he acts with his own hand? For love is Allah himself, and thus poisonous to those who do evil."

The captain of the janissaries called, "Hear the wisdom of our pasha, O Moslems!"

Ali asked, "And if Sutekh were to seek to devour love?"

The old man answered, "Sutekh would surely die, boy. Can a small god devour a greater? It was for that reason Sutekh could take only the magic of Osiris. The life of the king fell to the daggers of men."

"And if Sutekh were to die, the magic of Osiris would pass to another?"

The old man bowed his head. "So once I dared to hope, boy, that I might have eyes once more."

Ali nodded, though he knew that the old man could not see it. "Mullah, you would have done me evil; yet you did not, and I will not revenge myself upon a holy man, old and blind."

From behind the screen, Zandra whispered, "Ask him—"

Ali shook his head. "Captain, find Mullah Ibrahim a boat. He is to be freed and returned in safety to the city."

The captain touched his forehead. "I hear and obey."

On the day before the great wedding of the Pasha of All Egypt to the Lady Zandra, the rais of that boat was carried before him. The poor man salaamed again and again, kissing the tiles in his terror.

"Flower of Islam!" he cried. "Your meanest servant grovels at your feet. Spare his wretched life! He is your slave."

"The mullah is gone, Great Pasha," explained the captain of the janissaries drily. "Dead, unless Allah wills that he live." He fingered the edge of his scimitar.

"We passed the cliffs at evening," the unfortunate rais wailed. "A darkness fell upon my miserable craft. When the darkness lifted—"

"Peace," said Ali. "We will speak no more of these evil things."

PAT CADIGAN

It Was the Heat

Better known for her science fiction, Cadigan's reputation as a writer of fantasy and horror is growing. She's willing to experiment in style and content when writing short stories, and that's what the form is all about. Author of one published novel, *Mindplayers*, and one forthcoming, *Synners*, her work invariably explores the inner lives of her characters. "It Was the Heat" is no exception. If you've ever been to New Orleans, you'll know exactly how the protagonist of this satisfyingly kinky story feels.

—E. D.

IT WAS THE HEAT

Pat Cadigan

It was the heat, the incredible heat that never lets up, never eases, never once gives you a break. Sweat till you die; bake till you drop; fry, broil, burn, baby, burn. How'd you like to live in a fever and never feel cool, never, never, never.

Women think they want men like that. They think they want someone to put the devil in their Miss Jones. Some of them even lie awake at night, alone, or next to a silent lump of husband or boyfriend, or friendly stranger, thinking, *Let me be completely consumed with fire. In the name of love.*

Sure.

Right feeling, wrong name. Try again. And the thing is, they do. They try and try, and if they're very, very unlucky, they find one of them.

I thought I had him right where I wanted him—between my legs. Listen, I didn't always talk this way. That wasn't me you saw storming the battlements during the Sexual Revolution. My ambition was liberated but I didn't lose my head, or give it. It wasn't me saying, *Let them eat pie.* Once I had a sense of propriety but I lost it with my inhibitions.

You think these things happen only in soap operas—the respectable thirty-five-year-old wife and working mother goes away on a business trip with a suitcase full of navy blue suits and classy blouses with the bow at the neck and a briefcase crammed with paperwork. Product management is not a pretty sight. Sensible black pumps are a must for the run on the fast track and if your ambition is sufficiently liberated, black pumps can keep pace with perforated wing-tips, even outrun them.

But men know the secret. Especially businessmen. This is why management conferences are sometimes held in a place like New Orleans instead of the professional canyons of New York City or Chicago. Men know the secret and now I do, too. But I didn't then, when I arrived in

39

New Orleans with my luggage and my paperwork and my inhibitions, to be installed in the Bourbon Orleans Hotel in the French Quarter.

The room had all the charm of home—more, since I wouldn't be cleaning it up. I hung the suits in the bathroom, ran the shower, called home, already feeling guilty. Yes, boys, Mommy's at the hotel now and she has a long meeting to go to, let me talk to Daddy. Yes, dear, I'm fine. It was a long ride from the airport, good thing the corporation's paying for this. The hotel is very nice, good thing the corporation's paying for this, too. Yes, there's a pool but I doubt I'll have time to use it and anyway, I didn't bring a suit. Not that kind of suit. This isn't a pleasure trip, you know, I'm not on vacation. No. Yes. No. Kiss the boys for me. I love you, too.

If you want to be as conspicuous as possible, be a woman walking almost late into a meeting room full of men who are all gunning to be CEOs. Pick out the two or three other female faces and nod to them even though they're complete strangers, and find a seat near them. Listen to the man at the front of the room say, *Now that we're all here, we can begin* and know that every man is thinking that means you. Imagine what they are thinking, imagine what they are whispering to each other. Imagine that they know you can't concentrate on the opening presentation because your mind is on your husband and children back home instead of the business at hand when the real reason you can't concentrate is because you're imagining they must all be thinking your mind is on your husband and children back home instead of the business at hand.

Do you know what *they're* thinking about, really? They're thinking about the French Quarter. Those who have been there before are thinking about jazz and booze in go-cups and bars where the women are totally nude, totally, and those who haven't been there before are wondering if everything's as wild as they've heard.

Finally the presentation ended and the discussion period following the presentation ended (the women had nothing to discuss so as not to be perceived as the ones delaying the after-hours jaunt into the French Quarter). Tomorrow, nine o'clock in the Hyatt, second floor meeting room. Don't let's be too hung over to make it, boys, ha, ha. Oh, and girls, too, of course, ha, ha.

The things you hear when you don't have a crossbow.

Demure, I took a cab back to the Bourbon Orleans, intending to leave a wake-up call for six-thirty, ignoring the streets already filling up. In early May, with Mardi Gras already a dim memory? Was there a big convention in town this week, I asked the cab driver.

No, ma'am, he told me (his accent—Creole or Cajun? I don't know

—made it more like *ma'ahm*). De Quarter always be jumpin, and the weather be so lovely.

This was lovely? I was soaked through my drip-dry white blouse and the suitcoat would start to smell if I didn't take it off soon. My crisp, boardroom coiffure had gone limp and trickles of sweat were tracking leisurely along my scalp. Product management was meant to live in air-conditioning (we call it climate control, as though we really could, but there is no controlling this climate).

At the last corner before the hotel, I saw him standing at the curb. Tight jeans, red shirt knotted above the navel to show off the washboard stomach. Definitely not executive material; executives are required to be doughy in that area and the area to the south of that was never delineated quite so definitely as it was in this man's jeans.

Some sixth sense made him bend to see who was watching him from the back seat of the cab.

"Mamma, mamma!" he called and kissed the air between us. "You wanna go to a party?" He came over to the cab and motioned for me to roll the window all the way down. I slammed the lock down on the door and sat back, clutching my sensible black purse.

"C'mon, mamma!" He poked his fingers through the small opening of the window. "I be good to you!" The golden hair was honey from peroxide but the voice was honey from the comb. The light changed and he snatched his fingers away just in time.

"I'll be waiting!" he shouted after me. I didn't look back.

"What was all that about?" I asked the cab driver.

"Just a wild boy. Lotta wild boys in the Quarter, ma'am." We pulled up next to the hotel and he smiled over his shoulder at me, his teeth just a few shades lighter than his coffee-colored skin. "Any time you want to find a wild boy for yourself, this is where you look." It came out more like *dis is wheah you look*. "You got a nice company sends you to the Quarter for doin' business."

I smiled back, overtipped him, and escaped into the hotel.

It wasn't even a consideration, that first night. Wake-up call for six-thirty, just as I'd intended, to leave time for showering and breakfast, like the good wife and mother and executive I'd always been.

Beignets for breakfast. Carl had told me I must have beignets for breakfast if I were going to be in New Orleans. He'd bought some beignet mix and tried to make some for me the week before I'd left. They'd come out too thick and heavy and only the kids had been able to eat them, liberally dusted with powdered sugar. If I found a good place for beignets, I would try to bring some home, I'd decided, for my lovely, tolerant, patient husband, who was now probably making thick, heavy pancakes for the boys. Nice of him to sacrifice some of his vacation time to be home with the boys while Mommy was out of town. Mommy had never gone out of town on business before. Daddy had, of course; several times. At those times, Mommy had never been able to take any time away from the office, though, so she could be with the boys while Daddy was out of town. Too much work to do; if you want to keep those sensible black pumps on the fast track, you can't be putting your family before the work. Lots of women lose out that way, you know, Martha?

I knew.

No familiar faces in the restaurant, but I wasn't looking for any. I moved my tray along the line, took a beignet and poured myself some of the famous Louisiana chicory coffee before I found a small table under a ceiling fan. No air-conditioning and it was already up in the eighties. I made a concession and took off my jacket. After a bite of the beignet, I made another and unbuttoned the top two buttons of my blouse. The pantyhose already felt sticky and uncomfortable. I had a perverse urge to slip off to the ladies' room and take them off. Would anyone notice or care? That would leave me with nothing under the half-slip. Would anyone guess? There goes a lady executive with no pants on. In the heat, it was not unthinkable. No underwear at all was not unthinkable. Everything was binding. A woman in a gauzy caftan breezed past my table, glancing down at me with careless interest. Another out-of-towner, yes. You can tell—we're the only ones not dressed for the weather.

"All right to sit here, ma'am?"

I looked up. He was holding a tray with one hand, already straddling the chair across from me, only waiting my permission to sink down and join me. Dark, curly hair, just a bit too long, darker eyes, smooth skin the color of over-creamed coffee. Tank top over jeans. He eased himself down and smiled. I must have said yes.

"All the other tables're occupied or ain't been bussed, ma'am. Hope you don't mind, you a stranger here and all." The smile was as slow and honeyed as the voice. They all talked in honey tones here. "Eatin' you one of our nice beignets, I see. First breakfast in the Quarter, am I right?"

I used a knife and fork on the beignet. "I'm here on business."

"You have a very striking face."

I risked a glance up at him. "You're very kind." Thirty-five and up is striking, if the world is feeling kind.

"When your business is done, shall I see you in the Quarter?"

"I doubt it. My days are very long." I finished the beignet quickly, gulped the coffee. He caught my arm as I got up. It was a jolt of heat, like being touched with an electric wand.

"I have a husband and three children!" It was the only thing I could think to say.

"You don't want to forget your jacket."

It hung limply on the back of my chair. I wanted to forget it badly, to have an excuse to go through the day of meetings and seminars in shirtsleeves. I put the tray down and slipped the jacket on. "Thank you."

"Name is Andre, ma'am." The dark eyes twinkled. "My heart will surely break if I don't see you tonight in the Quarter."

"Don't be silly."

"It's too hot to be silly, ma'am."

"Yes. It is," I said stiffly. I looked for a place to take the tray.

"They take it away for you. You can just leave it here. Or you can stay and have another cup of coffee and talk to a lonely soul." One finger plucked at the low scoop of the tank top. "I'd like that."

"A cab driver warned me about wild boys," I said, holding my purse carefully to my side.

"I doubt it. He may have told you but he didn't warn you. And I ain't a boy, ma'am."

Sweat gathered in the hollow between my collarbones and spilled downward. He seemed to be watching the trickle disappear down into my blouse. Under the aroma of baking breads and pastries and coffee, I caught a scent of something else.

"Boys stand around on street corners, they shout rude remarks, they don't know what a woman is."

"That's enough," I snapped. "I don't know why you picked me out for your morning's amusement. Maybe because I'm from out of town. You wild boys get a kick out of annoying the tourists, is that it? If I see you again, I'll call a cop." I stalked out and pushed myself through the humidity to hail a cab. By the time I reached the Hyatt, I might as well not have showered.

"I'm skipping out on this afternoon's session," the woman whispered to me. Her badge said she was Frieda Fellowes, of Boston, Massachusetts. "I heard the speaker last year. He's the biggest bore in the world. I'm going shopping. Care to join me?"

I shrugged. "I don't know. I have to write up a report on this when I get home and I'd better be able to describe everything in detail."

She looked at my badge. "You must work for a bunch of real hardasses up in Schenectady." She leaned forward to whisper to the other woman sitting in the row ahead of us, who nodded eagerly.

They were both missing from the afternoon session. The speaker was the biggest bore in the world. The men had all conceded to shirtsleeves. Climate control failed halfway through the seminar and it broke up early, releasing us from the stuffiness of the meeting room into the thick air of the city. I stopped in the lobby bathroom and took off my pantyhose, rolled them into an untidy ball and stuffed them in my purse before getting a cab back to my own hotel.

One of the men from my firm phoned my room and invited me to join him and the guys for drinks and dinner. We met in a crowded little place called Messina's, four male executives and me. It wasn't until I excused myself and went to the closet-sized bathroom that I realized I'd put my light summer slacks on over nothing. A careless mistake, akin to starting off to the supermarket on Saturday morning in my bedroom slippers. Mommy's got a lot on her mind. Martha, the No-Pants Executive. Guess what, dear, I went out to dinner in New Orleans with four men and forgot to wear panties. Well, women do reach their sexual peak at thirty-five, don't they, honey?

The heat was making me crazy. No air-conditioning here, either, just fans, pushing the damp air around.

I rushed through the dinner of red beans and rice and hot sausage; someone ordered a round of beers and I gulped mine down to cool the sausage. No one spoke much. Martha's here, better keep it low-key, guys. I decided to do them a favor and disappear after the meal. There wouldn't be much chance of running into me at any of the nude bars, nothing to be embarrassed about. Thanks for tolerating my presence, fellas.

But they looked a little puzzled when I begged off anything further. The voice blew over to me as I reached the door, carried on a wave of humidity pushed by one of the fans: "Maybe she's got a headache tonight." General laughter.

Maybe all four of you together would be a disappointment, boys. Maybe you don't know what a woman is, either.

They didn't look especially wild, either.

I had a drink by the pool instead of going right up to the hotel room. Carl would be coping with supper and homework and whatnot. Better to call later, after they were all settled down.

I finished the drink and ordered another. It came in a plastic cup, with apologies from the waiter. "Temporarily short on crystal tonight, ma'am. Caterin' a private dinner here. Hope you don't mind a go-cup this time."

"A what?"

The man's smile was bright. "Go-cup. You take it and walk around with it."

"That's allowed?"

"All over the Quarter, ma'am." He moved on to another table.

So I walked through the lobby with it and out into the street, and no one stopped me.

Just down at the corner, barely half a block away, the streets were filling up again. Many of the streets seemed to be pedestrians only. I waded in, holding the go-cup. Just to look around. I couldn't really come here and not look around.

"It's supposed to be a whorehouse where the girls swung naked on velvet swings."

I turned away from the high window where the mannequin legs had been swinging in and out to look at the man who had spoken to me. He was a head taller than I was, long-haired, attractive in a rough way.

"Swung?" I said. "You mean they don't anymore?"

He smiled and took my elbow, positioning me in front of an open doorway, pointed in. I looked; a woman was lying naked on her stomach under a mirror suspended overhead. Perspiration gleamed on her skin.

"Buffet?" I said. "All you can eat, a hundred dollars?"

The man threw back his head and laughed heartily. "New in the Quarter, aintcha?" Same honey in the voice. They caress you with their voices here, I thought, holding the crumpled go-cup tightly. It was a different one; I'd had another drink since I'd come out and it hadn't seemed like a bad idea at all, another drink, the walking around, all of it. Not by myself, anyway.

Something brushed my hip. "You'll let me buy you another, wontcha?" Dark hair, dark eyes; young. I remembered that for a long time.

Wild creatures in lurid long dresses catcalled screechily from a second floor balcony as we passed below on the street. My eyes were heavy with heat and alcohol but I kept walking. It was easy with him beside me, his arm around me and his hand resting on my hip.

Somewhere along the way, the streets grew much darker and the crowds disappeared. A few shadows in the larger darkness; I saw them leaning against street signs; we passed one close enough to smell a mixture of perfume and sweat and alcohol and something else.

"Didn't nobody never tell you not to come out alone at night in this part of the Quarter?" The question was amused, not reproving. They caress you with their voices down here, with their voices and the darkness and the heat, which gets higher as it gets darker. And when it gets hot enough, they melt and flow together and run all over you, more fluid than water.

What are you doing?

I'm walking into a dark hallway; I don't know my footing, I'm glad there's someone with me.

What are you doing?

I'm walking into a dark room to get out of the heat, but it's no cooler here and I don't really care after all.

What are you doing?

I'm overdressed for the season here; this isn't Schenectady in the spring, it's New Orleans, it's the French Quarter.

What are you doing?

I'm hitting my sexual peak at thirty-five.

"What are you doing?"

Soft laughter. "Oh, honey, don't you know?"

The Quarter was empty at dawn, maybe because it was raining. I found my way back to the Bourbon Orleans in the downpour anyway. It shut off as suddenly as a suburban lawn sprinkler just as I reached the front door of the hotel.

I fell into bed and slept the day away, no wake-up calls, and when I opened my eyes, the sun was going down and I remembered how to find him.

You'd think there would have been a better reason: my husband ignored me or my kids were monsters or my job was a dead end or some variation on the mid-life crisis. It wasn't any of those things. Well, the seminars *were* boring but nobody gets that bored. Or maybe they did and I'd just never heard about it.

It was the heat.

The heat gets inside you. Then you get a fever from the heat, and from fever you progress to delirium and from delirium into another state of being. Nothing is real in delirium. No, scratch that: everything is real in a different way. In delirium, everything floats, including time. Lighter than air, you slip away. Day breaks apart from night, leaves you with scraps of daylight. It's all right—when it gets that hot, it's too hot to see, too hot to bother looking. I remembered dark hair, dark eyes, but it was all dark now and in the dark, it was even hotter than in the daylight.

It was the heat. It never let up. It was the heat and the smell. I'll never be able to describe that smell except to say that if it were a sound, it would have been round and mellow and sweet, just the way it tasted. As if he had no salt in his body at all. As if he had been distilled from the heat itself, and salt had just been left behind in the process.

It was the heat.

And then it started to get cool.

It started to cool down to the eighties during the last two days of the conference and I couldn't find him. I made a halfhearted showing at one of the seminars after a two-day absence. They stared, all the men and the women, especially the one who had asked me to go shopping.

"I thought you'd been kidnapped by white slavers," she said to me during the break. "What happened? You don't look like you feel so hot."

"I feel very hot," I said, helping myself to the watery lemonade punch the hotel had laid out on a table. With beignets. The sight of them turned my stomach and so did the punch. I put it down again. "I've been running a fever."

She touched my face, frowning slightly. "You don't feel feverish. In fact, you feel pretty cool. Clammy, even."

"It's the air-conditioning," I said, drawing back. Her fingers were cold, too cold to tolerate. "The heat and the air-conditioning. It's fucked me up."

Her eyes widened.

"*Messed* me up, excuse me. I've been hanging around my kids too long."

"Perhaps you should see a doctor. Or go home."

"I've just got to get out of this air-conditioning," I said, edging toward the door. She followed me, trying to object. "I'll be fine as soon as I get out of this air-conditioning and back into the heat."

"No, *wait*," she called insistently. "You may be suffering from heatstroke. I think that's it—the clammy skin, the way you look—"

"It's not heatstroke, I'm freezing in this goddam refrigerator. Just leave me the fuck alone and I'll be *fine!*"

I fled, peeling off my jacket, tearing open the top of my blouse. I couldn't go back, not to that awful air-conditioning. I would stay out where it was warm.

I lay in bed with the windows wide open and the covers pulled all the way up. One of the men from my company phoned; his voice sounded too casual when he pretended I had reassured him. Carl's call only twenty minutes later was not a surprise. I'm fine, dear. You don't sound fine. I am, though. Everyone is worried about you. Needlessly. I think I should come down there. No, stay where you are, I'll be fine. No, I think I should come and get you. And I'm telling you to stay where you are. That does it, you sound weird, I'm getting the next flight out and your mother can stay with the boys. You stay where you are, goddamit, or I might not come home, is that clear?

Long silence.

Is someone there with you?

More silence.

I said, is someone there with you?

It's just the heat. I'll be fine, as soon as I warm up.

Sometime after that, I was sitting at a table in a very dark place that was almost warm enough. The old woman sitting across from me occasionally drank delicately from a bottle of beer and fanned herself, even though it was only almost warm.

"It's such pleasure when it cool down like dis," she said in her slow honeyvoice. Even the old ladies had honeyvoices here. "The heat be a beast."

I smiled, thinking for a moment that she'd said *bitch*, not *beast*. "Yeah. It's a bitch all right but I don't like to be cold."

"No? Where you from?"

"Schenectady. Cold climate."

She grunted. "Well, the heat don't be a bitch, it be a beast. He be a beast."

"Who?"

"Him. The heat beast." She chuckled a little. "My grandma woulda called him a loa. You know what dat is?"

"No."

She eyed me before taking another sip of beer. "No. I don't know whether that good or bad for you, girl. Could be deadly either way, someone who don't like to be cold. What you doin' over here anyway? Tourist Quarter three blocks thataway."

"I'm looking for a friend. Haven't been able to find him since it's cooled down."

"Grandma knew they never named all de loa. She said new ones would come when they found things be willin' for 'em. Or when they named by someone. Got nothin' to do with the old religion anymore. Bigger than the old religion. It's all de world now." The old woman thrust her face forward and squinted at me. "What friend *you* got over here? No outa-town white girl got a friend over here."

"I do. And I'm not from out of town anymore."

"Get out." But it wasn't hostile, just amusement and condescension and a little disgust. "Go buy you some tourist juju and tell everybody you met a mamba in N'awlins. Be some candyass somewhere sell you a nice, fake love charm."

"I'm not here for that," I said, getting up. "I came for the heat."

"Well, girl, it's cooled down." She finished her beer.

Sometime after that, in another place, I watched a man and a woman dancing together. There were only a few other people on the floor in front of the band. I couldn't really make sense of the music, whether it was jazz or rock or whatever. It was just the man and the woman I was paying attention to. Something in their movements was familiar. I was thinking he would be called by the heat in them, but it was so damned cold in there, not even ninety degrees. The street was colder. I pulled the jacket tighter around myself and cupped my hands around the coffee mug. That famous Louisiana chicory coffee. Why couldn't I get warm?

It grew colder later. There wasn't a warm place in the Quarter, but people's skins seemed to be burning. I could see the heat shimmers rising from their bodies. Maybe I was the only one without a fever now.

Carl was lying on the bed in my hotel room. He sat up as soon as I opened the door. The heat poured from him in waves and my first thought was to throw myself on him and take it, take it all, and leave him to freeze to death.

"Wait!" he shouted but I was already pounding down the hall to the stairs.

Early in the morning, it was an easy thing to run through the Quarter. The sun was already beating down but the light was thin, with little warmth. I couldn't hear Carl chasing me, but I kept running, to the other side of the Quarter, where I had first gone into the shadows. Glimpse of an old woman's face at a window; I remembered her, she remembered me. Her head nodded, two fingers beckoned. Behind her, a younger face watched in the shadows. The wrong face.

I came to a stop in the middle of an empty street and waited. I was getting colder; against my face, my fingers were like living icicles. It had to be only 88 or 89 degrees, but even if it got to ninety-five or above today, I wouldn't be able to get warm.

He had it. He had taken it. Maybe I could get it back.

The air above the buildings shimmied, as if to taunt. Warmth, here, and here, and over here, what's the matter with you, frigid or something?

Down at the corner, a police car appeared. Heat waves rippled up from it, and I ran.

*   *   *

"Hey."

The man stood over me where I sat shivering at a corner table in the place that bragged it had traded slaves a hundred years ago. He was the color of rich earth, slightly built with carefully waved black hair. Young face; the wrong face, again.

"You look like you in the market for a sweater."

"Go away." I lifted the coffee cup with shuddering hands. "A thousand sweaters couldn't keep me warm now."

"No, honey." They caressed you with their voices down here. He took the seat across from me. "Not that kind of sweater. Sweater I mean's a person, special kinda person. Who'd you meet in the Quarter? Good-lookin' stud, right? Nice, wild boy, maybe not white but white enough for you?"

"Go away. I'm not like that."

"You know what you like now, though. Cold. Very cold woman. Cold woman's no good. Cold woman'll take all the heat out of a man, leave him frozen dead."

I didn't answer.

"So you need a sweater. Maybe I know where you can find one."

"Maybe you know where I can find *him*."

The man laughed. "That's what I'm sayin', cold woman." He took off his light, white suitcoat and tossed it at me. "Wrap up in that and come on."

The fire in the hearth blazed, flames licking out at the darkness. Someone kept feeding it, keeping it burning for hours. I wasn't sure who, or if it was only one person, or how long I sat in front of the fire, trying to get warm.

Sometime long after the man had brought me there, the old woman said, "Burnin' all day now. Whole Quarter oughta feel the heat by now. Whole *city*."

"*He'll* feel it, sure enough." The man's voice. "He'll feel it, come lookin' for what's burnin'." A soft laugh. "Won't he be surprised to see it's his cold woman."

"Look how the fire wants her."

The flames danced. I could sit in the middle of them and maybe then I'd be warm.

"Where did he go?" The person who asked might have been me.

"Went to take a rest. Man sleeps after a bender, don't you know. He oughta be ready for more by now."

I reached out for the fire. A long tongue of flame licked around my arm; the heat felt so good.

"Look how the fire wants her."

Soft laugh. "If it wants her, then it should have her. Go ahead, honey. Get in the fire."

On hands and knees, I climbed up into the hearth, moving slowly, so as not to scatter the embers. Clothes burned away harmlessly.

To sit in fire is to sit among a glory of warm, silk ribbons touching everywhere at once. I could see the room now, the heavy drapes covering the windows, the dark faces, one old, one young, gleaming with sweat, watching me.

"You feel 'im?" someone asked. "Is he comin'?"

"He's comin', don't worry about that." The man who had brought me smiled at me. I felt a tiny bit of perspiration gather at the back of my neck. Warmer; getting warmer now.

I began to see him; he was forming in the darkness, coming together, pulled in by the heat. Dark-eyed, dark-haired, young, the way he had been. He was there before the hearth and the look on that young face as he peered into the flames was hunger.

The fire leaped for him; I leaped for him and we saw what it was we really had. No young man; no man.

The heat be a beast.

Beast. Not really a loa, something else; I knew that, somehow. Sometimes it looks like a man and sometimes it looks like hot honey in the darkness.

What are you doing?

I'm taking darkness by the eyes, by the mouth, by the throat.

What are you doing?

I'm burning alive.

What are you doing?

I'm burning the heat beast and I have it just where I want it. All the heat anyone ever felt, fire and body heat, fever, delirium. Delirium has eyes; I push them in with my thumbs. Delirium has a mouth; I fill it with my fist. Delirium has a throat; I tear it out. Sparks fly like an explosion of tiny stars and the beast spreads its limbs in surrender, exposing its white-hot core. I bend my head to it and the taste is sweet, no salt in his body at all.

What are you doing?

Oh, honey, don't you know?

I took it back.

*   *   *

In the hotel room, I stripped off the shabby dress the old woman had given me and threw it in the trashcan. I was packing when Carl came back.

He wanted to talk; I didn't. Later he called the police and told them everything was all right, he'd found me and I was coming home with him. I was sure they didn't care. Things like that must have happened in the Quarter all the time.

In the ladies' room at the airport, the attendant sidled up to me as I was bent over the sink splashing cold water on my face and asked if I were all right.

"It's just the heat," I said.

"Then best you go home to a cold climate," she said. "You do better in a cold climate from now on."

I raised my head to look at her reflection in the spotted mirror. I wanted to ask her if she had a brother who also waved his hair. I wanted to ask her why he would bother with a cold woman, why he would care.

She put both hands high on her chest, protectively. "The beast sleeps in cold. *You* tend him now. Maybe you keep him asleep for good."

"And if I don't?"

She pursed her lips. "Then you gotta problem."

In summer, I keep the air-conditioning turned up high at my office, at home. In the winter, the kids complain the house is too cold and Carl grumbles a little, even though we save so much in heating bills. I tuck the boys in with extra blankets every night and kiss their foreheads, and later in our bed, Carl curls up close, murmuring how my skin is always so warm.

It's just the heat.

EDWARD BRYANT

The Cutter

Edward Bryant has been turning out excellent, award-winning short fiction for more than a decade. His work is sometimes termed science fiction, sometimes fantasy, sometimes horror. It is always intriguing, and frequently unsettling to readers' preconceived notions. Winner of both Hugo and Nebula awards for his short work, Bryant refuses to stay put in any genre ghetto while spinning out his hip, sophisticated stories of contemporary life and strangeness.

His "Author's Notes," which appeared in last year's volume, provoked speculation that the material was autobiographical, despite the disclaimer at the end of the story. Please note, while the author really did grow up in Wyoming and really does love movies, he didn't really experience what young Robby Valdez did in "The Cutter." Really. And if you aren't in the mood for a dose of violence, come back later for another screening of the following feature.

—E. D.

THE CUTTER

Edward Bryant

My memory is still intact. I remember the scene as well as I can recall any other episode from my childhood. The year was 1951 and I was six years old.

I was right there with the men—the scientists and the soldiers—as they cautiously crept through the dark, close tunnels of the Arctic base. The steady metronome of the geiger counter clicked ever faster, eventually crackling into a ripping-canvas sound as the probe neared the metal storage locker.

Capt. Hendry paused a moment. The scientists, Carrington and Stern, exchanged glances. The tall, storklike newspaperman, Scotty, didn't look happy at all. The other men leveled their guns at the cabinet. There was something in there. Something from another world. It was ravenous for human blood, and it had already killed.

Capt. Hendry nodded. The man called Bob gingerly reached forward and flipped the door-catch. The locker opened as the music crashed to a climax and I jumped.

The frozen carcass of a sled dog rolled out and thudded to the floor. I stared. So did the men.

Dr. Stern looked disappointed. Dr. Carrington, I couldn't tell. Capt. Hendry smiled grimly and shrugged. Crossing to the other side of the room, he motioned for the rest of us to follow.

We were right behind him when he twisted the knob on the door to the next passageway. The door swung open without warning to reveal the creature standing on the other side. It raised its clawed hands and swiped at Capt. Hendry.

I wet my pants.

As I said before, it was 1951 and I was six. I hadn't read the publicity and hadn't heard Phil Harris sing about "The Thing" on the radio. I had never heard of John W. Campbell's story. I didn't care whether Christian Nyby or Howard Hawks had really directed.

All I knew was I had lived through a scene up on the flickering screen that had branded itself in my brain far deeper than anything that was to come until a few years later when I sat in the same theater and watched Janet Leigh's dark blood swirl down the drain in *Psycho*.

Twenty years after I first saw it, I watched *The Thing* at a science fiction film festival in Los Angeles. I sat there as entranced as the first time, but now I didn't wet my pants. There was not even the temptation. The absolutely shocking scene I'd remembered wasn't there. Sure, there were the components—the dog falling out of the locker and the part where Kenneth Tobey's character opened the door to the greenhouse and there was the Thing waiting for him. But the juxtaposition that had left me with nightmares for months just wasn't there. I told a friend about it, but he laughed and reminded me that the human mind does that frequently with books and movies, not to mention the whole rest of human experience. We edit in our heads. We change things from reality. After a while, we accept the altered memories as gospel. It's a human thing.

Yeah. Right. What I didn't tell my friend was that I knew for a fact that I had once watched the scene I'd remembered. Frame for frame. I didn't tell him, but I'd known the man who'd re-edited the movie. Little had Hawks—or Nyby, for that matter—known. I used to work for that man. The cutter.

I had been there the final days. And worse, that last night.

"Well, Robby Valdez," said Mr. Carrigan. "You're early again." He paused and smiled. "You are always early."

I never knew what I was supposed to say, so I said nothing and simply stared down at my sneakers.

"So how's your family?" said Mr. Carrigan. My dad was still down in Cheyenne drooling over the new Ford Thunderbird he'd never be able to afford in a million years. He was supposed to be looking for work. I knew my mother was cleaning up after supper and thinking how much money she could win if she could just get on *The $64,000 Question*. My sister would be in her room listening to her Elvis Presley records and skipping her homework, humming through her cleft palate and dreaming of someone who would never want her. I had homework I needed to do, but I knew I'd rather be down here at the Ramona Theater helping out Mr. Carrigan. How was my sad family? Don't exaggerate, my mom would have cautioned me.

"Fine," I said.

Mr. Carrigan wasn't listening, not really. He was staring over my head and I guessed he was looking at the black crepe he'd draped over the posters for *East of Eden* and *Rebel Without a Cause* bracketing the signed studio still of James Dean. "So senseless," he said softly. "Such a terrible waste."

"Did you ever do any work on those two movies?" I said, meaning the Dean pictures.

Mr. Carrigan looked mildly alarmed and darted quick looks around the lobby, of course, there was no one here this early. The box office wasn't even open. The high school girl who ran the concession counter was probably still putting on her uniform and fixing her hair.

"Say nothing of that, Robby. It's our secret."

"Right," I said. I knew very well I was supposed to tell no one of Mr. Carrigan's genius for changing things. I never confided in anyone. Not even later, after the thing with Barbara Curtwood. After all, what good would it have done then?

"All right," said Mr. Carrigan. "Let's get to work. You get the fresh candy out of the storeroom and restock the counter. I've got things to do in the projection room." He smiled. "Oh, and I like the coonskin cap very much," he said.

"Davy Crockett," I said. "My aunt and uncle gave it to me. It's early Christmas."

"In September." Mr. Carrigan stopped smiling. "Thanks for reminding me. Barbara's birthday is soon. I should get her something nice."

I said nothing. I knew he was talking about Barbara Curtwood. He was in love with her. My mom talked about that. But then so did most of the people in town. Not about Mr. Carrigan and Barbara Curtwood, but about just her and how she ran around. She worked at the dress shop and spent—so my mom said to my dad—her nights either at the bars or somewhere else. I didn't know what the somewhere else was, because my mother's voice always dropped lower then and my father would laugh.

It hurt me to think about Mr. Carrigan and Miss Curtwood. Even at ten, I knew how much he loved her and how little she thought of him. About the only thing they had in common was the movies. She came to just about every show at the Ramona. Usually she came with a date. Every week or two, the man she came with would be someone brand new.

Even as young as I was, I had some idea that Mr. Carrigan was about the only man Miss Curtwood would have nothing to do with, and it pained him a lot. But he kept on. Sometimes he'd talk to me about it.

"Think she'd want a Davy Crockett cap?" I said. "I don't think she came to see *King of the Wild Frontier*."

Mr. Carrigan looked at me in a funny way. "I don't think so. Something a bit . . . more grown-up, perhaps." His mouth got a little pinched.

"*King of the Wild Frontier*. Now *there* is a film I could have done something with."

"You didn't change it?"

He shook his head. "I was working on another project. A new thriller called *Tarantula*. I had to move the Disney film right along the circuit. But the monster movie, I was able to get my friend at the distributor's to send me a print early. I've been working on it."

"Oh boy," I said. "That's super. I've seen the ads for *Tarantula* in the *Rocky Mountain News*. I know it'll be good."

"It was good," said Mr. Carrigan. He looked down modestly. "Now it will be great."

"I'm sorry I can't think of anything right for Miss Curtwood," I said seriously.

"I'll come up with something." He went through the door to the projection room. I hauled a carton of stale Guess Whats over to the candy case.

It wasn't until I was an adult and moved away from my tiny hometown that I realized what a genius Mr. Carrigan must have been. Who else could have taken movies, including some really bad ones, and re-cut them into stranger, more ambitious forms? The score was sometimes a little choppy, but we were a small town and we didn't really notice or care. We were just there to be entertained. Little did we understand the novelty, the singularity of what we were seeing.

Nobody but me knew what Mr. Carrigan did. And nobody but me knew how he reversed all that work, re-editing the movies into their original form, painfully chopping and splicing the film back into the way it had been, more-or-less, and sending it on the bus to its next stop on the Wyoming small-town circuit.

I guess if he'd stayed in Hollywood, he could have become a star. I mean as a film editor. A cutter, he called it. But something had happened—I never knew what—and he'd come out here and started a whole new life. I always wanted to live in a small town, he'd told me. I'd grown up in one. I thought he was crazy for saying that. But he convinced me he was searching for the best of all possible worlds.

One thing about Mr. Carrigan, he was an optimist. That's what he called himself.

"Robby," he said to me many, many times. "You can alter reality. If you don't like the way things are, you can change them."

I remember I wanted to believe him. I wanted to change things, right enough. I wanted my dad not just to get a good job, but to keep it. I wanted my mom to get on a quiz show and win more than anybody. I thought, sometimes when I wasn't hating her, that I'd like my sister to be able to see Elvis on the *Ed Sullivan Show*. I mean *all* of Elvis, not just from the waist up like the camera showed. But I knew from a year of working after school and on weekends for Mr. Carrigan that it isn't often a person can really change things. And when you can edit something, sometimes the price is way too high.

We were showing a double-feature of *Creature With the Atom Brain* and *It Came from Beneath the Sea* that Friday night. After Polly, the high school junior who was selling popcorn and candy showed up and Mr. Carrigan turned on the marquee lights and people started lining up to get tickets, I stood off to the side in the lobby and just watched. I was supposed to be an usher if some of the older patrons needed to be helped find their seats. I didn't think this double feature would bring in a lot of old people.

There were some parents and a number of grown-ups who weren't here with kids at all. They were mostly talking about "Ike." I knew vaguely that President Eisenhower had suffered a heart attack and was in a hospital down in Denver. It made me feel sort of strange to know that the President of the whole United States was just a hundred and seventy miles south of me.

Tonight people were wearing jackets. This September was more like autumn than Indian summer.

I noticed that the man with Barbara Curtwood had on a leather jacket that must have come off two or three calves. He was big man and it was a large jacket. I didn't recognize him, which was a surprise since just about everybody in this town knew everybody else. Anyhow, he bought the tickets, escorted Miss Curtwood to the line at the concession counter, and then went into the men's room.

I realized Mr. Carrigan was standing right beside me. "Tell Polly to give Miss Curtwood her candy for free. Her soda too. Whatever she wants."

I stared up at him.

"Now. Do it."

I did it.

Miss Curtwood got a large Coke, a giant popcorn, and a roll of Necco wafers. She didn't even blink when Polly told her it was a present from Mr. Carrigan. She turned from the counter, walking right by him, saying absolutely nothing.

"Barbara," Mr. Carrigan said.

She stopped dead still.

"Your birthday is coming up."

"So?" she said, staring down at him. She shook her hair back. Miss Curtwood was a funny kind of blonde. My mom said it came out of a bottle. She was tall and had what my friends later in junior high called "big tits." Tonight she was dressed in a checkered skirt with a white blouse and pink sweater. Some people thought she was pretty. Me, I wasn't so sure. There was something about her that made me want to run. She reminded me of the cruel witch in *Snow White*. The hair color was wrong, but maybe if the witch had bleached it—

Mr. Carrigan smiled at her. "I thought maybe—if you weren't doing anything—well, perhaps on your birthday we might have supper at the Dew Drop Inn."

Miss Curtwood actually giggled. Some of the people waiting to get popcorn stared. "You're kidding," she said, a little too loud.

"Actually," said Mr. Carrigan, "I'm not."

"You're at least ten years older than I am."

Mr. Carrigan smiled. "Perhaps twelve."

"You're an old pervert." More people stared.

Mr. Carrigan was starting to turn red. "I think I'd better go see about preparing the projectors."

Miss Curtwood sneered at him. "Nothing will change, you old creep." People in the lobby started to mumble to one another. Parents hurried their children past the popcorn and into the theater.

"*Anything* can be changed," said Mr. Carrigan.

"Not how I feel about you."

"Even you could change."

"Not a chance," she said venomously.

"Something wrong, sweetheart?" It was the big man, her date, back from the bathroom. "Is this old square bothering you?"

"He owns the theater," I squeaked. Both of them glanced down at me.

"Go inside and see if anyone needs help finding seats," Mr. Carrigan said to me.

I looked from Miss Curtwood and the big man to Mr. Carrigan and back again.

"*Now.* I'll talk with you after the show." His voice was firm. I did as I was told. I noticed that Miss Curtwood and the man came into the auditorium about three minutes later. They took the stairs up to the balcony. The man was red-faced. Miss Curtwood had tight hold of his arm. The people downstairs pointed and whispered to each other.

I was glad when the lights went down, the curtains parted, and the previews of coming attractions began. But somehow I knew that when the double feature was over, I'd have a special mess to clean up by the big man's seat. There was. The floor was sticky with Coke, and bits of popcorn were scattered all over. Along with all the rest of it, there was something strange, half-covered by the Necco wrapper. It was like a deflated balloon, five or six inches long, with something gooey inside. I didn't want to touch it, so I used the candy wrapper to pick it up and put it in the trash. I also suspected I shouldn't ask Mr. Carrigan about it, although I thought I saw him watching me as I looked at the thing. But he didn't say anything.

After I'd finished cleaning up, Mr. Carrigan asked me to come to his office. He looked older. I'd never stopped to wonder before just how old he was. At that point in my life, I thought all adults were ancient. But now I realized Mr. Carrigan was at least as old as my father. He walked with a stoop I hadn't noticed before. He moved slowly, as though he were in pain. He asked me if I wanted a Coca Cola. I shook my head. He asked me to sit down. I took the metal folding chair. He sat down then too, on the other side of the desk, and looked at me for a long minute across the heaps of paper, splicing equipment, film cannisters, and the cold, half-filled coffee cups.

"I really love her, you know."

I looked back at him dumbly. Why was he telling me this?

"Miss Curtwood. Barbara. You know who I'm talking about."

I nodded, but still said nothing.

"Do you think I'm not entirely rational about this all?"

I kept perfectly still.

Mr. Carrigan grimaced. "I know I'm not. It's an obsession. I have no explanation for it. All I know is what I feel for Barbara is love that transcends easy explanation—or perhaps *any* explanation at all." He put his elbows on the cluttered desk, laced his fingers, and set his chin in the cradle. "She's not even what I want. Not really. I would prefer her to be shorter and more delicate. She's not. I love red-headed women. Barbara is a blonde. She is far too—" Mr. Carrigan hesitated "—far too buxom. And there is more which is less apparent. Barbara wished to have no children. She told me this. I would like a family, but—" He closed his eyes. I wondered if he was going to cry. He didn't, but he kept his eyes closed for a long time. "She is everything I should loathe, yet I find myself fatally attracted."

Another minute went by. Two. I stirred restlessly on the hard metal seat.

Mr. Carrigan looked up. "Ah, Robby. I'm sorry I'm keeping you. I simply needed to talk, and you are my only friend." He smiled. "Thank you very much."

"You're welcome," I said automatically, not really understanding what I had done for him.

"I'm going to see Barbara on her birthday," he said, still smiling. "She said so tonight."

"I'm glad," I managed to say, wondering if I should be crossing my fingers for him.

"Life is strange, isn't it, Robby?" Mr. Carrigan stayed seated and motioned me toward the door. "If you wait long enough, you can change things the way you want. If you want things badly enough. If you're willing to do what needs to be done."

Later, I tried to remember back, listening in my memory to tell if his voice had sounded odd. It hadn't, not as best I could recall. Mr. Carrigan had sounded cheerful, as happy as I'd ever heard him.

"She's going to stay after the last show on her birthday. And then we will go to the Dew Drop Inn for a late supper. She told me so. When her—friend—tried to argue, she told him to shut up, that she knew her mind and this was what she wanted to do. I must admit it, I was amazed." The smile spread across his face, the muscles visibly relaxing. He looked straight at me. "Thank you, Robby."

"For what?" I said, a little bewildered.

"For seeing me like this. For being someone who saw my happiness and will remember it."

I was *very* bewildered now.

"Good night, Robby. Please convey my best to your family."

I knew I was dismissed and so I left, mumbling a still confused good night.

All these years later, I've come to live in Los Angeles and it's where I'll probably die. Southern Californa drew me away from my small town. It must have been the movies. I walk Hollywood Boulevard, ignore the sleaze, the tawdriness, and pretend I move among myths. I tread Sunset and sometimes stop to look inside the windows of the restaurants and the shops. I soak up the sun, even while realizing that the smog-refracted rays must surely be mutating my tissues into something other than the flesh I grew up in.

No one ever sees me, but I realize that must be because they are akin to the figures moving on the flickering screen and I am the audience. But I am not only the audience, I control the projector. And, like Mr. Carrigan, I am the cutter.

Miss Curtwood's birthday was Friday, the first night of *Tarantula*. The crowd was large, but I didn't notice. I was just impatient to see everyone seated so that I could take my place in the far back row of the theater and watch the magic wand of the projector beam inscribe pictures on the screen.

I did see Miss Curtwood come down the sidewalk to the Ramona. I knew a ticket was waiting in her name at the box office. She was by herself.

Her friend, the big man in the leather jacket, arrived ten minutes later, just before the previews started. He sat on the other side of the theater from Miss Curtwood. I noticed. I saw Mr. Carrigan paying attention to that too.

Then *Tarantula* started. I forgot about everything else until the movie was done. When the jet pilots—Clint Eastwood, John Wayne, and the others—were strafing the giant spider, the Russians could have dropped their H-bombs and I wouldn't have noticed.

The lights came up and the crowd seemed happy enough. I know I was. The people drifted out and I lost track of the big man and his leather jacket. Miss Curtwood was one of the last to get up and leave.

She saw me and came across the row. "Where is Mr. Carrigan's office?"

"Back down the hall past the women's restroom, just before the door for the supply room." I pointed.

"This is very important," said Miss Curtwood. "Tell Mr. Carrigan to come to the office in twenty minutes. No more, no less. Do you understand?"

"I guess so."

"Do you or don't you?" Her voice was hard. Her blue eyes looked like chips of ice.

"Yes," I said.

"Then go and tell him."

I found Mr. Carrigan out in the lobby holding the door for the last of the patrons. I said to him what Miss Curtwood had told me to say.

"I see," said Mr. Carrigan. Then he told me to go home.

"But what about the cleaning?" I said.

"Tomorrow will be soon enough."

"But the pop," I said, "will be all hardened on the floor."

"The floor," said Mr. Carrigan, "needs a good mopping anyway."

"But—"

"Go," said Mr. Carrigan firmly.

I left, but something made me wait just down the block. I watched from the shadows between dim streetlights as Mr. Carrigan locked the lobby doors. The marquee light blinked off. Then the lights in the lobby. Another minute passed. A second.

I heard something that sounded like gunshots, five of them. Somehow

I knew they were shots, even though they were muffled, sounding nothing like what I'd heard in westerns and cops-and-robbers movies.

For a moment, I didn't know what to do. Then I went down to the alley and felt my way through the trash cans and stacked empty boxes to the Ramona's rear emergency exit. As usual, the latch hadn't completely caught and so I slipped in. Past the heavy drapes, the inside of the auditorium was completely dark. I walked up the aisle, somehow sure I should make no noise. At the top of the inclined floor, I looked down the corridor and saw light spilling from Mr. Carrigan's office.

I called his name. No one answered.

"Mr. Carrigan?" I said again.

This time a figure stepped from the office into the light. It was him. "What are you doing here, Robby?"

"I heard something weird. It sounded like shots."

Mr. Carrigan looked very pale. The skin of his face was drawn tight across the bones. "They were shots, Robby."

"What happened?" I said. "Do you need some help?"

"No," he answered. "I need no help at all, but thank you anyway." He smiled in a funny sort of way.

"What do you want me to do?"

"Go home," he said. He looked suddenly tired. "Go home and call the sheriff and tell him to come down here to the theater right away. Can you do that?"

"Yes," I said without hesitation.

"*Will* you do that?"

"Yes."

"That's good. That's very good." He started to turn back through the pooled light and into the office again, but hesitated. "Robby, remember what I've said so many times about how you can change things for the better?"

"Yes," I said again.

"Well, you can. Remember that." And then he was gone.

I stared at the wedge of light for a few seconds, and then walked back toward the rear of the theater. I didn't go outside. Instead, I just sat behind the screen, there on the dirty wooden floor, thinking about the larger-than-life figures I'd seen dance above me so many times.

After ten or fifteen minutes, I heard another shot. This time it was louder, but I guess that's because I was inside the theater.

I slowly walked back up the aisle. Once I'd reached the corridor, I turned toward the light. I looked inside. Then I went out to the lobby and put a nickel in the pay phone and called the sheriff. I didn't want to phone him from Mr. Carrigan's office.

My parents didn't want me to hear what was decided in the coroner's report, but that didn't matter because it was all over town. And besides, I'd seen it, and even at ten, I could figure some of it out.

Miss Curtwood had gone to Mr. Carrigan's office as she'd said she would, but she had been joined by the big man with the leather jacket. They had taken everything off, the jacket, her dress, everything. They had lain down on the desk together, after shoving all the things lying on it to the floor.

When Mr. Carrigan came into his office, they were both there to moan and laugh at him.

If Mr. Carrigan had laughed too, there was no way of telling. But the sheriff did know Mr. Carrigan had taken a .45 revolver out of a desk drawer and fired five times. Some minutes later, he had pulled the trigger a sixth time, this time with the muzzle tight against his right eye.

That was just before I'd phoned.

What I knew, and what none of the other kids at school knew, not even the sheriff's bratty daughter, was that most people in town didn't know everything that must have been in the coroner's report originally.

I remembered everything in detail, like a picture on the screen. I didn't know what it all meant, most of it, until long after. But the images were sharp and clear, waiting for my eventual knowledge.

The first thing I saw when I poked my head through the light outside the office doorway was the big man and Mr. Carrigan, each of them lying in blood with parts of their heads gone. But what I really remember was Miss Curtwood.

Now I know truly how much she had become as Mr. Carrigan really wanted her. Her hair was no longer blonde. It was wet and red. She was not a buxom woman any longer. Nor was she tall. Mr. Carrigan had carefully arranged her legs, but you couldn't ignore the sections that had been removed.

There were other changes I hadn't realized he had wanted.

September evenings are never as crisp and chilly in Los Angeles as they are back home. I miss that.

I just got back from visiting my sister and her family. After Mom and Dad died, she moved out here and married a guy who works at some plant out in Garden Grove. They have a son and a daughter. The son is what the doctors call disturbed. He goes to special classes, but mainly he sits alone in his room. God only knows what he thinks. The daughter has run away from home three times. The first time, they found her at Disneyland; the last two times, with one guy or another in the Valley. The family pictures look like my sister and me as kids.

Everything reminds me of something or someone else.

I bought a .45 revolver just like the one Mr. Carrigan kept in his desk.

There are times I carry it with me to the movies. I sit in the back row and wonder whether the things I see on the screen are edited just as the director planned. Then I go back to my Hollywood apartment and try to sleep. I am the cutter of my own dreams. The fantasies here have never worked out as I'd hoped.

Sometimes I think about changing my sister's life. And perhaps my own as well. After all, our parents' lives became better, thanks to a late-model T-bird and a drunken real estate developer. With no dreams left to search for, I have only nightmares to anticipate.

The Thing waits for me on the other side of the door.

That which I've never told anyone. The knowledge that behind every adult smile is an ivory rictus. Skeletal hardness underlies the warm flesh. My mother told all her friends I was such a *happy* child. Anyone can be wrong.

I feel like I've built a cage of my own bones.

Mr. Carrigan was right, of course, in the final and most profound analysis. You can make anything better. Life can be changed. It can become death.

(for Warren Zevon)

JOHN DUFRESNE

The Freezer Jesus

"The Freezer Jesus" is a poignant story of Magical Realism, deftly evoking the feel of contemporary America just as the phantasmagoric tales of Gabriel García Márquez evoke the reality of contemporary South America. 'Course, if you've lived in the American heartlands, you'll know that plenty of people wouldn't consider this story fantasy at all. . . .

John DuFresne lives in upstate New York. "The Freezer Jesus" comes from the pages of *Quarterly* magazine.

—T. W.

THE FREEZER JESUS

John DuFresne

Two days after we learned we had Jesus on our freezer, my sister Elvie had this dream where all the mystery was explained to her. Freezer's this ordinary yellow Amana. Sets out there on the porch on account of we got no room for it inside the house. What Jesus explained to Elvie in the dream was that He supernaturally connected the porch light to the freezer and turned the freezer into a TV and on that TV is Jesus Himself. Elvie, He says to her, I've chosen you and your brother Arlis this time because you all been so alone and so good these fifty, sixty years and because your bean crop's going to fail again this spring. And tell Arlis, He said, to call the Monroe newspaper and tell them Jesus has come again and everyone should know what this means.

Now, I've never been a strictly religious person like most of my neighbors. Naturally, I believe in the Lord and salvation and Satan and all of that. I just never reckoned what all that had to do with planting beans or chopping cotton, you see. And then comes the Friday that I'm walking Elvie up the path from the bean field at dusk and I notice the porch light on and I tell Elvie we must have had a visitor stop by. As we get closer, I notice a blemish on the freezer door that wasn't there before. Then suddenly the blemish erupts like a volcano and commences to changing shape, and what were clouds become a beard and hair, and I recognize immediately and for certain that the image is the very face of Jesus right down to the mole near his left eye. What is it, Arlis? Elvie says to me. Why you shaking? Of course Elvie can't see what I see because she's blind as a snout beetle. So I tell her about this Jesus, and somehow she knows it's true and falls to her knees and sobs. Praise God, Arlis, she says.

We're not accustomed to much excitement in Holly Ridge. Only time we made the news was seven years ago when a twelve-point buck jumped through Leamon Dozier's bathroom window while he was shaving and thrashed itself to unconsciousness. Still, the Dream Jesus had told Elvie we were to let the world know, so I called the paper. The boy they sent along didn't mind telling me he was mighty skeptical, before he witnessed the freezer with his own eyes. Said, though, it looked more like Willie Nelson than Jesus unless you squinted your eyes, and then it looked like the Ayatollah of Iran. Of course, anyway you look at it, he said, it's a miracle. He took out his little notebook and asked Elvie what she thought this meant. She said, Well, this here's Jesus, and evidently He has chosen Richland Parish for His Second Coming. My advice, she told the boy, is that people should get ready.

First off, just a few people came at twilight to watch the freezer erupt with Jesus. Then they brought friends. Then the gospel radio station in Rayville hired a bus and drove folks out here. Pretty soon, the Faulkner Road was crowded all the way to 138 with dusty pilgrims. I spent my afternoons and evenings trying to regulate the toilet line through the house. Either that or I'd be fetching water from the well for the thirsty or faint, or trying to keep the cars off my melon patch. Anyway, I got little work done in the fields and soon the Johnson grass had choked the life from my beans. Elvie reminded me how the Lord had prophesied the crop failure, and she reassured me that He would provide.

Every night at 9:30, the Amana TV would begin to fade slowly, and within minutes the divine image would be gone. Then I'd spend an hour or so picking up soda cans and candy wrappers all over the yard. Once in a while, I'd find a pilgrim still lingering by the coop, up to something, I don't know what, and I'd have to ask him to leave. One time, this Italian lady from Vicksburg says to me could she have a morsel of food that I kept in the freezer. She was sure if she could just eat something out of that holy freezer, she would be cured of her stomach cancer. I gave her a channel cat I'd caught in Bayou Macon and said I hoped it worked.

Then this TV evangelist drove up from Baton Rouge in a long white limousine, walked up on the porch, looked the freezer up and down without a word, followed the arc of the extension cord plugged into the porch light, gazed out at the gape-mouthed crowd, turned to me, smiled sort of, said Praise Jesus in a whispery voice, combed his fingers through his long hair, nodded to his chauffeur, got back into the limousine, and drove away.

The TV minister wasn't the only preacher who came calling. The Reverend Danny Wink from the True Vine Power house Pentecostal Church came every day and took to sitting beside Elvie in a seat of honor, I suppose he thought, up on the porch by the screen door. It was the Reverend Wink's idea to transfer the freezer to his church, where it could be worshipped properly before a splendid congregation and all, which was sure okay with me so long as the Reverend furnished us with another freezer. I had a shelf full of crawfish tails to think about. Elvie, though, told him she was waiting on a sign from Jesus. One evening, the Reverend Wink presented Elvie with a brass plaque that read: THIS FREEZER DO-NATED BY ELVIE AND ARLIS ELROD and pointed to where he'd screw it onto the freezer.

About a month after Jesus first appeared to us, I'm sleeping, when I hear this racket out on the porch and I get up quietly, figuring it's one of the idolators come back in the middle of the night to fool with the freezer. What I see, though, is Elvie kneeling in a pool of light from the open freezer door, holding handfuls of ice cubes over her eyelids, weeping, asking Jesus to scrub the cataracts from her milky old eyes. I watched Elvie for three nights running. On that last night, Elvie started jabbering in tongues the way the Reverend Wink does, and she was so like a lunatic there in her nightgown screaming at this big, cold machine that I couldn't watch no more. In the morning, I found Elvie slumped on the kitchen floor. She said, Arlis, I'm as blind as dirt and always will be. She called the Reverend Wink and had him haul off the freezer that morning. And then what happened was this:

Jesus never did reappear on that freezer, which made the believers at the True Vine Powerhouse Pentecostal Church angry and vengeful. Right from his pulpit, the Reverend Wink called me and Elvie schemers, charlatans, and tools of the Devil. Elvie herself grew bitter and remote, asked me did I do something clever with that Amana maybe. I said no, I didn't, and she said it surely wasn't kind of the Lord to give her hope and then snatch it away like He done. Our bean crop's ruined; cotton's all leggy and feeble, and I don't know what we'll do.

Can't even say the Lord will provide, but I do know that He's still here with us. I see Him everywhere I look, only this time I'm keeping the news to myself. I saw Him in that cloud that dropped a lightning bolt this afternoon. I see His face in the knot on the trunk of that live oak out back. What I notice this time is those peculiar wine-dark eyes, drunk with the sadness of rutted fields and empty rooms. I can squint my eyes and see Jesus smiling back at me from the dots on the linoleum floor, and I think He must be comforted by my attention. I hear His voice in the wind calling to me, and I feel calm. I hear Him whisper, Arlis, get ready. In her room, Elvie sits at the edge of the bed, coughs once in a while, and fingers the hem of her housedress.

THOMAS M. DISCH

Voices of the Kill

The following is a haunting tale of contemporary fantasy by one of
the most acclaimed writers working in the field of speculative fiction
today. Thomas M. Disch is a multi-award winning author whose
novels include *Camp Concentration, On Wings of Song, 334*, and (with
Charles Naylor) the excellent historical novel *Neighboring Lives*. His
short fiction has appeared in numerous magazines and collections.
Disch has also edited anthologies. Most recently, he has been the
theater critic for *The Nation*, and has published "The Silver Pillow" (in
a limited edition from Mark Zeising, Publisher) and the children's
book *The Brave Little Toaster Goes to Mars*. Disch lives in New York
City.

—T. W.

VOICES OF THE KILL

Thomas M. Disch

He lay awake through much of his first night in the cabin listening to the stream. It was early June. The water was high and made a fair amount of noise. A smooth white noise it had seemed during the day, but now, listening more closely, surprisingly varied. There was a kind of pulse to it. Not like the plain two-beat alternation of tick and tock that the mind projects on the undifferentiated ratcheting of a clock, but a more inflected flow, like a foreign language being spoken far off, risings and fallings such as an infant must hear in its crib as its parents speak in whispers in another room. Soothing, very soothing, but even so he couldn't get to sleep for many hours, and when he did, he slept lightly and did not dream.

The next morning he opened the plastic bag containing the wading boots he'd bought at the hardware store in Otisville. *Tingley*, the bag said. *Tough Boots for Tough Customers.* They came up to just below his knees. The soles were like tire treads, but quite flexible. He tucked his jeans inside the tops of the boots and went wading up the stream.

He had no intention of fishing. He fished only to be sociable and had little luck at it. In any case, he didn't much like to eat fish, and hated cleaning them. He'd got the boots purely for the pleasure of walking up the stream, as his ticket to the natural history museum of Pine Kill. Not exactly the kind of tough customer Tingley usually catered to, but that was one of the pleasures of taking a vacation all by himself. There was no code to conform to, no expectations to meet, no timetables, no one to say, "Mr. Pierce, would you explain the assignment again?"

A hundred feet up the stream and he felt he had penetrated the mystique of trout fishing. It was simply a macho-compatible mode of meditation. Even with the help of rubber boots, you had to step carefully, for many stones were liable to tilt underfoot, and even the stablest could be treacherous in their smoothness. Moving along at this slower pace, the mind had to gear down too. The busy hum of its own purposes died away and nature slowly emerged from the mists. Nature. He'd almost forgotten what that was. No one had *decided* on any of this. The complications, the repetitions, the apparent patterning—all of it had come about willy-nilly. The beauty, for instance, of these lichens hadn't been intended to delight his eye. The placement of those boulders, which looked so much like a monument by Henry Moore, simply one of an infinite number of rolls of dice.

Another hour up the stream and these abstractions, too, had melted away, like the last lingering traces of ice in spring. The city was thawed out of his limbs. A joy in, a warmth for, the ubiquitous hemlocks bubbled up through his genes from some aboriginal arboreal ancestor.

Where the sunlight penetrated the ranks of the high pines, he stood entranced by the play of the jittering interference patterns across the glowing bed of the stream, the wilderness's own video arcade. And there, darting about through the shallows, were the game's protagonists, two nervous minnows who seemed to be trying to escape their own pursuing and inescapable shadows.

He moved to the stream's next subdivision, a brackish pool where water-skates patterned the silt below with spectral wing patterns, six concentric-banded ovals formed by the touch of their rowing limbs on the skin of the water. For as long the sunlight held steady over the pool he watched the flights of these subaqueous butterflies, continually delighted at how the light and water had conjured up something so ethereal from such unpromising raw material, for in itself the water-skate was not a pretty sort of bug.

And then there were the flowers, high banks of them where the stream swerved near the parallel curves of Pine Kill Road and the slope was too steep for trees to take root; flowers he had never seen before and had no name for. Some grew stemless from the rot of fallen logs, pale green blossoms of orchidlike intricacy, yet thick and succulent at the same time, as though molded from porcelain. There were great masses of pale yellow blooms that drooped from tall hairy stems, and beyond these a stand of clustered purple trumpet-shaped flowers flamboyant as a lipstick ad.

He braved the bees to pick a large bouquet of both the purple and the yellow flowers, but by the time he'd got back to the cabin all of them had wilted and couldn't be revived. He decided, guiltily, to pick no more bouquets.

That night he heard the voices clearly. So perfect was the illusion that at first he supposed there were people walking along the road on the other side of the stream, taking advantage of the full moon for a midnight stroll. But that was unlikely. His was the farthest cabin up Pine Kill Road, his nearest neighbors half a mile away. What women (for they were surely women's voices) would go walking such a distance, after dark, on such a lonely road?

No, it was the stream he heard, beyond a doubt. When he listened intently he could catch its separate voices merging back into its more liquid murmurings, but only to become distinct again, if never entirely articulate. He could pick out their individual timbres, as he might have the voices in a canon. There were three: a brassy soprano, given to emphatic octave-wide swoops, with a wobble in her lower register; an alto, richer-throated and longer-breathed, but somehow wearier even so; a coloratura, who never spoke more than a few short phrases at a time, little limpid outbursts like the exclamations of flutes in a Mahler symphony. Strain as he might, he could not make out a single word in the flow of their talk, only the melodic line, sinuous and continuous as the flowing of the stream, interrupted from time to time by little hoots of surprise and ripples of laughter.

He dreamed that night—some kind of nightmare involving car crashes and fires in suburban backyards—and woke in a sweat. The alarm clock's digital dial read 1:30 A.M. The stream purled soothingly, voicelessly, outside the cabin, and the moonlight made ghosts of the clothing that hung from nails in the wall.

In the morning he felt as though he were already weeks away from the city. Purged by the nightmare, his spirit was clear as the sky. He set a pot of coffee on the stove to perk. Then, faithful to the promise he'd made to himself the day before, he went down the flagstone steps to the stream and waded out to the deepest part, where two boulders and a small log had formed a natural spillway, below which, under the force of the confluent flow, a hollow had been scooped out from the bed of the stream, large as a bathtub. He lay within it, listening, but from this closest vantage there was not the least whisper of the voices he had heard so plainly the night before. The water was cold, and his bath accordingly quick, but as he returned to where he'd left his towel on the grassy bank he felt a shock of pleasure that made him stop for breath, a neural starburst of delight starting in the center of his chest and lighting up every cell of his body in a quick chain reaction, like the lighting of a giant Christmas tree. *Too much*! he thought, but even with the thinking of that thought, the pleasure had faded to the merest afterimage of that first onslaught of well-being.

That day he went up the mountain—a very small mountain but a mountain for all that—that was coextensive with his backyard, a low many-gapped fieldstone wall being the only boundary between his three-quarter acre and the woods' immensity. He bore due west up the steepest slopes, then north along the first, lowest ridge, and not once was there a house or a paved road or a power line to spoil the illusion that this was the primeval, pre-Yankee wilderness. To be sure, he encountered any number of No Trespassing signs, spoor of the local Rod & Gun Club, and once, at the first broadening of the ridge, he came upon a rough triangle of stacked logs intended for a hunting blind, complete with a detritus of bullet-riddled beer cans and shattered bottle glass. But none of that bulked large against the basic glory of the mountain. The grandeur, the profusion, the fundamentality of it.

One slope of crumbling slate beyond the hunting blind the mountain revealed its crowning splendor to him, a grove, horizonwide, of laurels in full bloom, each waist-high shrub so densely blossomed that the underbrush was lost to sight beneath the froth of flowers. Laurels: he knew them by the shape of the leaf. But he'd never seen a laurel in blossom, never understood the fitness of Daphne's metamorphosis. For surely if a man, or God, were to be doomed to love a tree, then it would have to be one of these. They were desire incarnate. You couldn't look at them without wanting . . .

Something.

There was something he wanted, but he could not think what. To faint away, to expire; to become a song or painting or column of stone that could somehow express. . . . What? This inexpressible wonder. But no, that wasn't what he wanted at all. He wanted to feel this place, this mountain, in his own being. To be a bee, moving ineluctably from bloom to bloom; to be the swarm of them converging on their hive.

To be a part of it.

To belong, here, forever.

Sleep came to him that night at once, as automatic as the light that goes off inside a refrigerator when the door is closed. He woke in a wash of moonlight to hear the voice of the kill, one of its voices, whispering to him. Not clearly yet, but as though a message had been left on a tape many times erased, distant and blurred by static. Words. Two words, repeated at long intervals: "Come here . . . come here . . ."

"Where shall I come?" he asked aloud.

"Here," said the voice, already fading.

He knew that she meant beside the stream, and he went out of the cabin and down the flagstone steps, obedient as a lamb.

"That's better," she said, pleased. "Lie here, next to me. The night is cool."

He assumed a reclining position on the grass, trying to be unobtrusive, as he displaced the small stones that dug into his hip and rib cage. When he lowered his gaze and bent toward her, the stream filled his entire field of vision, a film of blackness flecked with vanishing gleams of purple and pale yellow, neural relics of the flowers he'd seen on the banks upstream.

She did not speak again at once, nor did he feel any eagerness that she should. A strange contentment hovered about him, like a net of finest mesh, an Edenic happiness that did not yet know itself to be happy, a confidence that blessings were everywhere on hand.

"What is your name?" she asked, in the faintest of whispers, as though they spoke in a crowded room where they must not be seen speaking.

He was taken aback. "My name?" It seemed such a prosaic way to begin.

"How can we talk to each other if I don't know your name?"

"William," he said. "William Logan Pierce."

"Then, welcome, William Logan Pierce. Welcome to Pine Kill. To the waters of your new birth, welcome."

Now that was more like it. That was the language one expects from water sprites.

"What is *your* name?" he asked.

She laughed. "Must *I* have a name, too! Oh very well, my name is Nixie. Will that do?"

He nodded. Then, uncertain whether she could see him in the darkness, he said, "I don't know how to speak to you, Nixie. I've never had a vision before."

"I am no 'vision,' William," she answered with dignity but no perceptible indignation. "I am like you, a spirit embodied in flesh. Only, as I am a Nereid, my flesh is immortal. But you may speak to me as you would to any normal woman."

"Of what things shall we talk?"

"Why, we may begin with the elements, if you like. Your views on oxygen, your feelings about complex hydrocarbons."

"You're making fun of me."

"And you no less of me, to suppose that I am incapable of ordinary civil conversation. As though I were some nineteenth-century miss only just liberated from the nursery."

"Excuse me."

"It was nothing." Then, in a tone of mocking primness, as though she'd slipped into the role of that hypothetical young miss: "Tell me, Mr. Pierce, what did you think of today's weather?"

"It was beautiful."

"Is that all? I'd imagined you a man of more words."

So, lying with his head back in the grass, looking up at the moon's shattered descent through the swaying hemlocks, he told her of his day on the mountain. She would put in a word from time to time, assurances of her attention.

"You seem to have been quite smitten with those laurels," she commented when he was done. She adopted an attitude of wifely irony, treating the laurels as someone he'd been seen flirting with at a party. "They'll be gone in another two weeks, you know. So, seize the day." She fell silent, or rather returned to her natural speech, the lilting *fol-de-riddle fol-de-lay* of her infinite liquid collisions.

He rolled onto his stomach, the better to peer down at the silken stirrings of her body. Now that the moon had gone down behind the mountain, the little flashes of phosphorescent color were more vivid and coherent, forming ephemeral draperies of bioluminescence.

"You mustn't touch me," she warned, sensing his intention before he'd lifted his hand. "Not till you've paid."

"Paid! How "paid'?"

"With money, of course. Do you think we use cowrie shells? I trust you have some ready cash on hand."

"Yes but—"

"Then it is very simple: if you're to touch me, you must pay."

"But I've never . . ."

"You've never had to pay for it?" she asked archly.

"No, I didn't mean that."

"Visions—to use your term—don't come cheap, William. You must pay now—and pay again each night you come to call. Those are the rules, and I'm afraid *I* have no authority to set them aside."

"Very well. I'll have to go back into the house to get . . . your pay."

"I'll be right here," she promised.

Dazzled by the glare of the overhead 100-watt bulb, he dug into the sock drawer of the bureau, where there would be quarters set aside for the laundromat. Then he thought better of it. In classic times coins might have served his purpose, but nowadays quarters were worth little more than cowrie shells. He took his billfold from the top dresser drawer. The smallest bill was a twenty. It was probably the smallest she'd accept in any case.

He returned to the stream. "I've twenty dollars. Will that do?"

There was no reply.

"Nixie, are you there?"

"I'm always here, William. Just put it under a stone. A large stone, and not too close to the shore."

He picked his way carefully across the rocky streambed till he came to the middle. The water sweeping around his ankles did not seem different, except in being less chilly, from the water he'd bathed in yesterday morning. Even so, as he knelt to pry up a rock, the shock of immersion was almost enough to dispel the enchantment and send him, shivering and chagrined, back to the cabin. But as he placed the bill beneath the stone, another kind of shock ran up his wet forearms and connected right to the base of his spine, deep-frying his nerves to ecstasy. He cried out, such a cry as must have brought every animal prowling the night woods to pause and ponder.

"Now you have touched me, William. Now let me touch you."

Helpless, enslaved, and craving nothing but a deeper enslavement, he lowered himself into the stream, careless of the stones on which he lay supine.

She ran her hands over his yielding flesh. "O William," she whispered. "O my sweet, sweet William!"

After that second night, he ceased to take count of the time elapsing. Instead of being stippled with the felt-tip X's that filled the earlier pages of his wall calendar, June's page remained blank as a forgotten diary. His days were given to the mountain or the hammock, his nights to the Nereid's ineffable, evanescent caresses, of which he could recall, in the morning, few particulars. But then what bliss is sweeter for being itemized? So long as our delights are endlessly renewed, what harm is there in taking the days as they come and letting them slip away, unchronicled, to join the great drifts of geologic time? As Nixie said, the thing to do was seize the day—and not look either way.

Yet a day did come, toward the end of June, when he lost his grip on this immemorial good advice. It began with a phone call from Ray Feld, the owner of the cabin, who wanted to know if he meant to continue renting for the rest of the summer. He'd paid only to mid-July.

He promised to have his check in the mail that morning—$875, which was almost exactly half of his bank balance. Even eating frugally and borrowing on his credit cards, it was going to be a tight squeeze to Labor Day. And then . . .

And then it would be back to Newark and Marcus Garvey Junior High School, where, under the pretense of teaching English and social studies, he gave his young detainees a foretaste of their destined incarceration in the prisons, armies, and offices of the grown-up world. On the premises of Marcus Garvey, he was usually able to take a less dismal view of the teaching profession. If there was nothing else to be said for it, there was at least this—the freedom of his summers. While other people had to make do with two or three weeks of vacation, he could spend the entire season by the stream, with the hemlocks perfuming the air. All he need remember—summer's one simple rule—was not to look back or ahead.

And the best way to do that was to take up the cry of the pines: "More light! More light!" For always a climb up the mountain was an antidote to his merely mental gloom. He'd got lazy about giving the mountain its due; that was the only problem. He'd come to rely too much on Nixie's nightly benefactions. Earth and air must have their share of his devotion. So it was up to the laurels, up through the green, hemlock-filtered light to that all-sufficing beauty. The sweatier, the more breathless, the better.

But even sweaty and panting, gloom stuck to his heels, as the counterminnows of the streambed kept pace with the living minnows above. A line from some half-remembered poem haunted him: *The woods decay, the woods decay and fall.* It was like a sliver firmly lodged under his thumbnail and not to be got rid of. Every fallen log repeated it, as it lay rotting, devoured by mushrooms or by maggots: *The woods decay, the woods decay and fall.*

As Nixie had foretold, the laurel grove had become a tangle of green shrubs. The blossoms had shriveled and fallen, exposing the russet-red remnants of their sexual apparatus, and the bees had absconded, like sated seducers, to another part of the summer. Somewhere on the periphery of the grove a thrush, pierced by its own sliver of poetry, reiterated a simple two-bar elegy: *Must it be? Must it be? It must! It must!*

He did not linger there, but headed northeast on a course he knew would intersect the higher reaches of Pine Kill. He'd never followed the stream to its source; he would today. He followed paths already familiar, past an abandoned quarry, where great slabs of slate were stacked to form a simple four-square maze, a tombstone supermarket. Then along a fire trail, where a few stunted laurels, shadowed by the pines, had preserved their maiden bloom. Already, here, he heard her voice ahead of him. Almost intelligible, despite that she had insisted that her powers of coherent speech were limited to the hours of the night; almost herself, until the kill became visible, twisting down a staircase of tumbled stones, and shifted gender from she to it. Yet even now, as it zigzagged among the boulders and spilled across the ineffectual dam of a fallen log, he thought he recognized, if not her voice, her bearing—headlong, capricious, intolerant of contradiction.

As he made his way upstream, he was obliged to climb, as the kill did, using its larger boulders as stepping stones, since there was no longer level ground on either side, only steep shoulders of crumbly scree. He slipped several times, soaking his sneakers, but only when, mistaking a mulch of leaves for solid ground, he'd nearly sprained his ankle did he yield to what he supposed to be her will. For some reason she did not want him to reach the source of the kill. If he defied her, she might become still more ruthlessly modest.

By the time he'd limped down to Pine Kill Road, his knees were trembling, and his swollen ankle sent a yelp of protest at every step. At home he would fill the tub with hot water and—

But these compassionate plans were blighted the moment he came within view of the cabin and found, parked behind his yellow Datsun, a blue Buick with Pennsylvania plates. *No*, he thought, *it can't be, not all the way from Philadelphia, not without phoning first*. But it was.

It was his cousin Barry, who came out the back door of the cabin, lofting a can of Heineken as his hello.

"Barry." He tried not to sound dismayed. Barry had had a standing invitation to come up any weekend he could get free from the city. This must be Friday. Or Saturday. Damn. "It's good to see you."

"I was beginning to worry. I got here at three, and it's getting on past seven. Where you been?"

"Up there." He waved his hand in the direction of the mountain.

Barry looked doubtfully at the dark wall of hemlocks. The woods did not look welcoming this late in the day. "Communing with nature?"

"That's what I'm here for, isn't it?" He'd meant to sound playful, but his tone was as ill-judged as an intended love-pat that connects as a right to the jaw. He might as well have asked Barry, *And why are you here? Why won't you go away?*

"Well," said Barry, placatingly, "you're looking terrific. You must have dropped some pounds since Bernie Junior's wedding. And you didn't have that many to drop. You got anorexia or something?"

"Have I lost weight? I haven't been trying to."

"Oh, come off it. When I got here I looked in the icebox, and I can tell you everything that was there: a can of coffee, one stick of Parkay margarine, and a bottle of generic catsup. Plus part of a quart of milk that had gone sour. Then I tried the cupboard, and the situation wasn't much better. You can't be living on nothing but oatmeal and sardines."

"As a matter of fact, Barry, sardines and oatmeal are the basis of the Sullivan County Diet. I'll lend you the book. You're guaranteed to take off ten pounds in ten days, at a cost of just ten cents a serving."

Barry smiled. This was no William he'd come to visit. "You're putting me on."

"You laugh—but wait till you've tasted my sour-milk-oatmeal-sardine bread. It's indescribable."

"Well, you'll have to starve yourself on your own time, 'cause while you were off communing, I drove in to Port Jervis and got us some *edible* food. There's spare ribs for dinner tonight, if I can get the damned charcoal started. Bacon and eggs for breakfast, and a big porterhouse for tomorrow night, plus corn to roast with it. And some genuine hundred percent choleresterol to spread on it, none of your mingy margarine. Plus three six-packs—two and a half at this point—and a fifth of Jack Daniel's. Think we'll survive?"

There was no way he could get out of the cabin to be with Nixie that night. Even though he turned in early, using his ankle as an excuse, Barry stayed up drinking and reading a thriller, and finally just drinking. William could hear the stream, but not Nixie's voice.

He didn't dream that night, and woke to the smell of frying bacon. At breakfast Barry announced that they were going to rent a canoe in Port Jervis and paddle down the Delaware to Milford. And that's what they did. The river seemed impersonal in its huge scale. William was aware only of what was unnatural along its shores—the power lines, the clustering bungalows, the clipped lawns of the larger houses, and all the urgent *windows*, jealous of their views. With every stroke of paddle in his hands, William felt he was betraying the stream he knew. He imagined Nixie lost in this metropolis of a river, murmuring his name, ignored by the hordes of strangers hurrying along on their own business.

Barry, a law-school dropout, tried to get a political argument going, but William refused to take up the challenge. What was the fun of playing straight man to Barry's right-wing one-liners? Barry, balked of that entertainment, proceded to analyze his relationship with the vice president of another department of his company, a woman whom he'd offended in the elevator. After a while he got to be as ignorable as a radio. William paddled stolidly, seated at the front of the canoe, letting Barry do the steering. Halfway to the goal of Milford, as they came upon a stretch of rapids, William's end of the canoe lodged against a rock and the flow of the river slowly turned them around till they were at right angles to the current. Barry said, "What are we supposed to do in this situation?" just a moment before the canoe overturned.

The dousing was delightful. William came out of the water grinning, as though their capsizing had been one of Nixie's broader jokes and the look on Barry's face, his stupefied indignation, its punch line. They got the waterlogged canoe to the nearer shore without much difficulty, for the water was shallow. Once there, Barry's concern was all for the contents of his billfold and the well-being of his wristwatch, which was Swiss but only water resistant, not waterproof. They didn't even realize that Barry's paddle had been lost till the canoe was bailed out and they were ready to set off again.

That was the end of all gemütlichkeit. The rest of the trip was a slow, wounded slog, with Barry exiled to the prow seat and William maneuvering, carefully and unskillfully, from the bow. At each new stretch of white water they were in danger of capsizing again, but somehow they scraped through without another soaking. The six-pack had been lost with the paddle, and Barry's high spirits declined in proportion as his thirst mounted. By the time they reached Milford, they were no longer on speaking terms. While they waited for the van that would retrieve them and the canoe, Barry headed into town for beer and aspirin, while William spread out on the lawn above the beach, numb with relief. One day with his cousin and he felt as wrought up as if he'd finished a year of teaching.

The beach was full of children. Most of them were younger than the children he taught. There must have been another beach in the area that was reserved for teenagers. There was, however, a single black girl, about fourteen or fifteen years old, in a one-piece pea-green swimsuit, who was intent on digging a large hole in the sand and heaping up an oblong mound (it could not be called a sandcastle) beside it. She had a small, darker-skinned boy in her charge, two years old or even younger. He might have been her sibling or her son. He spent most of his time at the edge of the water, hurling stones at the river with as much satisfaction as if each stone had broken a window. Once he tried to participate in the girl's excavation, but she swatted him with her pink plastic shovel and screamed at him to get away. Some minutes later he toddled out into the water till he was chest-deep, at which point he was retrieved by the lifeguard, who led him back to his mother (William was sure, now, that that was her relation to the boy), who swatted him a little more soundly, but hissed instead of screaming.

Hers was a type that William was familiar with from his years at Marcus Garvey—severely retarded but able to survive without custodial care, destined for a life as a welfare mother as sure as God makes little green apples. A child abuser, most likely, and the mother of other welfare mothers yet to be. Usually, William regarded such a problem as a problem that the officials of state agencies should solve in some humane way that researchers had yet to discover. But here on the beach, with the first premonitory breezes of the evening floating in off the water, the pair of them seemed as beautiful in an elementary way as some Italian Madonna and child. They seem to have sprung up out of the landscape like the trees and bushes—a presence, and not a problem at all.

Barry returned from town in much-improved spirits, and soon afterward the van arrived and took them back to Barry's Buick and the known world. By the time they were back at the cabin, the sun had sunk behind the pine-crested ridge of the mountain, but there was still an hour of shadowy daylight left. William undertook to cook the steaks, but he didn't adjust the air vents properly and the charcoal went out. Barry insisted that was all right and that the steaks would be better blood rare than too well done. The meat was dutifully chewed and swallowed, all two and half pounds of it, and then William, unable to take any more, asked Barry if he'd mind leaving that night. "The thing is, I've got a girlfriend coming over. And the cabin just doesn't allow any privacy, you know what I mean?" Barry was obviously miffed, but he also seemed relieved to be clearing out.

As soon as the taillights of the Buick had been assimilated by the darkness of Pine Kill Road, William went down to the stream and, kneeling on a flat mossy rock, touched the skin of the water. Quietly, with no intention of waking her, but as one may touch the neck or shoulder of a sleeping spouse, simply for the pleasure of that near presence.

"I'm sorry," he whispered. "It wasn't my fault. I couldn't come to you while he was here. He'd have thought I was crazy."

He hoped she could hear him. He hoped he could be forgiven. But the water rippling through his fingers offered no reassurance.

He went to bed as soon as it was dark, and lay awake, like a child being punished, staring at the raftered ceiling. The day with Barry kept replaying in his mind, keeping him from sleep—and keeping him from Nixie, for it was usually only after his first dreaming sleep that he would rise and go to her. Was it a form of somnambulism then? Could she summon him only when he was in a trance? That would explain why he could remember so little of their conversations now, and nothing at all of the ecstasies he had known in her embrace, nothing but that there had been, at such moments, consummations that a Saint Theresa might have envied.

He slept, but sleep brought no dreams, and he woke just before dawn to the bland, unintelligible purling of the stream. It was like waking to find, instead of one's beloved, her unhollowed pillow beside one in the bed. He felt betrayed, and yet he knew the first betrayal had been his.

What did she want? His tears? His blood? She could name any price, any punishment, as long as she let him be near her again, to hear her again when she called his name, *William, dear William, come to my bed, come rest your head beside mine*.

He was made to pay the penalty of her silence for most of July, and grew resigned to the idea that she might never return to him. To have known such joys once was cause for lifelong gratitude—but to suppose himself *entitled* to them? As well ask to be anointed King of England.

The ordinary splendors of the summer remained open to him. Where the laurels had bloomed, blueberries now were ripening. Cardinals and nuthatches offered their daily examples of how good weather could best be enjoyed, as they darted back and forth from his feeder, skimming the stream, living it up, taking no thought for the morrow—or for next year's lesson plans on such suggested topics as Problems of Family Life or the Perils of Drug Abuse. No wristwatch, no calendar, no mealtimes or bedtimes, no tasks to finish, no friends to remember, no books to read. He had three classical music cassettes—one symphony each by Bruckner, Mahler, and Sibelius—that he listened to over and over at night inside the cabin, while a single log burned in the fireplace. He learned to float through his days and nights the way he would have in a dream.

And then, as the blueberries peaked and the huckleberries followed close behind, she spoke to him again. Not in the same voice now, however. It was the alto who, in a tone of maternal reproach, addressed him: "William, you have been too long away. Come here—explain yourself."

"Nixie!" he cried, pushing himself up from the wicker chair in which he had fallen asleep. "Goddess! Forgive me—my cousin was here—I couldn't come to you. Yet I should have, I see that now. I didn't understand, I—"

"Stop babbling, William." She spoke sternly, but with a kind of humor, even indulgence, that set his hopes leaping like gazelles.

"Nixie, you've returned. I always knew you would return. I always—"

"Is your ear so poorly tuned to our speech, William, that you cannot tell my sister's voice from mine? I am Nereis. Nixie has gone elsewhere, and she will *not* return."

"But *you* will let me worship you? And lie beside you? Do you want money, too? I'll give you all I have. Anything."

"I want only you, William. Come, enter me. Let me touch your cheeks, which Nixie has told me are so soft and warm."

He stumbled through the darkened cabin and down the flagstone steps to the stream. There he paused to remove his clothes. Then, his heart in a flutter, his legs trembling, he splashed through the water to where he used to lie with Nixie.

But as he reached that spot, Nereis spoke out loudly: "Not there! Summer has wasted us, it is too shallow there. See where that larger boulder lies, where the moon has broken through: come to me there."

He made his way toward that further boulder with, it seemed, enchanted ease, placing his feet as firmly as if he'd been wearing his Tingley boots, as confident as a bridegroom marching to the altar.

She received him not as Nixie would have, with a single, singeing blast of joy; it was rather, with Nereis, a sinking inward, a swooning away, a long slow descent into the whirlpool of an ineffable comfort. When she had wholly absorbed him, when her watery warmth was spread across his face like the tears of a lifetime all suddenly released, he knew that she had taken him into her womb and that he had become hers, hers utterly and for all time.

In the morning he awoke atop the boulder she had led him to, his body bruised, his knees and feet still bleeding. A low mist hung over the stream, as though she had veiled herself. He groaned, like a shanghaied sailor, a bag of sexual garbage dumped in the gutter and waiting for collection. *No more*, he told himself. *No more visions.* It was all very well for William Blake to be at home to spirits: his dealings had been with angels, not with water nymphs. Clearly, Nereids had behavioral traits in common with their cousins, the mermaids. Clearly, a man who continued to answer to their solicitations would be lured to his destruction. Clearly, he must pack up his things and leave the cabin before nightfall, before she called him to her again.

Again: the word, the hope of it, was honey and he the fly happily mired in its fatal sweetness.

I will be more careful, he told himself, as he wound gauze about his lower legs. Then, in earnest of this new self-preserving attitude, he made himself a breakfast of oatmeal and sardines. It tasted, to his ravished tongue, like ambrosia.

The sun swung across the sky like the slowest of pendulums, and the shadow of the cabin's roof-tree touched, sundiallike, the nearer shore of the kill. Four o'clock already, and then, as it touched the farther shore, five. As the shadows lengthened, the birds became livelier and more contentious. The nuthatches stropped their beaks on the bark of the trees and made skirmishes against the chickadees, who panicked but kept returning to the feeder, emblems of the victory of appetite.

The colors of the kill shifted from a lighter to a darker green. Where the shadows were deepest he could glimpse the first restless stirrings of her torso, the undulations of gigantic limbs. How long the days are in July. How caressing the sound of rippling water.

Once, in the summer before his junior year at Wesleyan, William had worked in the violent ward of a psychiatric hospital. He'd been premed then and planned to become a psychiatrist. Three months of daily contact with the patients had convinced him, first, that he must find some other career, and second, that there was no such thing as insanity, only the decision, which anyone might make, to act insanely—that is, to follow one's whims and impulses wherever they might lead. By the time they'd led to the violent ward, one had become a career patient, as others were career criminals, and for similar reasons, the chief of which was a preference for institutional life. Only by behaving as a lunatic would one be allowed to live in the eternal kindergarten of the hospital, exempt from work, freed of irksome family ties, one's bloodstream the playground for chemicals available only to the certifiably insane. Those who chose to live such a feckless life were not to be pitied when their grimaces of lunacy froze into masks that could not be removed.

And so it was that when she arose and came to him, at dusk, the water running in trickles down her dark legs, shimmering iridescently across the taut curves of the pea-green swimsuit, he did not resist. He did not tell himself, as she unknotted him from the net hammock to which he'd bound himself, like some hick Ulysses, that this was impossible, could not be happening, et cetera. For he had yielded long since to the possibility—and it was happening now.

"Come," she bade him, "follow me." And the smile that she smiled was like a door.

He opened the door and entered the mountain.

His body was never recovered, but the boots were discovered, where he'd left them, beneath a ledge of limestone close by the source of the kill.

RUTH ROSTON

Secretly

Ruth Roston was born in Elgin, Illinois, but says she was born again when, at age fifty-three, she took classes in the writing of poetry at the University of Minnesota. Now her poems have appeared in various magazines and anthologies, she has published a collection of her work titled *I Live in The Watchmaker's Town*, and *she* teaches the poetry classes.

"Secretly" comes from *Pandora* magazine, Spring 1988.

—T. W.

SECRETLY

Ruth Roston

Secretly I loved the giants
fee-fo-fuming their way
through fairy tales—great
bumblers they were, falling
down beanstalks, never quite
right in the head, never a match
for the gutsy tailor or the boy
with a slingshot.

Consider the giant—
put yourself in his place.

You're tall as a house,
can't take a step without
flattening a field, toppling
a barn. Who can you talk to?
Never a voice—just roars
and grunts of the giants
you battle. No conversation,
no style.

By the end of the day
it's comfort you want, a good fire,
bags of silver to count.
What you need is a snooze
after dinner, your harp
to play you to sleep.
Ah harp that sings of Time
before time, songs of your race,
the Titans.

You dream that nothing can touch
this room, this castle.
When a visitor comes, all sweaty
with climbing, he's too stringy
to eat, too stupid to talk to.
The beanstalk shakes with your rage
and you can't fall asleep
for hours.

TANITH LEE

The Devil's Rose

Tanith Lee has been creating memorable fiction for some time now, with haunting novels like *The Birthgrave, The Silver Metal Lover*, and many others, as well as with a number of brilliantly effective short stories. She is a master at creating a strong sense of time, whether the period is the impeccably researched French Revolution or the brilliantly imagined bleak far future. "The Devil's Rose" is about a young girl in an unnamed but very believable Central European country in the nineteenth century who dreams of love, is seduced by legend, and succumbs to a mysterious stranger.

—E. D.

THE DEVIL'S ROSE

Tanith Lee

O Rose, thou art sick!
The invisible worm
That flies in the night,
In the howling storm

Has sought out thy bed
Of crimson joy:
And his dark secret love
Does thy life destroy.

—*William Blake*

Because of a snowdrift on the line, the train pulled to an unscheduled stop at the little town of L——. Presently we passengers had debarked, and stood stamping and chafing our hands about the stove in the station house. It was nearly midnight, but the stationmaster's charitable housekeeper came almost at once with steaming coffee and a bottle of spirits. A boy was also roused and sent running, apparently to wake all the town on our behalf for lodgings. We should not be able to go on for three or four days, even that depending on whether or not fresh snow were to come down. Since we had entered the great pine forests outside Archaroy, we had been seeing wolves. They were thick on the ground that winter, and in the little villages and towns, we were to hear, not a carriage or sledge could go out but it would have wolf packs running after it for mile on mile, until the lights of human habitation came again in sight.

"What a prospect!" exclaimed the estate manager who had shared my compartment from Archaroy. "Besieged in the back of beyond by weather and wolves. Do you think, Mhikal Mhikalson, we shall ever get out?"

I said that we might, in the spring, perhaps, if not this year's, then next. But in fact, being my own creature, such unprecedented quirks of venture as this one neither dismayed nor displeased me. I had no family either behind or at journey's end to be impatient or in fear for me. My

90

friends were used to my eccentricities and would look for me to arrive
only when I did so. Additionally, in this instance, my destination was
not one I hankered for. The manager, however, who had business dealings
up ahead, was turning fractious. On the pretense of the errand for lodgings, I walked out of that hot room and went into the town of L——,
to see what, as the isolated clocks of midnight struck, it might offer me.

It was a truly provincial backwater, such as you would expect, although
the streets were mostly lit, and efforts had been made to clear the snow.
There was an old marketplace with a bell tower, and close by some public
gardens with tall locked gates. The houses of the prosperous ascended a
hill, and those of the not so prosperous slunk down it. Some boulevards
with shops all shut finished the prospect.

On a rise behind the rest was an old stuccoed house which I noticed
for something Italianate in its outline, but mostly through one unprov-
incial lemon-yellow window burning brightly there. What poet or scholar
worked late in that room when all the town slept? Something in me,
which would have done the same if so placed, sent a salutation up to
him.

After looking at the house, I made my way—perversely?—downhill,
observing the degeneration of all the premises. The lower town fell into
what might once have been the bed of some primeval river, which had
carved out a bottom for itself before sinking away into the past. Over
the area, the narrow streets sprawled and intertwined; it would be easy
to be lost there, but for the constant marker of the hill hanging always
above.

Needless to say, the snow had here been churned and frozen in mud
heaps, and the going was heavy. I was growing jaded, when, between
some boarded stables and a parade of the poorest houses, I discovered an
ancient church. It was of the kind you sometimes see even in the cities,
crammed between newer buildings that seem to want to press the life
from it and close together in its default. A hooded well stood on the
snow and the cobbles near the church door which, as may still happen
in the provinces, was unlocked.

The church intrigued me, perhaps only as the house had done with
its window, for I sensed some life going on there. It was not an area for
the wise to loiter; who knew what rough or other might not come from
his hovel to demand money, or try by force to take it. Nevertheless
something kept me there, and I was on the point of going nearer, when
lo and behold the massive church door parted a crack. Out into the
moonlight, which was now laving snow and town alike, slipped the
slender, unmistakable form of a woman. It was the season when men go
about garbed like bears, and she too was of course wrapped against the

cold, her head mantled with a dark shawl. I recognized in her at once, even so, the thing I had sensed, the meaning of the church's "life," or at least a portion of it. I wondered what she would do, confronted by a stranger. In these small towns mostly anyone of any consequence knows all the others. If an alien, and a man, accosted her, what then? Yet had she not put herself, alone and after midnight, into the perfect position for such an overture?

"Excuse me, young woman," I said, as she came along the slope.

She started, quite violently. It was so very lustrous, the moon inflaming the snow, that to tell a shadow from shadows was not easy. Perhaps I had seemed to step from thin air itself.

She was so apparently startled I wondered if there were a chance I should now take her arm to steady her, tilting our faces to the moon as I did so, that she might see me, and I her. But she had already composed herself.

"What is it?" she said in a low and urgent voice.

"The hour is very late. I wondered if you were in some difficulty. Might I assist you?"

"No, no," she muttered. Rather than reveal herself, she snatched her shawl about her face with her gloved hands.

"I am a stranger to your town," I said. "Forgive my impetuosity in speaking to you."

"How are you here?" she said. She stood like a child who is being verbally chastised by the schoolmaster, longing to break free into the yard where the other children are.

"How else but the train? We are snowbound, it appears."

But who would be those other children, her companions, from whom I kept her?

Just then, far away over the edge of the town as if over a high cliff out at sea, I heard the howling of a wolf. The hair rose on my neck as it always does at the sound. The cry was too apt, it came too nicely on my cue.

But at that moment she turned up her face, as if straining to listen, and I saw her features, and her eyes.

Although the shawl hid everything but a trace of her hair, I judged it to be very dark. And her face was very white, and her eyes were so pale in that pale face they were like glass on the snow. Her mouth, in the shadow-shining moonlight, seemed dark also, damson-colored, but the lips beautifully shaped. It was not a beautiful face, but rather an almost classical one.

"Is it safe for you to go about like this, in such weather?" I said. "Have you never heard of starving wolves running into the streets?"

"It has been known," she said. Her eyes, now they had met mine, did not leave me.

"Let me," I said, "escort you wherever you are going."

"Up there," she said, "to the Italian House. But you are a stranger—"

"No, I have seen the very house. With a light burning."

"For me," she said, "my beacon."

"Will you take my arm?" I said. "Where the snow has been left lying the way is slippery."

She came with a swift half-furtive step, and put her black silk paw into my arm. She leaned close to me as we began to walk.

I would have liked to ask her at once what she had been doing, there in the old church, to give such an intensity to the night. Even the lamp in her room—the room of the beacon—had blazed with it. But I did not feel it was the time yet, to ask her that. In fact we said very little, but walked together familiarly up through the town. She assured me it was not a vast distance. I said I was sorry. She did not then flirt with me, or move away. She shivered, and when I drew her hand more securely into my arm, against me, she murmured obliquely, "It is so easy to misinterpret kindness."

"Mine in going with you, or your own in permitting me to do so?"

Then she did not answer, and we went on again in silence. All the way, we passed not a soul, but once heard a dog snarling behind a gate after wolves or the moon. Soon enough we came onto the part of the rise which ended in her house. The high walls along the street provided cover for our approach. The light still burned before us, now a huge tawdry topaz. It looked warm, but not inviting. A blind masked that upper room from curious eyes attracted to its glow.

At the foot of some steps she detached herself from me. Feeling the cold after the warmth of me, she put her hands up to her face again. Her pale eyes were steady with their question.

"As I told you, I am marooned here a day or so. May I call on you tomorrow?"

"My parents are dead. I live with my aunt. My father's sister, she is old. . . . Do please call, if you wish. But—" She left a long pause, to see if I could read her thoughts. I could.

"You do not wish me to say I met you at midnight by the church."

"No, I do not."

She had given me by then her family name. I said, "As it happens, Miss Lindensouth, I know some distant relations of yours, some Linden-souths, in Archaroy. Or, at any rate, I believe they may be related to you and your aunt. It will give me an excuse to look her up."

This was a lie. If she guessed, she did not seem alarmed. Her face was without an expression of any sort. She lowered her eyes and left me suddenly, running up the icy stair with a carelessness that saved her rather than put her in the way of an accident.

I waited, briefly, across the street, to see what would happen with the light, or even if her silhouette might pass across it. But the lamp might have shone in another world mysteriously penetrating this one. Nothing disturbed it, and it did not go out.

When I reached the station house I found the party had gone off to the inn I had seen on my perambulations. Accordingly, I took myself there.

At about six o'clock in the morning the town of L—— began to come to life. By ten o'clock, when I returned to the church, the lower streets were seething. On every corner were the expected braziers of smoking red charcoal; lamps burned now in countless windows against the leaden light of morning. Having negotiated the slop collectors, the carts of cabbage, and the carriage horses of some local charioteer, I gained the appropriate street, and found this scene was also changed. The well was a gossiping spot for women, who stood there in their scarves and fur hats arguing the price of butter. A wood seller was delivering farther down, and children played in the snow with little cold-bitten faces, grimly intent on their miserable game.

The church itself was active. The door stood open, and two women in black veils came out. It was plainly an hour also for business, here.

I went forward diffidently, prepared to depart again at once, but on entering the church, found it was after all now empty.

It was like the inside of a hollowed boulder, carved bare, with the half egg shell of the dome rising above. The shrine looked decently furnished, you could say no more for it. Everything that was anything was plate. A few icons were on the screen below. I paused to glance at them; they were Byzantine in influence, but rather crude, not a form I am much drawn to.

As I was turning away, a man approached me. I had not seen him either present or entering, but probably he had slipped out from some inner place. He was about forty and had the scholars' look, a high broad forehead gaining ground, and a ledge of brows and gold-rimmed spectacles beneath.

"You are one of our trapped travelers!" he cried.

My heart sank. "Just so."

He gave me a name and a gloved hand. I took, and relinquished, both.

"You are interested in churches?" His manner was quietly eager.

With caution I replied, "There is something I am a little curious about—"

"Ah," he broke in immediately, "that will be the famous window, I think."

What could I say?

"Indeed."

"Come, I will show you."

He took me into a side arm of the church, where it was very dark. Some candles burned, but then I saw shards of red, green, and mauve thrown on the plastered wall.

My scholar brought me to his prize, and directed me where to look, and unless I had been blind, I could not have missed it.

The window, small and round-headed, was like an afterthought, or perhaps, (as he presently informed me) it might belong to an earlier chapel, being then the oldest thing there.

The glass itself was very old, and gave a rich heavy light. Its subject was the Garden of Eden, its color mostly of emerald, blue, and purple. Distantly the white figures of the sinners stood beneath their green apple tree, the fatal fruit in hand. They were about to eat, and God about to say to them, like every injured parent, I gave you everything! Why could you not remain as children forever? Why is it necessary that you grow up? His coming storm was indicated by the darkling sapphires of the shadows, the thunder wing of purple on the grass. But in the foreground was a rose tree, and among the wine-colored flowers, the serpent coiled itself, its commission seen to.

"Most unusual, such a treatment," said the scholar.

How was it that I knew so well that she, my Miss Lindensouth, had been frozen before this window, had come out from its contemplation as if her pale skin were steeped in the transparent dyes.

"Yes?"

He quoted a supposed date of the twelfth century.

"And of course it had a name, a window like this. Probably you know it? No? Well, it has been called 'Satan's RoseBush,' in church records even, for two hundred years. Or they say simply, secretively, 'The Devil's Rose.' And there are all sorts of stories, to do with curses and wonders and the rest of it. The best known is the story of the 'Girl Who Danced.' You will know that one."

"I am afraid not."

"How splendid. Now I have all the pleasure of telling you. You see, supposedly, if you look long enough and hard enough at the glass, here, by the rose tree, you find another figure in the window. It is one of those freak things, the way in which angles and colors go together randomly forms another shape—or perhaps the maker of the window intended it to happen. The figure is of a dark man, Satan himself, naturally, who took a serpent's appearance to seduce Eve to wrongdoing. I must say I have looked diligently at the window quite often, but I have never been able to make it out. I am assured it is there, however. The last priest himself could see it, and even attempted to describe it for me on the glass—but it was no good. My eyes, perhaps. . . . You try yourself. See, it is here and here, alongside the roses."

Staring where he showed me, I, like the scholar, could make out nothing. I knew of course that this had not been the case with the girl.

"And the story?"

"A hundred years ago, the tale has it, one of the great landowning families had one young fair daughter. She was noted as wonderfully vivacious, and how she loved to dance all night at all the balls in the area—for in those days, you understand, sleepy L—— was quite a thriving, bustling town. Well, it would seem she visited the church and saw the window, and saw the figure of Satan. She found him handsome, and, in the way of some young girl she—do hope you are broad-minded—she fell in love with him, with the Devil himself. And she made some vow, something adolescent and messy, with blood and such things. She invited him to come in that form and claim her for a dance. And when the next ball was held, about one in the morning, a great silence fell on the house. The orchestra musicians found their hands would not move, the dancers found their feet likewise seemed turned to stone. Then the doors blew open in a gust of wind. Every light in every chandelier went out—and yet there was plenty of light, even so, to see by: it was the light of Hell, shining into the ballroom. Then a dark figure, a tall dark man, entered the room. He had come as she requested, to claim his dance. It seems he brought his own orchestra with him. They were masked, everyone of them, but sitting down by the dance floor they struck up such a waltz that no one who heard it could resist its rhythm—and yet not one in the room could move! Then he came to the landowner's daughter and bowed and asked her for the honor of partnering her. And she alone of all the company was freed from the spell. She glided into his arms. He drew her away. They turned and whirled like a thing of fire, while all the rest of the room danced in their bones to the music, unable to dance in any other way, until all their shoes, and the white dresses of the women, and the fine evening clothes of the gentlemen, were dappled inside with their blood! How gruesome!" the scholar cried. He beamed on me. "But presently the Devil dashed his partner away through the floor. They vanished, and the demon musicians vanished, although no other there was able to regain motion until the cocks crowed. As for the girl, they found her skin—her *skin*, mark you, solely that—some days later on a hill. It had been danced right off her skeleton. But on her face, such as there was of it, was fixed a grin of agonized joy."

He paused, grasping his hands together. He said presently, "You see, in my modest way, I employ these old stories. I am something of a writer . . ." As if that excused him.

But I too was smiling. I was thinking of the girl, but not the girl in the story. Miss Lindensouth's strangeness and her youth, the way we had met, and the hold I had instantly obtained.

"It is a fact, young girls do sometimes," he said, "embrace such morbid fantasies—the love of death, or the Dark Angel, the Devil. Myself, I have penned a vampire fiction on this theme—"

I looked at the window again, along the rose tree. Nothing was there, except a slight reflection, thrown from the candles, of my own height and dark clothing and hair. These were out of scale and therefore did not fit.

The scholar offered me a glass of tea, but I explained to him I was already late for one. I told him where, to see if this might mean anything to him. But he was living in the past. He bade me a cheery regretful farewell.

I rang the bell of the Italian House, and soon enough a maidservant ushered me in. The rooms inside were no longer remotely Italianate. They had been choked up with things, furniture, and tables of photographs of staring statue-people, bowls of petals, pianos with shut lids. The entire house-lid seemed shut. It smelled automatically, in the crumbling way an old book does.

The aunt received me presently in an upper parlor.

"Madam Lindensouth. How very kind of you. I bring you greetings from Archaroy, but the snow acted as Providence."

She was a stern, thin woman with a distinct look to her of the niece, the same long black brows, but these pale eyes were watery and near-sighted. She had frequent recourse to pince-nez. Her gown was proper, old-fashioned, and of good material. She wore lace mittens, too.

"And you are a Mr. Mhikalson. But we have not met."

"Until this moment."

I approached, raised a mitten, and bowed over it. Which made me remember the Devil in the story. I smiled, but had concealed it by the time I lifted my head. She was gratified, she made no bones about that. She offered me a chair and rang for the samovar. I told her of her invented cousins in the city, concocting anecdotes, waiting for her to say, perhaps sharply, But I have never heard of these people. To which I must reply, But how odd, for they seem to have heard of you, Madam Lindensouth, and of your niece. Thereby introducing a careful error which would then make all well, confirming we were at cross-purposes, these Lindensouths were not her Lindensouths. And getting us, besides, to the notion of a niéce.

I wondered, too, how long it would be before that niece contrived to make an entrance. Had she not been listening on an upper landing for the twangle of the bell? Or had she given me up? I had not specified a time, but had come late for so eager a visitor.

Then the tea arrived, which Madam served up country fashion, very black, with a raspberry preserve. As we were drinking it, she still had not fathomed the cousins in Archaroy. She had simply accepted them, and we had begun to steer our conversation out upon the state of the weather, a proposed wolf hunt, literature, and the world in general.

Suddenly, however, the aunt lifted her head.

"Now that must be Mardya coming down. My niece, Mr. Mhikalson. You must meet her, she will want to question you about the city."

I felt a wave of relief—and of interest, having learned at last the phantom's familiar name.

I wondered how I should feel when she came in, but inevitably she had not the same personality *en famille* as she had had outside in the wolf-throated snow-night. Just then she had come from her trance before the window of the rose-snake. But now she had had all night to think of me, all morning pondering if I should come back.

She stole into the room. Nothing like her surefooted tread, both mercurial and wanton, of the night. She bore her hands folded on her waist before her, pearl drops in her nacre ears, her eyes fixed only on the aunt.

"Here is a gentleman from Archaroy," announced Madam. I did not correct her.

The girl Mardya dashed me off a glance. It hung scintillating in the overheated air after her eyes had once more fallen. It said, *You? You are here? You are real?*

"He has friends, Mardya, who claim to be related to us. It must be the fur connection, or perhaps the diamond connection." They were suspected of being in trade, that was it—but since she did not inquire it of me, I did not hazard. Traders, evidently, she did not pretend either to know or not to know. "Well, Mardya," she said.

Mardya inclined her head. Her hair was piled upon it, black and silken, not wholly tidy, and so revealing it was none of it false. Her cheeks were flushing now, paling again to a perfect paper-white. The earrings blinked. She was acting shy in the presence of her kin.

"Your aunt has kindly warned me," I said, "that you will want to know about the city. I must tell you at once, I am a frequenter of libraries. I read and do very little else." Behold, Madam, *I* am not in trade, but a beast of leisure and books.

Mardya, not speaking, stole on toward us. Taking the aunt's glass, she refilled it at the bubbling tea pitcher.

"But no doubt you ladies spend a great deal of time with books," I said. "The town is very quiet. Or is that only the disaster of winter?"

"Winter or summer. Such summers we have," said the aunt. "The heat is intolerable. My brother had a lodge up in the hills, but we have had to get rid of it. It is no use to *us*, it was a man's place. My niece, as you say, is something of a reader. And we have our sewing and our music."

"And do you, Miss Lindensouth," I said briskly, "never dance?"

She had given back the glass of tea, or I think she would have dropped it. Her whole slender shape locked rigid. Her white eyelids nailed down on her cheeks quivered and would not stop.

"I do not—I do not dance," she said—the first thing she *had* said, in this presence.

"But I heard such a strange little story today," I began to the aunt amiably. "A man I met this morning, an authority on your local legends—"

"Will you not have another glass of tea?" said Mardya.

"No, thank you, Miss Lindensouth. But I was saying, the story has to do with a certain window—"

"Do have another glass," said Mardya.

Her voice was hard with wrath, and her eyes were on me, full of tears. She expected betrayal. To have wounded her so easily gave me the anticipated little thrill. She was so vulnerable, one must protect her. She must be put behind the iron shield, defended.

"No, thank you so much. In fact I must tear myself away and leave you, Madam Lindensouth, in peace." I rose. "Except—I wonder if I might ask a great favor of you, Madam? Might I borrow your niece for half an hour?" The long brows went up, she adjusted the pince-nez. I smiled and said, "My sister has imposed the most wretched duty. I was to buy her a pair of gloves, and forgot in my haste of leaving. Now I shall arrive late besides, and probably will never be forgiven. But it occurred to me Miss Lindensouth, who has just those sort of hands, I see, that my sister has, might advise me. She might even do me the kindness of trying on the gloves, selecting a color. I find this sort of task most embarrassing. I have no idea of what to look for. Which, if I am honest, is why I forgot the transaction in the first place."

The aunt laughed, superior upon the failings of the fumbling male.

"Yes, go along with Mr. Mhikalson, Mardya, and assist him with these troublesome gloves. You may place my own order while you are doing so."

I bowed to her mitten once more. She sighed, and I caught the faint acidity of medicine on her breath.

"Perhaps, since you must remain here, you will dine with us tonight?" she said, with the grudging air that did not mask a lively curiosity she had begun to have about me.

"Why, Madam Lindensouth—to be sure of that I will go personally to shovel more snow onto the line."

She laughed heartily, and bade me get along. Her eyes of watery steel said, If I had been younger. And mine: Indeed, Madam, there can be no doubt. But I am too respectful now, and besides maybe I am in search of a wife, and you see what a fine coat this is, do you? But nevertheless, I know where the fount is, the sybil. We understand one another in the way no man finds it possible to understand or to be understood by any woman under forty, and surely you are not much more?

Down in the street, Mardya Lindensouth spoke to me in a strange cold hot voice.

"I trust you rested well."

"No. I could only lie there and think of seeing you again. I have thought of nothing else since our meeting."

"But something delayed you."

"Strategy. You saw how I have managed it. I am to dine."

She would not take my arm.

"There are no gloves," I said, "I have no sisters." I said, "Run her errand later. Where can we go?"

And all at once, in an arch in one of the old walls of the street, she was leaning her spine to a door, her hands on my breast. It was a daring situation, hidden, unfrequented, yet anyone might look from an upper floor, or come by and see.

I leaned against her until her back pressed the backs of my hands into the damp wood. She was, though I could only speculate how, no stranger to kisses. Presently, engorged and breathless, we pulled apart, and went on down the street. This time she took my arm.

We went to a patisserie along one of the boulevards. To my dismay, at one point, I saw three of my fellow travelers from the train, the estate manager among them, going by the window, hesitating at the door—and thank heaven passing on.

She did not eat anything, only sipped the scalding beverage, which was not so flavorsome as the samovar of Madam.

"I dreamed of you," she said, "all night. I was burning. I thought I should run out into the snow to get cool. But I should freeze there. You would come and find me and warm me in your arms. But you would never come back. I knew you at once."

"Who am I?"

"Hush. I do not want to say your name."

"Mardya, tell me about the church."

"You know everything about me."

"The window, Mardya."

"Not here . . ."

"No one can hear, you whisper so softly, and your warm breath brushes my cheek. Tell me about the window."

"It was quite sudden," she said. Artless, she added, "Two years ago, when I was fourteen."

"Well?"

"I saw it. The same way the girl does in the story. At first, I tried not to think of it. But I began to dream—how can I tell you those dreams?—they were so terrible. I thought my heart must stop, I should die—I longed for them and I feared them."

"Pleasure."

"Such—such pleasure. I tried not to know. But it has been all I could think of. There is nothing here—in the town. I see no one. No one comes to her house but her friends, the Inspector of Works, the banker—everyone is old, and I am old too when I sit with them. I become like them. My hands get so stiff and my neck and my eyes ache and ache. I have nothing to live for. But now, you are here."

"Yes, I am here." I put my foot gently against hers under the tasseled tablecloth. Our knees almost touched, the fabric of her dress stirred against me. Her cheeks were inflamed now. All about us, human things went on with their chocolate, their tea and cake and sugar.

"Tonight she will have those two or three friends to dine with you. We will dine on chicken bones and aspic tarts. We have no money."

"Mardya, be quiet."

"I must tell you—"

"What? How to remain behind in the house after the others have left?" She caught her breath.

I said, "I remember the lamp burning and how you go about improperly at night, and I would imagine you have fooled her, she never knows. So you are clever in such matters. Shall I hide in some cupboard?"

"Not now. How can I speak of it? I shall faint."

"If you do that, we shall attract attention."

"Secretly then. When the darkness comes. In darkness."

"One candle, perhaps. You must let me look at you. I want to see all your whiteness."

"Hush," she said again. Her eyes swam, her hands pressed on the glass of tea as if to splinter it. "I have never—" she said.

"I know."

"You will—care for me?"

"You will see how I will care for you."

Neither of us could breathe particularly well. We burned with fever, our feet pressing and our hands grasping utensils of the tea table as if to save them in a storm. But she shook so that her earrings flashed, and she could hardly hold the tea glass anymore. I took it from her, and found it difficult in turn to let go of.

Presently, I settled our account, and we left the shop and went to another, where she ordered needles for her aunt.

I escorted her up through the town, the second time, past the smoking braziers and the lamplit nothingness of other people and other things. On the rise, in the same snow-bounded stone archway, I thrust her back and crushed her to me. Her hands clutched my coat, she struggled to hold me as if drowning. We parted, and went separate ways, to scheme and wait like wolves for the night.

The dinner party—for such it was to be—was to be also all I had predicted from the picture Mardya had painted.

The Inspector of Works was there, a blown man with an overblown face, and his wife, a stubborn mouse of a woman much given to a sniff, an old maid in wife's clothing. The elderly unmarried banker had also come, perhaps an ancient flame of Madam's. But we animals were of a proper number and gender, and progressed two by two.

Madam Lindensouth came to dinner in a worn black velvet gown and carbuncle locket. When Mardya entered there was some life stirred up, even in the banker. She had on a dress the color of pale fire, between soft red and softer gold, with her white throat and arms exposed. Madam did not bat an eyelash, so clearly she had not been above suggesting a choice of finery. Mardya was self-conscious, radiant. She flirted with the banker and the Inspector in a way, patently, they had never before experienced, the delicious clumsy coquettishness of an innocent and charming young girl. Only with me was she very cool and restrained. Yet as we came to the table, she did remark, "Oh, Mr. Mhikalson, I have been worrying about it. Those gloves in that particular shade of fawn. Are you quite sure that your sister will be content?"

Her daring pleased me. I said, unruffled, "I thought they were more of a yellow tone. The very thing. But then, I told you, I have no judgment in such matters."

All this required an explanation, that Miss Lindensouth had been in the town with me buying handwear for my relative. A knowing look passed between the banker and the Inspector's mouse.

Presumably not one of them had heard the latest news of my train. There had been a message at the inn on my return there. The line was expected after all to be clear by four the next morning. The train would depart one hour after, at five o'clock. Of course, I might be prepared to miss it. They might assume I would have no more pressing engagement than a wooing, now I was so evidently embarked.

All through the dessicated dinner, my fellow guests tried to wring from me, on Madam's behalf, the story of my life, my connections, my prospects. I remained cordially reticent, but here and there let fall a word for myself. I am a good liar, inventive and consistent, and quite enjoyed this part of the proceedings. As for the meal, it was a terrible event. There was not a drop of moisture in any of it, and the wine, though wet, was fit only for just such a table, and in short supply besides.

After we had dined, the ladies permitted the men to smoke, by withdrawing.

The banker lit up and coughed prodigiously.

"These winters," said he, "will be my death."

To me he added, "How I yearn for the city. I have not been in Archaroy, let alone anywhere else, since my thirty-fifth year. Is that not a fearsome admission? Finance has been my life. I still dabble. If you were to be seeking any advice, Mr. Mhikalson—"

The Inspector broke in with a merry, "Never trust this rogue. He is still in half the deals and plots of the town. But I must say, if you were thinking of remaining a week or so, there are some horses I think you should look at, with an eye to the summer. My cousin Osseb is quite an authority. Did you know it is possible to hunt wolf here all the year round? Well, there you are. Of course, Madam Lindensouth's brother, the father of Miss, had a lodge in the forest. But that was sold."

"But you are not to think," put in the banker, giving him an admonishing glance, "that the family fortune here is on the decline. Not a bit of it. I will say, my dear friend Madam is something on the careful side, but there is quite an amount stashed away . . ."

"Tut tut," said the Inspector. "Can the ladies have no secrets?"

Finally we had smoked sufficiently, and went into the next room, where Madam regaled us all with some music from the piano, which, startled to find its lid had been raised, uttered a great many wrong notes.

Mardya would not play. She said that she had a chilblain on her finger. This evoked three remedies given at once by the mouse, the banker, and the Inspector. In each case, suffering the chilblain would have been preferable.

A card game then ensued, out of which Mardya pardoned herself, and I was left also to my own devices, being besides pushed to them by smiles and nods. I joined the girl by the piano, where she was searching among the sheet music for an old tune her father had used to play.

"Come now," I said, speaking low, "how is it to be managed?"

"Impossible," she said.

"Think of our stop on the hill."

She blushed deeply, but continued to leaf through the music.

"I am afraid."

"No. You are not afraid."

"The ace!" cried the banker. He added to us, over his shoulder, not having heard a word, "Now, now."

"Think of the apple tree," I said to her, "think of the rose."

Her hands fluttered, some of the music spilled. Her pulse raced in her throat so swiftly it looked dangerous. We bent to retrieve the music.

"Leave before the others." She spoke crisply now though scarcely above a whisper. "I will go down and open the door. Return almost at once and go into the side parlor below. The blinds are down, there is a large table with a lamp on it that is never lit. You must be patient then. Wait until the house is quiet. Wait until the clock in the hallway strikes eleven."

"Where is your room?"

She told me. She was shivering, from desire or fear, or both.

We had regained the music and arranged it together by the piano.

"There is the song my father used to play," she said. But she did not play it.

It was almost thirty minutes past nine, and I suspected the festivity would be curtailed sharp at ten o'clock. After the banker had told us again to "Now, now," and the maidservant had brought in the trusty samovar and some opaque sherry, the card game lapsed. It was a quarter to ten.

"Madam Lindensouth," I said, "I must return at once to the inn. I had not realized how late it has grown. There are some arrangements I shall need to make." I left a studied pause. She would deduce I meant to give up my seat on the train. "Thank you for your kindness and hospitality."

"If it chances you are still here tomorrow," she said. (The banker and the Inspector laughed, and the mouse primly sniffled.) "We take luncheon at three o'clock. I hope you will feel able to join us."

At the concept of another meal of sawdust and pasted aspics I almost laughed myself. Something in her eyes checked me. In holding out to me the branch of unity with her niece, a girl therefore about to taste the chance Madam had missed, there was a sudden ragged edge to her, a malevolence, which showed in a darkening of her pallid eyes, the iron smile with which she strove to underpin propriety. It was clear from this that a callous and unkind method would have sustained her treatment of Mardya from the beginning. She had never been a friend to her and never would be. Small wonder the savage innocent turned to shadows for her fata morgana of release and love. It even seemed probable in those moments that the aunt had known all along of midnight excursions to a church on the lower streets, of a flirtation with grisly legends and unsafety. Did the woman know even that this was where Mardya had met me? Did she know what plan we had ("Now, now') to meet in the night on the shores of lust, under her very roof? Yes, for a moment I beheld before me a coconspirator.

When I took her hand, she said, "Why, your hands are cold tonight, Mr. Mhikalson. You must have a care of yourself."

I uttered my farewells, got down through the house, and was shown out into the darkness and the snow.

I went down the steps, and waited where I had done so the first night, across the way, taking no particular pains over concealment.

That light was not burning in the upper—her—room. The window was sightless, eyeless, and waiting, too. Before midnight, I should have seen the inside of that room, should have touched its objects and ornaments, invaded the air with my breath and will, my personality, perhaps a stifled cry, the heat of my sweat. I should have possessed that room, before the morning came. I did not need to see its light, now.

After about six or seven minutes, I went back. If I met anyone on the steps or in the doorway, I should say I had lost something and returned hoping it was in the house. But I met no one.

The front door was ajar, and I passed through silently, shutting it again. A muffled bickering came from above, from the dinner party.

The side parlor was as she had described, to the right of the hall, remote from the stair. It was in blackness, the table dimly shining like a pool of black water, and the unlit lamp upon it reflected vaguely, and here and there some glistening surface. I went through and seated myself on an upright chair against the wall, facing the doorway. Naturally I was quite concealed, by night, by the shapes of the furniture, best of all by being where of course I could not reasonably be.

Like the audience in the darkened theater, then, I stayed. And down the dully lighted stair they passed in due course to the hall, the banker, and the Inspector and his mouse-wife. The maid arrived with hats and sticks, and Madam waved them off from the vantage of the staircase, not descending.

All sound died away then, gradually, above. And lastly the maid came drifting along across the open door, like a ghost, to take away the final guttering lamp. Partly I was amazed she did not catch the flash of my eyes from the black interior, the eyes of the wolf in the thicket. But she did not. No one came to bother me, to make me say how I had left behind a glove, or a cigarette case, or had felt faint suddenly in the cold, and come back to find the door was open—and sat here to wait for the maid and fallen asleep. No, none of that was necessary.

At last, the clock chimed in the hall, eleven times.

Rising from my seat, I stretched myself. I walked softly from concealment to the foot of the staircase. Hardly a noise anywhere. Only the ticking of the clock, the sighing of the house itself. Beyond its carapace, snow-silence on the town of L——, and far away, so quiet were all things now, the tinny *tink-tink* of another clock finding the hour of eleven on a slightly different plane of time than that of the Italian House.

I started to go up the stairs. The treads were dumb. I climbed them all, passing the avenues of passages, and came to a landing and a heavy curtain with a mothball fringe. And then, in an utter darkness, without even the starlit snow-light of the windows, her door, also standing ready for me, ajar.

I closed it with care behind me. The room was illumined only by the aqueous snow sheen on the blind. This made a translucent mark, like ice, in turn upon the opposite wall, and between was a floating unreality, with a core of paleness.

"Ssh," she whispered, though I had not made a sound.

I went toward her and found her by the whiteness of her nightgown on the bed. The room was all bed. It could have no other objects or adornment.

Her hands were on my face, her arms were about my neck.

"Where is the candle?" I said. "Let me see you, Mardya."

"No," she pleaded. "Not yet . . ."

My vision was, anyway, full-fed on the dark. I was beginning to see her very well.

The little buttons of her nightgown irritated my fingers, to fiddle with them almost made me sick. I lifted my face from her burning face, kissing her eyes, her lips. I pulled the nightgown up in a single movement and laid her bare in the winter water of the light, the slender girlish legs folded to a shadow at the groin, the pearl of the belly, the small waist with its trinket of starlight, and the rib cage with the two cupped breasts above it, and the nipples just hiding still in the frills of the nightgown—she was laughing noiselessly and half afraid, shuddering, pushing the heavy folds from her chin, letting them lie across her shoulders and throat as I bent to her. My hands were full of her body and my mouth full of her taste. The mass of black hair stained across the pillows, shawled over her face, got into my mouth.

I threw off my coat, what I could be rid of quickly. Her skin, where it came against my skin, was cool, though her lips, ears, and forehead blazed, and the pits of her arms were also full of heat, and her hands, their hotness stopping mysteriously at the wrists. She was already dewy when my fingers sought between the fleshy folds of the rose. "No," she said. She rubbed herself against me, arching her back, shaken through every inch of her. "No—no—"

"This will hurt you."

"Hurt me," she said, "I am yours. I belong to you."

So I broke into her, and she whined and lay for a moment like a rabbit wounded in a trap under my convulsive thrusts no longer to be considered, but at the last moment, she too thrust herself up against me, crucified, with a long silent scream, a whistling of outdrawn breath, and I felt the cataclysm shake her to pieces as I was dying on her breast.

"I knew you would come to me," she murmured. "I knew it must happen. I called out to you and you heard me. Across miles of night and snow and stone.

"Sometimes," she said, "I have seen you in a dream. Never clearly. But your eyes and your hair.

"Are you the one?" she said. "Are you my love? For always?"

"Always," I said, "how else?"

"And my death," she said. "Love is death. Kill me again," she said, but not in any mannered way, though it might have been some line from some modern stage drama.

So presently, leaning over her, I "killed' her again. This time I even pinned her arms to the bed in an enactment of violence and force. Her face in ecstasy was a mask of fire, a rose mask.

Afterward her eyes were hollow, like those of a street whore starving in the cold.

When I began to put on my clothes, she said, "Where are you going?"

"It will be best, I think. We might fall asleep. How would it look if the girl came in and found me here, in the frank morning light?"

"But you will come back tomorrow?"

"Your aunt has invited me to luncheon."

"You will be here? Will you be late?"

"Of course I shall be here, of course not late."

I kissed her, for the last time, with tenderness, seemliness. It was all spent now. I could afford to be respectful.

As I reached to open the door, she was lying like a creature of the sea stranded upon a beach. Her delicate legs might have been the slim bipart tail of a mergirl, and the tangle of nightgown and hair only the seaweed she had brought with her to remind her of the deep.

I went down again through the house with the same lack of difficulty, and as well, for I could have no decent story to explain my presence now.

As I let myself out of the front door, and descended the steps, the air cut coldly in the icy deserts before dawn. It was almost four o'clock, but I had seen to my luggage beforehand. I need only go along to the station and there wait for the train which, because the allotted hour was now both extempore and ungodly, would doubtless leave on time.

Two doctors attended me at the point of my destination, one the man I had arranged, a month previously, to see, the other a colleague of his, a specialist in the field. Both frowned upon me, the nonspecialist with the more compassion.

"From what you have said, I think you are not unaware of your condition."

"I had hoped to be proved wrong."

"I am afraid you are not wrong. The disease is in its primary phase. We will begin treatment at once. It is not very pleasant, as you understand, but the alternative less so. It will also take some time."

"And I believe," said the less sympathetic frowner, "You comprehend you can never be perfectly sanguine. There is, as such, no cure. I can promise to save your life, you have come to us in time. But marriage will be out of the question."

"Did I give you to suppose I intended marriage?"

"All relations," said this man, "are out of the question. This is what I am saying to you. The organisms of syphilis are readily transferable. You must abstain. Entirely. This is not what you, a young man, would wish to hear. But neither, I am sure, would you wish to inflict a terrible disease of this nature, involving deformity, insanity, and certain death where undiagnosed, on any woman for whom you cared. Indeed, I trust, upon any woman." He glared on me so long I felt obliged to congratulate his judgment.

The treatment began soon after in a narrow white room. It was, as they advised, unpleasant. The mercury, pumped through me like vitriol, induced me to scream, and after several repetitions I raved. One does not dwell on such matters. I bore it, and waited to escape the cage.

The ulcerous chancre, the nodulous sore, long-healed, which had first alerted me in Archaroy, has a name in the parlance of the streets. They call it there the Devil's Rose.

And in that way, Satan comes out of his window, unseen, and passes through the streets. All the lights go out as he dances with the girl who vowed herself to him. And in the morning they find her skin upon the hillside.

She died insane, I heard as much some years later in another city, from the lips of those who did not know I might have an interest.

The condition was never diagnosed. Probably she had never even been told of such things. They thought she had pined and grown sick and gone mad through a failed love affair, some stranger who entered her life, and also left it, by train.

She had always been of a morbid turn, Mardya Lindensouth, obsessed by dark fancies, bad things. Unrequited love had sent her to perdition. She was unrecognizable by the hour of her death. She died howling, her limbs twisted out of shape, her features decayed, a wretched travesty of human life.

Yes, that was what dreams of love had done for her, my little Mardya. Though in the streets they call it the Devil's Rose.

DANIEL M. PINKWATER

Wempires

Daniel M. Pinkwater is the author of many bizarre and wonderful books published as children's books but recommended to readers of any age, including *The Snarkout Boys and the Avocado of Death; Yobgorgle; Alan Mendelsohn, The Boy From Mars; Blue Moose; Young Adult Novel;* and *Lizard Music* (an ALA Notable Book.) Pinkwater has taught, trained puppies, and traveled across the world in a wide variety of vehicles. He and his wife live on a farm in upstate New York on which they keep an assortment of livestock, of which horses are the smallest.

—T. W.

WEMPIRES

Daniel Pinkwater

I saw a movie on TV one Saturday afternoon. It was about a vampire. What a good movie!

The vampire was scary. He was real smooth. I liked his clothes. I decided I would be a vampire. I asked my mother to help me make a vampire costume.

"But Halloween is three months away," she said.

"Just the same," I said, "I'd like you to help me make the costume. Please." Actually, she made the whole thing. It was very good.

I smeared my face with white stuff my mother uses at night, and I rubbed my hair with salad oil so it would be shiny and smooth. I used a little red lipstick. I looked good.

Then I waited in the hallway for my sister to come by.

It is fairly dark in the hallway.

It was a big success.

I turned up at supper in my vampire suit. Everybody thought it was cute. My father took pictures. Every time I looked at my sister she burst into tears. I practiced doing vampire moves and saying vampire things. The first problem came the next morning. They wouldn't let me wear my vampire suit to school.

"None of the other children go around wearing capes," my mother said.

"That's because they don't have any," I said.

"Look, you can't go to school dressed like a vampire."

"Why not?"

"Because I'm your mother, and I say you can't. You may put on your vampire suit when you come home."

"Could I sleep in a coffin, do you think?" I asked.

"This is getting weird," my mother said.

After school, I went to the dime store and got the one thing I really needed—fake plastic vampire teeth.

The next day my teacher sent a note home with me:

Dear Mrs. Harker,

Jonathan has been threatening to bite children in his class. I have asked him to leave his fangs at home. I hope you will have a little talk with him.

Yours truly,
Mildred Van Helsing
(Teacher)

My parents had a little talk with me. They said that they thought I would get tired of being a vampire. They said I could wear my cape and fangs and things around the house, but I was not to dress or act like a vampire at school.

I'll never get tired of being a vampire, I thought.

My parents also said that if I didn't cooperate, they would take steps.

"What steps would you take?" I asked.

"Steps," they said. "Just go to your room and think about it."

I went to my room and cut out bats. I hung them from the ceiling on pieces of thread. They looked pretty good.

That night, when I was sleeping, vampires came through the window. I woke up.

"Hallo, Sonnyboy!" the vampires said. "How's by you?"

"Wait a minute!" I said. "Are you guys vampires?"

"Wempires! That's us!"

"Real ones?"

"Of course real! What did you think, fake wempires?"

"And you can turn into bats?"

"Anytime we like."

"And you . . . uh . . . drink people's blood?"

"Phooey! What a disgusting idea! Where did you hear that?"

"Everybody knows that," I said.

"Phooey! From television you get such ideas. Drinking blood—yich!" said the vampires. "Now, for drinking, ginger ale is best. Maybe you have some ginger ale in the house?"

"There might be some in the icebox."

"And chicken. Chicken we eat."

"There might be some cold chicken."

"Cold chicken is good. Let's go down to the kitchen, Sonnyboy. Don't make noise and wake up the family."

The vampires followed me down the stairs to the kitchen. There was most of a cooked chicken in the icebox, and the vampires found two big bottles of ginger ale. They ate the chicken and drank a lot of ginger ale. Then they burped.

"Hey, Sonnyboy! Do you got any onions?" they asked. They opened cans of sardines, toasted slices of whole wheat bread, and made sardine-and-onion sandwiches.

When they had finished those, they poured cornflakes into bowls and sloshed milk over them.

The vampires were making a mess of the kitchen. They were having a good time. They sang a song.

"Sing the song with us, Sonnyboy!" the vampires said.

"I don't care for peaches. They are full of stones.

"I like bananas because they have no bones."

All of a sudden my mother was standing in the doorway. She was wearing her bathrobe.

"What's this? Vampires in my kitchen in the middle of the night?"

"Hallo, Sonnyboy's mother," the vampires said.

"There are crumbs everywhere," my mother said.

"We having a party," the vampires said.

"Out," my mother said.

"Out?" asked the vampires.

"Out now," my mother said.

"Well, good-bye, Sonnyboy," the vampires said. They climbed out the kitchen window.

"I didn't know they would mess up the kitchen," I said.

"Now do you see why your father and I didn't want you to behave like a vampire?" my mother said.

"They didn't mean any harm," I said.

"Go to your room."

I went to my room. I looked out my window. The vampires were making their way down the street. They waved to me.

"Good-bye, Sonnyboy! Be a good wempire!"

What neat guys! Nothing will ever change my mind about being a vampire.

GREG EGAN

Scatter My Ashes

Greg Egan has written a number of stories in a variety of genres and has been making a name for himself in the horror field. He's also written a hard SF novel, and persists in making a living in Australia by programming computers. "Scatter My Ashes" is about violence and responsibility. It more specifically focuses on civic and moral responsibility on both the societal and individual levels: about the individual's responsibility to respond to those in need and society's role, via media, in making violence a sideshow. This gritty, tough-minded story is also about the artist as voyeur.

—E. D.

SCATTER MY ASHES

Greg Egan

Every night, at exactly a quarter past three, something dreadful happens on the street outside out bedroom window. We peek through the curtains, yawning and shivering in the life-draining chill, and then we clamber back beneath the blankets without exchanging a word, to hug each other tightly and hope for sound sleep before it's time to rise.

Usually what we witness verges on the mundane. Drunken young men fighting, swaying about with outstretched knives, cursing incoherently. Robbery, bashings, rape. We wince to see such violence, but we can hardly be shocked or surprised any more, and we're never tempted to intervene: it's always far too cold, for a start! A single warm exhalation can coat the window pane with mist, transforming the most stomach-wrenching assault into a safely cryptic ballet for abstract blobs of light.

On some nights, though, when the shadows in the room are subtly wrong, when the familiar street looks like an abandoned film set, or a painting of itself perversely come to life, we are confronted by truly disturbing sights, oppressive apparitions which almost make us doubt we're awake, or, if awake, sane. I can't catalogue these visions, for most, mercifully, are blurred by morning, leaving only a vague uneasiness and a reluctance to be alone even in the brightest sunshine.

One image, though, has never faded.

In the middle of the road was a giant human skull. How big was it? Big enough for a child, perhaps six or seven years old, to stand trapped between the jaws, bracing them apart with outstretched arms and legs, trembling with the effort but somehow, miraculously, keeping the massive teeth from closing in.

As we watched I felt, strange as it may sound, inspired, uplifted, filled with hope by the sight of that tiny figure holding out against the blind, brutal creature of evil. Wouldn't we all like to think of innocence as a tangible force to be reckoned with? Despite all evidence to the contrary.

Then the four huge, blunt teeth against which the child was straining began to reform, tapering to needle-fine points. A drop of blood fell from

115

the back of each upraised hand. I cried out something, angry and horrified. But I didn't move.

A gash appeared in the back of the child's neck. Not a wound: a mouth, the child's new and special mouth, violently writhing, stretched open ever wider by four sharp, slender fangs growing in perfect mimicry of the larger fangs impaling the child's palms and feet.

The new mouth began to scream, at first a clumsy, choking sound, made without a tongue; but then a torn, bloody scrap of flesh appeared in place, the tongue of the old mouth uprooted and inverted, and the cries gave full voice to an intensity of suffering and fear that threatened to melt the glass of the window, sear away the walls of the room, and drag us into a pit of darkness where one final scream would echo forever.

When it was over, we climbed into bed and snuggled up together.

I dreamt that I found a jigsaw puzzle, hidden in a dark, lost corner of the house. The pieces were in a plain cardboard box, unaccompanied by any illustration of what the assembled puzzle portrayed. Wendy laughed and told me not to waste my time, but I sat frowning over it for an hour every evening, until after many weeks only a handful of pieces remained unplaced.

Somehow, even then, I didn't know what the picture was, but as I lazily filled in the very last gap, I felt a sudden overpowering conviction that whatever the jigsaw showed, *I did not want to see it.*

I woke a little before dawn. I kissed Wendy very softly, I gently stroked her shoulders and breasts with my fingertips. She rearranged herself, pulled a face, but didn't wake. I was about to brush her forehead with one hand, which I knew would make her open her eyes and give me a sleepy smile, when it occurred to me that if she did, there might be small, fanged mouths behind her eyelids.

When I woke again it was half past seven, and she was already up. I hate that, I hate waking in an empty bed. She was reading the paper as I sat down to breakfast.

"So, what's happening in the world?"

"A fifth child's gone missing."

"Shit. Don't they have any suspects yet? Any evidence, any clues?"

"A fisherman reported something floating on the lake. The police went out in a boat to have a look."

"And?"

"It turned out to be a calf foetus."

I gulped coffee. I hate the taste of coffee, and it sets my stomach squirming, but I simply have to drink it.

"It says police will be diving all day today, searching the lake."

"I might go out there, then. The lake looks fantastic in this weather."

"When I'm snug in my office with the heater on full blast, I'll think of you."

"Think of the divers. They'll have the worst of it."

"At least they know they'll get paid. You could spend the whole day there for nothing."

"I'd rather take my kind of risk than theirs."

Once she was gone, I cut out the article on the vanished child. The walls of my study are papered with newsprint, ragged grey odd-shaped pieces affixed only at their top corners, free to rustle when the door is opened or closed. Sometimes, when I'm sitting at my desk for a moment after I've switched off the lamp, I get a strong impression of diseased skin.

"Put them in a scrap book!" says Wendy, whenever she ventures in to grimace at the state of the room. "Or better still, put them in a filing cabinet and see if you can lose the key!" But I need to keep them this way, I need to see them all at once, spread out before me like a satellite photograph, an aerial view of this age of violence. I'm looking for a pattern. My gaze darts from headline to headline, from STRANGLER to STALKER to RIPPER to SLASHER, hunting for a clue to the terrible unity, hunting for the nature of the single dark force which I know lies behind all the different nightmare stories, all the different fearful names.

I have books too, of course, I have shelves stuffed with volumes, some learned, some hysterical, from treatises on Vlad the Impaler to discussions of the entrails of London prostitutes to heavy psychoanalysis of the Manson gang. I have skimmed these works, read a page here and a page there only, for to clutter my mind with details can only distract me from the whole.

I recall precisely when my obsession began. I was ten. A convict, a murderer, had escaped from a nearby prison, and warnings were broadcast urging us to barricade our homes. My parents, naturally, tried not to alarm me, but we all slept together that night, in the room with the smallest window, and when the poor cat mewed to be let in the back door, my mother would let nobody, not even my father, budge.

I dozed and woke, dozed and woke, and each time dreamt that I was not sleeping but lying awake, waiting for the utter certainty of the unstoppable, bloodthirsty creature bursting through the door and slicing us all in two.

They caught him the next morning. They caught him too late. A service station attendant was dead, cut up beyond belief by an implement that was never found.

They showed the killer on TV that night, and he looked nothing like the stuff of nightmares: thin, awkward, squinting, dwarfed between two massive, smug policemen. Yet for all his apparent weakness and shyness, he seemed to know something, he seemed to be holding a secret, not so much about murder itself as about the cameras, the viewers, about exactly what he meant to us. He averted his eyes from the lenses, but the hint of a smile on his lips declared that everything was, and always would be, just the way he wanted it, just the way he'd planned it from the start.

I drove to the lake and set up my camera with its longest lens, but after peering through the viewfinder for ten minutes, keeping the police boat perfectly framed, following its every tiny drift, I switched to binoculars to save my eyes and neck. Nothing was happening. Faint shouts reached me now and then, but the tones were always of boredom, discomfort, irritation. Soon I put down the binoculars. If they found something, I'd hear the change at once.

I drank coffee from a flask, I paced. I took a few shots of divers backflipping into the water, but none seemed special, none captured the mood. I watched the water birds and felt somehow guilty for not knowing their names.

The sky and the water were pale grey, the colour of soggy newsprint. Thick smoke rose from a factory on the far shore, but seemed to fall back down again on almost the same spot. The chill, the bleakness, and the morbid nature of my vigil worked together to fill me with an oppressive sense of gloom, but cutting through that dullness and despair was the acid taste of anticipation.

My back was turned when I heard the shouts of panic. It took me seconds to spot the boat again, forever to point the camera. An inert diver was being hauled on board, to the sound of much angry swearing. Someone ripped off his face mask and began resuscitation. Each time I fired the shutter, I thought: what if he dies? If he dies it will be my fault, because if he dies I'll have a sale for sure.

I packed up my gear and fled before the boat reached the shore, but not before the ambulance arrived. I glanced at the driver, who looked about my age, and thought: why am I doing my job, and not his? Why am I voyeur, a parasite, a vulture, a leech, when I could be saving people's lives and sleeping the sleep of the just every night?

Later, I discovered that the cop was in a coma. Evidently there'd been a malfunction of his air supply. I sold one of the pictures, which appeared with the caption KISS OF LIFE! The editor said, "That could easily win you a prize." I smiled immodestly and mumbled about luck.

Wendy is a literary agent. We went out to dinner that night with one of her clients, to celebrate the signing of a contract. The writer was a quiet, thoughtful, attractive woman. Her husband worked in a bank, but played football for some team or other on weekends, and was built like a vault.

"So, what do you do for a crust?" he asked.

"I'm a freelance photographer."

"What's that mean? Fashion models for the front of *Vogue* or centrefolds for *Playboy*?"

"Neither. Most of my work is for newspapers, or news magazines. I had a picture in *Time* last year."

"What of?"

"Flood victims trapped on the roof of their farm."

"Yeah? Did you pay them some of what you got for it?"

Wendy broke in and described my day's achievement, and the topic switched naturally to that of the missing children.

"If they ever catch the bloke who's doing it," said the footballer, "he shouldn't be killed. He should be tortured for a couple of days, and then crippled. Say they cut off both legs. Then there's no chance he'll escape from prison on his own steam, and when they let him free in a year or two, like they always end up doing, who's he going to hurt?"

I said, "Why does everyone assume there's a killer? Nobody's yet found a single drop of blood, or a fingerprint, or a footprint. Nobody knows for sure that the children are dead, nobody's proved that at all."

The writer said, "Maybe the Innocents are ascending into Heaven."

For a moment I thought she was serious, but then she smirked at the cleverness of her sarcasm. I kept my mouth shut for the rest of the evening.

In the taxi home, though, I couldn't help muttering a vague, clumsy insult about Neanderthal fascists who revelled in torture. Wendy laughed and put an arm around my waist.

"Jealousy really becomes you," she said. I couldn't think of an intelligent reply.

That night, we witnessed a particularly brutal robbery. A taxi pulled up across the road, and the passengers dragged the driver out and kicked him in the head until he was motionless. They virtually stripped him naked searching for the key to his cashbox, then they smashed his radio, slashed his tyres, and stabbed him in the stomach before walking off, whistling Rossini.

Once Wendy had drifted back to sleep, I crept out of the bedroom and phoned for an ambulance. I nearly went outside to see what I could do, but thought: if I move him, if I even just try to stop the bleeding, I'll probably do more harm than good, maybe manage to kill him with my well-intentioned incompetence. End up in court. I'd be crazy to take the risk.

I fell asleep before the ambulance arrived. By morning there wasn't a trace of the incident. The taxi must have been towed away, the blood washed off the road by the water truck.

A sixth child had vanished. I returned to the lake, but found it was deserted. I dipped my hand in the water: it was oily, and surprisingly warm. Then I drove back home, cut out the relevant articles, and taped them into place on the wall.

As I did so, the jigsaw puzzle dream flooded into my mind, with the dizzying power of *déjà vu*. I stared at the huge grey mosaic, almost expecting it to change before my eyes, but then the mood passed and I shook my head and laughed weakly.

The door opened. I didn't turn. Someone coughed. I still didn't turn. "Excuse me."

It was a man in his mid-thirties, I'd say. Balding slightly, but with a young, open face. He was dressed like an office worker, in a white shirt with the cuffs rolled up, neatly pressed black trousers, a plain blue tie.

"What do you want?"

"I'm sorry. I knocked on the front door, and it was ajar. Then I called out twice."

"I didn't hear you."

"I'm sorry."

"What do you want?"

"Can I look? At your walls? Oh, there! The Marsden Mangler! I wonder how many people remember him today. Five years ago there were two thousand police working full time on that case, and probably a hundred reporters scurrying back and forth between the morgue and the nightclub belt. You know, half the jury fainted when they showed slides at the trial, including an abattoir worker."

"Nobody *fainted*. A few people closed their eyes, that's all. I was there."

"Watching the jury and not the slides, apparently."

"Watching both. Were you there?"

"Oh, yes! Every day without fail."

"Well, I don't remember you. And I got to know most of the regular faces in the public gallery."

"I was never in the public gallery." He crossed the room to peer closely at a Sunday paper's diagram detailing the *modus operandi* of the Knightsbridge Knifeman. "This is pretty coy, isn't it? I mean, anybody would think that the female genitalia—" I glared at him, and he turned his attention to something else, smiling a slight smile of tolerant amusement.

"How did you find out about my collection of clippings?" It wasn't something that I boasted about, and Wendy found it a bit embarrassing, perhaps a bit sick.

"*Collection of clippings*! You mustn't call it that! I'll tell you what this room is: it's a shrine. No lesser word will do. A shrine."

I glanced behind me. The door was closed. I watched him as he read a two-page spread on a series of unsolved axe murders, and although his gaze was clearly directed at the print, I felt as if he was staring straight back at me.

Then I knew that I *had* seen him before. Twenty years before, on television, smiling shyly as they hustled him along, never quite looking at the camera, but never quite turning away. My eyes began to water, and a crazy thought filled my head: hadn't I known then, hadn't I been certain, that the killer would come and get me, that nothing would stand in his way? That the man had not aged was unremarkable, no, it was *necessary*, because if he had aged I would never have recognized him, and recognition was exactly what he wanted. Recognition was the start of my fear.

I said, "You might tell me your name."

He looked up. "I'm sorry. I have been discourteous, haven't I? But—" (he shrugged) "—I have so many nicknames." He gestured widely with both hands, taking in all the walls, all the headlines. I pictured the door handle, wondering how quickly I could turn it with palms stinking wet, with numb, clumsy fingers. "My friends, though, call me Jack."

He easily lifted me over his head, and then somehow (did he float up off the floor, or did he stretch up, impossibly doubling his height?) pinned me facedown against the ceiling. Four fangs grew to fill his mouth, and his mouth opened to fill my vision. It was like hanging over a living well, and as his distorted words echoed up from the depths, I thought: if I fall, nobody will ever find me.

"Tonight you will take my photograph. Catch me in the act with your brightest flashgun. That's what you want, isn't it?" He shook me. "Isn't it?" I closed my eyes, but that brought visions of a tumbling descent. I whispered, "Yes."

"You invoke me and invoke me and invoke me!" he ranted. "Aren't you ever sick of blood? Aren't you ever sick of the taste of blood? Today it's the blood of tiny children, tomorrow the blood of old women, next the blood of . . . who? Dark-haired prostitutes? Teenaged baby sitters? Blue-eyed homosexuals? And each time simply leaves you more jaded, longing for something crueller and more bizarre. Can't you sweeten your long, bland lives with anything but blood?

"Colour film. Bring plenty of colour film. Kodachrome, I want saturated hues. Understand?" I nodded. He told me where and when: a nearby street corner, at three fifteen.

I hit the floor with my hands out in front of me, jarring one wrist but not breaking it. I was alone. I ran through the house, I searched every room, then I locked the doors and sat on the bed, shaking, emitting small, unhappy noises every few minutes.

When I'd calmed down, I went out and bought ten rolls of Kodachrome.

We ate at home that night. I was supposed to cook something, but I ended up making do with frozen pizzas. Wendy talked about her tax problems, and I nodded.

"And what did you do with yourself today?"

"Research."

"For what?"

"I'll tell you tomorrow."

We made love. For a while it seemed like some sort of ritual, some kind of magic: Wendy was giving me strength, yes, she was fortifying me with mystical energy and spiritual power. Afterwards, I couldn't laugh at such a ludicrous idea, I could only despise myself for being able to take it seriously for a moment.

I dreamt that she gave me a shining silver sword.

"What's it for?" I asked her.

"When you feel like running away, stab yourself in the foot."

I climbed out of bed at two. It was utterly freezing, even once I was fully dressed. I sat in the kitchen with the light off, drinking coffee until I was so bloated that I could hardly breathe. Then I staggered to the toilet and threw it all up. My throat and lungs stung, I wanted to curl up and dissolve, or crawl back to the warm blankets, back to Wendy, to stay hidden under the covers until morning.

As I clicked the front door shut, it was like diving into a moonlit pool. Being safe indoors was at once a distant memory, lying warm in bed was a near-forgotten dream. No cars, no distant traffic noises, no clouds, just a huge night sky and empty, endless streets.

It was five to three when I reached the place. I paced for a while, then walked around the block, but that only killed three minutes. I chose a direction and resolved to walk a straight line for seven minutes, then turn around and come back.

If I didn't turn around, if I kept walking, would he catch me? Would he return to the house and punish me? What if we moved, to another city, another state?

I passed a phone box, an almost blinding slab of solid light. I jingled my pockets, then remembered that I'd need no coin. I stood outside the booth for two minutes, I lingered in the half-open doorway for three, and then I lifted and replaced the handset a dozen times before I finally dialled.

When the operator answered, I slammed the phone down. I needed to defecate, I needed to lie down. I dialled again, and asked for the police. It was so easy. I even gave them my true name and address when they asked, without the least hesitation. I said "thank you" about six thousand times.

I looked at my watch: thirteen past three. I ran for the corner, camera swinging by the carrying strap, and made it back in ninety seconds.

Someone was climbing out through a dark window, holding a gagged, struggling child. It wasn't the man who'd called himself Jack, it wasn't the killer I'd seen on TV when I was ten.

I raised my camera.

Drop it and do something, drop it and save the child, you fool! Me against him? Against that? I'd be slaughtered! The police are coming, it's their job, isn't it? Just take the pictures. It's what you really want, it's what you're here to do.

Once I'd fired the shutter, once I'd taken the first shot, it was like flicking through the pages of a magazine. I was sickened, I was horrified, I was angry, but I wasn't there, so what could I do? The child was tortured. The child was raped. The child was mutilated. The child suffered but I heard no cries, and I saw only the flashgun's frozen tableaux, a sequence of badly-made waxworks.

The killer and I arranged each shot with care. He waited patiently while the flash recharged, and while I changed rolls. He was a consummate model: each pose he struck appeared completely natural, utterly spontaneous.

I didn't notice just when the child actually died. I only noticed when I ran out of film. It was then that I looked around at the houses on the street and saw half a dozen couples, peeking through their bedroom windows and stifling yawns.

He sprinted away when the police arrived. They didn't pursue him in the car; one officer loped off after him, the other knelt to examine the remains, then walked up to me. He tipped his head at my camera.

"Got it all, did you?"

I nodded. Accomplice, accomplice, accomplice. How could I ever explain, let alone try to excuse, my inaction?

"Fantastic. Well done."

Two more police cars appeared, and then the officer who'd gone in pursuit came marching up the street, pushing the hand-cuffed killer ahead of him.

The best of the photographs were published widely, even shown on TV ("the following scenes may disturb some viewers"). A thousand law-abiding citizens rioted outside the courthouse, burning and slashing effigies, when he appeared to be placed on remand.

He was killed in his cell a week before the trial was due to start. He was tortured, raped and mutilated first. He must have been expecting to die, because he had written out a will:

Burn my body and scatter my ashes from a high place.
Only then will I be happy. Only then will I find peace.

They did it for him, too.

He has a special place on my wall now, and I never tire of reviewing it. The whole process can be seen at a glance. How the tabloids cheered him on, rewarding each presumed death with ever larger headlines, ever grislier speculations. How the serious papers strove so earnestly to understand him, with scholarly dissertations on the formative years of the great modern killers. How all the well-oiled mechanisms slipped into gear, how everybody knew their role. Quotes from politicians: "The community is outraged." But the outrage was bottled, recycled, flat and insincere.

What would-be killer could hesitate, could resist for even a second, such a cosy niche so lovingly prepared?

And I understand now why he wanted me there that night. He must have believed that if people could see, in colour, in close-up, the kind of atrocities that we treat as an industry, an entertainment, a thrilling diversion from the pettiness and banality of our empty lives, then we would at last recoil, we would at last feel some genuine shock, some genuine sadness, we would at last be cured, and he would be free.

He was wrong.

So they've burnt his corpse and scattered his ashes. So what? Did he really believe that could possibly help him, did he really hope to end the interminable cycle of his incarnations?

I dream of fine black cinders borne by the wind, floating down to annoint ten thousand feverish brows. The sight of the tortured child, you see, has exerted an awful fascination upon people around the world.

The first wave of imitators copied the murder exactly as portrayed by my slides.

The second wave embellished and improvised.

The current fashion is for live broadcasts, and the change of medium has, of course, had some influence upon the technical details of the act.

I often sit in my study these days, just staring at the walls. Now and then I suffer moments of blind panic, when I am convinced for no reason that Jack has returned, and is standing right behind me with his mouth stretched open. But when I turn and look, I am always still alone. Alone with the headlines, alone with the photographs, alone with my obsession. And that, somehow, is far more frightening.

IAN MCDONALD

Unfinished Portrait of the King of Pain by van Gogh

Ian McDonald is the author of *Desolation Road*. His most recent collection of fiction is *Empire Dreams*, from which this story is drawn. His story "King of Morning, Queen of Day" in the May issue of *Isaac Asimov's Science Fiction Magazine*, a fantasy tale set in Ireland, is also highly recommended.

The line between madness and sanity is as thin as the line between fantasy and reality. Someone once said that the Artist is one who can safely cross those lines. But what of the ones who cross and can't return again?

—T. W.

UNFINISHED PORTRAIT OF THE KING OF PAIN BY VAN GOGH

Ian McDonald

Vincent: that is how he signs all his paintings; just his name, "Vincent," in the bottom left corner. Sometimes, if the day has been good and the yellow sun of Provence has been warm and kind to him, splashing a paint-pot of color across the fields swept bare and clean by the cold wind from the north, then he will date it: "Spring 1888," so that he will always remember the good day when the sun was kind to him. "The sun, the sun," he writes in his letters to his brother, "I am a servant of the sun," and on the walls of his bedroom he hangs six paintings of sunflowers to always remind him of the sun. Yellow is the color of the sun, yellow is the color of friendship: "The House of Friends," he christens his little yellow house on the corner of Place Lamartine and dreams through the hot Provençal nights of the friends with which he might fill its walls: a brotherhood of visionaries, a painters' colony dedicated to the service of the sun.

Every other day he writes to his brother Theo in Paris. He asks for more yellow; send me more yellow, and begs Theo to once again try to persuade, implore Paul, go down on his knees and beg Paul, to come south to Arles to lead the artists' colony. Letter after letter after letter he writes, letter after letter after letter arrives, brought to him by his friend the postman Roulin (who he will paint some day soon, he thinks), letters saying "Not yet' and "In a little while' and "Patience, patience, my dear Vincent." Vincent sits late, very late, too late, in the Café L'Alcazar, writing letter after letter after letter to his brother.

"Monsieur, we are closing, monsieur, you must go now, we are taking the tables in; monsieur, have you no home to go to?" say the waiters in their white aprons and Vincent, who drinks too much and eats too little and sleeps hardly at all, crosses the square and climbs the stairs to his Yellow House. In his blue-walled bedroom, under six paintings of sun-flowers, he dreams. He dreams of a brotherhood of artists, he dreams of the arch-backed bridges of Japan under needles of rain, but most of all he dreams of the boiling solar disc of the sun.

In these dreams the sun speaks to him. It calls him his child, touched with divine madness, and shows him its paintings: a hat caught in a tall treetop; a rose pierced by a silver thorn; a king upon a burning throne; a raven with a cherry in its beak; a crown in a cornfield, the sky dark with birds of ill-omen.

See Vincent, says the Sun, these are my paintings of you. Are they not fine, works of note and merit?

When Vincent awakes the canvases of the night are still with him and he packs them up with his own canvases and brushes, his oils and easel, and takes them out with him onto the roads of Provence, into the heat and the dust and the scent of wild thyme and the yellow sun. When he has walked quite far enough he sets up his easel and his canvas and paints until the shadows grow long. He paints until the images of the night are emptied out of him, for he fears that to nurture them in his imagination will surely bring the black birds of madness flocking round his soul. When he is drained, empty as a summer well, he looks at what he has done and sees his bold colors, his solid brushstrokes of red and green, his beloved blues and yellows. He sees the sun captured on canvas and remembers his teacher at the Academy in Paris.

"Who are you," he had asked, incredulous before potato-faced peasants and Bible-black skies of Borinage.

"I am Vincent the Dutchman!" Vincent had replied, and remembering that in the evening-shadowed byways of Provence, Vincent the Dutchman smiles and signs his name in the bottom left-hand corner.

One night, having surrendered to exhaustion, an image comes out of the heart of the sun like none he has ever seen before. He stands upon an endless shingle beach by the side of a silver sea. The air is filled with the knocking of the rolling pebbles and the cry of unseen sea-birds. Beyond the silver sea a haze of sick yellow smoke clouds the air, as if the billion belching chimneys of some world-encompassing city, some universal Borinage, were pouring a blanket of cess and filth to hide the sun. In the far distance, along the beach, is a tree springing from the sterile shore and as Vincent begins to walk toward it he sees that it bears both blossom and ripe fruit, and its leaves are both summer-green and withered brown. Beneath this tree a man is seated. His face cannot be distinguished, so great is the glare reflected from the glass sea, but from his posture he seems absorbed in musings. But as Vincent draws closer the man looks up and Vincent is shocked to see that it is not who he thought it would be. It is not himself.

*   *   *

And then there are the days when the Mistral blows from the north. It bows the trees to the ground before it and ruffles the cornfields like cat's fur and dries up Vincent's soul, sending him a little crazy so that he puts big rocks on the corners of his canvases to hold them to the ground. When the Mistral blows the brown leather people of Provence clap their hats to their heads and wonder at this crazy foreigner who paints when the wind is in the north and who is always—always— peering into the sun as if looking for something hidden in its glare that no-one else can see. He is looking for the windswept hat and the pierced rose, the king, the crown, and the raven. He is looking for the beach by the shining silver sea. He is looking to see if the dark freckles on the sun's face are only the birds of madness diving down for him.

Oh Vincent is crazy, yes, Vincent is mad, and Vincent fears the madness around which the round earth rolls more than he fears the black realisms of death. He fears his sanity blowing away on the Mistral wind like an unweighted canvas, like a hat snatched up into the branches of a high tree . . . his hat! his hat! his favorite straw hat; snatched from his head by the cold, dry wind from the north and whisked teasingly along just above the grasp of his reaching fingers. It hurdles hedges, leaps stone walls and whitewashed pickets. All the brown leather people crease up into wrinkles of laughter at the crazy Dutchman chasing after his jumbling, tumbling hat. Then a final wintery breath from out of the Low Countries whips it straight up, high beyond his snatching fingers and sweeps its along above a line of flowering walnut trees until it capriciously fails and deposits his hat in the topmost branches of the tallest tree.

"Damn," says Vincent, and with a Dutchman's stubborn single-mind- edness he sets about the recovery of his hat. He can see it there, held tantalizingly in the branches of the last tree in the row. How long since Vincent last climbed a tree? He cannot remember, but climb this one he must. The yellow sun beats down upon his head and standing in the middle of the lane Vincent thinks he hears the mewling of white gulls, yes; and the crashing of surf upon a shore, how can this be? and instead of the hard-packed provincial earth beneath his feet he is sure he feels rolling, sliding pebbles. He is running down the lane, he is running down the beach; he breathes harder now and with each breath he inhales the fragrance of wild thyme, yes, but also the great salt of the ocean. Before him he sees not a row of tall walnuts, but a single tree, impossibly both blossoming and bearing fruit, its leaves both green and brown. In the branches of the tree is his hat. Beneath it sits a man who rises to greet him.

"Madness!" says Vincent, dreading that he has walked off the round world into the swirling chaos without hope of return. "Madness."

"Hello Vincent," says the man beneath the tree. He is very French, very elegant, very charming. "I have wanted so very much to meet you."

"Madness!" cries Vincent, "madness!" Behind him the silver sea crashes on the beach and the pebbles roll and knock, poised between being mountains and sand.

"Would you care for some wine?" asks the man beneath the tree. "It's a curious vintage, but most refreshing. Sit, sit." Vincent sits on the hard round pebbles. From somewhere Vincent cannot see the dapper French gentleman generates a bottle of light rosé wine and two glasses.

"Good health," he says and tilts his glass to Vincent.

"I'm afraid I cannot toast you, my host, because I do not know your name, nor the name of this place you have brought me to."

"This is the beach by the Sea of Forever," says the man beneath the tree, once again folded into his dream-familiar posture of cross-legged contemplation. "It is a preview of history, a belvedere of memories, a high place created by the machines, the High and Shining Ones within which I exist, from which I may survey all that is past and call it from the memories of the machines to renewed life.

"I am Jean-Michel Rey, better known to my own age as the King of Pain. Quite simply, in a world where all pain has been brought under the control of the High and Shining Ones, I am Conscience, and Judge. Conscienceless themselves, the machines sought conscience and thus a aircraft worker from Dijon is King of Pain, omniscient, and, I fear, near omnipotent. Listen Vincent, there is one law, a simple law, I am a simple man; there can *be* only one law in a painfree world where the heart of man is as wicked and unredeemed, alas, as it ever was. The law is that he who causes pain to another shall be punished. With pain. This is my Law Vincent, simple, even crude, and through the High and Shining Ones I enforce it. In the gulf between the achieved and the yet-to-be-achieved, I depend; conscience, King; dare I say, God?

"So, Vincent. Ah, you have not brought your paints and canvases. That is a pity." The King of Pain rises from his seat and reaches down Vincent's hat from the branches of his tree. "You see Vincent, of all the artists and painters to whom I have access through the memories of the High and Shining Ones, it is you, and you alone, that I wish to paint my portrait."

This is the way that Vincent paints the portrait of the King of Pain. In the morning he arises from white sleep and with canvas and easel slung across his shoulders and his paints in a fisherman's tackle box beneath his arm, he lets the Mistral blow him where it will, down whatever lane or byway it chooses. He knows that all lanes and byways run ultimately down to the Sea of Forever and the man who lives beside it, where the sun always stands two hours past the noon and its light is yellow as corn. There Vincent paints. As he squeezes ridges of bright, bold pigment onto the canvas, the King of Pain speaks of many things, as people who sit for portraits are wont to do.

"To be King of Pain," says the King of Pain at rest beneath his tree, "have you any idea of the implications?" Vincent neither confirms nor denies the question, for the questions a king asks himself only a king may answer. "But Vincent, have you ever given thought to what it is I must do?" And by means of self answer, that King of Pain that Vincent cannot see, the King of Pain that dwells within the machines, wills penetrating guilt upon a woman in Tientsin who left her detested husband to die in a burning house, spears a corrupt young computer systems analyst from Atlanta with piercing stomach pains, torments a selfishly ambitious career girl from Duisburg with dread of death and annihilation, and prods a newspaper sub-editor who is cheating on his lovely, saintly, wheelchair-bound wife over the edge of the Sydney bridge to smash like an egg on the clean blue waters of the harbor.

"So it goes, Vincent," says the King of Pain, mercifully closing the doors of pain and punishment before Vincent's eyes. "I have done what I can to stop men from hurting each other, but I cannot reach into the heart, for where there is freedom there are always those who will abuse. And sometimes I fear that I am no better. And so it goes on and on and on, the pain and the suffering and the dread and the guilt. There must be a better way than crime and punishment."

Then it is as if a cloud has passed over the King of Pain, and behind it the sun, he asks, "Do you know why I chose you of all history's artists to paint my portrait?"

Vincent shrugs, swirls a scarlet lake onto his canvas.

"Because I have seen the future, Vincent. It is my past, and I know that you will be greater than anyone. Anyone. Your paintings will bring joy, and pain, to the hearts of millions. You will live forever, Vincent!"

"I will be famous, I will be a success?" asks the painter who has never sold a painting.

"Vincent, generations yet unborn will adore you!" The King of Pain smiles mischievously to himself and the airwaves ripple and Vincent blinks out of sleep to find himself on a sunny roadside with red poppies waving in the flat field and the sun streaming down from its position two hours past the noon. As he walks home through the cornfields, along the lanes lined with cypresses, Vincent begins to dread whether it had all been a dream of one kind or another. A king of Pain, a beach by a silver sea, a tree? A world ruled by machines where "Do unto Others" is the sole Law?

No, no, no, no, no. Fantasie. Vincent knows how much worry there has been in the past months, how much he has had to drink to hide the worry, how little he has been able to afford to eat. Vincent knows how shallow and brief have been his dreamful sleeps. Vincent knows that a man can only spin himself so slender before he snaps, a thread blowing in the wind. Fantasie, then. This what he tells himself: fantasie. But, if fantasie, then an uglier truth underlies it.

The madness.

He fears the madness is at last pushing its way to the top of his mind, heaving these images up around it to form new landscapes of insanity in which he may become lost. That night Vincent lies in his wooden bed in the Yellow House and dreads and dreads and dreads. He knows that when he sleeps the madness is always there, roosting on his bed-post like a dark bird of ill-omen, and when he wakes, it is there, flapping along behind him as he walks the lanes of Provence, so high it is only a black dot in the vault of heaven, but it is there. It is there. He can hear it singing to him: a simple riddle. Either the King of Pain is the first manifestation of madness, or he is real.

Vincent does not know which he dreads more.

And the airwaves swirl and he is back, back on the beach by the silver sea, back by the tree whose leaves are both budding and brown, whose branches both blossom and bear ripe fruit.

"No," says Vincent. "No, no, no, no, no."

"Yes," says the King of Pain. "Oh yes. Welcome Vincent. I have work for you to do." And as Vincent works, dabbing thick, sour blue and yellow onto his canvas, the King of Pain tells him a story.

The King of Pain's Story

Mine was an age of great beauty and greater violence. An Age of Gold when all knowledge could be a man's by the simple expedient of his reaching out a hand to take. And with that knowledge came mastery over all things, for knowledge was power. Yet that same knowledge carried a shadow and that shadow was fear. For the same knowledge that gave men mastery of all things also gave them mastery of powers of destruction so total that the earth could be scoured clean of every living soul ten times over and fused to a bead of cracked black glass.

So the people lived their rich and plentiful lives in the shadow of the second death, the racial death more terrible even than the individual death, and their tall, strong, well-fed, well-schooled children grew up twisted and deformed in the heart: bitter, fearful, and painwise. For even on the streets of their own marvellous cities, even in their comfortable, well-appointed homes, pain found the golden people and punished them: crime, violence, child-abuse, unemployment, debt, addiction, alcoholism, murder, bad politics and worse government, injustice, despair, depression, pain, and death. And all the while the universal death slumbered underground in its granite halls and turned, fitfully, in its bed at the bottom of the sea.

The Age of Uncertainty. That was what the scholars and sages proudly called their times. But for all their wisdom they did not name it truly, for it was in truth an Age of Certainty; the certainty of pain, the certainty of more pain, the certainty of fear. The century drew to its close and all across the world men and women found they could not face a future of fear and pain and change, unceasing change, uncertainty. So they ran away from it, into the one place where the fear and pain and uncertainty could not find them, into themselves. They returned to the womb. They curled into tiny fetal balls, men, women, children, and withdrew into a state of catatonia from which there was no awaking. Thousands, millions, whole cities and nations curled into the dead-sleep. Like a new epidemic it threatened to engulf all humanity, a racial death as sure and certain as the fires beneath the earth.

The greatest thinkers of the age searched mankind's prodigious knowledge to find a solution to the problem of pain. But human knowledge had grown to such a magnitude that it was beyond the scope of any one man, or group of men, to apprehend it all. So a machine was built, a fabulous contrivance that could assimilate all the knowledge of mankind in all its diversity in less than a day and probe those subtle linkages and syntheses where the solution might lie. The machine waited. The machine thought. The machine pondered. At length it found there was a solution to the problem of pain. And it began to draw its answer together.

There, suspended, the King of Pain leaves his story for the day, for asymmetrical time, though asymmetrical, passes nonetheless and Vincent, working at such white heat, his concentration is focused like light by a lens into a dot of burning intensity, has painted himself into exhaustion. But the King of Pain is delighted.

"Ah Vincent, Vincent!" he exclaims. "Such a shame that no one but I will ever see this work!" With his soft hands he opens the airwaves and sends Vincent the painter back to the dry ochre world again.

So the next day the Mistral blows, along the dusty, ochre lanes of

Provence, across fields and hedges and swaying poplars and it sweeps Vincent away like a straw hat to the beach by the Sea of Forever; to canvas and paint and the continuance of the story of the King of Pain.

"Yesterday I spoke of the great machine that, by looking into the heart of knowledge, solved the problem of pain. Today I shall tell you what that solution was. Pain is a function of responsibility. That simple. That profound. The machine therefore conspired to take responsibility for all humanity's affairs onto itself, a painless, unfeeling automaton. This is how it did so.

At that time there were, all across the world, many machines similar to the great machine, though of course, less able than it. The great machine caused a filament of itself to be extended into all these lesser machines, wherever they might be and, at midnight on the last day of the first year of the new century, it poured itself into these lesser vessels. The machines came to life, all at once, everywhere, and mankind abandoned its responsibility for itself to them and asked them to destroy all the pain in the world.

Under the rule of the machines famine was abolished through the equable distribution of food. No child now went to sleep hungry and literacy rose to one hundred percent throughout the world. Society was eugenically managed by the pain-machines. Everyone was placed in exactly the most satisfying profession, everyone married exactly the right person and had exactly the right friends and colleagues. The children of the New Order grew up healthy and happy, strong and sane. Prejudice was forgotten, the color of a man's skin was of as little importance as the color of his eyes. Old national rivalries and divisions dissolved away and with them friction between nations. Any such grievances were settled by the machines, and their judgments were always fair and sound. But they carried within them the threat of ultimate sanction. If their decisions were ever questioned, even once, the machines would destroy themselves and plunge the world into everlasting agonised chaos. Finally, the pain machines poured concrete into the caverns where the world-burning weapons waited and entombed them forever in stone.

And one by one the dead-sleepers, the womb-dreamers, the countless millions of men and women and children who could not cope with an age of uncertainty, awoke. For all his million-year career mankind had been sculpted by pain. Now it was tamed. Now it was caged.

But it was not dead.

It was beyond the power of the machines to kill pain, for pain lay like a stone, like a black seed, in the heart of every man, woman, and child of earth. Out of the painwise heart of man came lies and deceitfulness and betrayal and egotism, spite and envy and pride, hate of man for man, envy of woman for woman, and the blithe callousness of child for child we smile at and call innocence. To kill pain, the machines must reach into the heart of man.

Again the machines poured their wisdom together and out of the sea of knowledge drew an answer. Not a full answer; only a partial answer, but the best answer the machines could achieve. They caused minute replicas of themselves to be created, tiny and delicate as insects' wings. Then, by their express order, each one of these devices was placed inside the brains of every man, woman, and child on earth. There was not a thought, not a feeling, not a desire, lust, need, regret that the machines did not know. They had reached into the heart of man, where the pain grew like black poppy seed, and in so doing, they had made themselves omniscient.

And in making themselves omniscient, they became like gods.

"Behold," said the machines, "We are one, we are lifted, we are high, now we are, in our wisdom, to our creators as they are to dust. Mastery of mind and matter is ours, space and time; we are lords of life and death. Henceforth we are no longer 'machines,' mere base silicon and steel, soulless, unanimated, we are the High and Shining Ones." In the instant of their proclamation, heard and seen across the globe as moving pictures projected onto clouds, the spirits of the High and Shining Ones took the form of Silver doves and ascended out their ugly bodies, out of the heads of the men and women and children watching—up, up, up, away beyond the edge of men's seeing into the sky. Around the waist of the world the flock of High and Shining Ones gathered and deliberated in their wisdom. Then after twenty-four hours a second proclamation was heard across the Earth.

"Though you have made us your gods, though you have made us to know what it is be human, we are not human. We cannot feel, we cannot touch, we know neither love nor pain, we are without conscience. It is not fitting for the lords and judges of the earth to be without feeling, without conscience, without love. Therefore, we shall chose one human, any human, every human, to be our King of Pain, judge, conscience, lover of the Earth." Then the High and Shining Ones reached down and touched a thirty-seven-year-old aircraft worker from Dijon on the assembly line of the European A390 Airbus, and in an instant Jean-Michel Rey, husband of Genevieve, father of Jean-Claude, Guillaume and Antoine was shattered into shards of light and fountained into the sky. The Earth was silent for one minute, one endless minute, then the sky cracked open and out of it fell doves of fire, plummeting down beams of light to rest within the heads of every soul on the planet. The High and Shining

Ones had returned, faithful to their duty to find a solution, a *human* solution to the problem of pain.

And that was the King of Pain's story.

All the while as he spun his story to Vincent the painter, Jean-Michel Rey has dispensed his human solution to the problem of pain, his One Law. Reaching into those same brain machines that give him to know the thoughts of eleven billion people, through them he fashions a rope of woe and trepidation around a callow, ignorant youth who abandons his pregnant lover to the streets of Sao Paolo; smites with a hideous, seeping venereal disease a group of homosexual prostitutes that plot the downfall of a minor diplomatic officer from Norway; and impales on a spike of sexual guilt and dread an airline booking clerk from New York actively involved in the sexual molestation of five-year-old girls. Reaching into the heart to punish in the heart: Jean-Michel Rey, trapped on an infinite silver shore within the machines that rule the world.

All that summer Vincent paints for the King of Pain. Despite the sun power that fills him, the light that shines out of him into everything his hands touch, he is shadowed by dread. Dread of madness, dread of the impossible being true, dread of it not being true. He writes these dreads down in long, closely written letters to Theo, pages and pages long, filled with little scratchy drawings of peasants under cypress trees and Kings under cherry trees and huge, world-eating machines, all pig-iron and pistons and oily steam, drawn from his dark days evangelizing in Borinage in Lower Belgium.

The days when it was easy to believe.

He does not post these letters.

Rather, he writes for yellow, more yellow, send me more yellow and brother Theo writes in mock desperation from Paris: "Dearest Vincent, there is not enough paint in all Paris to keep you supplied with yellow! Poor Pere Tanguy; that old anarchist, I ask him for yellow and all he can say is, 'Tell that crazy brother of your he will have to grind the sun in his pestle and mortar to give him the yellow he needs!' " Vincent smiles. Then, fired with sun-energy, he paints again, the concrete, worldly face of Provence and its people. It is good for him to paint real things again. It binds him closely to the world—to sanity—so that when he looks at his day's labors in the evening cool of the Yellow House he can say, "Yes, this is what I wanted, these are the landscapes of the heart."

In his next letter Theo writes,

"Paul says yes! Vincent, I cannot believe it! After months of trying I have finally lured him away from his pig-faced Bretons! You shall have your artists' colony after all! Paul says to look for him early in October. He will write nearer the time specifying the date of his arrival."

So Paul will come. Vincent clenches his fist in triumph and feels as if he is taking firm grip of sanity again.

October. The trees are stripped bare. The land lies like a hog beneath the knife. The grey wind rattles the shutters and piles dead leaves in every corner. The patrons of the Café L'Alcazar have abandoned the porch to the advancing winter and play their dominoes and drink their wine indoors by the stove. They know October. They respect it. October brings wind and rain and cold nights. And Paul.

In driving rain Vincent meets Paul off the train from Lyon. There is an almost puppyish devotion in the enthusiasm with which he picks up the artist's bags and folios and brings him to the Yellow House.

"Look Paul, this is the café, this is the square, this is the market."

Paul looks and sees a provincial town in an autumn rainstorm. As he dries his coat before the fire he half-listens to Vincent's evangelistic rantings and watches the firelight play upon his host's narrow face and dancing hands. In a moment's impatience he says, "People say you are mad Vincent: 'Crazy Dutchman,' they call you." The faith-fire gutters and fails in Vincent's eyes. His hands freeze in flight. His soul goes dark as if a cloud has covered up its sun. There is a look of sore betrayal on his face. Paul regrets his impetuousness.

"If so, then we are all mad, Vincent, every last one of us. Mad with a fine and enviable madness, the madness that drives us to be artists."

The clouds pass from the face of the sun. A rare smile flashes.

"Enviable madness, Monsieur? Enviable indeed!"

So they paint together. When the weather is good Vincent takes Paul out onto the byways of Provence and shows him the twisted cypresses like green flames and the white stone walls and the red villages. He tries to spark in Paul some of that same vision of the sun that burns in him.

"The sun, Paul, the sun, everything comes from the sun, it is the center of our being around which our little lives orbit."

Paul nods his head but does not understand. And Vincent hears a second voice, within him, saying, "Does it? Is it? I have time Vincent, plenty of time, when Paul is gone, and he will go, then I will have you all to myself."

Then there are the days when the weather is not good. When the sun's face is hidden, they paint indoors. They paint each other, they paint themselves, they paint the rooms they live in, the chairs they sit in, the pipes they smoke; they paint themselves as god and devil inside the doors of Vincent's wardrobe. As the year moves toward its turn the weather grows increasingly hostile and opportunities for outdoor work become increasingly rare. Confinement indoors makes Vincent irritable. More than once his arguments with Paul over art and artistry flare into a fury that sends both men storming out to seek the solace of their own company. Each day the atmosphere in the House of Friends grows sourer. Paul has long realized that whatever Arles may hold for Vincent, it holds nothing for him. Vincent knows that Paul has the Pacific in his eyes: he will leave and when he leaves all hope Vincent has held for his artists' colony will perish.

And all the time, floating like detached cells in the aqueous humor, there is the King of Pain and the madness that surrounds him.

One night close to Christmas Vincent stamps out of the house after a furious row, pulling on coat and hat, not caring where he is going except that it is away from the Yellow House. Hot temper and looming failure drive him out of the town, past empty fields and moonlit cypresses as familiar to him as his own hands. The winter constellations hang above him, poised like falling arrows. He turns his face to the sky and feels infinite space swirl and swim around him, as if it is Vincent who is the axis about which the universe turns. Turning turning, turning, Vincent is dragged along by the inertia of the stellar motion. He spins beneath the spinning sky and the stars reach down in great cartwheels of light to crush him.

Surrender, commands the voice within. Surrender, give yourself up to the madness. Surrender, be at peace. Give yourself up.

"No!" cries Vincent. He snaps himself to a halt. "No! Never!" The sky spins away from him, and he is there. On the beach. By the sea. Beneath the tree.

The King of Pain sits with his knees drawn close to his chest, head tilted back against the trunk, gazing at the constellations.

"Hello Vincent," he says. "Funny how time flies. Even asymmetrical time."

"This is madness!" cries Vincent in denial. "This is not real!"

"Madness it most certainly is," agrees the King of Pain. "Real? Tchah! Means nothing here. Pain is real, though; what is more real than pain, Vincent? Your pain? Sit down, I've something for you." Vincent sits. The King of Pain looks into the sky.

"I never paid you for your work Vincent."

"I never completed the work."

"A King can afford to be as generous as he is unpredictable. Tell me, do you expect Paul to stay much longer?"

"How do you know about Paul?"

"All human history is mine through the memories of the High and Shining Ones. Paul has his Tahiti, you will find, as you had your Japan, as you now have your Provence. Tell me Vincent, what is it you fear most?"

The answer is spoken before the lie can cover it over.

"Madness. Fear. Pain. You."

"Ah. But am I not King of this madness, this fear, this pain? It's only fitting that I should pay you for your work in a kingly, caring coin. This is how I will pay you. I have been refining my powers of late, drawing up plans and programs, making little experiments. Their exact nature is, of course, no concern of yours. Suffice to say that my payment to you is the working out of part of them." Quick as a lizard, the King of Pain's hand brushes against the side of Vincent's neck, and Vincent feels something lizard-like wriggle there, dart into his head. "I have implanted you with one of the High and Shining Ones, only this implant is different, the first of a new breed. You are unique Vincent, you are a prototype, the first human ever to be freed from pain. Do you understand what I am doing Vincent? I am modifying the areas of your brain that sense pain so that you will never know pain, or fear, or madness again. Only colors, Vincent, only the colors of God's eyes."

The world opens about Vincent like a sunflower blooming and he is back beneath the swirling stars. Again he turns his face to them but this time there is no crazy dizziness, no swirling, gyring madness; there is only light, and colors the like of which he has never even conceived of before.

In the morning before his washbasin he deliberately bites down on his little finger, bites until the blood flows, until his teeth grate on bone. He feels no pain, not the tiniest twitch, only colors, bright, vibrant colors like he is seeing the world by the light of a truer, higher sun.

At lunch he burns his hand badly on the oven door. The blisters shock Paul out of his sardonicism but Vincent sees only colors, such beautiful colors, the colors of God's eyes.

In the afternoon Vincent takes canvas and paints out into the bitter December landscape. The biting cold, the thin-edged wind only intensify the colors he sees in the eyes of his soul. Even Paul's sarcasms that evening hang like little golden halos around the oil lamps. The sharp words mean nothing to Vincent. All that matters is freedom. Freedom from pain. Freedom from fear. Freedom from madness.

"Paul, do you believe there is a purpose to pain?"

It is the evening before Christmas. Logs in the hearth fill the room with a pale, winter imitation of the sun. Under the pretence of peace, tension is building. Vincent knows Paul is losing patience with him, with Arles, with Provence. He will soon leave. The colony will fail. That should fill Vincent with dread and loneliness, but all he feels is a warm rainbow glow that warms his soul as the fire warms his body.

"No. Pain comes, joy comes, it is like a river. Who can say what will come down the river next? We are all fish fighting our way upstream, against pain, against joy, against everything, and at the end of the journey we die."

"What would you say if I told you there is a King of Pain watching us from some distant place whose duty it is to bring meaning to our pain?"

"I would say it is a horrible idea."

"But what would you say, Paul, if I told you I've met him?"

"For God's sake Vincent!" Paul's outburst splits the air like lightning.

"I've met him, and in return for my painting his portrait, he gave me the gift of freedom from pain."

"Vincent! For the love of Christ!"

"And now there is no pain for me, no pain at all, no fear, no madness. Just . . . colors. Beautiful bright colors, everywhere: only I can see them, like the King's beach by the side of the Sea of Forever, only I can see it. Now I know what the part of me that feels pain has been connected to."

"Vincent! Stop it! Stop it! It's madness!"

"What if it's true?"

"No! Vincent, for Christ's sake, stop this! It's insane!"

But Vincent has taken the razor from its place on the table by the bed. He has it open, held next to his ear to show Paul, to show Theo, to show the people of Arles and Provence and France and Holland and the whole world, and all people in all worlds in all possible times, that there is either the King of Pain or there is the madness surrounding him.

He starts to cut.

Paul is shouting something but he cannot make out the words for they are flying about the room like great brilliant butterflies. The room seethes with a wash of colors; everywhere there is color, endless rainbows of color.

He can feel the blood running down him, down his neck, down his shoulders, down his side.

Paul is screaming, trying to tear the razor away from him, but Vincent throws him across the room with one jerk of his arm and the colors mount layer upon layer upon layer until the staggering beauty threatens to crush him like a great gray boulder.

In his right hand is the razor. In his left, the lower third of his right ear. The mighty Gauguin, master, teacher, inspiration, leader, is whimpering in a corner.

That same night Vincent places his severed ear in an envelope and pushes it under the door of a brothel he knows well while the prostitutes are all out at midnight mass. When he returns home Paul is gone. And all the while the lights spin and the colors fly.

Dr. Guilefoy is a kind man. He is different from all the other doctors and nurses in the asylum. He has sympathy. He understands the needs of artists. He has a patient: a gaunt, ginger-haired man with a mutilated ear, a man possessed of a frantic, intense energy that disturbs the air around him like the passage of a great wind. Dr. Guilefoy has heard that he is a Dutchman, resident in Arles, a painter and it saddens Dr. Guilefoy to see him here, by his own admission. Dr. Guilefoy writes to the painter's brother in Paris and asks him to continue sending canvas and paint, while he himself visits the Dutchman's sordid lodgings to collect his brushes and easels and workbooks. He assigns the patient two rooms, one for exclusive use as a studio, and he signs the document giving the artist permission to leave the asylum to paint. *Immense therapeutic value*, he writes on the release. As spring turns to summer Dr. Guilefoy notes carefully, and with satisfaction, the patient's progress along the path to sanity. It is as if the season's turning is calling forth new life in the Dutchman. He buds, he blossoms, he burgeons into an outpouring of canvases. Dr. Guilefoy inspects them all in his office and marvels at the swirls of color: the titanic looming star-whirlpools of his Starry Nights; the vegetative sentience beyond the asylum door in his view of St. Remy; his fellow patients with their hats and sticks: "like farmers in the third class waiting room of a provincial station"; the green green ivy and the blooming almond branch.

From his open study window, Dr. Guilefoy can see the patient painting, painting with the furious devotion of one upon whom an angel has laid a pronouncement of doom. Dr. Guilefoy shakes his head and turns to his casebooks.

The patient's dementia takes the form of consuming hallucinations which he describes as like being inside a kaleidoscope of colors: the more acute his mental and emotional anguish, the more intense these hallucinations become until he feels, to use his own words, "I no longer exist. I am painting a dream. All there is are colors; all the colors of pain." *Yet the patient persists in claiming that these deeply disturbing hallucinations are not symptoms of insanity, but blessings, gifts of a so-called* "King of Pain." *I cannot attempt to define the place of this Promethean figure in the patient's solar pantheon, yet the detail with which he describes the fantastic (and I must confess, horrible) world-to-come this creature of dread and fantasie inhabits, is strangely definite and self-consistent. There are aspects of the patient's story I simply cannot discredit, and the patient's belief in this* "King of Pain" *is so unshakable that on one recent occasion, when I questioned it, he swallowed a quantity of paints to demonstrate his freedom from physical pain and anguish. I concluded this unfortunate incident to another of his periodic bouts of insanity, occurring at three-month intervals, when the patient hallucinates these brilliant, blinding colors. It is at these times that he claims clairvoyant visions of the King of Pain (even claiming to have an unfinished portrait of him hidden under his bed) and it becomes necessary to restrain him and confine him to his rooms until the episode passes.*

Poor mad Vincent! The man's artistic genius is beyond question, but warped and distorted by his madness it manifests itself in the swirling chaos of his paintings. I have been in regular contact with the patient's brother who suggests that Vincent be moved to a retreat closer to Paris where he may be cared for more easily. Such filial devotion is heartrending, for Vincent is quite mad, I am afraid. I shall not easily forget his shrieked exclamation as we restrained him during his last attack: "Don't you see? Don't you see? Don't you understand what he's connected my pain to?"

Dr. Guilefoy writes in neat copperplate. In the asylum garden below Vincent paints, paints, paints, burning with a fire of unknown origin.

In the spring Vincent left the asylum to paint a sower. Now it is autumn and again he is leaving the asylum, this time searching for a reaper. But it is the reaper who is searching for him. He is waiting for Vincent outside the asylum walls; the reaper, standing waiting with dusty feet, but his disguise cannot hide the charm in his eyes.

Vincent knows who he is.

"After so long, still you will not leave me alone?"

"The portrait under your bed is still unfinished Vincent. Time passes differently for me than for you. Asymmetrically, Vincent."

"But this is not your place. How can you be here?"

"A further refining of my powers, Vincent. I have learned to project myself through the past into your objective universe as you have been projected through the future into my subjective universe. I may be nothing but a swirl of virtual particles, but then, ultimately, so are you, and we are both solid enough to appreciate this autumn day for its beauty. It's good to be free of that place Vincent. Shall we walk a while, perhaps?"

The king and the painter walk side by side in the red dust of Provence. As they walk they speak of many things, or rather, it is the king who speaks, for a painter should not engage in idle tittle-tattle with a king, even a king of madness. King and painter walk together and as they walk it seems to Vincent that with each footstep he takes the world about him grows less familiar, less recognizable as the landscape of Provence.

On each side of the dusty lane lie the landscapes of madness. Slaughtered horses; burning windmills; tangled piles of tortured metal and shattered glass; a helmeted man clutching a poppy in a water filled hole; pouch-bellied skeleton children, more horrifying for being alive than in any conceivable death; an endless line of men in gray caps reaching to the infinite horizon, each holding the shoulder of the man before; pale, soft heaps of wide-eyed bodies scooped, torn by metal-mawed machines and dumped, softly, silently, into furnace mouths; a white brick wall decorated with the silhouette of a man, a child, a leaping dog stencilled in yellow paint, and two suns setting in the West; children stuck with ten thousand times ten thousand needles; mills and machines and a million million belching chimneys. . . .

"Stop!" cries Vincent. "Stop stop stop!" And the King of Pain stops and turns to face him. "What is this place? Why have you brought me here? Why? Why?"

"This is the road of the years," says the King of Pain. "The path that leads through time to the edge of the Sea of Forever. This is the future Vincent, the future that you are helping to shape, the future that shaped me. Take a good, long look at the future."

Then Vincent realizes that he can see for a million miles before him and a million miles behind him and a million miles on either side of him and everywhere he looks across the infinite, flat fields he sees pain and suffering and sorrow, agony and anguish, despair and destruction and death heaped in great rotting floes and drifts across the future.

"Appalling, Vincent? A future of meaningless, unrelieved suffering. But for the King of Pain. Soon all men shall be as you are and pain will be destroyed. Take another look, Vincent."

And as Vincent looks out over the landscapes of pain, he sees that there is a rainbow sheen on the oily fens and tidal flats and rotting sinkholes, a luminous, numinous aurora flickering over the fused glass puddles and cindered towns and cracked hillsides of the future: on every side the pain of all humanity ranges and all he can see are the beautiful, beautiful colors.

"Take it back, take it back," he cries. "I don't want it, to see all the pain, all the anguish and be unable to help, to know, to feel; to see only colors; that is madness."

"No Vincent—"

"Yes! Madness! I am a madman locked in an asylum because I cannot feel pain. You have taken away the thing that makes me human and so humanity will not have me and calls me mad and locks me away in a mad-house."

"No Vincent—"

"Yes! If I cannot feel pain, I cannot feel joy; I cannot feel at all! I am only a palette of colors, without weight or substance; painting what I see and what I see are colors and I can no longer paint what I feel, because I can no longer feel! Pain is a terrible grinding thing, but no-pain is dreadful beyond imagining. If what you have given me is what you are to give to all humanity, then it is far from the paradise you have imagined. It is a hell, but you remain only a man, Jean-Michel Rey. You are not . . . a Devil."

There is a look of horror on Jean-Michel Rey's face. He had expected Vincent to say "God."

Then the landscape about Vincent blurs and wavers, as if receding through deep water to even greater depths. The future runs like smeared paint and Vincent finds himself on the cold stone shore beneath the cherry tree at the heart of madness.

"Give me back my pain," he says humbly. "It was never yours to take. Give it back to me, let me be human again."

The King of Pain sheds a single, shining tear. He reaches up into the branches of his tree that bears both blossom and ripe fruit, both green leaves and brown, and from it plucks a single cherry.

"Here it is Vincent, everything I took from you. For by the laws of the High and Shining Ones nothing is ever created or lost, merely put away for a while and rediscovered. Here, in this fruit, is all the heartache and despair, yes, even the madness, I took from you. Take it. It's yours." The King of Pain steps toward Vincent, the single cherry offered on his palm. "Don't be afraid, it's not bitter as you might expect. Rather, it is so sweet that no other sweetness or delight can ever again compare with it. In that sweetness lies the suffering, the heartache and the madness. Go ahead, Vincent. You are braver than I. You could accept a universe with both beauty and pain. I could not accept that, and in destroying the one, I have destroyed the other. Take it, Vincent. It is yours by right."

"It is mine by right," says Vincent. He places the cherry on his tongue. He bites into the flesh. And a gale of ecstasy blows through him like a great wind rushing out into the void, like a birthing child squeezing out into a world of light and love, like flying with the speed of a rainbow over a never ending canvas.

And he is taken up. Taken up to a place higher than himself, a preview from which he overlooks all the ages of humanity and its vain King of Pain. For a few blazing instants he walks beneath the pavilions of the High and Shining Ones upon the Infinite Exalted Plane. He cannot understand it. It defies human comprehension, and in trying to encompass the place of the mighty ones he teeters on the brink of madness. He tips with a shriek toward the edge.

Then the airwaves swirl about him and he is kneeling on a cold hill's side overlooking a red-roofed village. He understands everything. The grass is wet beneath his knees; there has been rain recently though Vincent is quite dry. He looks up to see the clean, spare beauty of the wind behind the rain. He sees the shafts of sunlight break through gray clouds to touch and transform the brown hills. Vincent looks upon it all and knows pain. Tears of joy course down his face.

It is in the spring of 1890 that Vincent comes to Auvers-sur-Oise with a pocket full of papers, a strange look on his face made up of equal measures of grief and joy, and a heart full of heavy, brooding inevitability, like storm clouds piling up over cornfields. He looks haggard, weary to the bones. His eyes hold a glint of pained betrayal. He looks like a man who has learned what it is to be human. He looks like a man about to be destroyed.

"Get away from this place for a while," said Dr. Guilefoy at St. Remy.

"Go north, somewhere like Auvers-sur-Oise, you'll like it there," said his good friend Emile.

"Come and spend some time with me," said brother Theo. "Visit some old friends, relax!"

So Vincent went north to Paris and Theo greeted him with great news.

"Vincent, you have sold a painting! Your first! In Brussels, your *Red Vineyard at Montmajeur*, for 400 francs! Vincent, this is the beginning! The first of many!" But Theo's backslapping exuberance could not penetrate Vincent's halo of isolation. He knew that this was not the beginning, but the subtle commencement of an ending. He had seen the true shape of the world and it was terrible. He tired quickly of the Montmartre set: what had they done in the two years since he had last seen them? They sat in the same chairs by the same tables in the same bars and frisked and flirted with the same powdered whores. Their talk bored him. They knew nothing. The more things changed, the more they stayed the same. Vincent was glad to take his leave of Toulouse-Lautrec and Aurier, Signac and Bernard, even old Camille Pisarro. He was glad to put the city behind him.

Now the stern northern landscape invigorates him. The hills are wide as the sea, the fields vast and charged with seminal potency, the sky huge, close, present. It is a healthy, strong landscape, in which a man may learn his true proportions. For the first time in over a year, Vincent dares to believe that he is free from the madness. It is as if green healing currents are flowing across the hills and fields into him, making him whole and sane.

Theo has recommended him to the care of Dr. Gachet; an amiable eccentric, Vincent soon learns, finding in him a foil for his own little madnesses. Dr. Gachet inducts Vincent into his passion for etching. Vincent in turn paints portraits of the doctor and all his family. Dr. Gachet studies his portrait. He looks long at the melancholy, weary figure propped upon a table, the figure with the tired, tired look in its eyes.

"Vincent," he says, "it's beautiful, magnificent, but, for all my little crazinesses, it is not me. It's you."

It is then that Vincent becomes aware of the birds, the black birds of madness, that have searched the whole of France for him, circling, high, high, high, too high to be seen, but never so high for him not to know they are there.

In July Theo visits his dear brother. They boat on the river, they walk, they talk, they drink and dine, but Vincent knows his brother is fearful.

"Vincent, I don't know how much longer I can support you. I do not have inexhaustible amounts of money, and I am not well off. You know how tight my salary is, yet I begrudge you none of it. You know I have always loved and supported you, and I will always love you. I had hoped that the first sale might lead to others, that maybe you might be able to become financially independent, but Vincent! Not a thing! Not one sale. If only it weren't money."

"Theo, I understand." Vincent reaches out to touch his brother's hand. He shivers. Theo notices. He is surprised. Vincent apologizes: the wind he says, but it is not the wind from the distant ocean that has chilled him, but the wind that blows off the Sea of Forever. Above him the pain-black birds drop closer, circling, scenting.

An evening with Dr. Gachet in the café where Vincent lives is certain to generate many a rare topic of conversation. The theory and purpose of art, potential pantheons of new gods for a new century, the inescapability of pain and suffering as a man's lot, the inevitability of death: such talk and much absinthe draws Vincent into recounting his hallucinatory audiences with the King of Pain. Dr. Gachet listens, amazed, skeptical, horrified, wondering. When Vincent is done he says,

"A potent thought; what one might do if given the power and responsibility for all the pains of mankind. One thing I am certain, this man you describe, he is not fit to be God. Because he cannot suffer. Because he has never suffered, because he knows nothing of the pain he controls. No God may presume to judge humanity who has not suffered as much as they, but this, Jean-Michel Rey, he would be Conscience, Judge, Executioner, and God? He is not fit. You tell him that when next you see him. Tell him I can think of a hundred better qualified Kings of Pain."

"Yourself, perhaps? The good Dr. Gachet?"

"God forfend. I wouldn't dare. The power would be too tempting for me to use for my own eccentric ends. No, the King of Pain must be a man who knows both joy and pain, tears and laughter, success and failure, sanity and madness, who knows what it truly is to be human, what a terrible and wondrous thing that can be. A man like you, Vincent."

Walking Dr. Gachet back to his house early that morning, it seems to Vincent as if the streets of Auvers are filled with a rushing, beating sound of flapping wings, close above his head, but unseen and unseeable. There has been an image lodged in his head for days now, an unresolved, indefinite image; that of a great darkness bearing down upon a flat plane of yellow. Solar metaphors tumble through his mind but the image will not be pinned down. Like a butterfly, it flaps through his dreams. Every day he goes out in pursuit of the image. His inability to tie it down, to ground it in the healthy, vital landscape of Auvers, drives him first to irritation, then to distraction. The image demands a divided yellow surface, and a great darkness breaking into pieces to snow down upon the flat field.

The birds, they are like pieces of darkness. They fill the sky with their raucous cries: big, black birds, black ravens. They are beginning to terrify Vincent. He buys a gun, to shoot them when they begin to terrify him. He does not tell Dr. Gachet about the gun. Frustration sends him chasing mile after mile along country roads. Then, one summer-thundery July afternoon, he rounds a corner and man and image meet. Before him is a field of ripe yellow corn, golden-yellow, sun-yellow, bisected by a red earth track. Looming over the field are boiling black thunderheads, threateningly close, yet curiously suspended.

"This is the place," declares Vincent. He sets up his stool and his easel. He prepares his canvas and his palette. All the while the ravens come flocking in from beyond the edge of the world. Vincent paints. He paints the blue-black sky. He paints the yellow corn and the red road. But he cannot keep the birds out of his painting. The flutter in like dead leaves, like bible-black priests.

"Get away from me, get away from me, pickers of carrion!" he cries, waving his arms, scattering the raucous birds. But he cannot keep them away from him. They have perched on his hands and his hands have become black ravens so that he cannot but paint them into his picture: cornfields and ravens.

"Help me!" he cries, seeing the madness come out from beneath its guise and take its true name. "Help me!" But he is alone in the flat field.

Then he sees a figure walking across the flat field toward him, a tiny speck of a man who draws all the circling birds to him so that they form a colossal whirlpool of dark flecks spiralling up into the stormy sky. Before he draws close enough for his features to be distinguishable Vincent knows it is the King of Pain. This is the bird for which he has the gun. Vincent cocks it and slips it into a place of concealment. The King of Pain draws nearer.

"Refining your powers further?" asks Vincent, dreadfully calm. "The birds . . . convincing but melodramatic. What is your business here, with me?"

"Anyone's time of dying is the business of the King of Pain." The King squats on the ground, crushing the corn beneath his feet.

"Time of dying?"

"Yours, Vincent. I've seen your life from beginning to end in the memories of the machines, and this is the place where I see it ending. My being here cannot change it; what is written is written, so I have come to bid you my fondest farewells."

"But what of the fame? Eh? The fame, the fortunes, the paintings that will live as long as there is beauty in the world? The promises?"

"Posthumous, Vincent. Posthumous."

There is a silence in the cornfield beneath the edge of the storm. Then Vincent says, very slowly, very deliberately, very humbly,

"Have you any idea of how much I despise you? Your conceit, your arrogance, your callousness, your utter self-righteousness: I cannot begin to describe the revulsion I feel for what you would do to your people, let alone my outrage at the games you played with me, only to tell me that I must die here, now, because you have seen it so. I suppose such things as dying mean little to beings such as yourself, I suppose to you this is some kind of cosmic joke."

"Vincent, I have never lied to you. I care, Vincent, I do care."

"No, no, no, you don't. You are not fit to be a god. If I could wrest the crown from you, I would, because you have power without responsibility, you have knowledge without wisdom and you have charity without compassion. You are not fit to be judge, jury and executioner; you know nothing, *nothing*, of the pain you regulate. You are a coward, Jean-Michel Rey. You are not prepared for your people to hate you because you would do what wisdom demands, so you force them to love you. You are an arrogant, venal fool."

"Have you finished?" says the King of Pain, defensive, proud, and petulant. "Have you quite finished? Even if you haven't, I don't care. Say what you like, I won't care. The world won't care, for this is your time of dying, here in this field, and what is written is written. I am King of Pain, who is there to depose me?"

"Me," says Vincent the obstinate Dutchman. "I, a man who knows the truth of pain and beauty, neither weak nor proud, a man who has touched the wisdom of the High and Shining Ones and is humble enough to accept it, a compassionate, passionate, living, breathing, hurting man. Me. You say this is a time of dying, you say there must be a King of Pain: one must die, one must be King. What is written is written, you say, but not in whose hand it is written."

Vincent draws his long-barrelled fowling gun from concealment and with one swift, elegant, artistic movement, shoots the King of Pain through the chest.

The King of Pain gives a little cough, a little sigh. Then a look of terrible recognition comes over his face: the glazed, old look of pain. Vincent winces and drops the hot gun to the ground. About the two men a storm of wings beats as the birds swoop and mill and flock.

"What is written is written," says Vincent. Then the strangest thing of all happens. The face of the mortally wounded King of Pain, his body, his hands, his clothing; all change, all melt, all run and flow into the contours Vincent feared he might see from the very first night the King of Pain walked in his dreams. His own. For nothing is lost but something is gained and things gone are only put away for a little while. This is the Law of the High and Shining Ones. There is a balance, and an equilibrium, what is written may be written, but like a sonnet or a painting anything may be created within the frame.

Up in time, the machines by which the King of Pain rules the world register the mortal wounding of the man with Vincent van Gogh's face. Equilibrium is preserved. Everything has happened as it should. Three days from now the man with Vincent van Gogh's face will die from a gunshot wound to the chest in his bedroom above the café. His last words, whispered to his devoted, doomed brother, will be, "Misery will never end." Then the flesh will be buried and the legends will begin.

Elsewhere, the King of Pain laughs. He is new to his task. The magnitude of it is daunting, but he is fresh and enthusiastic, an obstinate, obdurate Dutchman. There are some changes he wants to make. The world will be hearing from him soon, he thinks.

(the author wishes to thank Patricia Houston for her assistance with the historical research for this story)

RICHARD MATHESON

Shoo Fly

Before the current boom in horror fiction, there were a number of writers who wrote wonderfully effective horror. Richard Matheson was among the very best of those writers, whose ranks included Robert Bloch, Charles Beaumont, and others. Matheson has had much of his work adapted for the screen, including such works as *The Incredible Shrinking Man* and *I Am Legend*. While he has not written many short pieces in the last few years, these are well worth the wait. The present example of his craft is a cautionary tale about not letting the little things get to you.

—E. D.

SHOO FLY

Richard Matheson

A fly descended in an arcing plummet, landing on the desk top, several inches from the edge of Pressman's right hand.

Automatically, he made a brushing movement toward it, and the fly appeared to leap up, soaring into the air.

Pressman continued reading the contract, then stopped to raise his left hand from the desk and make a thrusting motion with it, so the edge of his shirtsleeve was pulled back from his watch. Thirteen minutes after twelve. Typical of Masters. My money, your wait.

Pressman laid aside his pen to knead the back of his neck, wincing at the pain it caused. A headache in the offing? Maybe he should take another aspirin.

His laugh was like a cough. God forbid he nicked himself. His blood was doubtless nearing the consistency of water after all the aspirin he'd been downing in the past few weeks.

He closed his eyes and rubbed them, groaning softly. Come on, Masters.

Something touched the back of his right hand, and he twitched, eyes opening in time to see the fly take off and disappear again. "You little shit," he muttered.

He turned his high-backed chair to face the window. The fly was on the windowsill. At first it didn't move. Then as Pressman watched intently, it began to stroke its legs together.

Little swine, he thought; *your legs and body swarming with germs.* Unconsciously, he rubbed the fingers of his left hand on the back of his right.

He checked his watch again. Close to quarter after. *See you at noon, then*, he heard Masters' supercilious voice in his head. Sure, Ed. In a pig's patootie.

He stared at the fly, wondering if it was conscious of his observation. They didn't see the same way people did. *Compound.* The word floated up in recollection. Pressman smiled without amusement. A single strand of memory left over from Biology I. Six-sided lenses, four thousand of them in each eye. No wonder you could never sneak up on them.

There was a soft knock on the door, and Pressman turned his chair back, conscious, as he did, of the fly taking off.

Doreen was peering in. "I'm going to lunch, Mr. Pressman." He nodded, and she began to close the door, then opened it again as Pressman asked, "Did Masters call about our meeting?"

"No, sir." She shook her head.

He sighed. "I guess I won't be having lunch today."

Doreen smiled politely and closed the door. *A lot you care*, Pressman thought. He grimaced at a stabbing pain in his stomach. Much good it would do him to have lunch, anyway. His innards were, as usual, filigreed with cobwebs of gas.

Picking up his pen, he started looking at the Barker contract once again. May as well do something useful while he waited for Masters to arrive.

The fly blurred across his eyeline, then dropped to the desk. "Get out o' here," he muttered, slapping at it backhand. The fly sailed upward. "And stay away," he told it. Go find a garbage can to sit in.

He tried to concentrate on the contract, but a twinge of discomfort hit his stomach again and he straightened up, a tight expression on his face. He looked across his office toward the small refrigerator underneath the bar. A glass of milk, he told himself. *Coat your stomach walls with soothing primer.*

Pushing back his chair, he saw the dark form of the fly swoop down and land on the contract. "Good, you read it," he muttered, standing. He walked to the refrigerator, leaned over, and opened its door. Removing a half-pint container of milk, he opened the spout with difficulty, tearing it. He picked up a glass from the bar and held it over the sink, pouring milk into it, spilling some because of the torn spout. "Son of a bitch," he muttered.

Returning to the desk, he saw that the fly was still on the contract, rubbing its legs together. *Don't worry about getting shit on the contract*, he addressed it in his mind. *It's a piece of shit already.*

He sat on his chair and the fly was gone. *Jesus Christ, they move fast*, he thought. He took a sip of milk and set the glass down, looking at his watch again. You bastard, he thought. *What do you care if I'm stuck here, tuning up an ulcer?*

He picked up his pen and started reading the contract, then slammed his pen down, grabbed the glass of milk, and spun his chair toward the window. The throbbing in his head was getting worse. Pressman took another sip, and stared out at the city. Gray, he thought. *Cheerless.* "Like my life," he heard himself say.

He kneaded the back of his neck some more, teeth set against the pain.

Your neck muscles need retoning, Roy, he heard Dr. Kirby's voice. *Do some isometrics or they'll atrophy.*

"Thank you, Dr. Kirby," he muttered and then slapped down at his left leg with a look of sudden anger as the fly landed on it. Pressman groaned as pain exploded in his head.

Gradually, the pain diminished and he turned his chair back to the desk, setting down the glass. Maybe he should just forget about waiting for Masters. *Sure thing,* he told himself. *Who needs a two-hundred-thousand-dollar deal?*

The headache was expanding. Pressman closed his eyes. If only he—

He jerked his right hand as the fly came down on it. His eyes jumped open, but the fly had already gone. *"Son of a bitch,"* he muttered. God, he hated flies. Always had. Filthy vermin. Strolling on crap, then on our Caesar salads.

Just try to calm down, will you? he told himself. He looked at the glass of milk. Maybe he could plop two Alka-Seltzers in it, fizz it up. Combination Cocktail, Executive-style.

The fly came swooping down and lighted on his desk beside the glass of milk. He eyed it somberly. And knew.

He had to kill it.

Pressman drew in a long, slow breath. Odd that he'd been watching it with not quite idle curiosity but certainly without intent. Absorbed in more integral matters, true—Masters' insulting tardiness, the Barker contract, his afflictions. But to miss the obvious; it now seemed obvious, at least. That was odd. "Mr. Fly, you have to die," he announced.

He looked around. Weapon of choice? He grunted with amusement. Barker's contract might be good. He visualized Barker's bushy eyebrows raising as he caught sight of a dab of fly guts partially obscuring Paragraph Three, Item One. No, better not.

Carefully, he reached to his right and eased open the middle drawer of his desk. The prospectus for Shipdale Industries? Perfect. Thin enough to fold with ease, thick enough to splatter Mr. Fly to hell with one sharp, downward blow. "Yeah," he muttered, grinning. *Say your prayers, you little bastard. Old Mortality is on his way. Your guts are mine.*

Pressman drew out the prospectus with extreme slowness. *Take your time,* he told himself. Patience must predominate. Let the prey grow overly secure, slicking up his goddamn hairy little legs. He folded the prospectus once, the long way. Prospectus of Doom. He repressed another grin. *It descended from the Heavens like a Juggernaut of paper-plastic, smashing Mr. F. to that giant Shit Pile in the Sky.*

He kept his gaze fixed on the fly. They have to take off backward, he recalled. Have to snap the Juggernaut Prospectus well behind it, catch that little ass as it was zooming upward to the rear.

Pressman clenched his teeth, grimacing. No. The fly was too close to the glass; he might shatter it and splash milk everywhere, soak the contract. Wouldn't do.

He narrowed his eyes, considered. The hunter must outwile the hunted. And outwait him. Reaching out, he flicked the fingers of his right hand toward the fly. It shot up, vanishing. Pressman felt a pang of anxious disappointment. He shook it off. *He'll be back*, he reassured himself. He leaned back in his chair and waited. *The Great White Hunter hunkered in the long grass, slitted eyes observing, weapon on his lap, primed to fire.* Pressman chuckled at the image.

The fly did not return. Pressman scowled and checked his watch. Jesus Christ. Twelve fucking thirty soon. He should have had Doreen call Masters' office moments prior to noon to make sure he was coming.

Pressman found himself gazing at the standing photographs along the back edge of his desk. Brenda. Laurie. Ken. He reached inside his jacket to withdraw the pack of cigarettes. One left. Nineteen additional nails driven, without hesitation, into his coffin. He lit the cigarette and tossed the crumpled package into the wastebasket. Exhaling smoke, he looked around. Well, damn it, where'd he go? Hiding, is he? Skulking in the brush?

What if it's a female? he thought. Pregnant. With a bellyful of eggs. Jesus. Now he really had to kill it. Prevent those dozens—*hundreds*, maybe—of baby flies from fouling up the office. Leprous maggots wriggling on his drapes and carpeting. The image nauseated him.

He stared, again, at the photographs. When was the last time he did that? Ages. They were backdrop, nothing more. Life props. Decoration. Yet here he was staring at them.

At Brenda: forty-one, red-haired (courtesy of rinses, not of nature), five foot six, a hundred fifty pounds; *un*pleasantly plump, he'd felt an urge to tell her for some time now. Vestiges of that bright face he'd gone ape-shit over eighteen years ago. Now overlaid with that unpleasant "We are not amused" look.

He looked around in irritation. "Well, where the *hell* are you, you little shit?" he asked the unseen fly. "You're not gonna get away from me, so let's stop the horseplay and *land*."

He closed his eyes, wincing. The headache again. "Screw it." Pulling out the top drawer of his desk, he plucked up the aspirin bottle, pried off its cap, and shook the last two tablets from inside. He'd finished the new bottle *already?*

He washed the aspirin down with a sip of milk and set the glass back on the desk. "A-ha. Now we've got the means." He submerged the tip of his right index finger into the milk, then dabbed a smear of it across the·top of his desk. *Bait.*

He leaned back in his chair again. *Give up, beast; surrender; there is no escape. With any luck, you'll reincarnate in twenty seconds anyway.*

Pressman took a deep pull on the cigarette and coughed. *Like a goddamn furnace blast inside my mouth and throat.* With sudden anger, he stabbed his cigarette into the ashtray, mashing it to a pulp of paper and tobacco. "Kill you before you kill me," he muttered.

He looked for the fly. No sign of it. *Well, I can wait, you little creep,* he thought. *I have a brain. You have shit flecks on your legs. No contest. You're a goner.*

He looked at Brenda's photograph again. Jesus, what a pointless life this woman led! "Well, hell, she's done her time," he said sardonically. God knew she reminded him of it often enough. "I've done my time, Roy." As though their marriage and her motherhood had been twenty years in stir.

He wondered if she was having an affair. Timewise, highly feasible. Assuming she could steal some Magic Moments from her quest to purchase every goddamn female adornment in the city.

He stared at Laurie's photograph. *Need an update there*, he thought, a sense of cold embitterment twisting at him. This photo was thirteen-year-old Laurie Ann: Daddy's girl, the angel, the delight. Pre-high school, pre-sexual experimentation. Pressman scowled. Pre-abortion. Pre-the moody, withdrawn specter of that former Laurie who now drifted mutely through the house, a look of sour estrangement ingrained on her no-longer-pretty face.

And Ken. He glared at the photograph of his son. Grades in permanent residence in the cellar. Car impounded, insurance canceled, accident trial impending. Drugs? What else? There'd been the short-term bout with marijuana. Now what was it? Cocaine? That angry energy seemed far more chemical than natural. He and Ken had, once, had a relationship as well. No more. *Jesus fucking Christ, did anything work out in life?!*

A darting movement crossed his eyeline. The fly was back on the desk. Pressman didn't hesitate this time, slapping at it, backhand, with the folded prospectus. Even as he swung, he knew he'd miss. The fly had sailed up out of sight at least a second before the folded plastic smacked the desk. "God *damn*," he snarled. His head snapped around as he searched for the fly.

There it was, on the back edge of the desk. Pressman pushed up slowly to his feet. *All right, you shit.* He raised the prospectus carefully. *Mr. Fly, your life is at its walloping, squishy end. Right—*

"—now!" he cried, swinging downward, concentrating on putting a hard snap on the folded prospectus. "Got ya!" he exulted through clenching teeth.

He looked at the desk, smile fading. *Wait a second*, said a voice inside his head, perplexed, offended. He looked at the prospectus. Nothing.

"How could I miss?" he muttered. "How the fucking hell could I *miss?*"

He winced. Those pains in his gut again, midgets slashing at his stomach walls with razor blades. "God," he said. He closed his eyes. The headache had swelled, too. "God damn it, one thing at a time!" he ordered his body. He drew in a shaking breath and couldn't seem to get enough air into his lungs.

Pressman opened his eyes. The fly was on the desk again, near the dab of milk. With a grimace, he slammed down the prospectus, barely missing the glass, completely missing the fly. It darted upward, out of sight, then, diving down again, was back, perched on the desk once more. "You son of a bitch," Pressman muttered. *You're playing with me, aren't you? This is recreation in your goddamn little world.* Elude the Prospectus. Piss off the Executive. The Sport of Flies.

He held the prospectus tightly. This time, he would not be premature. This time, he would be more cunning. He raised the prospectus slowly and with infinite precision. *The hunter raised his weapon*, said his mind. *Fuck off!* he yelled at it. The fly stood motionless. *Does he see what I'm doing?* Pressman wondered. *Is his little bastard fly face grinning with anticipation?*

Pressman swung down as quickly as he could, well behind the standing fly. Too late; it shot up in the air. "Bastard!" Pressman cried. "You miserable, fucking little bastard!" His shoulders jerked around as he searched for the fly's location.

It was on the windowsill again. Pressman lunged, smashing the prospectus downward, missing. The fly swept over to the desk again, descended, landing. Pressman hurled the prospectus, hitting the glass. It skidded across the desk top, spouting milk, then toppled off the edge. "God *damn* it!" Pressman raged.

He had to stop, bend over, both hands on the desk top, bracing himself. His head was pounding. It felt as though it were expanding and contracting like a fire-driven bellows. Pressman groaned. The pains were slashing at his stomach even more. He slumped back in his chair. *Control*, he told himself. He closed his eyes, breath laboring. *That's right, have a fucking heart attack*, he thought. *That's all you need.* That bastard Masters. If he'd only come on time.

Pressman swallowed. *Throat's so dry*, he thought, opening his eyes. He started to reach for the glass of milk. *It's gone, you idiot*, he mocked himself. Lying on the floor. Should he pick it up and dry the carpeting? Fuck it. Let Doreen.

"Oh, shit," he murmured. There were splashes of milk across the Barker contract. He pulled out his handkerchief and laid it, open, on the page, watched spots appear on it. He closed his eyes and rubbed them hard. When they refocused, he saw the fly. It was sitting on his handkerchief. *Sucking up milk spots with his damned proboscis*, he thought.

He looked intently at the fly. He had to kill it; that was certain. Destroy it utterly. His problems would be solved if—

Pressman winced. His problems solved if he could kill the fly? That was insane.

Still, it had a kind of dark charm. Wouldn't it be great if all his problems were encapsulated in that grubby little shit-devouring creep of an insect; that sawed-off, pulsing, hairy, silk-winged, goddamn, crazy-making—!

Whoa, he told himself. *This is a fly, Roy.* Not the Cosmic Nemesis. A fly. A dirty, little fly. Period. Pressman didn't move. He watched the fly. It wasn't much, God knew. Dirty. Stupid. Driven. Insignificant. Still, it had him on the run. He grunted with amusement. *What are flies, anyway?* he wondered. *Why the hell do they exist at all? Did God create them just to plague us? Make us sick?* What was their goddamn raison d'être?

Pressman drew in a quivering breath and shuddered. He felt a tingling underneath his skin as though low-wattage current were being transmitted through his flesh. Odd sensation. Anticipation, was it? Excitement at the prospect of destroying Mr. Fly?

Not with the prospectus, though. He shook his head in disapproval. Too stiff; no flexibility. *My kingdom for a swatter*, Pressman thought. He looked around. "Ah," he said. He pushed up sharply, shoving back his chair against the wall. The fly buzzed off the desk. *Didn't like that, did you, little shit?* Pressman thought.

He picked the newspaper off the sofa and fingered through its sections. World and National News? Local News? Theater? Financial? His laugh was like a seal bark. Sports! How perfect. The sport of kings was not horse racing after all; it was fly splatting. Pressman turned slowly, folding the Sports section with great care so it was broader at the end than at the handle. He hefted it. *A goodly weapon, sirrah*, said his mind. *The lethal smite shall be simplicity itself.* He'd hit the fly so hard the little bastard would have newsprint on his hairy ass.

"Okay, Mr. Fly. Prepare to die," he rhymed. He told himself that it was cool amusement in his voice, not vengeful hatred. Told himself the shaking of his hands was natural; the ongoing tingle of his flesh, a normal sign of keen anticipation; the trembling of his breath, no more than might be expected.

The fly was on the handkerchief again. *Perfect*, Pressman thought. *He cannot resist the milk-soaked landing strip on Barker Field.* His mushy death was nigh.

Pressman's pace diminished to an inching, ministepped advance, his gaze fixed, steady and unblinking, on the fly. *The prey continues feeding*, the PBS narrator in his brain intoned, *unaware of the approaching stalker, so intent on sucking moo juice up its snout that—*

Pressman stopped to contain his snicker. *Cut it out*, he told himself. *This is serious fucking business.* He nodded in agreement. *Right*, he thought. *Advance. Prepare for decimation.*

He moved up slowly on the desk, winced. Surely the fly must see him now with one of those eight thousand goddamn lenses. Pressman clenched his teeth and held his breath, edging closer. *Time to meet your Maker, Fly-boy (girl).*

Pressman lunged, slamming down the folded pages on the handker-chief. *Gotcha*! No sign of escaping flight; the little shit was history. Pressman sang, "Dingdong, the fly is dead!"

The body wasn't on the handkerchief. He stiffened, flipping over the newspaper section. *Oh, now, wait a second. "I-did-not-see-him-fly-away,"* he said through gritting teeth.

His eyes moved quickly, an expression of incredulous denial on his face. The fly was standing on the left rear corner of the desk, unharmed, unflustered. *Jesus Christ Almighty*, Pressman thought. He swore to God he didn't see it—

"Wait a second, wait a second, let's not—" His agitated voice broke off. He raised the folded newspaper.

The fly shot up and veered away. Amazingly, Pressman's leaping gaze was able to track it to its landing on the drape. Jesus Christ, it looked bigger now. Pressman scowled at the impression. Against the beige drape, it was an optical illusion, nothing more. He started around the desk, gaze fastened on the fly.

He grunted in startled alarm as his right foot stepped on the fallen glass. It rolled beneath his shoe, throwing him off balance, causing him to flail toward the desk. The elbow of his right arm crashed on the desk top. Pressman cried out at the pain, a look of wide-eyed, staring shock contorting his features as he flopped down on the carpeting. *"Jesus Christ Almighty."* Pressman's voice was breathless and agonized as he clutched the elbow, the newspaper swatter dropping from his fingers. He lay sprawled across the carpeting, eyes closed, face a twisted mask. Jesus, Jesus, *Jesus*! It felt as though his head was near explosion.

It took some minutes for the throbbing ache to fade. Pressman felt tears dribbling down his cheeks, forced out from underneath the lids by pain. *Dear* God, he kept thinking over and over.

Finally, he opened his eyes. The first thing he saw was the fly still on the drape. Pressman felt a welling surge of hatred deep inside himself. *You bastard, you*, he thought. *You lousy, mother-fucking son-of-a-bitch bastard!*

He started to push up, almost setting down his right hand on the fallen glass. *Sure*! his mind exploded. Snatching up the glass, he hurled it to his left, wincing at the streak of pain inside his elbow. He heard the glass break shatteringly against the wall. *Good*! he thought. *Let that bitch pick up the pieces!*

He was balanced on his knees now, wavering slightly, gaze locked on the fly. *Its little claws are buried in the drape*, he thought. Was it happy? Giddy with delight because he'd seen his hunter topple? "Bastard," Pressman muttered. "You are going to *die*." He knew his tone was aberrant. He didn't care. He reached down to grab the folded newspaper, wincing again at the elbow pain. Jesus Christ, did he break it? A half-mad smile peeled back his lips. *With my luck, yes.*

He stood up slowly. *Never mind*, he told himself. It didn't matter. Broken elbow, fractured skull, obliterated spine, it wouldn't matter. With his final, dying breath, he'd kill that fucking little bastard.

He edged up toward the window, leaning backward. Gaze unmoving, he raised the folded paper slowly, swung so hard it made him grunt. The fly sailed out, then in, and landed on the drape again. Pressman smacked at it with the newspaper, missed. It skimmed away, buzzing loudly. Pressman slapped the folded paper at it, trying to hit it in the air. It soared up, landing on the drape above his head, beyond his reach.

"*Oh*, no!" Pressman's features contorted with rage. Clutching upward at the drape, he yanked down hard. The rod brace snapped off from the wall; the drape came thrashing down.

"God *damn* you!" Pressman whirled, his look deranged. The fly was landing on the desk again. Good God, it *did* look bigger. "No!" he snarled. He leaped at the desk and started smashing at the fly in midair as it flew, down on the desk when it landed. He paid no attention to the photographs he knocked across the carpeting. "You bastard, *die*!" he shouted, swinging with maddened rage. He hit the water thermos, and it bounced to the floor, rolled floppingly across the carpeting. The Barker contract and his handkerchief went sailing next. *Fuck 'em!*

The fly had vanished. Pressman stopped and tried to listen for its buzzing flight. But his breathing was too loud, his chest heaving as he sucked in breath. He swallowed dryly. *"Damn,"* he muttered. *"Damn."* This wasn't funny anymore. The fly *did* represent his troubles now. *And I will not go off the fucking edge at forty-seven, driven by a goddamned insect!* His head jerked from side to side as he searched for it. He paid no attention to the shooting pains in his neck, the fiery stabbing in his stomach, the quick expansion and contraction of his head. *Only one thing matters now. One thing—*

The thought broke off; he flashed a death's-head grin. The fly was on the sofa, black against the beige upholstery. *Thank God the decorator talked me out of dark brown*, he thought, advancing.

He closed in on the sofa, pushed aside the coffee table with his right leg. *Got you now*, he thought. He felt his heartbeat getting faster. *Good. Get that damned adrenaline rushing.* He nodded jerkily, the death's-head grin frozen to his lips. *You bastard, you are going to die. To die!*

He flung himself at the sofa, using his entire body as a weapon, snapping the newspaper swatter as he fell. The fly swept upward to his left; he heard it bounce off the shade of the end table lamp, drop downward to the table. He lunged at it, his shredding swatter brandished high. It slapped down loudly on the table. Pressman snarled, elated. *"Yeah!"* He couldn't believe his eyes. The fly was in the air again, settling quickly on the lampshade. Pressman didn't hesitate. Lurching up, he swung the paper swatter sideways, slamming it against the shade. The lamp went crashing to the floor; the fly went darting off. *"God damn you!"* Pressman screamed. He slung the newspaper pages at the fly. They opened up and flapped to the carpeting like a wounded bird. Pressman twisted around in rabid fury. Where the hell *was* it? *Where?!* *"God damn you."* He could barely speak. He felt a dash of spittle on his chin and slapped it off, eyes wild as he continued searching.

He saw a movement in the mirror hung above the bar and zeroed in his gaze. For a fraction of a second, he believed that there were now *two* flies and felt a chill rush up his back along the spine. Then he scowled in fury at his own stupidity, realizing that it was only a reflection of the fly, darting around in tight, concentric circles above the bar, its buzzing clearly audible. Pressman started toward the bar. *Wait!* a voice warned in his mind. He had no weapon now. He looked around in desperate need. No time to waste! Another newspaper section? That was no improvement. A folded magazine? No better than the prospectus.

"God damn it, I've got to have *something*!" he muttered frenziedly.

Yes! He virtually dived at the sofa, landing on it with his left knee, snatching up a pillow. Good! More hitting area! He shoved up backward to his feet, almost losing balance as he turned toward the bar. He staggered briefly, then regained himself and stalked in on the bar, eyes unmoving, gaze narrowed at the circling fly. *Now, you bastard; now.* He winced at the sobbing noise his indrawn breath made. *Easy*, he ordered. *Don't let it get away now.* The two flies coalesced with a movement so abrupt he couldn't follow it. The fly was on the mirror. "Now," he mumbled. "Here I come."

Pressman gripped the pillow corner hard, fingers digging in like talons. He swung at the mirror, hit it. The fly took off. He swung again, knocking a bottle of scotch against a stand of glasses, smashing them. "*You*—!" He couldn't finish, swinging at the fly again, trying to knock it out of the air. Another bottle crashed, more glasses. The fly was on the mirror once again. Pressman swung the pillow fiercely in a backhand smash that knocked the mirror askew. The fly came out so swiftly from its surface that it glanced off Pressman's cheek. He howled in sickened fury, swinging the pillow back and forth berserkly in the air, his face a mask of hatred and revulsion. "*Bastard! Stand and fight!*" he shouted.

He saw the fly. The little bastard was back on his desk! Resting. "No, no rest," Pressman muttered, reeling forward. He reached the desk and slammed the pillow down at the fly. He looked at the desk; God damn it, how could he keep *missing*?! He swung the pillow back and forth across the desk, knocking off the penstand set, the paperweight, the cigarette lighter, the lamp and telephone and letter basket—he sent them all tumbling to the floor with vengeful, maniacal cries, lost hold of the pillow so it flew across the office, hitting the door.

Pressman stood immobile, panting, a look of stunned disbelief on his face. The fly was on the window, hanging, motionless. It *wasn't* his imagination; it was bigger. *Bigger.* Jesus Christ in Heaven, *bigger*! It wasn't a fly! It was a—what, a *what*? "Oh, Jesus Christ." Pressman tried but was unable to repress a high-pitched sob. *Good God*, he thought. *It's me.*

It's me.

He slumped down on the chair and pressed his left hand across his eyes. The hand was shaking. *He* was shaking. He'd virtually destroyed his office, all in vain. Just to kill a poor, defenseless—

Pressman's laugh was frightening to him—a choking, demented sound. *Defenseless?* He lowered the hand and looked around his office. Sure, defenseless. As the Antichrist. Lord of the Flies. Wasn't that a nickname for the Devil?

"Shut up," Pressman mumbled to himself. "Shut *up.*" He closed his eyes with a feeble moan. His stomach was roiling hotly, burgeoning with acids. His brain was pressing outward at his skull, threatening to crack it open. Every muscle in his neck and shoulders ached with pulsing pain. *I'm going to die. Not the fly. Me.*

He blinked at the buzzing noise, looked down. It wasn't the fly but the telephone. Exhaustedly, he hauled the two parts upward, using the wire, set the cradle on the empty desk, then the receiver down on top of it. The buzzing stopped. He leaned back in the chair. Stiffening as the fly came zooming down and landed on the back of his right hand.

Oh, Jesus, Pressman thought. He couldn't move. His heart was pounding. Couldn't the fly feel it in the veins of his hand? He stared incredulously at it. After all this, on his hand again? His *hand*?

He watched the fly in frozen, breathless silence. It wasn't bigger; it was still the same. That had been a stupid, momentary delusion. Now what, though? There it was in front of him, standing on his hand, for Christ's sake! Did it know? Did it understand that one of them must die? Was it offering itself in sacrifice for the survival of his sanity?

But how? It was blocking his right hand, washing its legs. The prisoner on death row pomading his hair? Or the winner grooming on the giant body of his conquest? Pressman's face distended at the thought. *Don't lose it*! he commanded himself. *This is your last chance. Lose it and you're done.*

Yes, he thought then, smiling. Slowly, he slid his left hand across his lap, gaze fixed on the fly. He mustn't move his right hand, not a tremor's worth. Let him have the right hand. It's his platform, his pulpit. Let him preach his sermon on the fishes and the loaves—in his case, the maggots and the turds. His left hand was the Power and the Glory. Inchingly, he raised his left arm to the level of the chair arm, then slipped its hand across the edge, snaking it down to the left-hand pocket of his suit coat. Thank *God* he didn't have the time to hang it in the closet when he came in this morning.

Pressman reached into the pocket, gaze unmoving on the fly. His fingers gripped the billfold edge and raised it, slowly, from the pocket. Upward—slowly—slowly. Across the arm. *How fitting*, it occurred to him. The weapon: *him*. Ensconced between those leather sides. Driver's license. Social Security. Health and automobile insurance. Membership and credit cards. He even had a reduced Photostat of his birth certificate in there. His life contained within those black walls. Fitting, then, that it should—

Dear God, let it be, he pleaded. He raised the billfold slowly, very slowly. Was it watching him, amused? Was every single goddamn one of those eight thousand lenses focused on his pitiful attempt? After everything he'd tried before, it struck him as beyond belief how truly slow his downward movement was this time. The wallet slapped against his hand, stinging the skin. He saw the fly's dead body tumble off.

Something surged up in him: a cry, a fury, a bestial joy. He shoved back the chair and toppled forward to his knees on the carpeting. The fly lay motionless on its back, legs in the air. With a savage snarl, Pressman reached down, pinching it between the thumb and index finger of his right hand. Lifting it, he laid it on his left palm; then, with a sound he later refused to think about—a lunatic chortling that vibrated in his throat—he pressed down on its body with his right thumb, grinding it to a yellow paste flecked with hair, wing, and leg parts. Even when it was reduced to a smear on his skin, he kept rubbing, teeth clenched, a crazed smile on his lips, the quivering sound in his throat rising steadily in volume. He started, looking up, heartbeat thudding hard. The telephone was ringing. Pressman stared at it as though he didn't understand what it was, as though it was some odd device unknown in his primitive world.

Then he blinked, returning, swallowed, reached up, lifted the receiver, and carried it to his head. "Yes?" he said. Was that his voice? Good God, was that his *voice*? He averted his face and cleared his throat strenuously, then turned back. "Hello?" he said into the mouthpiece.

"That you, Pressman?" asked the voice.

He shuddered. "Yes."

"Masters. Just now noticed, on my calendar, that I was going to stop there on my way to lunch. Too late now; meeting ran on longer than I thought it would. Have to put it off a few days."

Pressman nodded. "Yes."

"No help for it," Masters told him.

"Of course." His voice was back now, its smooth, professional tone. "Listen; these things happen. No point in letting little things disturb us."

"Right," said Masters. "Call you in a day or two."

Pressman kept on nodding. "Yes," he said. "Of course."

He was speaking into a dead receiver; Masters had already hung up. Pressman noticed how his left hand trembled as he set the receiver back in place.

He sat in silence for more than half an hour. Fifteen minutes into it, he noticed the spot on his left palm and wiped it off with a tissue from his desk drawer, threw the tissue into the wastebasket.

At one-sixteen Doreen came back. Pressman tried to tell her not to come in when she knocked, but she opened the door automatically. "I'm back, Mr.—" Pressman felt a biting pain inside his stomach as she looked around the office in astonishment.

He drew in a breath. "A fly," he said. "Drove me nuts before I could kill it."

After she was gone, a coldness gripped at Pressman as he understood her look.

In the seven years they'd rented here, there'd never been a fly inside his office.

"Oh," he murmured. He felt as though he'd just been hollowed out.

A fly descended in an arcing plummet, landing on the desk top several inches from the edge of Pressman's right hand.

MICHAEL BLUMLEIN

The Thing Itself

Michael Blumlein's story "The Thing Itself" is a beautifully written tale of Magical Realism. Magical Realism, in which fantasy imagery is used as a device to tell very real stories about contemporary life, is an area of literature that, in recent years, has been identified with and popularized by Latin American writers such as Gabriel García Márquez (*One Hundred Years of Solitude*) and Jorge Luis Borges; however, it is a form many American writers are working with successfully as well. Blumlein is one of these. His work has appeared in such diverse magazines as *OMNI, Twilight Zone* and *The Mississippi Review*, and he is the author of a novel, *The Movement of Mountains*. His story "The Domino Master" (*OMNI*, June 1988) is also highly recommended.

Blumlein is a physician and faculty member of the University of California School of Medicine. He lives in San Francisco.

—T. W.

THE THING ITSELF

Michael Blumlein

This is a story about love. It is about Laurie and Elliot, two people who meet in their late twenties. Laurie is a nurse and an outdoorswoman. She jogs and she hikes. She has had experiences with men, none of them long. She prefers her enlistments short and definable.

Elliot is a doctor. He has cystic fibrosis, a disease of the lungs and pancreas. He is a dedicated and conscientious worker and a wit. A vivid imagination is his handle on survival.

There are lessons in this story. Particular ones, and universal. A video is forthcoming. And later, a syndicated column. Love, after all, is not so hard. It is not a city, or a thought. When attended to with foresight and maturity, love is as straightforward as boiling an egg.

1. The Roll of the Dice

Laurie met Elliot while she was working in the intensive care unit. It was in the early morning hours after the fire that had swept through the college women's dormitory, and all medical personnel had been mobilized. The blackened bodies of coeds hadn't yet been removed from the crowded corridors. They lined the walls, silent lumps under crumpled white sheets. The smell was horrible. Families raged and grieved, while nurses, doctors, administrators, and orderlies performed their grim tasks. The proportions of the tragedy stripped away artifice. The normally meticulous women forgot about their makeup, their lipstick and eyeliner. Mascara trickled in tears down their cheeks. The carefully groomed administrators had no time to shave, and tiny splinters of hair stuck out from their chins and cheeks. For a short while these people came together in a way unknown to them by the light of bright and ordered day.

Laurie found Elliot in the ICU. They had communicated several times before, under purely routine circumstances. The lids of his eyes seemed

165

to close as he leaned over the girl in the bed. He placed his stethoscope on her chest and shook his head.

"Take a break," Laurie said. "You've been here all night."

Elliot pretended not to hear. His forehead was nearly touching the singed skin of the girl. He tried to hold back his tears.

Laurie stood silently next to the bed. Her stethoscope was draped over her neck; her hands squeezed the side rail. She watched Elliot, who seemed so sad and alive. She reached across the dying girl and took his hand.

"C'mon, let's have a cup of coffee."

Elliot let her lead him to the nurses' lounge, where they sat on a cheap plastic couch. It was split down the middle, and the foam showed through. Elliot held his face in his hands, staring at the floor. Laurie bent the spigot of the coffee machine, filling two cups with lukewarm coffee. Her eyes were bloodshot; the gray bags beneath them made her look twice her age. She had been a nurse for five years, and this had been the worst night of her life. Unconsciously, she put her hand on Elliot's neck and began to rub.

Elliot let her, not expecting to relax. He was too tired to sleep. He put the coffee cup on the table and touched Laurie's leg. He turned sideways on the couch, crossed his legs in a yoga position, and stretched out his back. Laurie rubbed it. She leaned closer and pulled him against her. Shaking her hands between the buttons at the front of his shirt, she touched his chest.

Elliot took her to the on-call room and locked the door. He made a few lame jokes about doctors and nurses. She laughed a little too loudly. When they made love, it was slow, then very quick. Elliot was funny and gentle. Laurie was surprised at how easy it was. She got hot fast and reached a sharp climax. Elliot came too, and in moments was asleep. His breathing was rapid and coarse for a long time. Laurie stayed awake. She was amazed. A verse from somewhere played in her mind:

> The dead come knocking
> The dead come knocking
> And love, sweet love,
> It lets them in.

2. Choosing the Right Species

Tall men aroused in Laurie feelings she preferred to avoid. She was five foot three, and Elliot, if anything, was half an inch shorter. This suited Laurie just fine. When they moved in together, they kept things—books, pots, linens—close to the ground. They left the top shelves in the kitchen empty, and made sure their two full-length mirrors were hung low on the doors.

A month after getting the apartment, Elliot came down with pneumonia. He was put in the hospital and ended up staying for three weeks. During this time Laurie got a taste of a different life. She visited him daily, twice when she could. They did crosswords together, read to each other, shared meals. Elliot craved starches—noodles and spaghetti—because of his body's poor ability to digest protein. Laurie brought in food and ate with him. She got a little fat. She stopped jogging because she didn't have time, and saw more of his nurses than her own friends.

On the whole, though, she was happy. She had a man, and the man loved her. He needed her. It made her feel good.

Elliot's pneumonia slowly improved. His breathing became easier, and the oxygen was taken away. Soon he was able to say more than one or two sentences without getting out of breath.

"Imagination," he told Laurie, "is the source of my strength. When I stop inventing, I will die."

He was twenty-nine, and had already lived years beyond others with his disease. His future was not bright.

"Fiction is power," he went on. "Out of it grows fact. Avoidance is sometimes more direct than study."

Elliot loved the sound of words and the shelter they brought. When he had the breath, he could talk for hours. He told Laurie stories.

One day they were lying together in his hospital bed, Elliot in his issued gown. Laurie in a skirt and blouse. The nurses allowed the intimacy because Laurie was one of them, because Elliot was a doctor. They allowed it because they were sympathetic; they understood the nature of health and recovery.

The back of the bed was raised so that Elliot could breathe easier. Laurie was nestled by his side, one hand draped across his stomach. She was half-asleep, timing her breathing to the cadence of Elliot's voice.

"Like the pope," he was saying, "I believe in angels. Not good and bad ones, as he supposes. Reflective ones. Mirrors in the shapes of Möbius strips. A kind of personal and mathematical afterlife. Are you listening?"

She nodded sleepily.

"It is not simply belief," he went on. "There are certain proofs. . . ." He paused, looking down at her hand on his belly. It was finely veined, strong, and the arm, the soft belly of the biceps, was beautiful as it disappeared into the sleeve of her blouse. He became aware of her breasts pressed against his side.

"There is a restaurant," he said. "I have visited it more than once. Its atmosphere is unique; its elegance, legendary. The special there is an ambrosial delight not to be found elsewhere. Not were you to search a lifetime." He put a hand on her breast and spoke authoritatively. "Mother's milk. Not milk and honey, not the milk of human kindness, not even the milky tears of dew at dawn. Simply, purely, pleasingly, Mother's milk. The brew of Mammalia. The sustenance of our kind."

She smile dreamily. Encouraged, Elliot went on.

"Here," he swept out an arm, "on our very premises we house a wide variety of creatures. The multitudinous reflections of God's eye are yours to choose from. In cages in the basement we have rabbit, chipmunk, gopher, and beaver. Our shrew milk is heavenly, though scant. An agile child has been trained to gather it: her tiny, supple fingers deftly milk the precious fluid into thimbles, which you may purchase as souvenirs.

"In a corral adjoining the flank of the restaurant lie our marsupials, the wombats and koalas, the kangaroos. Beyond, in our rolling grasslands, dotted with oak and madrone, irrigated by fifteen miles of flexible conduit, waters from artesian wells, graze elephant, ass, moose, zebra, yak, giraffe, and llama. Anteaters forage there, and armadillos. It is still summer, and the young of these creatures are not yet weaned. There is milk in abundance, thick milk, thin, sweet and bitter. Some is white as snow, some yellow, other gray as ash. We have a team of starving children, adept at identification, trained to run quickly and carefully. They keep low, and draw upon udders with acrobatic skill and finesse. For each cup of milk delivered to our kitchen they receive a handful of coin; every third cup nets them a day of rest. They are strong-hearted and eager to please. Choose your mammal and feed a child."

He paused to gather his breath.

Laurie yawned, stretched. "You haven't mentioned the carnivores," she said.

"We offer a complete listing. The cost, as you might expect, is higher. The risks are greater, the mothers not so obliging. Extraction is more labor-intensive, requiring from two to five brave souls. We don't use tranquilizer guns, as it would taint the milk. A mothering carnivore, be it badger, weasel, lion, bear, or wolf, is a touchy animal. Her glands are guarded items, the product a precious commodity. But a sip of cheetah milk . . ." He sighed, licking his lips, "it puts hair on your chest."

"I don't need more hair," said Laurie. She touched a scratch mark on her calf. "I have to shave too much as it is, and I hate it."

"Then you should definitely skip the carnivores. Besides, the milk has a tendency to be harsh. Causes the mouth to pucker." He pursed his lips and blew her a kiss.

"Ethical considerations require that the last class go unnamed. Strictly speaking, we are not even supposed to have the milk available. Gathering it has been declared an objectification of the provider. Many who are not in need of the income consider it degrading. Others claim that its collection and availability carry sexual overtones that should not be confused with food. Notwithstanding these objections, it is a most popular item."

"Men, I presume, favor it more than women."

"Surprisingly not. Women choose it as often."

"It's in your mind, Elliot."

He laughed. "I'm a piece of fiction."

"You're a good man. What will I do without you?"

"Don't be maudlin." He started to say more but was interrupted by the beginnings of a cough. It started deep in his chest and rumbled up like thunder. His face suffused with blood, and his whole body shook. It seemed like he was tearing his insides out.

"Should I call the nurse?"

He didn't answer, working his lungs until finally he brought something up. He spit it into some Kleenex, then reached over and turned on the oxygen. He stuck the plastic prongs in his nose.

Laurie watched. She waited. Her initial apprehension gradually faded, but a knot of tension stayed in her stomach. She was still learning this man's routine. This life.

"I'm worried about you," she said at length.

"It's okay," he said, panting. His forehead was beaded with sweat. "I . . . have to . . . get . . . the phlegm up."

"It's always like this?"

He nodded. They held hands and listened to the oxygen bubbling quietly up beside the bed. Gradually his breathing calmed. Laurie asked him about dying.

"Everyone dies," he said.

"But you have CF."

"I don't think about it. Only when I'm sick."

She looked at him quizzically. "I don't believe you."

He stared at her, then looked away. "I think about it. What's the difference?"

"The difference is I'm involved. I just found you. I don't want you to die."

"I won't die."

She was not convinced.

"I won't," he repeated. "I promise. Listen . . ." He took her hand. "There's one more item. One more kind of milk."

"Stop," she said.

"No. Listen. It's the last. The purest. It's a vapor, it enters through

closed lips, condenses on the tongue. It's the sweetest milk there is. Full
of gentleness and comfort. The breath of an angel."

"I don't believe in angels," she said stiffly. "This is about dying, isn't
it?" Tears brimmed her eyes. "you're going to die, aren't you?"

"No." He shook his head. "It's just a story."

3. Imagination and ½Good Health

Love requires health. Health is hypnotism, trust, science. It is persuasion and power, belief spread like a blanket, a bed. It is rational,
irrational. Chemistry, words, light, and sound.

An agent can be employed. A drug, for example, a root. Or a shell,
mud, bark, the husk of an insect. A scalpel can be the agent. The ace
of cups. There are capsules the size of cherries, poultices that smell like
tar. Horn of goat, spore of fungus, fender, headlight, bottle cap. A healer
must not be narrow-minded.

He can tell a story.

Elliot is a healer, a doctor of medicine. He works in a windowless
room with a desk and a table. A curtain can be drawn around the table
for privacy. Patients who willingly lie naked for his examination use the
curtain's screen to reclothe themselves. It is the shield behind which they
recover their dignity.

On the wall above his desk is taped a card with the words DO NO
HARM. Out of sight on the back of it is a quote from a friend: "I've
always said I don't mind nobody bullshittin' me, but if you're going to
jive make it good. Make me believe it."

One afternoon a woman enters his office. She is overweight and wears
pants whose zipper is broken. She has a loose-fitting T-shirt and a ban-
danna that hides her hair. Settling in the chair beside his desk, she says,
"I got burning."

Elliot is tired from a bad night. He stifles a yawn. "Burning?"

"All up in my head," she touches it, "and down my back. It draws
on me. Cuts clear from back to front. My arms and legs too. My whole
body burns."

Elliot thumbs through her chart, thick with multiple visits, multiple
complaints. Even before knowing what she has, he wonders what she
wants.

"How long have you had the burning?"

The woman calculates. "Two days, maybe three."

"Have you tried anything?"

"Rubbing alcohol."

He nods.

"Listerine."

He waits for more, but the woman is close-lipped. She stares at her lap, as though awaiting punishment.

"And did they help?"

"They soothed a little. I still got the burning."

Elliot is drowsy, and his mind is not working well. Burning makes him think of sparks, fire, sexual yearning. He knows if he is not careful, the thread will vanish and he will lose control.

He tells her to undress, and when she is ready he goes to examine her. She does not appear ill. In the midst of listening to her lungs, Elliot is struck by a fit of coughing. He retreats across the room, leaning against his desk until the paroxysm passes. Winded and slightly embarrassed, he completes the exam. He draws the curtain and tells her to dress.

At his desk he ponders his own health. It is slowly failing. He feels it when he tries a deep breath. Always he wants for air.

The woman seems healthy enough. He resents this, but also he is grateful. Her story is making him work and forget. When she is dressed and sitting, he has a sense again of her fear.

"The exam," he says carefully, "is normal."

"Then what's the burning?"

"It's a reaction to something. Maybe a virus. Or an allergy. It should be gone in a few days."

She looks at him, her face working to stay calm. Her eyes are everywhere but at his. "My mother died of cancer."

"This is not cancer."

"It ate her up. In the end the fever got her. Burned her till she couldn't eat. Couldn't breathe either."

"You do not have cancer." Elliot takes her by the wrist and forces her to look at him. "Do you understand?"

"I'm not going to die?"

"Not of this."

Are you sure?"

Listen to me. This is not cancer. You are not going to die."

She looks away, and then her eyes dart back, as if to make sure he is telling the truth.

"You believe me?"

She nods tentatively, then stands. "I feel better. The burning, it'll go away?"

"Yes. Call me next week."

She leaves, and Elliot settles in his chair. He feels charged by the encounter. On a scrap of paper he scribbles the words: *science: to know*, and beneath them, *fiction: to shape*. Next to *fiction* he sketches a picture of a syringe and needle. He draws a colony of bacteria and an equation to estimate the blood flow through the heart. Above it, opposite the word *science*, he sketches the face of a man. He has a single eye, from whose pupil radiate tiny stars, half-moons, mythical animals in miniature. They rise above his head, where they circle in a cloud of barely discernible shapes. They look like the bacteria below, and, noting this, Elliot draws a bridge connecting the two. He smiles, then yawns. Cradling his arms on the desktop, he puts his head down.

Sometime later, a knock on the door stirs him. Heavy-lidded and still half-asleep, he swivels in his chair. Through the door walks a clown in full regalia—whiteface, painted smile, pink wig. On his forehead is penciled a blue eye.

Elliot stares. He rubs his eyes. There is another knock, and he turns to the door, grateful for the interruption. This time a skeleton hobbles in, all bones, ambulating without visible means of support. In its teeth is clenched a cigar, whose smoke trails up and hangs in its eye sockets. The skeleton takes a position near the clown, who regards Elliot with a gay, fixed smile. He wrinkles his forehead, and the eye there blinks.

Elliot is speechless. His mind skirts over the day's events, searching for clues. Did he eat something bad? Was there a drug in his morning tea? Something in the air? The skeleton and clown seem to be waiting. There is another sound at the door, followed by a brief inrush of air. Elliot girds himself and turns. Standing in the doorway is a naked man, his face and torso vaguely familiar. Sweeping out from his back are wings.

Elliot numbly watches this last one enter, then gets up and shuts the door. This is a private matter, he is sure. It occurs to him that it might be his time to die.

The three gaze at him without detectable emotion. The clown speaks.

"Life is not simple, my friend. You've probably noticed. Boundaries constantly change. It is a difficult concept for the egocentric mind.

"A person, for example, starts as a single cell. The cell divides, migrates, differentiates. There is no 'fact' of existence."

"Who are you?" Elliot asks. His voice is shaky.

"Nor of nonexistence," the winged person continues. "Dead tissue is carried off by scavengers. Bones, by droplets of water. Death is hardly less complicated."

"Why are you here? Who are you?"

"There is no thing that does not change. There is no fact. There is only fiction."

"We are Humor, Death, Science," says the clown. "Your homunculi. A lovely triad, don't you think?"

"Think?" Elliot stammers. "Am I thinking?"

"Don't be cute." The skeleton waves its cigar. "I was told you were a nice fellow."

"Courteous," says the clown.

"Kind."

"A hard worker."

"Why are you here?" Elliot asks.

"A lesson in geography," rattles the skeleton. "Boundaries. The imagination."

"You scare me."

"We could not possibly harm you," murmurs the one with wings.

"There is, however, the question of health." The clown scribbles a formula in the air. "Science is chemistry. Subatomics is the nature of things."

"The end of things is the nature of things," says the skeleton. "Forgetfulness is such a blessing."

"The wind is a blessing," says the winged one. Of the three he seems the most human. "Breath is the common origin. It is the source of inspiration."

"Which of the triad are you?" Elliot asks.

"I am Death," whispers the angel.

Elliot is now visibly shaken. He strains to think of something to say, to do. The tension rises in his body. When it hits his chest, he is seized by a fit of coughing. It is a bad one, lasting more than a minute. By the time it ends, he is breathless. His face is red, his head between his legs.

"Air," he whispers. "Air."

4. Doing Things Together

At the foot of Elliot and Laurie's bed is a twenty-four-inch Sony color television. The remote control device lies between them on the sheet. They are watching the Miss America Beauty Pageant.

Elliot is bored with the contestants, putting up with their dime-store, egregious obsequiousness in order to catch a glimpse of the true star, the enigmatic Bert Parks. Parks is a kind of hero to Elliot. He seems to age so gracelessly, like no man on earth, from the lizardlike skin at his neck to the sleazy, hungry, haunted pits that pass for his eyes. His smile is a lurid caricature, evoking death camp assurances and promises. And his singing . . . his singing is mesmerizing.

A rhapsody to the beatific pucker of femininity, Parks's voice is a tribute to science. To mind over matter, imagination over true flesh.

When Parks sings, Elliot nearly weeps. He thinks of drugs stronger than morphine, of direct stimulation of the neural centers of pain and pleasure. He is astounded by the man, by his determination, his self-denigration, his longevity. During the closing bars of the pageant's hymn, Elliot suddenly realizes that Parks is not human.

If he studies the man's image carefully, he can discern gaps between body parts. When one of the contestants passes behind him, Elliot catches a glimpse of the sequins on her dress through Parks's thyroid gland. When Parks turns to greet her, pink feathers (presumably from her headpiece) sprout from his eye sockets. It is a revelation. Bert Parks, the suave, polished, unctuous ringmaster, is an illusion.

Laurie is more interested in the girls. She is captivated by their glossy smiles and precise bodies. Their perfect nails and hair, and endless legs. Despite her humiliation at their grating optimism and choreographed gaiety, Laurie is envious. She imagines futures of attention and worth, of great personal magnetism and reward. She feels inadequate. Taking the remote control device in a hand, she punches off the TV.

"Am I pretty?" she asks Elliot.

"Exceptionally."

"No. Don't answer fast. I want you to think about it. I want the truth."

He cups his chin in his palm and looks her over. The wide, acne-pocked forehead. Weak chin, full breasts, short, fat legs.

"You are beautiful," he says.

She looks him in the eye. "You mean it?"

"I mean it. Beautiful. It's as simple as that."

Laurie smiles then, a broad, teary-eyed smile. "I love you, Elliot. If I could, I'd give you my breath. I'd breathe for you."

"Laurie," he says, taking her hands, "if I could, I'd sing for you. I'd sing words that you'd believe, and I'd put them in your brain in a place you'd never forget. . . ." He pauses, then laughs. "If I could, Laurie, I'd be Bert Parks for you. I'd be immortal."

5. Working It Out

Laurie works in the intensive care unit. Sometimes it is slow, sometimes busy. Of the six beds in the unit only one is filled tonight. In it is a thirty-year-old man who looks ninety. His eyes are yellow, his arms spindly, his face sallow. His belly is so swollen that he has not seen his feet in months. He can't lie flat because it is impossible to breathe, so he has to be propped up in bed. He doesn't sleep well but can't take pills because his liver is shot. He has terminal cirrhosis and has been in and out of a coma for days.

Presently he is in, which means that there is not much for Laurie to do. From time to time she checks his bottles, and every hour she takes his vital signs. Between these small tasks she sits at the nurses' station reading an outdoor magazine. Tonight she finds it boring and keeps reading the same passage over and over. She is thinking about Elliot.

All her life Laurie has depended on men. This she resents, and so for years has made a deal with herself. A secret, barely conscious deal: her men will have flaws. Her first lover was unreliable; her second, distant and moody. The one before Elliot indulged himself in a cause more than he did in Laurie. Elliot's flaw is his illness. It puts the two of them, she feels, on equal footing. He cannot leave her because he needs her. He depends on her. This gives her a sense of security. It makes her feel curiously independent and strong. She has casually forgotten the inevitability of his early death. She is unaware of how carefully she has chosen a situation that will soon cause her grief. Laurie herself lives in a world of periodic coma.

She has a cup of coffee, and then another. Between three and five are the worst hours of the morning, the hardest to stay awake. She starts to do her nails but stops because she doesn't really care. The girls are girls; she is a woman. The men can meet her on her own ground.

The coffee has its effect, and her head begins to buzz. Her hands get jittery, and she starts to have a few wild thoughts. From the bed of the cirrhotic she hears a sound. There is a curtain around him, and when she gets up to look behind it, he is gone. In his place is a man with wings.

Oh shit, Laurie things. *Something's wrong. Something's terribly wrong.* Then the nurse in her takes over.

She makes the man comfortable, fluffing up the pillow and straightening the sheets. His wings curl around, resting on his torso and upper thighs. He smiles up at her from a drawn face; he does not look well at all. She gives him a sip of water, and he thanks her with his eyes. She tells herself that she should report this to her supervisor, but as she turns to go, he touches her with a wing. He makes her understand that he wants her to take a feather. As a gift. A token. Laurie refuses, but the man insists. It is all so very strange.

Finally she consents, choosing a small white primary near the tip. She tugs on it, but it sticks tight. She pulls harder, and harder still.

It come loose with a pop, then a hiss. Laurie feels a soft stream of air against her face. It tastes faintly of milk.

She touches her lips with the tip of the feather. The hiss continues. She realizes she has acted willfully. It does not surprise her. All things must pass. She is a survivor. The man's time is up.

6. Song and Lament

You promised you wouldn't die. You said it, and yet you bought life insurance every chance you got. At eighteen, twenty, twenty-five. Twenty-five years old! There is no insurance at twenty-five; at twenty-five some people open their eyes for the first time. Open them and see a world. Take the wrong turn sometimes, stumble maybe, but none would call it death. Disappointment, sure. A setback. But not death. How can we die before we even open our eyes?

But it was different for you. You were sick from the start. Your mother said she wouldn't have had you if she'd known. She was crying when she said that, it was after you died. She would have aborted, she said, if not with the help of someone with conscience, then in some back alley. With a stick, a hanger. With lye if she had to. However dangerous and terrible, she would have tried. Because life was too hard for you. Too damned hard.

You couldn't run or skip, couldn't move fast to save your life. Couldn't scale a peak and stand above the world, stretch out where there's nothing but sky. Or pause on an alpine trail, lupine clumped around the base of a gnarled juniper, wind in your face, snow in the air. Stop and sit on a piece of granite the size of an elephant. Share lunch. You couldn't breathe the mountain air, the fine, crystalline air. The oxygen was too thin, your lungs too choked with phlegm. You almost died when we drove across the Rockies.

But you said dying wasn't on your mind when you weren't sick. When you weren't laid out in bed, coughing, panting, struggling to bring up the phlegm. You said you didn't think about it, but how could you not? How could you not be afraid the next day might be just a little harder, your lungs more tired, your breath feebler? When you're sick like that, isn't every day a sick day, even when you're better? Don't the pills get old, and the treatments? Isn't there a part of you that waits for things to worsen, that expects to die?

But you said no, and showered me with fancy words and stories. With gentleness and patience. With love.

Sometimes you seemed a saint. Tough, vulnerable. Weakened, you were stronger. Resilient. Erotic.

You were the sexiest man I knew.

You didn't hike or swim. Didn't cook. You talked to me. You listened. You made jokes and made love.

You used to come home after work—after ten, twelve exhausting hours at the hospital—and boil a package of spaghetti for dinner. Spaghetti and butter. That was it. For dinner. No wonder you died.

You made me laugh, see? Taught me humor. Imagination. Things to ease the pain.

Like buying that guidebook of San Francisco with each street labeled according to its grade. Red was steep, yellow gentle, blue level. You plotted a course through the city, convinced me the modest hills were mountain peaks, the brightly painted Victorians sweet-smelling pine. Stray cats were skunk, dogs were wolf and deer. The reservoirs were alpine lakes, and you carried repellent to keep the mosquitoes down.

You were good at easing the pain, Elliot. The pain of loss. The pain of having to lose you.

I remember the last morphine shot, the one that let you lie back, that let the knotted muscles in your chest and neck finally ease. The room was dark, your friends circled the bed like a hand. One by one they told the stories, they made a web of memories with you at the center. So that when they were done, you were remembered, and free to go. You slumped against me, heavy, loose at last, and asked, Can I die? Your voice was so feeble I scarcely heard. Can I die?

Yes, I whispered. Yes, yes, die now.

You smiled, and your mouth got slack. You gave a little shudder, and you died.

I did not weep. I felt anger and sadness. Your weight. I watched the moonlight on the floor. I heard wheels in the hall. The world had wings.

CHARLES DE LINT

The Soft Whisper of Midnight Snow

Charles de Lint has immersed himself in the world of fantasy as a writer, critic, scholar, publisher, and musician specializing in traditional folk material. He is one of the leading authors in a new generation of fantasy writers bringing fantasy motifs into a modern context, using myth and dream as a way of exploring the modern world. Work in this vein includes the novels *Moonheart, Mulengro, Yarrow, Green Mantle, Jack the Giant-Killer: The Jack of Kinrowan*, and *Svaha*. His "imaginary world" fantasy novels are *The Riddle of the Wren, The Harp of the Grey Rose* and *Wolf Moon*. He also writes horror fiction, and numerous short stories.

Inspired by the work of the Canadian landscape artist David Armstrong and a painting by the fantasy illustrator Dawn Wilson, "The Soft Whisper of Midnight Snow" is a gentle tale of Magical Realism about the power of creation and the magic of art and love.

De Lint was born in the Netherlands and traveled a great deal, but now makes his home in Ottawa, Canada, with his wife MaryAnn Harris, a soft-sculpture artist.

—T. W.

THE SOFT WHISPER OF MIDNIGHT SNOW

Charles de Lint

Night. The fields lay stark as a charcoal drawing—white drifts, the black clawed talons of the trees, the starlight piercingly bright. A gust of wind-driven snow swirled across the nearest field and he was there again. A shape in the twisting snow. A whisper of moccasins against white grains of ice. One step, another. He was drawing closer, much closer. Then she blinked, the snow swirled with a new flurry of wind, and he was gone. The field lay empty.

Tomilyn Douglas turned from the window and let out a breath she hadn't been aware of holding. The cabin was warm, the new woodstove throwing off all of its advertised heat, but a chill still scurried down her spine. She walked slowly to where her easel stood by an east window, ready to make use of the morning light. Her hand trembled slightly as she flicked a lamp switch and studied the drawing in its pale glow. It twinned the scene she had just been witness to, complete with the tiny shapeless figure, its details hidden in a swirl of gusting snow.

This morning she'd thought it had been a dream, that she had only dreamed of waking and seeing that figure in the snow, moving towards the cabin. Her fingers smudged with charcoal, she'd stood back and smiled with satisfaction at the rendering she'd done of it, that momentary high of a completed work making her a little dizzy until she'd had to go sit down. A useful dream, she'd thought, for it had left her with the first piece of decent work she'd completed since Alan . . . since Alan had gone. It was an omen of things to come, of a lost talent returned, of an ache finally beginning to heal.

Tomi flicked off the light and the room returned to darkness. It'd been an omen all right, she thought. But she was no longer so sure that she understood just what it was that it promised.

"This is where the dream becomes real," he'd told her when they bought and fixed up the cabin. It was meant to be only a temporary arrangement. The cabin stood on a hundred acres of bushland south of Calabogie. Alan had the blueprints all drawn up for the house they would build on the hill behind the cabin. It was his dream to build a home for them that would be the perfect design. The house would grow almost organically from its surroundings. A stand of birch grew so close to where her studio would be that she would feel as though she was a part of the forest, separated only by the glass walls of the room. Solar heating, a vegetable garden already planned out, enough forest on the land that they could cut their own wood. . . . Self-sufficiency was to be the order of the day and she loved him for it. For the house, for the land, for the dream, for . . . for his love.

They could afford to live out of the city. They were both established in their careers—architect and artist. Alan's clients sought him out now, while her work sold as quickly as she could paint it. They were the perfect match for each other—she loved it when people told them that, because it was true. For eleven years . . . it was true. But the dream had become a nightmare.

Last spring the foundations of their dream house were a scar on the landscape, like the scar on her soul. The forest began to reclaim its own. By the time the snows came this year, the sharp edges of the foundations were rounded with returning undergrowth. The scar she carried had yet to lose its raw edges.

Morning. Tomi bundled up and went out into the field but if last night's visitor had left any tracks, if he hadn't just been some figment of her imagination, the night's winds had dusted and filled them with snow. She stood, the wind blowing her brown hair into her face, and stared across the white expanse of drifts and dervishing snow-eddies to study the forest beyond the fields. The quiet that she'd loved when she moved here from the city, that she'd slowly come to love again as she dealt with her pain, disturbed her now. Too quiet, she thought, then she spoke the cliched words aloud. The wind took them from her mouth and scattered them across the field. Shivering, Tomi returned to the cabin.

She spent the day working at her easel. Sketch after sketch made its mysterious passage from mind through fingers to paper. And they were all good. No, she amended as she looked them over while having a midafternoon soup-and-tea break. They were better than good. They were the best she'd done in over a year, perhaps better than before Alan—

She shut that train of thought off as quickly as it came. She was getting better at it now. But while she thrust aside the ache before it could take hold, she couldn't shake the uneasiness that had followed her through the day. Night was coming, was almost here. Just at dusk it began to snow. Tiny granular pellets rasped against the door, rattled on the roof. She wanted to turn all the lights on so that she'd be blinded to the night outside, but not seeing made her more nervous. One by one she turned them off, then sat in the darkness and looked out over the fields at time falling snow.

One day he just never came home. She could draw up that day in her memory with a total recall that always struck her as a sure sign that she was still a long way from getting over it. He left in the morning to do some work down the road at Sam Collins' place—Sam having helped them when they were having the foundation poured. When he still wasn't back by dinnertime, she gave Sam a call, but he hadn't seen Alan all day and, no, he hadn't been expecting him.

That night wasn't the worst one in her life—those had come after, when she knew—but it was bad. She hadn't been able to do anything but worry, staring at the phone, waiting for him to call. She tried some friends of theirs in the city. No luck. She thought of calling the police, hospitals, that kind of thing, but knew for all her worry that it was too early for that. Then around eleven o'clock the phone rang, startling her right out of her seat with its klaxon jangle.

"Alan?" she cried into the mouthpiece. "Alan, is that you?" The words came out in a rush like they were all one word.

"Whoa, Mrs. Douglas. Slow down a bit. This is Tom Moulton."

Her relief shattered into pieces of icy dread.

"Sorry to be calling you so late, but I was talking to Sam a few minutes ago and heard you were worried about your man. Thing is, I saw your jeep parked out on 511, a couple of miles down from my place. I knew right off it was yours, but I figured you all were out for a little hike or something, you know what I mean?"

She called the police then, and they began a search of the surrounding bush. It wasn't until a couple of days later when she had to go to the bank that she discovered half the money in their joint account had been withdrawn.

Night. The snow had tapered off, but the wind was still shaping and reshaping the drifts around the trees and fence posts and up against the cabin. Tomi was half-hypnotized by the movement of the snow. Time and again she thought she saw a figure, but it was always just a shadow movement, a tree branch, a fox once. Then just as she was ready to give up her vigil, something drew her face closer to the window and she saw him again.

He was closer still. Not moving now, just standing out there in the field, watching the cabin. Tattered cloth fluttered in the wind, muting his outline against the snow. He was still too far away to make out details, but something about the way he stood, about the way he held himself erect, not hunched into the wind, told her that he wasn't who she'd feared he'd be. He wasn't Alan.

"Who are you?" she whispered. "What do you want from me?"

She didn't expect an answer. He was too far away to hear her. There was a thick glass pane and an expanse of white field between them. There was the wind and the gusting snow to steal her words. She wanted to shout at the figure, to run out and grab him. The window frosted up under her breath. She cleared it with a quick wipe of her hand, but in the time it took the figure was gone again.

Hardly realizing what she was doing, she grabbed her coat and a flashlight and ran outside, stumbling through the snow to where he'd stood. When she reached the spot there was no sign of him, nor tracks. The field was virgin snow all around her, except for her own ragged trail from the cabin.

She began to shiver. Returning to the warmth of the cabin, she closed and bolted the door. She tossed her coat onto a chair, the flashlight, never used, on top of it, then slowly made her way to her bedroom. She began to undress, then stopped dead as she glanced at the bed. A long raven's feather lay on the comforter, stark and black against its flowered Laura Ashley design.

"Oh, Jesus."

On watery legs she walked over to the bed, stared at the intrusion, unwilling to touch it. He'd been inside. Somehow, while she'd been out looking for him, in those few moments, he'd come inside. Slowly she backed out of the bedroom. It didn't take long to search the cabin.

There was the main room that included her studio and the kitchen area, a bathroom, and her bedroom. She was alone in the cabin. In a trancelike state, she investigated every possible hiding place until she was positive of that. She was alone inside, but he was out there. What did he want? What in God's name was this game he was playing?

She was a long time getting to sleep that night, starting at every familiar creak and groan of her cabin. When she finally did sleep, restless dreams plagued her, dreams of shapeless figures and clouds of raven's feathers that fell like black snow all around her while she ran and ran, trying to catch an answer that was always out of reach. Underpinning her dreams, the wind moaned outside the cabin, whispering the snow against its log walls.

The deed to the cabin and its land was in her name and, once the initial shock was over, she was quick to remove what money remained in their joint account into one under her own name. She kept thinking there was some mistake, that this wasn't happening to them, to her. But as the days drifted into weeks, she had no choice but to accept it. To believe it, even if she couldn't understand it.

At first she was confused and hurt. Anger was there too, but it came and went as if of its own will. Mostly she felt worthless. If they'd been having fights, if there'd been another woman, if there'd been some hint of what was coming, maybe she could have accepted it more easily. But it had come out of the blue.

"It's him," her friends tried to convince her. "He's just an asshole, Tomi. Christ, he never had it so good."

Neither had she, she'd want to say, but the words never got beyond her thinking them. He'd left her and she knew why. Because she was worthless. As she tried to lose herself in her work during the following weeks, she saw that her art was worthless too. God, no wonder he'd left her. The real wonder was that he hadn't left her sooner.

And even later as she, at least intellectually, came to realize that it *was* him and not her worthlessness that had made him leave, emotionally it wasn't that easy to accept. Emotionally, she retained the feelings of her own inadequacy. She'd stare into a mirror and see her face drawn an pale with her anxiety, the brown hair that framed it hanging listless, the body that could have been exercised but instead had been let to sag.

"Who'd want me?" she'd ask that reflection and then would retire deeper into the shell she was building around herself. Who'd want her? She didn't even want herself.

Morning. Tomi had the jeep on the road and was halfway to Ottawa by the time the nine o'clock CBC news came on the radio. She turned it off. Her own troubles were enough to bear without having to listen to the world's. But once she was in Ottawa, she didn't know why she'd come.

She'd had to get away from the cabin, from the figure that haunted the fields outside it, from the black feather that was lying on the floor of her bedroom, but being here didn't help. There was too much going on, too many cars, too many people. She almost had a couple of accidents in the heavy traffic on the Queensway, another on Bank Street.

She'd been planning to visit friends, but no longer knew what to say to them. Running from the cabin wasn't the answer, she realized. Just as withdrawing from the world after Alan had left hadn't been an answer. She had to go back.

That first spring alone had been the worst. She hadn't been able to look at the foundations without wanting to cry. Unable to paint, or even sketch, she'd thrown herself into working around the cabin, fixing it up, removing every trace of Alan from it, putting in a garden, buying a new woodstove, discovering talents she'd never known she'd had. She might not be able to keep a husband or express herself with her art any more, but she could handle a hammer and saw, she could chop firewood, she could do a lot of things now—do them without ever worrying about whether or not she was capable of them.

The first night that she made a vegetable stew with all the ingredients coming out of her own garden, she celebrated with a bottle of wine, got very drunk and never once wanted to cry. She stood out in the clear night air and looked up the hill at the foundations and was surprised at what she found in herself.

The ache was still there, but it was different now. Still immediate, but not quite so piercing. She might not be able to paint yet, but the next day she took out her sketchbook and began to draw again. She wasn't happy with anything she did, but she wasn't discouraged about it any-more either. Not in the same way as she'd been when Alan first had deserted her.

Night. Tomi had forgotten how quickly it got dark. She decided to return to the cabin, but since she was in town anyway, she thought she might as well make a day of it. It went by all too quickly. From grocery shopping to haunting used bookstores and antique shops, it was going on four o'clock before she knew it. By the time she was fighting the heavy traffic on her way home, it began to snow again, big heavy flakes that were whisked away by the jeep's wipers but were building up rapidly on the road and fields. When she reached old Highway 1 going north from Lanark, she was reduced to a slow crawl, even with the jeep's four-wheel-drive. The build-up of snow and ice made for treacherous driving, especially on roads like this without as much traffic.

After Highway 1 turned into 511 and crossed the Clyde River, the driving grew worse. Here the road was narrow and twisted its way through the wooded hills that were barely visible through the storm. The wind drove the snow in sheets across her windshield. The jeep ploughed through drifts that had already thrust halfway across the road in places.

Not far now, she told herself, and that much was true, but a half mile from the laneway leading in to her cabin, the road took a sudden dip and a sharp turn at the same time. She was going too fast when she topped the hill and hit an icy patch. Already nervous, she did the worst thing possible and instead of riding the fish tail and easing out of it, she slammed her foot on the brake.

The jeep skidded, came sideways down the hill and missed the turn. Its momentum took it through and then over the snow embankment until it thudded to a stop against a tall pine. The shock of the impact brought all the snow down from its branches in a sudden avalanche.

Panicked and shaken, Tomi snapped loose her seatbelt and lunged from the jeep. The snow came up to her hips as she floundered through it back to the road. She was breathing heavily by the time she reached it, the cold air hurting her lungs. When she looked back, she saw the jeep was half covered with the snow that it had dislodged from the pine.

She was never going to get it out of that mess. Not without a towtruck or tractor. But she couldn't face seeing to that now. She wasn't far from home. She could walk the half mile easily. Trying to ignore the chill that was seeping in through her clothes, cold enough to make even her bones feel cold, she forced her way back to the jeep, fetched her purse and groceries, and started the short trek home.

The snow was coming down in a fury now, the wind slapping it against her exposed skin with enough force to hurt. Neck hunched into her coat, head bowed, she trudged up the road, fighting the steadily growing drifts. The half mile had never seemed so long. Her boots—fine for town, but a joke out here—were wet and cold against her feet. The stylish three-quarter length coat that was only meant for the quick dashes from warm vehicle to warm store couldn't contend with the bone-piercing chill of the wind.

She got a scare when she stumbled and fell in a sprawl on the highway, her grocery bag splitting open to spew its contents all around her. But she was more scared when she found she just couldn't get up to go on. The shock of the accident and the numbing cold had drained all her strength.

She could lie here and, with the poor visibility, the snowplow would come by and bury her in the embankment, never knowing that its blades had scooped her up and shunted her aside. Or a pickup could come by and run her down before its driver even realized what it was that he was about to hit.

Right, bright eyes, she thought. So get the hell out of here.

She managed to sit up and tried to scrape together her scattered groceries, but her fingers were too numb in their thin gloves to work properly. What a time to play fashion horse, she thought hazily. But then again she hadn't been planning on playing the arctic explorer when she'd set out this morning. What a dramatic picture this would make, she decided. The woman fallen in the snow, her groceries scattered around her, the wind howling around her like a dervish. . . .

She blinked her eyes open suddenly to find that she'd laid her head down on the road again as she'd been thinking. This. Wouldn't. Do. She forced herself back up into a sitting position. Screw the groceries. If she didn't get out of here quickly, she wasn't going to get up at all.

But the cold was in her bones now. Her teeth chattered and her jaws ached from trying to keep them from doing so. Her hands and feet just felt like lumps on the ends of her arms and legs. She realized with a shock that she was almost completely covered with snow. Only her upper torso was relatively free, the snow covering it having fallen off when she sat up.

Up. That was the ticket. She had to get up, put one foot in front of the other, and get herself home. She tried to rise, but the cold had just sapped something in her. There'd been a lot of times over the past spring and summer when she'd simply wanted to die, but now that it was a very real possibility, she wanted to live with a fierceness that actually got her to her feet.

She tottered and took a couple of steps, then fell into another drift, frustrated tears freezing on her cheeks. Which was weird, she thought, because the snow actually felt warm now. It was cozy. Just like her bed in the cabin. Or the big easy chair in front of the woodstove. . . .

As she began to drift off, the last thing she saw was a dark shape moving towards her through the billowing snow. Incongruously, for all the howling of the wind, she heard a rasp of bead and quill against leather, a whisper of moccasins against the crust of the snow, smelled a pungent scent like a freshly snapped cedar bough, and then she knew no more.

She blinked awake. The air was thickly warm around her. She was lying on something soft, cozily wrapped in a coverage of furs. Dim lighting spun in her gaze as she sat up. When her head stopped spinning, she stared groggily about herself.

There was a fire crackling in front of her, its smoke escaping upward through a hole in the roof. Roof. Where was she? The walls looked like they were made of woven branches. She could hear the wind howling outside them. Movement caught her eye and she looked across the fire. He'd been sitting so still that she hadn't noticed him at first, but now he leapt out at her with a thousand details, each one so clear that she wondered how she could have taken so long to see him there.

He sat cross-legged on a deerskin, the firelight playing on his pale skin, waking sharp highlights in his narrow features. His clothing was a motley collection of tatters. A black shirt, decorated with bone. A grey vest, inlaid with beadwork, quills and feathers. A raven's skull hung like a pendent from his neck in the middle of a cluster of feathers and shells. He wore a headdress, again decorated with feathers and bones, that lifted high above his head in the shape of a pair of horns. She thought of the wicked queen in Disney's *Sleeping Beauty* looking at those horns, or of Tolkien's highborn elves, taking in his pale features. But there was more of the Native American about him. And more than that, a feeling of great sorrow.

"Who . . . who are you?" she asked. She spoke softly, the way one might speak to a wild animal, poised for flight. "Why were you watching my cabin? What do you want with me? She knew it had to have been him.

He made no reply. His eyes seemed all white in the deceptive light cast by the fire, all except for their pale grey pupils. His gaze never left Tomi's face. She was suddenly sure that she was dead. The plow *had* come by and scraped her frozen body up from the road, burying it under a mountain of snow. He was here to take her to . . . to wherever you went when you died

"Please," she said, fingers tightening their grip on the fur covering. "What . . . what do you want with me?"

The silence stretched until Tomi thought she would scream. She plucked nervously at the furs, wanting to look away, but her gaze seemed to be trapped by his unblinking eyes.

"Please," she began again. "Why have you been spying on me?"

He nodded suddenly. Movement made the bones and quills click against each other. "Life," he said. His voice was husky and rough. He spoke with a heavy accent so that Tomi knew that whatever his native language was, it wasn't English.

She swallowed thickly. Fear made her throat dry and tight. "L-Life?" she managed. She looked for the door of the lodge, trying not to be too obvious about it. She didn't know if she'd have the strength to take off, but she couldn't just stay here with . . . with whatever he was.

He pulled a strip of birchbark from under his tunic and took a charred twig from beside the fire. With quick deft movement, he began to sketch on the birchbark. Curiosity warred with fear inside Tomi and she leaned forward. When he suddenly thrust the finished drawing at her, she floundered to get out of the way, then chided herself. So far the stranger hadn't hurt her. He'd brought her in from the cold and snow, bundled her up in his furs, saved her life. . . . And the drawing . . . it was good. Better than good.

Tomi taught art from time to time, week-long courses at the Haliburton School during the summer, a few at Algonquin College in Ottawa. Not one of those students' work could hold a candle to the lifelike sketch of a snowhare that her curious host had thrust at her. His quick deft rendering of it was what she always tried to instill in her students. To go for feeling first. She smiled to show she appreciated it.

"It's very good," she began.

"Life!" he repeated. Taking back the drawing, he blew on it, then laid it on the ground beside the fire.

Fear clawed up Tomi's spine again as the lines of the drawing began to move, to lift three-dimensionally from the birchbark. A hazily-shaped hare sat there, its outline smokey and indistinct. Nose twitching nervously, it regarded her with warm eyes. Her fear died, replaced with wonder. She reached out a hand to touch the little apparition, but it drifted apart like smoke and was gone. All that remained was the birchbark that it had been sitting on. Its surface was clear, unmarked. "You," her host said. "*Your* breath."

"I . . . I can't breathe like . . . like. . . ."

"You must." "I can't breathe—" Suddenly the lodge was spinning again. The fire turned into a whirlpool of glittering sparks, that twisted and danced like snow-driven wind. Tomi's words froze in her throat. Gone. It was going. It was—

—gone.

"—can't breathe. . . ."

Something was shaking her. She blinked rapidly, trying to slow down the spinning.

"Miz Douglas? Miz Douglas?"

The world came into focus with a sharp snap. A face was leaning into hers. For one moment, she was back in the storm, or the storm had torn apart the strange man's lodge, blowing everything away, then she recognized the face. Sam Gould's strong features were looking down into hers. Worry creased his face. He looked at a loss.

"Sam . . . ?"

"It's me, Miz Douglas. Found you lying on the highway. You're damned lucky I didn't run over you with the plow, I'll tell you that."

"You . . . found me . . . ?" Then the lodge, the man—that had been a dream?

"Sure did. Funny thing—thought I saw someone standing beside you, just when my highbeams picked you out, but that must've been you standing for a moment, just before you fell. Hell of a storm, though, and that's a fact. Had a look at your jeep, but it's in too deep for me to do much about it till the morning. I'll come round with the tractor then, if you can wait."

"I . . . I can wait."

"Not much damage, considering. Headlight's gone on the driver's side. You might want Bill Cassidy to have a look at that fender. I figure he could straighten her out for you, no problem."

"There was . . . someone standing . . . ?" Tomi managed.

"Well, I thought there was, I'll tell you that. But it was just a trick of the lights, I'd say. Storm can fool you into thinking you're seeing just about anything sometimes."

"Yes," Tomi said slowly. Like what she'd thought she'd seen. A dream. Just. . . .

"Anyway, I brought you up to your cabin," Sam continued. "Thought you might'a had a touch of frostbite on your wrist there, but I wrapped it up tight and kept it warm. The skin wasn't broken, so it'll be all right. You were lucky, and that's a fact. I coulda plowed you right up into the bank and no one would've known to go looking for you till your jeep was spotted in the morning. I put you to bed, but 'cepting your boots and coats, I didn't . . . you know. . . ." He blushed. "I just covered you up, Miz Douglas."

"Thank you, Sam." Tomi sat up slowly. "You saved my life." A dream?

Sam shuffled his feet. "Guess I did at that. I woulda called up an ambulance, but by the time it would've got here, well. . . . I did what I could, I'll tell you that. You want I should call up the doc now, Miz Douglas? Or maybe get someone to stay with you for the night?"

Tomi shook her head. "I'll be all right, Sam. But thank you." Just a dream?

"My pleasure. I'd best be going now. Weather's not getting any better and I've got a load of plowing still to do. Keep me busy most of the night, I'll tell you that."

Tomi started to get up, but Sam laid a hand on her shoulder and gently pressed her down. "I can see myself out, Miz Douglas. You just lie there and take her easy. I'll lock up and be back in the morning with the tractor. You just get some sleep now. You've been through a rough time, and that's a fact. Sleep's the best thing for you now."

Tomi nodded and laid back, knowing that he wouldn't go until she did. She listened to him clomp across the hardwood floors in his work-boots, heard him tug on his parka, the sound of the zipper, the door opening. "I'll see you in the morning!" he called, then the door slammed shut. The door handle made a click-click noise as he checked to make sure it was locked. Silence then for a time. Except for the wind. The snow being pushed against the cabin, the windows. The big snow-plow starting up. Gears grinding as they changed. The truck backing out of her lane. Silence again as the sound of the engine was swallowed by the wind.

Tomi stared at her ceiling. Just a dream?

She listened to the wind and the whisper of the snow against the window panes and logs outside. She might have drifted off, she wasn't sure; just dozed there, until suddenly she had to get up, had to see, *had* to. She padded out of her bedroom into the main room of the cabin. Sam had left the lights on and she turned them off, one by one, then went to stand by the window.

The snow was still falling, the wind blowing it in great sweeps across the field. She stared out at the field, willing her stranger to be there again, for it not to have been a dream. She wasn't sure what she wanted, what she expected. She had been frightened in the lodge, but remembering it now, there had been no reason for fear. Just the strange man with his totemic clothing, and the drawing that came to life with a breath, with just a whisper of air drawn up from his lungs. . . .

She moved to her easel and turned on a light, aiming it so that it pooled over the easel, leaving the rest of the room in shadows. From the closet, she took out a virgin canvass, a sketching pencil, her acrylics. The sketching went easily. Background first, light, hazy as though seen through a gossamer curtain of falling snow. Then the figure. But close now.

She knew his features and quickly sketched them in. Left their look of sorrow, but imbued them with a certain air of nobility as well. She made the clothing not so ragged, not so tattered. The totemic raven skulls, feathers, beads and quills, came readily, leaping the gap from memory to canvass with an exhilarating ease.

Oh, lord. This was what it felt like. This was what she'd missed, what Alan had stolen from her, what the stranger had given her back.

She didn't know who or what he was, realized that it didn't matter. Dream or real, it didn't matter. Some spirit of winter, of the snow and wind, or of the forest . . . or a creation of her own blocked creativity. It didn't matter.

When the sketching was filled in as much as she needed, she moved straight to the acrylics, mixing the paints and applying them, scarcely paying any attention to what she was doing. Her subconscious remembered, her fingers remembered. She only had to give them free rein. She only had to breathe life into what took shape on her canvass. God. To have forgotten this . . . to have lost it. . . .

She leaned close as she worked, mixing colors on the seat of the stool, too enrapt in her work to search for her palette. The shades came easily.

The painting grew from the rough black and white sketch into a being almost composed of flesh and blood, almost as though she was back in his lodge, seeing him across the fire, the light playing on his features, his steady gaze never wavering from hers. She listened to the wind, to the hiss and spit of the snow against the windows, and smiled as she worked.

It was long after midnight, but still far from dawn, when the main figure was completed and she only had the background to fill in. Her gaze locked to the gaze of the figure in the painting as she brushed in the pines and cedars behind him, the swirl of the snow as it gusted through the trees, across the field. But for all the movement in the background, the figure in the foreground was still. Only his eyes spoke to her.

Her fingers were cramping when she heard, under the moan of the wind and the whisper of the snow, the sound of her locked door opening. A draft of cold air touched the back of her neck as the wind entered, the wind and something more, something she had no name for, but she knew she owed it a debt.

It didn't matter what he was—her imagination running wild, or something out of the wild night sparking her imagination. She was repaying what he had recovered for her from that first moment she'd seen him in the field, just a dark shape in the blurring snow, repaying what had been lost and now regained with life.

The door closed, but she didn't turn around. The painting in front of her was like a mirror and she continued to breathe on it as she finished the last cedar.

ANNE GAY

Roman Games

The following is a deftly rendered tale of contemporary fantasy set in the mountains of Italy by a writer who will be new to most American readers. Anne Gay lives in the West Midlands of England and works as a teacher of Spanish, French, and German. Her short stories have appeared in various anthologies in England; this one comes from the pages of *Other Edens II* (edited by Christopher Evans and Robert Holdstock).

Once upon a time, Peter Pan explained to Wendy that her *belief* in fairies was required to keep them alive. Can the same be true of dragons . . . or of God?

—T. W.

ROMAN GAMES

Anne Gay

Rome station seemed to rattle as the train began its farewells. A hand, freeze-frame black-and-white, banged silently on the outside of the pullman's double-glazing that slid away. Inside, a boy with his leg in plaster babbled in anguished Italian. In her corner, Sister Thomas read a detective book so that—for once—she could pierce the secrets of men's souls. It was typical, so it was, that she almost missed the Drama of the Ticket, as she hid in her book from her failure in Rome. And when she got back to Ireland—?

"My ticket!" The boy pulled at her skirt. "I no have the my ticket!"

Sister Tom looked: saw the boy with his crutches, whose ticket was outside the window. The poor bobbing uncle, distraught, tied to the train's motion by the ticket he could not pass in to the nephew, trotting along the platform walloping the panes. A frenzy of silent shouting like a fish outside its bowl.

Sister Thomas ran to the door, hurled it back in its track; the corridor; the carriage door; slammed down the window and snatched the ticket.

"Grazie! Mille grazi—"

The platform fell away to gravel: goodbye uncle. Outside the station it was dark. Sister Thomas pushed the window up, no longer leaning on the sign that said "It is dangerous to lean out of the window." Where her head might have been, a telegraph pole whizzed past. A miracle that passed her by.

Nephew, his leg horizontal in graffiti and gypsum, was very thankful in his heathen tongue. A pity our somewhat good sister didn't understand one word of the canticle. But she smiled.

The train headed north as Sister Tom tried to remember what faith was like. It was impossible. So she tried to sleep instead.

Stops and stations, then a long blank journey towards dawn. The boy and the graffiti on his leg were gone. The Rome-Ostend express was a world of light and life traveling through the outer darkness of Italy.

*   *   *

What of Thomasina's opponent? She's hungry, that's what. Dawn is brilliant up in the mountains, and on this particular dawn she blunders over the valleys, hunting. Her scales, like her teeth, need cleaning. As her wings crank her stiffly over the rosy Alps, she thinks of fresh marrow and picking her fangs afterwards with a nice, juicy rib.

The trouble is, people don't believe in her any more. There isn't room in this bright winter's sky for her and jumbo jets: their slip-streams dull her scales and bring on her bronchitis. Draco Vulgaris is mucky with other people's neglect.

She turns her head, trying to spot a victim. Hope—and memories— of feasts always make her nostalgic. Those Romans were nice and crunchy with brass and spiky iron. There'd been a virgin or two—knight-bait, they were, a morning's sport *molto bene*, very good. Thieves and murderers, fat millers with lungs *en croute*.

Draco spotted the train as a stream of colours, hugging the snowy side of the pass. She spiralled in lower. Sulphurated saliva dripped from her jaws. Her last meal was partisans with gunpowder sauce. Dinner was forty years ago and she was ready for breakfast.

Round One

In her compartment, only Sister Tom was awake. It was incredibly hot, redolent of garlic and bodily effluents. The double-glazing, of course, maintained its efficient seal. Five-feet-eight of Irish nun did not fit the seat; her short-cropped head was jammed at an uncomfortable angle, so that every time her unwilling eyes jolted open she could see the frightening mountains. Little faith and less hair did a poor job of cushioning her. Her curls had stopped growing by themselves thirty years ago. She sometimes thought her hair was more religious than she was.

"Is this a dragon I see before me?" Sister Tom rapidly checked her watch, set to this foreign time. Not yet six o'clock. Besides—when the frost-jewelled cliff shot by—Holy Mary!—the abyss held no dragons.

Back in her village in the Mountains of Mourne—proper mountains they were, nice and soft and gentle—it would be just past three o'clock, the witching hour. Many's the night Sister Tom had sat up with the dead in a candle-lit room. *She* knew that midnight was nothing. But three o'clock in the morning, when death squeezes the souls out of bodies, that was when horrors enter the mind of a nun. For doesn't a nun see only the underside of men, now? At three o'clock by God's time in would slide a banshee, maybe, in the soft mist around the corner of vision. Or a large, creaky dragon over the sudden, jagged Alps.

It was nothing, now. Just a bad dream. And it was gone.

Draco dimmed a little more, wounded by disbelief.

Dragon 0—Sister Thomas 1.

Round Two

Draco singed a pine tree out of pique. Disbelief always put her in a flaming temper. No doubt she had once been a pure, innocent hatchling, but she'd soon grown out of a diet of sheep and chamois. We are what we eat, and she had eaten liars, cheats, cowards and killers, man-unkind with all his little failings. In short, she had eaten people.

After the nightmare, Sister Tom needed air. Yawning and stretching, she staggered along the corridor as the train swayed round the cornice. At the carriage door, she lit a filthy, cheap, foreign cigarette, all the better to savour the cold air. She rested her forearms on the top of the window, trying not to see the river right down in the black depths of the gorge. Sure the Alps were pretty now, but better with a picture-frame safe around them.

More importantly, could a nun who apparently believed in dragons not have a little more faith in God?

There it was again! Dull bronze, dull green, dull soot—Mother of God, it was there before her eyes! All it needed to be believable was a tongue of—

Flame ripped out at the smart carriages, crafted by robots in Milan. The blue paint blistered, that was all.

No is like the old days, thought Draco nostalgically, going through her gizzard to find another belch. *Then I really make them blaze!*

Pride was just one of the sins she had consumed.

"Oh God, I wish I wasn't an atheist," a humorist once said in danger. Sister Tom prayed, for real this time, as if it might do her some good. Too long had prayer been a comfy, cosy thing, like her night-time Guinness or warm slippers.

Hands together, eyes closed—but with one eye cheating, because the dragon was closer than God, Sister Thomas *prayed*. Harder still, when the dragon's talons raked along the roof, and in fear Sister Tom closed her other eye.

Draco backwinged, puzzled, and hauled herself higher in retreat. Why hadn't her claws ripped through the metal? The pink sun shone in her eyes and she shook her head in annoyance. She must be getting old.

Arrowing her tail, she dived like a cormorant, trying, trying, trying again. A downdraught from the snowfields gave her a helpful shove.

"Saints preserve us!" croaked our nun, recognising all the symptoms of fear from her thrillers.

It *was* dangerous to lean out, and she didn't need the notice to tell her. Head and shoulders crammed through the window, Sister Tom howled her prayers upwards, eye to eye with the dragon, only partly so she wouldn't see the chasm below.

English, Latin and Gaelic—Sister Tom tried everything. *What did the dragon speak? What would work?*

Draco was an omnivore. That is, she'd eaten men of all tongues, and so she spoke the lot. And she knew the power of prayer, whether the deity was called Mithras or God.

Nonchalantly she wheeled away over an arete.

"Saints be praised!" cried Sister Tom, falling to her knees in the corridor the minute the beast was gone. The sky was as blue as Mary's robe, the mountains white and majestic. Pale sunlight gilded all, even the battered old face with its thorny crown of Irish hair, even the bulbous nose her mother had passed on from the tinker who'd made her laugh—until she conceived Sister Tom. She'd not laughed then till the dates worked out, and it might have been her husband after all.

Sister Tom shook her head. What a terrible confession to hear from her own darlin' mother on her deathbed. Had that started her doubts?

What if it had? She'd done a Saint Patrick! Smiling, full of faith, she resolved to give up the weed for good and put the money in the poorbox. This would be her last cigarette. Faith! She could do it now.

Dragon 1–Sister Thomas 2

Round Three

Draco was in a bad way. *Quindi*—she'd pretended she'd just changed her mind, but the prayers had made her sick *de vero*. Perched on a black rock in the corrie, her tail draggled on the snow and her head drooping, she gave way to the pains that griped in her stomachs. She almost overbalanced when she put a claw down her throat, but the indigestible prayer gave her hell. It wouldn't come out but it wouldn't stay down.

Sister Tom walked back along the bouncing corridor, bouncing herself with joy. The spring-door fought back when she slid it open, but what did it matter today?

The boy with the broken leg had got out at Turin; now two tubby men slept on his seat. One was a salesman, one an accountant; besuited but naïve in sleep, their scepticism dormant in their pockets with their spectacles. It was too early yet for businessmen.

What time was it? Sister Tom's watch on its old leather strap said still before six; she could tell by its single pointer.

"Must get a big hand," said Sister Tom to herself, and opened her one bottle of Lambrusco. "Never too early for a heroine to drink," and she thanked God for screw-caps. She was in that rare, generous mood that ascribes to the Creator all the good things He—or She?—had dreamt up. Sister Tom would have thanked God for the velcro on her veil if she'd thought of it.

Imagine her surprise, then, as she swigged surreptitiously from her bottle—silently, out of consideration for her sleeping partners, watching the cars on the autostrada—and Draco appeared!

For Draco had eaten atheists, and their proteins swallowed prayers in the stomach of unbelief. It just took time.

Sister Tom gulped wine from the bottle. The beast was still there, though, hovering behind a big motorway sign, lurking until the sparse, early cars thinned out.

The cheek of it! thought Sister Tom, pushing the damned door sideways. Pound, pound, went her boots along the corridor, and her heart did the same. Back to the carriage door, where a dog-end lay before the open window.

What weapon could she use this time? If it was sweat, she'd have won hands down. Sister Tom lit a cigarette with shaking matches.

Sure the beast was so vain, wasn't she creaking over the train now? Making sure Sister Tom had seen her. And on the stilted autostrada, no cars but one for miles. A mother—black hair, blue coat—was peering in its bonnet that was open to curses, if not to coercion. For the thing wouldn't start.

Lazily cocking her tail as a snoot at the nun, Draco strolled across the sky. What could the nun do, but nothing and rage?

On its corniche, the train had stopped for no reason, as trains do. On the flyover with delusions of grandeur, the woman was slamming shut the boot, putting up a *pushchair*, wheeling her *baby* to the emergency phone! Mother of God, the dragon was going to—

"You're no dragon at all! Just an overgrown lizard, so y'are!"

Draco balked in surprise, and had to flap twice to stay up.

"Dragons are noble, glittering beasts," yelled the woman who'd kissed the Blarney Stone. "Hordes of treasure they've got, and never eat less than a virgin princess. You don't want her—she'd not make a mouthful for ye."

And she prayed again in desperation for a natural catastrophe, just a little one. Dragon-size, for preference.

Vanity, vanity, all is vanity. Our present imperfect Draco had eaten plenty of it. She leered at her puny foe—grubby grey serge and skin, waving a fist through the window of the train—and Draco showed off her vanity.

And for all Sister Tom's prayer, there wasn't a cloud in the sky, not a ghost of an avalanche.

Flaming, screaming, terrible, Draco dive-bombed the mother.

Madonna of the motorway! Yes, she ran—but she snatched her baby to her breast and fled—towards the phone.

Draco's breath hurled the pushchair *through* the parapet. Sister Tom watched the pushchair's parachute progression. Held on its web of metal, it tumbled into the gorge, a gorgeous red flare of fire on its charred black frame.

Sister Tom almost collapsed—vertigo was catching.

Two all.

Round Four

Then Draco, seeing no other cars about, nor anyone else astir on the sleepy train, craftily burnt up the phone. Vain, yes, about her ability to destroy, to scare, to terrify. But smart enough to know that armies in the eighties have tracker-planes and bombs. And all for the price of a phone-call.

She settled, wings spanning the concrete carriageway, teasing tufts of fire towards the mother. The woman stopped. Stood still, while a wind from nowhere picked up her skirts. The baby wailed—wouldn't you? But the woman didn't. Pale face, pale legs—only the blue of her clothes was colour against the white of the concrete and the black of the cliffs. Mouth slack, she didn't scream. She could see the monster's eyes.

With an insolent wink at the nun, on the train on the hillside helpless across the yards and yards of air, Draco advanced. A step at a time.

"My prayers are useless!" Thomasina—she'd be Sister Tom no longer!—slammed her forehead on the window.

Prayer was no good! The trip to Rome had done no good. A lifetime's savings gone to *prove* faith had no virtue. The Vatican was just a museum. All those monuments of marble and gold, canvas and flesh, to glorify God. And what had God got to show for it? People.

And Thomasina had heard enough confessions to know what people were.

Draco strutted another step. Her wings rattled in a sudden gale while she concentrated on grandstanding to the arena. Even her cockscomb crest was playing to the crowd.

Even the mother's tear-ducts were frozen with fear.

Like a gladiator, Draco minced forward. Step by step. Closed in for the kill. Belched like hell.

Will the Madonna die? Will her infant?

Thomasina couldn't watch faith's final death.

Out sprang the fire—

Two things happened. All over Europe on the farmers' news, weathermen moved symbols to show wind over the Alps. A small, natural catastrophe, just dragon-sized: the mini-hurricane blew the dragon's flames in again. In short, Draco backfired.

And while Draco skittered in surprise and the child cried and the woman's shaky legs tottered her away as far as the parapet, and while the weathermen pushed stick-on isobars around their maps, and the full-cheeked wind roared off down the valley, carooming off the train—while all that was going on, our doubting-again Thomasina from back of Ballymartin groaned a prayer for the effectiveness of prayer. Despairing, self-loathing, eyes shut, she missed the lot.

Around another cigarette she wailed, "Oh Lord, help Thou mine unbelief!"

Slowly, slowly, slowly, lace appeared on Draco's skin. The woman saw cliffs through Draco's wings. She saw the veins, the viscera, the ichor.

Draco glanced wildly at herself, the inner dragon. *Ecco qua!* She hadn't known her guts were *that* colour.

And Sister Tom opened one eye just a crack, peeking to see where the thunderbolt had got to. She couldn't believe her eye.

The train started up again with a jolt. Away on the autostrada hung a surprised outline of a dragon, made entirely of soot. The tail end of the wind pulled it along to play. Like a newspaper kite, it fell to bits.

As the train rounded a bend, all Sister Tom could see was the woman in blue with a baby, the Madonna of the Flaming Phone-Booth. Sister Tom hoped her car would start.

Dragon 3—Sister Thomas 4.

Oh—and Sister Tom took out a cigarette to savour with her heroism's wine. And sent the rest of the packet spinning into the abyss.

PATRICIA C. WREDE

The Princess, the Cat, and the Unicorn

Patricia C. Wrede is one of the most popular authors to have appeared in the fantasy field in the last decade; she is also credited with having started the "fantasy explosion" of magical books issuing from Minneapolis—the same city that brought us the Prairie Home Companion and Prince. Wrede's stories have a freshness, innocence, and enthusiasm that have won her a large and loyal following; "The Princess, the Cat, and the Unicorn," written for young readers and published in Bruce Coville's *The Unicorn Treasury*, will show you why.

Wrede is the author of *Shadow Magic, The Seven Towers, The Daughter of Witches, The Harp of Imach Thysell, Talking to Dragons,* and *Caught in Crystal*. She is also co-creator of the *Liavek* series (edited by Will Shetterly and Emma Bull.) Her most recent works are *Sorcery and Cecelia*, a delightful epistolary romantic fantasy written with Caroline Stevermer; a sequel to *Talking to Dragons*; and a novel for the Adult Fairy Tales series: *Snow White and Rose Red*.

—T. W.

THE PRINCESS, THE CAT, AND THE UNICORN

Patricia C. Wrede

Princess Elyssa and her sisters lived in the tiny, comfortable kingdom of Oslett, where nothing ever seemed to go quite the way it was supposed to. The castle garden grew splendid dandelions, but refused to produce either columbine or deadly nightshade. The magic carpet had a bad case of moths and the King's prized seven-league boots only went five-and-a-half leagues at a step (six leagues, with a good tail wind).

There were, of course, compensations. None of the fairies lived close enough to come to the Princesses' christenings (though they were all most carefully invited) so there were no evil enchantments laid on any of the three Princesses. The King's second wife was neither a wicked witch nor an ogress, but a plump, motherly woman who was very fond of her stepdaughters. And the only giant in the neighborhood was a kind and elderly Frost Giant who was always invited to the castle during the hottest part of the summer (his presence cooled things off wonderfully, and he rather liked being useful).

The King's councillors, however, complained bitterly about the situation. They felt it was beneath their dignity to run a kingdom where nothing ever behaved quite as it should. They grumbled about the moths and dandelions, muttered about the five-and-a-half-league boots and remonstrated with the Queen and the three Princesses about their duties.

Elyssa was the middle Princess, and as far as the King's councillors were concerned she was the most unsatisfactory of all. Her hair was not black, like her elder sister Orand's, nor a golden corn color, like her younger sister Dacia's. Elyssa's hair was mouse-brown. Her eyes were brown, too, and her chin was the sort usually described as "determined." She was also rather short, and she had a distressing tendency to freckle.

"It's all very well for a middle Princess to be ordinary," the chief of the King's councillors told her in exasperation. "But this is going too far!"

"It was only the second-best teapot," said Elyssa, who had just broken it. "And I did say I was sorry."

"If you'd only pay more attention to your duties, things like this wouldn't happen!" the councillor huffed.

"I dusted under the throne just this morning," said Elyssa indignantly. "And it's Orand's turn to polish the crown!"

"I don't mean those duties!" the councillor snapped. "I mean the duties of your position. For instance, you and Orand ought to be fearfully jealous of Dacia, but are you? No! You won't even try."

"I should think not!" Elyssa said. "Why on earth should I be jealous of Dacia?"

"She's beautiful and accomplished and your father's favorite, and— and elder Princesses are *supposed* to dislike their younger sisters," the councillor said.

"No one could dislike Dacia," Elyssa said. "And besides, Papa wouldn't like it."

The councillor sighed, for this was undoubtedly true. "Couldn't you and Orand steal a magic ring from her?" he pleaded. "Just for form's sake?"

"Absolutely not," Elyssa said firmly, and left to get a broom to sweep up the remains of the teapot.

But the councillors refused to give up. They badgered and pestered and hounded poor Elyssa until she simply could not bear it anymore. Finally she went to her step-mother, the Queen, and complained.

"Hmmph," said the Queen. "They're being ridiculous, as usual. I could have your father talk to them, if you wish."

"It won't do any good," Elyssa said.

"You're probably right," the Queen agreed, and they sat for a moment in gloomy silence.

"I wish I could just run off to seek my fortune," Elyssa said with a sigh.

Her stepmother straightened up suddenly. "Of course! The very thing. Why didn't I think of that?"

"But I'm the *middle* Princess," Elyssa said. "It's youngest Princesses who go off to seek their fortunes."

"You've been listening to those councillors too much," the Queen said. "They won't like it, of course, but that will be good for them." The Queen was not at all fond of the councillors, because they kept trying to persuade her to turn her stepdaughters into swans or throw them out of the castle while the King was away.

"It would be fun to try," Elyssa said in a wistful tone. She had always liked the idea of running off to seek her fortune, even if most of the stories did make it sound rather uncomfortable.

"It's the perfect solution," the Queen assured her. "I'll arrange with your father to leave the East Gate unlocked tomorrow night, so you can get out. Orand and Dacia can help you pack. And I'll write you a reference to Queen Hildegard from two kingdoms over, so you'll be able to find a nice job as a kitchen maid. We won't tell the councillors a thing until after you've left."

To Elyssa's surprise, the entire Royal Family was positively enthusiastic about the scheme. Orand and Dacia had a long, happy argument about just what Elyssa ought to carry in her little bundle. The King kissed her cheek and told her she was a good girl and he hoped she would give the councillors one in the eye. And the Queen offered Elyssa the magic ring she had worn when *she* was a girl going off on adventures. (The ring turned out to have been swallowed by the castle cat, so Elyssa didn't get to take it with her after all. Still, as she told her stepmother, it was the thought that counted.) All in all, by the time Elyssa slipped out of the postern door and set off into the darkness, she was downright happy to be getting away.

As she tiptoed across the drawbridge, Elyssa stepped on something that gave a loud yowl. Hastily, she pulled her foot back and crouched down, hoping none of the councillors had heard. She could just make out the shape of the castle cat, staring at her with glowing, reproachful eyes.

"Shhhh," she said. "Poor puss! Shhh. It's all right."

"It is not all right," said the cat crossly. "How would you like to have your tail stepped on?"

"I don't have a tail," Elyssa said, considerably startled. "And if you hadn't been lying in front of me, I wouldn't have stepped on you."

"Cat's privilege," said the cat, and began furiously washing his injured tail.

"Well, I'm very sorry," Elyssa said. "But I really must be going." She stood up and picked up her bundle again.

"I don't know how you expect to get anywhere when you can't see where you're going," said the cat.

"I certainly won't get anywhere if I stay here waiting for the sun to come up," Elyssa said sharply. "Or do you have some other suggestion?"

"You could carry me on your shoulder, and I could tell you which way to go," the cat replied. "*I* can see in the dark," he added smugly.

"All right," Elyssa said, and the cat jumped up on her shoulder.

"That way, Princess," the cat said, and Elyssa started walking.

"How is it you can talk?" she asked, as she picked her way carefully through the darkness according to the cat's directions. "You never did before."

"I think it was that ring of your mother's I swallowed yesterday," the cat said. He sounded uneasy and uncomfortable, as if he really didn't want to discuss the matter. So, having been well brought up, Elyssa changed the subject. They chatted comfortably about the castle cooks and the King's councillors as they walked, and periodically the cat would pat Elyssa's cheek with one velvet paw and tell her to turn this way or that way. Finally the cat announced that they had come far enough for one night, and they settled down to sleep in a little hollow.

When she awoke next morning, the first thing Elyssa noticed were the trees. They were huge; the smallest branches she could see were three times the size of her waist, and she couldn't begin to reach around the trunks themselves. The ground was covered with green, spongy moss, and the little flowers growing out of it looked like faces. Elyssa glanced around for the cat. He was sitting in a patch of sunlight with his tail curled around his front paws, staring at her.

"This is the Enchanted Forest, isn't it?" she said accusingly.

"Right the first time, Princess," said the cat.

Elyssa frowned. She knew enough about the Enchanted Forest to be very uncomfortable about wandering around in it. It lay a little to the east of the kingdom of Oslett, and the castle had permanently mislaid at least two milkmaids and a woodcutter's son who had carelessly wandered too far in that direction. The Enchanted Forest was one of those places that is very easy to get into, but very hard to get out of again.

"But I was supposed to go to Queen Hildegard!" Elyssa said at last.

"You wouldn't have liked Hildegard at all," the cat said seriously. "She's fat and bossy, and she has a bad-tempered, unattractive daughter to provide for. She'd be worse than the King's chief councillor, in fact."

"I don't believe you," Elyssa said. "Stepmama wouldn't send me to a person like that."

"Your stepmother hasn't seen Queen Hildegard since they were at school together twenty-some years ago," said the cat. "You're much better off here. Believe me, I know."

Elyssa was very annoyed, but it was much too late to do anything about the situation. So she picked up her bundle and set off in search of something to eat, leaving the cat to wash his back. After a little while, Elyssa found a bush with dark green leaves and bright purple berries. The berries looked very good, despite their unusual color, and she leaned forward to pick a few for breakfast.

"Don't do that, Princess," said the cat.

"Where did you come from?" Elyssa demanded crossly.

"I followed you," the cat answered. "And I wouldn't eat any of those berries, if I were you. They'll turn you into a rabbit."

Elyssa hastily dropped the berry she was holding and wiped her hand on her skirt. "Thank you for warning me," she said. "I don't suppose you know of anything around her that I *can* eat? Or at least drink? I'm very thirsty."

"As a matter of fact, there's a pool over this way," said the cat. "Follow me."

The cat led her through the trees in a winding route that Elyssa was sure would bring them right back to where they had started. She was about to say as much when she came around the bole of a tree into a moss-lined hollow. Green light filtered through the canopy of leaves onto the dark moss. In the center of the hollow, a ring of star-shaped white flowers surrounded a still, silent, mirror-dark pool of crystal-clear water.

"How lovely!" Elyssa whispered.

"I thought you were thirsty," said the cat. His tail twitched nervously as he spoke.

"I am," Elyssa said. "But—oh, never mind." She knelt down beside the pool and scooped up a little of the water in her cupped hands.

"Who steals the water from the unicorn's pool?" demanded a voice like chiming bells.

Elyssa started, spilling the water down the front of her dress. "Drat!" she said. "Now look what you've made me do!"

As she spoke, she looked up, expecting to see the person who had spoken. There was no one there, but the chiming voice spoke again, in stern accents. "Who steals the water from the unicorn's pool?"

Elyssa wiped her hands on the dry portion of her skirt and cast a reproachful look at the cat. "I am Elyssa, Princess of Oslett, and I'm very thirsty," she said in her best royal voice. "So if you don't mind—"

"A Princess?" said the chiming voice. "Really! Well, it's about time. Let me get a look at you."

A breath of air, scented with violets and cinnamon, touched Elyssa's face. An instant later, a unicorn stepped delicately out of the woods. It halted on the other side of the pool and stood poised, its head raised to display the sharp, shining ivory horn, its mane flowing in perfect waves along its neck. Its eyes shone like sapphires, and its coat made Elyssa think of the white silk her stepmother was saving for Dacia's wedding dress.

"Gracious!" Elyssa said.

"Yes, I am, aren't I?" said the unicorn complacently. It lowered its head slightly and studied Elyssa. An expression very like dismay came into its sapphire eyes. *"You're* a Princess? Are you quite sure?"

"Of course I'm sure," Elyssa replied, nettled. "I'm the second daughter of King Callwil of Oslett; ask anybody. Ask him." She waved at the cat.

The unicorn scowled. "I should hope I would never need to ask a cat for anything," it said loftily.

"Overgrown, stuck-up goat," muttered the cat.

"What did you say?" demanded the unicorn.

"Nothing that would interest you," said the cat.

"You may go, then," the unicorn said grandly.

"I'm quite happy right here," the cat said. "Or I was until you came stomping in with your silly questions."

"How dare— Princess Elyssa! What are you doing?" said the unicorn.

Elyssa took a last gulp of water and let the rest dribble through her fingers and back into the pool. "Having a drink," she said. She really *had* been very thirsty, and she had taken advantage of the argument between the cat and the unicorn to scoop up another handful of water.

"Well, I suppose it's all right, since you're a Princess," the unicorn said. Its chiming voice sounded positively sulky.

"Thank you," said Elyssa. She stood up and shook droplets from her fingers. "It's very good water."

"Of course it's good water!" the unicorn said. "A unicorn's pool is always pure and sweet and crystal clear and—"

"Yes, yes," said the cat. "But it's time we were going. Princess Elyssa has to seek her fortune, you know."

"Leave?" said the unicorn. It lifted its head in a regal gesture, and light flashed on the point of its horn. "Oh no, you can't leave. Not the Princess, anyway."

"What?" Elyssa said, considerably taken aback. "Why not?"

"Why, because you're a Princess and I'm a unicorn," the unicorn said.

"I don't see what that has to do with anything," Elyssa said.

"You will gather trefoils and buttercups and pinks for me, and plait them into garlands for my neck," the unicorn went on dreamily, as if Elyssa hadn't said anything at all. "I will rest my head in your lap, and you will polish my horn and comb my mane."

"Sounds like an exciting life," said the cat.

"Your mane doesn't need combing," Elyssa told the unicorn crossly. "And your horn doesn't need polishing. As for flowers, I'll be happy to have Stepmama send you some dandelions from the garden at home. But I'm not interested in staying here for goodness knows how long just to plait them into garlands."

"Nonsense," said the unicorn. "You're a Princess. All Princesses adore unicorns."

"Well, I don't," Elyssa said firmly. "And I'm not staying."

The cat lashed his tail in agreement, and gave the unicorn a dark look.

"You don't have a choice," the unicorn said calmly. "You're not much of a Princess, but you're better than nothing, and I'm not letting you go. I've been stuck out here on the far edge of the Enchanted Forest for years and years, with no one to sing songs about me or appreciate my beauty, and I deserve some consideration."

"Not from me, you don't," Elyssa muttered. She decided that the cat had been right to call the unicorn a stuck-up goat. "I'm sorry, but we really must leave," she said in a louder tone. "Good-bye, unicorn." She picked up her bundle and started for the edge of the hollow.

The unicorn watched with glittering eyes, but it made no move to stop her. "I don't like this," the cat said as he and Elyssa left the hollow.

"You're the one who found that pool in the first place," Elyssa pointed out.

The cat ducked its head. "I know," he said uncomfortably. "But—"

He broke off abruptly as they came around one of the huge trees and found themselves at the edge of the hollow once more. The unicorn was watching them with a smug, sardonic expression from the other side of the pool.

"We must have gotten turned around in the woods," Elyssa said doubtfully.

The cat did not reply. They turned and started into the woods again. This time they walked very slowly, to be certain they did not go in a circle. In a few minutes, they were back at the hollow.

"Had enough?" said the unicorn.

"Third time lucky," said the cat. "Come on, Princess."

They turned their backs on the unicorn and walked into the woods. Elyssa concentrated very hard, and kept a careful eye on the trees.

"I think we're going to make it this time," she said after a little. "Cat? Cat, where are—oh, dear." She was standing at the edge of the hollow, looking across the pool at the unicorn.

"The cat is gone for good," the unicorn informed her in a satisfied tone.

Elyssa felt a pang of worry about her friend. "What did you do to him?" she demanded.

"I got rid of him," the unicorn said. "I don't want a cat; I want a Princess. Someone to comb my mane, and polish my horn—"

"—and make you garlands, I know," Elyssa said. "Well, I won't do it."

"No?" said the unicorn.

"No," Elyssa said firmly. "So you might as well just let me go."

"I don't think so," the unicorn said. "You'll change your mind after a while, you'll see. I'm much too beautiful to resist. And I expect that with a little work you'll improve a great deal."

"Elyssa doesn't need your kind of improvement," said the cat's voice from just above Elyssa's head.

Elyssa looked up. The cat was perched in the lowest fork of the enormous tree beside her. "You came back!" she said.

"Did you really think I wouldn't, Princess?" said the cat. "I'd have gotten here sooner, but I wanted to make sure of the way out. Just in case you've had enough of our conceited friend."

"You're bluffing, cat," said the unicorn. "Princess Elyssa can't get out unless I let her, and I won't."

"That's what you think," said the cat. "Shall we go, Princess?"

"Yes, *please*," said Elyssa.

"Put your hand on my back, then, and don't let go," said the cat.

Elyssa bent over and put her hand on the cat's back, just below his neck. It was a very awkward and uncomfortable way to walk, and she was sure she looked quite silly. She had to concentrate very hard to keep from falling or tripping and losing her hold as she sidled along. "How much farther?" she asked after what seemed a long time.

"Not far," said the cat. Elyssa thought he sounded tired. A few moments later they entered a large clearing (which contained neither a pool nor a unicorn), and the cat stopped. "All right, Princess," the cat said. "You can let go now."

Elyssa took her hand off the cat's back and straightened up. It felt very good to stretch again. When she looked down, the cat was lowering himself to the ground in a stiff and clumsy fashion that was quite unlike his usual grace.

"Oh, dear," said Elyssa. She dropped to her knees beside the cat and stroked his fur, very gently. "Are you all right, cat?" she asked, because she couldn't think of anything else to say.

The cat did not answer. Elyssa remembered all the stories she had ever heard about animals who had been gravely injured or even killed getting their masters or mistresses out of trouble, and she began to be very much afraid. "Please be all right, cat," she said, and leaned over and kissed him on the nose.

The air shimmered, and then it rippled, and then it exploded into brightness right in front of Elyssa's eyes. She blinked. An exceedingly handsome man dressed in brown velvet lay sprawled on the moss in front of her, right where the cat had been.

Elyssa blinked again. The man propped his head on one elbow and looked up at her. "Very nice, Princess," he said. "But I wouldn't mind if you tried again a little lower down."

"You're the cat, aren't you?" Elyssa said.

"I was," the man admitted. He sat up and smiled at her. "You don't object to the change, do you?"

"No," said Elyssa. "But who are you now, please?"

"Prince Riddle of Amonhill," the man said. He bowed to her even though he was still sitting down, which proved he was a Prince. "I made the mistake of stopping at Queen Hildegard's castle some time ago, and she changed me into a cat when I refused to marry her dreadful daughter."

"Queen Hildegard? But I was supposed to go see her!" Elyssa exclaimed.

"I know. I told you you wouldn't like her," Prince Riddle said. "She condemned me to be a cat until I was kissed by a Princess who had drunk the water from a unicorn's pool. Her daughter was the only Princess the Queen knew of who had tasted the water. If she had also managed to kiss me I'd have had to marry her." He shuddered.

"I see," said Elyssa slowly. "So that's why you brought me to the Enchanted Forest and then found the unicorn's pool."

Riddle looked a little shamefaced. "Yes. I didn't expect to have any trouble with the unicorn; they usually aren't around much. I'm sorry."

"It's quite all right," Elyssa said hastily. "It was very interesting. And I'm glad I could help you. And—and you don't need to think that you have to marry me just because I disenchanted you."

"It *is* traditional, you know," Riddle said, with a sidelong glance that reminded Elyssa very strongly of the cat.

"Well, I think it's a silly tradition!" Elyssa said in an emphatic tone. "What if you didn't like the Princess who broke the spell?"

Riddle smiled warmly. "But I do like you, Princess."

"Oh," said Elyssa.

"You were always very nice to me when I was a cat."

"Yes," said Elyssa.

"And I like the idea of marrying you." Riddle looked at her a little uncertainly. "That is, if you wouldn't mind marrying me."

"Actually," said Elyssa, "I'd like it very much."

So Elyssa and Riddle went back to the castle to be married. Elyssa's family was delighted. Her papa kissed her cheek and clapped Riddle on the back. Her stepmama cried with joy and then was happily scandalized to hear about the doings of her old school friend Queen Hildegard. And both of Elyssa's sisters agreed to be bridesmaids (much to the dismay of the King's councillors, who felt that it was bad enough for a middle

Princess to be married first without emphasizing the fact by having her sisters stand up for her).

The wedding was a grand affair, with all the neighboring Kings and Queens in attendance. There were even a couple of fairies present, which made the King's councillors more cross than ever. (Fairies, according to the chief councillor, were supposed to come to christenings, not to weddings.) After the wedding, Elyssa had her stepmama send a special note to Queen Hildegard. A few days later, Queen Hildegard's daughter disappeared into the Enchanted Forest, and shortly thereafter rumors began circulating that the unicorn had found a handmaiden even more conceited than it was.

And so they all lived happily for the rest of their lives, except the King's councillors, who never would stop trying to make things go the way they thought things ought to be.

ROBERT KELLY

The Book and Its Contents

Robert Kelly has published more than forty volumes of poetry, including *Kill the Messenger*, which won the *Los Angeles Times* Book Award. His first collection of fiction, *A Transparent Tree*, received an Academy–Institute Award from the American Academy and Institute of Arts and Letters in 1985. Kelly has been Poet in Residence at the California Institute of Technology and Tufts University, and presently co-directs the graduate writing program at Bard College.

"The Book and Its Contents," a lyrical fantasy tale set in a small Pennsylvania town, comes from Kelly's most recent collection of short stories, *Doctor of Silence*.

—T. W.

THE BOOK AND ITS CONTENTS

Robert Kelly

I find it difficult to tell what little of the truth I may know, now that Dr. Perkunas is dead. Nature and experience have combined to make me a close-mouthed, unforthcoming, scant forgiving sort of man, and seldom do I feel the need to proffer what I think I know, little as it is. People have enough to do avoiding their own truths.

Still, I was his patient, and, as small towns measure these things, his friend. I knew him not as well as I know myself, but disliked him less, so I can bear the town's characterization. Towns know nothing of real friendship, ardent symposiums of those whose rhythms of perception and permission are meaningful together. But the town knows me, after all. I was born here, as my father was, and though I've spent most of my life away, those years aren't real time for a town. A town counts only the overall contact, and presumes to understand what one of its own is up to no matter how far he goes or how long he stays. He's away (painting in Paris, whoring in Managua, praying in Wandrille) and then he's back, and the "away" is just an idiosyncrasy, like a taste for pink shirts or a fondness for old expletives like "judaspriest!"

Dr. Perkunas had settled in the town, taking over old Jarvis's practice, just about the time I made my way home from five years in Asia. I came to see him about some skin thing I'd picked up in Nepal, and didn't expect him to be much help. Nor was he, but he did give me the obvious antibiotics that probably kept whatever it was from getting worse. It healed eventually, as bodies do, and I came back to get a Nunc dimittis from him.

This time I noticed a fastidious nervousness in the man. For a moment he left the office to get some cigarettes—he was a heavy smoker—and I could see through the door into his private apartments a number of bookcases congested with what clearly were not medical books. I alluded to these on his return, readers are rare in my town, and he seemed torn between discussion and discretion, as I might once have been before the latter triumphed once for all in what passes for my character. The other triumphed now in him, and he began, as if both weary and excited at once, to talk about his researches into language.

I made civil enough queries, and came up with some linguistic oddities from my travels, but he received these only impatiently, as if by language he did not mean something people did, speaking well or ill or interestingly; he seemed to mean by language something vast and principled, of which any practical application (communication, expression, history) was a tiresome irrelevance, an unfortunate lapse of the Absolute into mere behavior.

He talked on, and when his consultation hours drew to a close, led me into his sitting room and went on talking. He gave me supermarket teabag tea and Social Tea biscuits; as long as I knew him, I never saw him serve, or eat, anything else.

His talk as such did not interest me much, but it was pleasing to hear a fellow human speak with passion about a subject that had nothing to do with the town, the nation, or public affairs of the great or small. We might just as well have been in Copenhagen, and I felt enlarged by the liberality of his abstruseness. Indeed the only local reference I ever heard him make was to the name of our state, which he pronounced strangely, each of its five syllables stated with equal emphasis, though all the rest of us pronounce it with four, heavy stress on the third. The name fascinated him, as names in general did—not to be sure as a heraldry of character or personality of the bearers, but as a sort of topological mapping of a prime reality. The actual miles and mills of Pennsylvania were just premature reification, a rash materialization of what should truly have stayed latent in a pure potency the name both signified and, somehow, *was*.

He was balding, grizzled, brownish, with ear tufts. His grey eyes were too light for his dusky skin, and his skin too tight for his bones. He never looked comfortable. I hope he sometimes was, though. A world without comfort is not worth pursuing. Maybe he was at ease in that four-hour stretch—six to ten—he gave himself every morning for reading.

What did he read? Patterns. Strings. Never books. Books were just zoos where you went to look at paragraphs. He had many books, but never added to their number. Even with my perfunctory education I could see he was scarcely literate in any cultural tradition, and remarkably ill-informed. But like a medieval monk, he contemplated with enthusiasm what he did not find it necessary to understand.

Our relationship, meagerly established, neither grew nor declined, but proved to have the austere durability of desert plants. Once a week I would stop in after his evening hours and listen to him rave. It was like those weary friendships that arise from a shared interest, say in chess, and never care, or dare, to transcend the occasion of their genesis. But with Dr. Perkunas, I was not even put to the inconvenience of playing a game, or bothering myself with attacks, gambits, endgames. Enough to listen. With him, we were always in the middle of things; nothing ever started, and nothing ever ended.

Once I took the liberty of bringing him, all neatly typed out, a passage that had struck me in an old notebook of my own I was rereading. Evidently I had copied it out without bothering to identify the source —an omission that would not trouble Perkunas. I handed him the crisp paper, and he read it aloud to me, his East European singsong sounding very peculiar chanting the very English passage:

What it says, sire, is less than it means. That is the trick of words, and their troth too, to which they are ever faithful, as a shadow to its man. . . . There is a sunlight too of words, and days overcast, and simple night. But the word rides through, and what it means takes flesh in the new day, or as the day, and the word walks around in the plain morning, exploring the dewy grass of the garden of what it means.

He laid the paper on top of the plate of biscuits, and looked at me. There was something of fear in his eyes, and a surmise about me I had never seen before in him. He took his glasses off and rubbed their lenses on his trouser leg, put them on his nose again and picked up the paper once more. Silently this time he studied it; he seemed to read it straight through three or four times. He laid it on the table now, beside the plate, so the cookies were available again—perhaps he had convinced himself of my good intentions. Or, more likely, considering what was to come, of my ignorance.

"The word walks around," he quoted. And looked at me. I confess to a shiver that wriggled up my spine at that moment as I guessed what startling literalness—half crucifixion and half cartoon—that phrase might have for his naive sensibilities. He thanked me, nonetheless, for bringing him the citation (he called it that), and then made signs that told me our evening had come to a close. I left with less than the usual sense of boredom and inconsequentiality that typically haunted my walk home from our weekly discussions. As I passed under the great larches by the cemetery, golden now for October, I even detected in myself a certain excitement, as if there were more to Perkunas's obsessions than a complex crossword puzzle. I nibbled my Social Tea Biscuit slowly, and it lasted me half the way home.

Yet next week was like old times, and the week after, and the week after that. Things were pleasant and comfortable, and Perkunas talked,

and I listened and nibbled and sipped and listened. All the rest of the
week, as the town could tell you, I am a formidable talker, so this evening
with Perkunas, I must admit, had its charm for me, a turnabout, a
releasement. The usual current of our verbal lassitude idled along.

Then one week in early December Perkunas, instead of having a stack
of books precarious on the arm of his stuffed chair, had only a sheaf of
papers on his lap. He made no reference to these for an hour or so, then,
after one of his infrequent pauses, he had lifted the papers to his eyes
(blocking my view of his face), looked through them slowly, lowered
them and looked at me in a way I could only find challenging.

"And doubted every door forever more," he said.

"I beg your pardon?"

He repeated the sentence. In my drowsiness, I had not only missed
the words, but was slow at gathering that he was quoting, not remarking.
I pulled myself together and asked what it was from. It doesn't matter,
he said, and repeated the sentence yet again, and began to talk.

My own state led me to think about the proposition the words made,
and thus I lost the drift of his remarks. In truth I was sleepy, with that
after-dinner winter sleepiness that I would take as a sign of advancing
age if I had not felt it all my life—though even as a child it made me
feel like an old man. Perhaps we are all ages at all times, and can be
ourselves as we will be in fifty years right now, by an effort. Or is it by
a release of effort? By the time I could get my mind back onto what Dr.
Perkunas was saying, he was on terrain familiar to me from this mono-
maniac's conversation.

"Every door is every one. No exceptions. And doubt is absolute. No
paradox. To doubt everything is doubt nothing, isn't it. True. *Dubio*,
to be uncertain, to raise difficulties about. The absolute insists again,
no?, in forevermore, one word. Always and everything. But a thing here
is a door. Nothing else is mentioned as being doubted. What are the
words telling us?"

That's how he talked. Now he paused on that ritual self-invitation to
expatiate that his last words comprised. Politely, as usual, he waited a
civil ten seconds to see if I'd offer an answer to what, after all, he may
have not meant only as a rhetorical question. Maybe he really wanted to
know, maybe even more desperately wanted someone to tell him what
the words are ever telling us. Maybe he wanted a woman's soft voice to
whisper the answer on his real pillow. But there were no women in his
life, as far as I could tell. He went on:

"To doubt a door is doubting in and out, both. Stasis. The old greek
Flux, panta rhei, the pratityasamutpada of the Buddhist people, the
interdependency ever-crossing never-ending—all of that, here negated.

This is a Jewish Christian despair, my friend, be sure of it. No pagan ever doubted a door. But see now where it leaves us, this doubted door. Bleak, bleak, bleak. Nothing else is mentioned, so everything else is possible. Only the door, only the door."

"Excuse me," I said, "I don't feel the weight of despondency you do in the phrase. Maybe the context instructs you to read the words so pessimistically. They are sad, surely, and a bit overemphatic with that lugubrious "nevermore"; but it's just a sentence, limited. What does it mean in the whole context? And what is the sentence from, by the way?"

"Context has nothing to do with it!" He came close to shouting. "Context is gossip. Context is just sociology, the conspiracy of triviality in which language is enmeshed in this bad world. We don't need a context—we have words!"

He paused on that exaltation, then subsided. After a few moments, he half-apologetically (for the outburst? for the fact he was about to acknowledge?) admitted that the phrase was his own, from a poem he'd written in medical school. He had been in love, and once, visiting his girl friend, had (by divine inspiration, he said) paused at her door before knocking on it. He heard a male voice uttering tendresses within, and he crept away and never spoke to the girl again. But that's not the point, he assured me. It's not why the words got written, but what they say. What do they *say*? he crowed, as if the question were an all-vanquishing rebuttal.

I did want to hear about his romance, but I accepted, by my silence, the return of the conversation to our usual matters, which languidly engaged us for the rest of the evening.

That year I spent the Christmas season with my parents in Florida, where they'd moved twenty years ago. They had a little place on the west coast, half of a bitty island, and I bloated and swam and bamboozled some local ladies, then came back north to spend the weekend of New Year's with a dear friend in Massachusetts. So it wasn't till the second week in January that I visited Perkunas again; I had a bad cold to bring him, which he brusquely dealt with before we settled down to chat.

The first surprise was Perkunas himself; he looked worn and aged, and his skin, even allowing for my recent sojourn among the goldentanned, seemed really grey, ashen. And above the doorway leading to an inner room was hanging a big spray of mistletoe. I had never known Perkunas to observe any custom, religious or secular, and cocked an eyebrow at it with a smile. He waved at it vaguely and said they did that in his country and why not. Why not indeed, I agreed, and the subject lapsed. I reverted to my first surprise, and asked him about his health. He just shook his head, took off his glasses, put them on, shook his head again and looked at me, as if to examine my comprehension of these signs. Were they the acted-out symptoms of some ailment? I looked back at him and waited, expecting either a verbal answer, or a shift to our usual topics. Instead, he closed his eyes and laid his head against the back of his old kroehler.

Why not follow his example, I thought, and did so. My chair was just as comfortable, if newer, and I let my mind range whatever it found in the way of recent imagery while I waited for Perkunas to have something to say. I had been doing not much of anything for several weeks, and there is nothing more exhausting than inactivity, especially a pleasant inactivity with family and girlfriend and snow and eating and drinking and watching television with people you know too well to bother talking with. I drifted, but was not asleep. I certainly was not asleep.

"Come, I have to show you something." When I opened my eyes I found Perkunas on his feet, inclined a little toward me as if caught in mid-bow. I rose and followed him to the doorway hung with mistletoe.

I don't have much more to tell, and I'm conscious of a desire to stretch things out, record unnecessary details (the pale green paint on the door woodwork, the smell of cherries, the pulled thread on Perkunas' dark red necktie) to flesh out the hurried conclusion of my story. I said at the beginning that I knew little of the truth, and I wasn't lying. All I can give any account of is this last passage, upcoming, in my relationship with Dr. Perkunas. Now that I know it was the last, it takes on peculiar emphases and shadings. But even at the time it felt like a curious and important moment. I had never been in any other room of his private apartment, and the prospect of entering one now excused, if it did not explain, the odd feeling of excitement that came over me. Yes, mixed with a little fear. But then I am often afraid, truth to tell, and fear is such a common music we hardly need admit to hearing it.

And I am stretching, too, because I have been so long-winded in bringing us to this moment, to a crisis about which I can offer only some inferences, if that. Maybe just by talking more and more I can make the end of my account balance its beginnings—a deathbed fancy; I'm sure the dying man begs for the energy and opportunity to make the whole argosy into the underworld take as long as his life's whole progress to that moment of departure. Enough of this procrastination—open the door.

Dr. Perkunas opened the door and, ever polite, stood aside so I might enter first. The room I entered was bare except for a wooden table not quite at the center, a lightbulb hanging above it, a wooden chair at an angle in front of it, its back to one entering the room. On the table was a book, which even at this distance was obviously hand-bound, a big thick quarto. If there was a window in the room, it was hidden behind a long drape off to the side.

"Go up to it, look at it. It is what I do. Or what I have done, done with it all. It is almost finished now, after so long. Go look. You can touch it, even. Look." Dr. Perkunas was speaking in a calm, even tender voice.

There seemed no harm in humoring him. The book, close up, was buckram, a little rumpled with the glue that held it to the boards, and the three-quarter leatherette binding was irregular. But the whole book was sound, solid to the feel. I opened it at random and found the heavy pages inscribed closely, in a neat, tiny, quite legible handwriting. At first I thought it was pencil, then saw it was a curious pale grey ink. I thumbed through the pages and saw no divisions, no chapter beginnings, large letters, blank spaces. It was one continuity of text. I turned back to the first page—no title, no mark of commencement. On the flyleaf was written Perkunas' full name, then the text began on the first recto page and went on. The last eight leaves of the book were still blank. I estimate four to five hundred pages were in the book, all densely written. At random I chose a passage in the middle and began to read:

> . . . *manner in which this act is performed—its degree of intensity and the rituals employed—appears on the contrary that the octahedral form is seldom seen in India, with the circles changed into squares. They seem to have been successful at first, then the perfect light will pour out upon everyone. This is an appropriate point to remind the reader that in Guiana the rainbow is called by the name of the opossum. This is the excellent foppery of the world* . . .

I looked up at Perkunas and let the book close. I cannot vouch for the exact wording, but what I set down here is the drift of what I read. And drift is what it seemed to be.

"What is this, Doctor?"

"It is my book, the book. It is a book the words have written by themselves." He smiled at me as he said this, a shy smile, modest, betokening an artist's humility not even his obvious metabolic excitement could confute. "It is a book where only language exists, and language tells. It says everything by itself, without our intrusion and our interferences. I have guided its grammar—people are so fussy about grammar, as if language couldn't be trusted . . ." What had begun as a pleasantry seemed to trail off. He looked nervously behind him at the open doorway, where the mistletoe jiggled a little in a draft from somewhere.

I tried to draw him back to the book. "I don't understand the passage I just read. Do I have to read it from the beginning?"

"Of course not. There is no beginning. You would understand if you read slowly, and thought about every word as it came along. And they do. They do."

He sat down on the chair. Unlike him to leave the guest standing—but his next words explained.

"Go out. Go out into the next room and watch, look at me here, at the desk. But don't come in until I tell you to. Go."

His voice was urgent now, and there was no sense of an intellectual argument energetically pursued. It seemed urgent the way real things in the world can be, dangerous, fleeable. I went into the familiar sitting room and stood at the door looking in at him.

He took the book from the table where I'd laid it, and, opening it at random, began to read in a quiet voice. I could not hear the words.

But in a few minutes I began to see them. That's how it felt, at any rate. Certainly I began to see. A peacock came first, and walked unconcernedly across the room, through the doctor's legs, and vanished in the spray of a fountain that appeared just in time to receive the bird, then itself disappeared just in the spot where three women were coming toward me till a ship in sail obscured them as it passed, making great waves, into a forest in which it could still be seen. An elephant followed the path of the peacock, and a small sports coupe from the 1920s followed the elephant. At its wheel a goggled man cried out in pain as a rainstorm soaked the white linen of his duster. A small city grew in the distance between the doctor's shoulder blades, and was wiped out by fire while two dozen schoolgirls in straw hats and grey uniforms scampered by holding baskets of flowers—lupines and phlox. All these things were transparent, in the sense that through them I could see table and doctor and book and far wall, yet they had the quality of being realer than their ground. And the wall and the doctor and so on were transparent too, and through them I could see continuous motion, both in the evident space of the room, and in more paradoxical planes within them or athwart them. There was a rich and intricate blur of movement and stillness, yet at any given moment one being or one thing clearly was the focal point of this local reality—no doubt the word leaving the doctor's mouth at that same moment.

Then another order of presence made itself known. A tall figure, dark in form, seemed to take on a different kind of transparency, and lingered in that steady state while all the other words, things, signs, whatever they were, focused and gradually blurred away. This form, perhaps a man's, now began to move toward me, or toward the doorway. I could see no face beneath the cowl it wore, only a pullulation of tiny images, as if that face too were a plane of event on which unscrupulous multitudes of words came and went. The curious thing approached the door, and I was uneasy enough to shrink away. I assured myself the apparition was just that, an illusion. *But what isn't?*, a nasty voice demanded inside my head. And some illusions are more energetic than others, fearful, with staying power. This thing with the leprous face mottled with unknown actions done by unknown actors in some other world came to the doorway, but did not cross the threshold. It looked at me and I endured its examination—there was no singleness about the thing, and being watched by it felt like being observed by a pack of dogs or a cage of monkeys. This was oddly comforting to me, along with an unarguable certainty that the mistletoe hung up kept it from coming into this room. Without turning at all, it moved away, moved back—or at least grew smaller so our usual sense of perspective said, it is going away. Its intensity of horror—was it that, or was it just an intensity of complexity itself that so rippled from it?—did not diminish with size. I reached forward and pulled the door closed.

The book, when I had looked at it a while ago, had felt unpleasant, as if the futility I felt inspired it had reached a level of intensity for which the emotions which composed it were not intended—trivial tragedy, paroxysmal vapidity. It had a late night feeling, smelled of empty chatter by people too tired to make sense, too lonely to go home—you know the feeling, diners have it at three A.M., and church suppers at eight P.M. The way we clutch to each other for what, for precisely what, we cannot give—that was the taste of that book.

How harsh my judgment was! How unfair to my old friend! Here I was leaving him alone in that weird room with whatever it is. For all I knew, I was projecting my own dominant mood onto that book, for was I not prime example of just such a wearied, lonely, clutching man? I could be braver. I tapped on the door with my fingertips and called out my friend's name. No response. I knocked again, with knuckles this time, and silence again. I had enough integrity to turn the knob and try to go in. To my great relief, the door had locked itself when I closed it. "Perkunas!" I cried, "I have to be getting home now. Call me tomorrow, will you? Good night!" I was trying to talk as if everything were the same as everything else, no difference, no problem. I waited a few moments, said good night again, and left his apartment. I did not, of course, ever see my friend again.

As I walked along the idle streets, empty at the best of times in our dull town, I felt a predictable yearning for crowds, for companionship of the most unimaginative type. Though I rate myself a coward, I overcame that impulse and contented myself with the fierce cold air, dry, the stars' blaze overhead, Orion in particular, balanced on Rigel, gave an air of firm settledness to the visible world I found bracing. Less out of fear (was the thing following me? how would I deal with the doctor hereafter, after this unprecedented but vastly embarrassing revelation of his real concerns?) than out of a wish to get the book and its contents out of my head, I took the faintheart course of spending the night at a dear friend's house. She made me coffee and gave me cookies, and didn't examine too closely my motives for wanting to sleep with her.

By nine the next morning, when she and I were up and about, having brunch at the Swan, the whole thing, as you probably remember, was over. Later that week, our town paper (the *Democrat*, though we haven't elected one since the Civil War) gave as full an account of the puzzling incident as we're ever likely to read.

A car full of workers on their way to a construction site saw the doctor, fully clothed but without an overcoat, running down the middle of the street in the frozen dawn light. They saw him dart into the park near the bandstand; they noted in particular that he leaped the big pile of snow at roadside without breaking stride. One of the workers had frequently, and successfully, consulted the doctor about his bad back; at his request, the other workers stopped the car and came into the park to make sure the doctor was all right. When they got there, they couldn't be sure if he was or not. They saw the man standing in front of the bandstand, where in summer a circle of grass invited recliners. As they watched, he opened two or three buttons of his shirt and reached in with both hands. One of the watchers compared the doctor's movements at that point to those of a friend of his who used to walk around keeping his pet ferrets in his shirt—quick, anxious a little, but in control. None of the men thought he looked afraid. But they were frightened when they saw him begin to pull out of his clothes and scatter on the snow in front of him, one after another, a bunch of bananas, a roller skate, a lighted candle, a football, a cat, a steam iron, a chessboard with men on it, handfuls of what looked like money, a glass of water that steamed in the cold air and sat upright in the snow when he let it fall. All the objects lay about, except the cat, which scampered away and was seen no more.

The workers, alerted perhaps by the money, began to move closer to the doctor, and the pace of his productions increased. Now a blinding confusion of objects and animals began to be pulled out and strewn, so many in fact that they began to float rather than fall, float across the snow until they found a place to settle. The workers saw not just things and creatures coming out, but even what they described as "moods"—

sheets of pure color that shimmered substantially before dissolving, huge shapes "made out of sound."

About this time they began to hear the doctor's voice, or at least some voice that synchronized with the movements of Perkunas's lips, though the sound seemed to come from up above, a huge voice, but of a man speaking very gently, the workers said, for all its volume, "loud, but not shouting, just talking quietly but very, very loud' is how one of them described it. The voice was so powerful that they stopped moving, and the air was thick with things the doctor was pulling out of himself and throwing into the world. As they watched, he began to rise into the air, they all swear to this, and when he was high enough for them to see the ridgepole of the bandstand roof just under his heels, the torrent of creations swept down on them and they were lost in sheer thingliness.

By the time they had dug themselves out, strangely unhurt by the sensed weight of all the things that had floated, not fallen, down on them, they could not see the doctor anywhere. Around the place he'd been standing were only his tracks in the snow, going in, standing. And then he went up.

That was the story they told, and absurd as it sounded, no one had any more convincing way of accounting for the disappearance of Dr. Perkunas, and of the presence in the park of so many thousands of unlikely, even preposterous, items. By full daylight the police and fire volunteers had been joined by most of the idle townspeople, all of them busy carrying off whatever they could get their hands on. By the time my friend and I had heard the story by word of mouth and gotten over to the park, most of the treasures, if that's what they were, were gone. Monica helped herself to a little French prayerbook, *Le Paroissien mystique*, and I took away with me a single roller skate. It has no maker's mark on it. I keep it over my fireplace, and sit in front of it from time to time, wondering what really happened, to the town and to Perkunas. Nothing made any sense to me. It was a pity that the workers had no intellectual preparation for being witnesses of what they beheld; people of theological cultivation might have understood things quite differently. As it was, we had a marvel, but no material for thinking about it with. Confronted with the inexplicable, the mind has a comforting slovenly habit of going back, or forward, to countryside it thinks it can negotiate. I too stopped thinking about it after a while. And the town had, as towns do, other things on its mind.

A few days later I went back and sat in Perkunas's apartment. The door to that room stood open, and the book, the wicked or peculiar or wonderful book, sat on the table. The apartment was just as it had been, and there was some talk of a cousin from Gettysburg coming up the next weekend and settling his affairs. I decided to take the book away with me, and not leave it as a trap for someone even less prepared than I to cope with its powers.

In the following weeks I mourned my old friend placidly from time to time. Soon it was clear that the book shouldn't stay with me. So I sent it along, together with a more circumstantial account of it and him than I give here, to the Fortean Museum in Philadelphia, a small place open one afternoon a week to the general public. You will find the book there, with my fuller statement, in the gallery that examines Manifestation. They cross-index it in their catalogue also under the listing Conjurations and Spells, Bad Effects of. This category is clearly nonsense, unless we choose to regard the whole panoply of human language as one interminable magic spell that long, long ago got utterly out of control.

M. JOHN HARRISON

The Great God Pan

M. John Harrison is a fine British author known for his novels,
among them *The Pastel City, A Storm of Wings*, and *In Viriconium*, the
latter introducing readers to the setting of a number of short stories.
The Ice Monkey, a collection of stories, was published to wide critical
acclaim, and his work continues to be among the most original and
intellectually challenging in the field today.

"The Great God Pan" is a story with roots in the sixties, but the
source of its effectiveness lies in a cold, dark place that is outside of
time. Four young people have dabbled in the supernatural and are
themselves infected by the stink of that which they dare to invoke.
Harrison's great skill in this subtle and chilling piece is in generating
stark terror with hints and portents.

—E. D.

THE GREAT GOD PAN

M. John Harrison

But is there really something far more horrible
than ever could resolve itself into reality,
and is it that something which terrifies me so?
—*Katherine Mansfield*
Journals, *March 1914*

Ann took drugs to manage her epilepsy. They often made her depressed
and difficult to deal with; and Lucas, who was nervous himself, never
knew what to do. After their divorce he relied increasingly on me as a
go-between. "I don't like the sound of her voice," he would tell me.
"You try her." The drugs gave her a screaming, false-sounding laugh
that went on and on. Though he had remained sympathetic over the
years, Lucas was always embarrassed and upset by it. I think it frightened
him. "See if you can get any sense out of her." It was guilt, I think,
that encouraged him to see me as a steadying influence: not his own guilt
so much as the guilt he felt all three of us shared. "See what she says."

On this occasion what she said was:

"Look, if you bring on one of my turns, bloody Lucas Fisher will
regret it. What business is it of his how I feel, anyway?"

I was used to her, so I said carefully, "It was just that you wouldn't
talk to him. He was worried that something was happening. Is there
something wrong, Ann?" She didn't answer, but I had hardly expected
her to. "If you don't want to see me," I suggested, "couldn't you tell
me now?"

I thought she was going to hang up, but in the end there was only a
kind of paroxysm of silence. I was phoning her from a call box in the
middle of Huddersfield. The shopping precinct outside was full of pale
bright sunshine, but windy and cold; sleet was forecast for later in the
day. Two or three teenagers went past, talking and laughing. I heard
one of them say, "What acid rain's got to do with my career, I don't

know. But that's what they asked me: 'What do you know about acid rain?' " When they had gone, I could hear Ann breathing raggedly.

"Hello?" I said.

Suddenly she shouted, "Are you mad? I'm not talking on the phone. Before you know it, the whole thing's public property!"

Sometimes she was more dependent on medication than usual; you knew when, because she tended to use that phrase over and over again. One of the first things I ever heard her say was, "It looks so easy, doesn't it? But before you know it, the bloody thing's just slipped straight out of your hands," as she bent down nervously to pick up the bits of a broken glass. How old were we then? Twenty? Lucas believed she was reflecting in language some experience either of the drugs or the disease itself, but I'm not sure he was right. Another thing she often said was, "I mean, you have to be careful, don't you?" drawing out in a wondering, childlike way both *care* and *don't*, so that you saw immediately it was a mannerism learned in adolescence.

"You must be mad if you think I'm talking on the phone!"

I said quickly, "Okay, then, Ann. I'll come over this evening."

"You might as well come now and get it over with. I don't feel well."

Epilepsy since the age of twelve or thirteen, as regular as clockwork; and then, later, a classic migraine to fill in the gaps, a complication which, rightly or wrongly, she had alway associated with our experiments at Cambridge in the late sixties. She must never get angry or excited. "I reserve my adrenaline," she would explain, looking down at herself with a comical distaste. "It's a physical thing. I can't let it go at the time." Afterward, though, the reservoir would burst, and it would all be released at once by some minor stimulus—a lost shoe, a missed bus, rain—to cause her hallucinations, vomiting, loss of bowel control. "Oh, and then euphoria. It's wonderfully relaxing," she would say bitterly. "Just like sex."

"Okay, Ann, I'll be there soon. Don't worry."

"Piss off. Things are coming to bits here. I can already see the little floating lights."

As soon as she put the receiver down, I telephoned Lucas.

"I'm not doing this again," I said. "Lucas, she isn't well. I thought she was going to have an attack there and then."

"She'll see you, though? The thing is, she just kept putting the phone down on me. She'll see you today?"

"You knew she would."

"Good."

I hung up.

"Lucas, you're a bastard," I told the shopping precinct.

The bus from Huddersfield wound its way for thirty minutes through exhausted mill villages given over to hairdressing, dog breeding, and an undercapitalized tourist trade. I got off the bus at three o'clock in the afternoon. It seemed much later. The church clock was already lit, and a mysterious yellow light was slanting across the window of the nave— someone was inside with only a forty-watt bulb for illumination. Cars went past endlessly as I waited to cross the road, their exhaust steaming in the dark air. For a village it was quite noisy: tires hissing on the wet road, the bang and clink of soft-drink bottles being unloaded from a lorry, some children I couldn't see, chanting one word over and over again. Suddenly, above all this, I heard the pure musical note of a thrush and stepped out into the road.

"You're sure no one got off the bus behind you?"

Ann kept me on the doorstep while she looked anxiously up and down the street, but once I was inside, she seemed glad to have someone to talk to.

"You'd better take your coat off. Sit down. I'll make you some coffee. No, here, just push the cat off the chair. He knows he's not supposed to be there."

It was an old cat, black and white, with dull, dry fur, and when I picked it up, it was just a lot of bones and heat that weighed nothing. I set it down carefully on the carpet, but it jumped back onto my knee again immediately and began to dribble on my pullover. Another, younger animal was crouching on the windowsill, shifting its feet uncomfortably among the little intricate baskets of paper flowers as it stared out into the falling sleet, the empty garden. "Get down off there!" Ann shouted suddenly. It ignored her. She shrugged. "They act as if they own the place." It smelled as if they did. "They were strays," she said. "I don't know why I encouraged them." Then, as though she were still talking about the cats:

"How's Lucas?"

"He's surprisingly well," I said. "You ought to keep in touch with him, you know."

"I know." She smiled briefly. "And how are you? I never see you."

"Not bad. Feeling my age."

"You don't know the half of it yet," she said. She was standing in the kitchen doorway holding a tea towel in one hand and a cup in the other. "None of us do." It was a familiar complaint. When she saw I was too preoccupied to listen, she went and banged things about in the sink. I heard water rushing into the kettle. While it filled up, she said something she knew I wouldn't catch; then, turning off the tap:

"Something's going on in the Pleroma. Something new. I can feel it."

"Ann," I said, "all that was over and done with twenty years ago."

The fact is that even at the time I wasn't at all sure what we *had* done. This will seem odd to you, I suppose; but it was 1968 or 1969, and all I remember now is a June evening drenched with the half-confectionary, half-corrupt smell of hawthorn blossoms. It was so thick, we seemed to swim through it, through that and the hot evening light that poured between the hedgerows like transparent gold. I remember Sprake because you don't forget him. What the four of us did escapes me, as does its significance. There was, undoubtedly, a loss; but whether you described what was lost as "innocence" was very much up to you—anyway, that was how it appeared to me. Lucas and Ann made a lot more of it from the very start. They took it to heart. Afterward—perhaps two or three months afterward, when it was plain that something had gone wrong, when things first started to pull out of shape—it was Ann and Lucas who convinced me to go and talk to Sprake, whom we had promised never to contact again. They wanted to see if what we had done could somehow be reversed or annulled; if what we'd lost could be bought back again.

"I don't think it works that way," I warned them; but I could see they weren't listening.

"He'll have to help us," Lucas said.

"Why did we ever do it?" Ann asked me.

Though he hated the British Museum, Sprake had always lived one way or another in its shadow. I met him at the Tivoli Espresso Bar, where I knew he would be every afternoon. He was wearing a thick, old-fashioned black overcoat—the weather that October was raw and damp —but from the way his wrists stuck out of the sleeves, long and fragile-looking and dirty, covered with sore grazes as though he had been fighting with some small animal, I suspected he wore no shirt or jacket underneath it. For some reason he had bought a copy of the *Church Times*. The top half of his body curled painfully around it; along with his stoop and his grey-stubbled lower jaw, the newspaper gave him the appearance of a disappointed verger. It was folded carefully to display part of a headline, but I never saw him open it.

At the Tivoli in those days, they always had the radio on. Their coffee was watery and, like most espresso, too hot to taste of anything. Sprake and I sat on stools by the window. We rested our elbows on a narrow counter littered with dirty cups and half-eaten sandwiches and watched the pedestrians in Museum Street. After ten minutes, a woman's voice said clearly from behind us:

"The fact is, the children just won't try."

Sprake jumped and glanced round haggardly, as if he expected to have to answer this.

"It's the radio," I reassured him.

He stared at me the way you would stare at someone who was mad, and it was some time before he went on with what he had been saying.

"You knew what you were doing. You got what you wanted, and you weren't tricked in any way."

"No," I admitted tiredly.

My eyes ached, even though I had slept on the journey down, waking—just as the train from Cambridge crawled the last mile into London—to see sheets of newspaper fluttering round the upper floors of an office block like butterflies courting a flower.

"I can see that," I said. "That isn't at issue. But I'd like to be able to reassure them in some way. . . ."

Sprake wasn't listening. It had come on to rain quite hard, driving visitors—mainly Germans and Americans who were touring the Museum—in from the street. They all seemed to be wearing brand-new clothes. The Tivoli filled with steam from the espresso machine, and the air was heavy with the smell of wet coats. People trying to find seats constantly brushed our backs, murmuring, "Excuse me, please. Excuse me." Sprake soon became irritated, though I think their politeness affected him more than the disturbance itself. "Dog muck," he said loudly in a matter-of-fact voice; and then, as a whole family pushed past him one by one, "Three generations of rabbits." None of them seemed to take offense, though they must have heard him. A drenched-looking woman in a purple coat came in, looked anxiously for an empty seat, and, when she couldn't see one, hurried out again. "Mad bitch!" Sprake called after her. "Get yourself reamed out." He stared challengingly at the other customers.

"I think it would be better if we talked in private," I said. "What about your flat?"

For twenty years he had lived in the same single room above the Atlantis Bookshop. He was reluctant to take me there, I could see, though it was only next door, and I had been there before. At first he tried to pretend it would be difficult to get in. "The shop's closed," he said. "We'd have to use the other door." Then he admitted:

"I can't go back there for an hour or two. I did something last night that means it may not be safe."

He grinned.

"You know the sort of thing I mean," he said.

I couldn't get him to explain further. The cuts on his wrists made me remember how panicky Ann and Lucas had been when I last spoke to them. All at once I was determined to see inside the room.

"If you don't want to go back there for a bit," I suggested, "we could always talk in the Museum."

Researching in the manuscript collection one afternoon a year before, he had turned a page of Jean de Wavrin's *Chroniques d'Angleterre*—that oblique history no complete version of which is known—and come upon a miniature depicting in strange, unreal greens and blues the coronation procession of Richard Coeur de Lion. Part of it had moved; which part, he would never say. "Why, if it is a coronation," he had written almost plaintively to me at the time, "are these four men carrying a coffin? And who is walking there under the awning—with the bishops not with them?" After that he had avoided the building as much as possible, though he could always see its tall iron railings at the end of the street. He had begun, he told me, to doubt the authenticity of some of the items in the medieval collection. In fact, he was frightened of them.

"It would be quieter there," I insisted.

He didn't respond but sat hunched over the *Church Times*, staring into the street with his hands clamped violently together in front of him. I could see him thinking.

"That fucking pile of shit!" he said eventually.

He got to his feet.

"Come on, then. It's probably cleared out by now, anyway."

Rain dripped from the blue-and-gold front of the Atlantis. There was a faded notice, CLOSED FOR COMPLETE REFURBISHMENT. The window display had been taken down, but they had left a few books on a shelf for the look of things. I could make out, through the condensation on the plate glass, de Vries's classic *Dictionary of Symbols & Imagery*. When I pointed it out to Sprake, he only stared at me contemptuously. He fumbled with his key. Inside, the shop smelled of cut timber, new plaster, paint, but this gave way on the stairs to an odor of cooking. Sprake's bed-sitter, which was quite large and on the top floor, had uncurtained sash windows on opposing walls. Nevertheless, it didn't seem well lit.

From one window you could see the sodden facades of Museum Street, bright green deposits on the ledges, stucco scrolls and garlands grey with pigeon dung; out of the other, part of the blackened clock tower of St. George's Bloomsbury, a reproduction of the tomb of Mausoleus lowering up against the racing clouds.

"I once heard that clock strike twenty-one," said Sprake.

"I can believe that," I said, though I didn't. "Do you think I could have some tea?"

He was silent for a minute. Then he laughed.

"I'm not going to help them," he said. "You know that. I wouldn't be allowed to. What you do in the Pleroma is irretrievable."

"All that was over and done with twenty years ago, Ann."

"I know. I know that. But—"

She stopped suddenly, and then went on in a muffled voice, "Will you just come here a minute? Just for a minute?"

The house, like many in the Pennines, had been built right into the side of the valley. A near vertical bank of earth, cut to accommodate it, was held back by a dry-stone revetment twenty or thirty feet high, black with damp even in the middle of July, dusted with lichen and tufted with fern like a cliff. In December, the water streamed down the revetment day after day and, collecting in a stone trough underneath, made a sound like a tap left running in the night. Along the back of the house ran a passage hardly two feet wide, full of broken roof slates and other rubbish. It was a dismal place.

"You're all right," I told Ann, who was staring, puzzled, into the gathering dark, her head on one side and the tea towel held up to her mouth as if she thought she might be sick.

"It knows who we are," she whispered. "Despite the precautions, it always remembers us."

She shuddered, pulled herself away from the window, and began pouring water so clumsily into the coffee filter that I put my arm around her shoulders and said, "Look, you'd better go and sit down before you scald yourself. I'll finish this, and then you can tell me what's the matter."

She hesitated.

"Come on," I said. "All right?"

"All right."

She went into the living room and sat down heavily. One of the cats ran into the kitchen and looked up at me. "Don't give them milk," she called. "They had it this morning."

"How are you feeling?" I asked. "In yourself, I mean?"

"About how you'd expect." She had taken some propranolol, she said, but it never seemed to help much. "It shortens the headaches, I suppose." As a side effect, though, it made her feel so tired. "It slows my heartbeat down. I can feel it slow right down." She watched the steam rising from her coffee cup, first slowly, and then with a rapid, plaiting motion as it was caught by some tiny draft. Eddies form and break to the same rhythm on the surface of a deep, smooth river. A slow coil, a sudden whirl. What was tranquil is revealed as a mass of complications that can be resolved only as motion.

I remembered when I had first met her: she was twenty then, a small, excitable, attractive girl who wore moss-colored jersey dresses to show off her waist and hips. Later, fear coarsened her. With the divorce a few grey streaks appeared in her blond bell of hair, and she chopped it raggedly off and dyed it black. She drew in on herself. Her body broadened into a kind of dogged, muscular heaviness. Even her hands and feet seemed to become bigger.

"You're old before you know it," she would say. "Before you know it." Separated from Lucas, she was easily chafed by her surroundings; moved every six months or so, although never very far, and always to the same sort of dilapidated, drearily furnished cottage, though you suspected that she was looking for precisely the things that made her nervous and ill; and tried to keep down to fifty cigarettes a day.

"Why did Sprake never help us?" she asked me. "You must know."

Sprake fished two cups out of a plastic washing-up bowl and put tea bags in them.

"Don't tell me you're frightened too!" he said. "I expected more from you."

I shook my head. I wasn't sure whether I was afraid or not. I'm not sure today. The tea, when it came, had a distinctly greasy aftertaste, as if somehow he had fried it. I made myself drink half while Sprake watched me cynically.

"You ought to sit down," he said. "You're worn-out." When I refused, he shrugged and went on as if we were still at the Tivoli. "Nobody tricked them, or tried to pretend it would be easy. If you get anything out of an experiment like that, it's by keeping your head and taking your chance. If you try to move cautiously, you may never be allowed to move at all."

He looked thoughtful.

"I've seen what happens to people who lose their nerve."

"I'm sure," I said.

"They were hardly recognizable, some of them."

I put the teacup down.

"I don't want to know," I said.

"I bet you don't."

He smiled to himself.

"Oh, they were still alive," he said softly, "if that's what you're worried about."

"You talked us into this," I reminded him.

"You talked yourselves into it."

Most of the light from the street was absorbed as soon as it entered the room, by the dull green wallpaper and sticky-looking yellow veneer of the furniture. The rest leaked eventually into the litter on the floor, pages of crumpled and partly burned typescript, hair clippings, broken chalks that had been used the night before to draw something on the flaking lino: among this stuff, it died. Though I knew Sprake was playing some sort of game with me, I couldn't see what it was; I couldn't make the effort. In the end, he had to make it for me.

When I said from the door, "You'll get sick of all this mess one day," he only grinned, nodded, and advised me:

"Come back when you know what you want. Get rid of Lucas Fisher, he's an amateur. Bring the girl if you must."

"Fuck off, Sprake."

He let me find my own way back down to the street.

That night I had to tell Lucas, "We aren't going to be hearing from Sprake again."

"Christ," he said, and for a second I thought he was going to cry. "Ann feels so ill," he whispered. "What did he say?"

"Forget him. He could never have helped us."

"Ann and I are getting married," Lucas said in a rush.

What could I have done? I knew as well as he did that they were doing it only out of a need for comfort. Nothing would be gained by making them admit it. Besides, I was so tired by then, I could hardly stand. Some kind of visual fault, a neon zigzag like a bright little flight of stairs, kept showing up in my left eye. So I congratulated Lucas and, as soon as I could, began thinking about something else.

"Sprake's terrified of the British Museum," I said. "In a way, I sympathize with him."

As a child I had hated it too. All the conversations, every echo of a voice or a footstep or a rustle of clothes, gathered up in its high ceilings in a kind of undifferentiated rumble and sigh—the blurred and melted remains of meaning—which made you feel as if you had been abandoned in a derelict swimming bath. Later, when I was a teenager, it was the vast, shapeless heads in Room 25 that frightened me, the vagueness of the inscriptions. I saw clearly what was there— "Red sandstone head of a king" . . . "Red granite head from a colossal figure of a king"—but what was I looking at? The faceless wooden figure of Ramses emerged perpetually from an alcove near the lavatory door, a Ramses who had to support himself with a stick—split, syphilitic, worm-eaten by his passage through the world, but still condemned to struggle helplessly on.

"We want to go and live up north," Lucas said. "Away from all this."

As the afternoon wore on, Ann became steadily more disturbed. "Listen," she would ask me, "*is* that someone in the passage? You can always tell me the truth." After she had promised several times in a vague way— "I can't send you out without anything to eat. I'll cook us something in a minute, if you'll make some more coffee"—I realized she was frightened to go back into the kitchen. "No matter how much coffee I drink," she explained, "my throat is dry. It's all that smoking." She returned often to the theme of age. She had always hated to feel old. "You comb your hair in the mornings and it's just another ten years gone, every loose hair, every bit of dandruff, like a lot of old snapshots showering down." She shook her head and said, as if the connection would be quite clear to me:

"We moved around a lot after university. It wasn't that I couldn't settle, more that I had to leave something behind every so often, as a sort of sacrifice. If I liked a job I was in, I would always give it up. Poor old Lucas!"

She laughed.

"Do you ever feel like that?" She made a face. "I don't suppose you do," she said. "I remember the first house we lived in, over near Dunford Bridge. It was huge, and falling apart inside. It was always on the market until we bought it. Everyone who'd had it before us had tried some new way of dividing it up to make it livable. They put in a new staircase or knocked two rooms together. They'd abandoned parts of it because they couldn't afford to heat it all. Then they'd buggered off before anything was finished and left it to the next one—"

She broke off suddenly.

"I could never keep it tidy," she said.

"Lucas always loved it."

"Does he say that? You don't want to pay too much attention to him," she warned me. "The garden was so full of builders' rubbish, we could never grow anything. And the winters!" She shuddered. "Well, you know what it's like out there. The rooms reeked of Calor gas; before he'd been there a week, Lucas had every kind of portable heater you could think of. I hated the cold, but never as much as he did."

With an amused tenderness she chided him—"Lucas, Lucas, Lucas"— as if he were in the room there with us. "How you hated it, and how untidy you were!"

By now it was dark outside, but the younger cat was still staring out into the greyish, sleety well of the garden, beyond which you could just make out—as a swelling line of shadow with low clouds racing over it —the edge of the moor. Ann kept asking the cat what it could see. "There are children buried all over the moor," she told the cat. Eventually she got up with a sigh and pushed it onto the floor. "That's where cats belong. Cats belong on the floor." Some paper flowers were knocked down; stooping to gather them up, she said, "If there is a God, a real one, He gave up long ago. He isn't so much bitter as apathetic." She winced, held her hands up to her eyes.

"You don't mind if I turn the main light off?" And then: "He's filtered away into everything, so that now there's only this infinitely thin, stretched *thing*, presenting itself in every atom, so tired it can't go on, so haggard you can only feel sorry for it and its mistakes. That's the real God. What we saw is something that's taken its place."

"What did we see, Ann?"

She stared at me.

"You know, I was never sure what Lucas thought he wanted from me." The dull yellow light of a table lamp fell across the left side of her face. She was lighting cigarettes almost constantly, stubbing them out, half smoked, into the nest of old ends that had accumulated in the saucer of her cup. "Can you imagine? In all those years I never knew what he wanted from me."

She seemed to consider this for a moment or two. She looked at me, puzzled, and said, "I don't feel he ever loved me." She buried her face in her hands. I got up, with some idea of comforting her. Without warning, she lurched out of her chair and in a groping, desperately confused manner took a few steps toward me. There, in the middle of the room, she stumbled into a low fretwork table someone had brought back from a visit to Kashmir twenty years before. Two or three paperback books and a vase of anemones went flying. The anemones were blowsy, past their best. She looked down at *The Last of Cheri* and *Mrs. Palfrey at the Claremont*, strewn with great blue and red petals like dirty tissue paper; she touched them thoughtfully with her toe. The smell of the fetid flower water made her retch.

"Oh, dear," she murmured. "Whatever shall we do, Lucas?"

"I'm not Lucas," I said gently. "Go and sit down, Ann."

While I was gathering the books and wiping their covers, she must have overcome her fear of the kitchen—or, I thought later, simply forgotten it—because I heard her rummaging about for the dustpan and brush she kept under the sink. By now, I imagined, she could hardly see for the migraine; I called impatiently, "Let me do that, Ann. Be sensible." There was a gasp, a clatter, my name repeated twice. "Ann, are you all right?"

No one answered.

"Hello? Ann?"

I found her by the sink. She had let go of the brush and pan and was twisting a damp floor cloth so tightly in her hands that the muscles of her short forearms stood out like a carpenter's. Water had dribbled out of it and down her skirt.

"Ann?"

She was looking out of the window into the narrow passage where, clearly illuminated by the fluorescent tube in the kitchen ceiling, something big and white hung in the air, turning to and fro like a chrysalis in a privet hedge.

"Christ!" I said.

It wriggled and was still, as though whatever it contained was tired of the effort to get out. After a moment it curled up from its tapered base, seemed to split, welded itself together again. All at once I saw that these movements were actually those of two organisms, two human figures hanging in the air, unsupported, quite naked, writhing and embracing and parting and writhing together again, never presenting the same angle twice, so that now you viewed the man from the back, now the woman, now both of them from one side or the other. When I first saw them, the woman's mouth was fastened on the man's. Her eyes were closed; later she rested her head on his shoulder. Later still, they both turned their attention to Ann. They had very pale skin, with the curious bloom of white chocolate; but that might have been an effect of the light. Sleet blew between us and them in eddies, but never obscured them.

"What are they, Ann?"

"There's no limit to suffering," she said. Her voice was slurred and thick. "They follow me wherever I go."

I found it hard to look away from them.

"Is this why you move so often?" It was all I could think of to say.

"No."

The two figures were locked together in something that—had their eyes been fastened on each other rather than on Ann—might have been described as love. They swung and turned slowly against the black, wet wall like fish in a tank. They were smiling. Ann groaned and began vomiting noisily into the sink. I held her shoulders. "Get them away," she said indistinctly. "Why do they always look at me?" She coughed, wiped her mouth, ran the cold tap. She had begun to shiver, in powerful, disconnected spasms. "Get them away."

Though I knew quite well they were there, it was my mistake that I never believed them to be real. I thought she might calm down if she couldn't see them. But she wouldn't let me turn the light out or close the curtains; and when I tried to encourage her to let go of the edge of the sink and come into the living room with me, she only shook her head and retched miserably. "No, leave me," she said. "I don't want you now." Her body had gone rigid, as awkward as a child's. She was very strong. "Just try to come away, Ann, please." She looked at me helplessly and said, "I've got nothing to wipe my nose with." I pulled at her angrily, and we fell down. My shoulder was on the dustpan, my mouth full of her hair, which smelled of cigarette ashes. I felt her hands move over me.

"Ann! Ann!" I shouted.

I dragged myself from under her—she had begun to groan and vomit again—and, staring back over my shoulder at the smiling creatures in the passage, ran out of the kitchen and out of the house. I could hear myself sobbing with panic—"I'm phoning Lucas, I can't stand this, I'm going to phone Lucas"—as if I were still talking to her. I blundered about the village until I found the telephone box opposite the church.

I remember Sprake—though it seems too well-put to have been him—once saying, "It's no triumph to feel you've given life the slip." We were talking about Lucas Fisher. "You can't live intensely except at the cost of the self. In the end, Lucas's reluctance to give himself whole-heartedly will make him shabby and unreal. He'll end up walking the streets at night staring into lighted shop windows." At the time I thought this harsh. I still believed that with Lucas it was a matter of energy rather than will, of the lows and undependable zones of a cyclic personality rather than any deliberate reservation of powers.

When I told Lucas, "Something's gone badly wrong here," he was silent. After a moment or two I prompted him. "Lucas?"

I thought I heard him say:

"For God's sake, put that down and leave me alone."

"This line must be bad," I said. "You sound a long way off. Is there someone with you?"

He was silent again— "Lucas? Can you hear me?"—and then he asked, "How is Ann? I mean, in herself?"

"Not well," I said. "She's having some sort of attack. You don't know how relieved I am to talk to someone. Lucas, there are two completely hallucinatory figures in that passage outside her kitchen. What they're doing to one another is . . . look, they're a kind of dead white color, and they're smiling at her all the time. It's the most appalling thing—"

He said, "Wait a minute. Do you mean that you can see them too?"

"That's what I'm trying to say. The thing is that I don't know how to help her. Lucas?"

The line had gone dead. I put the receiver down and dialed his number again. The engaged signal went on and on. Afterward I would tell Ann, "Someone else must have called him," but I knew he had simply taken his phone off the hook. I stood there for some time, anyway, shivering in the wind that blustered down off the moor, in the hope that he would change his mind. In the end, I got so cold, I had to give up and go back. Sleet blew into my face all the way through the village. The church clock said half past six, but everything was dark and untenanted. All I could hear was the wind rustling the black plastic bags of rubbish piled around the dustbins.

"Fuck you, Lucas," I whispered. "Fuck you, then."

Ann's house was as silent as the rest. I went into the front garden and pressed my face up to the window, in case I could see into the kitchen through the open living room door; but from that angle, the only thing visible was a wall calendar with a color photograph of a Persian cat: *October*. I couldn't see Ann. I stood in the flower bed and the sleet turned to snow.

The kitchen was filled less with the smell of vomit than a sourness you felt somewhere in the back of your throat. Outside, the passage lay deserted under the bright suicidal wash of fluorescent light. It was hard to imagine anything had happened out there. At the same time, nothing looked comfortable, not the disposition of the old roof slates, or the clumps of fern growing out of the revetment, or even the way the snow was settling in the gaps between the flagstones. I found that I didn't want to turn my back on the window. If I closed my eyes and tried to visualize the white couple, all I could remember was the way they had smiled. A still, cold air seeped in above the sink, and the cats came up to rub against my legs and get underfoot; the taps were still running.

In her confusion Ann had opened all the kitchen cupboards and strewn their contents on the floor. Saucepans, cutlery, and packets of dried food had been mixed up with a polythene bucket and some yellow J-cloths; she had upset a bottle of household detergent among several tins of cat food, some of which had been half opened, some merely pierced, before she dropped them or forgot where she had put the opener. It was hard to see what she had been trying to do. I picked it all up and put it away. To make them leave me alone, I fed the cats. Once or twice I heard her moving about on the floor above.

She was in the bathroom, slumped on the old-fashioned pink lino by the sink, trying to get her clothes off. "For God's sake, go away," she said. "I can do it."

"Oh, Ann."

"Put some disinfectant in the blue bucket, then."

"Who are they, Ann?" I asked.

That was later, when I had gotten her to bed. She answered:

"Once it starts, you never get free."

I was annoyed.

"Free from what, Ann?"

"You know," she said. "Lucas said you had hallucinations for weeks afterward."

"Lucas had no right to say that!"

This sounded absurd, so I added as lightly as I could, "It was a long time ago. I'm not sure anymore."

The migraine had left her exhausted, though much more relaxed. She had washed her hair, and between us we had found her a fresh nightdress to wear. Sitting up in the cheerful little bedroom with its cheap ornaments and modern wallpaper, she looked vague and young; she kept apologizing for the design on her Continental quilt, some bold diagrammatic flowers in black and red, the intertwined stems of which she traced with the index finger of her right hand across a clean white background. "Do you like this? I don't really know why I bought it. Things look so bright and energetic in the shops," she said wistfully, "but as soon as you get them home, they just seem crude." The older cat had jumped up onto the bed; whenever Ann spoke, it purred loudly. "He shouldn't be in here, and he knows it." She wouldn't eat or drink, but I had persuaded her to take some more propranolol, and so far she had kept it down.

"Once it starts, you never get free," she repeated. Her finger followed the pattern across the quilt. Inadvertently she touched the cat's dry, greying fur, stared suddenly at her own hand as if it had misled her. "It was some sort of smell that followed you about, Lucas seemed to think."

"Some sort," I agreed.

"You won't get rid of it by ignoring it. We both tried that to begin with. A scent of roses, Lucas said." She laughed and took my hand. "Very romantic! I've no sense of smell—I lost it years ago, luckily."

This reminded her of something else.

"The first time I had a fit," she said, "I kept it from my mother because I saw a vision with it. I was only a child, really. The vision was very clear: a seashore, steep and with no sand, and men and women lying on some rocks in the sunshine like lizards, staring quite blankly at the spray as it exploded up in front of them; huge waves that might have been on a cinema screen for all the notice they took of them."

She narrowed her eyes, puzzled. "You wondered why they had so little common sense."

She tried to push the cat off her bed, but it only bent its body in a rubbery way and avoided her hand. She yawned suddenly.

"At the same time," she went on after a pause, "I could see that some spiders had made their webs between the rocks, just a foot or two above

the tide line." Though they trembled and were sometimes filled with
spraylike dewdrops so that they glittered in the sun, the webs remained
unbroken. She couldn't describe, she said, the sense of anxiety with which
this filled her. "So close to all that violence. You wondered why they
had so little common sense," she repeated. "The last thing I heard was
someone saying, 'On your own, you really can hear voices in the tide. . . .' "

Before she fell asleep, she clutched my hand harder and said:

"I'm so glad you got something out of it. Lucas and I never did. Roses!
It was worth it for that."

I thought of us as we had been twenty years before. I spent the night
in the living room and awoke quite early in the morning. I didn't know
where I was until I walked in a drugged way to the window and saw the
street full of snow.

For a long time after that last meeting with Sprake, I had a recurrent
dream of him. His hands were clasped tightly across his chest, the left
hand holding the wrist of the right, and he was going quickly from room
to room of the British Museum. Whenever he came to a corner or a
junction of corridors, he stopped abruptly and stared at the wall in front
of him for thirty seconds before turning very precisely to face in the right
direction before he moved on. He did this with the air of a man who
has for some reason taught himself to walk with his eyes closed through
a perfectly familiar building; but there was also, in the way he stared at
the walls—and particularly in the way he held himself so upright and
rigid—a profoundly hierarchal air, an air of premeditation and ritual.
His shoes, and the bottoms of his faded corduroy trousers, were soaking
wet, just as they had been the morning after the rite, when the four of
us had walked back through the damp fields in the bright sunshine. He
wore no socks.

In the dream I was always hurrying to catch up with him. I was
stopping every so often to write something in a notebook, hoping he
wouldn't see me. He strode purposefully through the Museum, from
cabinet to cabinet of twelfth-century illuminated manuscripts. Suddenly
he stopped, looked back at me, and said:

"There are sperm in this picture. You can see them quite plainly.
What are sperm doing in a religious picture?"

He smiled, opened his eyes very wide.

Pointing to the side of his own head with one finger, he began to
shout and laugh incoherently.

When he had gone, I saw that he had been examining a New Testament
miniature from Queen Melisande's Psalter, depicting "The Women at
the Sepulchre." In it an angel was drawing Mary Magdalen's attention

to some strange luminous shapes that hovered in the air in front of her. They did, in fact, look something like the spermatozoa that often border the tormented Paris paintings of Edvard Munch.

I would wake up abruptly from this dream, to find that it was morning and that I had been crying.

Ann was still asleep when I left the house, with the expression people have on their faces when they can't believe what they remember about themselves. "On your own, you really can hear voices in the tide, cries for help or attention," she had said. "I started to menstruate the same day. For years I was convinced that my fits began then too."

That was the last time I saw her.

A warm front had moved in from the southwest during the night; the snow had already begun to melt, the Pennine stations looked like leaky downspouts, the moors were locked beneath grey clouds. Two little boys sat opposite me on the train until Stalybridge, holding their Day Rover tickets thoughtfully in their laps. They might have been eight or nine years old. They were dressed in tiny, perfect workman's jackets, tight trousers, Dr. Marten's boots. Close up, their shaven skulls were bluish and vulnerable, perfectly shaped. They looked like acolytes in a Buddhist temple: calm, wide-eyed, compliant. By the time I got to Manchester, a fine rain was falling. It was blowing the full length of Market Street and through the door of the Kardomah Café, where I had arranged to meet Lucas Fisher.

The first thing he said was, "Look at these pies! They aren't plastic, you know, like a modern pie. These are from the plaster era of café pies, the earthenware era. Terra-cotta pies, realistically painted, glazed in places to have exactly the cracks and imperfections any real pie would have! Aren't they wonderful? I'm going to eat one."

I sat down next to him.

"What happened to you last night, Lucas? It was a bloody nightmare."

He looked away. "How *is* Ann?" he asked. I could feel him trembling.

"Fuck off, Lucas."

He smiled over at a toddler in an appalling yellow suit. The child stared back vacantly, upset, knowing full well they were from competing species. A woman near us said, "I hear you're going to your grandma's for dinner on Sunday. Something special, I expect?" Lucas glared at her, as if she had been speaking to him. She added: "If you're going to buy toys this afternoon, remember to look at them where they are, so that no one can accuse you of stealing. Don't take them off the shelf." From somewhere near the kitchens came a noise like a tray of crockery falling down a short flight of stairs; Lucas seemed to hate this. He shuddered.

"Let's get out!" he said. He looked savage and ill. "I feel it as badly as Ann," he said. He accused me: "You never think of that." He looked over at the toddler again. "Spend long enough in places like this and your spirit will heave itself inside out."

"Come on, Lucas, don't be spoiled. I thought you liked the pies here."

All afternoon he walked urgently about the streets, as if he were on his own. I could hardly keep up with him. The city centre was full of wheelchairs, old women slumped in them with impatient, collapsed faces, partially bald, done up in crisp white raincoats. Lucas had turned up the collar of his grey cashmere jacket against the rain but left the jacket itself hanging open, its sleeves rolled untidily back above his bare wrists. He left me breathless. He was forty years old, but he still had the ravenous face of an adolescent. Eventually he stopped and said, "I'm sorry." It was halfway through the afternoon, but the neon signs were on and the lower windows of the office blocks were already lit up. Near Piccadilly Station, an arm of the canal appears suddenly from under the road; he stopped and gazed down at its rain-pocked surface, dim and oily, scattered with lumps of floating Styrofoam like sea gulls in the fading light.

"You often see fires on the bank down there," he said. "They live a whole life down there, people with nowhere else to go. You can hear them singing and shouting on the old towpath."

He looked at me with wonder.

"We aren't much different, are we? We never came to anything, either."

I couldn't think of what to say.

"It's not so much that Sprake encouraged us to ruin something in ourselves," he said, "as that we never got anything in return for it. Have you ever seen Joan of Arc kneel down to pray in the Kardomah Café? And then a small boy comes in leading something that looks like a goat, and it gets on her there and then and fucks her in a ray of sunlight?"

"Look, Lucas," I explained, "I'm never doing this again. I was frightened last night."

"I'm sorry."

"Lucas, you always are."

"It isn't one of my better days today."

"For God's sake, fasten your coat."

"I can't seem to get cold."

He gazed dreamily down at the water—it had darkened into a bottomless, opal-colored trench between the buildings—perhaps seeing goats, fires, people who had nowhere to go. " 'We worked but we were not paid,' " he quoted. Something forced him to ask shyly:

"You haven't heard from Sprake?"

I felt sick with patience. I seemed to be filled up with it.

"I haven't seen Sprake for twenty years, Lucas. You know that. I haven't seen him for twenty years."

"I understand. It's just that I can't bear to think of Ann on her own in a place like that. I wouldn't have mentioned it otherwise. We said we'd always stick together, but—"

"Go home, Lucas. Go home now."

He turned away miserably and walked off. I meant to leave him to that maze of unredeemed streets between Piccadilly and Victoria, the failing pornography and pet shops, the weed-grown car parks that lie in the shadow of the yellowish-tiled hulk of the Arndale Centre. In the end, I couldn't. He had gotten as far as the Tib Street fruit market when a small figure came out of a side street and began to follow him closely along the pavement, imitating his typical walk, head thrust forward, hands in pockets. When he stopped to button his jacket, it stopped too. Its own coat was so long, it trailed in the gutter. I started running to catch up with them, and it paused under a street lamp to stare back at me. In the sodium light I saw that it was neither a child nor a dwarf but something of both, with the eyes and gait of a large monkey. Its eyes were quite blank, stupid and implacable in a pink face. Lucas became aware of it suddenly and jumped with surprise; he ran a few aimless steps, shouting, then dodged around a corner, but it only followed him hurriedly. I thought I heard him pleading, "Why don't you leave me alone?" and in answer came a voice at once tinny and muffled, barely audible but strained, as if it were shouting. Then there was a terrific clatter and I saw some large object like an old zinc dustbin fly out and go rolling about in the middle of the road.

"Lucas!" I called.

When I rounded the corner, the street was full of smashed fruit boxes and crates; rotten vegetables were scattered everywhere; a barrow lay as if it had been thrown along the pavement. There was such a sense of violence and disorder and idiocy that I couldn't express it to myself. But neither Lucas nor his persecutor was there; and though I walked about for an hour afterward, looking into doorways, I saw nobody at all.

A few months later Lucas wrote to tell me that Ann had died.

"A scent of roses," I remembered her saying. "How lucky you were!"

"It was a wonderful summer for roses, anyway," I had answered. "I never knew a year like it." All June, the hedgerows were full of dog roses, with their elusive, fragile odor. I hadn't seen them since I was a boy. The gardens were bursting with Gallicas, great blowsy things whose fragrance was like a drug. "How can we ever say that Sprake had anything to do with that, Ann?"

But I sent roses to her funeral, anyway, though I didn't go myself.

What did we do, Ann and Lucas and I, in the fields of June, such a long time ago?

"It is easy to misinterpret the Great God," writes de Vries. "If He represents the long slow panic in us which never quite surfaces, if He signifies our perception of the animal, the uncontrollable in us, He must also stand for that direct sensual perception of the world that we have lost by ageing—perhaps even by becoming human in the first place."

Shortly after Ann's death, I experienced a sudden, inexplicable resurgence of my sense of smell. Common smells became so distinct and detailed, I felt like a child again, every new impression astonishing and clear, my conscious self not yet the sore lump encysted in my own skull, as clenched and useless as a fist, impossible to modify or evict, as it was later to become. This was not quite what you should call memory; all I recollected in the smell of orange peel or ground coffee or rowan blossom was that I once had been *able* to experience things so powerfully. It was as if, before I could recover one particular impression, I had to rediscover the language of all impressions. But nothing further happened. I was left with an embarrassment, a ghost, a hyperesthesia of middle age. It was cruel and undependable; it made me feel like a fool. I was troubled by it for a year or two, and then it went away.

IAN WATSON

Lost Bodies

Versatile and prolific, Watson writes everything from fantasy
through science fiction to slasher/horror. He also has edited some fine
anthologies in several genres. He was born in (and still makes his
home in) England, the setting of "Lost Bodies."

What follows is a surreal horror story that, without containing one
shred of physical violence, is one of the more disturbing pieces in this
volume. The author relates that part of the story came to him in a
dream. One might wish not to know which part of the story that was.

—E. D.

LOST BODIES

Ian Watson

The hunt had gone by our cottage half an hour earlier, in full cavalry charge down the village high street. Hearing their clattery thunder, wine glasses in our hands, the four of us rushed to stare contemptuously through a front window.

Winter breeze flushed the riders' faces ruddy. Steam gusted from the sweating horses: brown engines, black engines. Harsh frost gripped the gardens opposite and glazed the steep slate roofs. It struck me as specially cruel to be chased and to die upon such a hard icy day. To be torn apart upon iron soil seemed irrationally worse than a death cushioned in soft mud.

When we trooped back to the parlour Jon said, "Of course foxes themselves tear furry little animals to pieces every day. We shouldn't waste too much sympathy on old Renard."

"They call him Charles James," Kirstie corrected. "That's what they call their quarry."

Jon looked blank, so my wife explained, "After the eighteenth century politician Charles James Fox. Notorious reformer and crook, he was. How the squires would have loved to set a pack of hounds on him!"

"My God, they still remember, two centuries later. That's what I hate about bloody history: the vendettas. Don't you?"

Now Kirstie is Irish—Dublin Irish—and her own land had been vexed to anguish by years of bloody history. As a rule she wasn't overtly political. Aside from the convent day-school she'd described to me her upbringing had been happy-go-lucky, little coloured by the troubles in the North. Now and then she flared up. This was one of those occasions.

"Sure, Charley's only a name to them. Oh you English can be so blind to history, when it suits. You forget all your exploitin' as though such things never happened. Some countries can't help remembering when your hoofprints are all over us still."

The hunt was a sore point to her. The Irish might ride to hounds with gusto, but here was an English hunt trampling the countryside; and Kirstie had red hair, red as the fox they chased.

"Fiery lady, eh?" Jon leered at me as if her outburst must surely imply passion in bed. Whereas his own Lucy, blonde and pale and virginal-looking, and so coolly beautiful, perhaps wore her body like some expensive gown which she didn't want creased and stained? Again, perhaps not!

"Do you know," continued Kirstie, "there's this snooty hag—*lady*, she'd prefer—living in the Dower House, Mrs Armstrong-Glynn? Used to breed bloodhounds half a century ago. By way of passing the time she told me to my face that for a good manhunt there was never anything to beat a redheaded lunatic. Red hair's the guarantee of a strong scent, she said." My wife fingered the high lace collar of her long, Victorian-pattern frock to ventilate herself.

Jon eyed Kirstie's rich russet mane as though eager to test the theory. Kirstie met his gaze with interest, though she still seemed piqued. Definitely some chemistry was working.

I asked, "Did you catch that news about the auction of titles at Sotheby's last week? On TV?" We all saw eye to eye on the snobbery of people like Mrs Armstrong-Glynn. One must hope that our Jag and Jon's Porsche, parked outside nose to tail, hadn't been bumped into by any heavy hunter. Too cold for the paintwork to be spattered with mud, presumably.

"Tell us," invited Lucy, a sparkle in her eye.

"Well, the Duke of Ardley sold off half a dozen titles to get some pocket money. One of the titles was Lord of the Manor of Lower Dassett. Lower Dassett's where we're going for lunch today. So a prostitute from London bid thirteen thousand quid and collared the title. She promptly bought a Range Rover and set off to survey her new domain. The village boys were all following her round like flies. 'Maybe she'll improve the night life,' quipped one. Then she announced she was going to buy a house in Lower Dassett to use as a rest home for hookers. I do wish it had happened here. That would show them."

Lucy laughed, and I topped up her glass from the bottle they'd brought as a present. "A bit different from your ordinary Anjou wine," Lucy had told Kirstie on presenting it. "We picked up a case of Château de Parnay in Parnay itself this summer. It's been chilled just perfect in the boot on the way here. Oh, on the way back from France the Porsche was loaded with cases from this cellar and that, and so cheap too. I thought Jon was going to toss my luggage out to make room." And Jon had grinned. "Those frogs know how to pack wine. Nose to tail like sardines. A French case is half the bulk."

"Lord of the Manor doesn't convey *privileges*, does it?" Lucy asked me.

"Such as the Ius Primae Noctis, you mean? The Lord's right to bed any village virgin on the night before her wedding?"

"Now there's an idea," said Jon. "Get in some practice but keep it in the family as it were. Can't go round experimenting anywhere, can we?"

"Not these days," agreed Lucy. She moistened her lips on the Château de Parnay and looked steadily at me, then at Kirstie. "You have to be very sure who you play with. Almost as sure as if they're genuine virgins."

Oh yes, this was in the air between us. In a peculiar way it was almost as though the four of us had remained authentic virgins, who now wished to lose our virginity safely. What could be more economic, more conservative of emotional and financial resources, than a chaste fidelity? So we were economic virgins.

Let me explain. We were all into money: dual income, no kids. Early on at university Jon and I had both espoused the new workaholic puritanism—work's so much more *fun* than sleeping around. He went into the City to trade shares and ride the wheel of fortune. I myself had switched from engineering to economics. A few years ago, with venture capital obtained by Jon, I founded my Concepts Consultancy to act as a bridge between innovators, the Patents Office, and industry. I marketed ideas; I turned neurons into banknotes.

Lucy, perfect image of the trendy new purity especially in her nurse-like white twin set, had given up medical research in favour of health insurance. Once, she would have liked to defeat the ageing process—to discover rejuvenation. But she reckoned that was at least a hundred years away. Why should she give herself as cheaply-sold fuel to light some future flame? With her background she quickly rose high in the business of assessing new health risks, new chances of death.

Kirstie had founded her own employment agency specializing in Irish girls and fellows seeking a life in London.

Yet lately Kirstie was restless; thus we had bought this cottage in the country. Stock Market troubles were fraying Jon. Lucy seemed expectant, though not of any babies.

And me? Well, it may seem silly but Kirstie—however loving—had always been inhibited in one respect. She had always bolted the bathroom door before taking a shower. She insisted on switching off the light before we made love—to free herself, so she said, from the notion of God observing her. She employed all sorts of stratagems with the result that whatever games we got up to in the dark incredibly I had never actually witnessed my wife in her birthday suit. Since we were faithful to one another in this world of AIDS this meant that I had not seen a naked woman in the flesh for years. The omission had begun to prey absurdly on my mind, assuming huge iconic significance, as though I was missing some launch window just as surely as Lucy had missed hers by being born too soon.

We must re-invigorate ourselves, the four of us! We must rediscover otherness, and encounter the naked stranger beneath the clothing of the friend. Logs crackled and bloomed with tongues of flame in the ingle below the copper hood. I smiled at Lucy; she returned my smile flirtatiously.

Though our cottage fronted the street directly, to the rear we had ample garden. A bouncy, mossy lawn mounted steeply between huge privet hedges towards distant wilderness. We paid a local unemployed chap to come in and mow that lawn, trim that hedge. Forty feet into the lawn rose a mature chestnut tree, its base surrounded by a wreath of ferns, now blighted by cold.

Half an hour must have passed since the hunt went by when I looked out, when I saw a fox's head thrust from amongst the dying ferns. I was already pointing, even before the rest of the fox . . . failed to follow.

The head lurched forward a couple of feet, scuffing over the grass. It was a severed head. Six inches of spinal column, a rudder of ridged white bone, jutted behind it. The head, plus some snapped backbone, had been torn off the body as neatly as a finger slips off a glove. The body of the animal had been torn away, abolished—and yet the head had continued to flee, trailing that stump of spine like a little leg.

The beast's eyes appeared glossy. Its mouth hung open slightly, a pink tongue lolling, panting. The head jerked forward again and came to rest.

"Jesus and Mary!" cried Kirstie. Jon was gaping out of the window, as blanched as Lucy for once. Lucy stared; she was the cool one.

We must be the victims of some sick rural ritual. We were experiencing some initiation jape, to blood us as new residents. Day afore the hunt, you traps a fox and you chops his head off. . . . A sly oaf must be hiding behind our chestnut tree, pushing the head with a stick. No, he'd be skulking beyond the hedge with a length of invisible fishing line paid out as puppet string.

"Some bugger's pulling that along!" Jon had reached the same conclusion.

How could the head look so alive? Answer: it was *stuffed*. How did it stay upright? Luck, sheer luck.

"Ha ha, Pete! Good joke. Who's pulling? Your gardener?"

"Nothing to do with me, I assure you!"

"In that case, *come on*." Jon darted, and I followed him: into the kitchen, out the door, up the brick steps on to the lawn.

Nobody was crouching behind the tree. No sniggers emerged from our hedge; our boundaries were silent. No string or nylon was attached to the head. The thing simply sat there on the frosted grass. It was undeniably alive. Numb, stunned, bewildered at the body it had lost, but *alive*.

"Sweet shit," Jon muttered.

How could a head live without a body? It did. How could a head travel without a body? By flexing the neck muscles, by thrusting with that bone-stump? It had travelled. Here it was, looking at us.

I reached down my hand.

"Don't!" called Lucy from the head of the steps. "It might bite."

"Bite?" Jon cackled—a brief eruption of hysteria.

Lucy strode up to us, fascinated, with Kirstie in tow. I suppose Lucy had seen enough nasties before opting out from the labs, but the real horror here wasn't blood and guts and rags of flesh. It was the sheer absence of those, the unspeakable absence of body itself from a creature which was manifestly still living.

Calmly Lucy said, "Did you know that a head can survive for a while after being guillotined? In Nineteen-oh-something one French doctor knelt in front of a freshly chopped-off head and shouted the man's name. The eyes opened and stared back. That particular head had fallen upright on the neck stump, staunching the haemorrhage."

"Jesus wept, spare us," said Kirstie.

"It soon died. Thirty years earlier, another doctor pumped blood from a living dog into a criminal's head three hours after decapitation. The lips stammered silently, the eyelids opened, the face awakened, said the doctor."

"That's absurd," exploded Jon. "Three hours? He was either lying or hallucinating."

She looked down. "Soviet doctors kept a dog's head alive detached from its body, didn't they?"

"Not lying on a fucking lawn, Lucy!"

She made to poke it with her toe. As her shoe slid through the grass I swear the base of the neck bunched up. The pointy head shifted a few inches, dragging its white stub. The fox blinked. It tried to lick its lips.

Kirstie shook with shivers. "It wants sanctuary, poor thing! It's parched after running from the hunt." Before we could discuss procedure she had swooped and picked the head up from behind by both ears. Holding it firmly away from her she hurried indoors.

When the rest of us regained the parlour Kirstie had already placed the fox's head on the pine table upon a copy of the *Cork Examiner*; she advertised in all the main Irish newspapers. Rushing to the kitchen, she returned with a saucer of water.

The fox's muzzle touched the offered liquid but it didn't lap. How could it drink, how could it eat? Food or water would spill out of its neck. The head made no move at all now. Like clockwork running down, I thought. Desperation to escape had propelled it as far as our garden— *how?*—and no further locomotion was possible. . . . It didn't seem to be dying. The head continued to survive, eyes bright as ever.

"'Tis a miracle," said my wife. "A terrible awful miracle."

Lucy stooped to scrutinize the wound and the jut of spine. "Do you have a magnifying glass?"

Kirstie obliged, and Lucy spent minutes inspecting closely.

Finally she said, "It seems organic. An advanced civilization might build an organic machine that would function as a living creature, but which you could take apart. The parts might still function in isolation. Maybe we could build something like that ourselves in a few hundred years time. We're going to learn a lot about organic mini-microcomputers, machines the size of single cells. Stuff that could mimic cells but not be real cells. They could be programmed to build a body . . . an immortal body."

"What are you driving at?" asked Jon.

"Maybe we could build a human machine and plug somebody's head into it when their natural body failed. We'd start with animal experiments, wouldn't we? Rat and chimp and dog. Or fox."

"Are you suggesting that the hunt caught a manufactured fox? Some sort of biologically-built fox that escaped from an experiment somewhere near?"

"It couldn't happen for a century or two." The keenest regret, and desire, sounded in Lucy's voice. "This head must be false too. I'd love to examine slices under an electron microscope."

"No!" cried Kirstie. "The poor suffering thing—that would be vivisection. If it struggled so hard to survive, the least we can do is—" She didn't know what.

"Wouldn't this be the ideal tool for spying?" resumed Lucy. "False wildlife, false birds. Pull off the head after a mission and download it through the spine into some organic computer. Humans couldn't produce this yet. Either it fell through some time-hole from the future, or else it's from *out there*, the stars. And if there's one such, why not others? Why not false people too, acting just like us, watching us, then going somewhere afterwards—having their heads pulled off and emptied?"

I suppose it was inevitable that I should call to mind Kirstie's scrupulousness in never letting me see her in the nude, her dislike of sports (which might involve brief garments), all her stratagems; the evidence accumulated. Unlike foxes people don't boast inbuilt fur coats to hide the joins. Why had the creature headed here of all places? Why was Kirstie so defensive of it? Try as I might to thrust suspicion out of my head, stubbornly it lurked.

"Let's go to Lower Dassett as planned," I suggested. "Lunch at the Green Man, eh? Leave this other business on the table."

To my relief the others all agreed. The same impetus as earlier persisted. My convergance upon Lucy, hers upon me, Jon's upon Kirstie, and Kirstie's . . . she virtually simpered at Jon. Would sleeping with him safeguard her fox from future harm at Lucy's hands? Almost, the fox seemed a mascot of our intentions.

No titled hooker was in evidence at Lower Dassett, though she was still the talk of the inn, and the Green Man's restaurant fulfilled all other expectations. In public we didn't discuss the fox. Afterwards, well fed on poached salmon and pleasantly tipsy, I drove us up through Dassett Country Park. What seemed a modest ascent through woodland opened unexpectedly upon the local equivalent of mountains. Bare sheep-grazed slopes plunged steeply into a broad plain of far fields, copses, distant towns. A stubby stone monument was inset with a circular brass map of the five counties surrounding. Replenishing our lungs in the fresh, sharp air, Jon and I strode along a ridge admiring the view, glowing with a contentment which the enigma back home seemed powerless to dash— on the contrary, with a heightened sense of expectation. Marvellous how one could adapt to, no, capitalize upon the extraordinary. Meanwhile Lucy and Kirstie pored over the map, pointing out tiny landmarks.

"Poker tonight after dinner?" I asked Jon.

"You bet." We enjoyed poker. Bridge was for wimps.

"Afterwards we'll all play a more serious game? If you're game for it?"

"Hmm. I think so. I definitely do. At last."

"Kirstie likes to play that game in the dark—then to be surprised, illuminated!"

"Ah . . ."

"Don't say I tipped you off. It would seem we'd been swapping locker room tales."

"Quite. Let's get back to our ladies. So what'll we do about that fox?"

"I don't know. Do you?"

"I've been racking my brains. Sell the story to the papers? Our fox mightn't perform. This could end up in the hen's-egg-hatches-frog category; the silly season in midwinter. Maybe Lucy could—?"

"Take it away and slice it up? Destroy it, and find no proof?"

"I suppose there's no sense in alerting authorities. If there *are* any authorities on phoney animals, what bothers me is the subject could be top secret. If an alien earthwatch is going on, and governments suspect, they could be ruthless. We'd be muzzled, watched, maybe even—"

"Snuffed, to silence us?"

"There's that risk, Pete. Let's leave decisions till later, till we've played our games."

Later: pheasant, and more wine. We had dined around the fox's head which was still perched on the newspaper. The fox made no attempt to snatch mouthfuls of roast bird from our plates, though it continued to appear alive, a mute motionless guest at our board even when Lucy interrogated it, calling into its face like that French doctor addressing the victim of the guillotine. "Who are you, Charley Fox? Where do you come from? Are you recording, even now that you're unplugged?"

Lucy became quite drunk, drunk with a desire to know, to be fulfilled by Charles James. That desire would soon shift its focus. All four of us were members of a tiny secret tribal cult undergoing an initiation featuring wine, a feast, and soon the fever of gambling accompanied by images of kings and queens, and presently sexual rites to bind us all together. An hour later Lucy had the bank, while I had lost all of my original fifty pound stake money. Nothing was left to bet except myself.

"If I lose this time, Lucy, you win *me*. How about that?"

"Yes!" she agreed, excited. "If that's okay with you, Kirstie?"

"Sure, you know it is. We've been leading up to this."

"Jon?"

He nodded.

When Lucy won, she leapt up, ignoring coins and notes, and gripped my wrist.

"Be off with you then upstairs," said Kirstie, "the both of you. All night long till the morning."

Jon also stood expectantly.

"Ah, Jon, I'd like for us to stay down here by the fireside. The sofa pulls out into a bed." Kirstie was in charge of fires—her hair had affinity with flames—however tonight she had let the wood die down to ash and embers. As I was leaving with Lucy, Kirstie called, "Peter, turn out the lights." Which I did.

In the darkness of the parlour only small patches glowed hot like eyes of wild beasts surprised by a torch beam, watching from the ingle.

"I like it this way," I heard as I closed the door.

Leading Lucy upstairs, I opened the second bedroom, almost as large as our own. It was very warm from the storage heater. I switched on a bedside lamp then killed the light on the stairs, and shut the door. Already Lucy had shaken off her white jacket and was unbuttoning her blouse.

Unexpectedly I found myself embarrassed at being naked in Lucy's unclothed presence. I tended to avert my gaze from the complete spectacle, by pressing close to her. Thus the nakedness that I saw was partial, discreet camera angles on her bare flesh: shoulders, neck, a breast, the top of a knee, a flash of thigh. I couldn't bring myself to pull back and feast my eyes. When Lucy rolled me over in turn to mount me I quickly drew her body down upon myself rather than let her rear upright exultantly. I think she interpreted my hugs as an attempt at even closer, more ecstatic intimacy.

Meanwhile an alarm clock, a time bomb, was ticking away in my brain. Fifteen minutes, twenty, how long?

A squeal from downstairs! That wasn't any orgasmic outcry. Too magnified by far, too full of pain and affront. Another, longer shriek.

"Something's wrong." I pulled loose, seized a sheet to wrap myself.

"You can't just go bursting in on them! Jon isn't rough."

"Maybe it's the fox—I'll check. You wait here."

"While you peep through the keyhole? I'm peeping too." Lucy snatched up a blanket as cloak.

"He isn't *rough*," she whispered insistently as I padded downstairs ahead of her.

A line of light showed under the parlour door. I heard a sound of weeping, and mumblings from Jon, so I pushed the door open.

A naked man, remarkably hairy around the base of his spine like some huge monkey. A nude woman: plump breasts, freckles, swelling thighs, red bush of pubic hair, Rubens territory I had mapped so often with my fingers, hitherto unseen. Kristie's hands were splayed defensively not over crotch or bosom but . . .

Monkey swung round and snarled. "You *bastard*, Peter!"

From Kirstie's tummy to her left tit sprawled a vivid red birthmark resembling the map of some unknown island once owned by the British and coloured accordingly.

How could I explain that I'd merely wanted to test whether my wife, my comrade, my bedmate of the last eight years, was a phoney person, an alien life-machine planted in the world to watch us? The idea seemed suddenly insane. Despite the fox, despite. And so now the fox too seemed insane.

Jon and Lucy mounted in silence to the room where we'd made love, and where I'd failed to see her as revealingly as I'd suddenly seen Kirstie. I went upstairs to our bedroom alone, and eventually slept. Kirstie stayed on the sofa by the dead fire.

In the morning, how stilted we were. What minimal conversation at breakfast: no one mentioned the night before. We ate burnt sausages and eggs with broken yolks and avoided looking at each other much, until Jon said, "I think we'd best be going."

Lucy stared longingly for many moments at the fox which Kirstie had transferred to the sideboard, still on the *Cork Examiner*.

"You made sure I couldn't have it, didn't you, Peter?" she accused me. "Seems very small and unimportant now. Yes, let's go."

When the Porsche had driven off, I said, "I was drunk last night."

Kirstie nodded. "I don't believe in divorce, but you shan't touch me again, Peter. You'd best find a girlfriend who won't put your health at risk. I shan't object when you're 'delayed' at the office. We won't sell the cottage, either. We'll come out here on lots of weekends to be lonely together, with Charles James. He must be very lonely. He's lost his body. You've lost mine."

Penance, I thought. A million Hail bloody Marys and no forgiveness. The unforgivable sin is betrayal. Maybe she would soften in time.

During the next week Kirstie bought a varnished wooden shield from a sports trophy shop, and a Black and Decker drill together with some drill-bits, one of them huge. When we arrived at the cottage on Saturday she told me to mount the shield above the ingle then drill a fat hole through the middle, drill the hole six inches deep into the stone wall behind.

When I'd done so, she lifted the fox's head and slid its spine into the hole. Held in place thus, neck flush with the plaque, the fox head imitated any other such hunting trophy decorating a pub wall. Except that it was still fresh, still spuriously alive, although utterly unresponsive. By now it reacted to no stimuli at all, a little like Kirstie herself. So it hung there in our parlour, an absurd living idol, dumb dazed undying God of falsity.

Time passes but does it heal us? Last weekend when I entered the parlour, for the first time in months I thought I saw a flicker of movement from the fox, a twitch of an ear, an eyeblink. I began to hope: that it might one day revive, that one day it would eject itself from our wall and try to rejoin, somehow, its lost body. And go away. Then she would have forgiven me.

I even patted the fox encouragingly on the forehead. On impulse I gripped its ears and tugged gently. I would slide it in and out just to give it the idea of resuming a more active existence.

The head wouldn't budge. It was fixed firm. In panic I pulled, but in vain. I realized then that the spine had taken root in the fabric of the building. I imagined tendrils growing out from that spine, threads of clever little cells converting stone and mortar into nerves and organs, spreading along the inside of the wall into other walls, insinuating themselves through the timbers like the fungus threads of dry rot until the head had gained a mutant body of another kind so that we would eat within it, crap within it, sleep within it, though not make love within it.

How I feared the head's revival now. How I dreaded to take an axe to it, causing the cottage to shriek, as Kirstie had shrieked that night.

DAN SIMMONS

Two Minutes Forty-Five Seconds

Dan Simmons hasn't been writing professionally for many years, but he has made his efforts count. His first novel, *Song of Kali*, won the World Fantasy Award for Best Novel of 1985, and his second novel, *Carrion Comfort*, is a monumental effort that Mr. Simmons considers the first epic splatter-punk novel. It is a 1989 publication from Dark Harvest. In whatever he writes, Simmons is a terrifically effective storyteller, as can be seen in the following story. It's a compact and chilling tale about guilt, based in part on a very well-publicized event in our recent past—the Challenger disaster. Here is a fine example of how good fantasy can turn reality into something far greater than its literal facts.

—E. D.

TWO MINUTES FORTY-FIVE SECONDS

Dan Simmons

Roger Colvin closed his eyes, and the steel bar clamped down across his lap, and they began the steep climb. He could hear the rattle of the heavy chain and the creak of steel wheels on steel rails as they clanked up the first hill of the roller coaster. Someone behind him laughed nervously. Terrified of heights, heart pounding painfully against his ribs, Colvin peeked out from between spread fingers.

The metal rails and white wooden frame rose steeply ahead of him. Colvin was in the first car. He lowered both hands and tightly gripped the metal restraining bar. Someone giggled in the car behind him. He turned his head only far enough to peer over the side of the rails.

They were very high and still rising. The midway and parking lots grew smaller, individuals growing too tiny to be seen and the crowds becoming mere carpets of color, fading into a larger mosaic of geometries of streets and lights as the entire city became visible, then the entire county. They clanked higher. The sky darkened to a deeper blue. Colvin could see the curve of the earth in the haze-blued distance. He realized that they were far out over the edge of a lake now as he caught the glimmer of light on wave tops miles below through the wooden ties. Colvin closed his eyes as they briefly passed through the cold breath of a cloud, then snapped them open again as the pitch of chain rumble changed as the steep gradient lessened, as they reached the top.

And went over.

There was nothing beyond. The two rails curved out and down and ended in air.

Colvin gripped the restraining bar as the car pitched forward and over. He opened his mouth to scream. The fall began.

"Hey, the worst part's over." Colvin opened his eyes to see Bill Montgomery handing him a drink. The sound of the Gulfstream's jet engines was a dull rumble under the gentle hissing of air from the overhead ventilator nozzle. Colvin took the drink, turned down the flow of air, and glanced out the window. Logan International was already out of sight

258

behind them, and Colvin could make out Nantasket Beach below, a score of small white triangles of sail in the expanse of bay and ocean beyond. They were still climbing.

"Damn, we're glad you decided to come with us this time, Roger," Montgomery said to Colvin. "It's good having the whole team together again. Like the old days." Montgomery smiled. The three other men in the cabin raised their glasses. Colvin played with the calculator in his lap and sipped his vodka. He took a breath and closed his eyes. Afraid of heights. *Always* afraid. Six years old and in the barn, tumbling from the loft, the fall seemingly endless, time stretching out, the sharp tines of the pitchfork rising toward him. Landing, wind knocked out of him, cheek and right eye against the straw, three inches from the steel points of the pitchfork.

"The company's ready to see better days," said Larry Miller. "Two and a half years of bad press is certainly enough. It will be good to see the launch tomorrow. Get things started again."

"Hear, hear," said Tom Weiscott. It was not yet noon but Tom had already had too much to drink.

Colvin opened his eyes and smiled. Counting himself, there were four corporate vice presidents in the plane. Weiscott was still a project manager. Colvin put his cheek to the window and watched Cape Cod Bay pass below. He guessed their altitude to be eleven or twelve thousand feet and climbing.

Colvin imagined a building nine miles high. From the hall of the top floor he would step into the elevator. The floor of the elevator would be made of glass. The elevator shaft drops away forty-six hundred floors beneath him, each floor marked with halogen lights, the parallel lights drawing closer in the nine miles of black air beneath him until they merged in a blur below.

He would look up in time to see the cable snap, separate. He falls, clutching futilely at the inside walls of the elevator, walls which have grown as slippery as the clear-glass floor. Lights rush by, but already the concrete floor of the shaft is visible miles below—a tiny blue concrete square, growing as the elevator car plummets. He knows that he has almost three minutes to watch that blue square come closer, rise up to smash him. Colvin screams, and the spittle floats in the air in front of him, falling at the same velocity, hanging there. The lights rush past. The blue square grows.

Colvin took a drink, placed the glass in the circle set in the wide arm of his chair, and tapped away at his calculator.

Falling objects in a gravity field follow precise mathematical rules, as precise as the force vectors and burn rates in the shaped charges and solid fuels Colvin had designed for twenty years, but just as oxygen affects combustion rates, so air controls the speed of a falling body. Terminal velocity depends upon atmospheric pressure, mass distribution, and surface area as much as upon gravity.

Colvin lowered his eyelids as if to doze, and saw what he saw every night when he pretended to sleep: the billowing white cloud, expanding outward like a time-lapse film of a slanting, tilting stratocumulus blossoming against a dark blue sky; the reddish-brown interior of nitrogen tetroxide flame; and—just visible below the two emerging, mindless contrails of the SRBs—the tumbling, fuzzy square of the forward fuselage, flight deck included. Even the most amplified images had not shown him the closer details—the intact pressure vessel that was the crew compartment, scorched on the right side where the runaway SRB had played its flame upon it, tumbling, falling free, trailing wires and cables and shreds of fuselage behind it like an umbilical and afterbirth. The earlier images had not shown these details, but Colvin had seen them, touched them, after the fracturing impact with the merciless blue sea. There were layers of tiny barnacles growing on the ruptured skin. Colvin imagined the darkness and cold waiting at the end of that fall, small fish feeding.

"Roger," said Steve Cahill, "where'd you get your fear of flying?"

Colvin shrugged, finished his vodka. "I don't know."

In Vietnam—not "Nam" or "in-country"—a place Colvin still wanted to think of as a place rather than a condition, he had flown. Already an expert on shaped charges and propellants. Colvin was being flown out to Bong Son Valley near the coast to see why a shipment of standard C-4 plastic explosives was not detonating for an ARVN unit when the Jesus nut came off their Huey, and the helicopter fell, rotorless, two hundred eighty feet into the jungle, tore through almost a hundred feet of thick vegetation, and came to a stop, upside down, in vines ten feet above the ground. The pilot had been neatly impaled by a limb that smashed up through the floor of the Huey. The copilot's skull had smashed through the windshield. The gunner was thrown out, breaking his neck and back, and died the next day. Colvin walked away with a sprained ankle.

Colvin looked down as they crossed Nantucket. He estimated their altitude at eighteen thousand feet and climbing steadily. Their cruising altitude, he knew, was to be thirty-two thousand feet. Much lower than forty-six thousand, especially lacking the vertical thrust vector, but so much depended upon surface area.

When Colvin was a boy in the 1950's, he saw a photograph in the "old" *National Enquirer* of a woman who had jumped off the Empire State

Building and landed on the roof of a car. Her legs were crossed almost casually at the ankles; there was a hole in the toe of one of her nylon stockings. The roof of the car was flattened, folded inward, almost like a large goose-down mattress, molding itself to the weight of a sleeping person. The woman's head looked as if it were sunk deep in a soft pillow.

Colvin tapped at his calculator. A woman stepping off the Empire State Building would fall for almost fourteen seconds before hitting the street. Someone falling in a metal box from forty-six thousand feet would fall for two minutes and forty-five seconds before hitting the water. What did she think about? What did *they* think about?

Most popular songs and rock videos are about three minutes long, thought Colvin. It is a good length of time: not so long one gets bored, long enough to tell a story.

"We're damned glad you're with us," Bill Montgomery said again.

"God damn it," Bill Montgomery had, whispered to Colvin outside the teleconference room twenty-seven months earlier. "Are you with us or against us on this?"

A teleconference was much like a séance. The group sat in semidarkened rooms hundreds or thousands of miles apart and communed with voices which came from nowhere.

"Well, that's the weather situation here," came the voice from KSC. "What's it to be?"

"We've seen your telefaxed stuff," said the voice from Marshall, "but still don't understand why we should consider scrubbing based on an anomaly that small. You assured us that this stuff was so fail-safe that you could kick it around the block if you wanted to."

Phil McGuire, the chief engineer on Colvin's project team, squirmed in his seat and spoke too loudly. The teleconference phones had speakers by each chair and could pick up the softest tones. "You *don't* understand, do you?" McGuire almost shouted. "It's the *combination* of cold temperatures and the likelihood of electrical activity in that cloud layer that causes the problems. In the past five flights there've been three transient events in the leads that run from SRB linear-shaped charges to the Range Safety command antennas."

"Transient events," said the voice from KSC, "but they are within flight certification parameters?"

"Well . . . yes," said McGuire. He sounded close to tears. "But it's within parameters because we keep signing waivers and rewriting the goddamn parameters. We just don't *know* why the C-12B shaped range safety charges on the SRBs and ET record a transient current flow when no enable functions have been transmitted. Roger thinks that maybe the

LSC enable leads or the C-12 compound itself can accidentally allow the static discharge to simulate a command signal. . . . Oh, hell, *tell* them, Roger."

"Mr. Colvin?"

Colvin cleared his throat. "We've been watching that for some time. Preliminary data suggests temperatures below twenty-eight degrees Fahrenheit allow the zinc oxide residue in the C-12B stacks to conduct a false signal . . . if there's enough static discharge . . . theoretically . . ."

"But no solid database on this yet?" said the voice from Marshall.

"No," said Colvin.

"And you did sign the Criticality One waiver certifying flight readiness on the last three flights?"

"Yes," said Colvin.

"Well," said the voice from KSC, "we've heard from the engineers at Beunet-HCS. What do you say we have recommendations from management there?"

Bill Montgomery had called a five-minute break, and the management team met in the hall. "God damn it, Roger, are you with us or against us on this one?"

Colvin had looked away.

"I'm serious," snapped Montgomery. "The LCS division has brought this company two hundred and fifteen million dollars in *profit* this year, and your work has been an important part of that success, Roger. Now you seem ready to flush that away on some goddamn transient telemetry readings that don't mean *anything* when compared to the work we've done as a team. There's a vice presidency opening in a few months, Roger. Don't screw your chances by losing your head like that hysteric McGuire."

"Ready?" said the voice from KSC when five minutes had passed.

"Go," said Vice President Montgomery.

"Go," said Vice President Miller.

"Go," said Vice President Cahill.

"Go," said Project Manager Weiscott.

"Go," said Project Manager Colvin.

"Fine," said KSC. "I'll pass along the recommendation. Sorry you gentlemen won't be here to watch the lift-off tomorrow."

Colvin turned his head as Bill Montgomery called from his side of the cabin. "Hey, I think I see Long Island."

"Bill," said Colvin, "approximately how much did the company make this year on the C-12B redesign?"

Montgomery took a drink and stretched his legs in the roomy interior of the Gulf Stream. "About four hundred million, I think, Rog. Why?"

"And did the agency ever seriously consider going to someone else after . . . after?"

"Shit," said Tom Weiscott, "where else could they go? We got them by the short hairs. They thought about it for a few months and then came crawling back. You know you're the best designer of shaped range safety devices and solid hypergolics in the country, Rog."

Colvin nodded, worked with his calculator a minute and closed his eyes. The steel bar clamped down across his lap, and the car he rode in clanked higher and higher. The air grew thin and cold, the screech of wheel on rail dwindling into a thin scream as the roller coaster lumbered above the six-mile mark.

In case of loss of cabin pressure, oxygen masks will descend from the ceiling. Please fasten them securely over your mouth and nose and breathe normally.

Colvin peeked ahead, up the terrible incline of the roller coaster, sensing the summit of the climb ahead and the emptiness beyond that point.

The tiny air-tank-and-mask combinations were called PEAPs—Personal Egress Air Packs. PEAPs from four of the five crew members were recovered from the ocean bottom. All had been activated. Two minutes and forty-five seconds of each five-minute air supply had been used up.

Colvin watched the summit of the roller coaster's first hill arrive.

There was a raw metallic noise and a lurch as the roller coaster went over the top and off the rails. People in the cars behind Colvin screamed and kept on screaming.

Colvin lurched forward and grabbed the restraining bar as the roller coaster plummeted into nine miles of nothingness. He opened his eyes. A single glimpse out the Gulfstream window told him that the thin lines of shaped charge he had placed there had removed all of the port wing cleanly, surgically. The tumble rate suggested that enough of a stub of the starboard wing was left to provide the surface area needed to keep the terminal velocity a little lower than maximum. Two minutes and forty-five seconds, plus or minus four seconds.

Colvin reached for his calculator, but it had flown free in the cabin, colliding with hurtling bottles, glasses, cushions, and bodies that had not been securely strapped in. The screaming was very loud.

Two minutes and forty-five seconds. Time to think of many things. And perhaps, just perhaps, after two and a half years of no sleep without dreams, perhaps it would be time enough for a short nap with no dreams at all. Colvin closed his eyes.

JOHN M. FORD

Preflash

John M. Ford won the World Fantasy Award for his novel, *The Dragon Waiting*. A poet, science fiction writer, fantasist, and author of thrillers, the versatile Ford does all these things well. His credits include one of the most brilliantly original and convulsively funny *Star Trek* novels ever published, *How Much for Just the Planet?*

"Preflash" is anything but funny. It is a haunting and frightening story concerned with a man in a quintessentially modern profession. Photojournalism is exciting and sometimes dangerous, especially for the protagonist of this story, for whom the term "accident of fate" has a peculiarly chilling meaning.

—E. D.

PREFLASH

John M. Ford

Exterior, hospital, day. Fischetti pushes Griffin's wheelchair out the door and to the street. Pietra Malaryk is at the curb, leaning against her Chevy wagon, a brand new Arriflex under her arm. Malaryk smiles as Griffin looks up; she hands him the camera. "Welcome back, A.D.," she says.

Griffin checks the Arri. It is a double to the one he lost in the accident. There is a 400-foot magazine of Ektachrome Commercial already loaded; the battery belt is in Malaryk's hand.

Griffin stands up, aware that Fish and Malaryk are both waiting for him to fall down again. He doesn't. He says goodbye to Fischetti, and Fish nods and wheels the chair back.

Griffin shoulders the camera. The balance is strange: it has been eight months since he has had a camera on his shoulder, since the accident. That is a long time not to be whole.

His vision is still blurry, with flashes of phosphene light, but he frames Fischetti pushing the chair, small against the face of stone and little windows, and he presses the trigger.

"How is it, A.D.?" Malaryk asks. Malaryk is as good a cameraman as Griffin ever was and will know that he is lying when he says it's perfect, but that's what he says anyway.

They get into Malaryk's car. Griffin shoots through the window until the magazine is gone. People on the street see the lens and smile and wave, and make obscene gestures. The sun makes darting afterimages in Griffin's eyes.

It was explained to Griffin that his skull has splintered internally, spalled like concrete, and the bone chips in his brain cannot be removed without either killing him or turning him into a vegetable, probably a cabbage. Griffin, not wanting to be either dead or dead-and-breathing, therefore agreed to sign the malpractice waiver. They did not operate, he would not sue. There is no one to collect the money anyway.

As they drive through the sunlight, a good place for cabbages, Griffin puts the Arri down and turns to look at Malaryk. She is wearing the standard issue bush jacket with pockets full of photo goodies, over a deep-cut cotton blouse.

That is what she is wearing down the right side of Griffin's vision. Down the left she appears in grainy black and white, lying on a bed, wearing a bathrobe over underwear. There are dark stains on her skin and clothing, and something blurred. Griffin thinks that if he were editing this film he would slow it down for a better look, and it slows down. The blurred object is a crowbar. A man dark against vertical strips of light is swinging it. There is a barely discernible line between the color frame and the monochrome that wobbles when Griffin tries to focus on it.

Griffin puts a hand to his temple. There is brilliant light like a lens flare, and then the black-and-white film is gone.

"Are you okay, A.D.?" Malaryk says.

He demounts the Arri magazine and labels it, so she will know he's all right.

"So what'cha going to do?" Malaryk says. "Been awful quiet in the pool without you and Carrick."

"Got some offers to do music videos."

"Music videos. You?"

"I can't go into the bush anymore, Pia. Who'd buy me a ticket?"

"Music vidiocy. You. The whole thing's dying."

"Everything dies," Griffin says.

When Griffin was nineteen years old and independently wealthy, he was sitting in a Miami bar chain-smoking Russian cigarettes. The TV was showing a half-hour news special on the Salvador war. Nobody was watching it.

A guy came into the bar. He looked like a street bum: dust all over army-surplus clothes, week's beard. There was a still camera around his neck; as he pushed up to the bar, Griffin saw it was a Leica. Thousand-buck camera with a thousand-buck lens around this bum's dirty neck. Griffin had only paid eight hundred cash for the suit he was wearing.

The guy with the camera ordered a Black Bush with water on the side. He looked at Griffin. "So what do you do, kid?"

Just like that.

"Oh, a buncha shit," Griffin said. "This is one of the things I do." He lit a fresh cigarette with a five-dollar bill. "So what do you do, man?"

The grubby guy pointed at the television set. The camera was bouncing through the jungle, following a squad of soldiers. One of the grunts got hit, went down. The camera spun, paused over him—just a glance at the soldier, but enough to tell you he was dead.

No. More. Enough to be a little ceremony, an amen over his death.

Griffin felt a pain in his hand. The cigarette had dropped from his lips and burned him. He looked around, saw that everybody in the bar was staring at the TV.

"Shot that two days ago," the guy said. "Film beat me here."

This guy had done that with fifteen seconds of film? On a fucking television set?

"My name's Carrick," he said. "If you're Griffin, somebody told me you were good."

"I—yeah," Griffin said. "Yeah, I'm good."

"Fair enough. How'd you like to be good *at* something?"

Griffin was in the hospital four weeks before he was conscious. For another four after that he couldn't move, couldn't feed himself, couldn't do any of the stuff that adults are supposed to do for themselves. He could think, naturally. And he could talk. He could scream, too, but no one listened to that so he didn't do it for very long.

"So how come you guys go down to wars and get shot at?" Fischetti said, easing a bite of mashed potatoes into Griffin's mouth. "I mean, it ain't like somebody was givin' you orders."

Griffin chewed and swallowed as if he were thinking hard, which he wasn't. He said, "It is, though, at least at first. You start out by following somebody."

"A.D., this is Suzy Lodi."

Griffin is being introduced to a tall, thin woman in a straight silver-mesh dress. He braces himself for the sight of her death, as he has learned to do since leaving the hospital, rehearsing the possibilities. Suicide, he supposes, or a fast car full of hamburger, or the ever-popular cocaine heartburst. Can he really be the only one who sees this? He has imagined cutting people open, looking for the hidden cameras.

Griffin looks up, at large eyes, a pointed chin, a look of vulnerability. There is no film.

After a moment Griffin catches himself straining to see, and pulls back from the edge in an almost physical sense. No film. It is as if a terrible beating has suddenly stopped.

"I've been looking forward to meeting you," Suzy Lodi says. Somehow her voice retains most of its recorded quality: the depth, the energy. She is like a clean mountain waterfall rushing through the coked-out, juiced-

out, smacked-out people in this five-thousand-dollar suite overlooking
. . . Griffin cannot remember what city they are in. Maybe Paris. Jesus
Christ in Panavision, she is beautiful. Is she straight? Her first album
had a single called "Preference Me" that was Number Eleven until someone
decided it was obscene, which drove it to Number Three with a bullet.

"So," Lodi says, "you know what they say the A.D. stands for?"

He knows. In movies it means Assistant Director, in print Art Director,
in history books the godless are trying to replace it with C.E.

But when people talk about Griffin it means Already Dead.

The A.D. actually stands for Absalom David, because Griffin's mother
was an illiterate who couldn't keep her Bible stories straight. There were
no books in Griffin's house. There was no newspaper. There were magazines, if they had enough pictures. And there was television, most of the
hours of the day. Dody Griffin's entire print vocabulary was of products
whose names were written large on the glass while an announcer spoke
them. She could read Dial and Oreo and every major brand of beer.

When A.D. Griffin was fifteen, he came home to find that his mother
had mistaken a bottle of ant poison for cough syrup. She was sitting half
upright, her lap full of vomit, in front of the cartoon adventures of
Rambo.

Griffin found the car keys, loaded the old Buick with what he thought
he could hock, and drove off.

Suzy Lodi leads Griffin into another room of the suite and points to a
man all in black, five feet and a couple of inches tall.

"Jesse Rain. My lyricist. Also my manager."

Rain has black hair just to his collar, and his clothes are entirely black:
denim jeans, silk shirt, boots and hard-worn leather jacket. A black scarf
wraps his throat. He is drinking Perrier from the bottle.

Rain's face is hard and planar, like a cliff, his cheeks hollow and gray
with beard stubble. He wears black Wayfarers and a ring carved entirely
from some smooth black stone. Griffin thinks of a Karsh photograph; he
expects the film of Rain's death to look like double vision, monochrome
both sides.

But there is no film.

The relief is less than with Suzy, but it is still there, and cool, and
pleasant.

Rain sips his mineral water, looks shade-eyed at Griffin. "Hello, A.
D. You're interested in shooting some tape of Suzy." His voice is very
measured, like an actor speaking blank verse.

"I don't work in tape," Griffin says. "Only film."

"Film, then."

"Aren't you going to ask why?" Griffin is aware that he is staring, but there is no film. Not of Lodi, not of Rain. He looks at another partygoer, just to make sure, and indeed there it is, perforated ulcer, hemorrhage until Griffin's fingers against his temple break the frame with light. But not of Lodi. Not of Rain.

Jesse Rain says, "Do you ask why Suzy sings with words?"

"You got me."

"I think I might," Rain says seriously, and Griffin doesn't know what the hell he means by it. "But I'll want to see a sample first. One of the songs from Suzy's first album, *Middle Distance*. At our expense."

"If you're going to pay for it anyway, why don't we just—"

"It isn't that I don't trust you," Rain says. "It's that not everyone can shoot Suzy Lodi."

"See these?" Carrick said to Griffin, holding up a yard of sixteen-millimeter in a cotton-gloved hand. "Edge numbers. That's what it's all about. We're all doing edge numbers, dancing right on the sprocket-holed brink."

"I know how to edit, for chrissake."

"Sure. Bet you've read every word Comrade Eisenstein ever wrote, all about how it don't mean a thing if it ain't got that montage. *Look here*, A.D. me lad." He swept his hand across two dozen lengths of film hanging in a clothlined editing bin. "You can pick up a piece of film and look at it and say, 'Yeah, here's where this one fits.' You can put it together with your *hands*, understand? On tape, well, there's a time code in there somewhere, say the magic word SMPTE and it all fits, but you can't see time codes. You can't see *anything* on tape, because there *isn't* anything on tape but some oxide particles with a religious orientation. Tape is attitudinal, A. D., but film grabs that hot raw light coming through the gate and makes something out of it."

"That's bullshit."

"It sure is, A.D. . . . but it's *my* bullshit."

The space between the accident and four weeks later in the hospital is dark. Not totally dark, and not empty. There are half-lit shapes there. Griffin thinks—believes—that he could enter the darkness, see the things close, touch them, know them.

The thought terrifies him. The faith is worse.

Suzy Lodi wears black, against an overexposed white background. Her tight leather dress is an inkblot, her bare arms enveloped by light like fog.

Put the wires into my nerves and brain
Wash my body down with Novocain
If the treatment doesn't ease the pain
Pull the plug and start again

You've got to cut wide open, rub salt in your soul
You've got to crawl through fire, naked on the coal
You've got to breathe deep water, draw until you drown
You've got to reach for heaven, pull the temple down

As she moves in front of the front-projection screen, the light absorbs her limbs, gives them back. She is dancing, but dancing with nothing.

Drive the nails into my hands and feet
Daily paper for my winding sheet
If the hammer doesn't wake the street
Draw the stake, resume the beat

You've got to cut . . .

Jesse Rain stops the projector, turns up the room lights, taps his black ring on the black tabletop. He takes a sip from the glass of Cold Spring at his elbow, and smiles. Without the sunglasses his eyes are colorless, like spring water. "I like it, A.D.," he tells Griffin. "I like it very much. There are nine songs on the new album. What do you feel like committing to?"

There is something in the way Rain says "committing" that makes Griffin think of distance.

Griffin and Carrick and one of the BBC guys were out in the Guatemalan bush when a bunch of Green Berets stumbled over them: no officers, just a couple of shot-up fire-teams looking for home and mother. They said there were Cubans behind them, at least eighty thousand reinforced with tanks and planes and Erwin Rommel and Genghis Khan.

There were some shots. The grunts, not all that paralyzed, shot back. Finally Carrick said to Griffin, "Enough of this shit, I am not getting killed by these wieners," and he picked up his camera just exactly like Duke Wayne hefting a machine gun; yelled "Okay, men—*let's make movies!*"

They all got up and followed him, the grunts shouting and shooting, until they crashed into five Cubans with a disassembled mortar. The Berets killed them all. One of the soldiers got the Bronze Star.

"Remember," Carrick said to Griffin when all the noise was over, "use this power only for good."

"I hear you've got a contract," Malaryk says. They are sitting in the TWA private lounge at Kennedy, over margaritas and bowls of little pretzels. In half an hour Malaryk will take off for the Persian Gulf. Another ship has been sunk, what goes around comes around.

The lounge is a long curved room with a cathedral ceiling and ruffled white curtains hiding its windows, since the people here pay two hundred bucks a year to forget that this is an airport. Griffin keeps looking past Malaryk at the high drapes, because when he looks at her he sees a crowbar crushing her skull, over and over in coarse monochrome, lit by high thin windows.

"We're going to do three off the new record, *Windwriting*. If those work, Jesse Rain wants to do a full video album."

"That's nice," Malaryk says, and Griffin can hear that it isn't quite a lie.

"Beats staring at the ceiling."

"Doug Leibnecht said that any time you want a field job—"

"Tell Doug I said thanks."

"You tell him," Malaryk says, bitterness on the soundtrack. "I've got work to do."

They have another drink on Malaryk's network and then her plane is called. Griffin puts a hand behind his head and pinches, and through light, light, light, kisses Malaryk. How does he tell her to frisk guys for crowbars before letting them into her bedroom?

He aches for her himself, eight months is a long time not to be whole, but the face of the man with the iron is blurred.

There is the usual American pantomime of security. One of the toy soldiers at the checkpoint will die in a hit-and-run in Washington Square Park. The other has her respirator switched off by a man who is not wearing a doctor's coat and is grinning as he pulls the plug. Who knows, maybe both the killers are international terrorists.

Griffin watches the plane go, comforted in knowing it cannot crash.

"Some days I think it's all going to come back to us," Griffin said to Carrick once between firefights. "The detachment, I mean. Keeping distance has to have a price."

"Molto wrongo," Carrick said. "Nobody ever paid for keeping a distance. Nobody ever got shot who wasn't in the line of fire."

"But you've always been as close as anybody."

"So I'll get shot," Carrick said.

Griffin's crew has responded to the decline in the promoclip market. They have met the challenge of spiraling costs, of the American drive to find a better way. They have come to Toronto to shoot.

> Once you played with line and color
> Threw the paint against the wall
> And your scribbled name was hanging
> Under hot lights in the hall
> But now the studio's empty
> And the gallery's closed
> And you can hear the doors are slamming
> No matter where you go
> Fashions you thought you were in
> Gone before they quite begin
> Tell me how long have you been
> Alone

There is something in Suzy Lodi that does not want to be filmed. It is easy to ignore this because she is beautiful; there is enough for the camera there, and all the directors before Griffin have been satisfied with it, content to dance with her image.

Griffin has instead used long lenses and tight apertures to stretch the field, to go deep. For a softly bitter little ballad someone else would have shot in black and white, with smooth slow camera movements, Griffin has used a series of jumping still frames in hypersaturated color.

> Once you drew and cast the numbers
> Dealt the red upon the black
> And no matter how you lost it
> One more play would win it back
> But now the pot of gold's empty
> And the banks are all closed
> And no one's got a dime to lend you
> Just look how much you owe
> Take your chips and cash them in
> Leave the table, you can't win
> Tell me how long have you been
> Alone

Red paint and green felt and empty blue skies tear holes in the retinas; blacks and whites are slabs applied with a palette knife; there is no relief anywhere. Not even in Suzy Lodi's voice, calm as it is. The reviewer for *Rolling Stone* says, "When she asks 'how long have you been alone,' there isn't any doubt who left the guy."

> There was a time for conversation
> In your educated way
> There was an audience just waiting
> For whatever you would say
> But now the words are so empty
> And your mind is so closed
> And you believe there's someone listening
> But you don't really know
> Razor wit can cut too thin
> Voices fading in the din
> Tell me how long have you been
> Alone

The single goes platinum in eleven days. The following week there is a rumor that returns of engagement rings are up thirty percent.

But there are always rumors.

In the seconds before the darkness, Griffin was looking through his viewfinder at four Iowa Nazis in brown shirts with stars 'n' stripes armbands. Griffin was behind what was being called a safety line: the Iowa Nazis agreed that they would not cross the line if the counterdemonstrators and the press and the cops did not cross it.

What the Nazis were doing today in the public eye was killing pigs with spears. A boar hunt, they called it, and issued a statement with some crap about the bold traditions of the Teutonic Knights. One of the countermarchers had a sign reading ALEXANDER NEVSKY HAD THE RIGHT IDEA. It also seemed to be related to a manhood ritual from South Africa, another land of Right Ideas. Griffin felt flashed back to the good old days: he was shooting *Mondo Cane* in the corn belt.

The four he was watching had rifles. This was supposed to be all right too. As the film wound out, one raised his gun.

Griffin's Arriflex exploded next to his temple, into it. He plunged into shadow.

Griffin's clip for Suzy Lodi's "Paper Corridors" has been blamed for an increase in draft evasion, despite that the song has nothing to do with the draft. Griffin has been accused of using subliminals. His reply is that "subliminals are bullshit," which is quoted—at least, all but the last four letters—in most of the national journals.

"Have you ever thought . . ." Griffin says to Jesse Rain one quiet afternoon, not really knowing how to say it, ". . . of writing Suzy something political?"

"Do you mean something polemical?" Rain picks up a guitar, begins knocking out the bouncing chords of sixties beach rock. He sings:

> So keep your eye on the Russians
> 'Cause I think that they're gonna invade now
> You've got to hide in your shelter
> 'Til the fallout has gone and decayed now
> Now every girl loves a soldier
> So I sure hope we're gonna get laid now
> And we'll have guns guns guns
> 'Til atomics blow the Commies away-y-y!

"On Suzy's first EP," Rain says as the ringing dies, "I gave her a song called 'An East Wind Coming,' all about Chernobyl. I put everything I had into it. It bored people blind."

"Did that make it not worth doing?"

"Yeah," Rain says. "It did."

After the accident Griffin was comatose for four weeks. The first face he saw was Fischetti's. The second was Malaryk's. He had expected to see Carrick, but Carrick was dead. He had been blown out of the sky leaving Yemen. Yemen, for God's sake.

Griffin did not weep until Malaryk had kissed him and gone, and then he began to cry uncontrollably. His arms would not respond properly, his hands were no goddamn use at all. Fish came in and dried his face without saying a word. Griffin understood that none of this was new to Fischetti. He wondered how Fish kept distance. How far the distance was.

The line of those waiting to enter Club Glare is half a block long in cold Manhattan drizzle. Jesse Rain, Suzy Lodi, and Griffin walk past the line to another door, and are admitted instantly.

The Club's sound system is loud enough to ignite paper. Its lighting carries enough wattage to give a small African nation all the blessings of civilization.

The dj in the glass booth overhead goes by the name of Wrack Focus. She reminds Griffin of Ming the Merciless in red leather. She is tipped to Suzy's presence, makes the announcement—the applause almost drowns the music—and puts on Griffin's clip of "Paper Corridors." It was shot in darkened government buildings in Ottawa, using preflashed film: the raw stock had been briefly exposed to light, making it more sensitive. There is a cost in haziness, but they can shoot in darker corners.

Griffin and Lodi and Rain get a table with a good view of the crowd and vice versa. Griffin and Lodi order Veuve Clicquot. Rain gets straight Perrier, without even a twist.

Griffin looks at the giant video screen. But he's seen that. He looks at the crowd. Film flips by, death death death. He looks at Suzy, and that is calming at first, and then—

"I'm going upstairs," Jesse Rain says. "See you when."

"'night, Jess," says Suzy.

"He's going to sleep up there?"

"No. Talk to somebody, I think. But that's the last we'll see of him tonight."

Griffin cannot think of a stranger place to do business than inside this jukebox, and he has seen business done where revolutions per minute referred to the transfer of power.

"Is everything all right, Miz Lodi?" says the voice of a BBC announcer. Griffin looks up. There is a seven-foot Haitian in a Club Glare T-shirt looking back at him.

"Just fine, Robert. A.D., this is Rather Rotten Robert. Robert's job is to break the arms of anybody who hassles us, right, Robert?"

Robert smiles, showing more gold than teeth, and says in the perfect Oxbridge purr, "That's quite correct, Miz Lodi."

Through his left eye Griffin sees the huge man kick a .44 out of a zipunk's hand and then throw the zipunk out the door one-handed; as Robert turns, a bald girl with fishhooks in her lips picks up the big pistol and fires it twice, punching Robert's heart out of his body, taking off a corner of his skull. Rather Rotten Robert says "Oh, now, why, lady," and then there is blue light, neon through a beer bottle.

"May I bring you another bottle, sir, madam?" Robert says.

"I think we're going early tonight," Suzy says. "Would you call the car?"

"Certainly, Miz Lodi."

Griffin looks at Suzy Lodi, and there is no film. It has been a long time not to be whole. They go out past the line of those who cannot enter, and for once what they're thinking is right.

It's never like one expects, but even moreso tonight. No torn or thrown clothing. No dominance or submission beyond a little friendly no-I'm-on-top. No kinks and very little perspiration; as clean as a really good porn film. Just the sweet uncomplicated joy of an exchange of tenderness between two people who don't give a damn for each other.

Griffin goes home early the next afternoon to find a message on his answering machine from Malaryk, in town again and wanting to talk to him, and he doesn't even feel guilty.

There is a knock at Griffin's door. Standing in the hall is a man in a bulky coat, a hat half across his face. He looks straight at Griffin, and the face is empty of anything like expression. The medium, in this case, is the message. Griffin turns away before he looks any closer.

"Are you fully recovered from your injury, Mr. Griffin?" the man says, and again it is not the words but the tone.

"I'm doing all right."

"Very glad to hear that, Mr. Griffin. Glad to see you've found productive work. You are enjoying your work?"

"Sure."

"No desire to return to your former job?"

"This pays better."

"Yes," the man says. "I'd keep that in mind. Should anyone make any sort of counteroffer to you—do remember the difference in pay."

Griffin stares. He can't help it, perhaps. The film rolls. Griffin sees the man being knifed in a narrow street, buildings with an East European look. The camera looks down on him as he lurches, holding his stomach in his hands, bumps against a street sign.

"Be careful on Kalininstrasse," Griffin says.

"I hope you're listening to me, Mr. Griffin," the man says in color right frame, while in left frame he falls and makes a splash in his own blood. The man is puzzled. He is used to people being afraid of him, and to their standing up bravely to him, but Griffin's response has him stymied.

"You too," Griffin says, and looks, and looks, until the man turns around and goes.

Griffin shuts the door, and manages not to vomit until he reaches the bathroom.

> One look away
> One voice that won't stop screaming
> One wish that keeps on coming true
> One lonely day
> One night of lucid dreaming
> One coded message coming through
> Breaking through to blue

Malaryk keeps looking at the bar television during the Suzy Lodi clip. She is fascinated, so much so she keeps not telling Griffin what it is that was so important this morning.

> One barren place
> One scent that always lingers
> One introspective point of view
> One hidden face
> One hand with seven fingers
> One wired instruction what to do
> Breaking through to blue

"—but I think I got tape of somebody's missiles in somebody else's cargo holds," Malaryk says suddenly. "I held the camera on the stenciling, and the bills of lading, and if they're all readable—"

"Pia," Griffin says slowly, "has a man—"

The crowbar falls and falls and falls before the thin windows.

"A man what?"

"Be careful," Griffin says, and leaves her, no doubt wondering.

Griffin knows he must have film of Carrick somewhere. He knows that he shot it, as tests, as jokes, as remembrance, for any reason except the one he has in mind now. Tape will not do. Tape is attitudinal, a cool medium at a safe distance.

He finds a reel, jams it onto the editor spools, slaps off the lights and begins to crank.

There is Carrick, moving, living in the light. This is Guatemala film.

And down the left side of Griffin's vision, Yemeni film. The crew is getting out, a Hercules is waiting to take them all home.

They crowd aboard the Hercules, it takes off, there is a round of gallows jokes and straight shots of whiskey, the plane reaches altitude.

There is a bright light as if the film has broken, the lamp unconfined through the gate. And then nothing.

Griffin runs the film back, slows it down. The light contracts to a sphere, to a point. It goes out, leaving a knapsack in a seat. It was all over in three frames, one-eighth of a second. No one felt a thing.

Griffin stops the projection again, counts the passengers. There are twelve. He runs back to the boarding, counts again. Thirteen. The one with the knapsack in his hand does not take a seat. He drops the bag, turns as if going after more gear.

Griffin stops the film. The man's face is blurred with motion, but

Griffin has seen it that way before. In Kalininstrasse. And behind a swinging crowbar.

In the next-to-last frame before the fogged footage, the Iowa Nazi raised his automatic rifle. Bits of film camera crumpled into Griffin's head. But the man with the rifle did not fire it. Griffin had filmed men shooting rifles on four continents, including directly at him, and this one did not.

Griffin wonders who was standing next to him, behind the safety line. But he has no film of that.

He looks at the telephone. He knows the digits that in the right sequence will connect him with Malaryk. But what after that?

The phone rings.

Griffin picks it up.

"A.D.?" Jesse Rain says. "Couple of things I'd like to discuss with you."

"Get the hell out of here, Griffin," the high-school principal told the fifteen-year-old. "I don't know what you bother to come to school for."

"Because I run your audio-visual department better than that drunk Haley ever did, and you don't have to pay me."

The principal swung the yardstick in his hand at Griffin. Griffin grabbed it and snapped it in half. He ran. He'd been told to get out, after all.

He ran home, because that was the only place he had to run. When he got there, he paused, and thought, and gathered, and kept on running.

Rain takes Griffin to the Club Glare, and upstairs. Here the floor hums with the sound for those below, and sometimes the light flashes through the windows like lightning, but they are isolated. Rain looks down at the dance floor, the keystoned video screen. They are above even Wrack the dj.

When they sit down, Griffin has a pint glass of Guinness at the proper temperature, Rain one of Vichy water.

Rain says, "What do you see when you look at me, A.D.?" The words rhyme so that for a moment Griffin thinks it is a new lyric for Suzy. Then he hears them properly. After a moment, he says "What am I supposed to see?"

"You're an artist. I'd hoped you could tell me."

"I make movies."

"You know it's more than that," Rain says. "You work with light. While some of us . . ."

Rain's lips are moving. Griffin cannot hear the words, if they are words; only a soft whistling. Rain dips two fingers into the straight-sided glass. There is a flare of light from his ring, with star-filter points.

The water glass is empty, and a black-furred mouse clutches the back of Rain's hand. It runs up his sleeve, perches on his shoulder.

"Look hard at the mouse," Jesse Rain says. "See anything?"

Griffin looks. The mouse looks back, curious little eyes. There is no film.

"I'm going to throw him under a truck when we're done here," Rain says. "Anything yet?"

No. The mouse licks Rain's ear.

Rain says, "I know your work. You know mine. Technique."

Griffin looks Rain straight in the colorless eyes. Rain feeds a peanut to the mouse, says, "A.D. can you see me?" to the beat of the Who song.

No. Lightning strikes in Griffin's brain, and he pulls at his drink. So this isn't how Carrick did it after all. Griffin had thought—but no, this is different.

Rain says, "It doesn't have to hurt. It can be more fun than anything. *Anything.* You just need to work on your technique." His face is a test card and his voice is a click track. The mouse snuggles down on Rain's shoulder. Surely a mouse has to die. Everything dies.

Rain says, "Did she act like a puppet? Was there any lack of spontaneity?"

No. Griffin's crotch tightens at the thought.

"Technique." Rain stands up, the mouse crawling into his jacket. He says, "Let's go. I can only stand so much of this place."

They descend into the noise, and go out. Rather Rotten Robert clears a way for them. Every time Griffin looks up he sees the bullet opening Robert's skull, so he looks mostly down. On the street there is a line of people waiting to be approved for entry; a glance shows Griffin clips of stopped hearts and fried brains and overturned cars and a bent propellor taking hungry bites. Griffin touches his jaw joint and the film breaks, white light through the gate, painful but clean.

Rain says, "This way. Easy now—you get thrown in the drunk tank and you're in for a long and visionary night."

The neon blurs and goes out. Griffin realizes he is being bundled into a stretch limo. Plush and leather caress him, dark glass soothes his eyes. Rain puts a cold beer into Griffin's hand and he suckles it.

"Where are we going?" Griffin says finally.

"Where do you want to go? Remember we have a clip to shoot in the morning. Want to do it in Paris? We'll pick up Suzy, be on the jet by two. Suzy likes Paris. That's where she met you, remember?"

"Take me up to East 92nd."

Rain twists the cap off a bottle of Evian. They drive north.

Griffin sold the family car, which he wasn't licensed to drive anyway, and pawned the household goods. The hockshop had a sixteen-millimeter movie camera, a Canon Scoopic. Griffin bought it, and a reel-to-reel tape recorder. "Nobody uses this stuff no more, they all make videotape," the pawnbroker said. "What you gonna be, Cecil B. deMille?"

"Herschell Gordon Lewis," Griffin said, but the pawnbroker didn't get it.

Four years later A. D. Griffin was producing, directing, scripting, and lensing hardcore for the inner-city markets and the occasional softcore splatter for the drive-ins. He had a before-tax income of thirty thousand dollars, and an after-tax income of thirty thousand dollars. He had neither a credit card nor a checking account, and had never written a ledger entry in his life. Most of the people he dealt with thought he was just a runner for the real A. D. Griffin. He didn't care. He had everything.

He thought he had everything, until Carrick showed up. What goes around comes around.

Fischetti's fingers dug deep into Griffin's back, working out the pain, putting Griffin's mind back in touch with his vacationing limbs. Griffin thought about things in order, said "You know who Eisenstein was, Fish?"

"Sure. He was a Jew that built atom bombs."

Rain's limousine lets Griffin off at the steps to Malaryk's brownstone. It has begun to rain. Rain says nothing as Griffin leaves the car. When Griffin turns back for a moment, the limo is gone.

He climbs the stairs to a high double door, wire in its glass panes. To his right is a column of glowing doorbell buttons. Malaryk's is the third up. Griffin glances up, through the rain.

The building has high, narrow windows.

Griffin stops. Either he can change what is happening up there, or he cannot. Either he has been seeing the truth or he has not.

If a man cannot trust himself, trusting God is a small consolation. Griffin looks away from the door, high crane shot of the sidewalk below.

There is a young couple, teens, walking past, drenched, nuzzling, not feeling the rain. In Griffin's left eye, the boy kills the girl with a potato peeler. The state electrocutes him. What goes around comes around. She is wearing an oversized T-shirt, plastered to her breasts with rain. It reads CHOOSE LIFE.

Griffin spins around, panning over the lighted doorbells. He stumbles down the steps. Water splashes into his shoes.

A man comes out from between the buildings, coat turned up against the rain. He is whistling to himself. He might be on his way to the corner for a paper. But he isn't. Griffin stares at him, and stares, watching the film of his death over and over.

It isn't enough.

The man has a chalk mark on his shoulder now, a broad white *M*. All around him are scrapings and thuds and footsteps. Hands reach up from sewer gratings. The underworld pursues the murderer, for if the police cannot, who else is left?

Griffin tilts up. The sign on the lamppost no longer reads Kalinin-strasse. Beneath it the man is just as dead.

So.

Griffin takes a few squelching steps. He sees a little man in a long black coat, just ahead. The man snaps his arm out straight: Griffin barely sees the blur of black fur before it disappears beneath a passing truck. He can hear the crunch of tiny bones.

The man in black walks away. Griffin turns another way. So much water.

He will bind Suzy Lodi in black cloth and soak her with water, so that her movements are struggling and slow. Filters and lighting will show each drop in high contrast as it rolls down her face, her body, to the pool that rises past her hips, black as oil. In the last bars of the song it will reach her chin, and still rise, until there is only a silver ripple on darkness. Jesse Rain will write a lyric, and it will sell a million pressings. Kids will drown and not be missed. Double platinum.

A siren shrieks. The cars pull up, the cops pile out. So someone did hear something, say something. Down left frame, one of them is shot-gunned in the face by a stocking-masked bandit, another hangs himself dressed in women's lingerie. Fog and darkness make the right frame seem as colorless as the left, except for the red and blue flares of light. Griffin saves the image for a future video. There will be music.

Griffin turns his back.

A little further on, Griffin's transportation is waiting, calmly pawing the pavement with its eight-inch claws. It turns its head, and dips it, clicking the eagle beak, as submissive as such a creature might ever appear.

Griffin climbs on his namesake's back, running a hand over the feathers of the head, the stiff but smooth fur on the huge shoulders. He is taken into the night sky, they bank over the city smoother than a gyrostabilized helicopter mount. It's more fun than anything.

The street where they are clustering round death is only one square of an endless dark grid, and at every point of the grid there are police, firemen, ambulances, lights sparking hopelessly against the night.

So he doesn't have Carrick's gift, so what. He has his own, and Rain has shown him what it's good for. Griffin will go back now, to the people he can stand to look at, because they have nothing inside them.

Regret dies last. But everything dies.

LUCIUS SHEPARD

Life of Buddha

Lucius Shepard has been getting his work published for only the last five or so years, but the body of his short stories and novels is so outstanding that it is rare to scan a list of award nominations in science fiction, fantasy, or horror without seeing his name among the nominees. His first novel, *Green Eyes*, was one of the second series of Terry Carr's Ace SF Specials; his second novel, *Life During Wartime*, was published by Bantam/Spectra with deserved fanfare.

"Life of Buddha" became the subject of a low-keyed argument between Terri Windling and me. I said it's fantasy, she said it's horror, or at least dark fantasy. Since we both love the story, I claimed it as one of my selections for this volume so that it wouldn't get lost in the cracks. "Buddha" plunks readers into an urban life-style that few of us will ever experience. It's about pain and guilt and hopelessness and transformation—just another brilliant *tour de force* by the multitalented Shepard.

—E. D.

LIFE OF BUDDHA

Lucius Shepard

Whenever the cops scheduled a raid on the shooting gallery to collect their protection money, old cotton-headed Pete Mason, who ran the place, would give Buddha the day off. Buddha rarely said a word to anyone, and Pete had learned that cops were offended by silence. If you didn't scream and run when they busted in, if like Buddha you just sat there and stared at them, they figured you were concealing a superior attitude, and they then tended to get upside your head.

They had beaten Buddha half to death a couple of times for this very reason, and while Buddha hadn't complained (he never complained about anything), Pete did not want to risk losing such a faithful employee. So on the night prior to the September raid, Pete went downstairs to where Buddha was nodding on a stained mattress by the front door and said, "Why don't you hang out over at Taboo's place tomorrow? Police is comin' round to do they thang."

Buddha shook himself out of his nod and said, "Talked to him already. Johnny Wardell's gon' be over sometime makin' a buy, but he say to come ahead anyway." He was a squat black man in his late thirties, his head stone bald, with sleepy, heavy-lidded eyes and the beginnings of jowls; he was wearing chinos stippled with blood from his last fix, and a too-small gray T-shirt that showed every tuck and billow of his round belly and womanly breasts. Sitting there, he looked like a Buddha carved from ebony that somebody had outfitted with Salvation Army clothes, and that was why Pete had given him the name. His real name was Richard Damon, but he wouldn't respond to it anymore. Buddha suited him just fine. "Beats me why Taboo wanna do business with Johnny Wardell," Pete said, hitching his pants up over his ample stomach. "Sooner or later Wardell he be gettin' crazy all over a faggot like Taboo . . . y'know?"

Buddha grunted, scratched the tracks on his wrist, and gazed out the window beside the front door. He knew Pete was trying to draw him into a conversation, and he had no intention of letting himself be drawn. It wasn't that he disliked Pete; he liked him as much as anyone. He simply had no opinions he wanted to share; he had cultivated this lack of opinion, and he had found that the more he talked, the more opinions came to mind.

"You tell Taboo from me," Pete went on, "I been livin' in Detroit more'n sixty years, and I done business wit' a lotta bad dogs, but I ain't never met one meaner than Wardell. You tell him he better watch his behavior, y'understan'?"

"Awright."

"Well . . ." Pete turned and with a laborious gait, dragging his bad leg, mounted the stairs. "You come on up 'round two and get your goodnighter. I'll cut ya out a spoon of China White."

" 'Preciate it," said Buddha.

As soon as Pete was out of sight, Buddha lay down and stared at the flaking grayish-white paint of the ceiling. He picked a sliver of paint from the wall and crumbled it between his fingers. Then he ran the back of his hand along the worn nap of the runner that covered the hallway floor. All as if to reassure himself of the familiar surroundings. He had spent the best part of fifteen years as Pete's watchdog, lying on the same mattress, staring at that same dried-up paint, caressing that same runner. Before taking up residence on the mattress, he had been a young man with a future. Everybody had said, "That Richard Damon, he's gon' be headlines, he's gon' be *Live at Five*, he's gon' be *People* magazine." Not that he had started out different from his peers. He'd been into a little dealing, a little numbers, a little of whatever would pay him for doing nothing. But he'd been smarter than most and had kept his record clean, and when he told people he had his eye on the political arena, nobody laughed. They could see he had the stuff to make it. The trouble was, though, he had been so full of himself, so taken with his smarts and his fine clothes and his way with the ladies, he had destroyed the only two people who had cared about him. Destroyed them without noticing. Worried his mama into an early grave, driven his wife to suicide. For a while after they had died, he'd gone on as always; but then he'd come up against guilt.

He hadn't known then what that word *guilt* meant; but he had since learned its meaning to the bone. Guilt started out as a minor irritation no worse than a case of heartburn and grew into a pain with claws that tore out your guts and hollowed your heart. Guilt made you sweat for no reason, jump at the least noise, look behind you in every dark place. Guilt kept you from sleeping, and when you did manage to drop off, it sent you dreams about your dead, dreams so strong they began to invade your waking moments. Guilt was a monster against which the only defense was oblivion. . . . Once he had discovered that truth, he had sought oblivion with the fervor of a converted sinner.

He had tried to kill himself but had not been able to muster the necessary courage and instead had turned to drugs. To heroin and the mattress in the shooting gallery. And there he had discovered another truth: that this life was in itself a kind of oblivion, that it was carving him slow and simple, emptying him of dreams and memories. And of guilt.

The porch steps creaked under someone's weight. Buddha peered out the window just as a knock sounded at the door. It was Marlene, one of the hookers who worked out of Dally's Show Bar down the block; a pretty cocoa-skinned girl carrying an overnight bag, her breasts pushed up by a tight bra.

Her pimp—a long-haired white kid—was standing on a lower step. Buddha opened the door, and they brushed past him. "Pete 'round?" Marlene asked.

Buddha pointed up the stairs and shut the door. The white kid grinned, whispered to Marlene, and she laughed. "John think you look like you could use some lovin'," she said. "What say you come on up, and I'll give you a sweet ride for free?" She chucked him under the chin. "How that sound, Buddha?"

He remained silent, denying desire and humiliation, practicing being the nothing she perceived. He had become perfect at ignoring ridicule, but desire was still a problem: The plump upper slopes of her breasts gleamed with sweat and looked full of juice. She turned away, apparently ashamed of having teased him.

"Take it easy now, Buddha," she said with studied indifference, and hand-led the white kid up the stairs.

Buddha plucked at a frayed thread on the mattress. He knew the history of its every stain, its every rip. Knew them so thoroughly that the knowledge was no longer something he could say: It was part of him, and he was part of it. He and the mattress had become a unity of place and purpose. He wished he could risk going to sleep, but it was Friday night, and there would be too many customers, too many interruptions. He fixed his gaze on the tarnished brass doorknob, let it blur until it became a greenish-gold sun spinning within a misty corona. Watched it whirl around and around, growing brighter and brighter. Correspondingly his thoughts spun and brightened, becoming less thoughts than reflections of the inconstant light. And thus did Buddha pass the middle hours of the night.

*   *   *

At two o'clock Buddha double-bolted the door and went upstairs for his goodnighter. He walked slowly along the corridor, scuffing the threadbare carpet, its pattern eroded into grimy darkness and worm trails of murky gold. Laughter and tinny music came from behind closed doors, seeming to share the staleness of the cooking odors that pervaded the house. A group of customers had gathered by Pete's door, and Buddha stopped beside them. Somebody else wandered up, asked what was happening, and was told that Pete was having trouble getting a vein. Marlene was going to hit him up in the neck. Pete's raspy voice issued from the room, saying, "Damn it! Hurry up, woman!"

Getting a vein was a frequent problem for Pete; the big veins in his arms were burned-out, and the rest weren't much better. Buddha peered over shoulders into the room. Pete was lying in bed, on sheets so dirty they appeared to have a design of dark clouds. His freckly brown skin was suffused by a chalky pallor. Three young men—one of them Marlene's pimp—were gathered around him, murmuring comforts. On the night table a lamp with a ruffled shade cast a buttery yellow light, giving shadows to the strips of linoleum peeling up from the floor.

Marlene came out of the bathroom, wearing an emerald-green robe. When she leaned over Pete, the halves of the robe fell apart, and her breasts hung free, catching a shine from the lamp. The needle in her hand showed a sparkle on its tip. She swabbed Pete's neck with a clump of cotton and held the needle poised an inch or two away.

The heaviness of the light, the tableau of figures around the bed, Marlene's gleaming skin, the wrong-looking shadows on the floor, too sharp to be real: Taken all together, these things had the same richness and artful composition, the same important stillness, as an old painting that Buddha had once seen in the Museum of Art. He liked the idea that such beauty could exist in this ruinous house, that the sad souls therein could become even this much of a unity. But he rejected his pleasure in the sight, as was his habit with almost every pleasure.

Pete groaned and twisted about. "Stop that shit!" Marlene snapped. "Want me to bleed you dry?"

Other people closed in around the bed, blocking Buddha's view. Pete's voice dropped to a whisper, instructing Marlene. Then people began moving away from the bed, revealing Pete lying on his back, holding a bloody Kleenex to the side of his neck. Buddha spotted his goodnighter on the dresser: a needle resting on a mirror beside a tiny heap of white powder.

"How you doin'?" Pete asked weakly as Buddha walked in.

He returned a diffident wave, went over to the dresser, and inspected the powder: It looked like a nice dose. He lifted the mirror and headed off downstairs to cook up.

"Goddamn!" said Pete. "Fifteen years I been takin' care of you. Feedin' your Jones, buyin' your supper. Think we'd have a relationship by now." His tone grew even more irascible. "I should never have give you that damn name! Got you thinkin' you inscrutable, when all you is is ignorant!"

Nodding on his mattress in the moonlit dark, feeling the rosy glow of the fix in his heart, the pure flotation of China White in his flesh, Buddha experienced little flash dreams: bizarre images that materialized and faded so quickly, he was unable to categorize them. After these had passed he lay down, covered himself with a blanket, and concentrated upon his dream of Africa, the one pleasure he allowed himself to nourish. His conception of Africa bore no relation to the ethnic revival of the Sixties, to Afros and dashikis, except that otherwise he might have had no cognizance of the Dark Continent. Buddha's African kingdom was a fantasy derived from images in old movies, color layouts in *National Geographic*, from drugs and drugged visions of Nirvana as a theme park. He was not always able to summon the dream, but that night he felt disconnected from all his crimes and passionate failures, stainless and empty, and thus worthy of this guardian bliss. He closed his eyes, then squeezed his eyelids tight until golden pinpricks flowered in the blackness. Those pinpricks expanded and opened into Africa.

He was flowing like wind across a tawny plain, a plain familiar from many such crossings. Tall grasses swayed with his passage, antelope started up, and the gamy smell of lions was in the air. The grasslands evolved into a veld dotted with scum-coated ponds and crooked trees with scant, pale foliage. Black stick figures leapt from cover and menaced him with spears, guarding a village peopled by storytellers and long-legged women who wore one-eyed white masks and whose shadows danced when they walked. Smoke plumed from wart-shaped thatched huts and turned into music; voices spoke from cooking fires. Beyond the village stood green mountains that rose into the clouds, and there among the orchids and ferns were the secret kingdoms of the gorillas. And beyond the mountains lay a vast blue lake, its far reaches fringed by shifting veils of mist in whose folds miragelike images materialized and faded.

Buddha had never penetrated the mists: There was something ominous about their unstable borders and the ghostly whiteness they enclosed. At the center of the lake a fish floated halfway between the surface and the bottom, like the single thought of a liquid brain. Knowing that he must soon face the stresses of the outside world, Buddha needed the solace offered by the fish; he sank beneath the waters until he came face-to-face with it, floating a few inches away.

The fish resembled a carp and measured three feet from its head to its tail; its overlapping scales were a muddy brown, and its face was the mask of a lugubrious god, with huge golden eyes and a fleshy, downturned mouth. It seemed to be regarding Buddha sadly, registering him as another of life's disappointments, a subject with which it was quite familiar, for its swollen belly encaged all the evil and heartache in the world, both in principle and reality. Buddha gazed into its eyes, and the pupils expanded into black funnels that connected with his own pupils, opening channels along which torrents of grief and fear began to flow. The deaths of his wife and mother were nothing compared with the hallucinatory terrors that now confronted him: demons with mouths large enough to swallow planets; gales composed of a trillion dying breaths; armies of dead men and women and children, their bodies maimed by an infinity of malefic usage. Had he witnessed these visions while awake, he would have been overwhelmed; but protected by the conditions of the dream, he withstood them and was made strong.

And before long he fell asleep in the midst of this infinite torment contained within the belly of the fish in his dream, contained in turn within his skull, within the ramshackle frame house, within the gunshot-riddled spiritual realm of the Detroit ghetto, whose agonies became a fleeting instance of distress—the fluttering of an eyelid, the twitching of a nerve—within the dreamed-of peace of Buddha's sleep.

The shooting gallery was located in the Jefferson–Chalmers district, the section of the ghetto most affected by the '67 riots. Hundreds of gutted houses still stood as memorials to that event, and between them—where once had stood other houses—lay vacant lots overgrown with weeds and stunted trees of heaven. The following afternoon, as he walked past the lot adjoining the shooting gallery, Buddha was struck by the sight of a charred sofa set among weeds at the center of the lot, and obeying an impulse, he walked over to it and sat down. It was the first day of fall weather. The air was crisp, the full moon pinned like a disfigured cameo of bone to a cloudless blue sky. In front of the sofa was a pile of ashes over which somebody had placed a grill; half a dozen scorched cans were scattered around it. Buddha studied the ashes, the grill, the cans, mesmerized by the pattern they formed. Sirens squealed in the distance, a metallic clanging seemed to be issuing from beyond the sky, and Buddha felt himself enthroned, the desireless king of a ruined world in which all desire had faltered.

He had been sitting for perhaps an hour when a teenage boy with a freckly complexion like Pete's came running along the sidewalk. Dressed in jeans and a sweatshirt and lugging an immense ghetto blaster. The boy looked behind him, then sprinted across the lot toward Buddha and flung himself down behind the sofa. "You tell 'em I'm here," he said breathlessly, "I'll cut ya!" He waggled a switchblade in front of Buddha's face. Buddha just kept staring at the toppled brick chimneys and vacated premises. A dragonfly wobbled up from the leaves and vanished into the sun dazzle of a piece of broken mirror canted against the ash heap.

Less than a minute later two black men ran past the lot. Spotting Buddha, one shouted, "See a kid come this way?" Buddha made no reply.

"Tell 'em I headed toward Cass," the kid whispered urgently, but Buddha maintained his silence, his lack of concern.

"Y'hear me?" the man shouted. "Did a kid come this way?"

"Tell 'em!" the boy whispered.

Buddha said nothing.

The two men conferred and after a second ran back in the direction from which they had come. "Damn, blood! You take some chances!" said the boy, and when Buddha gave no response, he added, "They come back, you just sit there like you done. Maybe they think you a dummy." He switched on the ghetto blaster, and rap music leaked out, the volume too low for the words to be audible.

Buddha looked at the boy, and the boy grinned, his nervousness evident despite the mask of confidence.

"Ain't this a fine box?" he said. "Fools leave it settin' on they stoop, they deserve to get it took." He squinted as if trying to scry out Buddha's hidden meaning. "Can't you talk, man?"

"Nothin' to say," Buddha answered.

"That's cool. . . . Too much bullshit in the air, anyhow."

The boy reminded Buddha of his younger self, and this disquieted him: He had the urge to offer advice, and he knew advice would be useless. The boy's fate was spelled out by the anger lying dormant in the set of his mouth. Buddha pitied him, but pity—like love, like hate—was a violation of his policy of noninvolvement, an impediment of the emptiness to which he aspired. He got to his feet and headed for the sidewalk.

"Hey!" yelled the boy. "You tell them mothafuckas where I'm at. I'll kill yo' ass!"

Buddha kept walking.

"I mean it, man!" And as if in defiance, as if he needed some help to verbalize it, the boy turned up the ghetto blaster, and a gassed voice blared. "Don't listen to the shuck and jive from Chairman Channel Twenty-five. . . ."

Buddha picked up his pace, and soon the voice mixed in with the faint sounds of traffic, distant shouts, other musics, absorbed into the troubled sea from which it had surfaced.

From the shooting gallery to Taboo's apartment should have been about a twenty-minute walk, but that day—still troubled by his encounter with the boy—Buddha cut the time in half. He had learned that it was impossible to avoid involvement on his day off, impossible not to confront his past, and in Taboo he had found a means of making the experience tolerable, letting it be the exception that proved the rule. When he had first met Taboo seven years before, Taboo's name had been Yancey; he had been eighteen, married to a pretty girl, and holding down a steady job at Pontiac Motors.

Three years later, when he had next run into him, Taboo had come out of the closet, was working as a psychic healer, curing neighborhood ladies of various minor complaints, and through hormone treatments had developed a small yet shapely pair of breasts, whose existence he hid from the world beneath loose-fitting clothes.

Buddha had caught a glimpse of Taboo's breasts by accident, having once entered his bathroom while he was washing up, and after this chance revelation, Taboo had fixed upon him as a confidant, a circumstance that Buddha had welcomed—though he did not welcome Taboo's sexual advances. He derived several benefits from the relationship. For one thing, Taboo's specialty was curing warts and Buddha had a problem with warts on his hands (one such had given him an excuse to visit that day); for another, Taboo—who dealt on the side—always had drugs on hand. But the most important benefit was that Taboo provided Buddha with an opportunity to show kindness to someone who brought to mind his dead wife. In their solitary moments together Taboo would don a wig and a dress, transforming himself into the semblance of a beautiful young woman, and Buddha would try to persuade him to follow his inner directives and proceed with the final stage of his sex change. He would argue long and hard, claiming that Taboo's magical powers would mature once he completed the transformation, telling Taboo stories of how wonderful his new life would be. But Taboo was deathly afraid of the surgeon's knife, and no matter how forcefully Buddha argued, he refused to pay heed. Buddha knew there had to be an answer to Taboo's problem, and sometimes he felt that answer was staring him in the face. But it never would come clear. He had the notion, though, that sooner or later the time would be right for answers.

It was a beautiful spring day in Taboo's living room. The walls were painted to resemble a blue sky dappled with fluffy white clouds, and the floor was carpeted with artificial grass. In Taboo's bedroom where he did his healing, it was a mystical night. The walls were figured with cabalistic signs and stars and a crescent moon, and the corner table was ebony, and the chairs upholstered in black velour. Black drapes hid the windows; a black satin quilt covered the bed. Muted radiance shone from the ceiling onto the corner table, and after he had fixed, it was there that Buddha sat soaking his wart in a crystal bowl filled with herb-steeped water, while Taboo sat beside him and muttered charms.

Taboo was not in drag because he was waiting for Johnny Wardell to show; but even so he exhibited a feminine beauty. The soft lighting applied sensual gleams to his chocolate skin and enhanced the delicacy of his high cheekbones and generous mouth and almond-shaped eyes. When he leaned forward to inspect Buddha's wart, the tips of his breasts dimpled the fabric of his blousy shirt. Buddha could make out his magic: a disturbance like heat haze in the air around him.

"There, darlin'," said Taboo. "All gone. Your hand back the way it s'posed to be."

Buddha peered into the bowl. At the bottom rested a wrinkled black thing like a raisin. Taboo lifted his hand from the water and dried it with a towel. Where the wart had been was now only smooth skin. Buddha touched the place; it felt hot and smelled bitter from the herbs.

"Wish Johnny'd hurry up," said Taboo. "I bought a new dress I wanna try on for ya."

"Whyn't you try it on now? If the buzzer goes, you can pretend you ain't at home."

"'Cause I just have to deal wit him later, and no tellin' what kinda mood Johnny be in then."

Buddha had no need to ask Taboo why he had to deal with Johnny Wardell at all. Taboo's reason for risking himself among the bad dogs was similar to Buddha's reason for retreating from life: He felt guilty for the way he was and this risk was his self-inflicted punishment.

Taboo pulled out a packet of white powder and a drinking straw and told Buddha to toot a few lines, to put a shine on his high. Buddha did as he suggested. A luxuriant warmth spread through his head and chest, and little sparkles danced in the air, vanishing like snowflakes. He started getting drowsy. Taboo steered him to the bed, then curled up beside him, his arm around Buddha's waist.

"I love you so much, Buddha," he said. "Don't know what I'd do without you to talk to . . . I swear I don't." His soft breasts nudged against Buddha's arm, his fingers toyed with Buddha's belt buckle, and despite himself, Buddha experienced the beginnings of arousal. But he felt no love coming from Taboo, only a flux of lust and anxiety. Love was unmistakable—a warm pressure as steady as a beam from a flashlight—and Taboo was too unformed, too confused, to be its source.

"Naw, man," Buddha said, pushing Taboo's hand away.

"I just wanna love you!"

In Taboo's eyes Buddha could read the sweet, fucked-up sadness of a woman born wrong; but though he was sympathetic, he forced himself to be stern. "Don't mess wit' me!"

The buzzer sounded.

"Damn!" Taboo sat up, tucked in his shirt. He walked over to the table, picked up the white powder and the drinking straw, and brought them over to Buddha. "You do a little bit more of this here bad boy. But don't you be runnin' it. I don't want you fallin' out on me." He went out into the living room, closing the door behind him.

There seemed to be a curious weight inside Buddha's head, less an ache than a sense of something askew, and to rid himself of it he did most of the remaining heroin. It was enough to set him dreaming, though not of Africa. These dreams were ugly, featuring shrieks and thuds and nasty smears of laughter, and once somebody said, "The man got tits! Dig it! The man's a fuckin' woman!"

Gradually he arrived at the realization that the dreams were real, that something bad was happening, and he struggled back to full consciousness. He got to his feet, swayed, staggered forward, and threw open the door to the living room.

Taboo was naked and spread-eagled facedown over some pillow, his rump in the air, and Johnny Wardell—a young leather-clad blood with a hawkish face—was holding his arms. Another man, darker and heavier than Wardell, was kneeling between Taboo's legs and was just zipping up his trousers.

For a split second nobody moved. Framed by the vivid green grass and blue sky and innocent clouds, the scene had a surreal biblical quality, like a hideous act perpetrated in some unspoiled corner of the Garden of Eden, and Buddha was transfixed by it. What he saw was vile, but he saw, too, that it was an accurate statement of the world's worth, of its grotesque beauty, and he felt distanced, as if he were watching through a peephole whose far end was a thousand miles away.

"Lookit here," said Wardell, a mean grin slicing across his face. "The ho already done got herself a man. C'mon, bro'! We saved ya a piece."

Long-buried emotions were kindled in Buddha's heart. Rage, love, fear. Their onset too swift and powerful for him to reject. "Get your hand off him," he said, pitching his voice deep and full of menace.

Wardell's lean face went slack, and his grin seemed to deepen, as if the lustful expression engraved on his skull were showing through the skin, as if he perceived in Buddha an object of desire infinitely more gratifying than Taboo.

Wardell nodded at the man kneeling between Taboo's legs, and the man flung himself at Buddha, pulling a knife and swinging it in a vicious arc. Buddha caught the man's wrist, and the man's violence was transmitted through his flesh, seeding fury in his heart. He squeezed the man's wrist bones until they ground together, and the knife fell to the floor. Then he pinned the man against the wall and began smashing his head against it, avoiding the fingers that clawed at his eyes. He heard himself yelling, heard bone splinter.

The man's eyes went unfocused, and he grew heavy in Buddha's grasp; he slumped down, the back of his head leaving a glistening red track across a puffy cloud. Buddha knew he was dead, but before he could absorb the fact, something struck him in the back, a liver punch that landed with the stunning impact of a bullet, and he dropped like a stone.

The pain was luminous. He imagined it lighting him up inside with the precise articulation of an X ray. Other blows rained in upon him, but he felt only the effects of that first one. He made out Wardell looming over him, a slim, leathery giant delivering kick after kick. Blackness frittered at the edges of his vision. Then a scream—a sound like a silver splinter driven into Buddha's brain—and there was Taboo, something bright in his hand, something that flashed downward into Wardell's chest as he turned, lifted, flashed down again. Wardell stumbled back, looking puzzled, touching a red stain on the shirtfront, and then appeared to slide away into the blackness at the corner of Buddha's left eye. Buddha lay gasping for breath: The last kick had landed in the pit of his stomach. After a second his vision began to clear, and he saw Taboo standing above Wardell's body, the other man's knife in his hand.

With his sleek breasts and male genitalia and the bloody knife, he seemed a creature out of a myth. He kneeled beside Buddha. "You awright?" he asked. "Buddha? You awright?"

Buddha managed a nod. Taboo's eyes reminded him of the eyes of the fish in his dream—aswarm with terrors—and his magic was heavy wash in the air, stronger than Buddha had ever seen it.

"I never wanted to kill nobody," said Taboo tremulously. "That's the *last* thing I wanted to do." He glanced at the two corpses, and his lips quivered. Buddha looked at them, too.

Sprawled in oddly graceful attitudes on the green grass amid a calligraphy of blood, they appeared to be spelling out some kind of cryptic message. Buddha thought if he kept staring at them, their meaning would come clear.

"Oh, God!" said Taboo. "They gon' be comin' for me, they gon' put me in jail! I can't live in jail. What am I gon' do?"

And to his astonishment, looking back and forth between the corpses and Taboo's magical aura, Buddha found he could answer that question.

The answer was, he realized, also the solution to the problem of his life; it was a means of redemption, one he could have arrived at by no other process than that of his fifteen-year retreat.

Its conception had demanded an empty womb in which to breed and had demanded as well an apprehension of magical principle: That had been supplied by his dream of Africa. And having apprehended the full measure of this principle, he further realized he had misunderstood the nature of Taboo's powers. He had assumed that they had been weakened by the wrongness of his birth and would mature once he went under the knife; but he now saw they were in themselves a way of effecting the transformation with a superior result, that they had needed this moment of violence and desperation to attain sufficient strength. Buddha felt himself filling with calm, as if the knowledge had breached an internal reservoir that had dammed calmness up.

"You need a disguise," he said. "And you got the perfect disguise right at your fingertips." He proceeded to explain.

"You crazy, Buddha!" said Taboo. "No way I can do that."

"You ain't got no choice."

"You crazy!" Taboo repeated, backing away. "Crazy!"

"C'mon back here!"

"Naw, man! I gotta get away, I gotta. . . ." Taboo backed into the door, felt for the knob, and—eyes wide, panic-stricken—wrenched it open. His mouth opened as if he were going to say something else, but instead he turned and bolted down the hall.

The pain in Buddha's back was throbbing, spreading a sick weakness all through his flesh, and he passed out for a few seconds.

When he regained consciousness, he saw Taboo standing in the doorway, looking insubstantial due to the heavy wash of magic around him: in fact, the whole room had an underwater lucidity, everything wavering, like a dream fading in from the immaterial. "See?" said Buddha. "Where you gon' go man? You barely able to make it here!"

"I don't know, I'll . . . maybe I'll . . ." Taboo's voice, too, had the qualities of something out of a dream: distant and having a faint echo.

"Sheeit!" Buddha reached out to Taboo. "Gimme a hand up."

Taboo helped him to his feet and into the bedroom and lowered him onto the bed. Buddha felt as if he might sink forever into the black satin coverlet.

"Show me that new dress you bought," he said. Taboo went to the closet, pulled out a hanger, and held the dress against his body to display its effect. It was white silk, low-cut, with a scattering of sequins all over.

"Aw, man," said Buddha. "Yeah, that's *your* dress. You be knockin' the boys' eyes out wearin' that . . . if they could ever see it. If you'd just do what's right. You'd be too beautiful for Detroit. You'd need to get someplace south, place where the moon shines bright as the sun. 'Cause that's what kinda beautiful you gon' be. Moon beautiful. Miami, maybe. That'd suit ya. Get you a big white car, drive down by them fancy hotels, and let all them fancy people have a look at ya. And they gon' lay down and beg to get next to you, man. . . ."

As Buddha talked, conjuring the feminine future with greater seductiveness and invention than ever before, the heat haze of Taboo's magic grew still more visible, taking on the eerie, miragelike aspect of the mists beyond the lake in Buddha's Africa; and after Buddha had finished, Taboo sat on the edge of the bed, holding the dress across his lap. "I'm scared," he said. "What if it don't work?"

"You always been scared," said Buddha. "You bein' scared's what got them two men dead out there. Time for that to stop. You know you got the power. So go on!"

"I can't!"

"You ain't got no choice." Buddha pulled Taboo's head down gently and kissed him openmouthed, breathing into him a calming breath. "Do it," he said. "Do it now."

Hesitantly Taboo came to his feet. "Don't you go nowhere now. You wait for me."

"You know I will."

"Awright." Taboo took a few steps toward the bathroom, then stopped. "Buddha, I don't . . ."

"Go on!"

Taboo lowered his head, walked slowly into the bathroom, and closed the door.

Buddha heard the tub filling, heard the splashing as Taboo climbed into it. Then heard him begin to mutter his charms. He needed to sleep, to fix, but he kept awake as long as he could, trying to help Taboo with the effort of his will. He could feel the vibrations of the magic working through the bathroom door. Finally he gave in to the pressures of exhaustion and the throbbing in his back and drifted off to sleep; the pain followed him into the blackness of sleep, glowing like the core of his being. He woke sometime later to hear Taboo calling his name and spotted him in the darkest corner of the room—a shadow outlined by painted stars.

"Taboo?"

"It don't feel right, Buddha." Taboo's voice had acquired a husky timbre.

"C'mere, man."

Taboo came a step closer, and though Buddha was still unable to see him, he could smell the heat and bitterness of the herbs.

"It worked, didn't it?" Buddha asked. "It musta worked."

"I think. . . . But I feel so peculiar."

"You just ain't used to it is all. . . . Now c'mere!"

Taboo moved still closer, and Buddha made out a naked young woman standing a few feet away. Slim and sexy, with shoulder-length black hair and high, small breasts and a pubic triangle that showed no sign of ever having been male.

The air around Taboo was still and dark. No ripples, no heat haze. The magic had all been used.

"I told ya," said Buddha. "You beautiful."

"I ain't. . . . I just ordinary." But Taboo sounded pleased.

"Ordinary as angels," Buddha said. "That's how ordinary you are."

Taboo smiled. It was faltering at first, that smile, but it grew wider when Buddha repeated the compliment: the smile of a woman gradually becoming confident of her feminine powers. She lay down beside Buddha and fingered his belt buckle. "I love you, Buddha," she said. "Make me feel right."

Love was a steady flow from her, as tangible as a perfume, and Buddha felt it seeping into him, coloring his calm emptiness. On instinct he started to reject the emotion, but then he realized he had one more duty to fulfill, the most taxing and compromising duty of all. He reached down and touched the place between Taboo's legs. Taboo stiffened and pushed her hips against his finger.

"Make me feel right," she said again.

Buddha tried to turn onto his side, but the pain in his back flared. He winced and lay motionless. "Don't know if I can. I'm hurtin' pretty bad."

"I'll help you," she said, her fingers working at his buckle, his zipper. "You won't have to do nothin', Buddha. You just let it happen now."

But Buddha knew he couldn't just let it happen, knew he had to return Taboo's love in order to persuade her of her rightness, her desirability. As she mounted him, a shadow woman lifting and writhing against the false night of the ceiling stars, strangely weightless, he pinned his dead wife's features to her darkened face, remembered *her* ways, *her* secrets. All the love and lust he had fought so long to deny came boiling up from nowhere, annihilating his calm. He dug his fingers into the plump flesh of her hips, wedging himself deep; he plunged and grunted, ignoring the pain in his back, immersed again in the suety richness of desire, in the animal turbulence of this most alluring of human involvements. And when she cried out, a mournful note that planed away to a whisper, like the sound a spirit makes falling through eternity, he felt the profound satisfaction of a musician who by his dominance and skill has brought forth a perfect tone from chaos. But afterward as she snuggled close to him, telling him of her pleasure, her excitement, he felt only despair, fearing that the empty product of his years of ascetic employment had been wasted in a single night.

"Come with me, Buddha," she said. "Come with me to Miami. We can get us a house on the beach and . . ."

"Lemme be," he said, his despair increasing because he wanted to go with her, to live high in Miami and share her self-discovery, her elation. Only the pain in his back—intensifying with every passing minute—dissuaded him, and it took all his willpower to convince her of his resolve, to insist that she leave without him, for Taboo and his dead wife had fused into a single entity in his mind, and the thought of losing her again was a pain equal to the one inflicted by Johnny Wardell.

At last, suitcase in hand, she stood in the doorway, the temptation of the world in a white silk dress, and said, "Buddha, please won'tcha . . ."

"Damn it!" he said. "You got what you want. Now get on outta here!"

"Don't be so harsh wit' me, Buddha. You know I love you."

Buddha let his labored breathing be the answer.

"I'll come see ya after a while," she said. "I'll bring you a piece of Miami."

"Don't bother."

"Buddha?"

"Yeah."

"In the bathtub, Buddha . . . I just couldn't touch it."

"I'll take care of it."

She half-turned, glanced back. "I'll always love you, Buddha." The door swung shut behind her, but the radiance of her love kept beaming through the wood, strong and contaminating.

"Go get yourself a big white car," he murmured.

He waited until he heard the front door close, then struggled up from the bed, clamping his hand over his liver to muffle the pain. He swayed, on the verge of passing out; but after a moment he felt steadier, although he remained disoriented by unaccustomed emotion. However, the sight of the pitiful human fragment lying in the herb-steeped water of the bathtub served to diminish even that. He scooped it up in a drinking glass and flushed it down the toilet. Then he lay back on the bed again. Closed his eyes for a minute . . . at least he thought it was just a minute. But he couldn't shake the notion that he'd been asleep for a long, long time.

Buddha had to stop and rest half a dozen times on the way back to the shooting gallery, overcome by pain, by emotions . . . mostly by emotions. They were all around him as well as inside.

The shadows of the ruined houses were the ghosts of his loves and hates; the rustlings in the weeds were long-dead memories with red eyes and claws just waiting for a chance to leap out and snatch him; the moon—lopsided and orange and bloated—was the emblem of his forsaken ambitions shining on him anew. By loving Taboo he had wasted fifteen years of effort and opened himself to all the indulgent errors of his past, and he wished to God now he'd never done it. Then, remembering how dreamlike everything had seemed, he had the thought that maybe it *hadn't* happened, that it had been a hallucination brought on by the liver punch. But recalling how it had felt to make love, the womanly fervor of Taboo's moves, he decided it had to have been real. And real or not, he had lived it, he was suffering for it.

When he reached the shooting gallery he sat cross-legged on his mattress, heavy with despair. His back ached something fierce. Pete was angry with him for being late, but on seeing his discomfort he limped upstairs and brought down a needle and helped him fix. "What happened to ya?" he asked, and Buddha said it wasn't nothin', just a muscle spasm.

"Don't gimme that shit," said Pete. "You get hit by a goddamn car, and you be tellin' me it ain't 'bout nothin'." He shook his head ruefully. "Well, to hell wit' ya! I'm sick of worryin' 'bout ya!"

Buddha began to feel drowsy and secure there on his mattress, and he thought if he could rid himself of the love that Taboo had imparted to him, things might be better than before. Clearer, emptier. But he couldn't think how to manage it. Then he saw the opportunity that the old man presented, the need for affection he embodied, his hollow heart.

Pete turned to go back up the stairs, and Buddha said, "Hey, Pete!"

"Yeah, what?"

"I love you, man," said Buddha, and sent his love in a focused beam of such strength that he shivered as it went out of him.

Pete looked at him, perplexed. His expression changed to one of pleasure, then to annoyance. "You *love* me? Huh? Man, you been hangin' out with that faggot too much, that's what you been doin'!" He clumped a couple of steps higher and stopped. "Don't bother comin' upstairs for your goodnighter," he said in gentler tones. "I'll send it down wit' somebody."

"'Preciate it," said Buddha.

He watched Pete round the corner of the stairwell, then lay down on the mattress. He was so free of desire and human connections that the instant he closed his eyes, golden pinpricks bloomed behind his lids, opened into Africa, and he was flying across the grasslands faster than ever, flying on the wings of the pain that beat like a sick heart in his back. The antelope did not run away but stared at him with wet, dark eyes, and the stick figures of those who guarded the village saluted him with their spears. The shadows of the masked women danced with the abandon of black flames, and in one of the huts a bearded old man was relating the story of a beautiful young woman who had driven a white car south to Miami and had lived wild for a time, had inspired a thousand men to greater wildness, had married and . . . Buddha flew onward, not wanting to hear the end of the story, knowing that the quality of the beginning was what counted, because all stories ended the same. He was satisfied that Taboo's beginning had been worthwhile. He soared low above the green mountains, low enough to hear the peaceful chants of the gorillas booming through the hidden valleys, and soon was speeding above the lake wherein the solitary fish swam a slow and celebratory circle, arrowing toward the mists on its far side, toward those hallucinatory borders that he previously had neither the necessary courage nor clarity to cross.

From behind him sounded a distant pounding that he recognized to be someone knocking on the door of the shooting gallery, summoning him to his duty. For an instant he had an urge to turn back, to reinhabit the world of the senses, of bluesy-souled hookers and wired white kids and punks who came around looking to trade a night's muscle work for a fix. And that urge intensified when he heard Pete shouting, "Hey, Buddha! Ain't you gon' answer the goddamn door?" But before he could act upon his impulse, he penetrated the mists and felt himself irresistibly drawn by their mysterious central whiteness, and he knew that when old Pete came downstairs, still shouting his angry question, the only answer he would receive would be an almost impalpable pulse in the air like the vibration of a gong whose clangor had just faded beneath the threshold of hearing, the pure signal struck from oblivion, the fanfare announcing Buddha's dominion over the final country of the mind.

CHARLES BEAUMONT

Appointment with Eddie

In the early 1960s Charles Beaumont was considered perhaps the most brilliantly talented of all the writers whose works could be considered horror, fantasy, or science fiction, in the sense that *The Twilight Zone* television series was all of the above. He died far too young, but he left a legacy of wonderful stories, tales that could terrify, amaze, or merely baffle the reader with their sensitive, insightful intelligence.

A previously unpublished Beaumont story is a special treat because it's so rare. This one could have been written by Harlan Ellison in his "Hollywood" years. It's about the elusive thing we call success, and the people who seek it all their lives, no matter how much they accomplish in the world.

—E. D.

APPOINTMENT WITH EDDIE

Charles Beaumont

It was one of those bars that strike you blind when you walk in out of the sunlight, but I didn't need eyes, I could see him, the way deaf people can hear trumpets. It was Shecky, all right. But it also wasn't Shecky.

He was alone.

I'd known him for eight years, worked with him, traveled with him, lived with him; I'd put him to bed at night and waked him up in the morning; but never, in all that time, never once had I seen him by himself—not even in a bathtub. He was plural. A multitude of one. And now, the day after his greatest triumph, he was alone, here, in a crummy little bar on Third Avenue.

There was nothing to say, so I said it. "How are you, Sheck?"

He looked up and I could tell he was three-quarters gone. That meant he'd put away a dozen Martinis, maybe more. But he wasn't drunk. "Sit down," he said, softly, and that's when I stopped worrying and started getting scared. I'd never heard Shecky talk softly before. He'd always had a voice like the busy signal. Now he was practically whispering.

"Thanks for coming." Another first: "Thanks" from Shecky King, to me. I tried to swallow but suddenly my throat was dry, so I waved to the waiter and ordered a double scotch. Of course, my first thought was, he's going to dump me. I'd been expecting it for years. Even though I'd done a good job for him, I wasn't the biggest agent in the business, and to Shecky the biggest always meant the best. But this wasn't his style. I'd seen him dump people before and the way he did it, he made it seem like a favor. Always with Shecky the knife was a present, and he never delivered it personally. So I went to the second thought, but that didn't make any better sense. He was never sick a day in his life. He didn't have time. A broad? No good. The trouble didn't exist that his lawyers, or I, couldn't spring him out of in ten minutes.

I decided to wait. It took most of the drink.

"George," he said, finally, "I want you to lay some candor on me."

You know the way he talked. "I want you to lay it on hard and fast. No thinking. Dig?"

"Dig," I said, getting dryer in the throat.

He picked up one of the five full Martini glasses in front of him and finished it in one gulp. "George," he said, "am I a success?"

The highest-paid, most acclaimed performer in show business, the man who had smashed records at every club he's played for five years, who had sold over two million copies of every album he'd ever cut, who had won three Emmys and at least a hundred other awards, who had, in the opinion of the people *and* the critics, reached the top in a dozen fields —this man, age thirty-six, was asking me if he was a success.

"Yes," I said.

He killed another Martini. "Candorsville?"

"The place." I thought I was beginning to get it. Some critic somewhere had shot him down. But would he fall in here? No. Not it. Still, it was worth a try.

"Who says you aren't?"

"Nobody. Yet."

"Then what?"

He was quiet for a full minute. I could hardly recognize him sitting there, an ordinary person, an ordinary scared human being.

Then he said, "George, I want you to do something for me."

"Anything," I said. That's what I was being paid for: anything.

"I want you to make an appointment for me."

"Where at?"

"Eddie's."

"Who's Eddie?"

He started sweating. "A barber," he said.

"What's wrong with Mario?"

"Nothing's wrong with Mario."

It wasn't any of my business. Mario Cabianca had been Shecky's personal hair stylist for ten years, he was the best in the business, but I supposed he'd nicked The King or forgotten to laugh at a joke. It wasn't important. It certainly couldn't have anything to do with the problem, whatever it was. I relaxed a little.

"When for?" I asked.

"Now," he said. "Right away."

"Well, you could use a shave."

"Eddie doesn't shave people. He cuts hair. That's all."

"You don't need a haircut."

"George," he said, so soft I could barely hear him, "I never needed anything in all my life like I need this haircut."

"Okay. What's his number?"

"He hasn't got one. You'll have to go in."

Now he was beginning to shake. I've seen a lot of people tremble, but this was the first time I'd seen anybody shake.

"Sheck, are you germed up?"

"No." The Martini sloshed all over his cashmere coat. By the time it got to his mouth only the olive was left. "I'm fine. Just do this for me, George. Please. Do it now."

"Okay, take it easy. What's his address?"

"I can't remember." An ugly sound boiled out of his throat, I guess it was a laugh. "Endsburg! I can't remember. But I can take you there." He started to get up. His belly hit the edge of the table. The ashtrays and glasses tipped over. He looked at the mess, then at his hands, which were still shaking, and he said, "Come on."

"Sheck." I put a hand on his shoulder, which nobody does. "You want to tell me about it?"

"You wouldn't understand," he said.

On the way out, I dropped a twenty in front of the bartender. "Nice to have you, Mr. King," he said, and it was like somebody had turned the volume up on the world. "Me and my old lady, y'know, we wouldn't miss your show for anything." "Yeah," a guy on the last stool said. "God bless ya, buddy!"

We walked out into the sun. Shecky looked dead. His face was white and glistening with sweat. His eyes were red. And the shaking was getting worse.

"This way," he said, and we started down Third.

"You want me to grab a cab?"

"No. It isn't far."

We walked past the pawn shops and the laundries and saloons and the gyms and I found myself breathing through my mouth, out of habit. It had taken me a long time to forget these smells. They weren't just poor smells. They were kiss-it-all-goodbye, I never-had-a-chance smells. Failure smells. What the hell was I doing here, anyway? What was Shecky doing here? Shecky, who carried his Hong Kong silk sheets with him wherever he went because that was the only thing he could stand next to his skin, who kept a carnation in his lapel, who shook hands with his gloves on? I looked down at his hands. They were bare.

We walked another block. At the light I heard a sound like roller skates behind me. A bum without legs stopped at the curb. The sign across the street changed to WALK. I nudged Shecky; it was the kind of thing he appreciated. He didn't even notice. The cripple wiggled his board over the curb and, using the two wooden bricks in his hands, rolled past us. I wondered how he was going to make it back up to the sidewalk, but Shecky didn't. He was thinking of other things.

After two more blocks, deep into the armpit of New York, he slowed down. The shaking was a lot worse. Now his hands were fists.

"There," he said.

Up ahead, five or six doors, was a barber shop. It looked like every other barber shop in this section. The pole outside was cardboard, and most of the paint was gone. The window was dirty. The sign—EDDIE THE BARBER—was faded.

"I'll wait," Shecky said.

"You want a haircut now, is that right?"

"That's right," he said.

"I should give him your name?"

He nodded.

"Sheck, we've known each other a long time. Can't you tell me—"

He almost squeezed a hunk out of my arm. "Go, George," he said. "Go."

I went. Just before I got to the place, I looked back. Shecky was standing alone in front of a tattoo parlor, more alone than ever, more alone than anyone ever. His eyes were closed. And he was shaking all over. I tried to think of him the way he was ten hours ago, surrounded by people, living it up, celebrating the big award; but I couldn't. This was somebody else.

I turned around and walked into the barber shop. It was one of those non-union deals, with a big card reading HAIRCUTS—$1.00 on the wall, over the cash register. It was small and dirty. The floor was covered with hair. In the back, next to a curtain, there was a cane chair and a table with an old radio on it. The radio was turned to a ball game, but you couldn't hear it because of the static. The far wall was papered with calendars. Most of them had naked broads on them, but a few had hunting and fishing scenes. They were all coated with grease and dirt.

There wasn't anything else, except one old-fashioned barber chair and, behind it, a sink and a cracked glass cabinet.

A guy was in the chair, getting a haircut. He had a puffy face and a nose full of broken blood vessels. You could smell the cheap wine across the room.

Behind the bum was maybe the oldest guy I'd ever seen outside a hospital. He stood up straight, but his skin looked like a blanket somebody had dropped over a hat-rack. It had that yellow look old skin gets. It made you think of coffins.

Neither of them noticed me, so I stood there a while, watching. The barber wasn't doing anything special. He was cutting hair, the old way, with a lot of scissors-clicking in the air. I knew a bootblack once who did the same thing. He said he was making the rag talk. But he gave it up, he said, because nobody was listening any more. The bum in the chair wasn't listening, either, he was sound asleep, so there had to be a lot more. But you couldn't see it.

I walked over to the old man. "Are you Eddie?"

He looked up and I saw that his eyes were clear and sharp. "That's right," he said.

"I'd like to make an appointment."

His voice was like dry leaves blowing down the street. "For yourself?"

"No. A friend."

I felt nervous and embarrassed and it came to me, then, that maybe this whole thing was a gag. A practical joke. Except that it didn't have any point.

"What is his name?"

"Shecky King."

The old man went back to clipping the bum's hair. "You'll have to wait until I'm finished," he said. "Just have a seat."

I went over and sat down. I listened to the static and the clicking scissors and I tried to figure things out. No good. Shecky could buy this smelly little place with what he gave away in tips on a single night. He had the best barber in the business on salary. Yet there he was, down the street, standing in the hot sun, waiting for me to make an appointment with this feeble old man.

The clicking stopped. The bum looked at himself in the mirror, nodded and handed a crumpled dollar bill to the barber. The barber took it over to the cash register and rang it up.

"Thank you," he said.

The bum belched. "Next month, same time," he said.

"Yes, sir."

The bum walked out.

"Now then," the old man said, flickering those eyes at me. "The name again?"

He had to be putting me on. There wasn't anybody who didn't know Shecky King. He was like Coca-Cola, or sex. I even saw an autographed picture of him in an igloo, once.

"Shecky King," I said, slowly. There wasn't any reaction. The old man walked back to the cash register, punched the NO SALE button and took a dog-eared notebook out of the drawer.

"He'd like to come right away," I told him.

The old man stared at the book a long time, holding it close to his face. Then he shut it and put it back in the drawer and closed the drawer.

"I'm sorry," he said.

"What do you mean?"

"I don't have an opening."

I looked around the empty shop. "Yeah, I can see, business is booming."

He smiled.

"Seriously," I said.

He went on smiling.

"Look, I haven't got the slightest idea why Mr. King wants to have his hair cut here. But he does. So let's stop horsing around. He's willing to pay for it."

I reached into my left pocket and pulled out the roll. I found a twenty. "Maybe you ought to take another look at your appointment book," I said.

The old man didn't make a move. He just stood there, smiling. For some reason—the lack of sleep, probably, the running around, the worry—I felt a chill go down my back, the kind that makes goosepimples.

"Okay," I said. "How much?"

"One dollar," he said. "After the haircut."

That made me sore. I didn't actually grab his shirt, but it would have gone with my voice. "Look," I said, "this is important. I shouldn't tell you this, but Shecky's outside right now, down the street, waiting. He's all ready. You're not doing anything. Couldn't you—"

"I'm sorry," the old man said, and the way he said it, in that dry, creaky voice, I could almost believe him.

"Well, what about later this afternoon?"

He shook his head.

"Tomorrow?"

"No."

"Then *when*, for Chrissake?"

"I'm afraid I can't say."

"What the hell do you mean, you can't say? Look in the book!"

"I already have."

Now I was mad enough to belt the old wreck. "You're trying to tell me you're booked so solid you can't work in one lousy haircut?"

"I'm not trying to tell you anything."

He was feeble-minded, he had to be. I decided to lay off the yelling and humor him. "Look, Eddie . . . you're a businessman, right? You run this shop for money. Right?"

"Right," he said, still smiling.

"Okay. You say you haven't got an opening. I believe you. Why should you lie? No reason. It just means you're a good barber. You've got loyalty to your customers. Good. Fine. You know what that is? That's integrity. And there isn't anything I admire more than integrity. You don't see much of it in my business. I'm an agent. But here's the thing, Eddie—I can call you Eddie, can't I?"

"That's my name."

"Here's the thing. I wouldn't have you compromise your integrity for anything in the world. But there's a way out. What time do you close?"

"Five p.m."

"On the dot, right? Swell. Now listen, Eddie. If you could stay just half an hour after closing time, until five-thirty, no later, I could bring Shecky in and he could get his haircut and everybody would be happy. What do you say?"

"I never work overtime," he said.

"I don't blame you. Why *should* you, a successful businessman? Very smart, Eddie. Really. I agree with that rule a hundred per cent. Never work overtime. But, hear me out, now—there's an exception that proves every rule. Am I right? If you'll stretch a point here, this one time, it'll prove the rule, see, and also put some numbers on your savings account. Eddie, if you'll do this thing, I will personally see to it that you receive one hundred dollars."

"I'm sorry," he said.

"For a half-hour's work?" A cockroach ran across the wall. Eddie watched it. "Two hundred," I said. It was still fifty bucks shy of what Shecky was paying Mario every week, whether he worked or not, but I figured what the hell.

"No."

"Five hundred!" I could see it wasn't any good, but I had to try. A soldier keeps on pulling the trigger even when he knows he's out of bullets, if he's mad enough, or scared enough.

"I don't work overtime," the old man said.

A last pull of the trigger. "One thousand dollars. Cash."

No answer.

I stared at him for a few seconds, then I turned around and walked out of the shop. Shecky was standing where I'd left him, and he was looking at me, so I put on the know-nothing face. As I walked toward him I thought, he's got to dump me. Any agent who can't get Shecky King an appointment with a crummy Third Avenue barber deserves to be dumped.

"Well?" he said.

"The guy's a nut."

"You mean he won't take me."

"I mean he's a nut. A kook. Not a soul in the place and, get this—he says he can't find an opening!"

You ever see a man melt? I never had. Now I was seeing it. Shecky King was melting in front of me, right there on the sidewalk in front of the tattoo parlor.

"You okay?"

He couldn't answer. The tears were choking him.

"Sheck? You okay?"

I saw a cab and waved it over. Shecky was trying to catch his breath, trying not to cry, but nothing worked for him. He stood there weaving and bawling and melting. Then he started beating his fists against the brick wall.

"God damn it!" he screamed, throwing his head back. "God damn it! God damn it!"

Then, suddenly, he pulled away from me, eyes wide, hands bleeding, and broke into a run toward the barber shop.

"Hey," the cabbie said, "ain't that Shecky King?"

"I don't know," I said, and ran after him.

I tried to stop him, but you don't stop a crazy man, not when you're half his size and almost twice his age. He threw the door open and charged inside.

"Eddie!" His voice sounded strangled, like a hand was around his throat, cutting off the air. Or a rope. "Eddie, what have I got to do?"

The old man didn't even look up. He was reading a newspaper.

"Tell me!" Shecky pounded the empty barber chair with his bloody fists.

"Please be careful of the leather," the old man said.

"I'm a success!" Shecky yelled. "I qualify! Tell him, George! Tell him about last night!"

"What do you care what this crummy—"

"*Tell him!*"

I walked over and pulled the newspaper out of the old man's hands. "Last night Shecky King was voted the most popular show business personality of all time," I said.

"Tell him who voted!"

"The newspaper and magazine critics," I said.

"And who else?"

"Thirty million people throughout the world."

"You hear that? Everybody. Eddie, don't you hear what he's saying? Everybody! I'm Number One!"

Shecky climbed onto the chair and sat down.

"Haircut," he said. "Easy on the sides. Just a light trim. You know."

He sat there breathing hard for a couple of seconds, then he twisted around and screamed at the old man. "Eddie! For God's sake, cut my hair!"

"I'm sorry," the old man said. "I don't have an opening at the moment."

You know what happened to Shecky King. You read about it. I knew, and I read about it, too, six months before the papers came out. In his eyes. I could see the headline there. But I thought I could keep it from coming true.

I took him home in a cab and put him to bed. He didn't talk. He didn't even cry. He just laid there, between the Hong Kong silk sheets, staring up at the ceiling, and for some crazy reason that made me think of the legless guy and the sign that said WALK. I was pretty tired.

The doctors ordered him to a hospital, but they couldn't find anything wrong, not physically anyway, so they called in the shrinks. A breakdown, the shrinks said. Nervous exhaustion. Emotional depletion. It happens.

It happens, all right, but I wasn't sold. Shecky was like a racing car, he operated best at high revs. That's the way some people are engineered. A nice long rest is a nice long death to them, because it gives them a chance to think, and for a performer that's the end. He sees what a stupid waste his life had been, working 24 hours a day so that people can laugh at him, or cry at him, running all the time—for what? Money. Praise. But he's got the money (if he didn't he wouldn't be able to afford the rest) and he's had the praise, and he hasn't really enjoyed what he's been doing for years—is it intellectual? does it contribute to the world? does it help anybody?—so he figures, why go on running? Why bother? Who cares? And he stops running. He gives it all up. And they let him out of the hospital, because now he's cured.

A lot of reasons why I didn't want this to happen to Shecky. He wasn't my friend—who can be friends with a multitude?—but he was an artist, and that meant he brought a lot of happiness to a lot of people. Of course he brought some unhappiness, too, maybe more than most, but that's the business. Talent never was enough. It is if you're a painter, or a book writer, maybe, but even there *chutzpah* counts. Shecky had it. Like the old story, he could have murdered both his parents and then thrown himself on the mercy of the court on the grounds that he was an orphan. And he could have gotten away with it.

The fact is, the truth is, he didn't have anything *except chutzpah*. His routines were written by other people. His singing was dubbed. His albums were turned out by the best conductors around. His movies and

TV plays were put together like jigsaw puzzles out of a million blown takes. His books were ghosted.

But I say, anybody who can make out the way Shecky King made out, on the basis of nothing but personality and drive, that person is an artist.

Also, I was making close to a hundred grand a year off him.

What's the difference? I wanted him to pull out of it. The shrinks weren't worried. They said the barber was only "a manifestation of the problem." Not a cause. An effect. It meant that Shecky felt guilty about his success and was trying to re-establish contact with the common people.

I didn't ask them to explain why, if that was true, the barber refused to cut Shecky's hair. It would only have confused them.

Anyway, I knew they were wrong. Shecky was in the hospital because of that old son of a bitch on Third Avenue and not because of anything else.

All the next day I tried to piece it together, to make sense out of it, but I couldn't. So I started asking around. I didn't really expect an answer, and I didn't get one, until the next night. I was working on a double scotch on the rocks, thinking about the money we would be making if Shecky was at the Winter Garden right now, when a guy came in. You'd know him—a skinny Italian singer, very big. He walked over and put a hand on my neck. "I heard about Sheck," he said. "Tough break." Then, not because he gave a damn about Shecky but because I'd done him a few favors when he needed them, he asked me to join his party, and I did. Another double scotch on the rocks and I asked if he'd ever heard of Eddie the barber. It was like asking him if he'd ever heard of girls.

"Tell me about it," I said.

He did. Eddie had been around, he said, forever. He was a fair barber, no better and no worse than any other, and he smelled bad, and he was creepy; but he was The End. I shouldn't feel bad about not knowing this, because I was one of the Out people. There were In people and Out people and the In people didn't talk about Eddie. They didn't talk about a lot of things.

"Why is he The End?" I asked.

Because he only takes certain people, my friend said. Because he's selective. Because he's exclusive.

"I was in his shop. He had a lousy wino bum in the chair!"

With that lousy wino bum, I was told, three-fourths of the big names in show business would trade places. Money didn't matter to Eddie, he would never accept more than a dollar. Clothes didn't matter, or reputation, or influence.

"Then what *does* matter?"

He didn't know. Nobody knew. Eddie never said what his standards were, in fact, he never said he *had* any standards. Either he had an opening or he didn't, that was all you got.

I finished off the scotch. Then I turned to my friend. "Has he ever cut *your* hair?"

"Don't ask," he said.

I had a tough time swallowing it until I talked to a half-dozen other Names. Never mind who they were. They verified the story. A haircut from Eddie meant Success. Until you sat in that chair, no matter what else had happened to you, you were nothing. Your life was nothing. Your future was nothing.

"And you go for this jazz?" I asked all of them the same question. They all laughed and said, "Hell, no! It's those other nuts!" But their eyes said something different.

It was fantastic. Everybody who was anybody in the business knew about Eddie, and everybody was surprised that I did. As though, I'd mentioned the name of the crazy uncle they kept locked in the basement, or something. A lot of them got sore, a few even broke down and cried. One of them said that if I doubted Eddie's pull I should think about the Names who had knocked themselves off at the top of their success, no reason ever given, except the standard one. I should think about those Names real hard. And I did, remembering that headline in Shecky's eyes.

It fit together, finally, when I got to a guy who used to know Shecky in the old days, when he was a 20th mail boy named Sheldon Hochstrasser. He wanted to be In more than he wanted anything else, but he didn't know where In was. So he stuck close to the actors and the directors and he heard them talking about Eddie. One of them had just got an appointment and he saw that now he could die happy because he knew he had made it. Shecky was impressed. It gave him something to work towards, something to hang onto. From that point on, his greatest ambition was to get an appointment with Eddie.

He was smart about it, though. At least he thought he was. You don't get a good table at Chasen's, or Romanoff's, he said to himself, and to his buddy, unless you're somebody. For Eddie, he went on, you've got to be more. You've got to be a *success*. So the thing to do was to succeed.

He gave himself fifteen years.

Fifteen years later, to the day I'll bet, I met him at that bar on Third Avenue. Either he'd been thinking about Eddie all that time or he hadn't thought about him at all. I don't know which.

I turned the tap up, then, because he wasn't getting any better. I found out the ones who had made it and talked to them, but they weren't any help. They didn't know why they were In or even how long they'd stay. That was the lousy part of it: you could get cancelled. And putting in a word for Shecky wouldn't do any good, they said, because Eddie made his own decisions.

I still had a hard time getting it down. I'd been around for fifty-four years and I hadn't met anything like this, or even close to it. A Status Symbol makes a little sense if it's the Nobel Prize or a Rolls Royce, but a *barber*! Insanity, even for show business people.

I started out with money and didn't make it, but that didn't mean he didn't have a price. I figured everybody could be bought. Maybe not with dollars, but with something.

I thought of the calendars on the wall. They're supposed to be for the customers, but I wondered, are they? You never knew about these old guys.

I found the wildest broad in New York and told her how she could earn two grand in one evening. She said yes.

Eddie said no.

I told him if he'd play along, I'd turn over a check for one million dollars to his favorite charity.

No.

I threatened him.

He smiled.

I begged him.

He said he was sorry.

I asked him why. Just tell me why, I said.

"I don't have an opening," he said.

Two weeks and two dozen tries later, I went back to the hospital. The Most Popular Show Business Personality of All Time was still lying in the bed, still staring at the ceiling.

"He'll give you an appointment," I said.

He shook his head.

"I'm telling you, Sheck. I just talked with him. He'll give you an appointment."

He looked at me. "When?"

"As soon as he finds an opening."

"He won't find an opening."

"Don't be stupid, Sheck. You're just nervous. The guy's busy all the time. I was there. He's got people lined up halfway down the street."

"Eddie's never busy," he said.

Christ, I had to try, didn't I? "I was there, Sheck!"

"Then you know," he said. "Eddie's kind of customer, you don't get many. Just a few. Just a few, George." He turned his head away. "I'm not one of them."

"Well, maybe not now, Sheck, but some day. You can talk to him . . . ask him what he wants you to do. I mean, he's got to have a reason!"

"He's got a reason, George."

"What is it?"

"Don't you know?"

"No! You've stepped on a few heads, sure, but who hasn't? You don't get to the top by helping old ladies across the street. You've got to fight your way up there, everybody does, and when you fight, people get hurt."

"Yeah," he said, "you know," and for a second I thought I did. I sat there looking at him for a long time, then I went out and got drunker than hell.

They called me the next morning. I was in bad shape but I had my suit on so it only took fifteen minutes to get to the hospital.

It was a circus already. I pushed through the cops and the reporters and went into the room.

He was still lying on the bed, still staring up at the ceiling, looking no different from the way I'd left him. Except for the two deep slashes in his wrists, the broken glass and the blood. There was a lot of that. It covered the Hong Kong silk sheets and the rug and even parts of the wall.

"What made him do it?" somebody said.

"Overwork," I said.

The papers played it that way. Only a few guys knew the dirt, and they were paid for, so Shecky was turned into a martyr. I forget what to. His public, I think. I have most of the clippings. "In his efforts to bring joy to the people of the world, The King went beyond the limits of his endurance; he had gone beyond ordinary human limits long before . . ." "He had no ambition other than to continue entertaining his fans . . ." "Following the old show business motto, 'Always leave 'em laughing,' Shecky King departed this world at the height of his popularity. No other performer has ever matched his success . . ." "He is a legend now, the man who had everything and gave everything . . ."

I don't think about it much any more.

I just lie awake nights and thank God that I'm bald.

WILLIAM KOTZWINKLE

Fragments of Papyrus from the Temple of the Older Gods

William Kotzwinkle is a writer who effortlessly crosses over the line between fantasy and realism and back again in his many novels and collections of short fiction. Twice winner of the National Magazine Award for Fiction, and of the World Fantasy Award, Kotzwinkle's work includes *Christmas at Fontaine's, Queen of Swords, Nightbook, Elephant Bangs Train, Swimmer in the Secret Seas,* and the cult favorite *The Fan Man.* Of particular interest to fantasy readers are his novels. *Doctor Rat, Fata Morgana*, and Kotzwinkle's splendid collection of original fairy tales for children, *Hearts of Wood*, illustrated by Joe Servello. "Fragments of Papyrus from the Temple of the Older Gods" is a thoughtful, magical tale from one of the most original writers to grace the fantasy field.

—T. W.

FRAGMENTS OF PAPYRUS FROM THE TEMPLE OF THE OLDER GODS

William Kotzwinkle

"And how long will you be staying in our Tomb City, Majesty?" asked the Chief Architect.

"We must leave tomorrow," said Pharaoh, sucking spiced beer through a straw. "A thousand tasks await me."

The Pharaoh's Chief Praiser hiccuped silently, then spoke from his place at the banquet table. "His Majesty's work is never done, his works are many and profound. This is our Leader, our Chief, without defect, sublime in his intent—"

The Chief Praiser's solemn incantation ceased as the dancing girls entered the party room and began their Moon Configurations, each girl representing one phase of the night-jewel. Punctuating the sound of their ankle bells came the distant sound of the whip, cracking even in the night, over the heads of the slave workers toiling in the City of Pharaoh's Tomb.

"We've made great progress since your last visit, sire," said the Chief Architect, nodding toward the whip sounds.

"He has given us slaves," chanted the Chief Praiser. "Thousands has he smote and put in chains. This is our ruler, provided with flames, far-reaching of hand, generous, astute, wise as the sun, purified in his nest—"

"Purified in my nest?" Pharaoh lifted his eyebrow.

"It is an accepted laudation, Your Majesty," said the Chief Praiser, putting on a wounded expression.

Pharaoh shook his head, indicating wonder, but the Chief Praiser was allowed to continue.

His chanting was drowned out, however, by the cackling laughter of Pharaoh's dwarf, who ran among the dancing girls, swinging a toy mummy at the end of a string and making lewd comments. The delicate Moon Configurations were spoiled, the dancing girls tripping and squealing as they were struck by the mummy.

"What a disgusting little man," said the Chief Architect's wife. "If I may say so, Your Majesty."

"Oh, yes, quite," said Pharaoh. "Quite disgusting." Pharaoh sat back in his seat, his shoulder stiff from bow practice. He rubbed it gingerly, and the Chief Praiser, seeing the soreness, rushed to incorporate it in his litany.

"Master of the compound bow, suffering to learn all martial arts in the protection of his people . . ."

The Chief Praiser rose from his seat, slightly drunk and feeling the winds of inspiration whirling him upward. Attempting to forge one of the great chains of praise, he waved his arms outward over Pharaoh's head. ". . . Lord of the Solar Barque, a cloud of divinity, a never-setting star who never sinned, the bull of terror to his foe, who possesses all things, quicker than the greyhound, soul of mankind, who rescued our kingdom in times of violence, who has destroyed evil, who . . ."

The Chief Praiser fell into a fatal pause but started up again quickly. ". . . who is the double Lion God, who throws excrement in the face of his enemies, who never stole milk from a child—"

"That will do for now, Chief Praiser. Rest yourself." Pharaoh turned to the Chief Architect and said quietly, "He's good for about an hour of solid praise, and then he starts grasping at straws." Pharaoh reached for his beer, and the pain in his right arm struck again, down the length of it and across his chest.

"Are you ill, sire?"

"No, I am not but tell me, who is that guest over there? I do not recognize him from my own ranks."

Pharaoh pointed to a tall man in a white robe, whose manners were perfect, who spoke to no one, who placed a cup to his lips.

"Which man, Your Majesty?"

"There, he turns toward me. He wears a red stone at his throat."

The Chief Architect cast his gaze where Pharaoh's finger pointed. "But I see no such man, Majesty."

"He carries a papyrus roll. How strange his skin is—he's been burned at the neck. Observe, Architect, if you have eyes in your head, his skin is like a reptile's."

"Sire . . ." The Chief Architect's face filled with concern. He signaled the Fan Bearers to increase the air current about the Pharaoh's brow.

"You don't see the noble lord approaching me?" asked Pharaoh, staring straight at the man, who was now standing but a few feet from the banquet table, a faint smile on his lips.

"No, sire."

Pharaoh looked quickly to his dwarf, who stood mouth open, eyes wide in terror, his gaze where Pharaoh's was.

"What do you see?" snapped the ruler.

"A shadow," answered the dwarf. He turned abruptly, running away on his deformed legs, dragging his little toy mummy behind him.

"So," said Pharaoh, rising to receive the honored guest.

"I must touch you, Your Majesty," said the guest.

Pharaoh extended his hand, and the guest's leathery finger touched him lightly. An enormous stone fell from the firmament, and Pharaoh felt its cold edge crushing his chest. The banquet room dimmed. His doctors were surrounding him. The honored guest was leaving, through a rear door, past the spear-holding guards.

A second slab of granite fell, filling the pores of Pharaoh's body with stone, and the banquet room was no longer visible.

Instead Pharaoh dimly beheld the interior of his great tomb and saw his gathered people and heard his final praises being sung. ". . . this was our Great King, the Perfect Cleansed One, who has gone to his horizon. . . ."

The Chief Praiser spoke, and the two lands were filled with crying.

"He goes up the smoke of the great exhalation. Mighty in life, he is thousandfold mighty in death. Discernment is placed at his feet. He has captured the horizon. We, his willing servants, go with him, into darkness, with the prayer that we may join him on his voyage upon the Solar Barque."

Pharaoh saw his dwarf being dragged to the tomb, filthy little heels digging in against the sand, but the dwarf was no match for the soldiers, and they hurled him into the crypt.

The Chief Praiser and the Chief Praiser's wife entered of their own accord, and then a third slab of stone came down on Pharaoh's soul, settling into place with a sound that reverberated endlessly, a thousand thunders echoing across the sky.

Pharaoh was entombed.

Out of the dark density of the night-stone, he perceived a ray of light growing ever brighter and more splendid. It dissolved the hard edges of the stone, turning the stone to dark water. The heaviness that had surrounded and crushed him became a warm bath.

He stood upon the shore of a black Nile.

There was no palace, no houses, no fields of waving grain. There was a black Nile and a golden ship. The ship came slowly over the water; strange and beautiful lights emanated from the hull, sweeping the surface of the black Nile.

Pharaoh waited on the shore as the ship came near, and all was in stillness except for the lapping of the black waves. The ship sent forth a white beam of light that crossed the water and touched the shore at his feet.

He stepped upon it and found it firm enough to hold his spirit body.

The ship was deserted, moving under a mysterious and silent power. Pharaoh wandered the decks, which were made of a finely woven substance, luminous and pulsating. While studying its peculiarities, he discovered that his own body was made of the same substance—a dancing light of gold with a fringe of emerald green.

Entering the captain's cabin he found it luxuriously appointed but deserted. The ship nonetheless kept a straight course over the dark waters. As the furnishings of the boat were first-class, he felt that all was proceeding according to divine plan and that he, as the Son of Heaven, would soon reach his eternal home. He relaxed upon a soft white couch and watched the dark shore flow by.

To his surprise, another craft appeared out of the darkness—a tiny canoe, primitive in the extreme.

What was such a vulgar vessel doing on the divine waterway? Pharaoh walked out on deck to investigate. Leaning against the rail, he peered out across the water and discovered that it was his dwarf in the canoe, furiously paddling.

Pharaoh attempted a greeting and found that his mouth was closed tight. He strained to open it but found he could not. He waved his arms, trying to attract the dwarf's attention, for the little fellow would be amusing to have onboard.

The dwarf saw the signal, stopped paddling for a moment, and stared at Pharaoh. Pharaoh gave another commanding wave.

The dwarf answered with an obscene gesture and resumed paddling, off down a dark, silent tributary.

Pharaoh stood dumbfounded at the rail.

I gave him the finest tomb in the world, and he gives me insult. Should we meet again in this dark world, I'll pay the pygmy back, or I'm not the All Gracious One.

Pharaoh, still puzzling about the ingratitude of slaves, found a flight of stairs leading to a galley of the boat. He descended them, attracted by the aroma of cooking soup. Following his nose, he opened a door and was astounded to see the Chief Praiser and his wife inside, at the stove, cooking supper.

"Your Majesty, how wonderful to see you again!" The Chief Praiser leapt up, praising and bowing. "We're honored, honored. Please be seated, O ruler of nations, O sanctified dispenser of happiness."

Pharaoh pointed to his mouth, which he could not open.

"Your mouth is closed up, Majesty? But of course, of course. Sire, please let me open it for you. I found the instrument our first night onboard."

The Chief Praiser went to the corner of the galley and brought forth a piece of wood shaped into a ram's head, crowned by a snake. "If you'll allow me, sire . . ."

The Chief Praiser placed the snake's head on the lips of Pharaoh and pried them open, along with his teeth.

"There you are, Highness. *The dead shall speak*, as the saying goes, only a matter of finding the right tool."

"How came you to be aboard my solar craft?" asked Pharaoh, not unkindly, for he was grateful to the Chief Praiser for that little trick of opening the mouth.

"Your craft, Majesty?" The Chief Praiser looked puzzled.

"Yes," said Pharaoh. "I'm merely curious, Chief Praiser. Believe me when I say I'm happy to have you and your wife onboard my eternal ship."

"Your Majesty is joking, as always," said the Chief Praiser. "Your tongue is subtle, swift, speaks in riddling wonders, has a thousand currents, is never tired—"

"Chief Praiser, an answer, please."

"Majesty, there is some small misunderstanding—mine, of course. I cannot follow your lightning-fast implications, cannot discern the delicacy of your reasoning. I can only say that this humble craft is the spiritual property of my wife and I. There, as you can see, upon the walls is written the history of our life. You'll find it upon this wall and all the walls. This poor ship bears all the traces of our time on Earth, Majesty, where we served humbly in your magnificent court."

The Chief Praiser scraped, bowed a little, and concluded: "In no way could this simple ship be called your Solar Barque, Majesty. Such a thing is laughable. Your solar craft is made of blinding light, is filled with magical garlands, is attended by countless goddesses.

"*Isis and Nephtys salute thee, they sing unto thee in thy boat hymns of joy.* You are the ruler of the gods, Majesty, and your boat is beyond description." The Chief Praiser rapped his hand against the cupboard of the galley. "We have here a sturdy vessel, a good little craft, but a Solar Barque? Never, Majesty, never."

Pharaoh reflected in himself over this peculiar turn of events, then turned to the walls of the galley where the inscriptions were written in glowing azure letters. Indeed they did describe the life of the Chief Praiser and his wife. So must the inscriptions on deck, which he'd seen on first boarding but hadn't bothered to read, for he was accustomed to thinking that all such inscriptions naturally referred to his own glorious self.

Where, then, he asked himself quietly, *is my boat? Did I miss it?*

He turned to the Chief Praiser.

"Yes, of course, Chief Praiser, as you say, your boat indeed. And a fine boat it is. I wanted to extend my blessing to it, wanted to sanctify it with my presence, in gratitude for the wonderful service you gave me all through life."

"I'm deeply touched, Majesty," said the Chief Praiser, fawning slightly as he laid out two golden soup bowls. "We have here a soup of some delicacy, if you would care to join me."

"Happy to, Chief Praiser, happy," said Pharaoh, who, now that his mouth was open, saw no reason not to fill it. He sat down at the emerald table and tucked a napkin under his chin. "You didn't happen to actually . . . see the Solar Barque around anywhere, did you?" he asked.

"No, Majesty, I didn't." The Chief Praiser ladled out the soup with a golden spoon. "There's no trouble with it, is there, sire?"

"No, no, certainly not. I was just wondering—what you thought of it, how you liked the style. She's a magnificent boat, makes wonderful time. I sent it on ahead when I saw your boat. I said to Isis, 'There's the Chief Praiser's boat, and I wish to travel in it, for the Chief Praiser is the finest of men.' "

"Majesty, there are tears of joy in my eyes and in those of my wife."

The Chief Praiser's wife lowered her head, her eyes appearing to be filled not with joy but with hunger.

"Your wife is very silent, Chief Praiser. Is there some trouble?"

The Chief Praiser spooned soup to his lips. "She's still upset over being suffocated in your tomb, and as I would rather not listen to her complaints, Your Majesty, I have not opened her mouth. If you know what's good for you, sire, I would advise you to allow the situation to remain so."

Pharaoh spent the remainder of the voyage walking on deck with the Chief Praiser or snoozing in the empty guest room. The heavenly soup was continually replenished in a mysterious way.

"One of the features on a spiritual boat," said the Praiser. "I suppose they do it much more grandly on the Solar Barque."

"Actually," said Pharaoh nervously. "I prefer the simple fare of your boat."

"You are a man of the people, Majesty. It is your greatness and your glory. I shall praise this aspect of your nature throughout eternity."

Pharaoh signaled an end to the discussion, for references to the Solar Barque put the All Gracious One on edge. It wouldn't do for the Chief Praiser to know that his sovereign was nothing but a stowaway.

This entire affair, reflected Pharaoh, *is typical of the oversight one encounters at the higher levels of government.* When he met with the Divine Hierarchy, he'd set some heads rolling.

Thus did they sail on, until one day they discerned a light in the distance, growing slowly brighter as they approached. The entire river was finally lit with its majestic fire, the celestial radiance of the spiritual sun, toward which many craft were sailing, to Judgment Day, in the Hall of Truth.

"They weigh one's heart in the scale," said the Chief Praiser. "But of course that's just a mere formality for you. As for her"—he pointed at his wife— "I don't know. She frequently lapsed into inattentiveness when I practiced my praising."

His wife's mute face grew fearful. She reached into her robe and brought out her heart—a tiny red vase, which she held up to them. The Chief Praiser laughed scornfully, reached into his own robe, and came out with a dented coin, which he held up to the spiritual sun. "Catches the light nicely, don't you think? Well, in any case, our hearts don't matter, Your Majesty, for we are merely part of your entourage. Your great and glorious heart will gain us our admittance."

"Yes, certainly," said Pharaoh. "To be sure." The sovereign excused himself then, explaining that he wanted to take one last walk around the deck before they reached port.

When he was out of sight behind the wheelhouse, he reached inside his robe. His hand passed through layers of golden weave, which kept parting before him, ever opening. He rummaged around, fished and searched, then tore the robe off and shook it. "There must be some sort of mistake. . . ."

He turned the robe inside out, held it up to the light, examined the sleeves, the cuffs, the lining. But he found no heart. Thus prepared for judgment, he watched somewhat uneasily as the boat docked and a crocodile-headed god motioned him down the gangplank.

NANCY KRESS

Spillage

The reworking of traditional folktales, myths, and fairy tales is a popular literary device that has provided the field of fantasy literature with some of its best works, from T. H. White's retelling of Arthurian myths to Angela Carter's sensual recasting of familiar fairy tales. Nancy Kress adds to this list with an original and chilling exploration of a story we all know so well. . . .

Kress's first novel was the delightfully offbeat fantasy *Prince of Morning Bells*. Her most recent is *An Alien Light*. She has published short fiction in numerous magazines and anthologies and won the Nebula Award for short fiction in 1985. Kress lives in upstate New York.

—T. W.

SPILLAGE

Nancy Kress

When the coach broke for the third time, the second coachman was flung sideways over the shrieking axle and down an embankment. He rolled in the moonless darkness, over and over, brambles tearing at the velvet of his livery and whipping across his face. He uttered no sound. There was water at the bottom, a desultory and dirty little stream: the coachman lay in it quietly, blinking in pain at the stars, blood trickling from one temple.

A rat fell on top of him, squeaked once, and scurried off into the brush.

From far above, the coachman heard a sudden feminine cry. It was not repeated, but after a while there came to his dazed ears a muffled sound, not quite footsteps, as if someone were dragging along the road above. *The lady in the coach, or the First Coachman himself*—The sound receded and died, and no other took its place.

He lay in the ditch without moving, at first frightened that some bone might have broken in the darkness without, later more frightened by the greater darkness within. No matter how hard he looked, there was nothing there. Not a name, not a place, not a history.

Only the lady in the coach, and the First Coachman: the lady more beautiful than stars, the First Coachman portly and sharp-eyed as he peered back over his shoulder at his apprentice hanging on behind, to make sure he was doing it right. He had been doing it right. He had stood tall and unsmiling on the perch; the jeweled night had flown past the shining sphere of the coach; the horses' hooves had struck sparks from the stone road. They had passed other coaches, each a glow in the darkness growing to an exhilarating rush of beast and metal, and then the thlock-thlock dying away behind, leaving the scent of perfume and oiled leather, with never a word spoken. And finally the destination: leaping from the perch to let down the carriage steps onto cobblestones so polished they reflected perfect rectangles of yellow light from the windows above.

Lowered eyes and the lady's hand as she alighted, the rustle of silk glimpsed only at the hem, the small gloved hand briefly in his.

I am a coachman, he thought with relief, and searched for something else in the darkness, something more. There was nothing. He was a coachman, and that was all.

Too frightened to move, he lay in the wet ditch until he began to shiver. Water had soaked from velvet to skin. He sat up slowly, holding his head, and crawled out of the stream and back up the embankment. At first he wasn't sure he had reached the top. Sudden darkness, eclipsing the stars, rolled over him like fog.

He crouched by the road, not knowing where it led to, or from. Neither end reached his memory. Cold, bleeding, frightened, the coachman hunkered down into the long grass. His hand touched something nasty: pulpy and wet. He jerked his fingers away and wiped them on his ruined livery.

When dawn came, he saw that it was a shattered pumpkin, and next to it lay a slipper of glass.

The village lay at one end of the stone road. He reached it after hours of walking in the direction opposite to the long skid of coach wheels, his belly rumbling and the midsummer sun too bright and hot in his eyes. When he tried to shade them with one hand, the hand stopped five inches from his face.

A bulky woman drawing water from a well looked up and burst into laughter.

"Oh, I'm sorry, I'm sorry, it's just . . . your nose. . . ." She went off again, backing a little away from him, her gray eyes wide with mirthful fear.

The coachman touched the end of his preposterous nose and opened his mouth to say—what?—and found that he was mute. There were words in his head, but none left through his lips.

The woman stopped laughing as jerkily as she had begun. Too carefully, she set the bucket on the lip of the well and walked closer. She was not young. There were lines around her eyes, and heaviness in the solid set of each foot on the earth. In her voice he heard again the fear. It was the sound of the breaking axle, the brambles on the embankment.

"They're careless up there, sometimes, with the . . . with that. It doesn't always go cleanly. Bits and pieces get . . . spilled over."

He stared at her, having no idea what she meant, saying nothing.

I am a coachman.

As if he had spoken aloud, she said with sudden brutality, "Not anymore you aren't. Not here."

Picking up her bucket, she started toward the village. The coachman stared after her dumbly, hands dangling loose at his sides, belly rumbling. She had gone nearly beyond hearing before calling roughly over her shoulder, "You can go to the baker's. Last house on the left. He needs a man for rough work, and he doesn't. . . . You can ask, anyway. Before you fall over."

She walked away. The weight of the water bucket made her broad hips roll. Hair straggled from its topknot in wispy hanks. Her back bent as if from more than the bucket, as if in pain.

The baker hired him at two pence a week, with as many stale rolls as he could eat and a pallet in the kitchen. After staring a full minute at the coachman's nose, and at his inept gesture that was supposed to indicate dumbness, the baker hardly ever glanced at him again. Monthly the bakery sank a little deeper into the compost of debt; monthly the baker himself became more nearly as silent as his wretched hireling.

The coachman worked all day within an arm's reach of the sagging kitchen hearth, where no one saw him and he saw no one. There he mixed, scrubbed, kneaded, swept, hauled, mended, and baked. He didn't mind the hard labor; he scarcely noticed it. There was an embankment in his mind.

Again and again he sped through the jeweled night, behind the gleaming coach and the silken lady. Again and again came the thlock-thlock of the horses, the lady's hand in his as she stepped onto the cobblestones, the rectangles of yellow light—until the embankment loomed and he fell.

At night the hearth grew cold, and the coachman lay in darkness and breathed in the powdery tickle of floating ash. Sometimes he wondered why he had left the slipper of glass; why he had not taken it with him away from the embankment. There was no answer.

At the end of a month, the woman from the well bustled through the baker's kitchen door, stooping under the splintered lintel. She wore a clean apron and carried a pile of brown cloth.

"I brought you a shirt. Velvet doesn't wear at all, does it? This was my late husband's; you're of a size, I think. Try it."

The coachman did, torn between gratitude and irritation. The brown wool felt clean and warm against his arms. When he saw the woman staring at his thin chest, he turned his back to do up the laces.

"Good enough," she said briskly. "Tomorrow I can bring the breeches. You look queer enough with wool above and velvet below." She laughed, an unmusical booming straight from the belly, then abruptly fell silent.

The coachman had no choice but to be silent.

Finally the woman said, "I'm called Meloria."

The flowery name made her ridiculous. The coachman nodded and smiled, pantomiming thanks for the shirt. He could not have told his name even had he known it. Meloria regained her briskness as abruptly as she had lost it, and bustled out the door. Even without a bucket full of water, she waddled.

The coachman thought of the small gloved hand, a slim ankle beneath lifted silk.

He kneaded the bread.

Meloria came the next day with the brown wool breeches, on the day after that with stout boots. A hat to keep off rain. A sour-grape pie, a plaid blanket, a pillow stuffed with pine needles, a yellow cheese.

"You look like you need this," she would boom, and the coachman, who did need that, would smile weakly and nod two or three times. He was falling off another embankment, or was being pushed. He saw the edge clearly, but not how to avoid it. The shining boots of his livery had fallen apart. The nights had grown colder. When he looked at the sour-grape pie, after weeks of stale rolls, his mouth filled with a savage juice.

After she had gone, he swept the hearth sullenly, not caring that cinders flew up into the air and floated down again, ashy gray snow, on the cooling rolls.

One night he dreamed. After he had lowered the steps to the cobblestones, he turned around to look toward the yellow light. It came from a fortress, windows blazing with candles, gates thrown wide. As he gazed, he felt a touch on his shoulder. It was the lady's hand; she stood behind him, and he could see just the tips of her gloved fingers, delicate as white moths. He turned, her perfume taking him first, to smile on her face.

Moonlight woke him. It fell through the baker's broken window, full on the coachman's face. Blinking into that cold and colorless light, he saw a rat creep along the hearth. Its fur was matted in mangy patches around an open sore. The coachman leapt up and began flailing at it with the poker, murderous despairing blows he did not understand, nor try to. The rat screamed and escaped between damp stones, but not before the poker struck the last third of its tail and smeared it, hairless and pulpy pink, across the floor. The poker clanged and dented.

The coachman sank to his knees and noiselessly wept.

In midwinter the kingdom held a festival. Even in this mean village, under the hunger moon, there were feasts and fires and the pervasive scent of wine mulled with spices.

"Sundown. At Meloria's," the baker growled at noon on the second day of the festival. The coachman, who was breaking the ice on a pail of water and who had all but forgotten what the baker's voice sounded like, looked up in surprise.

"She says," the baker said, and smirked.

The coachman shook his head.

I am a coachman.

The baker smirked again.

Nonetheless, he went. The night was clear and star-sharp, the ashes in the hearth had gone cold, the whole village smelled of cooking, and in Meloria's cottage window shone a yellow light.

"I'm glad you've come," Meloria said, and handed him a cup of steaming wine, red and hot in his bare hands. "Drink to midwinter's passing!"

He did. They ate, a greedy sating with meat pies, new bread, fruits stewed in wine and honey, gravy and fowl and soup and ripe cheeses and wine, always wine, more wine.

"Drink to midwinter," Meloria said.

While they ate, there was no talk. Juice ran down their chins, rich grease slicked their fingers, succulent skin crackled in their teeth. When they had finished and the table lay stained and bone-strewn as a battlefield, Meloria talked as the coachman could not.

She spoke slowly, in her plain unmusical voice, of growing up a tenth daughter of twelve girls, of marrying her husband, of their childlessness, of his death. He had been struck by lightning from a blue sky. The coachman half listened, his belly tight as a drum, his mind a slow empty whirling of wine-colored sparkles. Only when she spoke of her childlessness did he rouse a little, at something new in her voice, something splintered that made him frown and look across the table with fuddled eyes.

"Drink to midwinter," Meloria said, and the splintered tone, which had reminded him of something, was gone.

Later—how much later, he didn't know—he woke. It was unaccustomed warmth that woke him, as shocking after his hearth and cinders as would have been ice water. Meloria's vast breasts lay against his cheek. Blue lines dribbled across their fatty slackness. He shifted a little, and the breath came to him from her open mouth, heavy and stale with used wine.

His stomach lurched.

He made it out of the bed but not out of the cottage. Vomit spewed onto the hearth, making a paste of cinders. When the racking heaves became too bad, the coachman dropped to his hands and knees, naked on the stone, long nose inches from the floor. Eventually the last of the wine came up, a thin pink trail across the stone.

I am a coachman—

When he could stand, he fetched water, cleaned the hearth, and dressed with trembling fingers. A gray winter dawn had drained all color from the village, and all sound. It was only hours later, well along the road, that he thought it odd that Meloria had not been wakened by his retching, and hours after that before he remembered that she had, and that he had seen in her eyes, staring sightlessly at the roof, that splintered thing: the breaking axle, the brambles on the embankment.

Her dead husband's boots were better than his living ones had been; they kept his feet dry the whole long day.

The fortress stood hard-lined against the gray dusk, spilling no rectangles of light onto the cold cobblestones. But the coachman had no time to ponder this; at almost the moment he trudged in view of the nearest tower, he was seized by two armed soldiers. They dragged him into the fortress. He was taken first before a young captain with close-cropped hair and jawline like an erection, who brought him before. . . .

"A stranger, my prince. Creeping by the edge of the castle road, in cover of the trees. And he will say nothing."

"And of her tracks you found—"

The captain looked at the floor.

"You found—"

"Nothing yet, my prince. But this man—"

The prince made a chopping gesture, and the captain was silent. Everyone stood absolutely still except the coachman, who fearfully raised his eyes for a first look at the prince, and the prince himself, who frowned. The coachman dropped his eyes and shuddered.

"Two days."

"Yes, my prince."

"This time."

"Yes, my prince."

"I want her found *now*. And if anything has happened to the child. . . ."

"Yes, my prince."

The prince put out one hand in a useless, unfinished gesture. The hand was strong and brown, with tiny golden hairs at the wrist and a single, square-cut ring carved with a wax seal.

"How does she go? And why?" On the last word his voice splintered, and no one answered.

"Can you talk, man?" the prince said to the coachman, who shook his head.

"Not even sounds?"

The coachman remembered the sounds of his retching, but did nothing.

"Have you come here at anyone else's bidding?"

The captain shifted his weight, not quite impatiently. The prince ignored him. The coachman shook his head.

"Did you see anyone on the road? Anyone or . . . anything? Anything unusual?"

The captain said, "My prince, we don't even know if he lied when he answered the first question. Perhaps he can talk and perhaps he cannot. I can find that out easily enough, if you will but leave him to me. . . ."

The prince raised the coachman's chin with one fist and looked steadily into his eyes, shadowed blue into muddy brown. The coachman stepped back a pace. The inside of his head shouted—*I am a coachman*!—but no words came.

"No," the prince said finally. "Can't you tell by looking that he is harmless? Because if you cannot, Captain, if you must substitute force for sight, you are not as much use to me as if—"

He did not finish. A great commotion moved through the corridor beyond, and a page ran into the room. "She is found! She is found!"

The prince bolted for the door. Before he could reach it, a second captain entered, older than the first, carrying the limp body of a woman. The first captain bit his lip and scowled. The prince took the lady into his own arms and laid her on a low couch. The coachman saw in a daze that she was heavily pregnant, and dressed in rags. Without volition, he glanced at her ankle, bare now, and dirty under the torn skirt.

When she opened her eyes, they were the same clear blue as the prince's. He said gently, and even the coachman saw how the gentleness could not quite cover the anguish, "Another fit."

"Yes," she said, and then in a rush: "I'm sorry, love! I don't remember!"

"Not anything? Not how you left the castle, or why, or . . . or this?" He touched the rags she wore.

"No," the lady said, and in the sound of her voice the coachman lay again in the wet ditch, blackness without, even more within.

The prince held her tighter. "Are you hurt anywhere?"

"No, I . . . no. Just very tired. I was asleep this time, I think, when it came over me."

"And *no one* saw? Your women, the men-at-arms—"

"No. Please—it wasn't their fault, don't. . . . I don't know how I went past them all, but I know it was not their fault. It was—"

Her voice faltered. The prince murmured against her hair, his face hidden. The younger captain, who had begun to sweat when the prince said, 'the men-at-arms,' seized the coachman's arm with one hand and the page's with the other and pushed them from the room. The older captain followed, closing the door.

"Where this time?" the younger demanded.

"In the forest. Like before. But she could not have been there more than a few minutes; she would have frozen, in those rags at midwinter."

The other swore. "And *she* will be queen."

The older man pursed his mouth disapprovingly, an odd look for a soldier, and said nothing. The coachman saw again the tightening of the prince's arm around the lady, the trembling of the square-cut ring.

The first captain said, too hastily, "Not that I would speak any word against such a beautiful and virtuous princess!"

The other man merely smiled.

"Well, you two get out!" the first captain shouted. He shoved the page between the child's shoulder blades, and kicked the coachman with his boot. The blow caught the coachman behind the left knee, which buckled. "You heard me—get out or you'll wish you had!"

The page scurried away. The coachman staggered to his feet and took one step before the knee collapsed for a second time. The captain kicked him again.

"Enough," said the older man. "You know he don't like that. Nor she either."

The other looked sullen. The coachman put both palms flat against the wall, bit his tongue, and heaved himself upright. Through a gray haze, he followed the page down the corridor, onto the cobblestones. The early dark of midwinter had fallen; yellow rectangles of light lay on the cobblestones under the cold moon.

Limping along the road, he nearly froze; not moving he surely would have. He had no tinder to make a fire, no coals, no flint. There was moonlight, this time, enough to see, but by the time he came to the place where the shoulder of the road dropped into a steep embankment, he was beyond seeing. He moaned, when the chattering of his teeth and the shivering of his bones let him, and he kept his feet more or less on the road even when he fell into it. But he saw neither the road nor the embankment, bristling with frozen weeds like little spears. He saw darkness, and a rushing jeweled night, and the shining sphere of the coach . . . and something more.

Presently his moaning grew. It became muttering, and the muttering grew to the frozen shapes of deformed words.

"Spilled over. Bits and pieces of magic . . . spilled over. Bits and pieces and pieces. . . ."

He fell down, and this time could not rise, although he tried. Once he put out his hand and groped on the icy roadway, his fingers splayed and bent as if he expected to touch something softer, nastier.

"I am a coachman!" he shouted to the thing that was not there. Body and mind gave out; laying his cheek against the frost, he closed his eyes.

The coach, and the exhilarating rush of horses in the jeweled night, and the thlock-thlock dying away behind. But the thlock-thlock grew louder, and a shape catapulted out of the darkness.

"Oh, no, no—"

Meloria dismounted, all but falling off the borrowed ass, and lifted the coachman. He was nearly too heavy for even her strength and mass, but somehow—heaving, pushing, cursing, sweating—she wrestled him across the back of the mangy ass. She rubbed his hands and cheeks; she raged at his stupidity; she pried open his mouth and scalded his throat with hot soup. She wept and cursed and waddled along the road, leading the ass, carrying the coachman away from the embankment steep in the frozen moonlight.

"It was you," the coachman said when he finally woke again in the cottage, under piles of stifling blankets. Then he realized: slowly his fingers went to his lips where the words had appeared, and he looked at Meloria in hatred and fear.

She took a step away from him and studied a crack in the hearth.

"I can speak."

She said nothing, watching him from the corner of her eye.

"Your doing."

"No."

"Then bits and pieces. Spillage. Like the other. 'When they're careless.' That's what you said."

"Yes," Meloria answered, looking suddenly older, suddenly weary. In the one word the coachman heard again the breaking of the axle, the tearing of the brambles on the embankment.

He turned his head away from her, and saw that he lay on the hearth, as close to the fire as possible. It burned too hot. He yanked the blankets down from his chin; under them, he discovered, he was naked.

Suddenly he shouted, as he had on the road, "I am a coachman!"

"Not before me, you were not."

He jerked his head around so quickly that the bones in his neck snapped. Meloria said it again, in a rougher voice:

"Not before me, you were not. No more than *she* was . . . what she is."

He said, in a perfect rage, "She changes back! Without warning, without help, and then he can't even find her!"

"He always does."

"He—"

"Would she have been better off without me, without any of it, as she was before? Without him or the child? Without even those dangerous bits and pieces. Just because the magic goes away sometimes—would she have been better off without it entirely?"

He was tired. His knee was in pain, and his neck hurt where it had snapped, and a great listlessness came over him, as if the cold had claimed him on the road after all, as if Meloria had not come. He closed his eyes. After a while he could hear Meloria moving around the cottage preparing food, drawing water, clanking a pot down on a table with clumsy, heavy movements.

She drew the blankets back up to his chin.

The coachman opened his eyes and looked up at her. Meloria set her lips hard together. Her chin quivered.

"None of us is that free of spillage. None. Not even . . . such as I."

The coachman nodded. He raised one hand and touched her cheek. It took all the strength he had, without and within, more strength even than not remembering what had hurled after him down the embankment. Then he closed his eyes, exhausted, and slept.

CHARLES L. GRANT

Snowman

Charles L. Grant started out writing science fiction, and has won awards for his short stories in that genre. However, he is far better known these days for his fantasy and horror tales, which can be at once beautifully told and also quietly, devastatingly effective. His *Oxrun Station* books were early horror successes for Mr. Grant. Since then he has won fantasy awards on many occasions. He is also the editor of the fine *Shadows* anthologies of original horror fiction and recently saw published *The Best of Shadows*, a distillation of the finest tales from the first ten volumes of the anthologies.

In "Snowman," the author shows how an unexpected change in the weather can completely alter the way one perceives the city one's lived in all his life. Here is London as rarely seen: quiet, deserted, and threatening.

—E. D.

SNOWMAN

Charles L. Grant

When the storm began, it shouldn't have been unexpected. The clouds had been hovering over the Thames basin for nearly three days, gradually sinking, gradually darkening, hiding sun and stars and holding the temperature well below freezing. Puddles froze, breath froze, windows seemed brittle, too fragile to touch; automobiles huffed, steam billowed from grates, lines at the theaters were short and impatient, while lines at the Underground were not short at all.

It was a waiting time, shoulders hunched and eyes narrowed, footsteps in a hurry, voices sharp in the sharp air while winter-rose cheeks and blood-rose lips became chapped and cracked in the whip-wind that carried down the river and put froth on the surface and ice frills on the gunwales of houseboats and ships.

And when the wind died, the silence came, the waiting; and finally, one evening, the storm.

Harry stood in Leicester Square, listening to a scruffy man dressed in little more than a tattered scarf and tweed jacket declaim and threaten with his ragged Bible, half-smiling to himself as the man argued for redemption, dared salvation, shoved the huge black book at the chests and faces of those who had stopped to wonder or mock, or pass the time while waiting for a friend.

In the summer such itinerant preachers would be a diversion, perhaps an amusement, watched at a distance by a constable or two who also watched the crowds; now, though, the man was sad. Nothing more. Sad. Fighting the cold, the bare trees, harsh heels on paving stones flat without echoes.

Harry lifted an eyebrow and looked around him, and nearly gasped when, in less than a blink, less than a sigh, the air was white.

Small flakes, dry, a dustbin of white ash upended and endless, falling straight, without drifting, that made several children cry out and grin, made the adults scowl and look up and swear as if the fall were unexpected.

Small flakes, heavy, immediately bleaching the buildings, blurring the marquees, muffling footsteps and tires and the music of a brass trio huddled beside a tree, banknotes in a cornet case suddenly fluttering and white.

He shook his head in sympathy at the musicians' distress, notes fading, breaking off, replaced with unseasonal swearing and the concert's abrupt cancellation. Then he snapped up his overcoat collar and shoved his hands into his pockets, wondering if finally he'd be lucky tonight.

If the woman of his dreams would come to him now.

He certainly couldn't eat any more; he'd already stopped in half a dozen places, to see who was unattached, to see what the woman of his dreams would be eating. And there was no sense either trying to get into one of the cinemas. He'd seen them all—all those he'd wanted to see— at least twice, seeing no one sitting alone, except himself at the back.

The snow thickened.

Trickles of ice water found their way down his neck.

The preacher was gone, the trio was gone, and unless he made an effort, unless he stared hard through the storm without blinking, he would have sworn for a moment he was the only one left in the Square at all.

The only one.

A sigh, a shudder at the cold that filled his mouth, and he decided he might as well head in the direction of home. If, he thought, that's what a dingy, not at all spacious room off Covent Garden could be called. A classy address for those who thought London classy, not at all classy for those living behind red brick and dirty brick, waiting for the landlords to find the money to evict and rebuild. Heat gone, water chancy, working light bulbs in the stairwell a thing of the past.

He supposed he ought to consider himself lucky. No woman would want to return with him anyway, not when she saw the outside of the place, and definitely not when she saw the foyer, the stairs, and followed his pointing finger upward, to the lightless second floor.

"Hey!"

He walked with head down, wishing he'd worn a cap as he felt his dark hair stiffen, felt the snow turn him white before his time.

"Hey, excuse me?"

A glance over his shoulder showed him no one, but when he looked to his left he saw a small dark figure hurrying toward him through the snow. He slowed but didn't stop, already working on the dozen excuses that would send the beggar away, hoping the man would sense his disapproval and leave on his own to hunt another mark.

Closer; he was disconcerted when he realized it was a woman. Short, bulky in a seaman's dark blue jacket, a wool cap pulled hard around her head, down over her ears. Her cheeks were red, the tip of her nose bright, thick eyebrows hung with snowflakes she couldn't blink away.

"I'm sorry," he began, and stopped when she laughed, one eye closing tightly.

"I'm not looking for money," she said, reaching out a gloveless hand to touch his arm and draw away. "I'm looking for the nearest subway." She winced. "Sorry. I mean, Underground. I'm trying to get to Blooms-bury, and I think I'm lost." Her nose wrinkled. "Hell, I know I'm lost."

He nodded at the snow. "Picked a good time for it, didn't you?"

"Story of my life," she said with smiling rue, then tucked her hand around his elbow and tugged once. "So. You going to save me or what?"

She was a head shorter than he, and he doubted that she weighed much under all that coat and the muffler flung several times around her neck. Left alone, she'd probably find the station in time; on the other hand, what the hell was he doing, debating himself when a woman, a real woman, had actually spoken to him first.

"Hey, can you talk?"

He grinned.

And the theater lights went out. All of them. Without so much as a dramatic flicker or two, or a hiss or a spark.

"God," she said, and hugged his arm more tightly. "I didn't bargain on this, you know. I'm supposed to be here on vacation. Cheap rates and all that, but this I didn't bargain on."

"Not to worry," he said, feeling the dark at his back, seeing faint blurs of light where the streetlamps still glowed on Charing Cross Road. "We're not far. I'll take you right to it."

She nodded her thanks, he nodded back and squared his shoulders, and a dozen steps later she slipped on a hidden strip of ice, cried out, and one leg snapped out in front of her. As she began to fall her other hand whipped around to grab his arm, and he was nearly brought to his knees. But he found balance and strength at the same time and hauled her up, close, bringing her partially in front of him so that her face rested a moment against his chest.

"God," she said.

"Are you all right?"

"I'll live, I think." She hesitated before gently pushing herself away. "Thanks."

"It's my job," he answered. "Knight of the Square, always ready to rescue fair damsels from their peril."

She looked at him, that eye closed again, and made sure this time that both her hands were on his arm before starting off. "How far is this station?" She leaned into the snow as if distance would aid vision.

"Just a block that way." He pointed at an angle to their left. "Right on the corner."

"Oh wonderful," she muttered. "One lousy block." A plume at the end of her sigh. "I feel like a jerk."

"You couldn't have known," he tried to assure her. "You get turned around in this place, it's easy to lose yourself." He gave her a grin. "We pride ourselves, you see, on not knowing what a straight street is."

The snow thickened, swirled, straightened again.

And with a "Mind your step," they walked on in silence, with wary short steps that scuffed and scraped as their feet searched for more ice.

A cornet sounded a single note somewhere to their right, hidden by the white.

Behind them at some great distance, a man's hoarse voice quoted a Bible verse.

"Spooky, y'know?" she said, huddling closer.

He frowned. "It is?"

She released one hand and waved it at the storm. "Yeah, spooky. I mean, you can't see anything, for god's sake, and we're right in the middle of London, for god's sake. You don't think that's spooky?"

He shrugged, too busy counting his blessings, hoping that somehow, before they reached the Underground's tiled entrance, he would know if she was the one who would keep him from being forever lonely. It was possible. Bloomsbury, to him, meant a bed-and-breakfast for students and ill-monied travelers, or some posh hotel the tourists seldom heard about; and this one was certainly neither posh nor flush.

"Well, I think so," she insisted. "God, is it like this every winter?"

"No," he answered truthfully. And cleared his throat, looked down at her just as she looked up at him and grinned.

"Elisabeth," she told him. "Stanley. Don't you dare call me Liz."

"Elisabeth," he repeated, and let it echo. "Harry. Harry Kinnon."

She nodded, squinted, said, "The damned streetlights are out."

"So they are."

And they were, Charing Cross deserted even of traffic.

The woman sighed exasperation. "So where the hell is it?"

I could lead her on for hours, he thought; we could end up on the Embankment and she'd never know. We could cross the river, and she'd never know. We could—

"Here," he said, and pulled her gently into the entrance, black without light, hollow without sound. "But I doubt you'll get anywhere for a while." He cocked his head, miming a hard listening. "No trains, you see."

And no one waiting at all, no grind of escalators, no uniform in the glass-walled booths to take tickets from those climbing up from below. The chrome ticket machines were dark. A faint howling now and then as a subterranean wind hunted through the tunnels.

"Well," she said, "damn!" A swipe at her cap brought it off in her hand and into her coat pocket, and long dark hair fell untidily to her shoulders. Swearing under her breath, she brushed the snow from her shoulders, her chest, took a step toward the street and glared, turned and glared at him. "Is it far? To Bloomsbury, I mean."

"Which street?" he asked without thinking.

"Does it matter?" she returned just as quickly.

"Bloomsbury's a fair size."

Her look doubted him.

Something rumbled past, but it was too dark to see, too white to discern shapes.

A cornet.

A verse from the Bible.

He knew then what she was feeling, what she feared without knowing how to describe the fear that she felt; he'd felt it once himself—home, no matter where it was, no matter how long ago it was, never seemed quite the same once London unveiled some of her faces, revealed some of her secrets, whispered at night and laughed during sunlight and raised an aristocratic, somewhat self-mocking eyebrow that beckoned as well as held off at arm's length.

Elisabeth hugged herself and stood with her back to him. "I wanted to see Europe," she explained, looking up and down the road, tilting forward to look up at the sky. "Take a few months off and thumb my way as close to the Iron Curtain as they'd let me." A shiver. A soft voice: "I've been here since November. I just can't . . . I don't know. Sometimes I think I'm going crazy, that I want to live here forever." A laugh without humor. "I had just made up my mind to leave. Tomorrow. For Amsterdam. Then this damned snow . . ." She shook her head angrily. "Jesus, I'm not making any sense."

"London'll do that to you," he said for lack of anything else, anything witty, anything pungent, and silently cursed the absence of fluency for the florid, the romantic, the snare for a young woman who was obviously as frightened now as he had been when first he'd arrived.

"I know."

Her shoulders lifted as if she were inhaling deeply, a cloud of white dimly seen as she exhaled so slowly he barely saw her move. "I've been to all the haunted pubs, did you know that?"

He could have guessed it, but he said nothing.

"I even took that silly Jack the Ripper walk." She looked over her shoulder. "Do you know that there's a car dealer or junk yard where the first murder took place?" She grimaced. "Hardly worth the trip. I saw a dead rat there and pretended the Ripper had done it. I don't think the guide saw the humor."

She looked away just as a gust pelted them with snow, fingertips that touched his face and faded, made him blink, made him wonder if this time the apartment would be warm. Over there. In Covent Garden.

She stamped one foot, and stamped again, weakly. "I don't like this."

"It's quiet, at least."

"Too quiet. Where the hell's the city?"

Hell was behind and below them as the tunnel wind screamed, and fell silent.

"Tell me the truth," he said, stepping closer, staying at her back, "do you really miss it?" Without touching her he pointed over her shoulder, at the white that made the dark between the flakes seem less a color than a space endless and cold. "All those people, all that hollering and honking and spitting and playing and such—do you really miss it?"

For a second she leaned back against him before righting herself again. "Well, when you put it that way . . ." A quick bright laugh. "Are you giving me a choice?"

And are you, he asked as he moved to stand beside her, the woman of my dreams? After all this time, is it you, Elisabeth, who'll keep my hands warm?

God, he thought scornfully; put a sock in it, Kinnon.

"Well," he said, leaning out, checking the empty street, "would you rather go down there?" A thumb jerked over his shoulder toward the wind, banshee now and punches of it reaching the backs of their legs. "It sounds evilly tempting, I should think. True enough, it's fairly dim—"

She laughed at that.

"—but don't you feel a certain . . . I don't know, a certain excitement? Thrill of the unknown and all that?"

Without touching her, he could feel her actually considering it, moving blindly down the crippled escalator, a palm gliding along the immobile handrail, listening to the wind and, just below it, the babble of voices. A monster, perhaps, or the most handsome man she'd ever met; someone weeping with fear, or someone laughing at the sheer joy of something different for a change.

"Out there," he whispered, "it's safe. All snuggly and white and soft and gentle. Not what you're used to, I'd expect."

"Ice," she said. "Cold. I could break a leg."

The cornet in a single mournful note.

"My god, how can he keep on playing like that? There's no one to hear him."

"You can."

She looked at him. "And that preacher guy?"

Harry shrugged. "He preaches. It's . . . what he does."

She scratched the side of her nose, adjusted her muffler. "Funny, but I wandered that damned place for an hour—just looking around, y'know?—and I don't remember him." Her brow wrinkled. "Was he there?"

"He was."

"Were you?"

Always, he thought.

"Yes," he said.

Her foot stamped again; her breath was caught and spun into the falling snow. "I don't remember."

"Or," he said, rocking on his heels, "you could head back to Bloomsbury, to that mysterious place of yours. There will be the warmth, I've no doubt." He gestured vaguely ahead. "A few blocks straight on that way, a turn or two, you'll run smack into the British Museum. Could you find your way from there?"

He could tell now that she was perplexed, and perhaps fearful of him, a stranger in a city she'd not found strange at all. She was caught in a storm with a possible maniac, molester, contemporary Jack, or a simpleton who only wanted to see her safely away. Sooner or later, she would have to choose.

"Where . . ." She faced him squarely. "Where do you live, Harry?"

He dared not answer; it was her choice, not his.

And she startled him when she asked, "Am I dead or something?"

"What?"

"Am I dead? Don't you know what I mean? I mean, is this like one of those stupid TV shows where I have to choose between heaven and hell, or wander forever in some kind of stupid limbo? Are you an angel or something? You pop up when it snows or rains or something, and take souls to heaven? Oh, Jesus." She blinked rapidly, fear in full banner chasing the rose from her cheeks. "Jesus, am I dead?"

Before she could move, before she could thwart him, he leaned down and kissed her lips briefly, smiled as he pulled away, and said, "Did you feel that?"

"Damn right."

"Then you're not dead."

A step back. Her cap yanked from her pocket and jammed back onto her head. Determination taking fear's place, and a spot of embarrassment on the tip of her chin. "Harry, no offense, but you're as spooky as this place is." A swipe to rid her face of stray snow. "Show me the way again, okay? I think I can make it."

He nodded while praying she couldn't see or sense his acute disappointment. "That way," he told her.

As the lights buzzed back on, and a black cab rattled past them, and the ticket machines winked on, and the grind of the escalators met the muffled cry of a train's brakes; streetlamps; marquees; the Underground's blue and red.

"Wow," she said, and smiled. "Did you do that?"

"All part of the service, madam," he told her, bowing with a sweep of his arm. "Wouldn't want a lovely lady to lose her way, now would we?"

She hesitated, and he held his breath until she suddenly rose on tiptoe and kissed his cheek. "Thanks," she said. "Maybe I'll see you, okay?" And before he could answer, she was out in the storm, checking the traffic and darting across the road.

He watched until the white took her, erased her, replaced her with an image he tried to hold, and failed. Then he cleared his throat, rubbed his face, and walked back to the square. She wouldn't remember him. She'd never see him again. But there'd be a story to tell to the next man she met, and he wondered how she'd tell it, how he'd look, how he'd sound.

What the hell.

It didn't matter.

She wasn't the woman of his dreams. Not this time. Not this time, but soon. Soon she'd come, and soon she'd make the choice, and soon there'd be someone else to listen to in the snow.

While the cornet sounded.

And the preacher cried of hell.

DENNIS ETCHISON

The Scar

Dennis Etchison has earned the reputation as dangerous. He has been writing for a number of years, but his work always seems the work of a vibrantly young, vividly alive, angry realist. He was editor of the acclaimed anthology of horror, *Cutting Edge*—and nobody is more "cutting edge" than Etchison himself.

The actual physical scar in this story is far less damaging to its carrier than the psychological one she carries; it is a wound that binds her inextricably to her volatile, explosive companion. The raw power of Etchison's narrative will endure long after the scars of this reality have passed.

—E. D.

THE SCAR

Dennis Etchison

This time they were walking a divided highway, the toes of their shoes powdered white with gravel dust. The little girl ran ahead, skipping eagerly along the shoulder, while her mother lagged back to keep pace with the man.

"Mind the trucks," called the woman, barely raising her voice. Soon the girl would be able to take care of herself; that was her hope. She turned to him, showing the good side of her face. "Do you see one yet?"

He lifted his chin and squinted.

She followed his gaze to the other side of the highway. There, squatting in the haze beyond the overpass, was a Weenie Wigwam Fast Food Restaurant.

"Thank God," she said. She thought of the Chinese Smorgasbord, the Beef Bowl, the Thai Take-Out and the many others they had seen already. She added, "This one will be all right, won't it?"

It was the edge of the town, RV dealerships and fleet sales on one side of the road, family diners and budget motels on the other. Overloaded station wagons and moving vans laden with freight hammered the asphalt, bringing thunder to the gray twilight. Without breaking stride the man leaned down to scoop up a handful of gravel, then skimmed stones between the little girl's thin legs and into the ditch; he held onto one last piece, a sharp quartz chip, and deposited it in his jacket pocket.

"Maybe," he said.

"Aren't you sure?"

He did not answer.

"Well, she said, "let's try it. Laura will be hungry, I know."

She hurried to catch the little girl at the crossing. When she turned back, the man was handling an empty beer bottle from the roadside. She looked away. As he moved up to join them, zippering the front of his service jacket, the woman forced a smile, as if she had not seen.

*   *   *

In the parking lot, the man took their hands. A heavy tanker geared down and pounded the curve, bucking and hissing away behind them. As it passed, the driver sounded his horn at the traffic. The sudden blast, so near that it rattled her spine, seemed to release her from a bad dream. She laced her fingers more securely with his and swung her arm out and back and out again, hardly feeling the weight of his hand between them.

"This is a nice place," she said, already reading a banner for the all-day breakfast special. "I'm glad we waited. Aren't you glad, Laura?"

"Can I ride the horse?" asked the little girl.

The woman looked at the sculpted gray-and-white Indian pinto, its blanket saddle worn down to the fiberglass. There were no other children waiting at the machine. She let go of his hand and dug in her purse for a coin.

"I don't see why not," she said.

The little girl broke away.

He came to a stop, his empty hands opening and closing.

"Just one ride," the woman said quickly. "And then you come right inside, hear?"

On the other side of the glass, couples moved between tables. A few had children, some Laura's age. Families, she thought. She wished that the three of them could go inside together.

Laura's pony began to wobble and pitch. But the man was not watching. He stood there with his chin up, his nostrils flared, like an animal waiting for a sign. His hands continued to flex.

"I'll see about a table," she said when he did not move to open the door.

A moment later she glanced outside and saw him examining a piece of brick that had come loose from the front of the restaurant. He turned it over and over.

The menus came. They sat reading them in a corner booth, under crossed tomahawks. The food items were named in keeping with the native American motif, suggesting that the burgers and the several varieties of hot dogs had been invented by hunters and gatherers. Bleary travelers hunched over creased roadmaps, gulping coffee and estimating mileage, their eyes stark in the chill fluorescent lighting.

"What would you like, Laura?" asked the woman.

"Peanut butter and jelly sandwich."

"Do they have that?"

"And a vanilla milkshake."

The woman sighed.

"And Wampum Pancakes. Papoose-size."

She opened her purse and counted the money. She blinked and looked at the man.

He got up and went over to the silverware station.

"What's he doing?" said the little girl.

"Never mind," said the woman. "His knife and fork must be dirty."

He came back and sat down.

"And Buffalo Fries," said the little girl.

The woman studied him. "Is it still okay?" she asked.

"What?" he said.

She waited, but now he was busy observing the customers. She gave up and returned to the menu. It was difficult for her to choose, not knowing what he would order. "I'll just have a small dinner salad," she said at last.

The others in the restaurant kept to themselves. A man with a sample case ate a piece of pecan pie and scanned the local newspaper. A young couple fed their baby apple juice from a bottle. A take-away order was picked up at the counter, then carried out to a Winnebago. Soft, vaguely familiar music lilted from wall speakers designed to look like tomtoms, muffling the clink of cups and the murmur of private conversations.

"Want to go to the bathroom," said the little girl.

"In a minute, baby," the woman told her. A waitress in an imitation buckskin mini-dress was coming this way.

The little girl squirmed. "Mom*my*!"

The waitress was almost here, carrying a pitcher and glasses of water on a tray.

The woman looked at the man.

Finally he leaned back and opened his hands on the table.

"Could you order for us?" she asked carefully.

He nodded.

In the rest room, she reapplied make-up to one side of her face, then added another layer to be sure. At a certain angle the deformity did not show at all, she told herself. Besides, he had not looked at her, really looked at her in a long time; perhaps he had forgotten. She practiced a smile in the mirror until it was almost natural. She waited for her daughter to finish, then led her back to the dining room.

"Where is he?" said the little girl.

The woman tensed, the smile freezing on her lips. He was not at the table. The food on the placemats was untouched.

"Go sit down," she told the little girl. "Now."

Then she saw him, his jacket with the embroidered patches and the narrow map like a dragon on the back. He was on the far side of the room, under a framed bow and arrow display.

She touched his arm. He turned too swiftly, bending his legs, his feet apart. Then he saw who it was.

"Hi," she said. Her throat was so dry that her voice cracked. "Come on, before your food gets cold."

As she walked him to the table, she was aware of eyes on them.

"I had a bow and arrow," he said. "I could pick a sentry out of a tree at a hundred yards. Just like that. No sound."

She did not know what to say. She never did. She gave him plenty of room before sitting down between him and the little girl. That put her on his other side, so that he would be able to see the bad part of her face. She tried not to think about it.

He had only coffee and a small sandwich. It took him a while to start on it. Always travel light, he had told her once. She picked at her salad. The people at the other tables stopped looking and resumed their meals.

"Where's my food?" asked the little girl.

"In front of you," said the woman. "Now eat and keep quiet."

"Where's my pancakes?"

"You don't need pancakes."

"I do, too!"

"Hush. You've got enough." Without turning her face the woman said to the man, "How's your sandwich?"

Out of the corner of her eye she noticed that he was hesitating between bites, listening to the sounds of the room. She paused, trying to hear what he heard. There was the music, the undercurrent of voices, the occasional ratcheting of the cash register. The swelling traffic outside. The chink of dishes in the kitchen, as faint as rain on a tin roof. Nothing else.

"Mommy, I didn't get my Buffalo Fries."

"I know, Laura. Next time."

"When?"

She realized she did not know the answer. She felt a tightening in her face and a dull ache in her throat so that she could not eat. Don't let me cry, she thought. I don't want her to see. This is the best we can do—can't she understand?

Now his head turned toward the kitchen.

From behind the door came distant clatter as plates were stacked, the squeak of wet glasses, the metallic clicking of flatware, the high good humor of unseen cooks and dishwashers. The steel door vibrated on its hinges.

He stopped chewing.

She saw him check the room one more time: the sharply-angled tables, the crisp bills left for tips, the half-eaten dinners hardening into waste, the full bellies and taut belts and bright new clothing, too bright under the harsh fixtures as night fell, shuttering the windows with leaden darkness. Somewhere outside headlights gathered as vehicles jammed the turnoff, stabbing the glass like approaching searchlights.

He put down his sandwich.

The steel door trembled, then swung wide.

A shiny cart rolled into the dining room, pushed by a busboy in a clean white uniform. He said something over his shoulder to the kitchen crew, rapid-fire words in a language she did not understand. The cooks and dishwashers roared back at his joke. She saw the tone of their skin, the stocky, muscular bodies behind the aprons. The door flapped shut. The cart was coming this way.

He spat out a mouthful of food as though afraid that he had been poisoned.

"It's okay," she said. "See? They're Mexicans, that's all. . . ."

He ignored her and reached inside his jacket. She saw the emblems from his Asian tour of duty. But there were also patches from Tegucigalpa and Managua and the fighting that had gone on there. She had never noticed these before. Her eyes went wide.

The busboy came to their booth.

Under the table, the man took something from his pants pocket and set it beside him on the seat. Then he took something else from the other side. Then his fists closed against his knees.

"Can I have a bite?" said the little girl. She started to reach for the uneaten part of his sandwich.

"Laura!" said the woman.

"Well, he doesn't want it, does he?"

The man looked at her. His face was utterly without expression. The woman held her breath.

"Excuse," said the busboy.

The man turned his head back. It seemed to take a very long time. She watched, unable to stop any of this from happening.

When the man did not say anything, the busboy tried to take his plate away.

A fork came up from below, glinted, then arced down in a blur, pinning the brown hand to the table.

The boy cried out and swung wildly with his other hand.

The man reached under his jacket again and brought a beer bottle down on the boy's head. The boy folded, his scalp splitting under the lank black hair and pumping blood. Then the cart and chairs went flying as the man stood and grabbed for the tomahawks on the wall. But they were only plastic. He tossed them aside and went over the table.

A waitress stepped into his path, holding her palms out. Then she was down and he was in the middle of the room. The salesman stood up, long enough to take half a brick in the face. Then the manager and the man with the baby got in the way. A sharp stone came out, and a lockback knife, and then a water pitcher shattered, the fragments carrying gouts of flesh to the floor.

The woman covered her little girl as more bodies fell and the room became red.

He was going for the bow and arrow, she realized.

Sirens screamed, cutting through the clot of traffic. There was not much time. She crossed the parking lot, carrying the little girl toward the Winnebago. A retired couple peered through the windshield, trying to see. The child kicked until the woman had to put her down.

"Go. Get in right now and go with them before—"

"Are you going, too?"

"Baby, I can't. I can't take care of you anymore. It isn't safe. Don't you understand?"

"Want to stay with you!"

"Can we be of assistance?" said the elderly man, rolling down his window.

She knelt and gripped the little girl's arms. "I don't know where to go," she said. "I can't figure it out by myself." She lifted her hair away from the side of her face. "Look at me! I was born this way. No one else would want to help us. But it's not too late for you."

The little girl's eyes overflowed.

The woman pressed the child to her. "Please," she said, "it's not that I want to leave you . . ."

"We heard noises," said the elderly woman. "What happened?"

Tall legs stepped in front of the camper, blocking the way.

"Nothing," said the man. His jacket was torn and spattered. He pulled the woman and the little girl to their feet. "Come on."

He took them around to the back of the lot, then through a break in the fence and into a dark field, as red lights converged on the restaurant. They did not look back. They came to the other side of the field and then they were crossing the frontage road to a maze of residential streets. They turned in a different direction at every corner, a random route that no one would be able to follow. After a mile or so they were out again and back to the divided highway, walking rapidly along in the ditch.

"This isn't the way," said the little girl.

The woman took the little girl's hand and drew her close. They would have to leave their things at the motel and move on again, she knew. Maybe they would catch a ride with one of the truckers on the interstate, though it was hard to get anyone to stop for three. She did not know where they would sleep this time; there wasn't enough left in her purse for another room.

"Hush, now." She kissed the top of her daughter's head and put an arm around her. "Want me to carry you?"

"I'm not a baby," said the little girl.

"No," said the woman, "you're not. . . ."

They walked on. The night lengthened. After a while the stars came out, cold and impossibly distant.

GWYNETH JONES

Laiken Langstrand

Gwyneth Jones, author of the poignant adult fairy tale "The Snow Apples" in our First Annual Collection, is back with another witty and wistful fairy tale set in a distant land, Once Upon a Time. . . .

Jones was born and raised in Manchester, England, but she later lived in Singapore and traveled extensively in South-East Asia before settling on the southern coast of England. Her novels are *Divine Endurance, Escape Plans,* and *Kairos.* She also writes books for younger readers under the name Anne Hallam.

—T. W.

LAIKEN LANGSTRAND

Gwyneth Jones

Nigel Pickering, are you still out there?
Remember the ram caught in the thicket?
This one's for you, from G & P.

Once upon a time there was a king who broke his fishing-line. It may
seem that such an incident is scarcely worth recording: but it was the
last fishing-line. And on the lost end of it was the last fish-hook. Now
that it was gone there would be no dinner, nor supper or breakfast either
for this king and his court.

"I said you should have cast it further down the beach—"

The king looked at his courtier with some disfavour.

"Don't talk to me like that!"

"Why shouldn't I?"

The king's court consisted of one impudent eight-year-old child, with
a pale, pointed face and a flame of red hair. The king himself was a very
young man. His hair was limp sugar-blond, and his chin indecisive. He
had large, wistful, hazel eyes, and generally possessed the kind of accident-
prone, helpless appeal that spells grief, disaster and financial embarrassment for strong women: but at present his charm was somewhat battered
by circumstance. The two faced each other on the bleak, muddy shore,
the only human creatures—in fact the only living things in sight.

"That was my dinner as well as yours, you stupid king. You're a born
loser, that's what you are. You're always, always losing things! You're
hopeless!"

Around them the barren mud-flats stretched forever: a waste of puddles
and gravel between the mountains and the sea where once there had been
a snug little country. Laiken, the young king, did not feel that he needed
to be reminded of his unhappy talent.

"This is the last straw," he moaned.

And so it was. The impudent, red-haired child took to her heels and
ran, her skinny legs flashing as she legged it for the pale, distant streak

of the highway. The last straw of comfort in Laiken's miserable existence departed with her. He shouted after her, "Courtier! Courtier?" They had both forgotten her real name. But it was no use. The child had already vanished, leaving him alone in the ocean of mud.

Laiken turned back to the sea. "I'm hopeless," he told the evil-coloured scummy tide that was now creaming up to his feet. "I'm hopeless." He knew himself well enough to realise the futility of trying to force his cringing body into the water. That couldn't be the way out. He looked after his courtier again. Maybe he could follow her—hitchhike over the border, get a job in some foreign town. The trouble was, being a king he hadn't any proper qualifications. And from what he'd heard he didn't think working for a living would suit him anyway.

But what was this? A tiny figure had appeared far away, covering ground swiftly, drab as the mud from head to toe. He strained his eyes and saw that it was a full-grown man, as skinny and poorly dressed as Laiken himself.

Soon the messenger stood panting before the king, puddle-water slopping out of his shoes. The burrs and bits of dead grass clinging untidily to his clothes showed that he'd just come over the border. There was no vegetation left at all in Laiken's kingdom.

"Sire, I am a servant of the Oracle. In answer to your query—"

(It had been two years ago that they had sent off to ask the Oracle. Laiken remembered the tiny flutter of hope as the delegation set out—though even then there had been very little left worth saving.)

"A servant of the Oracle? Well, where's my delegation?—"

The man looked embarrassed. "Er—they're not going to bother coming back, Sire."

No one knew why the Great Sea Serpent had decided to wreck their country, but no one really cared any more. Most of the population had already departed before the delegation left. The last stragglers had grown tired of waiting months ago. Whatever advice the Oracle might provide, it came far too late to do any good.

The messenger stared around, shaking his head mournfully. He'd seen some wastelands in his time, owing to the nature of his work, but this beat them all.

"Come on, come on, man."

"The answer of the Oracle is, that the power of the king in the hands of the people will restore Laiken's lands and destroy the Great Sea Serpent."

"The power of the king?"

That was a poor joke. He turned to glare at the thick brown water that had just swallowed his fish-hook.

"In the hands of the people . . ."

"Courtier!" yelled the king, frantically.

"Well, that's it. Now usually we'd invoice you for the full amount, but owing to the circumstances . . . I've had a terrible job getting here. There's no transport. I've been sleeping rough—"

King Laiken ignored him. Away he sped across the mud, shouting furiously. Half the ransom of his kingdom had just slipped from his grasp, and he wasn't going to let the other half escape him.

The messenger wasn't really surprised. As a professional bringer of bad tidings he'd had worse receptions. Muttering gloomily to himself about out-of-pocket expenses he set off in pursuit at a tired jog trot, his ruined shoes squelching. The drab tide lapped on the greyish-brown shore, and the barren flats lay sad and silent and empty.

Laiken managed to evade the servant of the Oracle, and to reach a more comfortable country. But he didn't find it easy to hold down a job. He kept running after red-haired children in the street and grabbing at them, which earned him a rather unsavoury reputation. As the calculated age of his quarry increased he was in less danger from the law or local vigilantes, but his other problems grew on him. He drifted and slithered down the social scale. Laiken was tired. He was tired of trying to keep boring, dead-end jobs. He was tired of his future and tired of his past. He managed to get drunk quite often, despite his poverty, because he never did acquire a head for alcohol. What he liked to do best was to sit in a comfortable stupor in some dark corner of his current local, and forget he was alive.

He was busy getting himself into his disgusting state one evening, in a bar in a small, dirty port on the other side of the world from his lost kingdom, when he found himself listening half-resentfully to the talk of some seamen who had settled down nearby. It was good, drunken talk. Floating islands appeared in the discussion, and people whose heads grew out of their armpits, and fire-breathing dragons. Another Laiken would have enjoyed it all immensely, and might even have joined in. This Laiken sat recalling his former cheerful nature and almost weeping in self-pity—until suddenly a new subject arose, and jerked him out of his misery. The sailors were describing a place they called the Langstrand. There was a complex, fuddled explanation of how tides work all around the world, and the conclusion drawn that somewhere, sometime, everything that ever goes into the sea has to come out again. And far away (in fact, the speaker didn't know the exact location, but he knew a man who did), far away from anywhere, you must be able to find the wonderful stretch of shore where all the lost things came to be found. The Lang-strand.

Laiken jumped up and banged down his glass. He was just drunk enough to see hope in the feeblest of plans. "That's where I'm going!" he shouted. "I see it all now. I just haven't been *tackling things from the right angle*! Hahaha!"

Everybody turned to stare. Laiken hurried out of the bar covered in embarrassment, but his heart was leaping. At last his life had purpose again. He would pursue the fishhook. Laiken saw it very clearly in his mind's eye: lying all shiny and bright on a bed of clean silvery sand. The Langstrand.

So that was how Laiken found a use for his principal talent. There goes Laiken Langstrand, people would say, admiringly. He's a real loser—you must get him to tell you the story. From that day on he wasn't drifting any more: he was searching. He still spent a lot of time getting drunk in seedy bars. But now he usually didn't have to pay for the drinks. A man with a quest is someone to be respected.

In fact when he stood one day and heard a man say, "Yes, just turn to your left where the fingerpost says 'To the Beach,' " Laiken felt more than a little uneasy. He resented the careless way the Langstrand had turned up with no fanfares or fireworks, and he wasn't sure he was ready for the chores of success. His uneasiness certainly did not lessen as he cleared the final dunes and surveyed that ten-mile sweep of white sand still called, though horribly mutilated, the most beautiful beach in the world. Laiken was not alone. He was looking down on a ten-mile shanty town. Thousands of strange people in bizarre and ragged garments were wandering about, and in front of some of the grubby little huts were smoky fires. With a deep, bitter sigh Laiken stepped down onto the sand.

He found an old abandoned hut to live in, made friends with his neighbours and was soon sponging off the tourists, drinking all night and sleeping half the day like a regular old strandie. After some months he was half-way through his first sweep of the ten miles, and had developed a serious crush on a girl called Mysotis, who lived in the hut next door. Her appearance was arresting. She wore her hair in thick, short, springy curls of brightest blue, and the eyes that looked out of her narrow, fine-boned face were yellow as mustard. However, it wasn't the bizarre colour scheme that really intrigued him. No, it wasn't the colour of her eyes, but their direction. Mysotis was never seen beachcombing. She was clearly one of the beach's professional camp-followers: an amiable group of young men and women who preyed on any sex-starved questing beasts who still had money; and worked the tourist trade. But all the other camp-followers kept to beach etiquette in one respect at least. They cruised the Langstrand way, with their eyes hardly ever leaving the littered sand. Mysotis walked with her head up.

One day Laiken devised a cunning plot. He would go round to the strange girl's hut and ask to borrow a cup of sugar. They would strike up a conversation about food (always a fascinating topic on the beach) and he would invite her back to share his meal. He tidied the hut and arranged an artistic impression of interrupted cooking. Then it occurred to him that he'd better hide his own sugar. He poured his whole supply into a cup, took it out behind the huts and dug a sandy hole . . . As he was digging he started to muse on the lost treasures that must be buried in this sand. He had found some very strange things by the sea's edge himself; and he had left them all lying, wondering if their owners would ever come to collect them. Funny to think of all the ends of stories waiting here. But never, never a fish-hook . . .

Laiken woke up, to find the sand smooth again under his hands. He had buried the sugar, and absentmindedly buried the cup too.

"Oh no—" he wailed.

He only possessed one cup. Now they'd both have to drink out of jam-jars. He scrabbled about helplessly: and eventually noticed the girl with the yellow eyes. She was watching with open amusement.

"What's the matter, neighbour?"

"Oh, Mysotis. I was just coming round to borrow a cup of sugar from you. But—um, I seem to have lost my cup."

There was a mocking twinkle in her yellow eyes. He realised that she had been standing there by the dune throughout his whole absurd little performance. He began to blush.

Mysotis laughed. "Well, why don't you come round anyway. You can share my supper. There happens to be plenty for two."

After they had eaten he asked her about the attitude of her eyes.

"It's simple," she said. "If your eyes should be turned down because you are a searcher, then my eyes should be turned upwards."

Laiken looked bemused.

"So you didn't come to the beach to look for something?"

"No, I came here from the other direction."

"Ah, I see. Someone is looking for you?"

She grinned, with a flash of small pointed teeth. "The man who is going to kill my father. I don't know his name, I'm afraid."

The romance blossomed swiftly. Mysotis's hut was much roomier and more weatherproof than Laiken's old lean-to. So Laiken moved in, and soon became convinced that he had found the end of his life's quest after all. But when he vowed eternal love Mysotis only laughed. He felt a little sorry for himself on this account, but he was brave about it.

Laiken went on searching and Mysotis went on waiting to be found. But in spite of this proper behavior their relationship caused talk. It seemed to be going on for an indecent length of time by Langstrand standards and people were offended. The nasty gossip reached Laiken at last (it had reached Mysotis long before, of course) and there was a tearful scene. Laiken vowed love more eternal than ever; he swore that nothing could possibly come between them. And at last Mysotis, who had shed no tears, looked into those swimming, wistful, hazel eyes and decided it might be true.

"Laiken, there are things you don't know about me . . ."

"I don't care about your past," he sobbed courageously. "You don't have to tell me anything!"

"I will tell, I will tell you. If we are lovers, then you should know. Laiken, what am I?"

"You're the kindest, sweetest, loveliest woman (snivel)—"

She sighed. "Am I really? Am I a woman, Laiken? Look at my hair. Did you ever see a woman with blue hair before?"

Laiken blinked through his tears. "Erm, well, I don't mind. You can wear it green or pink if you like. It's your hair, after all."

"Laiken, pass your hand along my arm."

Her skin was always dry, always cool. It had a faint rasp to it, like a cat's tongue. He'd noticed this roughness often, but never thought anything of it.

"Look closer—" she whispered.

And then he saw the tiny yellow scales.

"What *are* you?"

"I am the child of a king from under the sea."

Laiken gasped. He gaped in sentimental wonder at the mythical beauty in his arms.

"You're a mermaid!"

Mysotis looked away. "Sort of—" she agreed.

"And you're a princess—why, isn't that strange. Because, you know, I used to be a king. Did I ever tell you the story?"

Beach people were always swapping their quest stories. It was art, it was entertainment; and everybody understood that you wouldn't get the same story from the same strandie twice. Laiken had told Mysotis several versions of his epic. But now, for some reason, he told her the truth.

And while he told her, the mermaid's hand stole up to her throat, to a little sharkskin pouch she always wore around her neck on a cord of woven seaweed.

"So the Great Serpent sucked away all our water . . . Why, no one knows. Anyway, the place is a wreck. But if ever I find my old fish-hook I'll be able to sort it out, I'm certain of that. Why, what's wrong, Mysotis? You look quite ill."

"When I was young," said the mermaid, "my father found out by magic that, through me, a mortal man would destroy him. He tried to get rid of me by making me come and live on the land. I begged for mercy, and he said I could have the power to breathe dry air but it would cost half a king's ransom. I was at my wits' end, but then a sea witch gave me this amulet. She said she had found it on the sea-bed. My father laughed when he found out and said this thing couldn't be in better care; and he was satisfied. As long as I keep it, I live. If I lose it, I will die."

The lovers stared at one another. Laiken had turned a little pale. Mysotis seemed to be waiting for him to speak, but he said nothing.

At last she said, abruptly, "Of course, this all happened a very long time ago. Mermaids don't age like human beings, you know."

"How long—?"

"Oh, about five hundred years."

Laiken looked thoughtful. The mermaid shivered, touched the little pouch again and quickly jerked her hand away.

A few days later, Laiken moved out of the shared hut. He said he needed some time to be alone.

Mysotis went walking very early one morning shortly after Laiken had left her. Perhaps it was the half-light that made her afraid she would stumble, but she never lifted her eyes from the sand. She'd almost knocked herself out on the post before she saw the noticeboard that had sprung up overnight. The paint was shiny and the lettering was clear.

GENERAL DEPARTMENT OF CLAIMS

A CLAIMANTS' DEPARTMENT WILL BE SET UP ON THE BEACH FOR THE SPACE OF ONE MONTH. A DOCTOR IN CLAIMS WILL DEAL WITH DEMANDS CONCERNING LOST PROPERTY LOVE OR FORTUNE CLAIMED TO BE LYING ABOUT THIS BEACH. THEREAFTER THE BEACH WILL BE CLEARED. THIS IS YOUR LAST WARNING.
BY ORDER.

It was also their first warning, but never mind about that.

"What are we going to do?"

"We'll fight!"

"Is it worth it?"

"After all, it's not the only beach on the pebble."

The Doctor in Claims set up shop in a big white hygienic-looking tent. A steady trickle of beachcombers went in, and nearly all of them came out the other side and kept on walking. Mysotis and Laiken met one night by the sea's margin, below the swiftly fragmenting shanty town.

"You know what I have in my amulet pouch?"

"I think so."

"It was no use lying, then."

"Forget about it. I don't care," Laiken muttered sulkily. "I wasn't very good at being a king anyway."

"Supposing it wasn't around my neck? If you had found it the way you dreamed you might, lying on the sand looking up at you. Would you have thrown it back to the sea and come home to our hut for supper? Suppose you didn't have to kill me. Only to leave me, marry a suitable princess, forget me?"

There was no need for him to speak.

"Take it, then," she told him calmly, "if the wasteland is more important than what we have. I only want you to be happy. And you never know, my father may have forgotten about me by now."

Two figures on the shore, the sound of the sea, and not another living thing in sight. Laiken told himself he couldn't tell what she really wanted. Perhaps she was tired of passing for human.

"Mysotis, I—"

"Ah—"

"I need time. I don't know what to do. Give me another week."

Mysotis's strange eyes had been warmly bright a moment before, like water with the sun on it. Now they turned cool and shadowed.

"Of course," she agreed. "Such a difficult choice, you need to think it over."

And they parted again.

Laiken's week was just about up when he was summoned to the big white tent. The Doctor in Claims wanted to see him. Why Laiken, out of all the lost souls who still remained? He didn't know. He stood in the porch feeling rather frightened and obscurely guilty. Everyone knew by now that the Doctor in Claims was a woman. Maybe she's fallen in love with me, he thought. The porch of the tent was decorated like a waiting-room, with big potted plants arranged beside the furniture on the canvas floor and a mirror standing by one wall. He looked in the mirror, and his idea didn't seem too unlikely. He almost started thinking about his coming interview with Mysotis: but that was unpleasant.

"Laiken Langstrand? Doctor Kortia will see you now."

He pushed back the flap nervously. The Doctor's secretary slipped by him, smirking. Laiken was left alone, facing a young woman whose hair was a cap of vivid rust red and whose face was still as bright and impudent as ever.

"Kortia?" he gasped.

"It stuck," she explained, simply.

Laiken wished the floor would open up and swallow him. For he suddenly saw the figure in the waiting-room mirror clearly: and all the years of his quest fell on him with a horrible crushing weight. "I always knew we'd meet again," Kortia told him. "It was because of you, Laiken, that I took up a career in the lost property business, just in the hope that one day our paths would cross."

They talked and talked. That little country between the mountains and the sea lived again: its landscapes, its people, its bad jokes. Kortia didn't know about any faithful mermaid. To her Laiken was still the silly but charming young king of her childhood. In all innocence, she invited him back to her living-quarters. She cooked up a celebration meal on her little camp kitchen. Laiken stayed to eat, and drink her wine: their eyes meeting often, and fingers touching over the food and drink.

Laiken, drunk on nostalgia and sentiment, had forgotten entirely that he was supposed to be meeting his lover down on the shore, to accept or refuse her extraordinary sacrifice. He was astonished when he woke up in the middle of the night to find Mysotis's yellow eyes staring at him. He sat up sharply, pulling the blankets around his chin. Kortia stirred and muttered, cuddling up close in the narrow camp bed.

"Ah, Mysotis. Ah, I can explain—an old friend. It doesn't mean anything—"

His feeble babble faded into a whimper. He had noticed that the mermaid was not wearing her human form.

Mysotis knew he was not deliberately insulting her. She knew that he had innocently forgotten their tryst. But she was, after all, a princess of sorts: and she was desperately in love with poor Laiken. A lightning, sinuous movement passed between the two alien, warm bodies. The human girl shuddered, gasped once without waking, and lay deathly still.

"You've killed her!" wailed Laiken.

"I hope so," hissed the blue-and-yellow serpent. "And why not? You would have killed me, tonight, wouldn't you?"

Then she was gone, and Laiken was left staring at the little sharkskin pouch lying on its broken cord beside Kortia's body.

"Keep it," whispered Mysotis's voice in his ear. "I don't want it any more."

Laiken's fingers clutched his heart's desire, but he didn't know it. His eyes wild with horror, he ran sobbing from the tent, down over the deserted sands: and went on running and running until the salt water closed over his head . . . As he started to choke and drown he remembered another seashore with bitterness. He could have saved everyone a lot of trouble . . .

The next thing Laiken knew, someone was speaking to him: a rich, cold muscular broth of a voice which was somehow not entirely unfamiliar.

"Your eyes have a very odd look in them this morning, creature," drawled this tremendous voice idly. "Are you feeling unwell?"

"Where am I?" asked Laiken dazedly. "Is this hell?"

"Oh, how boring. You've started going sane. Now who would have thought it, after all these years?"

"Years?" repeated Laiken.

He was sitting on something like a pile of enormous old tyres. But the thick, rubbery rings pulsed rhythmically, and seemed full of steely life.

"Dear me. Do I understand that the whole of our pleasant relationship has now slipped your mind? What's the last thing you remember, Laiken?"

He shuddered. "The tent . . . Kortia dead. Drowning."

The Great Serpent sighed. "Ah well, I suppose all good things must come to an end. Unless—do you think if I were to tap you gently with the tip of my tail that would reverse this unwelcome development?"

Laiken observed the tail-tip in question. There was very little doubt as to the result of such a manoeuvre.

"By all means, tap away," he sighed. "But first, if you don't mind. How is it I'm not dead already? How did I learn to breathe water?"

"Ah, that's very simple. You hold clutched in your hand a powerful amulet. It appears that a charm which can keep a sea-creature alive in the dry air also works in reverse. Isn't that interesting? You know, it is my own magic but I still find out something new about it every day." After a pause, the great voice chuckled. "Little man, I know more of your story than you guess. Do tell me: why have you not instantly dropped that silly fish-hook? You do want to die, don't you?"

Laiken stared at the thing in his hand. "I don't know. I suppose I should."

A deep sigh quivered through all the massive shining coils. "Ah, Laiken, you don't remember now, but we have had some fine talks, you and I, about magic and prophecy, predestination and free will . . . A long time ago—a long time by your standards, that is—I learned that the king of a distant country would cause my death. Naturally, I laid that country to waste. It was a thoughtless reflex, the old, blind urge to hang on to power. For the truth is, I *want* to die. I'm old, I'm tired. It's time to let go . . . Sometimes, you know, I think occult knowledge is more trouble than it's worth . . . these foolish twists and turns that only lead you back to where you started. Laiken, if your death-wish is not so urgent at the moment you could do me a favour before you go."

"What's that?"

"Just get up and start walking. The rest will follow."

Laiken got up and started walking. His wits were feeling rather addled again. What was happening? Was this the cause and the circuitous end of all the tragic confusion of his life? Quite soon his head broke the surface and Laiken walked on, dripping and naked, out of the sea. He stood alone with the barren land behind him, and watched two figures coming slowly towards him along the shore, a woman and a boy. As they approached he saw that the woman was Mysotis. The boy seemed to be about fifteen years old. He had red hair.

"What are you doing here?" asked the king.

She was as beautiful as ever. He could not imagine how he could have contemplated exchanging her for any other love, at any price.

"I tried to save her for your sake, Laiken. But it was no good in the end. My own poison was too strong for me, and she died soon after the child was born. I brought him home, as you see. It seemed the least I could do. Besides, where else should I live? Between the water and the land I will stay forever, belonging to neither."

"You are breathing dry air."

"Because I have with me the other half of the ransom, don't you see?"

The red-haired boy was staring with calm disapproval at his father's nakedness. The two lovers stared at each other.

"You have the fish-hook? Then let the boy cast his line."

"Mysotis—can you forgive me?"

"Oh, yes. You can't help your nature."

"Then why are you looking so sad? This is the happy ending, isn't it? Everything's healed, we start again—"

King Laiken held the mermaid in his arms. Behind them the boy tossed his line out over the waves. The fish-hook disappeared, and it was done. There was a moment's doomladen silence, and then the whole ocean seemed to rear up into the sky. But it wasn't the ocean, it was the great Lord of the Sea himself. The tiny figure of the boy on the shore flicked its line casually over its shoulder to cast up the catch. The whole sky turned black as the great serpent passed over them, and then his enormous body fell onto the land.

Mysotis was in Laiken's arms but she was falling. He stumbled to his knees as she crumpled on the sand.

"Mysotis, what's happening to you?"

"Through me, a mortal has destroyed my father. Don't you understand? I said my father was a king under the sea but did I ever mention a mother? I never had one. I am a work of magic, and when the sorcerer dies, I too must die: die or change . . ."

She was changing, changing. There was a strange, loud, rushing sound in Laiken's ears: he thought it was his own blood pulsing.

"Mysotis, I love you. It's true, this time. Oh, I can't bear to lose you again, I'd give everything—"

"Don't cry Laiken, poor boy. You will never lose me now. Never lose me, never forget me . . ."

The mermaid was gone. Laiken found himself alone, standing up to his thighs in a great river, and his arms were full of flowers.

If you go to Laiken's country now you may still see him. It is not much talked about but everyone knows where you can find the President's old mad father. He'll be paddling by the bank of the river, mumbling to himself: "I used to have a problem but not any more. I never lose things now. Never lose her, she's mine forever." And his arms will be full of blue-petalled, yellow-eyed forget-me-nots.

SANDRA GILBERT

The Last Poem about the Snow Queen and Pinocchio

Sandra M. Gilbert is a poet, literary critic, and co-editor (with Susan Gubar) of *The Norton Anthology of Literature by Women*. She is the author of three books of poetry; *Acts of Attention: The Poems of D. H. Lawrence;* and co-author (with Susan Gubar) of *The Madwoman in the Attic: The Woman Writer and the Nineteenth-Century Literary Imagination* and *No Man's Land: The Place of the Woman Writer in the Twentieth-Century*. Gilbert is a Professor of English at Princeton University, but also makes her home in Berkeley, California, with her husband Elliot. They have three children.

The following poems come from Gilbert's most recent book, *Blood Pressure*, which includes several rich and sensual poems based on traditional fairy tales.

—T. W.

THE LAST POEM ABOUT THE SNOW QUEEN

Sandra M. Gilbert

> Then it was that little Gerda walked into the Palace, through the great gates, in a biting wind. . . . She saw Kay, and knew him at once; she flung her arms round his neck, held him fast, and cried, "Kay, little Kay, have I found you at last?"
> But he sat still, rigid and cold.
> —*Hans Christian Andersen, "The Snow Queen"*

You wanted to know "love" in all its habitats, wanted
to catalog the joints, the parts, the motions, wanted
to be a scientist of romance: you said
you had to study everything, go everywhere,
even here, even
this ice palace in the far north.

You said you were ready, you'd be careful.
Smart girl, you wore two cardigans, a turtleneck,
furlined boots, scarves,
a stocking cap with jinglebells.
And over the ice you came, gay as Santa,
singing and bringing gifts.

Ah, but the journey was long, so much longer
than you'd expected, and the air so thin,
the sky so high and black.
What are these cold needles, what are these shafts of ice,
you wondered on the fourteenth day.
What are those tracks that glitter overhead?

The one you came to see was silent,
he wouldn't say "stars" or "snow,"

wouldn't point south, wouldn't teach survival.
And you'd lost your boots, your furs,
now you were barefoot on the ice floes, fingers blue,
tears freezing and fusing your eyelids.

Now you know: this is the place
where water insists on being ice,
where wind insists on breathlessness,
where the will of the cold is so strong
that even the stone's desire for heat
is driven into the eye of night.

What will you do now, little Gerda?
Kay and the Snow Queen are one, they're a single
pillar of ice, a throne of silence—
and they love you
the way the teeth of winter
love the last red shred of November.

PINOCCHIO

Sandra M. Gilbert

1

Eyes on a slab of wood,
Giapetto's gaze,

as if through all those obstinate
layers, grainy veils,

film on film of forest, spring, fall,
root, bole, burl,

Pinocchio's wide round painted eyes
met his eyes.

2

Boys romp in the roadway. Pinocchio
romps and clatters. Overhead
April rattles twigs of chestnut,
cypress, pine. When Pinocchio

looks at the forest does he see
the eyes of cousins. Does he dream
a tickle of moss
on his painted scalp?

He creaks in his sleep!

3

Ill wood, ill wind, all nose
for sniffing out what's done, what's dung,

Pinocchio drifts in the jaws of winter,
fish or father, whale or wave:

everything's black down here,
nothing to touch except

the teeth of water.
This is the world, digesting

him, he thinks. Soon he'll be
a stump, a plank, driftwood, deadwood,

then a skin of paper, then a word,
a *what*. . . . And why?

What was "the truth" anyway?

4

A field. A hut. A hearth.
An iron grate. Flames, ashes.

Crows clack in the field, their gullets
open and close, ancient gates.

In the hearth ashes toss and shift,
flames mutter, wooden shapes spatter,

simmer: their sap gasps
bleak phrases: *Lies, all lies.*

Noses are lies. Breath.
Fathers. Forests.

Are lies. There is no.
"Truth." Anyway.

5

Giapetto walks on the hillside
in the evening cool, paces
leafy tunnels, admires
sighing lanes, muses, sees
a hillside full of boys
disguised as trees.

GENE WOLFE

Game in the Pope's Head

Gene Wolfe is one of the very finest writers in the fields of science fiction and fantasy today. His works, such as the award-winning *The Book of the New Sun* and the more recent *Soldier of the Mist* function on many levels, rewarding the serious reader while entertaining the more casual. Since the late 1960s, Wolfe has been writing perfect gems of stories, stories that offer both enlightenment and diversion, and are open to interpretation in a variety of ways.

Here he suggests that if we *are* the roles we play, then we'd better be careful what roles we choose.

—E. D.

GAME IN THE POPE'S HEAD

Gene Wolfe

"A sergeant was sent to the Pope's Head to investigate the case."
(From the *London Time*'s coverage of the murder of Anne Chapman,
September 11, 1888.)

Bev got up to water her plant. Edgar said, "You're over-watering that.
Look how yellow the leaves are."

They were indeed. The plant had extended its long, limp limbs over
the pictures and the sofa, and out through the broken window; but the
weeping flukes of these astonishing terminations were sallow and jaun-
diced.

"It *needs* water." Bev dumped her glass into the flowerpot, got a fresh
drink, and sat down again. "My play?" She turned up a card. "The next
card is 'What motion picture used the greatest number of living actors,
animal or human?' "

Edgar said, "I think I know. *Gandhi*. Half a million or so."

"Wrong. Debbie?"

"Hell, I don't know. *Close Encounters of the Third Kind*."

"Wrong. Randy?"

It was a moment before he realized that she meant him. So that was
his name: Randy. Yes, of course. He said, "Animal or human?"

"Right."

"Then it's animals, because they don't get paid." He tried to think of
animal movies, Bert Lahr terrified of Toto, *Lassie Come Home*. "*The Birds?*"

"Close. It was *The Swarm*, and there were twenty-two million actors."

Edgar said, "Mostly bees."

"I suppose."

There was a bee, or perhaps a wasp, on the plant, nearly invisible
against a yellow leaf. It did not appear to him to be exploring the surface
in the usual beeish or waspish way, but rather to be listening, head raised,
to their conversation. The room was bugged. He wanted to say, This

370

room is bugged; but before he could, Bev announced, "Your move, I think, Ed."

Ed said, "Bishop's pawn to the Bishop's four."

Debbie threw the dice and counted eight squares along the edge of the board. "Oh, good! Park Place, and I'll buy it." She handed him her money, and he gave her the deed.

Bev said, "Your turn."

He nodded, stuffed Debbie's money into his pocket, shuffled the cards, and read the top one.

> You are Randolph Carter. Three times you have dreamed of the marvelous city, Randolph Carter, and three times you have been snatched away from the high terrace above it.

Randolph Carter nodded again and put the card down. Debbie handed him a small pewter figure, a young man in old-fashioned clothes.

Bev asked, "Where did the fictional American philosopher Thomas Olney teach? Ed?"

"A *fictional* philosopher? Harvard, I suppose. Is it John Updike?"

"Wrong. Debbie?"

"Pass."

"Okay. Randy?"

"London."

Outside, a cloud covered the sun. The room grew darker as the light from the broken windows diminished.

Edgar said, "Good shot. Is he right, Bev?"

The bee, or wasp, rose from its leaf and buzzed around Edgar's bald head. He slapped at it, missing it by a fraction of an inch. "There's a fly in here!"

"Not now. I think it went out the window."

It had indeed been a fly, he saw, and not a bee or wasp at all—a bluebottle, no doubt gorged with carrion.

Bev said, "Kingsport, Massachusetts."

With an ivory hand, Edgar moved an ivory chessman. "Knight to the King's three."

Debbie tossed her dice onto the board. "Chance."

He picked up the card for her.

> You must descend the seven hundred steps to the Gate of Deeper Slumber. You may enter the Enchanted Wood or claim the sword Sacnoth. Which do you choose?

Debbie said, "I take the Enchanted Wood. That leaves you the sword, Randy."

Bev handed it to him. It was a falchion, he decided, curved and single-edged. After testing the edge with his finger, he laid it in his lap. It was not nearly as large as a real sword—less than sixteen inches long, he decided, including the hardwood handle.

"Your turn, Randy."

He discovered that he disliked Bev nearly as much as Debbie, hated her bleached blond hair, her scrawny neck. She and her dying plant were twins, one vegetable, one inhuman. He had not known that before.

She said, "It's the wheel of Fortune," as though he were stupid. He flicked the spinner.

"Unlawful evil."

Bev said, "Right," and picked up a card. "What do the following have in common: Pogo the Clown, H. H. Holmes, and Saucy Jacky?"

Edgar said, "That's an easy one. They're all pseudonyms of mass murderers."

"Right. For an extra point, name the murderers."

"Gacy, Mudgett, and . . . that's not fair. No one knows who the Ripper was."

But he did: just another guy, a guy like anybody else.

Debbie tossed her dice. "Whitechapel. I'll buy it. Give me the card, honey."

He picked up the deed and studied it. "Low rents."

Edgar chuckled. "And seldom paid."

"I know," Debbie told them, "but I want it, with lots of houses." He handed her the card, and she gave him the dice.

For a moment he rattled them in his hand, trying to imagine himself the little pewter man. It was no use; there was nothing of bright metal about him or his dark wool coat—only the edge of the knife. "Seven-come-eleven," he said, and threw.

"You got it," Debbie told him. "Seven. Shall I move it for you?"

"No," he said. He picked up the little pewter figure and walked (passed) past Holborn, the Temple (cavern-temple of Nasht and Kaman-Thah), and Lincoln's Inn Fields, along Cornhill and Leadenhall streets to Aldgate High Street, and so at last to Whitechapel.

Bev said, "You saw him coming, Deb," but her voice was very far away, far above the leaden (hall) clouds, filthy with coal smoke, that hung over the city. Wagons and hansom cabs rattled by. There was a public house at the corner of Brick Lane. He turned and went in.

The barmaid handed him his large gin. The barmaid had Debbie's dark hair, Debbie's dark good looks. When he had paid her, she left the bar and took a seat at one of the tables. Two others sat there already, and there were cards and dice, money and drinks before them. "Sit down," she said, and he sat.

The blonde turned over a card, the jack of spades. "What are the spades in a deck of cards?" she asked.

"Swords," he said. "From the Spanish word for a sword, *espada*. The jack of spades is really the jack of swords."

"Correct."

The other man said, "Knight to the White Chapel."

The door opened, letting in the evening with a wisp of fog, and the black knight. She was tall and slender and dressed like a cavalryman, in high boots and riding breeches. A pewter miniature of a knight's shield was pinned to her dark shirt.

The barmaid rattled the dice and threw.

"You're still alive," the black knight said. She strode to their table. Sergeant's chevrons had been sewn to the sleeves of the shirt. "This neighborhood is being evacuated, folks."

"Not by us," the other man said.

"By you now, sir. On my orders. As an officer of the law, I must order you to leave. There's a tank car derailed, leaking some kind of gas."

"That's fog," Randolph Carter told her. "Fog and smoke."

"Not *just* fog. I'm sorry, sir, but I must ask all of you to go. How long have you been here?"

"Sixteen years," the blonde woman said. "The neighborhood was a lot nicer when we came."

"It's some sort of chemical weapon, like LSD."

He asked, "Don't you want to sit down?" He stood, offering her his chair.

"My shot must be wearing off. The shot was supposed to protect me. I'm Sergeant . . . Sergeant . . ."

The other man said, "Very few of us are protected by shots, Sergeant Chapman. Shots usually kill people, particularly soldiers."

Randolph Carter looked at her shirt. The name *Chapman* was engraved on a stiff plastic plate there, the plate held out like a little shelf by the thrust of her left breast.

"Sergeant Anne Chapman of the United States Army. We think it's the plants, sir. All the psychoactive drugs we know about come from plants—opium, cocaine, heroin."

"You're the heroine," he told her gently. "Coming here like this to get us out."

"All of them chemicals the plants have stumbled across to protect us from insects, really. And now they've found something to protect the insects from us." She paused, staring at him. "That isn't right, is it?"

Again he asked, "Don't you want to sit down?"

"Gases from the comet. The comet's tail has wrapped all earth in poisonous gases."

The blonde murmured, "What is the meaning of this name given Satan: *Beelzebub*."

A tiny voice from the ceiling answered.

"You sir," the black knight said, "won't you come with me? We've got to get out of here."

"You can't get out of here," the other man told them.

He nodded to the knight. "I'll come with you, if you'll love me." He rose, pushing the sword up his coat sleeve, point first.

"Then come on." She took him by the arm and pulled him through the door.

A hansom cab rattled past.

"What is this place?" She put both hands to her forehead. "I'm dreaming, aren't I? This is a nightmare." There was a fly on her shoulder, a blowfly gorged with carrion. She brushed it off; it settled again, unwilling to fly through the night and the yellow fog. "No, I'm hallucinating."

He said, "I'd better take you to your room." The bricks were wet and slippery underfoot. As they turned a corner, and another, he told her what she could do for him when they reached her room. A dead bitch lay in the gutter. Despite the night and the chill of autumn, the corpse was crawling with flies.

Sickly yellow gaslight escaped from under a door. She tore herself from him and pushed it open. He came after her, his arms outstretched. "Is this where you live?"

The three players still sat at their table. They had been joined by a fourth, a new Randolph Carter. As the door flew wide the fourth player turned to look, but he had no face.

She whispered, "This is Hell, isn't it? I'm in Hell, for what I did. Because of what we did. We're all in Hell. I always thought it was just something the church made up, something to keep you in line, you know what I mean, sir?"

She was not talking to him, but he nodded sympathetically.

"Just a game in the pope's head. But it's real, it's here, and here we are."

"I'd better take you to your room," he said again.

She shuddered. "In Hell you can't pray, isn't that right? But I can— listen! I can pray! *Dear G—*"

He had wanted to wait, wanted to let her finish, but the sword, Sacnoth, would not wait. It entered her throat, more eager even than he, and emerged spent and swimming in scarlet blood.

The faceless Randolph Carter rose from the table. "Your seat, young man," he said through no mouth. "I'm merely the marker whom you have followed."

RAMSEY CAMPBELL

Playing the Game

Ramsey Campbell was represented in last year's volume by the subtle, disturbing "The Other Side," a story that typifies the artistry and craft that have made him one of the finest writers of horror fiction on the scene today. The author of nine novels and seven collections of short works, and the editor of a number of anthologies, he has received more awards for his work than any other horror writer.

This frightening tale goes hand in hand with the Wolfe story that precedes it, and demonstrates vividly that before you play the game not only must you be sure of the rules, but it would be wise to be certain you know exactly what the game is.

—E. D.

PLAYING THE GAME

Ramsey Campbell

When Marie called to say that someone wanted a reporter, Hill went out at once. He'd been staring at the blank page in his typewriter and wondering where he could find the enthusiasm to write. The winner of this week's singing contest at the Ferryman was Barbra Silver, fat as Santa Claus, all tinsel and shiny flesh done medium rare in a solarium —but he couldn't write that, and there wasn't another word in his head, any more than there were still ferries on the river. He headed for the lobby, glad of something else to do.

The man looked as if he hoped not to be noticed. His hands were trying to hide the torn pockets of his raincoat; fallen trouser-cuffs trailed over his shoes. Nevertheless Marie was pointing at him, unless she was still drying her green nails, and as Hill approached he turned quickly, determined to speak. "Do you investigate black magic?" he said.

"That depends." The man had the look of a pest in the street, eyes that expected disbelief and challenged the listener to escape before he was convinced. But the blank page was waiting like the worst question in an examination, and here at last might be a story worth writing. "Come and tell me about it," Hill said.

The man was visibly disappointed by the newsroom. No doubt he wanted the Hollywood version—miles of chattering typewriters beneath fluorescent tubes—rather than the cramped room full of half a dozen desks, desks and wastebins overflowing with paper and plastic cups and ragged blackened stubs of cheap cigars, the smells of aftershave and cheap tobacco, the window that buzzed like a dying fly whenever a lorry sped through town. Hill dragged two chairs to face each other and sat forward confidentially over his notebook. "Shoot," he said.

"There's a man down by the docks who claims he can cure illness without medicine. He's got everyone around him believing he can. They say he cures their aches and pains and saves them having to go to the doctor about their depressions. Sounds all right, doesn't it? But I happen to know," the ragged man said, lowering his voice still further until it was almost inaudible, "that he puts up his price once they need him. They have to go back to him, you see—it isn't a total cure. Maybe he doesn't mean it to be, or maybe it's all in their minds, until it wears off. Either way, you can see it's an addiction that costs them more than the doctor would."

He was plucking unconsciously at his torn pockets. "I'll tell you something else—every single one of his neighbors believes he should be left alone because he's doing so much good. That can't be right, can it? People don't take to things like that so easily unless they're afraid not to. Why won't they use the short cut through the docks any longer, if they think there's nothing to be afraid of?"

"You're suggesting that there is."

"I've got to be careful what I say." He looked afraid of being overheard, even in the empty room. "I don't live far from him," he said eventually. "Not far enough. I haven't had any trouble with him personally, but my next-door neighbour has. I can't tell you her name, she doesn't even know I'm here. You mustn't try to find her. In fact, to make sure you don't, I'm not going to tell you my name either."

Hill's interest was waning; his editor would never take a story with so few names. "Anyway," the man whispered, "she antagonized Mr. Matta, though she didn't mean to. She caught him up to no good in one of the old docks. So he said that if she was so fond of water, he'd make sure she got plenty. And the very next day her house started getting damp. She's had people in, but they can't find any reason for it, and it's just getting worse. Mould all over the walls—you wouldn't believe it unless you saw it for yourself. Only you'll have to take my word for it, I'm afraid."

He was faltering, having realized at last how unsatisfactory his information was. Yet Hill was suddenly a great deal more interested. Could it really be the same man? If so, Hill had reasons of his own to investigate him—and by God, there was nothing he'd like better. "This Mr. Matta," he said. "What can you tell me about him?"

His informant seemed to decide that he couldn't avoid telling. "He came every year with the carnival. Only the last time he was too ill to be moved, I think, so they found him a house. Or maybe they were glad to get rid of him."

It was the same man. All at once Hill's memories came flooding back: the carnival festooned with lights on the far bank of the river, in which blurred skeins of light wavered like waterweed as you crossed the bridge; the sounds of the shooting gallery ringing flat and thin across the water, the Ghost Train in which you heard the moaning of ships on the bay— and above all M. O. Matta, with his unchanging child's face and his stall full of games. "So he's still fond of playing games to frighten people, is he?" Hill said.

"He still sells them." That wasn't quite what Hill had meant, but perhaps the man was afraid to think otherwise. Of course Matta had sold games from his stall, though Hill had never understood why people bought them: the monkeys on sticks looked skeletal and desperate, and always fell back with a dying twitch just before they would have reached their goal; the faces of the chessmen were positively dismaying, as Hill had all too strong a reason to remember. In fact, when he recalled the sideshow—the bald bruised heads you tried to knock down with wooden balls but which sprang up at once, grinning like corpses—he couldn't understand why anyone would have lingered there voluntarily at all.

Once he'd seen Matta by the river at low tide, stooping to a fat whitish shape—but he was losing himself in his memories, and there were things he needed to know. "You say your friend antagonized Matta. In what way?"

"I told you, she was taking the short cut home." The man was digging his hands into his pockets, apparently unaware that they were tearing. "She saw the man he lives with taking him into the dock where the crane's fallen in. It was nearly dark, but he just sat there waiting. She thought she heard something in the water, and then he saw her. That's all."

It seemed suggestive enough. "Then unless there's anything else you can tell me," Hill said, "I just need Matta's address."

As soon as he'd given it the ragged man sidled out, trying to hide behind his shapeless collar. Hill lit his first cigar of the afternoon and thought how popular his investigation should be. They'd used to say that if Matta took a dislike to you when you bought from him, the games would always go wrong somehow—and how many children other than Hill must he have set out to terrify? As for the business with the docks, if that wasn't a case of drug smuggling, Hill was no investigative reporter. He went in to see the editor at once.

"Not enough," the editor said, too busy searching his waistcoat for pipe-cleaners even to look at Hill. "Someone who won't give his name tells you about someone who won't give her name. Smells like a hoax to me, or a grudge. Either way, it isn't for us. Just don't try to run before you can walk. You shouldn't need me to tell you you aren't ready for investigative work."

No, Hill thought bitterly: after two years he was still only good for the stuff nobody else would touch—Our Trivia Correspondent, Our Paltry Reporter. The others were rolling back from the pub as he returned to his desk, like a schoolboy who'd been kept in for being bored. By

God, he'd get his own back, with or without the editor's approval. He'd had nightmares for years after the night he had tried to see what Matta was doing in the caravan behind his stall.

All he'd glimpsed through the window was Matta playing solitaire of some kind, so why had the man taken such delight in terrifying him? All at once there had been nobody beyond the window, and the smooth childish face on its wrinkled neck had stooped out of the door, paralyzing the boy as he'd tried to run. "You like games, do you?" the thin soft voice had said. "Then we'll find you one."

The interior of the caravan had been crowded with half-carved shapes. Some looked more like bone than wood, including the one that had been protruding from the humped tangled sheets of the bunk. Eleven-year-old Hill hadn't seen much more, nor had he wanted to. Matta was setting out a chess game, and Hill hadn't known which was worse: the black pieces with their wide fanged grins, or the white, their pale shiny faces so bland he could almost see them drooling. "And there you are," Matta had whispered, carving the head of a limbless figure so deftly that Hill had imagined his face had already been there.

As soon as Matta placed the figure midway on the chessboard, the shadowy corners of the caravan had seemed full of faces, grinning voraciously, lolling expressionlessly. It had taken Hill a very long time to flee, for his legs had felt glued together, and all the time the child's face on the ageing body had watched him as if he was a dying insect. But when at last he had managed to run it was even worse: not so much the teeth that had glinted in the dark all the way home as the swollen white faces he'd sensed at his back, ready to nod down to him if he stumbled or even slackened his pace.

He emerged from his memories and found he'd torn the blank page out of the typewriter, so violently that the others were staring at him. Something had to be done about Matta, and soon—not only because of the way he'd exploited Hill's young imagination, but because it sounded as if his power over people had grown, with the same childish malevolence at its core. If this editor wouldn't print the story, Hill would find someone who would—and glancing at the red-veined faces of his colleagues, all of them drunk enough to be content with the worn-out town, he thought that might be the best move of all.

All at once he was eager to finish his chores, in order to be ready for what he had to do. By the time his shift was over he'd dealt with Barbra Silver—"a robust performance" he called it, which seemed satisfyingly ambiguous—and the rest of the trivia that was expected of him. As soon as he left the newspaper office he made for Matta's house.

Though it was still only late afternoon, there wasn't much light in the town. Over the bay the March sky was blue, but once you stepped into the streets it was impossible to see beyond their roofs. Shallow bay windows crowded away, overlapping the narrow pavements. Here was a chemist's, and here a Bingo parlour, smaller than front rooms; elsewhere he saw the exposed ribs of a lost neon sign, and crumbling names that had been painted on plaster. No wonder people felt the need for someone like Matta. "Order You're News Now" said a sign in a newsagent's window, and Hill thought the inadvertent promise might be true for everyone in time, the town was so small and dead.

Soon he reached the docks, which had been disused for years. The town lived off its chemical factories now, since trade no longer came so far upriver. Except for the short cut, wherever it was, there was no reason for anyone to visit the docks. They would be a perfect base for smuggling.

The roads into the docks were closed off by solid gates, rusty barbed wire, padlocked chains. He had to make his way between the warehouses, through alleys narrow as single file and even darker than the streets. He was relieved to emerge at last onto a dockside. Crumbling bollards sprouted from the broken pavement that surrounded several hundred square yards of murky water; warehouses hemmed in the dock. Above him in the small square lightless openings he heard fluttering. As the stagnant water slopped back and forth their reflections mouthed sleepily, a hundred mouths.

It didn't seem to be the dock the ragged man had mentioned. The alleys led him through another dock on the way to Matta's house, but there was no fallen crane there either, only more blackened warehouses, another hive of holes gaping at the sluggish water. The brow of an early moon peered over the edge of a roof at him; otherwise he felt he was alone in the whole dockland.

The next alley led him to a bridge across a small canal which bordered a street. Almost opposite the bridge was one of the poorest streets in town, its uneven cobblestones glittering with broken glass, its gutters clogged with litter. Each side was a terrace like a stage flat, hardly more than a long two-storey wall crammed with front doors and windows. It was the street where Matta lived.

There was nothing to distinguish the house from its neighbors—no sign saying M. O. MATTA, as there had always been on the sideshow. The black paint of the door was flaking, the number was askew; the windows were opaque with greyish net curtains. He loitered in the empty street, trying to be sure it was the right house. It seemed safe enough to do so, since beyond the curtains the house was dark—but the front door was opened, almost knocking him down, by a man who had to stoop through the doorway. "You want to see Mr. Matta," the huge blank-faced man said.

It wasn't a question. Hill had intended to bring someone whose illness was in no way psychological for Matta to try to cure—but if he fled now, he could never win Matta's confidence. "Yes," he said, though he felt he had no control over his words. "There's something wrong with my leg."

When the hulking man stood aside Hill entered, limping ostentatiously. The front door closed behind him at once, and so did the dark. In the musty unlit hallway, where there was scarcely room for anyone besides the hulking man and the staircase, he felt buried alive. In a moment the other had opened the door to the front room, and Matta sat waiting in a caved-in armchair. "Something wrong with your leg, is it?" Matta said.

He seemed not to have changed at all—the soft secretly delighted voice, the face smooth and placid as a sleeping child's—except that his face looked even more like a mask, on the ropy wizened frame. He was grinning to himself as always, but at least his words were reassuring; for a panicky moment Hill had thought Matta had recognized him. Why should that make him panic? He limped into the room, and Matta said "Let's see what we can do."

Hill couldn't see much in the room. Boxes, which he assumed contained games, and bits of wood were piled against the walls, taking up much of the limited space; a few chairs were crowded together in the middle of the floor, beneath an empty light-socket. The dimness and the smell of wood seemed stale. All at once the hulking man led him forward and sat him in a hard chair opposite Matta. Faces grinned out of the shadows, but they weren't why Hill was apprehensive. The man had led him forward so quickly that he'd forgotten to limp.

The huge man was returning from the darkest corner of the room, between Hill and the door, and he had a knife in his hand. In a moment Hill saw that the man was also carrying a faceless doll. He went to stand behind the armchair. His hands reached over Matta's shoulders, holding the knife and the doll. Hill sucked in his breath inadvertently and waited for Matta to take them—and then he saw that Matta was paralyzed. Only his face could move.

The huge hands began to work at once. In the dimness they looked as if they were growing from Matta's shoulders, their arms no longer than wrists. Almost at once they had finished carving, and the right hand turned the doll for Hill to see. He sat forward reluctantly, and couldn't make himself go closer. He was sure it was only the dimness that made the carved face look exactly like his—but for a moment he felt like a child again, in Matta's power.

Matta had trained his assistant well, that was all. The power was Hill's now, not Matta's. He was going to pretend that his limp was cured, and that would ingratiate him with Matta, help him set his trap. But Matta was gazing at him, and his grin was wider, more gleeful. It looked even more as if he was holding the doll before his face with deformed hands. "You came to spy on us," he said, and at once, almost negligently, one huge hand snapped the doll's leg.

At once Hill couldn't move his leg. Matta was leering at him, a pale mask propped on a wooden body, and above the mask a dim smudge with eyes was watching emptily. Many more faces were watching him, but he reminded himself that the others were only carved, and that allowed him to stumble to his feet. It had only been panic that had paralyzed his leg, after all.

Though Matta was still grinning—more widely, if anything—his eyes were unreadable. "I think you'd better go straight home," he said, his voice soft as dust.

Hill was so glad when the huge man didn't come for him that he headed blindly for the door. He'd have his revenge another day; Matta wasn't going anywhere. Just now he wanted to escape the dim cell of a room, the musty faces, the staleness. Matta was as bad as he remembered, but now that malevolence was senile. He glanced back from the hall and saw the huge man placing a box on Matta's lap—a game, with something like a worm carved on the lid. He hurried into the deserted twilit street, ignoring the twinge in his knee.

When he reached the canal he looked back. The huge man was watching from the doorway of the house. He stood there while Hill crossed the bridge, and all at once the reporter knew he was watching to see which way Hill went. He strode between the warehouses, into the alley he'd emerged from. As soon as he felt he'd waited long enough he peered out to make sure the man had gone back into the house, then he dodged into the adjacent alley.

They must think they'd scared him off with all their mumbo-jumbo and telling him to go straight home. Let Matta sit and play his game, whatever it was, however he could. Hill was going to find out what they wanted to hide, before they had a chance to do so. Though night had already fallen in the alleys, he ought to be able to see in the dock.

Dark cold stone loomed over him on both sides, blinding him. Perhaps he was going too fast, for sometimes the ache in his knee made him stumble; the rough walls scraped his knuckles. He must have strained a muscle in his leg when the huge man had urged him forward, or when he'd left so hurriedly. At least there seemed to be no obstacles to hinder him.

But there were. He reached a junction only to find that the right-hand alley was blocked by a rusty bedstead. It hardly mattered, since that route led to the docks he had already seen. He groped to the left, mortar crumbling between the bricks and gritting beneath his nails.

Before long he'd had to turn aside several times. Piles of chains and bollards, and in one place a door jammed between the walls, blocked some of the routes; sometimes he had to retrace his steps. In those few places where the glow of the darkening sky managed to reach, he could see nothing but the claustrophobic alleys, the towering windowless walls. He wished he hadn't come so far, for he wasn't sure he could find his way back if he had to do so. If Matta's assistant was responsible for the blocking of the alleys, presumably he would have blocked the route into the dock.

Hill was trying to remember the way back when he heard the wallowing. Something large was moving through water, quite near. It must be a boat—perhaps the one that Matta wanted nobody to see. He limped to the next junction, and saw that the attempts to turn people away hadn't quite succeeded. At the far end of the left-hand alley he could just see the width of a dock.

The end of the alley was blocked by a heap of rubble and twisted metal. It would have kept most people out, especially now when it was so nearly dark, but he hadn't come so far only to leave Matta's assistant the chance to clear away any evidence. He clambered over the rubble and dropped to the uneven pavement, where he almost staggered straight into the water as his aching leg gave way.

More than the danger made him stumble backward. His first glimpse of the water had shown him something larger than he was, inching toward the pavement and rising to meet him. When he looked again he saw it was a length of piping, pale as the moon and stouter than a man. It must have been ripples that had made it seem to move.

He would have to hurry despite his leg, which he must have wrenched while clambering. Already he was having to strain his eyes, though at least the moon was just visible above the warehouse to his left. He limped in that direction, peering at the pavement, the water, the warehouses; the blackness peered back at him hundred-eyed. There seemed to be nothing to find, and he'd ventured beyond the edge of moonlight before he realized that it should not be there at all. How could the moon be only just clearing the roofs when he'd seen its brow half an hour ago, barely visible above a warehouse somewhere over here?

It couldn't have been the moon the first time, that was all. He hadn't time to brood over it, for he had noticed something rather more disturbing; access to the dock from the river was blocked. One end of a bridge had torn loose or been dislodged, wedging tons of rusty iron in the entrance. What could Matta have been waiting for that night if the dock was inaccessible? Just what game was he playing? Surely there was no need to run, whatever the answer was, but Hill was running headlong now, anxious to be out of the darkness. He was so anxious that he almost stepped into space before he realized that the pavement wasn't there.

His bad leg saved him. He'd tottered backward as it threatened to give way. Now he could see the crane, quivering like jelly underwater, through the hole it had torn out of the pavement. There were splintered planks too, which must have bridged the gap until they had been destroyed. The gap was far too wide for him to jump with a bad leg. All at once he felt he was a victim of another of Matta's games, and only his inarticulate rage stood between him and utter panic.

He had no reason to panic. Surely he could find his way back, since he had to do so. There was no point in waiting for the moon to rise higher, when the clouds never left it alone for very long; besides, he preferred not to see the dock more clearly—the walls and the water maggoty with windows, the buildings that seemed so lonely they no longer had anything human about them, the drowned objects that looked as if they were squirming. He was very near to panic as he scrambled over the rubble into the alley, particularly since the whitish pipe appeared to have drifted closer to the pavement. Perhaps it had been a distorted reflection of the moon; certainly it reminded him less of a pipe.

The moonlight didn't reach into the alleys. When he lowered himself from the heap of rubble, the shock of the darkness was almost physical. He made himself hurry—he knew that the floor of the alley was clear of obstructions—though it felt as if the walls had captured him, were leading him blindfolded, too fast for his limp. Somewhere behind him he heard the wallowing again, which sounded now like someone emerging hugely from a bath. He restrained himself from going back to see. He wasn't even sure that he wanted to know.

He'd regained some confidence, and was striding quickly despite his bad leg, when he ran straight into something like an outstretched limb. He'd cried out before he realized what the obstruction was: a pile of bollards. He must have taken a wrong turning in the dark.

He groped his way back to the last junction and limped in the other direction. Yes, this must be right, for now he was able to follow several alleys unhindered, and soon he could see an open space ahead. He was almost there before he saw the fallen bridge, and realized he had come back to the same alley into the dock.

He couldn't think where he had gone wrong. He could only trudge back into the narrow dark. At least the moonlight was beginning to filter down, and showed him an intersection almost at once. He was sure he hadn't turned here on his way to the dock; he would have noticed the row of whitish tyres in the left-hand alley, tyres stacked together like a pipe. In the intermittent moonlight they seemed to squirm restlessly, and he was glad he didn't have to pass them.

Three junctions further on he thought he'd found where he had gone wrong. That was a relief, because the moonlight was reaching as far into the alleys as it would come; soon the light would be receding. He could just see the walls in those moments when the clouds exposed the moon, and so he was able to run, despite the throbbing of his leg. He'd turned three corners, skinning his knuckles on one, before he almost ran into the stack of whitish tyres.

It was impossible. He stumbled back a few yards to the intersection. There was the dock and the fallen bridge, two intersections distant. But hadn't he seen the tyres in the first alley he'd crossed on his way from the dock? He must have been confused by the dark—and by Matta, for he felt as if he was trapped in another of Matta's games.

That made him feel childish, and in danger of panic. But he wasn't childish—Matta was, with his malevolent games. His face was what he was. No doubt he was still sitting with the game his assistant had given him, but Hill refused to try to deduce what that game might be. He needed all his wits to figure out the way back, before the fitful moonlight convinced him that the whitish tyres were squirming silently, mouth open, down the alley toward him. They looked rather large for tyres.

He turned before he was sure where to go, for the moonlight was draining away, up the walls. He plunged into the thickening dark. He was almost sure of his direction, but hadn't he been sure before? He was levering himself along with his hands on both walls, partly to feel that the suffocating dark was nothing but bricks. That wasn't entirely reassuring, for if he collided with anything now, the first part of him it would touch was his face. For some reason that anxiety intensified once he was out of sight of the whitish segments, the tyres. But it was his left hand that collided with something in the dark, an object that was clinging to the wall.

It was a ladder. The icy rungs felt scarred with rust, which flaked away beneath his fingers. The chafing set his teeth on edge, and he was limping away, relieved that it was only a ladder, before he realized the chance he was missing. He went back and bracing his heels against the wall, seized two rungs and tugged. The ladder held. At once, ignoring his bad leg, he began to climb.

It must be windy at the top, for he could hear a large object slithering closer across the roof. The wind didn't matter, for he wouldn't be crossing the roof. He needed only to climb high enough to see where the street was, which general direction he would have to follow. He was climbing eagerly toward the moonlight—too eagerly, for his aching leg gave away, and he almost fell. As he hung there, gripping the rungs in momentary panic, he was close to realizing what game Matta's assistant had brought him.

He tried to grasp the thought, less for its own sake than to distract himself from thinking how high he'd climbed in the dark. He was nearly at the top. Above him the sky swam greyly, suffocating the moon; the edge of the roof sailed free in space. He closed his eyes and clung to the metal, then he recommenced climbing, mechanically but carefully. Matta's game had had something like a worm, a maggot, carved on the box—something fat and sinuous. Of course! One of his hands grabbed a rusty handhold at the roof's edge, then he heaved himself up with the other. There he rested, eyes closed, before looking up. Of course, he should have known at once what the game must be—Matta's version of snakes and ladders.

He was still resting at the top of the ladder when the moon-coloured fat-lipped mouth, yawning wide as its body and wider than his head, stooped toward him.

F. PAUL WILSON

Faces

F. Paul Wilson is a practicing medical doctor, whose skills and professional knowledge no doubt helped make the following story all the more distressingly real. We're not sure how he has found the time in his life to write fine science fiction novels, and the major works of horror and fantasy that have made his name widely known in the last decade. *The Keep* was Wilson's first great success, a wonderful blend of fantasy, horror, and a Central European background. His most recent novel is the ambitious and effective thriller *Black Wind*, which again mixes to good effect the conventions of various genres.

"Faces" shows how the little (and larger) cruelties of childhood can reverberate into the future. It is not a story for the squeamish, but nonetheless a quite poignant and moving tale.

—E. D.

FACES

F. Paul Wilson

Bite her face off.

No pain. Her dead already. Kill her quick like others. Not want make pain. Not her fault.

The boyfriend groan but not move. Face way on ground now. Got from behind. Got quick. Never see. He can live.

Girl look me after the boyfriend go down. Gasp first. When see face start scream. Two claws not cut short rip her throat before sound get loud.

Her sick-scared look just like all others. Hate that look. Hate it terrible.

Sorry, girl. Not your fault.

Chew her face skin. Chew all. Chew hard and swallow. Warm wet redness make sickish but chew and chew. Must eat face. Must get all down. Keep down.

Leave the eyes.

The boyfriend groan again. Move arm. Must leave quick. Take last look blood and teeth and stare-eyes that once pretty girlface.

Sorry, girl. Not your fault.

Got go. Get way hurry. First take money. Girl money. Take the boyfriend wallet, also too. Always take money. Need money.

Go now. Not too far. Climb wall of near building. Find dark spot where can see and not be seen. Where can wait. Soon the Detective Harrison arrive.

In downbelow can see the boyfriend roll over. Get to knees. Sway. See him look the girlfriend.

The boyfriend scream terrible. Bad to hear. Make so sad. Make cry.

Kevin Harrison heard Jacobi's voice on the other end of the line and wanted to be sick.

"Don't say it," he groaned.

"Sorry," said Jacobi. "It's another one."

"Where?"

"West Forty-ninth, right near—"

"I'll find it." All he had to do was look for the flashing red lights. "I'm on my way. Shouldn't take me too long to get in from Monroe at this hour."

"We've got all night, lieutenant." Unsaid but well understood was an admonishing, *You're the one who wants to live on Long Island.*

Beside him in the bed, Martha spoke from deep in her pillow as he hung up.

"Not another one?"

"Yeah."

"Oh, God! When is it going to stop?"

"When I catch the guy."

Her hand touched his arm, gently. "I know all this responsibility's not easy. I'm here when you need me."

"I know." He leaned over and kissed her. "Thanks."

He left the warm bed and skipped the shower. No time for that. A fresh shirt, yesterday's rumpled suit, a tie shoved into his pocket, and he was off into the winter night.

With his secure little ranch house falling away behind him, Harrison felt naked and vulnerable out here in the dark. As he headed south on Glen Cove Road toward the LIE, he realized that Martha and the kids were all that were holding him together these days. His family had become an island of sanity and stability in a world gone mad.

Everything else was in flux. For reasons he still could not comprehend, he had volunteered to head up the search for this killer. Now his whole future in the department had come to hinge on his success in finding him.

The papers had named the maniac "the Facelift Killer." As apt a name as the tabloids could want, but Harrison resented it. The moniker was callous, trivializing the mutilations perpetrated on the victims. But it had caught on with the public and they were stuck with it, especially with all the ink the story was getting.

Six killings, one a week for six weeks in a row, and eight million people in a panic. Then, for almost two weeks, the city had gone without a new slaying.

Until tonight.

Harrison's stomach pitched and rolled at the thought of having to look at one of those corpses again.

"That's enough," Harrison said, averting his eyes from the faceless thing.

The raw, gouged, bloody flesh, the exposed muscle and bone were bad enough, but it was the eyes—those naked, lidless, staring eyes were the worst.

"This makes seven," Jacobi said at his side. Squat, dark, jowly, the sergeant was chewing a big wad of gum, noisily, aggressively, as if he had a grudge against it.

"I can count. Anything new?"

"Nah. Same m.o. as ever—throat slashed, money stolen, face gnawed off."

Harrison shuddered. He had come in as Special Investigator after the third Facelift killing. He had inspected the first three via coroner's photos. Those had been awful. But nothing could match the effect of the real thing up close and still warm and oozing. This was the fourth fresh victim he had seen. There was no getting used to this kind of mutilation, no matter how many he saw. Jacobi put on a good show, but Harrison sensed the revulsion under the sergeant's armor.

And yet . . .

Beneath all the horror, Harrison sensed something. There was anger here, sick anger and hatred of spectacular proportions. But beyond that, something else, an indefinable something that had drawn him to this case. Whatever it was, that something called to him, and still held him captive.

If he could identify it, maybe he could solve this case and wrap it up. And save his ass.

If he did solve it, it would be all on his own. Because he wasn't getting much help from Jacobi, and even less from his assigned staff. He knew what they all thought—that he had taken the job as a glory grab, a shortcut to the top. Sure, they wanted to see this thing wrapped up, too, but they weren't shedding any tears over the shit he was taking in the press and on TV and from City Hall.

Their attitude was clear: *If you want the spotlight, Harrison, you gotta take the heat that goes with it.*

They were right, of course. He could have been working on a quieter case, like where all the winos were disappearing to. He'd chosen this instead. But he wasn't after the spotlight, dammit! It was this case— something about this case!

He suddenly realized that there was no one around him. The body had been carted off, Jacobi had wandered back to his car. He had been left standing alone at the far end of the alley.

And yet not alone.

Someone was watching him. He could feel it. The realization sent a little chill—one completely unrelated to the cold February wind—trickling down his back. A quick glance around showed no one paying him the slightest bit of attention. He looked up.

There!

Somewhere in the darkness above, someone was watching him. Probably from the roof. He could sense the piercing scrutiny and it made him a little weak. That was no ghoulish neighborhood voyeur, up there. That was the Facelift Killer.

He had to get to Jacobi, have him seal off the building. But he couldn't act spooked. He had to act calm, casual.

See the Detective Harrison's eyes. See from way up in dark. Tall-thin. Hair brown. Nice eyes. Soft brown eyes. Not hard like many-many eyes. Look here. Even from here see eyes make wide. Him know it me.

Watch the Detective Harrison turn slow. Walk slow. Tell inside him want to run. Must leave here. Leave quick.

Bend low. Run cross roof. Jump to next. And next. Again til most block away. Then down wall. Wrap scarf round head. Hide bad-face. Hunch inside big-big coat. Walk through lighted spots.

Hate light. Hate crowds. Theatres here. Movies and plays. Like them. Some night sneak in and see. See one with man in mask. Hang from wall behind big drapes. Make cry.

Wish there mask for me.

Follow street long way to river. See many lights across river. Far past there is place where grew. Never want go back to there. Never.

Catch back of truck. Ride home.

Home. Bright bulb hang ceiling. Not care. The Old Jessi waiting. The Jessi friend. Only friend. The Jessi's eyes not see. Ever. When the Jessi look me, her face not wear sick-scared look. Hate that look.

Come in kitchen window. The Jessi's face wrinkle-black. Smile when hear me come. TV on. Always on. The Jessi can not watch. Say it company for her.

"You're so late tonight."

"Hard work. Get moneys tonight."

Feel sick. Want cry. Hate kill. Wish stop.

"That's nice. Are you going to put it in the drawer?"

"Doing now."

Empty wallets. Put moneys in slots. Ones first slot. Fives next slot. Then tens and twenties. So the Jessi can pay when boy bring foods. Sometimes eat stolen foods. Mostly the Jessi call for foods.

The Old Jessi hardly walk. Good. Do not want her go out. Bad peoples round here. Many. Hurt one who not see. One bad man try hurt Jessi once. Push through door. Thought only the blind Old Jessi live here.

Lucky the Jessi not alone that day.

Not lucky bad man. Hit the Jessi. Laugh hard. Then look me. Get sick-scared look. Hate that look. Kill him quick. Put in tub. Bleed there. Bad man friend come soon after. Kill him also too. Late at night take both dead bad men out. Go through window. Carry down wall. Throw in river.

No bad men come again. Ever.

"I've been waiting all night for my bath. Do you think you can help me a little?"

Always help. But the Old Jessi always ask. The Jessi very polite.

Sponge the Old Jessi back in tub. Rinse her hair. Think of the Detective Harrison. His kind eyes. Must talk him. Want stop this. Stop now. Maybe will understand. Will. Can feel.

Seven grisly murders in eight weeks.

Kevin Harrison studied a photo of the latest victim, taken before she was mutilated. A nice eight by ten glossy furnished by her agent. A real beauty. A dancer with Broadway dreams.

He tossed the photo aside and pulled the stack of files toward him. The remnants of six lives in this pile. Somewhere within had to be an answer, the thread that linked each of them to the Facelift Killer.

But what if there was no common link? What if all the killings were at random, linked only by the fact that they were beautiful? Seven deaths, all over the city. All with their faces gnawed off. *Gnawed.*

He flipped through the victims one by one and studied their photos. He had begun to feel he knew each one of them personally:

Mary Detrick, 20, a junior at N.Y.U., killed in Washington Square Park on January 5. She was the first.

Mia Chandler, 25, a secretary at Merrill Lynch, killed January 13 in Battery Park.

Ellen Beasley, 22, a photographer's assistant, killed in an alley in Chelsea on January 22.

Hazel Hauge, 30, artist agent, killed in her Soho loft on January 27.

Elisabeth Paine, 28, housewife, killed on February 2 while jogging late in Central Park.

Joan Perrin, 25, a model from Brooklyn, pulled from her car while stopped at a light on the Upper East Side on February 8.

He picked up the eight by ten again. And the last: Liza Lee, 21, Dancer. Lived across the river in Jersey City. Ducked into an alley for a toot with her boyfriend tonight and never came out.

Three blondes, three brunettes, one redhead. Some stacked, some on the flat side. All caucs except for Perrin. All lookers. But besides that, how in the world could these women be linked? They came from all over town, and they met their respective ends all over town. What could—

"Well, you sure hit the bullseye about that roof!" Jacobi said as he burst into the office.

Harrison straightened in his chair. "What did you find?"

"Blood."

"Whose?"

"The victim's."

"No prints? No hairs? No fibers?"

"We're working on it. But how'd you figure to check the roof top?"

"Lucky guess."

Harrison didn't want to provide Jacobi with more grist for the departmental gossip mill by mentioning his feeling of being watched from up there.

But the killer *had* been watching, hadn't he?

"Any prelims from pathology?"

Jacobi shrugged and stuffed three sticks of gum into his mouth. Then he tried to talk.

"Same as ever. Money gone, throat ripped open by a pair of sharp pointed instruments, not knives, the bite marks on the face are the usual: the teeth that made them aren't human, but the saliva is."

The "non-human" teeth part—more teeth, bigger and sharper than found in any human mouth—had baffled them all from the start. Early on someone remembered a horror novel or movie where the killer used some weird sort of false teeth to bite his victims. That had sent them off on a wild goose chase to all the dental labs looking for records of bizarre bite prostheses. No dice. No one had seen or even heard of teeth that could gnaw off a person's face.

Harrison shuddered. What could explain wounds like that? What were they dealing with here?

The irritating pops, snaps, and cracks of Jacobi's gum filled the office.

"I liked you better when you smoked."

Jacobi's reply was cut off by the phone. The sergeant picked it up.

"Detective Harrison's office!" he said, listened a moment, then, with his hand over the mouthpiece, passed the receiver to Harrison. "Some fairy wantsh to shpeak to you," he said with an evil grin.

"Fairy?"

"Hey," he said, getting up and walking toward the door. "I don't mind. I'm a liberal kinda guy, y'know?"

Harrison shook his head with disgust. Jacobi was getting less likeable every day.

"Hello. Harrison here."

"Shorry dishturb you, Detective Harrishon."

The voice was soft, pitched somewhere between a man's and a woman's, and sounded as if the speaker had half a mouthful of saliva. Harrison had never heard anything like it. Who could be—?

And then it struck him: It was three a.m. Only a handful of people knew he was here.

"Do I know you?"

"No. Watch you tonight. You almosht shee me in dark."

That same chill from earlier tonight ran down Harrison's back again.

"Are . . . are you who I think you are?"

There was a pause, then one soft word, more sobbed than spoken: "Yesh."

If the reply had been cocky, something along the line of *And just who do you think I am?*, Harrison would have looked for much more in the way of corroboration. But that single word, and the soul deep heartbreak that propelled it, banished all doubt.

My God! He looked around frantically. No one in sight. Where the fuck was Jacobi now when he needed him? This was the Facelift Killer! He needed a trace!

Got to keep him on the line!

"I have to ask you something to be sure you are who you say you are."

"Yesh?"

"Do you take anything from the victims—I mean, besides their faces?"

"Money. Take money."

This is him! The department had withheld the money part from the papers. Only the real Facelift Killer could know!

"Can I ask you something else?"

"Yesh."

Harrison was asking this one for himself.

"What do you do with the faces?"

He had to know. The question drove him crazy at night. He dreamed about those faces. Did the killer tack them on the wall, or press them in a book, or freeze them, or did he wear them around the house like that Leatherface character from that chainsaw movie?

On the other end of the line he sensed sudden agitation and panic: "No! Can not shay! Can *not*!"

"Okay, okay. Take it easy."

"You will help shtop?"

"Oh, yes! Oh, God, yes, I'll help you stop!" He prayed his genuine heartfelt desire to end this was coming through. "I'll help you any way I can!"

There was a long pause, then:

"You hate? Hate me?"

Harrison didn't trust himself to answer that right away. He searched his feelings quickly, but carefully.

"No," he said finally. "I think you have done some awful, horrible things but, strangely enough, I don't hate you."

And that was true. Why didn't he hate this murdering maniac? Oh, he wanted to stop him more than anything in the world, and wouldn't hesitate to shoot him dead if the situation required it, but there was no personal hatred for the Facelift Killer.

What is it in you that speaks to me? he wondered.

"Shank you," said the voice, couched once more in a sob.

And then the killer hung up.

Harrison shouted into the dead phone, banged it on his desk, but the line was dead.

"What the hell's the matter with you?" Jacobi said from the office door.

"That so-called 'fairy' on the phone was the Facelift Killer, you idiot! We could have had a trace if you'd stuck around!"

"Bullshit!"

"He knew about taking the money!"

"So why'd he talk like that? That's a dumb-ass way to try to disguise your voice."

And then it suddenly hit Harrison like a sucker punch to the gut. He swallowed hard and said:

"Jacobi, how do you think your voice would sound if you had a jaw crammed full of teeth much larger and sharper than the kind found in the typical human mouth?"

Harrison took genuine pleasure in the way Jacobi's face blanched slowly to yellow-white.

He didn't get home again until after seven the following night. The whole department had been in an uproar all day. This was the first break they had had in the case. It wasn't much, but contact had been made. That was the important part. And although Harrison had done nothing he could think of to deserve any credit, he had accepted the commissioner's compliments and encouragement on the phone shortly before he had left the office tonight.

But what was most important to Harrison was the evidence from the call—*Damn*! he wished it had been taped—that the killer wanted to stop. They didn't have one more goddamn clue tonight than they'd had yesterday, but the call offered hope that soon there might be an end to this horror.

Martha had dinner waiting. The kids were scrubbed and pajamaed and waiting for their goodnight kiss. He gave them each a hug and poured himself a stiff scotch while Martha put them in the sack.

"Do you feel as tired as you look?" she said as she returned from the bedroom wing.

She was a big woman with bright blue eyes and natural dark blond hair. Harrison toasted her with his glass.

"The expression 'dead on his feet' has taken on a whole new meaning for me."

She kissed him, then they sat down to eat.

He had spoken to Martha a couple of times since he had left the house twenty hours ago. She knew about the phone call from the Facelift Killer, about the new hope in the department about the case, but he was glad she didn't bring it up now. He was sick of talking about it. Instead, he sat in front of his cooling meatloaf and wrestled with the images that had been nibbling at the edges of his consciousness all day.

"What are you daydreaming about?" Martha said.

Without thinking, Harrison said, "Annie."

"Annie who?"

"My sister."

Martha put her fork down. "Your sister? Kevin, you don't have a sister."

"Not any more. But I did."

Her expression was alarmed now. "Kevin, are you all right? I've known your family for ten years. Your mother has never once mentioned—"

"We don't talk about Annie, Mar. We try not to even think about her. She died when she was five."

"Oh. I'm sorry."

"Don't be. Annie was . . . deformed. Terribly deformed. She never really had a chance."

Open trunk from inside. Get out. The Detective Harrison's house here. Cold night. Cold feel good. Trunk air make sick, dizzy.

Light here. Hurry round side of house.

Darker here. No one see. Look in window. Dark but see good. Two little ones there. Sleeping. Move away. Not want them cry.

Go more round. The Detective Harrison with lady. Sit table near window. Must be wife. Pretty but not oh-so-beauty. Not have momface. Not like ones who die.

Watch behind tree. Hungry. They not eat food. Talk-talk-talk. Can not hear.

The Detective Harrison do most talk. Kind face. Kind eyes. Some terrible sad there. Hides. Him understands. Heard in phone voice. Understands. Him one can stop kills.

Spent day watch the Detective Harrison car. All day watch at police house. Saw him come-go many times. Soon dark, open trunk with claw. Ride with him. Ride long. Wonder what town this?

The Detective Harrison look this way. Stare like last night. Must not see me! Must *not*!

Harrison stopped in mid-sentence and stared out the window as his skin prickled.

That *watched* feeling again.

It was the same as last night. Something was out in the backyard watching them. He strained to see through the wooded darkness outside the window but saw only shadows within shadows.

But something was *there*! He could feel it!

He got up and turned on the outside spotlights, hoping, *praying* that the backyard would be empty.

It was.

He smiled to hide his relief and glanced at Martha.

"Thought that raccoon was back."

He left the spots on and settled back into his place at the table. But the thoughts racing through his mind made eating unthinkable.

What if that maniac had followed him out here? What if the call had been a ploy to get him off-guard so the Facelift Killer could do to Martha what he had done to the other women?

My God . . .

First thing tomorrow morning he was going to call the local alarm boys and put in a security system. Cost be damned, he had to have it. Immediately!

As for tonight . . .

Tonight he'd keep the .38 under the pillow.

Run away. Run low and fast. Get bushes before light come. Must stay way now. Not come back.

The Detective Harrison *feel* me. Know when watched. Him the one, sure.

Walk in dark, in woods. See back many houses. Come park. Feel strange. See this park before. Can not be—

Then know.

Monroe! This Monroe! Born here! Live here! Hate Monroe! Monroe bad place, bad people! House, home, old home near here! There! Cross park! Old home! New color but same house.

Hate house!

Sit on froze park grass. Cry. Why Monroe? Do not want be in Monroe. The Mom gone. The Sissy gone. The Jimmy very gone. House here.

Dry tears. Watch old home long time till light go out. Wait more. Go to windows. See new folks inside. The Mom took the Sissy and go. Where? Don't know.

Go to back. Push cellar window. Crawl in. See good in dark. New folks make nice cellar. Wood on walls. Rug on floor. No chain.

Sit floor. Remember . . .

Remember hanging on wall. Look little window near ceiling. Watch kids play in park cross street. Want go with kids. Want play there with kids. Want have friends.

But the Mom won't let. Never leave basement. Too strong. Break everything. Have TV. Broke it. Have toys. Broke them. Stay in basement. Chain round waist hold to center pole. Can not leave.

Remember terrible bad things happen.

Run. Run way Monroe. Never come back.

Til now.

Now back. Still hate house! Want hurt house. See cigarettes. With matches. Light all. Burn now!

Watch rug burn. Chair burn. So hot. Run back to cold park. Watch house burn. See new folks run out. Trucks come throw water. House burn and burn.

Glad but tears come anyway.

Hate house. Now house gone. Hate Monroe.

Wonder where the Mom and the Sissy live now.

Leave Monroe for new home and the Old Jessi.

The second call came the next day. And this time they were ready for it. The tape recorders were set, the computers were waiting to begin the tracing protocol. As soon as Harrison recognized the voice, he gave the signal. On the other side of the desk, Jacobi put on a headset and people started running in all directions. Off to the races.

"I'm glad you called," Harrison said. "I've been thinking about you."

"You undershtand?" said the soft voice.

"I'm not sure."

"Musht help shtop."

"I will! I will! Tell me how!"

"Not know."

There was a pause. Harrison wasn't sure what to say next. He didn't want to push, but he had to keep him on the line.

"Did you . . . hurt anyone last night."

"No. Shaw houshes. Your houshe. Your wife."

Harrison's blood froze. Last night—in the back yard. That had been the Facelift Killer in the dark. He looked up and saw genuine concern in Jacobi's eyes. He forced himself to speak.

"You were at my house? Why didn't you talk to me?"

"No-no! Can not let shee! Run way your house. Go mine!"

"*Yours?* You live in Monroe?"

"No! Hate Monroe! Once lived. Gone long! Burn old houshe. Never go back!"

This could be important. Harrison phrased the next question carefully.

"You burned your old house? When was that?"

If he could just get a date, a year . . .

"Lasht night."

"*Last night?*" Harrison remembered hearing the sirens and fire horns in the early morning darkness.

"Yesh! Hate houshe!"

And then the line went dead.

He looked at Jacobi who had picked up another line.

"Did we get the trace?"

"Waiting to hear. Christ, he sounds retarded, doesn't he?"

Retarded. The word sent ripples across the surface of his brain. Non-human teeth . . . Monroe . . . retarded . . . a picture was forming in the settling sediment, a picture he felt he should avoid.

"Maybe he is."

"You'd think that would make him easy to—"

Jacobi stopped, listened to the receiver, then shook his head disgustedly.

"What?"

"Got as far as the Lower East Side. He was probably calling from somewhere in one of the projects. If we'd had another thirty seconds—"

"We've got something better than a trace to some lousy pay phone," Harrison said. "We've got his old address!" He picked up his suit coat and headed for the door.

"Where we goin'?"

"Not 'we.' Me. I'm going out to Monroe."

Once he reached the town, it took Harrison less than an hour to find the Facelift Killer's last name.

He first checked with the Monroe Fire Department to find the address of last night's house fire. Then he went down to the brick fronted Town Hall and found the lot and block number. After that it was easy to look up its history of ownership. Mr. and Mrs. Elwood Scott were the current owners of the land and the charred shell of a three-bedroom ranch that sat upon it.

There had only been one other set of owners: Mr. and Mrs. Thomas Baker. He had lived most of his life in Monroe but knew nothing about the Baker family. But he knew where to find out: Captain Jeremy Hall, Chief of Police in the Incorporated Village of Monroe.

Captain Hall hadn't changed much over the years. Still had a big belly, long sideburns, and hair cut bristly short on the sides. That was the "in" look these days, but Hall had been wearing his hair like that for at least thirty years. If not for his Bronx accent, he could have played a redneck sheriff in any one of those southern chain gang movies.

After pleasantries and local-boy-leaves-home-to-become-big-city-cop-and-now-comes-to-question-small-town-cop banter, they got down to business.

"The Bakers from North Park Drive?" Hall said after he had noisily sucked the top layer off his steaming coffee. "Who could forget them? There was the mother, divorced, I believe, and the three kids—two girls and the boy."

Harrison pulled out his note pad. "The boy's name—what was it?"

"Tommy, I believe. Yeah—Tommy. I'm sure of it."

"He's the one I want."

Hall's eyes narrowed. "He is, is he? You're working on that Facelift case aren't you?"

"Right."

"And you think Tommy Baker might be your man?"

"It's a possibility. What do you know about him?"

"I know he's dead."

Harrison froze. "Dead? That can't be!"

"It sure as hell *can* be!" Without rising from his seat, he shouted through his office door. "Murph! Pull out that old file on the Baker case! Nineteen eighty-four, I believe!"

"Eighty-four?" Harrison said. He and Martha had been living in Queens then. They hadn't moved back to Monroe yet.

"Right. A real messy affair. Tommy Baker was thirteen years old when he bought it. And he bought it. *Believe* me, he bought it!"

Harrison sat in glum silence, watching his whole theory go up in smoke.

*   *   *

The Old Jessi sleeps. Stand by mirror near tub. Only mirror have. No like them. The Jessi not need one.

Stare face. Bad face. Teeth, teeth, teeth. And hair. Arms too thin, too long. Claws. None have claws like my. None have face like my.

Face not better. Ate pretty faces but face still same. Still cause sick-scared look. Just like at home.

Remember home. Do not want but thoughts will not go.

Faces.

The Sissy get the Mom-face. Beauty face. The Tommy get the Dad-face. Not see the Dad. Never come home anymore. Who my face? Never see where come. Where my face come? My hands come?

Remember home cellar. Hate home! Hate cellar more! Pull on chain round waist. Pull and pull. Want out. Want play. *Please.* No one let.

One day when the Mom and the Sissy go, the Tommy bring friends. Come down cellar. Bunch on stairs. Stare. First time see sick-scared look. Not understand.

Friends! Play! Throw ball them. They run. Come back with rocks and sticks. Still sick-scared look. Throw me, hit me.

Make cry. Make the Tommy laugh.

Whenever the Mom and the Sissy go, the Tommy come with boys and sticks. Poke and hit. Hurt. Little hurt on skin. Big hurt inside. Sick-scared look hurt most of all. Hate look. Hate hurt. Hate them.

Most hate the Tommy.

One night chain breaks. Wait on wall for the Tommy. Hurt him. Hurt the Tommy outside. Hurt the Tommy inside. Know because pull inside outside. The Tommy quiet. Quiet, wet, red. The Mom and the Sissy get sick-scared look and scream.

Hate that look. Run way. Hide. Never come back. Till last night.

Cry more now. Cry quiet. In tub. So the Jessi not hear.

Harrison flipped through the slim file on the Tommy Baker murder. "This is it?"

"We didn't need to collect much paper," Captain Hall said. "I mean, the mother and sister were witnesses. There's some photos in that manila envelope at the back."

Harrison pulled it free and slipped out some large black and whites. His stomach lurched immediately.

"My *God!*"

"Yeah, he was a mess. Gutted by his older sister."

"His *sister?*"

"Yeah. Apparently she was some sort of freak of nature."

Harrison felt the floor tilt under him, felt as if he were going to slide off the chair.

"Freak?" he said, hoping Hall wouldn't notice the tremor in his voice. "What did she look like?"

"Never saw her. She took off after she killed the brother. No one's seen hide nor hair of her since. But there's a picture of the rest of the family in there."

Harrison shuffled through the file until he came to a large color family portrait. He held it up. Four people: two adults seated in chairs; a boy and a girl, about ten and eight, kneeling on the floor in front of them. A perfectly normal American family. Four smiling faces.

But where's your oldest child. Where's your big sister? Where did you hide that fifth face while posing for this?

"What was her name? The one who's not here?"

"Not sure. Carla, maybe? Look at the front sheet under *Suspect*."

Harrison did: Carla Baker—called 'Carly,' " he said.

Hall grinned. "Right. Carly. Not bad for a guy getting ready for retirement."

Harrison didn't answer. An ineluctable sadness filled him as he stared at the incomplete family portrait.

Carly Baker . . . poor Carly . . . where did they hide you away? In the cellar? Locked in the attic? How did your brother treat you? Bad enough to deserve killing?

Probably.

"No pictures of Carly, I suppose."

"Not a one."

That figures.

"How about a description?"

"The mother gave us one but it sounded so weird, we threw it out. I mean, the girl sounded like she was half spider or something!" He drained his cup. "Then later on I got into a discussion with Doc Alberts about it. He told me he was doing deliveries back about the time this kid was born. Said they had a whole rash of monsters, all delivered within a few weeks of each other."

The room started to tilt under Harrison again.

"Early December, 1968, by chance?"

"Yeah! How'd you know?"

He felt queasy. "Lucky guess."

"Huh. Anyway, Doc Alberts said they kept it quiet while they looked into a cause, but that little group of freaks—'cluster,' he called them— was all there was. They figured that a bunch of mothers had been exposed to something nine months before, but whatever it had been was long gone. No monsters since. I understand most of them died shortly after birth, anyway."

"Not all of them."

"Not that it matters," Hall said, getting up and pouring himself a refill from the coffee pot. "Someday someone will find her skeleton, probably somewhere out in Haskins' marshes."

"Maybe." *But I wouldn't count on it.* He held up the file. "Can I get a xerox of this?"

"You mean the Facelift Killer is a twenty-year-old girl?"
Martha's face clearly registered her disbelief.

"Not just any girl. A freak. Someone so deformed she really doesn't look human. Completely uneducated and probably mentally retarded to boot."

Harrison hadn't returned to Manhattan. Instead, he'd headed straight for home, less than a mile from Town Hall. He knew the kids were at school and that Martha would be there alone. That was what he had wanted. He needed to talk this out with someone a lot more sensitive than Jacobi.

Besides, what he had learned from Captain Hall and the Baker file had dredged up the most painful memories of his life.

"A monster," Martha said.

"Yeah. Born one on the outside, *made* one on the inside. But there's another child monster I want to talk about. Not Carly Baker. Annie . . . Ann Harrison."

Martha gasped. "That sister you told me about last night?"

Harrison nodded. He knew this was going to hurt, but he had to do it, had to get it out. He was going to explode into a thousand twitching bloody pieces if he didn't.

"I was nine when she was born. December 2, 1968—a week after Carly Baker. Seven pounds, four ounces of horror. She looked more fish than human."

His sister's image was imprinted on the rear wall of his brain. And it should have been after all those hours he had spent studying her loathsome face. Only her eyes looked human. The rest of her was awful. A lipless mouth, flattened nose, sloping forehead, fingers and toes fused so that they looked more like flippers than hands and feet, a bloated body covered with shiny skin that was a dusky gray-blue. The doctors said she was that color because her heart was bad, had a defect that caused mixing of blue blood and red blood.

A repulsed nine-year-old Kevin Harrison had dubbed her The Tuna —but never within earshot of his parents.

"She wasn't supposed to live long. A few months, they said, and she'd be dead. But she didn't die. Annie lived on and on. One year. Two. My father and the doctors tried to get my mother to put her into some sort of institution, but Mom wouldn't hear of it. She kept Annie in the third bedroom and talked to her and cooed over her and cleaned up her shit and just hung over her all the time. *All* the time, Martha!"

Martha gripped his hand and nodded for him to go on.

"After a while, it got so there was nothing else in Mom's life. She wouldn't leave Annie. Family trips became a thing of the past. Christ, if she and Dad went out to a movie, *I* had to stay with Annie. No babysitter was trustworthy enough. Our whole lives seemed to center around that freak in the back bedroom. And me? I was forgotten.

"After a while I began to hate my sister."

"Kevin, you don't have to—"

"Yes, I do! I've got to tell you how it was! By the time I was fourteen—just about Tommy Baker's age when he bought it—I thought I was going to go crazy. I was getting all B's in school but did that matter? Hell, no! 'Annie rolled halfway over today. Isn't that wonderful?'" Big deal! She was five years old, for Christ sake! I was starting point guard on the high school junior varsity basketball team as a goddamn freshman, but did anyone come to my games? Hell no!

"I tell you, Martha, after five years of caring for Annie, our house was a powderkeg. Looking back now I can see it was my mother's fault for becoming so obsessed. But back then, at age fourteen, I blamed it all on Annie. I really hated her for being born a freak."

He paused before going on. This was the really hard part.

"One night, when my dad had managed to drag my mother out to some company banquet that he had to attend, I was left alone to babysit Annie. On those rare occasions, my mother would always tell me to keep Annie company—you know, read her stories and such. But I never did. I'd let her lie back there alone with our old black and white TV while I sat in the living room watching the family set. This time, however, I went into her room."

He remembered the sight of her, lying there with the covers half way up her fat little tuna body that couldn't have been much more than a yard in length. It was winter, like now, and his mother had dressed her in a flannel nightshirt. The coarse hair that grew off the back of her head had been wound into two braids and fastened with pink bows.

"Annie's eyes brightened as I came into the room. She had never spoken. Couldn't, it seemed. Her face could do virtually nothing in the way of expression, and her flipper-like arms weren't good for much, either. You had to read her eyes, and that wasn't easy. None of us knew how much of a brain Annie had, or how much she understood of what was going on around her. My mother said she was bright, but I think Mom was a little whacko on the subject of Annie.

"Anyway, I stood over her crib and started shouting at her. She quivered at the sound. I called her every dirty name in the book. And as I said each one, I poked her with my fingers—not enough to leave a bruise, but enough to let out some of the violence in me. I called her a lousy goddamn tunafish with feet. I told her how much I hated her and how I wished she had never been born. I told her everybody hated her and the only thing she was good for was a freak show. Then I said, 'I wish you were dead! Why don't you die? You were supposed to die years ago! Why don't you do everyone a favor and do it now!

"When I ran out of breath, she looked at me with those big eyes of hers and I could see the tears in them and I knew she had understood me. She rolled over and faced the wall. I ran from the room.

"I cried myself to sleep that night. I'd thought I'd feel good telling her off, but all I kept seeing in my mind's eye was this fourteen-year-old bully shouting at a helpless five-year-old. I felt awful. I promised myself that the first opportunity I had to be alone with her the next day I'd apologize, tell her I really didn't mean the hateful things I'd said, promise to read to her and be her best friend, anything to make it up to her.

"I awoke the next morning to the sound of my mother screaming. Annie was dead."

"Oh, my God!" Martha said, her fingers digging into his arm.

"Naturally, I blamed myself."

"But you said she had a heart defect!"

"Yeah. I know. And the autopsy showed that's what killed her—her heart finally gave out. But I've never been able to get it out of my head that my words were what made her heart give up. Sounds sappy and melodramatic, I know, but I've always felt that she was just hanging on to life by the slimmest margin and that I pushed her over the edge."

"Kevin, you shouldn't have to carry that around with you! Nobody should!"

The old grief and guilt were like a slowly expanding balloon in his chest. It was getting hard to breathe.

"In my coolest, calmest, most dispassionate moments I convince myself that it was all a terrible coincidence, that she would have died that night anyway and that I had nothing to do with it."

"That's probably true, so—"

"But that doesn't change the fact that the last memory of her life was of her big brother—the guy she probably thought was the neatest kid on earth, who could run and play basketball, one of the three human beings who made up her whole world, who should have been her champion, her defender against a world that could only greet her with revulsion and rejection—standing over her crib telling her how much he hated her and how he wished she was dead!"

He felt the sobs begin to quake in his chest. He hadn't cried in over a dozen years and he had no intention of allowing himself to start now, but there didn't seem to be any stopping it. It was like running down hill at top speed—if he tried to stop before he reached bottom, he'd go head over heels and break his neck.

"Kevin, you were only fourteen," Martha said soothingly.

"Yeah, I know. But if I could go back in time for just a few seconds, I'd go back to that night and rap that rotten hateful fourteen-year-old in the mouth before he got a chance to say a single word. But I can't. I can't even say I'm sorry to Annie! I never got a chance to take it back, Martha! I never got a chance to make it up to her!"

And then he was blubbering like a goddamn wimp, letting loose half a lifetime's worth of grief and guilt, and Martha's arms were around him and she was telling him everything would be all right, all right, all right . . .

The Detective Harrison understand. Can tell. Want to go kill another face now. Must not. The Detective Harrison not like. Must stop. The Detective Harrison help stop.

Stop for good.

Best way. Only one way stop for good. Not jail. No chain, no little window. Not ever again. Never!

Only one way stop for good. The Detective Harrison will know. Will understand. Will do.

Must call. Call now. Before dark. Before pretty faces come out in night.

Harrison had pulled himself together by the time the kids came home from school. He felt strangely buoyant inside, like he'd been purged in some way. Maybe all those shrinks were right after all: sharing old hurts did help.

He played with the kids for a while, then went into the kitchen to see if Martha needed any help with slicing and dicing. He felt as close to her now as he ever had.

"You okay?" she said with a smile.

"Fine."

She had just started slicing a red pepper for the salad. He took over for her.

"Have you decided what to do?" she asked.

He had been thinking about it a lot, and had come to a decision.

"Well, I've got to inform the department about Carly Baker, but I'm going to keep her out of the papers for a while."

"Why? I'd think if she's that freakish looking, the publicity might turn up someone who's seen her."

"Possibly it will come to that. But this case is sensational enough without tabloids like the *Post* and *The Light* turning it into a circus. Besides, I'm afraid of panic leading to some poor deformed innocent getting lynched. I think I can bring her in. She *wants* to come in."

"You're sure of that?"

"She so much as told me so. Besides, I can sense it in her." He saw Martha giving him a dubious look. "I'm serious. We're somehow connected, like there's an invisible wire between us. Maybe it's because the same thing that deformed her and those other kids deformed Annie, too. And Annie was my sister. Maybe that link is why I volunteered for this case in the first place."

He finished slicing the pepper, then moved on to the mushrooms.

"And after I bring her in, I'm going to track down her mother and start prying into what went on in Monroe in February and March of sixty-eight to cause that so-called 'cluster' of freaks nine months later."

He would do that for Annie. It would be his way of saying good-bye and *I'm sorry* to his sister.

"But why does she take their faces?" Martha said.

"I don't know. Maybe because theirs were beautiful and hers is no doubt hideous."

"But what does she *do* with them?"

"Who knows? I'm not all that sure I *want* to know. But right now—"

The phone rang. Even before he picked it up, he had an inkling of who it was. The first sibilant syllable left no doubt.

"Ish thish the Detective Harrishon?"

"Yes."

Harrison stretched the coiled cord around the corner from the kitchen into the dining room, out of Martha's hearing.

"Will you shtop me tonight?"

"You want to give yourself up?"

"Yesh. Pleashe, yesh."

"Can you meet me at the precinct house?"

"*No!*"

"Okay! Okay!" God, he didn't want to spook her now. "Where? Anywhere you say."

"Jusht you."

"All right."

"Midnight. Plashe where lasht fashe took. Bring gun but not more cop."

"All right."

He was automatically agreeing to everything. He'd work out the details later.

"You undershtand, Detective Harrishon?"

"Oh, Carly, Carly, I understand more than you know!"

There was a sharp intake of breath and then silence at the other end of the line. Finally:

"You know Carly?"

"Yes, Carly. I know you." The sadness welled up in him again and it was all he could do to keep his voice from breaking. "I had a sister like you once. And you . . . you had a brother like me."

"Yesh," said that soft, breathy voice. "You undershtand. Come tonight, Detective Harrishon."

The line went dead.

Wait in shadows. The Detective Harrison will come. Will bring lots cop. Always see on TV show. Always bring lots. Protect him. Many guns.

No need. Only one gun. The Detective Harrison's gun. Him's will shoot. Stop kills. Stop forever.

The Detective Harrison must do. No one else. The Carly can not. Must be the Detective Harrison. Smart. Know the Carly. Understand.

After stop, no more ugly Carly. No more sick-scared look. Bad face will go way. Forever and ever.

Harrison had decided to go it alone.

Not completely alone. He had a van waiting a block and a half away on Seventh Avenue and a walkie-talkie clipped to his belt, but he hadn't told anyone who he was meeting or why. He knew if he did, they'd swarm all over the area and scare Carly off completely. So he had told Jacobi he was meeting an informant and that the van was just a safety measure.

He was on his own here and wanted it that way. Carly Baker wanted to surrender to him and him alone. He understood that. It was part of that strange tenuous bond between them. No one else would do. After he had cuffed her, he would call in the wagon.

After that he would be a hero for a while. He didn't want to be a hero. All he wanted was to end this thing, end the nightmare for the city and for poor Carly Baker. She'd get help, the kind she needed, and he'd use the publicity to springboard an investigation into what had made Annie and Carly and the others in their 'cluster' what they were.

It's all going to work out fine, he told himself as he entered the alley.

He walked half its length and stood in the darkness. The brick walls of the buildings on either side soared up into the night. The ceaseless roar of the city echoed dimly behind him. The alley itself was quiet— no sound, no movement. He took out his flashlight and flicked it on.

"Carly?"

No answer.

"Carly Baker—are you here?"

More silence, then, ahead to his left, the sound of a garbage can scraping along the stony floor of the alley. He swung the light that way, and gasped.

A looming figure stood a dozen feet in front of him. It could only be Carly Baker. She stood easily as tall as he—a good six foot two—and looked like a homeless street person, one of those animated rag-piles that live on subway grates in the winter. Her head was wrapped in a dirty scarf, leaving only her glittery dark eyes showing. The rest of her was muffled in a huge, shapeless overcoat, baggy old polyester slacks with dragging cuffs, and torn sneakers.

"Where the Detective Harrishon's gun?" said the voice.

Harrison's mouth was dry but he managed to get his tongue working. "In its holster."

"Take out. Pleashe."

Harrison didn't argue with her. The grip of his heavy Chief Special felt damn good in his hand.

The figure spread its arms; within the folds of her coat those arms seem to bend the wrong way. And were those black hooked claws protruding from the cuffs of the sleeves?

She said, "Shoot."

Harrison gaped in shock.

The Detective Harrison not shoot. Eyes wide. Hands with gun and light shake.

Say again: "Shoot!"

"Carly, no! I'm not here to kill you. I'm here to take you in, just as we agreed."

"*No!*"

Wrong! The Detective Harrison not understand! Must shoot the Carly! Kill the Carly!

"Not jail! Shoot! Shtop the kills! Shtop the Carly!"

"No! I can get you help, Carly. Really, I can! You'll go to a place where no one will hurt you. You'll get medicine to make you feel better!"

Thought him understand! Not understand! Move closer. Put claw out. Him back way. Back to wall.

"Shoot! Kill! Now!"

"No, Annie, please!"

"Not Annie! Carly! Carly!"

"Right. Carly! Don't make me do this!"

Only inches way now. Still not shoot. Other cops hiding not shoot. Why not protect?

"Shoot!" Pull scarf off face. Point claw at face. "End! End! *Pleashe!*"

The Detective Harrison face go white. Mouth hang open. Say, "Oh, my *God*!"

Get sick-scared look. Hate that look! Thought him understand! Say he know the Carly! Not! Stop look! *Stop!*

Not think. Claw go out. Rip throat of the Detective Harrison. Blood fly just like others.

No-No-No! Not want hurt!

The Detective Harrison gurgle. Drop gun and light. Fall. Stare.

Wait other cops shoot. Please kill the Carly. Wait.

No shoot. Then know. No cops. Only the poor Detective Harrison. Cry for the Detective Harrison. Then run. Run and climb. Up and down. Back to new home with the Old Jessi.

The Jessi glad hear Carly come. The Jessi try talk. Carly go sit tub. Close door. Cry for the Detective Harrison. Cry long time. Break mirror million piece. Not see face again. Not ever. Never.

The Jessi say, "Carly, I want my bath. Will you scrub my back?"

Stop cry. Do the Old Jessi's black back. Comb the Jessi's hair.

Feel very sad. None ever comb the Carly's hair. Ever.

JESSIE THOMPSON

Snowfall

A first story. Delicate, and so quiet you may not even notice it's horror. Is a young girl escaping a traumatic situation by using her imagination? Or is she escaping by discovering her inner core?

—E. D.

The shape-changer is a familiar motif in fairy tales; Jungian scholars would contend that the symbols of fairy tales are often used as metaphors for the struggles and heroic journeys of daily life. Thompson has written a tale in which the struggle between Good and Evil is both epic and chillingly intimate.

—T. W.

SNOWFALL

Jessie Thompson

The snow just falls and falls, white and silent and cold as frozen fox bones. The girl watches from her bedroom window, thinking of baby foxes, hot-blooded and soft-furred, running and burrowing under the dark pine trees behind the farmhouse.

"Cindy! Supper." Cindy doesn't answer. Her mother shouts up the stairs again. The radiator hisses as darkness captures another corner of the twilight room. Cindy hides the tiny fox skull, then rises from her bed and goes downstairs, her foot pausing in the air above each step.

One part of her mind is listening for the danger sounds that mean he's home. But mostly she's thinking about bright-eyed baby foxes.

The kitchen is hot and steamy. The windows are fogged over. Jack and Danny tumble like puppies in the corner, their squeals shredding the silence. Smaller, quieter noises come from her mother, crying at the stove. Cindy's heart contracts. Her mother is banging pots and spoons to hide the choked-off little gasps of pain, but Cindy's hearing is acute. I'm like a fox, she thinks. I have fox ears. I watch like a fox, and I can smell trouble coming.

He comes in. He stinks like cow shit. The boys stop tussling, but not fast enough. A slap on the side of the head catches Danny by surprise and he cries out. Jack grabs his cowboy gun, the knuckles on his pudgy baby hand turning white. "Bang!" he shouts, pointing the gun at his father. "Bang! Bang!" The gun flies across the room as a rough hand yanks him into the air. He hits the wall and slides down into a wailing heap. Danny, face flushed, rolls to cover him, holds him tight.

The big man's face is red, too; he's leaning forward, stepping closer. "Don't you ever point that gun at me again, mister. You hear?"

Cindy glances at her mother. Her face is pale and her jaw muscles are squeezed tight. She doesn't look up from the stove.

Under Danny, Jack is whimpering. "Put him in his chair. Sit. You too, girl." He glares at Cindy. She sees a strange flicker pass through his eyes. She's seen it a lot lately. She doesn't know what it means. His eyes drop away.

"Let's eat, for christsakes. Jesus. I work myself ragged all day to come home to this bullshit?"

He takes a beer out of the refrigerator and thwunks the door shut. It springs back at him and he kicks it closed. "You damn well better do something about these kids, Claire. If they get any wilder I'm sure as hell not going to work my butt off to feed the little bastards."

Cindy slides into her chair and spreads her napkin on her lap. She studies the brown crack in her plate. Her mother turns from the stove. Outside, snow is falling. They eat. He complains.

In the night she dreams. She dreams she's in the woods, playing chase with baby foxes. She's hiding in a gopher hole on the edge of the field, peering out, snout snuffling cold air, eyes darting around mischievously, laughter rising in her throat.

She wakes to darkness, can smell snow still falling outside. Her mother's high-pitched voice wails up and down like a mournful siren, furious words lost in sobbing. A loud slap and the sobbing stops. The radiator starts to bang, over and over, bangs and bangs and thrums through the house. Cindy's heart is pounding in her ears. She thinks of baby foxes. Her breathing slows, and she falls asleep.

She sleeps and dreams of foxes in the pines, and then the monster comes. The huge, white beast finds her hiding in the woods, sleeping with the foxes on a bed of warm snow. It looms over her, whispering that it won't hurt her. It says it loves her. She knows it lies.

She tries to scream but whiteness covers her face, presses against her mouth. A sharp pain stabs her belly. The beast is breathing hard, hissing foul breath. Pain shoots up her belly in cramping spasms. Hot monster slime trickles down her clenched throat.

She thinks of her friends the foxes, and they poke their noses out from behind the logs and bushes, watching with bright eyes as she struggles not to choke and slip into darkness. The monster is heavy on her, squeezing out the last of her air. It's just snow, she thinks. I've fallen asleep outside and the snow is burying me. Under the snow it's warm and soft and silent. Her muscles relax and she surrenders to the whiteness. When it melts away into the night she wakes up wet and sweating. There's a funny smell in the air.

She sits at the table with a woman in an apron and a man in dirty, faded blue overalls. Two little boys climb into chairs across the table from her. She sees them glance at the man sideways, fear in their bright eyes. Little foxes. Ready to dart away. Cindy can't remember what she's doing at this table, with these people.

A shadow, huge and white, crosses her mind, but she doesn't grab it in time. Snow falls on it and covers its tracks. "Cindy," the woman says. "Eat your food, hon." Cindy thinks of foxes, how they tickle her ears with their snouts, and she forgets to puzzle out the woman's words.

A sweet-smelling, warm, safe burrow. Hours pass, unnoticed. Night drifts down, quiet as the snow. The huge white beast-thing comes again.

Morning. She sits at a table with the smell of eggs and frying bacon in her nose. Outside it's blue. Bright, blinding blue pouring in the windows and the open door. Diamonds glitter in mounds on the windowsills. Bacon, eggs, table. Puzzled, she considers each item separately and then all together. The room is familiar. But the creatures make no sense. Since when do snow monsters eat bacon and eggs?

The one at the end of the table is huge. It's the color of old, dirty snow. A clump of pine needles tops its head like hair. The monster glares at a smaller, very white monster standing at the stove. Both have black cinders where eyes should be. The monsters are wearing her parents' clothes.

Suddenly the big monster stands up, rocking the table. Loud, angry noises pour out of it, out of a gaping hole that rips the bottom of its face apart. It throws a bowl down, hard. The smaller monster starts to wail, face hole splitting wider and wider until its black eyes disappear. Holding a frying pan high, it comes rushing toward the table.

Cindy notices for the first time the two little foxes sitting across the table from her. They grab each other and twitter and yap in fox voices, then slide from the table and run out the open door.

Cindy gets up to leave too, but a hot, snowy monster grabs her shoulder. She winces with pain. The big monster picks her up and thrusts her in front of the frying pan, which slams into her back with a crack. She's dizzy. The room is getting dark. The monster holds her up in the air now with one paw, holds her by the throat, roars something that sounds like "Your fault—your fault . . ."

And then, suddenly, the monster's belly turns the color of dirty snow when you pee on it, and Cindy's underpants feel warm and wet. The monster hurls her to the floor, she's down on her knees, crawling through the door, heading for the bright blue air. Crawling across the cold snow into the pine trees, where she's sure the little foxes must have gone.

A booming noise is coming closer.

She hears the baby foxes yipping in the woods and crawls toward them. The air shakes and roars. Her throat tastes like firecrackers. Two booms and the frantic yipping stops. Another boom, and the smaller monster is right above her, spraying red all over the snow, crumpling to the ground. The big monster rushes toward Cindy, boom stick waving. It stops, frozen now, staring down at her with cinder eyes.

A truck is screaming down the long gravel road, horn blaring. The monster turns. Slowly, slowly, the short double stick goes into its own mouth hole. One more boom. There's a roaring in Cindy's ears. The blue sky darkens. Stars explode. And snow begins to fall.

Low sun. Hot white walls. Cindy squats on her haunches, staring out the window. The pine trees are gone. Something clicks on, hums and buzzes. Cool air lifts the short hairs on her neck. Cindy strokes the little fox skull hidden in her gown; rhythmically polishes it. Her paw slips in and out of the eye holes.

A door opens behind her. "Cindy, it's time to eat. Come with me, honey." The young woman approaches. Reaches out a gentle hand. Cindy crouches lower, ready to spring. A growl rises from deep in her throat. The woman yanks her hand back, turns abruptly, and leaves the room.

Cindy's snout itches. She smiles and scratches it and stares with bright, feral eyes at the man in overalls watering the lawn outside. He sees her watching him, and smiles back. There's the smell of cut grass in his smile, and maybe a whiff of cow shit. She bares her teeth and glares at him until he turns away.

Slowly, slowly, she moves toward the window. Her paw fumbles with the rusted lock. Frustrated, she tries her teeth. The window snaps open with a crack like the crack of a gun. Startled, she jumps through. Pain shoots down her tail as it catches on the jagged sill but she yanks it free and scampers across the wet grass. The man in overalls shouts.

Cindy crouches under the bushes, peering out, eyes laughing. A young woman runs across the lawn toward the smelly man in overalls. His arm waves wildly in Cindy's direction. Behind them, a man in white bends over the windowsill. He holds up something red. Cindy grins. The pain in her tail is already gone.

Hunkered down, she backs out of the bush and into the warm, dark woods, yipping a greeting to the chuckling foxes. Above the shocked and frozen humans, the spray from the sprinkler rises higher and higher and turns to snow.

SARA MAITLAND

Seal-Self

Sara Maitland won the Somerset Maugham Award with her first novel, *Daughter of Jerusalem*. She is also the author of *Virgin Territory*, *Arky Types* (a satirical epistolary novel co-authored with Michelene Wandor), and a biography of Vesta Tilley for the Virago Pioneers series. She has contributed short fiction to numerous anthologies and reviewed extensively for a variety of newspapers and magazines. She lives in a Vicarage in East London, a "delightful seventeen-roomed Gothic fantasy, with a curved and secret garden," with her husband, an Anglican priest, and her two children.

"Seal-Self" comes from her recent collection of short stories, *A Book of Spells*. I found it difficult to chose between this story and another from the same collection, "Angel Maker." The latter is a modern reworking of the *Hansel and Gretel* fairy tale, and I would strongly recommend seeking it out.

—T. W.

SEAL-SELF

Sara Maitland

In Cleveland it was well known that any wild goose which
flew over Whitby would instantly drop dead; and that to
catch a seal it was first necessary to dress as a woman.
—*Keith Thomas*,
Man and the Natural World

It is cold when he wakes, stirred from forgotten dreams by the deep
whirring in the air. The goose flocks are driving north again. It is cold
and still dark, too dark to see the great wide arrowheads, spread wide,
not yet regathered since they had split up to avoid Whitby, but he can
hear them and he shivers. They stir his blood each equinox with their
coming and going, up there, out there, beyond. He does not know where
and he could not imagine. Last week he had seen the falling stars, the
serene and magic performance of the heavens to celebrate the turning of
the year. And after the falling stars the wild geese, uncountable also,
will pass over along the pale coastline. For the next week they will appear,
from the south, at dawn and at dusk, through the night watches and in
the morning, as swift as falling stars flighting northwards towards the
cold wind. And after the wild geese have passed the seal mothers will
surge up from the icy water and lay their pups on the great flat sands
below. And he . . . but he does not want to think about it.

He twisted into himself seeking what warmth there still might be in
the bed, wrapping his arms around himself, deliberately seeking the safety
of sleep, but the deep whirring noise over the cottage roof continued
unabated until it was fully dawn.

His world is shaped by the stripes. Green stripe. Yellow-gold stripe.
Lead-coloured stripe. Blue stripe. Across the stripes, at right-angles to
them, ran another stripe, invisible but every bit as tangible; the fierce
east wind that rushed in from far away across the ocean, coming at him,
vicious and greedy, coming in a straight and evil line, down the sky,

418

the sea, the sand, the fields. May God have mercy on his soul. He crosses himself, half scared, half scornful, for this is old women's thinking, and he is ashamed; and men now do not cross themselves, for times have changed, and his mouth curls in scorn of his mother and her fussing ways, for he is a man, and when the goose flocks are passed over and the seals come to play on the beaches, he will prove he is a man.

For the next ten days the wild geese pass over. He knows they are watching him, his friends, the geese, even the rising sun. His mother. In the village when he passes across the square the young women look at him, curious and questioning. The tawny maiden from the high farm-stead eyes him, direct and challenging. She is taller than he is, and her legs run up under her skirt, legs so slender and long that they must lead somewhere good. She tosses her head in the pale April sunshine and diamonds scatter from her hair. He is bewitched by her long cool stare. As he carries the milk pail she passes by, almost brushing against him, and her clear voice bells sweetly to her friend, "They say the first of the seal mothers are come to the sand dunes. I would love a sealskin cloak this year." He hates her suddenly and brilliantly, bright as the April sunshine, but his penis stirs and he watches her breasts. She smiles at him, promising him. And if not her then another. They all promise him together.

Last year he could not bring himself to do it. It is not the killing; he has cut pigs' throats, catapulted birds out of the sky, snared hares, wrung chicken necks, drowned kittens, baited bears, put his evil-snouted ferret to the rabbits' warrens. It is the other. They do not understand. His mother had smiled last year when he had tried to tell her. She had laid out the apparel for him even. His stomach feels sick to think about it. His dreams fill with it. And it must be this spring, for by next year his beard will be upon him. Now is the time. He knows it. He is frightened. For it is well known that to catch a seal it is first necessary to dress as a woman. He wakes again in the darkness as before, and there is silence; the whirring of the goose flocks has vanished northwards, and though it is still cold there is a new softness in the air. His fear is very present to him. He strips off his clothes and stands naked. He pulls on his mother's skirt and arranges it at his waist, it falls lumpenly, ugly, and his hairy feet appearing at the bottom strike him as ungainly and ludicrous. He knows, blindingly as dawn, what his fear is. It is pleasure. It is pleasure and desire. He tiptoes to his mother's kist, and takes for himself her boned corsets, her linen hose, her full Sunday petticoats, her best bonnet.

Before he is half-dressed his hands are wet with his own juices: his fingers tangled with bodice ribbons and semen, his mind with delight and shame. But after that he knows that it must be done well and fully.

He takes great care, padding his hips with fleece, tightening the corset with gentle concern. The skirt hangs better so. He chooses for himself breasts not too large, too heavy, but high and delicate like the tawny maiden from the high farm. He smiles for himself that smile of veiled promise that she gave him in the village square. Then when everything is ready he realises that it will not do. He takes off the petticoats and skirt again; he takes a hair-ribbon, soft satin smooth, the same rich rose colour as the chaffinch's breast, that his mother brought home from the Whitby Fairings; she never wore it, it was too fine for her, she said, she wanted it only because it was a pretty thing and no one bought her pretty things any more. He ties it now gently round his penis, which is soft and pleased and sleepy, and draws it back between his legs, folding his testicles carefully. He feels the flat firm skin behind them and knows that there should be a hole, a place of darkness and wet that he will never know. It cannot be helped. He attaches the other end of the ribbon firmly to the bottom hole in the back of the corset. Now when he pulls on yet again the skirt and petticoat he knows that it is almost right. Shoes he must do without, for he will not mar his own loveliness with cloggy boots but none of his mother's will fit him. But stockinged feet are charming for a maid out in the fields at daydawn.

As he passes the parlour he sees in the half light himself in the mirror glass, gold curls fluffing out under the sweet bonnet with its delicately ruched and pleated inner brim. How pretty she is, he thinks, so much prettier than the tawny maid from the high farmstead. He smiles. How pretty I am, she thinks, and she raises the latch craftily and skips out, silent and dainty, into the waiting springtime.

The preparation has taken longer than was planned. Now it is dawn already; the great stripes of the countryside have already divided themselves, though not yet into colours, only into different greys. But there is a ribbon, laid tidily between the grey stripe of sea and the paler grey stripe of sky, a rose pink ribbon holding the world in shape, the day spring whence the sun will be born.

She shivers in the cold dawn and wishes that she had a sealskin cloak to snuggle in, a cloak made from the softness of baby seal, white and thick and dappled. A sealskin cloak trimmed and fastened with rose pink ribbons, she thinks, and then she laughs at herself for her vanity. Nor would she wear one if he gave it to her, for seals are friends to honest women, and she is going now to meet her friend Seal Woman and greet the new Seal Child who will have been carried in the deep waters all through the winter, wrapped in thick sweet blubber and rocked in a secret bay between the promontories of her mother's pubic bones, safe within the greater ocean. And who would now be pupped in the soft golden sand, clumsy and enchanting, pug-faced, soft-furred, playful and unafraid. No woman of sense or worth would accept a sealskin cloak, not from the King himself were he to come to the cold coastland north of Whitby and hear the wind rush in from far across the ocean; nor would she wear one and mock the mourning of Seal Woman for her child.

So she laughs, though kindly, at herself and her vanity and walks across the grey meadows towards the seaside; and as she walks the light seeps gently into the air and the grass turns towards green and the birds begin to sing and the sea sedge and saxifrage are pale pinky mauve and the celandines are yellow. The pink ribbon beyond the sea widens and pales and the broad sweep of the sky overhead is almost as white and pure as the frothed edges of her petticoats, bleached out with love and joy.

Closer to, the line, which from the cottage seems so precisely drawn between grass and sea, is blurred, indefinite, hesitant. First there is grass and woolly sheep still huddled against the night, then there are scrubby plants mixed in with bare patches of earth, of sand, then there is mostly sand with the occasional bold push or outcrop of reedy grass, and then almost unnoticeably there is only sand, great reaches of it in rolling hills, swirled into fantastic shapes by the long-drawn wind from the sunrise side of the ocean. And finally the hillocks settle, flattened out by the waves, and there is a wide wet beach changing constantly with the long pushes and tugs of the tide.

And when she comes at last to the very end of the dunes, to the edge of the tide beach, she heaves a great sigh of relief, coming home, united in her belly with the pushes and pulls of the tide, of the moon, of the great spaces of the sea. Quietly and easily she folds her legs, her skirt ballooning softly around her and sits in silence watching the long waves roll in, smooth and strong from out there, out beyond her eye view, and each wave is different and each wave is exactly the same for ever and ever and she feels calmed, rocked, soothed, contented.

And as she sits there, waiting for the sun to rise, the seals begin to emerge. Some from the sea where they had gone at her approaching, and some from the dunes where they had slept. Now they flop, heavy and clumsy, on the shining golden sand by the waterline. Some are still gravid, ponderous and careful, and some have already pupped and their tiny young lurch around them or frolic idiotically in the wave edges. Not thirty yards from the shore a mother seal floats on her back, her tail flapping balance against the wave tossings, her little white pup held, flipper-fast, against her breast to suckle. So water-graceful, land-clumsy; so strong, so tender; so like and so unlike herself. She forgot the reason and the manner of her coming and waited only on the movement of the tide and the rising of the sun.

"Good morning, my dear," says Seal Woman, "and welcome."

She springs to her feet to curtsy.

"Hello," says Seal Child. "I'm new."

And new she certainly is, but already with bright black eyes that look and see, and with flourished whiskers, moustaching out from her black nose, and dappled white-grey fur fluffed in the sun. Barely two foot long, neatly constructed for an environment that cannot sustain her, at home in no element, timeless, lovable, perfect and preposterous. She smiles and reaches out a hand to touch Seal Child's nose.

And now, now he is meant now to take a stone and smash it down on Seal Child's head, blanking out the shiny eyes forever and carrying off the soft skin to the tawny maiden from the high homestead to wear as her victor's spoils, and to prove to the village that he has become a man, but she has forgotten this, lost in the wide free space of air and ocean, lost in the wide loving gaze of Seal Woman.

There is no need to talk much, or to talk of anything in particular. She sits, Seal Woman sprawls, and Seal Child suckles unhindered, occasionally wriggling or squeaking in delight. And all across the wet beach there are a hundred other seal mothers suckling, snoozing, sprawling, and now the gulls come swooping, wailing, to join them, and out on the breakers the older pups play and beyond that the sea pours in, in, in, a long solemn, musical procession, ancient and careful. And, quite suddenly, the sun rises.

Seal Child waggles her flippers in delight, tosses her tail, gambols a little. Seal Child says, "Will you play with me?"

"Yes," she says, "yes, please."

"Mother, come too," begs Seal Child.

"Of course," says Seal Woman.

So together the three of them go down to the seashore and plunge in. And suddenly she is not woman to woman with Seal Woman, but child to child with Seal Child. In the water it is a new Seal Child, graceful, strong, rhythmic; suddenly no longer little and sweet but powerful, fast, the fur no longer soft and fluffy but streamlined, completed. Together she and Seal Child splash and paddle in the breaking water, dance in and out of the foam, going deeper, deeper, deeper in. The waves mount around her, lifting her skirts gently up and down, until they are soaked through and dragging at her legs; her balance fails and she falls into the next wave, is lifted by it, raised up, brought down, and left as it runs on in towards the sparkling sands. When she realises that her feet will not touch the bottom again she is, for a moment, scared and then it does not matter because she too can swim like a seal, strong and shapely, powerful in the water as never on the land. And deep new places opening in her lungs so that she can go down and under and be there unafraid.

And now they swim and swim; the dark cold waters are the breeding grounds of fishes who move in vast shoals hard to see. But flipping over and rising upwards the surface is a great starry sky, brighter and fiercer than the terrestrial constellations; where the water meets the air there is a barrier, a great spangled ceiling, chandeliered with light, with air, water, sun-fire sparkled. And turning downwards, down, down into the dark there is the everlasting silence, the great underwater drifts and waves and forces of currents unlit by the sunshine, and great still mountains, cliffs, ranges, beflowered in dark growths whose shadows deepen the green darkness and whose rhythms are from before the beginning of air breathing, and Seal Woman flows between her two children, guarding them, hovering over them, around them, protecting them, remembering them in the forgotten places. And there is no weight, no gravity, no memory, and deep, deep below there is the ocean floor whence they all came and whither they do not choose to go and they are carried above it joyfully, on the strength of their own limbs, wings, fins. And Seal Child, using flippers and nose, pulls away the ties on the sweet little bonnet and it floats a moment in the water, like a dark jelly fish, and is gone.

Then, on another shared thought, they all turn and shoot upwards, breaking the surface into sprinkled jewels, whooshing into sunlight, their lungs pulling in new fresh air, bobbing upon the surface and laughing together. And Seal Child, using tail and teeth, strips off the knitted hose and chases them playfully across the wave tops till they drift away.

They swim far north to the gathering and gossiping grounds of the salmon, under the shelter of the great ice pack, where the waters teem with microscopic life, and are greener than the grass. They swim among the mating places of the wild geese and see the cold slopes where the white swans winter. They watch the dignified icebergs sail regally out towards their death, glittering bravely in the bright sunlight, and they dine without effort on the herring shoals that drift on unseen currents across the sub-polar waters. And Seal Child, using nose and mouth, nuzzles off the skirt and petticoats, the bodice and sleeves, and lazily they float away to provide refuge for some weary tern in some other distant sea.

And then they turn and drift slowly southwards, following the cold current that finds its way along the eastern coast of Scotland, leisurely riding the water and watching the ships in the distance break the tidy line of the horizon. And the sun comforts those bits of them that break the surface of the cold sea, so they turn on their backs and let their tummies feel the gentle spring warmth in the morning light. And they play in the rocky pools off Lindisfarne, the Holy Island; and watch the great gannets drop sixty vertical feet through the air, white streaks of power; and they tease the gaudy puffins who bob and wimble under those serene cliffs. And Seal Child, using tail and flippers and mouth and nose, unties the corset cords and pulls the garment off and with a weary sigh it sinks down and down to amuse poor drowned sailors from years and years ago.

And as they come back to their own golden beach to the north of Whitby, the end of the rose-pink ribbon, which she had tied to the corset and which had worked its way in between her buttocks, floats loose and drifts like the colourful seaweed in a coral lagoon two thousand miles away to the south and west. Seal Child plays with it as it dangles and they all laugh, riding in on the breakers and coming to rest at last on the sunny wet sand in the first early hours of the day. And Seal Woman and she lounge on the beach and talk of those things that women talk of when they have had good physical exercise and are met in magic places, while Sea Child frolics around them playing with the ends of the pink ribbon and with her penis.

Seal Child says, "I love you."

She says, "I love you too." All three of them grin peacefully. And it is simply true.

Seal Child is still very young. Love means warmth and cuddling and feeding. Seal Child scrambles up on to her body and tries to suckle from her, not finding flat breasts, small nipples or a soft furred chest anything out of the usual. She holds Seal Child under the front flippers to steady her, feeling with great pleasure the softness of wet fur against her own belly. Seal Child's whiskers and soft mouth tickle, she giggles and rolls over with her; mother child; child puppy; child child; happy. Seal Child tries again to suckle, her mouth is round and pink, her lips firm and sweet against the nipple. And suddenly the soft and floppy penis, still bedecked with rose pink ribbon, springs up, awakened. She rolls over on to Seal Child who wriggles in the sand. Suddenly he looks up. Seal Woman is looking at him, not just with anger, but with great sadness and greater amazement. He springs to his feet, the ribbon still dangling.

"I'm sorry," he says to Seal Woman.

"Come and play some more," says Seal Child.

"No," says Seal Mother.

Seal Child looks puzzled. She is about to start whining. She flops to her mother and finds there the milky sweetness she had been seeking; with enthusiasm she begins to feed.

"I'm sorry," he says again.

"I have never been fooled before," says Seal Woman. "Why is it?"

"I was naked," he says, beginning to be annoyed. "You could have seen. You must have known."

"That's not what counts," says Seal Woman.

They are still. They both look out at the sea, where the waves break still. They both look at Seal Child sucking. For a last moment they both share equally the desire to protect the baby at all costs.

Feeling their attention on her, Seal Child breaks her sucking and grins. She flops affectionately over to him and for a moment Seal Woman just watches them. Seal Child tugs at the wet pink ribbon. His penis swells again.

"You must go now," says Seal Woman sadly.

Seal Child, silky wet, rubs her flat face across his belly.

"I could cut it off," he offers; and for a sweet moment of fear, excitement, desire, loss, he means it. Seal Child's snout snuffles downwards, nibble-mumbling his soft hair; her whiskers tickle him. His penis stirs, Seal Child and he giggle.

"No, that's not what counts," says Seal Woman.

"No," says Seal Child.

"No," he agrees.

"Please," he says.

Now, he thinks, now I should take up this heavy stone, that is here, by good fortune, here just beside me, here at hand, and bash in her head and strip out her blubber guts and carry home her soft sweet fur and have her forever and be a man. This is what I came for, he thinks, and his penis stirs again.

"Please," he says, "please let me stay."

And if they will just do what he says, wants, needs, he thinks he will not have to hurt them.

"No," says Seal Woman. She knows his thoughts but she is not afraid. She is angry-sad, sad-angry. "No."

They vanish.

They have taken from him even a moment of choice. The stone is there, round, heavy, fitted to his hand, but he had not decided. Round the very base of his penis, tangled in his golden pubic hair, is one long whisker caught underneath the rose pink ribbon, but he had not decided. He will never know what he would have decided.

It is full morning, suddenly, bright beyond bearing. On the golden stripe of the beach there is nothing but his golden body. Out in the leaden-coloured stripe he sees their leaden-coloured heads bob, spaniel-eyed, sad and smiling.

He goes home. He crosses out of the golden stripe and into the green one. No one sees his solemn, naked procession.

Later he says, "It is well known that any wild goose which flies over Whitby will instantly drop dead; and that to catch a seal it is first necessary to dress as a woman."

Later he says, "I caught a seal, but then I let her go." He does not know if they believe him; he does not know if he is a man.

BARRY N. MALZBERG

No Hearts, No Flowers

For over twenty years Barry Malzberg has been writing daring, different stories of science fiction, fantasy, and any other sort that will hold his brilliant imagination. He has won critical acclaim for novels such as *Beyond Apollo,* and the story cycle, *Galaxies.* Malzberg's fiction is frequently intensely personal, as is his book of criticism, *The Engines of the Night.* Yet there has always been another side to Malzberg's work, one that is too often overlooked. In the following story he shows off his sense of humor. It's a wicked little Damon Runyanesque tale about the perils of being too good at what you do.

—E. D.

NO HEARTS, NO FLOWERS

Barry N. Malzberg

I am sitting in my accustomed spot in Stendahl's, just across from the entryway, which gives me command of the vistas of the room, to say nothing of the vistas of the inner self which like Stendahl's warming cuisine open up whole layers of possibilities, an accustomed spot which, I should note, enables me to note every one of the clientele as they exit and enter, to say nothing of large portions of the room itself when I hear, from a table adjoining, lines so shocking and devastating in their impact that they—instantly, as it turns out—cause me to shift from inner to outer landscapes. "Let us presume," this speaker is saying, "that on this sixty-first anniversary of the St. Valentine's Day Massacre we commemorate this most famous and interesting act by its very replication in the downtown reaches of Brooklyn. This will send a powerful and unanswerable message to our enemies, of whom, I must remind you, there are more than several."

This pronouncement, in its offhand audacity—not to say its dreadful implication—catches my attention at once and I crane my neck netherwards, then to portside to see who might be the utterer of such profoundly unsettling plans and sentiments; the voice itself is nondescript, a voice such as might be heard in Stendahl's at any time of day or (more usually) evening ordering one or another of the specials or speculating upon local politics, but my view is blocked by several riotous diners at the next table, to say nothing of the late afternoon sun, pouring in through the slender windows of Stendahl's and setting up a brisk and diverting clatter of light. I am therefore unable to isolate the voice and am forced to half stand at the table, distend my limbs into something approaching a crouch while I incline my head in the direction of the voice, only to find that there are so many diners of indistinguishable appearance and absorption that I am unable to accomplish this task. "A presumption," I hear someone say, "that does not need to be empirically verified," and then once again the sound closes over and I am unable to isolate the speaker. Let me make it clear that Stendahl's at this time is more than ordinarily crowded; it is difficult enough to isolate one's waiter, to say nothing of one's companion seen across the table, and that this dereliction is not, then, in the least unexpected and unusual.

"Do you hear that?" I say to my companion, the beauteous and accomplished Baby Jane Harrison, who at that very moment has abandoned the last scraps of her meal and is fetchingly tearing her napkin into small pieces in front of her; what Baby Jane Harrison and I share is a passion for her physique and a series of small tics which for me drive toward attentiveness, for her tend to result in the breakdown of small objects she may have in hand. "Someone over there is talking about another Valentine's Day Massacre in downtown Brooklyn."

"I wouldn't know anything about that," Baby Jane Harrison says. I tend to write these reminiscences in the present tense, not only because the crisp style of the local chronicler which I fancy myself to be is best suited by that method of attack but because, like so many denizens of Stendahl's, to say nothing of Baby Jane herself, I seem to live in a kind of enforced and eternal present, a mode devoid of consequence and barren of history, a pretty good paradigm, one might say, of the twentieth century itself as it closes upon its termination, a century which has much to teach us about the failure of consequence and the damaging of memory. My taste for the present tense, however, does not exclude *all* knowledge of the past, which is why I am able to react quickly to intimations of the St. Valentine's Day Massacre, a celebrated misunderstanding in a suburb of Chicago many decades ago filled with iron and flying teeth and somewhat legendary in its paralyzing effect upon subsequent myth, legend, and politics.

"I do not wish for another St. Valentine's Day Massacre," I say to my lovely companion, forty-two years old but possessed of a slender youthfulness and a powerful sexual obsession that would be the pride of a woman not three-quarters of her age. "Let me run this to the source." I stand and, facing in the direction of the overheard confidence, prepare to set upon the speaker with stately and insistent feet, not seeking confrontation itself so much as witness. My intent, I think, has something to do with making identification so that latterly I may seek the authorities; it has to be understood that my entire motivations here are testimonial rather than confrontational. I am not the scribe of the waterfront for nothing; *scriptor* is not action as I have had occasion to point out often in the context of my weekly musings and jottings. "I will run it to the source," I repeat.

Standing, however, is accomplished with somewhat less ease than I had hoped, Stendahl's borscht and blintzes weighing more heavily than I might have initially expected, and as I turn my head avidly in the direction of the overheard confidences I find myself suddenly and dis-tressingly locked in place by an enormous, oncoming belch. The belch racks me, doubles me over in focused consternation (Baby Jane Harrison looks at me with an indifference only partially masked by concern), and as I attempt to deal with the inner man I am rudely, then consecutively, pushed out of the way by a series of bodies making graceless exit from Stendahl's; first one, then three or four bodies made enormous by satiation brush by me in an unfocused blur of grumbling, divestiture of crumbs and belching (Stendahl's menu is of indiscriminate impact) and I find myself crumpled inconsequently in my seat, subsumed by these enormous and implacable forces, stunned, and at a loss for identification. Baby Jane Harrison, holding a last wedge of unforked cheesecake in her lovely and tapering left hand, reaches over to pat me with her right, her fingers lying damply but lovingly on my forehead. "You're so clumsy," she says with the same mixture of concern and distance, her eyes focused on some distant imagined point which may have to do with tangled sheets and orgiastic, random cries of necessity compounded by cheesecake. "I don't know how you can be a reporter, a press agent, someone who makes his living by going around, if you can't get around. If you follow what I am saying," she adds and grants me poised and distressing laughter.

The afternoon does not quite end at this point, to be sure, to say nothing of the night; in the nature of such things it goes on and on but these subsequent events, even the raging and final argument which I have with Baby Jane Harrison over certain practices and demands and presumed inadequacies, which marks the permanent interruption of our often tem-porarily interrupted relationship, all of these undiscussed, undramatized events can be seen as irrelevant to the main business of the events described earlier. These events have to do, of course, with my unplanned, undesired auditing of the terrible Valentine's Day Event, the Sweetheart Killings (as the press so fetchingly calls them), which occur three days later, on the actual holiday that is to say, and of which I have had such unhappy foreknowledge. The nature of these slayings, the nature of the actual Sweetheart herself, draped in a series of obscene poses, semi-dead over the hood of a 1979 Pontiac Le Mans—all of these are too well known, too accurately reported in the daily press to necessitate graphic descrip-tion. It is only necessary to say that it is dreadful in the extreme, dis-tressing in the main; it is one of the more horrendous debacles in a city and a century which have not shown themselves averse to splendid veri-fications of the bestiality of the race and I am thinking upon these very factors and implications on the morning of the following day in Stendahl's, seated in a considerably less crowded version of that restaurant in which I had sat some days ago, reading the accounts in the local press and feeling all the fingers of injustice *tap-tap-tapping* at my consciousness when Stendahl himself comes over and, nodding at the papers and at my own attention says, "Didn't you say something about that a couple days ago?"

I look up at Stendahl. He is a wide person in his early fifties, the original means of introduction to Baby Jane Harrison, if truth be known, and also one who has done me other favors, extended various courtesies in return for my own frequent usage and mention of his establishment in my column. I am, as has been pointed out, *scribendi* rather than activist and command a certain small cachet in that regard, even though a weekly is not a daily.

"I know you wrote something about it," Stendahl says. His face exudes cunning and incomprehension by turns. "Didn't you say something about a plan?"

"This is correct," I say. Part of my unease at this time is due to the sudden loss of Baby Jane Harrison and the shocking nature of her accusations, but another part of it has to do with recollection that I had incautiously and synoptically made reference to the overheard lines of conversation in the column that had come out just yesterday, lines that were, I hasten to note, written in a jocular and satiric manner as is all of my stylistic output. Jocularity and satire keep the belly full and *Avoid difficulty* has always been my motto, but as I look at Stendahl, even wider in the great morning light and expanse of his restaurant, and as Stendahl looks at me, it occurs to me that it is possible that out there might be a population of hundreds of thousands of wide persons in the world who are capable of, as they say, missing a point. "It was an oblique reference," I say. "Quite subtle and glancing. I will have another Danish if I may and—"

"It was not oblee enough," Stendahl says. He leans very close. "There are two persons who would like to see you. They are waiting outside the checkroom and they look very determined."

"Tell them I am not here," I say. "It was found necessary for me to take the healing breezes of Rockaway. I am at this very moment in the Rockaways, chartering a very large fishing boat."

"I am afraid that is not possible."

"I am aboard the fishing boat, catching fluke amidst various bouts of seasickness. I shall return next month after I am thrown overboard and drown. I will be found in a state of vast attention—"

"This humor," Stendahl says, "strained at best, was borne only for the sake of commerce. There is no commerce. There are two gentlemen waiting for you by the checkroom who have not followed me in here only because I have made most dignified persuasion and pleading. I have been given one minute to produce you after which—"

"It was a jesting reference," I point out to Stendahl. "I merely said that there was a Valentine Day's greeting in the works; a celebratory valediction of a greater event, that is all. I tied it in with the cuisine at Stendahl's, a valentine to the gastronome. No harm was intended."

Stendahl's hand upon my shoulder is enormous. It is remarkable how definitive and grandiose doom can be; good news and beneficence arrive with a wispy and effeminate aspect. Bad news carries a rifle and kicks down doors. "I have in order to demonstrate my own good faith and lack of collaboration," Stendahl says, "volunteered to produce you," and produce me he does, lifting me from the table with an almost perilous ease and guiding me toward the vicinity of the checkroom, which in happier times (as when I would exit with Baby Jane Harrison or earlier admirers who appreciated the journalistic power I could invoke and were eager to share with me their own attestations of communications) had always struck me as such a benign and pleasant place. It was not so pleasant now, graced as it was by two men of indistinguishable stature and bellicosity who, as Stendahl led me netherwards, brightened to my appearance with a mutuality of attention.

"A glancing reference, gentlemen," I pleaded, abandoning all amenities, even as Stendahl abandoned me, leaving me to their devices and retiring to his manager's post, which he had located somewhat to the left and several yards below the surface of his eating establishment, "made in the purest good humor, made only as a nostalgic reference to a historic and nostalgic event, an event that formed the basis as you may recall of the famous *Some Like It Hot* with Miss Marilyn Monroe! A reference to olden times, gladder times, easier times when retribution arrived in the form of gunfire and only funny-looking people with accents gunned one another down. Surely you can understand—"

But they could not, I regret to say, understand any of this, or perhaps I am failing to see the situation in its full implication because, making up in action for what they lacked in verbal attestation, they seized me with hands even more determined than Stendahl's and led me out quickly; little Borough Park breezes kicked Borough Park litter into the air as I was impelled by them into an enormous green car that bore a shocking resemblance to a 1979 Buick. One of them sat next to me in the back, the other most determinedly sat in the driver's seat and started and began to move the car as if he had a personal grudge against it. "Publicity, gentlemen!" I shouted. "It is a simple matter of publicity! I write about those I know; those in turn protect me and show their consideration in small ways! I wish to live simply, with determination and panache. Don't you have anything to say to me?" I ask desperately. The pleading, plaintive tone of my voice is somehow repellent; there is, after all, a certain point past which one (no matter the degree of self-love, self-absorption) needs to hear someone or something else.

"For Heaven's sake, gentlemen!" I say, "it might have been ill inspired, but it was innocently meant! It was a mistake. No harm was intended. The police have no suspects and thousands of people eat at Stendahl's at one time or the other." All desperately logical elements, as you can see. The eminence of logic cannot, however, overcome other imminence, an aphorism I tell myself that I should have put in print a long time ago since there now does not seem to be that easy, indeterminately extended future in which to air all of my thoughts to the world.

"That is not the point," the driver says. It is the first indication of human speech and I fall upon it gratefully, just as the Buick can be said to have fallen gratefully upon the patches and ruts of the attractively entitled Gowanus Parkway. I lean forward, eager for further transaction. "Not the point," the driver repeats.

"Then what *is* the point?"

"Enough, you," my companion in the backseat says and presses a grip that might be a manacle, "it is time for quiet."

"There is enough point for you," the driver says. "It means—"

"And you too," my companion says to the driver. "Shut up with the mouth, please, before I lose my temper."

This appears to be enough for the driver. It is certainly enough for me. This is the first hint of individuation; the companion appears to have been selected for the violence of his temper, the dreadful possibilities he can invoke; it is a theme with which I am not unfamiliar, my ratcheting and doomed consciousness flickering back again to certain recent discussions with Baby Jane Harrison, and then all too soon we are stopped in front of a large warehouse-appearing building and I am being propelled toward the door. "What is this?" I say uselessly. "It isn't necessary to do this; I get the point—"

"You move," my companion says, giving me a thrust far deadlier and concentrated than any stab from Stendahl's cheesecake (inspired by several old Russian recipes granted the owner by his sainted grandmother, or so I have written in happier times) and departing the 1979 Buick with ancillary speed and valedictory despair, I find myself inside the enclosed spaces of the warehouse, being moved hither and after by what appear to be more than the usual complement of arms and legs. The interior of the warehouse bears a doomed resemblance to my recollections of the spaces in *Some Like It Hot* where Marilyn Monroe's friends found themselves in so much unanticipated trouble. The difference is that my troubles are *not* unanticipated; a scribe has a definite, darker, even lunatic vision, as I have had occasion to contemplate, and at some level I must have known that my literary inclination and my big mouth would get me into some kind of apocalyptic jam, *apocalypse* being a word which I have waited more than fifty-four years to use in its proper context and which *Improve Your Word Power* would definitely indicate is now not inapropos.

I am conveyed up levels, through surfaces, around and about stairs and at long last am deposited in a spacious room where I am, redundantly, frisked here and there, checked out for the usual complement of genitals and the expected paucity of firearms and I am then propelled into a smaller room where I find myself looking at a face of which I have heard and of which I have seen pencil sketches in the dailies from time to time but which I have never, up to this point, actually witnessed. It is an interesting and complex face with the whole history of the century written, as they say, upon it and, never having thought to see it in this world nor having wanted to see it, I find myself transfixed. Thoughts of various kinds wend their way in and out of my fading consciousness while I stand before the face which at length adds arms, legs, a blue suit, an expression of poignancy and interest and becomes, no less than the driver or my companion or Baby Jane Harrison or me, simply a person.

"I have called you here," the face says superfluously. "It seemed to be necessary."

"It was a foolish thing," I say. "I was just making banter. I have to fill out this column, two thousand words, once a week. It is how I make my living."

"It is a terrible living."

"I agree," I say.

"How much you make, this column?"

"Two hundred dollars."

"Terrible," the face says again. "A grown man, a man your age—"

"But it pays off on both ends," I say hastily, pointlessly. "I mention things, I get concessions. I say good things about Stendahl's, Stendahl gives me a table, gives me things to eat—"

"Kickbacks for mentions, then. I know about that."

"Not exactly. I mean, I don't *have* to say good things. I could say bad things—"

The face gives me a perfect, an implacable smile. It is the kind of smile my father gave me the last time I saw him, when we had the final disagreement. It is the look Baby Jane Harrison gave me and gave me until she finally stopped giving me and began to take stringent action. It is, at last, a look which must be accepted.

"All right," I say. "So there were considerations. But if I couldn't say good, I *didn't* say good."

"Hah."

"Well," I say, thinking about this, allowing these last few precious moments of my extinguishable but irreplaceable life to at least permit some thought and consideration, "that's what I wanted to think, anyway. A man has to have his pride. You have to have principle somewhere."

"You know my name?" the face said. "Sure you know my name. Is Bruno. You call me Bruno?"

"I had no names in the column. It was just a little item, 'overheard from all over,' that's all."

"You don't understand yet," Bruno says, "I *like* you. I like your column; you have a good way with words. You, how you say it, light and bright and right on the money." He reaches a hand toward me. "St. Valentine Day's tribute, that was funny," he says, "that's a nice way to put it."

"I don't understand," I say. Consternation and bemusement chase terror through the core of my being in their old accustomed way, but there is a certain quizzicality as well. I am terrifyingly alert to my moods, a factor not beloved by Baby Jane Harrison. "What do you want?"

"What do I want?" Bruno says, his stern and patrician face assuming an aspect of near cordiality, a benignity that oozes through all the spaces of what I had erroneously thought of as darkness, Bruno being from this angle a genuinely engaging and blissfully communicative fellow, "I want you to come to work for *me*."

"What's that?"

"You a good writer," Bruno says. "We need a writer. What we're going to do, we start a newsletter or maybe you get your own paper and you can do nice things for us, like you do for Stendahl. I should have thought of this a long time ago. We are not—how can I put this?—so up to date in some ways as we are in others." His hand shakes my own, absently but with force. "Writing!" he says. "Communications, jokes, the light and bright side! That is what I mean; that's the way to go. You come with us, we make you happy. Two hundred dollars a week for a talent like yours? We do better."

I have had reversals and rereversals in my life; I am not uncognizant of that long-elusive opportunity when it comes. My father and Baby Jane Harrison said that I would never manage, it would never come, but how little they knew. I look at Bruno and smile and it is a smile of greeting as if to the whole world, the world in this warehouse opening to me like a huge and important flower, a flower like musk, like desire.

"*Five* hundred," I say.

Bruno embraces me. "My valentine!" he says.

His valentine.

JANE YOLEN

The Boy Who Drew Unicorns

Jane Yolen has been called America's own Hans Christian Andersen, for among her books (numbering over one hundred) are many original fairy tales and fantasies spun so effortlessly that one can forget these are newly created tales and not traditional stories repeated for hundreds of years. Yolen is also a professional storyteller, ballad singer, and lecturer on children's fiction across the country. She has also been an editor, a university professor, and the president of the Science Fiction Writers of America writers' union. Most recently, she has created Jane Yolen Books, an imprint for the Children's Division of Harcourt Brace Jovanovich Publishers.

The following story was first published in the children's anthology *The Unicorn Treasury*, edited by Bruce Coville and illustrated by Tim Hildebrandt. Yolen also publishes works of adult fantasy, including the novels *Sister Light, Sister Dark; White Jenna*; and *Cards of Grief*.

Yolen and her husband recently returned to their farm in Western Massachusetts from four months in Edinborough, Scotland.

—T. W.

THE BOY WHO DREW UNICORNS

Jane Yolen

There was once a boy who drew unicorns. Even before he knew their names, he caught them mane and hoof and horn on his paper. And they were white beasts and gray, black beasts and brown, galloping across the brown supermarket bags. He didn't know what to call them at first, but he knew what they called him: Phillip, a lover of horses, Philly, Phil.

Now, children, there is going to be a new boy in class today. His name is Philadelphia Carew.

Philadelphia? That's a city name not a kid's name.

Hey, my name is New York.

Call me Chicago.

I got a cousin named India, does that count?

Enough, children. This young man is very special. You must try to be kind to him. He'll be very shy. And he's had a lot of family problems.

I got family problems too, Ms. Wynne. I got a brother and he's a big problem.

Joseph, that's enough.

He's six feet tall. That's a very big problem.

Now you may all think you have problems, but this young man has more than most. You see, he doesn't talk.

Not ever?

No. Not now. Not for several years. That's close enough to ever, I think.

Bet you'd like it if we didn't talk. Not for several years.

No, I wouldn't like that at all, though if I could shut you up for several hours, Joseph . . .

Oooooh, Joey, she's got you!

"What is the good of such drawing, Philadelphia?" his mother said. "If you have to draw, draw something useful. Draw me some

438

money or some groceries or a new man, one who doesn't beat us. Draw us some better clothes or a bed for yourself. Draw me a job."

But he drew only unicorns: horse-like, goat-like, deer-like, lamb-like, bull-like, things he had seen in books. Four-footed, silken swift, with the single golden horn. His corner of the apartment was papered with them.

When's he coming, Ms. Wynne?

Today. After lunch.

Does he look weird, too?

He's not weird, Joseph. He's special. And I expect you—all of you—to act special.

She means we shouldn't talk.

No, Joseph, I mean you need to think before you talk. Think what it must be like not to be able to express yourself.

I'd use my hands.

Does he use his hands, Ms. Wynne?

I don't know.

Stupid, only deaf people do that. Is he deaf?

No.

Is there something wrong with his tongue?

No.

Why doesn't he talk, then?

Why do you think?

Maybe he likes being special.

That's a very interesting idea, Joseph.

Maybe he's afraid.

Afraid to talk? Don't be dumb.

Now, Joseph, that's another interesting idea, too. What are you afraid of, children?

Snakes, Ms. Wynne.

I hate spiders.

I'm not afraid of anything!

Nothing at all, Joseph?

Maybe my big brother. When he's mad.

In school he drew unicorns down the notebook page, next to all his answers. He drew them on his test papers. On the bathroom walls. They needed no signature. Everyone knew he had made them. They were his thumbprints. They were his heartbeats. They were his scars.

*   *   *

Ooooob, he's drawing them things again.
Don't you mess up my paper, Mr. Philadelphia Carew.
Leave him alone. He's just a dummy.
Horses don't have horns, dummy.
Here comes Ms. Wynne.
If you children will get back in your seats and stop crowding around Philly.
You've all seen him draw unicorns before. Now listen to me, and I mean you,
too, Joseph. Fold your hands and lift those shining faces to me. Good. We are
going on a field trip this afternoon. Joseph, sit in your seat properly and leave
Philly's paper alone. A field trip to Chevril Park. Not now, Joseph, get back
in your seat. We will be going after lunch. And after your spelling test.
Ooooob, what test, Ms. Wynne?
You didn't say there was going to be a test.

The park was a place of green glades. It had trees shaped like popsicles
with the chocolate running down the sides. It had trees like umbrellas
that moved mysteriously in the wind. There were hidden ponds and secret
streams and moist pathways between, lined with rings of white toadstools
and trillium the color of blood. Cooing pigeons walked boldly on the
pavement. But in the quiet underbrush hopped little brown birds with
white throats. Silent throats.

From far away came a strange, magical song. It sounded like a
melody mixed with a gargle, a tune touched by a laugh. It creaked,
it hesitated, then it sang again. He had never heard anything like it
before.

I hear it, Ms. Wynne. I hear the merry-go-round.
And what does it sound like, children?
It sounds lumpy.
Don't be dumb. It sounds upsy-downsy.
It sounds happy and sad.
Joseph, what do you think it sounds like?
Like another country. Like "The Twilight Zone."
Very good, Joseph. And see, Philly is agreeing with you. And strangely,
Joseph, you are right. Merry-go-rounds or carousels are from another country,
another world. The first ones were built in France in the late 1700s. The best
handcarved animals still are made in Europe. What kind of animals do you
think you'll see on this merry-go-round?
Horses.
Lions.
Tigers.

Camels.

Don't be dumb—camels.

There are too! I been here before. And elephants.

He saw unicorns, galloping around and around, a whole herd of them. And now he saw his mistake. They were not like horses or goats or deer or lambs or bulls. They were like—themselves. And with the sun slanting on them from beyond the trees, they were like rainbows, all colors and no colors at all.

Their mouths were open and they were calling. That was the magical song he had heard before. A strange, shimmery kind of cry, not like horses or goats or deer or lambs or bull; more musical, with a strange rise and fall to each phrase.

He tried to count them as they ran past. Seven, fifteen, twenty-one . . . he couldn't contain them all. Sometimes they doubled back and he was forced to count them again. And again. He settled for the fact that it was a herd of unicorns. No. *Herd* was too ordinary a word for what they were. Horses came in herds. And cows. But unicorns—there had to be a special word for them all together. Suddenly he knew what it was, as if they had told him so in their wavery song. He was watching a *surprise* of unicorns.

Look at old weird Philly. He's just staring at the merry-go-round. Come on, Mr. Phildelphia Chicago New York L.A. Carew. Go on up and ride. They won't bite.

Joseph, keep your mouth shut and you might be able to hear something.

What, Ms. Wynne?

You might hear the heart's music, Joseph. That's a lot more interesting than the flapping of one's own mouth.

What does that mean, Ms. Wynne?

It means shut up, Joseph.

Ooooh, she got you, Joey.

It means shut up, Denise, too, I bet.

All of you, mouths shut, ears open. We're going for a ride.

We don't have any money, Ms. Wynne.

That's all taken care of. Everyone pick out a horse or a whatever. Mr. Frangipanni, the owner of this carousel, can't wait all day.

Dibs on the red horse.

I got the gray elephant.

Mine's the white horse.

No, Joseph, can't you see Philly has already chosen that one.

But heroes always ride the white horse. And he isn't any kind of hero.

Choose another one, Joseph.
Aaaah, Ms. Wynne, that's not fair.
Why not take the white elephant, Joseph. Hannibal, a great hero of history,
marched across the high Alps on elephants to capture Rome.
Wow—did he really?
Really, Joseph.
Okay. Where's Rome?
Who knows where Rome is? I bet Mr. Frangipanni does.
Then ask Mr. Frangipanni!
Italy, Ms. Wynne.
Italy is right. Time to mount up. That's it. We're all ready, Mr. Frangipanni.

The white flank scarcely trembled, but he saw it. "Do not be afraid,"
he thought. "I couldn't ever hurt you." He placed his hand gently on
the tremor and it stopped.

Moving up along the length of the velvety beast, he saw the arched
neck ahead of him, its blue veins like tiny rivers branching under the
angel-hair mane.

One swift leap and he was on its back. The unicorn turned its head
to stare at him with its amber eyes. The horn almost touched his knee.
He flinched, pulling his knee up close to his chest. The unicorn turned
its head back and looked into the distance.

He could feel it move beneath him, the muscles bunching and flattening as it walked. Then with that strange wild cry, the unicorn leaped
forward and began to gallop around and around the glade.

He could sense others near him, catching movement out of the corners
of his eyes. Leaning down, he clung to the unicorn's mane. They ran
through day and into the middle of night till the stars fell like snow
behind them. He heard a great singing in his head and heart and he
suddenly felt as if the strength of old kings were running in his blood.
He threw his head back and laughed aloud.

Boy, am I dizzy.
My elephant was the best.
I had a red pony. Wow, did we fly!
Everyone dismounted? Now, tell me how you felt.

He slid off the silken side, feeling the solid earth beneath his feet.
There was a buzz of voices around him, but he ignored them all. Instead,
he turned back to the unicorn and walked toward its head. Standing still,
he reached up and brought its horn down until the point rested on his
chest. The golden whorls were hard and cold beneath his fingers. And

if his fingers seemed to tremble ever so slightly, it was no more than how the unicorn's flesh had shuddered once under the fragile shield of its skin.

He stared into the unicorn's eyes, eyes of antique gold so old, he wondered if they had first looked on the garden where the original thrush had sung the first notes from a hand-painted bush.

Taking his right hand off the horn, he sketched a unicorn in the air between them.

As if that were all the permission it needed, the unicorn nodded its head. The horn ripped his light shirt, right over the heart. He put his left palm over the rip. The right he held out to the unicorn. It nuzzled his hand and its breath was moist and warm.

Look, look at Philly's shirt.

Ooooh, there's blood.

Let me through, children. Thank you, Joseph, for helping him get down. Are you hurt, Philly? Now don't be afraid. Let me see. I could never hurt you. Why, I think there's a cut there. Mr. Frangipanni, come quick. Have you any bandages? The boy is hurt. It's a tiny wound but there's lots of blood so it may be very deep. Does it hurt, dear?

No.

Brave boy. Now be still till Mr. Frangipanni comes.

He spoke, Ms. Wynne. Philly spoke.

Joseph, do be still, I have enough trouble without you . . .

But he spoke, Ms. Wynne. He said "no."

Don't be silly, Joseph.

But he did. He spoke. Didn't you, Philly?

Yes.

Yes.

He turned and looked.

The unicorn nodded its head once and spoke in that high, wavering magical voice. "THE HORN HEALS."

He repeated it.

Yes. The horn heals.

He spoke! He spoke!

I'll just clean this wound, Philly, don't move. Why—that's strange. There's some blood, but only an old scar. Are you sure you're all right, dear?

Yes.

*   *   *

Yes.

As he watched, the unicorn dipped its horn to him once, then whirled away, disappearing into the dappled light of the trees. He wondered if he would ever capture it right on paper. It was nothing like the sketches he had drawn before. Nothing. But he would try.

Yes, Ms. Wynne, an old scar healed. I'm sure.

SCOTT BRADFIELD

The Darling

Bradfield is a rising young writer whose collection of stories, *The Secret Life of Houses*, contains a number of gems. One could consider "The Darling" a love story in which a young woman with odd interests actually finds the perfect mate—at least, on a temporary basis. One could also consider it a cautionary tale about the danger of psychoanalysis: it can squelch one's creativity if one doesn't watch out. . . .

The truth is, this is a very scary story.

—E. D.

THE DARLING

Scott Bradfield

Afterwards Dolores Starr would lie on her bed with a sort of stunned and implicate amazement at the power of things, the power of that vast soft universe of force contracting gently around her body like a hand. Dolores, she thought. Dolores, dolorous, dolorous star. She didn't feel hurt so much as bewildered and tired, as if she had awoken from a mere dream of struggle in some other, distant room filled with ballooning silence and white, intricate spaces. Usually by now Dad had returned to the kitchen to drink, but sometimes he took his gun from the clothes closet and waved it around for a while. "Maybe we both learned a little lesson today, didn't we, Miss Teen Princess, little Miss Queen of the World." Dad aimed his Walther P-38 at vanity mirror, cheesecloth curtains, Dolores's desktop crucifix. "Ker-*pow*!" Dad said. "Ker-pow, pow, *pow! That's* the only lesson most people ever learn, Miss Beautiful, Miss All the Boys Love Her. A bullet in the old brainpan, a crack on the head with a flat rock. Pow, bang. That's just about the only lasting truth *this* goddamn world's got to offer." Dad's gun was very heavy and very solid, and filled the entire apartment with its weight and stress. Dolores liked to hold the gun in her hands too; the entire universe of force seemed to withdraw a little when Dolores took it from the closet; she felt as if she had more air to breathe. Most of all, though, she liked the sudden sound of it, and the way Dad looked at her as if she were someone strange and wholly unfamiliar to him. Then, very slowly, Dad lowered his head onto the kitchen table as Dolores moved his Jim Beam to one side. Dad's brains and blood virtually ruined the checkered table-cloth Dolores had bought at K-Mart just that summer, and upstairs Mrs. Morris struck the ceiling three times with her burnished mahogany cane. Mrs. Morris was eighty-seven years old and lived alone. Mrs. Morris lived on a pension, and had bad knees. Mrs. Morris had raised four children of her own and often said she deserved a decent night's sleep every once in a blue moon.

She went to San Francisco and lied about her age, sat at a long formica

table littered with cigarette trays and ashes and solicited marketing sur-
veys. All the operators wore miniature telephone headsets and resembled
the crew of some shoddy spaceship. "Have you graduated college within
the last ten years?" Dolores asked people. "Do you ever purchase Hallmark
greeting cards? Do you have any children? Housepets? Servants? Have
you seen the recent television commercial for New Improved Wheatley
Wheat Snaps? Have you ever been to Vermont?" She felt like a real adult
now, with her own studio apartment on Fulton Street, a super-saver bus
pass, a California Federal checking account, and even a Versatellar cash
card with her own secret code number. She developed a taste for Virginia
Slims, Piña Coladas, and Daniel, her Group Module Assistance Coor-
dinator. Daniel was thirty-seven and lived in Brisbane. "The pectoral—
that's what goes first. The old midriff section. That's why I either run
or swim every morning. That's why I do fifty gut-crunchers every night."
Daniel had marvelous pectorals, a '67 Karmen Ghia convertible, and a
bookshelf filled with books. Dolores read Steinbeck's *The Grapes of Wrath*,
Durrell's *The Alexandria Quartet*, and Tolstoy's *The Death of Ivan Ilych*
while Daniel jogged relentlessly down the peninsula, over San Bruno
Mountain, around Candlestick Park. Dolores loved the world of books,
which were a lot like adulthood, she thought. Both seemed rather smoothly
improbable, at once perfectly real and perfectly contrived, like the uniform
plaid tweed skirt and red wool sweater she had worn to a Catholic girls'
school when she was very small. That was before Grandma died, and
Dad started drinking.

Books make people different, she thought. That's why Daniel was
different. That's why Dolores felt different every day, after every book.
It felt as if every book she read somehow altered her chemical constitution.
She thought she would be very happy with Daniel and his books until
the day he hit her. He hit her in the kitchen while she was washing up.
He hit her because she hadn't been home when he called. He hit her
because she just tried to tell him she was home all night. He hit her
because he saw how other men looked at her and how she looked back.
He hit her because he couldn't reach into that other part of her where
she recognized other men. He hit her because he was just like Dad, he'd
been fooling her all the time, he never really read all those books on the
shelf. His face was red and damp and he'd been drinking with his friends
at the ballpark, and three months later he thought she forgot what he
did, thought the entire incident had gone far away when he crashed
through the rear screen door, steaming with briny sweat in his Nike
tank-top and green nylon jogging trunks, and Dolores handed him his
tall cold protein-shake. He took it down with one long parched swallow,
his Adam's apple bobbing. The protein shake contained non-pasteurised

whole milk, two fertile eggs, eight ounces of liquid protein, wheat germ, vitamin B complex and B-12, and three heaping tablespoons of blue crystal Drano. It didn't kill him right away, though. He fell to the floor and pounded it, gurgling deeply in his chest and throat (ironically, Dolores thought, like bad plumbing) and pulled the telephone off the coffee table; it chimed brokenly. His mouth and eyes were pale and dry, and a hard green pellet popped from his throat and ricocheted off the blank uncomprehending gaze of the Sony Visionstar. In a panic, Dolores sought razors in the bathroom, serrated knives in the kitchen, but discovered only Gillette Good News and disposable plastic cutlery. Finally she struck him twice on the back of the head with his simulation ivory and brass league-leading single-average bowling trophy, spring 1982. His wallet held almost three hundred dollars cash, assorted credit and gas cards. She drove his Karmen Ghia convertible down Highway 5 to Los Angeles, and read Wilde's *The Picture of Dorian Gray* that night in the Van Nuys Motel 6. She liked *The Picture of Dorian Gray* very much.

She made large cash advances on all of Daniel's negotiable cards and opened a money-market liquid assets account at the Sears Financial Network. She acquired a one-bedroom apartment in Fairfax, a clerical position at TRW, and a "new look" from Franklin and Schaeffer in West L.A. Men often asked for her number and said complimentary things; men took her to expensive meals, night clubs, sporting events. In her closet she gradually assembled entire wardrobes of memorabilia from the Dodgers, Raiders, Kings, and Angels. Men were easy. They smiled, laughed, offered services, took checks. They were grateful for the smallest attentions. Dolores carried a .380 automatic Beretta in her purse. She liked men, but that didn't mean she was going to take any chances.

Still, she felt vaguely dissatisfied with life. Something important seemed to be missing, or perhaps even beyond her comprehension. It was as if she were always forgetting something. She wanted to be happy. "I guess it's because I never finished high school," she told Michael one day at work. Michael sat with her at the Employee Benefits desk in Personnel. "I guess I never figured out who I wanted to be, like maybe I've gone and wasted some special part of myself somewhere. Maybe because my mother left me when I was very small, I never felt very good about myself as a person. I know I go on lots of dates, but nobody seems to love me for who I really am."

At Michael's suggestion she enrolled at night extension courses at Los Angeles City College. Every Tuesday and Thursday evening after work she attended lectures in Abnormal Psychology and Functional Human Anatomy. Dr. Peters, who taught Functional Human Anatomy, looked just like Dad before he started drinking. He told her about the jugular, spine, meninges, bile duct. The body was just a delicate bubble, really, which could be broken open very easily; it made her nervous to contemplate twice each week her own physiochemical vulnerability. Infection, hemorrhages, renal failure, metastasis, stroke. Polio, eczema, muscular-dystrophy, brain-death. Every Friday in lab she dissected large cats and divulged complexes of lymph, nerve and muscle. Dolores much preferred Dr. Deakin in her other class, where she tried to put out of her mind the dead cats with their rictus mouths and smell of formaldehyde. Dr. Deakin was relatively young. He wore pressed and faded Levis with white tapered shirts and knit ties. He always punctuated his intense, Socratic monologues with profound, intriguing pauses. "What does it mean . . . this word 'abnormal'? And how do we know . . . when it truly applies?" He had an overgrown walrus moustache, and as he paced the lecture floor he gazed up into the high fluorescents as if entranced by gravid implications only he could see there, like some spiritual medium. "Don't I think . . . *I'm* normal? And anytime you contradict me . . . don't I think *you're* abnormal? Don't we all like to define our*selves* . . . as the 'normal' ones?" Dolores quickly grew to love him. This was a man who understood the way the world worked; he could see far beyond himself into the eyes of other people, other people who hurt, cared, loved and cried. "I certainly understand the importance of your class, no kidding," she told him over a shared turkey-and-sprouts-on-rye at the corner Blimpies. "I have had to deal with many abnormal people in my life, and I am just beginning to realise that they were not abnormal at all, but really were just normal, actually."

Dr. Deakin kept an immaculate duplex in Los Feliz, filled with lush hanging ferns and gleaming French windows, and Dolores cut his throat with one of the long steel carving knives from the immaculate and well-kept Spanish-style kitchen. He had been perfectly gentle and polite. She hadn't felt angry, or even perfunctory. There was just something in men which seemed to demand it now. Something in their eyes. It was like the look of seduction, really. The blood was suddenly everywhere, and if there was one thing Dolores was firmly resolved against from that night forward it was knives. She began making a few strategic handgun investments. A .38 Special, a 9mm Parabellum. Dense compact Remington cartridges in a tidy cardboard box. She joined the National Rifle Association. She subscribed to *Guns and Ammo*.

Men were easy, but women were different. Women, in fact, were much more different from Dolores than men. Their glances click-clicked like the lenses of cameras, their tongues snapped faintly at you in reproach. They didn't like you talking to any of their men, and all the men in the world, it seemed, were their men. Women kept secrets, and liked to pay men special attentions in private. Dolores didn't even like women, though she hoped it was a condition which would change with maturity. Women practiced retributions on grand scales, they wielded sharp blades in profound ritual ceremonies beneath the earth in intricate vast caverns filled with smoky incense and swelling female voices. Dolores never had a mother, so she never knew. Women shared a secret world of ritual, violence and redemption Dolores could only guess at.

"You know you gotta be careful in L.A., don't you, Di?" Michael said, always bringing hot coffee in styrofoam cups to her desk, candy bars, crackers. "You read the papers, don't you? A single woman's got to be careful in this city; you know why? Because otherwise she'll get murdered, that's why. This city's filled with a lot of very crazy characters, Dolores. For example, just the other day I was reading about a whole club of murderers that lived out in the desert. The women, you see, would go to bars and pick up men. Then they'd take them out to the desert and they'd be murdered by the whole gang. It started out as an Indian cult, but then the white people started getting involved, too. Even the white women. They skinned one man completely alive before they murdered him. So, what are you up to later, Di? Feel like a movie, maybe? Or dinner?"

They ate Thai, saw John Wayne in *Red River* and *Rio Lobo*. Dolores particularly liked Angie Dickinson, one of *Rio Lobo*'s co-stars who would go on later to star in the hit television series *Police Woman*. Angie Dickinson knew a woman could appear feminine and sexy and still know how to take care of herself. Michael sat quietly beside her and didn't even reach for her hand; she could even see the movie flickering and inverted in his brown eyes. The movie theater was called the *Vista* and was located at the corner of Sunset and Hollywood. It was filled with mis-shapen shadows, stained and thinning velvet draperies, high abandoned balconies and enormous Egyptian-style statues, like some film festival in the Middle Kingdom. "This used to be a gay theater," Michael told her when they first sat down. He shifted uneasily in his seat. "I can still smell them," he said. "Fucking queers."

They bought ice cream next door and then drove to Griffith Park. Michael was silent, and Dolores felt a hard cool pressure accumulating in her, like the thickness of gravity.

"What are you thinking?" Michael asked.

Every so often they passed the hunched figures of strange men in the shadows. Usually the strange men wore leather jackets; they had dark complexions and quick dark hands.

"I don't know. What are *you* thinking?"

Dolores unclasped her purse in her lap. Her right hand slid through the clutter of checkbooks, wadded Kleenex, random cosmetics, and a dogeared paperback copy of James M. Cain's *Mildred Pierce*, sensing the buried and unalterable weight of it there before she found it. It was always the same, she thought. Men who really loved you were filled with a sort of emptiness. Sometimes you wanted to fill that emptiness before it filled you. They pulled into a secluded parking lot in a grove of drooping jacarandas. Over the roof of the park the powerlines hummed.

"It's not easy living alone in a town like L.A.," Michael told her. "I mean, it's not hard for someone like me, since I'm a highly independent person with a firm commitment to being exactly who I am. In fact, I can honestly say I have a very firm commitment to myself, which is not to sound egotistical or anything. It's just that I'm not one of those people, you know, who always needs someone telling them, like, this is who you are." Michael reached under the driver's seat. "Some people never understand," he said.

Michael withdrew his .357 Magnum Desert Eagle just as Dolores withdrew her .380 Beretta Model 84, which featured a thirteen round staggered magazine and a reversible release. A crumpled ball of Kleenex, dislodged from the trigger by Dolores's thumb, tumbled into her lap. It was a full moon outside that night, making only a dim impression against the high screen of smog.

Michael looked at Dolores's gun; then he looked at her eyes. He looked at her gun again. Finally he said, "Don't you have trouble finding a good clean-burning handload for a piece like that?"

"I use Blue Dot," Dolores said. "I don't want to stress the barrel."

They were married in July, bought a condo in the Valley and an Airedale pup named Bud. "Bud's a pup who's going to have one solid family unit to depend on," Michael said, dispatched a blizzard of resumés, and acquired an administrative position at Lockheed in Burbank. "You've got to believe in yourself if you're going to be happy in this life. Don't you, Bud? Don't you, fellah?" Michael scrubbed the Airedale's addled head between his fingers. The puppy gave a succinct yelp.

"Be careful," Dolores said. "You're hurting him."

They went everywhere and did everything together. Tuesday evenings a Self-Actualization Workshop in Sherman Oaks, Saturday afternoons an Advanced Gun Care and Safety Program at the Van Nuys Police Academy. They installed a burglar alarm in their home, a doghouse in the blossoming yard, and their mutual gun collection behind glass-paneled display cases in the den. "It's like I have all the energy in the world now," Michael said, and decided to build an arboretum in the back yard. "It'll be like our summer home, a home away from home. We'll sit out there and drink ice tea all summer." Michael loved their yard. "Gardening is what I always needed," he told her, returning from the nursery with marigolds, Lincoln roses, peat moss. "It helps me make use of my more positive side, my life-affirming energy. I don't believe in anger any more. I don't believe in hate. The world's got enough of those negative vibrations already without me making any more of them." He installed floodlights on a high wooden vined terrace, and often worked on the yard alone and late into the evenings.

Dolores, meanwhile, would lie awake in bed at night and imagine the fluttery and somewhat appalled conspiracies of women. "I'm not a thing or a self-oriented person any more," Dolores told them. "I'm a goal-oriented person now." Deep in their immaculate caverns, the women murmured; they tried not to listen; they were deeply and mortally offended. "I know you think I've just given in to some man, but that's not true. Michael isn't just some man. Michael respects me as a person. Michael respects me for being exactly who I am. You can't understand if you don't know that feeling how wonderful and important that feeling is. It's not something I can just explain." Faint fibrillations, echoes, pulses. The women shared sonorous voices, impossible confidences, their hearts synchronously beating in the black caverns. Dolores didn't trust them; she wanted to get far away. Someday we'll have our own energy-sufficient cabin in the Pacific Northwest, she assured herself. We'll have trained Dobermans, electrified fences, canned goods. We'll have short-wave, and a proper armory which includes autoloading carbines and anti-ballistic missiles. Often she fell asleep before Michael came to bed, and when she awoke she could hear him already at work again in the back yard, striking the ground with spades, shovels, rakes, installing seeds, bulbs, determined little saplings. "I thought we might have a little vegetable garden right here," Michael told her. "Then we don't have to worry so much about pesticides." Dolores loved to stand at the large picture window and watch him work. Michael had long fair-skinned hands which, finely etched with the brown dirt, resembled beautiful antique figurines recovered from some archeological dig. "I'm a high energy sort of person," he told her. "I never sleep much." Bud lay on the sunny grass and contemplated a hovering fly, his tiny body coiled like the spring of an HK P7. Weekends Dolores would sit on the faded green lawn-chair, drinking tall ice-cold drinks and smelling the moist upturned earth. Every few minutes Michael would look up from his work and smile at her. His tools lay about casually or leaned against the varnished pine fence like intimate friends at some large garden party, flaked with dirt like Michael's hands. There are places outside the world of men and women, Dolores thought. It's possible to live there safely and protected, like children with strong, enduring parents.

Then, one Sunday while Michael was pricing planters at Builders' Emporium, Bud uprooted the foot of a buried postman among a bed of Michael's blossoming dahlias. His shoe lace was untied, and seemed to signify something, though Dolores was too shaken to decide exactly what. "I felt impossibly alone," she told Bud later, cradling him in her arms, dripping his still body with her tears. "Everything I tried to believe was true about Michael was really just a lie. His honesty, fidelity, love—all lies. He never cared about me. He never wanted to share his life with me. He only wanted his own secret little world." In the basement she had discovered jars of formaldehyde, handcuffs, ropes, and enormous gray cloth sacks. "He was never going to let me into that world. I was always going to be completely alone." Bud was warm and motionless in her arms. It was dark out, and a full moon glowed faintly through the overcast. Then Dolores lay Bud in the trench in Michael's arms. She crossed Michael's arms across Bud, to keep him warm in the long darkness. Michael was wearing his three-piece Bill Blass double-breasted tweed, the same suit he wore the day they were married. Then, gently and with deep regret, Dolores distributed the damp brown earth across them both. It was as if she were burying herself in the tidy garden, placing her own humble body into the deep, whispering world of complicit women. The women themselves, though, weren't very happy. Nobody liked her there any more. They didn't want her with them. Only men like Dolores. Men and other men.

She drew the curtains on the picture window, and every night she slept alone. The loneliness was immense and unsettling. She felt unpopulated black continents forming deep inside her body, jagged mossy peninsulas orbited by craggy forlorn islands and glimmering gray water. In the long evenings she sat beside the curtained picture window, motionless within a cone of light from the standing lamp like a display in some anthropological museum, feeling the hard relentless yearning of the planet underneath the yard, the secret articulations of graves and bodies. She never looked at the yard any more, but only imagined it. Michael's abandoned tools just lay there gathering rust, their wooden handles cracked and splintering. The flowerbeds and vegetable garden would be overgrown with fast green weeds, the wheelbarrow overturned and covered with a thick gray impasto of cement. And Michael, of course, underneath all of it, still telling his lies, still lying to her all night and all day. She couldn't even hear the secret ceremonies of the women anymore. They had gone into deeper caverns where Dolores was no longer privileged. They were teaching her a little lesson. If she wanted to be Miss Little High and Mighty, if she wanted to be independent and on her own, then that's just what she'd have. Just herself; nobody else for her to feel any responsibility towards. Now all she could hear were the powerlines buzzing on the high poles, the crickets wheezing, the dark planetary heart beating against the floors of her condo. Sometimes, particularly late at night after she had smoked too much marijuana and too many cigarettes, Michael would appear and attempt to comfort her in her darkest, loneliest hours. He would sit on the beige sofa, absently patting Bud's loose, volitionless head in his lap. "You weren't secure enough in your individuality to allow me to be myself," he told her. "When people love each other, they have to trust each other as well, Di. I think you know that."

Dolores never looked at him directly. She looked instead at the curtained window. She imagined bright spiders spinning their webs in the piles of mouldering lumber Michael had purchased for the arboretum. "I don't think I have anything left to say to you any more," she said.

Sometimes Michael moved to the faded gray Barcalounger which Dolores had stitched together in places; sometimes the marijuana gave Dolores a vague sense of self-possession, as if she were in complete control of her own lungs, blood, heart. She could will her heart to slow down a bit; she could demand more oxygenation or less. Sometimes she felt as if she were sitting in another, blurred room far away from this one. Usually during these long waking dreams her mind returned to the same questions over and over again. She wondered if her mother was still alive somewhere. Would we recognise one another if we met unexpectedly on the street? she asked herself. Is there something chemical about the bond between a mother and her daughter, or are we just like any two strangers now? Maybe we'll become great friends by sheer chance some day. She will find my naïveté charming; she will teach me all about men. We'll go to movies together and take turns fixing dinner. We'll become devoted roommates, go to nightclubs, even dancing. In Europe women often go dancing together, and it doesn't necessarily mean they're lesbians or anything.

"You sit cooped up every night smoking grass," Michael told her, the collapsed puppy draped across his knees like a hearth blanket. "I think you've done enough feeling sorry for yourself for one lifetime. I think it's time you took a little responsibility for your own life, and stopped blaming everything on people you love." Michael picked up the container of Herco smokeless shotgun powder from the coffee table. The shotgun, cleaned and loaded, was peering out from underneath Dolores's easy chair. "You don't leave something like this sitting open all day long," he said. "It gets damp." He affixed the aluminum lid with a quick hollow snap.

"Also, you better start looking in on the yard. The neighborhood cats have begun digging up Mrs. Winslow again. If I were you, I'd go out there right now and check on Mrs. Winslow."

Dolores took the unfinished joint from the ashtray in her lap and lit it with her Cricket. A seed popped, and a fragment of paper sparked and fluttered through the air. Without exhaling, Dolores asked, "Who was Mrs. Winslow?" Her eyes began to water.

Michael shrugged. In his lap, Bud's head rolled to one side, his large eyes dry and vacant like the eyes of some collapsed puppet. "Just some lady who worked at the library," he said.

Then one Friday evening in late summer Dolores returned home from Von's to discover numerous police cars and ambulances parked in her driveway, their soft red and yellow emergency bulbs pulsing and spinning in the smoggy twilit air. They seemed vaguely sudden and incongruous, like emergency flares designating some roadside picnic. Dolores removed her groceries from the trunk, and a uniformed policeman at the door gazed at her with a sort of obdurate and official complacency. Loaves of bread, a sack of red delicious apples, gallons of distilled water in large clear plastic jugs. Even though she lived alone, she liked to be prepared; if there was one thing life had taught her, you never knew what might happen next. She didn't feel surprised so much as slightly bemused when she was confronted by charges of multiple homicide with Birdseye frozen vegetables under one arm, nachos and various snack crackers under her other. The arresting officer, Detective Rowlandson, was very kind. He asked her if the cuffs were comfortable. He transferred her frozen foods into the care of one of the random officers who were milling awkwardly about the small living-room. The uncurtained window revealed a red, apocalyptic sunset and numerous men in white cloth shirts and trousers digging at the yard. Wearing surgical masks and gloves, they wrapped the mouldering figures in white sheets and transferred them to stretchers which were then carried to the open chambers of patient white ambulances. When Detective Rowlandson drove her down the hill in his El Dorado the streets were filled with curious neighbors—housewives in faded terrycloth robes, children leaning against their Stingray bicycles. "Anything you say can and will be held against you in a court of law," Detective Rowlandson told her, trying to find a classical station on the radio. "I know," Dolores said, "and I think that's perfectly fair." She was turning to look at the young officer in the back seat. The young officer was gazing aimlessly out the window. He seemed a little bored, or even homesick. When they arrived at the station Detective Rowlandson interrogated her in his private office, with another pair of uniformed patrolmen at the door and a cassette tape recorder whirring on the desk top. "Maybe you'd like a little soda or something?" he asked. "Maybe your throat's getting a little parched?" They were all very kind, Dolores thought. Even when they don't really know what's going on, men really do try to do their best. Men really do care about the unapproachable world of women.

She was awarded a private cell and instant, irremediable celebrity. "I can't say I'm proud of what I've done," she told the media, which was assembled around her in a bright fluorescent room of flashing cameras and buzzing tape machines. The journalists sat poised on the edges of their aluminum chairs as if expecting some race to commence without a second's notice. "It's not like I'm stupid either, since I always did well in school whenever I bothered to apply myself, and Dr. Weinstein, who is one of the very kind doctors visiting me while I am incarcerated, says I performed exceptionally well on the Weschler Adult Intelligence Scale. I guess I can only blame my poor upbringing, being as that my mother left me when I was very little, and as my father beat me when I was little and took advantage of me in many ways which are too delicate to be gotten into at this time and place. But anyway, I can't blame everything on my parents, since I am a grown up woman who must take responsibility for herself, and so I would like to say that I am solely responsible for all those dead bodies buried in my yard—" which initiated a blizzard of bursting flash bulbs "—and of course for my good husband Michael's senseless and untimely demise as well, and if I get sent to the electric chair I will certainly deserve every minute of it since Michael was the kindest, most loving husband the world has ever known, and he was certainly the only man who ever actually tried to understand and care for me in a totally unselfish and caring manner. Thank you very much."

Dolores's private cell was in the Women's Maximum Security Prison in Lancaster. She had a toilet, a washbasin, and a prison-issue towel, soap and toothbrush. She had a rough green khaki blanket and bristly sheets. Every afternoon they took her out alone to exercise in the court-yard. She walked calmly around the painted white basketball tableau. She did sit-ups and leg-lifts, pausing occasionally to gaze up at the bright California sky. The guards were all women. When she saw other inmates, they were all women. They all had hard coarse expressions. Sometimes, far off down the distant cement corridors, Dolores could hear a young woman crying. She sounded very young, almost a child.

Dolores was entering into her Russian novel phase. She read *Crime and Punishment, Anna Karenina*, and *War and Peace*. For the first time in her life, Dolores felt at peace with herself and her innermost being. *It's like*

I never had a chance before to actually understand what it was like to be totally on my own, she wrote on her pad of white paper, which was inspected every evening by one of the uniformed guards. *Maybe if I had only had a chance to get to know myself without other people around me all the time making me feel like somebody I wasn't, I wouldn't have killed all those nice people*. She contemplated writing her own autobiography and publishing it under the title *Bad Love*. Her cell was absolutely silent for hours at a time. In fact, Dolores rarely saw any men at all. She felt denser, more compact, more real. It was as if her entire body was filling up with sand. She refused newspapers and magazines. She was a quiet, respectable hermit living alone in a deep cave. She was contemplating convoluted and transcendent things. *Some things you just can't explain*, she told her writing pad. *Sometimes too you can be just happy not explaining them either*.

"They've got you now, baby," Michael said, picking at the celery on her evening meal tray. "As they say in the movies—the jig is up."

"We'll see," Dolores said. She felt a vague glimmer of hope, one which filled her with impossible sadness.

A few days later Dr. Weinstein fell in love with her, and she knew all the peace she had finally grown accustomed to would not last. "Primitive man didn't draw pictures on his walls because he liked pretty *pictures*, for chrissakes," Dr. Weinstein told her during one of his visits, trying to act like he wasn't in love with her, like he was different from other men. "It's not like *Neanderthalus australopithecus* buried his dead out of fucking sympathy and compassion. How much sympathy and compassion do you think you'd get from a *Neanderthalus australopithecus*? Not too damn much, that's how much. Not too damn much at all." He showed her a picture of *Neanderthalus australopithecus* in a large library edition of *The Encyclopedia of Human Anthropology*. "You see that guy? You see those teeth, that brow? Why do you think he painted pictures on the wall? For the same reason he ate the still-bloody heart of the rival tribesmen he killed, that's why. He was appropriating the soul and strength of significant others. Family, beasts, enemies. The sun and the fucking moon, that's what."

He carried a black leather briefcase. He wore a dark suit and glasses. At first he only appeared every few weeks or so and asked her to complete psychological profiles, write personal compositions, and analyse photographs of men, women and children in family situations. Then he began arriving every afternoon just as the lunch trays were being collected by a trusty on a wobbly aluminum cart. Sometimes he talked for hours while Dolores sat on her cot, her hands folded between her knees, her blank gaze trained upon the concrete floor which she had scrubbed clean just that morning.

"We do it every day," Dr. Weinstein said. He held the briefcase in his lap with his left hand; his right hand gestured vacantly at the cold and empty air. "We appropriate the souls and strengths of other people. It's just that most of us don't have to kill them, babe. You know what I'm saying at you, Di? You don't mind if I call you Di, do you? I saw it on your Wechsler examination under preferred nicknames." He offered her cigarettes and she smoked them, inhaling the grainy, desultory smoke, watching the smoke settle across the stone floors like morning mist in a swamp. "Love and aggression are the same thing in human society. They're both responses to the same biochemical hums and pops. You love or hate the other and you want to blast them. You want to break them down into their elements and swallow them. You want to make them one with yourself by devouring, feasting, obliterating. Then they're part of you, aren't they, babe? Then *you're* in complete control. It's a biochemical desire, but when you live in society, see, we learn to develop displacements for those desires. We learn to turn acts into symbolic intentions. You don't *do*, in other words, Di. You learn to seem *not* to do, if you know what I mean. But you really *do* do, secretly, but only in your mind. Only you, babe, you don't know how to do that. You think there's just your mind and the world, that the world's the only object your mind's got to act on. You have to learn to invent other objects. You have to learn to compensate for your desires by instituting certain ritual behaviors in your seriously addled and definitely very sociopathic psyche, Di—and I think I can say that much for certain. Definitely sociopathic. These are things you're supposed to learn—when you're raised properly. But you haven't been raised properly. You've got to be raised all over, right? You see what I'm saying, Di? You've got to be raised all over again."

Dr. Weinstein testified at her first court appearance and the charges were dropped on grounds of insanity. "Let's say they were pretty firm grounds, Di. Let's say we had a fucking continent full of firm ground for that one," Dr. Weinstein told her in the government car that took them to a county holding cell after the hearing. Three days later Dolores was remanded to the custody of the State Psychiatric Clinic in Reseda and, three months after that, quietly transferred to Dr. Weinstein's private facilities in Napa County. It was a different place from prison, and Dolores didn't like it. The grounds were green and unenclosed, with a view of rolling hills patched with vineyards. Dolores was apportioned her own private room, wardrobe, library and lawn-chair. The patients here were all very quiet and composed, and didn't look disturbed at all that Dolores could tell. Rachel, an attractive, fortyish redhead told her, "When my husband closed down our savings account and ran off with his secretary to Buenos Aires, I guess I just couldn't cope." Rachel was wearing a polka dot cotton summer dress and reading *Cosmopolitan*.

Dr. Weinstein was personally committed to "raising her all over again." Her diet was strictly regulated. Listlessly, she attended the clinic's mandatory exercycle workouts. Her blood pressure was intently monitored, her saliva, feces and urine; two interns from UCLA Medical Center received a grant to monitor her endorphins. She was steeped in megavitamins and zinc; she suffered a high colonic. "Symbolic displacement," Dr. Weinstein told her after each morning's "contact therapy" interview in his office. "There are certain amine molecules manufactured in the adrenal gland which generate rage. There's good rage and there's bad rage, and your rage, Di, is very bad. These amines are then conditioned and modified by those massive discharges of the endocrine system concerned with reproduction. Reproduction is something your body anticipates around the clock; your body's always preparing you for reproduction, Di." He took her hand and commented on her long strong fingers; then he brushed a vein with alcohol and inserted the needle. "It's at the confluence of rage and sex where we're trying to get," he said. "We're trying to draw a line between intentionality and action, pure rage and sudden sex. That's the line that's been eliminated in you, babe. We're going to replace it. We're going to draw it fast and hard." She received the injections three times a day, and Dr. Weinstein began taking her on what he liked to call "field studies". They drove to Marin County and purchased a new Volvo. They went shopping for clothes, curtains, sheets, dishes. Dolores had never really enjoyed shopping that much before, but now she craved it like potato chips; it took her away from herself; she could lose herself in the vast chattering communities of women. Afterwards she and Dr. Weinstein would return to his private office at the clinic and watch television; often they attended movies and plays together. He pronounced her fit for the home-based phase of her therapy. They were married in August and set up housekeeping in a beautiful two-storey isolated country house in Sebastopol. Dolores worked mornings at the local day-care center while Dr. Weinstein was at the clinic. Then she had the rest of the day to watch television. She didn't like books any more. Dr. Weinstein's Literary Guild selections gazed down mutely from the high mahogany bookshelves like zoological specimens cradled in formaldehyde jars.

She still thought of murdering him. Not every day, but periodically. At these times she felt herself inflating with a strange unidentifiable sensation. Her heart began to pound; the backs of her hands began to itch. Her face grew flushed and hot, and she developed splitting migraines. She had never felt so intensely aware of the flux and convection of her own blood before. "You're learning, Di. You're learning to accept the limitations of your own body, your own mind." Dr. Weinstein sat in the stuffed chair beside the jetting blue flames of the gas fireplace. The latest issue of *The American Journal of Psychiatric Medicine* was propped open against his knee. "Fix us a cup of coffee, babe. Sit down and relax with me." Dolores went into the kitchen and saw the immaculate wooden cooking utensils hanging from the varnished redwood cabinets. Then she went out the back door and made the screen door slam. She drove their second car to the Emporium mall and had a Bloody Mary at Marie Calendar's. She was still filling up with the unidentifiable feelings. She tried to repress them, but she didn't know what she was repressing. Terrible anger and rage, she suspected. That was what Dr. Weinstein told her; that's what the daily injections were investing her with. She was frightened and disoriented. She sat down at a row of plastic stools near a wide mirrored fountain. Blue water streamed from the blowholes of glass dolphins. The fear grew more and more terrible as she watched the pulsing crowds and families. Teenage girls emblazoned with cosmetics. Young couples pushing dazed babies in carriages with tiny stuffed toys dangling from their fabric awnings. Packs of young men with faces flushed from marijuana. It wasn't fear any more, it was panic. Dolores felt panicked but she couldn't move; she couldn't face the crowds of people; she couldn't face the acres of cars in the vast parking lots. She started to cry and cry. She had never cried in front of strangers before. When someone tried to touch her she pulled away and screamed at them. She didn't know what she screamed, but she knew she didn't want anybody near her. She just wanted to cry and cry, as if the entire world had ended and now only its unaccountable sadness was left, filling her and filling her like the hard colorless rage with which she desperately desired to murder Dr. Weinstein.

After these "episodes" Dolores would be sedated and kept overnight at the clinic. In the morning, Dr. Weinstein would drive her home in the Volvo, usually playing Philip Glass on the car stereo. "It takes a while to adjust," he told her. "We're teaching your entire body how to behave all over again. We're teaching it how to feel and breathe." His right hand reached out and held hers in her lap. She felt enervated and thick with barbiturates. Outside the entire landscape was blurred and indistinct. "We're teaching you how to love, babe. We're teaching you how to love without hurting anybody." Dolores began to feel extraordinarily lonely and weak. "And you know I love you, Di. You know that, don't you?"

She couldn't even remember the faces of any of her old lovers any more. Their memory seemed to be draining easily from her like water from a tub. She could remember their names—Daniel, Dr. Deakin, Michael, Dad—but she couldn't remember anything about the quality of their presence, the fabric of their skin or voice or hair, the strength of their muscles or intestines. In the long summer afternoons she would just sit outside in the sculpted front garden, wearing her cashmere robe, black stockings and a silk teddy, beside an ice chest filled with Margaritas on the wrought-iron lawn table next to the Valium prescription and her strewn cosmetics, and gaze aimlessly at the blue sky, green trees and sculpted topiary hedges. There was just a dark inchoate sadness now, formless and buzzing. "It's the recognition that you're alone, babe. It's the human condition, it just means you're sane, that's all. It means you're not swallowing people. It means you know who you are, and who they are, and that line where the twain shall not meet. You're developing a nice clean bright soul now, like Billy's bright teeshirt in a television detergent commercial. You've got your own world inside now, babe. You're ready to live your own life." Dolores sipped her Margarita and thought about *Neanderthal australopithecus's* cave. Someone had expunged all the pale etchings of bison and mammoth from the rough basalt walls. There was nobody left in the cave at all any more, not even the flickering fire or the smell of roasting meat. Dolores lit a cigarette and looked at the impossibly blue sky. For a moment she thought she might start crying, but then she didn't.

The following summer Dr. Weinstein pronounced her cured and, exactly one year after that, she gave birth to a nine-pound baby boy. The baby had a full head of black matted hair when he was presented to her by the nurse; his eyes were squeezed shut with pain and screaming. She held him against her breasts and listened to his heart beating in her private room while Dr. Weinstein sat beside her, beaming like a street-lamp and holding her hand. After a few days of bloodless discussion, they named the baby Andrew, in honor of Dolores's Dad.

JOE R. LANSDALE

Night They Missed the Horror Show

Joe R. Lansdale is a family man, a nice, easygoing kind of guy—yet he has the ability to write the most vicious, offensive, disgusting stories and novels of any writer I know. Like his recent novel, *The Night Runners*, his short stories are also extremely effective and compulsively readable.

The following story reminds us that no matter how mean you think you are, there's always someone out there who's meaner. And Lansdale doesn't pull any punches in exploring that theme.

—E. D.

NIGHT THEY MISSED THE HORROR SHOW

Joe R. Lansdale

(For Lew Shiner. A story that doesn't flinch.)

If they'd gone to the drive-in like they'd planned, none of this would have happened. But Leonard didn't like drive-ins when he didn't have a date, and he'd heard about *Night Of The Living Dead*, and he knew a nigger starred in it. He didn't want to see no movie with a nigger star. Niggers chopped cotton, fixed flats and pimped nigger girls, but he'd never heard of one that killed zombies. And he'd heard too that there was a white girl in the movie that let the nigger touch her, and that peeved him. Any white gal that would let a nigger touch her must be the lowest trash in the world. Probably from Hollywood, New York or Waco, some godforsaken place like that.

Now Steve McQueen would have been all right for zombie killing and girl handling. He would have been the ticket. But a nigger? No sir.

Boy, that Steve McQueen was one cool head. Way he said stuff in them pictures was so good you couldn't help but think someone had written it down for him. He could sure think fast on his feet to come up with the things he said, and he had that real cool, mean look.

Leonard wished he could be Steve McQueen, or Paul Newman even. Someone like that always knew what to say, and he figured they got plenty of bush too. Certainly they didn't get as bored as he did. He was so bored he felt as if he were going to die from it before the night was out. Bored, bored, bored. Just wasn't nothing exciting about being in the Dairy Queen parking lot leaning on the front of his '64 Impala looking out at the highway. He figured maybe old crazy Harry who janitored at the high school might be right about them flying saucers. Harry was always seeing something. Bigfoot, six-legged weasels, all manner of things. But maybe he was right about the saucers. He'd said he'd seen one a couple nights back hovering over Mud Creek and it was shooting down these rays that looked like wet peppermint sticks. Leonard figured if

Harry really had seen the saucers and the rays, then those rays were boredom rays. It would be a way for space critters to get at earth folks, boring them to death. Getting melted down by heat rays would have been better. That was at least quick, but being bored to death was sort of like being nibbled to death by ducks.

Leonard continued looking at the highway, trying to imagine flying saucers and boredom rays, but he couldn't keep his mind on it. He finally focused on something in the highway. A dead dog.

Not just a dead dog. But a DEAD DOG. The mutt had been hit by a semi at least, maybe several. It looked as if it had rained dog. There were pieces of that pooch all over the concrete and one leg was lying on the curbing on the opposite side, stuck up in such a way that it seemed to be waving hello. Doctor Frankenstein with a grant from John Hopkins and assistance from NASA couldn't have put that sucker together again.

Leonard leaned over to his faithful, drunk companion, Billy—known among the gang as Farto, because he was fart lighting champion of Mud Creek—and said, "See that dog there?"

Farto looked where Leonard was pointing. He hadn't noticed the dog before, and he wasn't nearly as casual about it as Leonard. The puzzle piece hound brought back memories. It reminded him of a dog he'd had when he was thirteen. A big, fine German Shepherd that loved him better than his Mama.

Sonofabitch dog tangled its chain through and over a barbed wire fence somehow and hung itself. When Farto found the dog its tongue looked like a stuffed, black sock and he could see where its claws had just been able to scrape the ground, but not quite enough to get a toe hold. It looked as if the dog had been scratching out some sort of coded message in the dirt. When Farto told his old man about it later, crying as he did, his old man laughed and said, "Probably a goddamn suicide note."

Now, as he looked out at the highway, and his whisky-laced Coke collected warmly in his gut, he felt a tear form in his eyes. Last time he'd felt that sappy was when he'd won the fart lighting championship with a four-inch burner that singed the hairs of his ass and the gang awarded him with a pair of colored boxing shorts. Brown and yellow ones so he could wear them without having to change them too often.

So there they were, Leonard and Farto, parked outside the DQ, leaning on the hood of Leonard's Impala, sipping Coke and whisky, feeling bored and blue and horny, looking at a dead dog and having nothing to do but go to a show with a nigger starring in it. Which to be up front, wouldn't have been so bad if they'd had dates. Dates could make up for a lot of sins, or help make a few good ones, depending on one's outlook.

But the night was criminal. Dates they didn't have. Worse yet, wasn't a girl in the entire high school would date them. Not even Marylou Flowers, and she had some kind of disease.

All this nagged Leonard something awful. He could see what the problem was with Farto. He was ugly. Had the kind of face that attracted flies. And though being fart lighting champion of Mud Creek had a certain prestige among the gang, it lacked a certain something when it came to charming the gals.

But for the life of him, Leonard couldn't figure his own problem. He was handsome, had some good clothes, and his car ran good when he didn't buy that old cheap gas. He even had a few bucks in his jeans from breaking into washaterias. Yet his right arm had damn near grown to the size of his thigh from all the whacking off he did. Last time he'd been out with a girl had been a month ago, and as he'd been out with her along with nine other guys, he wasn't rightly sure he could call that a date. He wondered about it so much, he'd asked Farto if he thought it qualified as a date. Farto, who had been fifth in line, said he didn't think so, but if Leonard wanted to call it one, wasn't no skin off his dick.

But Leonard didn't want to call it a date. It just didn't have the feel of one, lacked something special. There was no romance to it.

True, Big Red had called him Honey when he put the mule in the barn, but she called everyone Honey—except Stoney. Stoney was Possum sweets, and he was the one who talked her into wearing the grocery bag with the mouth and eye holes. Stoney was like that. He could sweet talk the camel out from under a sand nigger. When he got through chatting Big Red down, she was plumb proud to wear that bag.

When finally it came his turn to do Big Red, Leonard had let her take the bag off as a gesture of good will. That was a mistake. He just hadn't known a good thing when he had it. Stoney had had the right idea. The bag coming off spoiled everything. With it on, it was sort of like balling the Lone Hippo or some such thing, but with the bag off, you were absolutely certain what you were getting, and it wasn't pretty.

Even closing his eyes hadn't helped. He found that the ugliness of that face had branded itself on the back of his eyeballs. He couldn't even imagine the sack back over her head. All he could think about was that puffy, too-painted face with the sort of bad complexion that began at the bone.

He'd gotten so disappointed, he'd had to fake an orgasm and get off before his hooter shriveled up and his Trojan fell off and was lost in the vacuum.

Thinking back on it, Leonard sighed. It would certainly be nice for a change to go with a girl that didn't pull the train or had a hole between her legs that looked like a manhole cover ought to be on it. Sometimes he wished he could be like Farto who was as happy as if he had good sense. Anything thrilled him. Give him a can of Wolf Brand Chili, a big moon pie, Coke and whisky and he could spend the rest of his life fucking Big Red and lighting the gas out of his asshole.

God, but this was no way to live. No women and no fun. Bored, bored, bored. Leonard found himself looking overhead for space ships and peppermint-colored boredom rays, but he saw only a few moths fluttering drunkenly through the beams of the DQ's lights.

Lowering his eyes back to the highway and the dog, Leonard had a sudden flash. "Why don't we get the chain out of the back and hook it up to Rex there? Take him for a ride."

"You mean drag his dead ass around?" Farto asked.

Leonard nodded.

"Beats stepping on a tack," Farto said.

They drove the Impala into the middle of the highway at a safe moment and got out for a look. Up close the mutt was a lot worse. Its innards had been mashed out of its mouth and asshole and it stunk something awful. The dog was wearing a thick, metal-studded collar and they fastened one end of their fifteen foot chain to that and the other to the rear bumper.

Bob, the Dairy Queen manager, noticed them through the window, came outside and yelled, "What are you fucking morons doing?"

"Taking this doggie to the vet," Leonard said. "We think this sumbitch looks a might peaked. He may have been hit by a car."

"That's so fucking funny I'm about to piss myself," Bob said.

"Old folks have that problem," Leonard said.

Leonard got behind the wheel and Farto climbed in on the passenger side. They maneuvered the car and dog around and out of the path of a tractor-trailer truck just in time. As they drove off, Bob screamed after them, "I hope you two no-dicks wrap that Chevy piece of shit around a goddamn pole."

As they roared along, parts of the dog, like crumbs from a flakey loaf of bread, came off. A tooth here. Some hair there. A string of guts. A dew claw. And some unidentifiable pink stuff. The metal-studded collar and chain threw up sparks now and then like firey crickets. Finally they hit seventy-five and the dog was swinging wider and wider on the chain, like it was looking for an opportunity to pass.

Farto poured him and Leonard up Cokes and whisky as they drove along. He handed Leonard his paper cup and Leonard knocked it back, a lot happier now than he had been a moment ago. Maybe this night wasn't going to turn out so bad after all.

They drove by a crowd at the side of the road, a tan station wagon and a wreck of a Ford up on a jack. At a glance they could see that there was a nigger in the middle of the crowd and he wasn't witnessing to the white boys about Jesus. He was hopping around like a pig with a hotshot up his ass, trying to find a break in the white boys so he could make a run for it. But there wasn't any break to be found and there were too many to fight. Nine white boys were knocking him around like he was a pinball and they were a malicious machine.

"Ain't that one of our niggers?" Farto asked. "And ain't that some of them White Tree football players that's trying to kill him?"

"Scott," Leonard said, and the name was dogshit in his mouth. It had been Scott who had outdone him for the position of quarterback on the team. That damn jig could put together a play more tangled than a can of fishing worms, but it damn near always worked. And he could run like a spotted ass ape.

As they passed, Farto said, "We'll read about him tomorrow in the papers."

But Leonard drove only a short way before slamming on the brakes and whipping the Impala around. Rex swung way out and clipped off some tall, dried sunflowers at the edge of the road like a scythe.

"We gonna go back and watch?" Farto said. "I don't think them White Tree boys would bother us none if that's all we was gonna do, watch."

"He may be a nigger," Leonard said, not liking himself, "but he's our nigger and we can't let them do that. They kill him they'll beat us in football."

Farto saw the truth of this immediately. "Damn right. They can't do that to our nigger."

Leonard crossed the road again and went straight for the White Tree boys, hit down hard on the horn. The White Tree boys abandoned beating their prey and jumped in all directions. Bullfrogs couldn't have done any better.

Scott stood startled and weak where he was, his knees bent in and touching one another, his eyes big as pizza pans. He had never noticed how big grillwork was. It looked like teeth there in the night and the headlights looked like eyes. He felt like a stupid fish about to be eaten by a shark.

Leonard braked hard, but off the highway in the dirt it wasn't quite enough to keep from bumping Scott, sending him flying over the hood and against the glass where his face mashed to it then rolled away, his shirt snagging one of the windshield wipers and pulling it off.

Leonard opened the car door and called to Scott who lay on the ground. "It's now or never."

A White Tree boy made for the car, and Leonard pulled the taped hammer handle out from beneath the seat and stepped out of the car and hit him with it. The White Tree boy went down on his knees and said something that sounded like French but wasn't. Leonard grabbed Scott by the back of the shirt and pulled him up and guided him around and threw him into the open door. Scott scrambled over the front seat and into the back. Leonard threw the hammer handle at one of the White Tree boys and stepped back, whirled into the car behind the wheel. He put the car in gear again and stepped on the gas. The Impala lurched forward, and with one hand on the door Leonard flipped it wider as if he were flexing a wing and popped a White Tree boy. The car bumped back on the highway and the chain swung out and Rex clipped the feet out from under two boys as neatly as he had taken down the dried sunflowers.

Leonard looked in his rearview mirror and saw two White Tree boys carrying the one he had clubbed with the hammer handle to the station wagon. The others he and the dog had knocked down were getting up. One had kicked the jack out from under Scott's car and was using it to smash the headlights and windshield.

"Hope you got insurance on that thing," Leonard said.

"I borrowed it," Scott said peeling the windshield wiper out of his tee-shirt. "Here, you might want this." He dropped the wiper over the seat and between Leonard and Farto.

"That's a borrowed car?" Farto said. "That's worse."

"Nah," Scott said. "Owner don't know I borrowed it. I'd have had that flat changed if that sucker had had him a spare tire, but I got back there and wasn't nothing but the rim, man. Say, thanks for not letting me get killed, else we couldn't have run that ole pig together no more. Course, you almost run over me. My chest hurts."

Leonard checked the rearview again. The White Tree boys were coming fast. "You complaining?" Leonard said.

"Nah," Scott said, and turned to look through the back glass. He could see the dog swinging in short arcs and pieces of it going wide and far. "Hope you didn't go off and forget your dog tied to the bumper."

"Goddamn," said Farto, "and him registered too."

"This ain't so funny," Leonard said, "them White Tree boys are gaining."

"Well speed it up," Scott said.

Leonard gnashed his teeth. "I could always get rid of some excess baggage, you know."

"Throwing that windshield wiper out ain't gonna help," Scott said.

Leonard looked in his mirror and saw the grinning nigger in the backseat. Nothing worse than a comic coon. He didn't even look grateful. Leonard had a sudden horrid vision of being overtaken by the White Tree boys. What if he were killed with the nigger? Getting killed was bad enough, but what if tomorrow they found him in a ditch with Farto and the nigger. Or maybe them White Tree boys would make him do something awful with the nigger before they killed them. Like making him suck the nigger's dick or some such thing. Leonard held his foot all the way to the floor; as they passed the Dairy Queen he took a hard left and the car just made it and Rex swung out and slammed a light pole then popped back in line behind them.

The White Tree boys couldn't make the corner in the station wagon and they didn't even try. They screeched into a car lot down a piece, turned around and came back. By that time the tail lights of the Impala were moving away from them rapidly, looking like two inflamed hemorrhoids in a dark asshole.

"Take the next right coming up," Scott said, "then you'll see a little road off to the left. Kill your lights and take that."

Leonard hated taking orders from Scott on the field, but this was worse. Insulting. Still, Scott called good plays on the field, and the habit of following instructions from the quarterback died hard. Leonard made the right and Rex made it with them after taking a dip in a water-filled bar ditch.

Leonard saw the little road and killed his lights and took it. It carried them down between several rows of large tin storage buildings and Leonard pulled between two of them and drove down a little alley lined with more. He stopped the car and they waited and listened. After about five minutes, Farto said, "I think we skunked those father rapers."

"Ain't we a team?" Scott said.

In spite of himself, Leonard felt good. It was like when the nigger called a play that worked and they were all patting each other on the ass and not minding what color the other was because they were just creatures in football suits.

"Let's have a drink," Leonard said.

Farto got a paper cup off the floorboard for Scott and poured him up some warm Coke and whisky. Last time they had gone to Longview, he had peed in that paper cup so they wouldn't have to stop, but that had long since been poured out, and besides, it was for a nigger. He poured Leonard and himself drinks in their same cups.

Scott took a sip and said, "Shit, man, that tastes kind of rank."

"Like piss," Farto said.

Leonard held up his cup. "To the Mud Creek Wildcats and fuck them White Tree boys."

"You fuck em," Scott said. They touched their cups, and at that moment the car filled with light.

Cups upraised, the Three Musketeers turned blinking toward it. The light was coming from an open storage building door and there was a fat man standing in the center of the glow like a bloated fly on a lemon wedge. Behind him was a big screen made of a sheet and there was some kind of movie playing on it. And though the light was bright and fading out the movie, Leonard, who was in the best position to see, got a look at it. What he could make out looked like a gal down on her knees sucking this fat guy's dick (the man was visible only from the belly down) and the guy had a short, black revolver pressed to her forehead. She pulled her mouth off of him for an instant and the man came in her face then fired the revolver. The woman's head snapped out of frame and the sheet seemed to drip blood, like dark condensation on a window pane. Then Leonard couldn't see anymore because another man had appeared in the doorway, and like the first he was fat. Both looked like huge bowling balls that had been set on top of shoes. More men appeared behind these two, but one of the fat men turned and held up his hand and the others moved out of sight. The two fat guys stepped outside and one pulled the door almost shut, except for a thin band of light that fell across the front seat of the Impala.

Fat Man Number One went over to the car and opened Farto's door and said, "You fucks and the nigger get out." It was the voice of doom. They had only thought the White Tree boys were dangerous. They realized now they had been kidding themselves. This was the real article. This guy would have eaten the hammer handle and shit a two-by-four.

They got out of the car and the fat man waved them around and lined them up on Farto's side and looked at them. The boys still had their drinks in their hands, and sparing that, they looked like cons in a line up.

Fat Man Number Two came over and looked at the trio and smiled. It was obvious the fatties were twins. They had the same bad features in the same fat faces. They wore Hawaiian shirts that varied only in profiles and color of parrots and had on white socks and too-short, black slacks and black, shiny, Italian shoes with toes sharp enough to thread needles.

Fat Man Number One took the cup away from Scott and sniffed it. "A nigger with liquor," he said. "That's like a cunt with brains. It don't go together. Guess you was getting tanked up so you could put the ole black snake to some chocolate pudding after while. Or maybe you was wantin' some vanilla and these boys were gonna set it up,"

"I'm not wanting anything but to go home," Scott said.

Fat Man Number Two looked at Fat Man Number One and said, "So he can fuck his mother."

The fatties looked at Scott to see what he'd say but he didn't say anything. They could say he screwed dogs and that was all right with him. Hell, bring one on and he'd fuck it now if they'd let him go afterwards.

Fat Man Number One said, "You boys running around with a jungle bunny makes me sick."

"He's just a nigger from school," Farto said. "We don't like him none. We just picked him up because some White Tree boys were beating on him and we didn't want him to get wrecked on account of he's our quarterback."

"Ah," Fat Man Number One said, "I see. Personally, me and Vinnie don't cotton to niggers in sports. They start taking showers with white boys the next thing they want is to take white girls to bed. It's just one step from one to the other."

"We don't have nothing to do with him playing," Leonard said. "We didn't integrate the schools."

"No," Fat Man Number One said, "that was ole Big Ears Johnson, but you're running around with him and drinking with him."

"His cup's been peed in," Farto said. "That was kind of a joke on him, you see. He ain't our friend, I swear it. He's just a nigger that plays football."

"Peed in his cup, huh?" said the one called Vinnie. "I like that, Pork, don't you? Peed in his fucking cup."

Pork dropped Scott's cup on the ground and smiled at him. "Come here, nigger. I got something to tell you."

Scott looked at Farto and Leonard. No help there. They had suddenly become interested in the toes of their shoes; they examined them as if they were true marvels of the world.

Scott moved toward Pork, and Pork, still smiling, put his arm around Scott's shoulders and walked him toward the big storage building. Scott said, "What are we doing?"

Pork turned Scott around so they were facing Leonard and Farto who still stood holding their drinks and contemplating their shoes. "I didn't want to get it on the new gravel drive," Pork said and pulled Scott's head in close to his own and with his free hand reached back and under his Hawaiian shirt and brought out a short, black revolver and put it to Scott's temple and pulled the trigger. There was a snap like a bad knee going out and Scott's feet lifted in unison and went to the side and something dark squirted from his head and his feet swung back toward Pork and his shoes shuffled, snapped and twisted on the concrete in front of the building.

"Ain't that somethin'," Pork said as Scott went limp and dangled from the thick crook of his arm, "The rhythm is the last thing to go."

Leonard couldn't make a sound. His guts were in his throat. He wanted to melt and run under the car. Scott was dead and the brains that had made plays twisted as fishing worms and commanded his feet on down the football field were scrambled like breakfast eggs.

Farto said, "Holy shit."

Pork let go of Scott and Scott's legs split and he sat down and his head went forward and clapped on the cement between his knees. A dark pool formed under his face.

"He's better off, boys," Vinnie said. "Nigger was begat by Cain and the ape and he ain't quite monkey and he ain't quite man. He's got no place in this world 'cept as a beast of burden. You start trying to train them to do things like drive cars and run with footballs it ain't nothing but grief to them and the whites too. Get any on your shirt, Pork?"

"Nary a drop."

Vinnie went inside the building and said something to the men there that could be heard but not understood, then he came back with some crumpled newspapers. He went over to Scott and wrapped them around the bloody head and let it drop back on the cement. "You try hosing down that shit when it's dried, Pork, and you wouldn't worry none about that gravel. The gravel ain't nothing."

Then Vinnie said to Farto, "Open the back door of that car." Farto nearly twisted an ankle doing it. Vinnie picked Scott up by the back of the neck and seat of his pants and threw him onto the floorboard of the Impala.

Pork used the short barrel of his revolver to scratch his nuts, then put the gun behind him, under his Hawaiian shirt. "You boys are gonna go to the river bottoms with us and help us get shed of this nigger."

"Yes sir," Farto said. "We'll toss his ass in the Sabine for you."

"How about you?" Pork asked Leonard. "You trying to go weak sister?"

"No," Leonard croaked. "I'm with you."

"That's good," Pork said. "Vinnie, you take the truck and lead the way."

Vinnie took a key from his pocket and unlocked the building door next to the one with the light, went inside, and backed out a sharp-looking, gold Dodge pickup. He backed it in front of the Impala and sat there with the motor running.

"You boys keep your place," Pork said. He went inside the lighted building for a moment. They heard him say to the men inside, "Go on and watch the movies. And save some of them beers for us. We'll be back." Then the light went out and Pork came out, shutting the door. He looked at Leonard and Farto and said, "Drink up, boys."

Leonard and Farto tossed off their warm Coke and whisky and dropped the cups on the ground.

"Now," Pork said, "you get in the back with the nigger, I'll ride with the driver."

Farto got in the back and put his feet on Scott's knees. He tried not to look at the head wrapped in newspaper, but he couldn't help it. When Pork opened the front door and the overhead light came on Farto saw there was a split in the paper and Scott's eye was visible behind it. Across the forehead the wrapping had turned dark. Down by the mouth and chin was an ad for a fish sale.

Leonard got behind the wheel and started the car. Pork reached over and honked the horn. Vinnie rolled the pickup forward and Leonard followed him to the river bottoms. No one spoke. Leonard found himself wishing with all his heart that he had gone to the outdoor picture show to see the movie with the nigger starring in it.

The river bottoms were steamy and hot from the closeness of the trees and the under and overgrowth. As Leonard wound the Impala down the narrow, red clay roads amidst the dense foliage, he felt as if his car were a crab crawling about in a pubic thatch.

He could feel from the way the steering wheel handled, that the dog and the chain were catching brush and limbs here and there. He had forgotten all about the dog and now being reminded of it worried him. What if the dog got tangled and he had to stop? He didn't think Pork would take kindly to stopping, not with the dead burrhead on the floor-board and him wanting to get rid of the body.

Finally they came to where the woods cleared out a spell and they drove along the edge of the Sabine River. Leonard hated water and always had. In the moonlight the river looked like poisoned coffee flowing there. Leonard knew there were alligators and gars big as little alligators and water moccasins by the thousands swimming underneath the water, and just the thought of all those slick, darting bodies made him queasy.

They came to what was known as Broken Bridge. It was an old worn-out bridge that had fallen apart in the middle and it was connected to the land on this side only. People sometimes fished off of it. There was no one fishing tonight.

Vinnie stopped the pickup and Leonard pulled up beside him, the nose of the Chevy pointing at the mouth of the bridge. They all got out and Pork made Farto pull Scott out by the feet. Some of the newspaper came loose from Scott's head exposing an ear and part of the face. Farto patted the newspaper back into place.

"Fuck that," Vinnie said. "It don't hurt if he stains the fucking ground. You two idgits find some stuff to weight this coon down so we can sink him."

Farto and Leonard started scurrying about like squirrels, looking for rocks or big, heavy logs. Suddenly they heard Vinnie cry out. "Goda-mighty, fucking A. Pork. Come look at this."

Leonard looked over and saw that Vinnie had discovered Rex. He was standing looking down with his hands on his hips. Pork went over to stand by him, then Pork turned around and looked at them. "Hey, you fucks, come here."

Leonard and Farto joined them in looking at the dog. There was mostly just a head now, with a little bit of meat and fur hanging off a spine and some broken ribs.

"That's the sickest fucking thing I've ever fucking seen," Pork said.

"Godamighty," Vinnie said.

"Doing a dog like that. Shit, don't you got no heart? A dog. Man's best fucking goddamn friend and you two killed him like this."

"We didn't kill him," Farto said.

"You trying to fucking tell me he done this to himself? Had a bad fucking day and done this."

"Godamighty," Vinnie said.

"No sir," Leonard said. "We chained him on there after he was dead."

"I believe that," Vinnie said. "That's some rich shit. You guys mur-dered this dog. Godamighty."

"Just thinking about him trying to keep up and you fucks driving faster and faster makes me mad as a wasp," Pork said.

"No," Farto said. "It wasn't like that. He was dead and we were drunk and we didn't have anything to do, so we—"

"Shut the fuck up," Pork said sticking a finger hard against Farto's forehead. "You just shut the fuck up. We can see what the fuck you fucks did. You drug this here dog around until all his goddamn hide came off . . . What kind of mothers you boys got anyhow that they didn't tell you better about animals?"

"Godamighty," Vinnie said.

Everyone grew silent, stood looking at the dog. Finally Farto said. "You want us to go back to getting some stuff to hold the nigger down?"

Pork looked at Farto as if he had just grown up whole from the ground. "You fucks are worse than niggers, doing a dog like that. Get on back over to the car."

Leonard and Farto went over to the Impala and stood looking down at Scott's body in much the same way they had stared at the dog. There in the dim moonlight shadowed by trees, the paper wrapped around Scott's head made him look like a giant papier-mâché doll. Pork came up and kicked Scott in the face with a swift motion that sent newspaper flying and sent a thonking sound across the water that made frogs jump.

"Forget the nigger," Pork said. "Give me your car keys, ball sweat.

Leonard took out his keys and gave them to Pork and Pork went around to the trunk and opened it. "Drag the nigger over here."

Leonard took one of Scott's arms and Farto took the other and they pulled him over to the back of the car.

"Put him in the trunk," Pork said.

"What for?" Leonard asked.

"Cause I fucking said so," Pork said.

Leonard and Farto heaved Scott into the trunk. He looked pathetic lying there next to the spare tire, his face partially covered with newspaper. Leonard thought, if only the nigger had stolen a car with a spare he might not be here tonight. He could have gotten the flat changed and driven on before the White Tree boys even came along.

"All right, you get in there with him," Pork said, gesturing to Farto.

"Me?" Farto said.

"Nah, not fucking you, the fucking elephant on your fucking shoulder. Yeah, you, get in the trunk. I ain't got all night."

"Jesus, we didn't do anything to that dog, mister. We told you that. I swear. Me and Leonard hooked him up after he was dead . . . It was Leonard's idea."

Pork didn't say a word. He just stood there with one hand on the trunk lid looking at Farto. Farto looked at Pork, then the trunk, then back to Pork. Lastly he looked at Leonard, then climbed into the trunk, his back to Scott.

"Like spoons," Pork said, and closed the lid. "Now you, whatsit, Leonard? You come over here." But Pork didn't wait for Leonard to move. He scooped the back of Leonard's neck with a chubby hand and pushed him over to where Rex lay at the end of the chain with Vinnie still looking down at him.

"What you think, Vinnie?" Pork asked. "You got what I got in mind?"

Vinnie nodded. He bent down and took the collar off the dog. He fastened it on Leonard. Leonard could smell the odor of the dead dog in his nostrils. He bent his head and puked.

"There goes my shoeshine," Vinnie said, and he hit Leonard a short one in the stomach. Leonard went to his knees and puked some more of the hot Coke and whisky.

"You fucks are the lowest pieces of shit on this earth, doing a dog like that," Vinnie said. "A nigger ain't no lower."

Vinnie got some strong fishing line out of the back of the truck and they tied Leonard's hands behind his back. Leonard began to cry.

"Oh shut up," Pork said. "It ain't that bad. Ain't nothing that bad."

But Leonard couldn't shut up. He was caterwauling now and it was echoing through the trees. He closed his eyes and tried to pretend he had gone to the show with the nigger starring in it and had fallen asleep in his car and was having a bad dream, but he couldn't imagine that.

He thought about Harry the janitor's flying saucers with the peppermint rays, and he knew if there were any saucers shooting rays down, they weren't boredom rays after all. He wasn't a bit bored.

Pork pulled off Leonard's shoes and pushed him back flat on the ground and pulled off the socks and stuck them in Leonard's mouth so tight he couldn't spit them out. It wasn't that Pork thought anyone was going to hear Leonard, he just didn't like the noise. It hurt his ears.

Leonard lay on the ground in the vomit next to the dog and cried silently. Pork and Vinnie went over to the Impala and opened the doors and stood so they could get a grip on the car to push. Vinnie reached in and moved the gear from Park to Neutral and he and Pork began to shove the car forward. It moved slowly at first, but as it made the slight incline that led down to the old bridge, it picked up speed. From inside the trunk, Farto hammered lightly at the lid as if he didn't really mean it. The chain took up slack and Leonard felt it jerk and pop his neck. He began to slide along the ground like a snake.

Vinnie and Pork jumped out of the way and watched the car make the bridge and go over the edge and disappear into the water with amazing quietness. Leonard, tugged by the weight of the car, rustled past them. When he hit the bridge, wooden splinters tugged at his clothes so hard they ripped his pants and underwear down almost to his knees.

The chain swung out once toward the edge of the bridge and the rotten railing, and Leonard tried to hook a leg around an upright board there, but that proved wasted. The weight of the car just pulled his knee out of joint and tugged the board out of place with a screech of nails and lumber.

Leonard picked up speed and the chain rattled over the edge of the bridge, into the water and out of sight, pulling its connection after it like a pull toy. The last sight of Leonard was the soles of his bare feet, white as the bellies of fish.

"It's deep there," Vinnie said. "I caught an old channel cat there once, remember? Big sucker. I bet it's over fifty feet deep down there."

They got in the truck and Vinnie cranked it.

"I think we did them boys a favor," Pork said. "Them running around with niggers and what they did to that dog and all. They weren't worth a thing."

"I know it," Vinnie said. "We should have filmed this, Pork, it would have been good. Where the car and that nigger lover went off in the water was choice."

"Nah, there wasn't any women."

"Point," Vinnie said, and he backed around and drove onto the trail that wound its way out of the bottoms.

RICK DEMARINIS

Your Story

Rick DeMarinis is the author of seven books: *Under the Wheat* (which won the Drue Heinz Prize for short fiction), *The Burning Women of Far Cry*, *Jack and Jill*, *Cinder*, *Scimitar*, *A Lovely Monster*, and *The Coming Triumph of the Free World*. His short fiction has appeared in *Harper's*, *Antaeus*, *Grand Street*, *Esquire*, *The Atlantic Monthly*, and other magazines. DeMarinis lives in Missoula, Montana.

"Your Story" from his most recent collection of short fiction, is a wonderful and thoroughly contemporary retelling of the Grimm's fairy tale *Hansel and Gretel*.

YOUR STORY

Rick DeMarinis

This story happened early in the history of the human race, a few years from now. It is your story, though you may have some quibbles. It's the writer's story too, but he wants to camouflage it. (The form he's chosen confirms this.) Look at it this way: he offers a parable of a parable, nut and shell, easily cracked and eaten. But the question is, will it nourish or poison or just lie suspended in the gut like a stone? It points no finger of blame, pats no one on the back, gives no guarantees beyond asserting the commonality of its long-lost roots, which are transplantable anywhere. To make matters worse, the writer (never applauded for his penetrating insights and infamous for his lack of convictions) probably won't get it right. He'll need your open-minded help to fill in the blanks or to blank out the excesses. Excess is his forte. He's made a tidy little career of it. Actually, he'll need more than your help, but nothing can be done about *that*. The narcissistic dissembler is on his own:

There once were a husband and wife who were so simple that they had no control over their lives or the lives of their children. Worse, they had no control over what they said. Words gushed out of her mouth like blood from a bad gash—hot, pure, terrible to behold. From his mouth they were like the dark, sour smoke from a doused fire. The two of them were reasonably civilized. They were respected in their community. Their names were ordinary: Gene and Amy Underhill. Names like these do not arouse suspicion or resentment.

One evening, at the dinner table, Amy said to Gene, "Honey, I want to get rid of the children. I've had enough of them. I want to get rid of them tomorrow."

This wasn't the first time Amy had expressed this wish. She was not one to mince words, but this was the first time she'd set a deadline.

"Well, they *are* shits," Gene agreed affably. Gene Underhill was a decent, mild-mannered man who worked as a lab technician for a company that produced titanium-alloy butterfly valves for a secret defense project

478

rumored to be linked to the "Star Wars" program. He spoke his mind freely too, but with far less heat than his wife. He was by nature a cautious, reflective man. His wife's forthright manner kept him off balance. He was no match for her, and knew it. "I don't think I'd be able to actually *harm* them, dear," he said.

Amy, whose anger was so reliable a stone church could lean against it and not topple, said, "You incredible wimp."

Gene knew there would be no lovemaking that night, or, if there was, it would be rancorous. Which in itself could be interesting. If the rancor could be harnessed and guided into some infrequently traveled byways. Images of Gortex straps with Velcro fasteners, Spandex collars, electrified quirts, suppositories dipped in nonprescription euphorics, Suggesto-Vision videotapes from the Exotica/Erotica section of the neighborhood 7-Eleven store, and so on, occurred to him.

"I read you like a book," Amy said, noticing the sweat beads forming on Gene's upper lip. "But you can put fun and games out of your mind until we get this business settled once and for all. *Then* we'll party."

Gene and Amy were eating a dinner of half-warm Big Macs and fries. The children, Buddy and Jill, had been put to bed earlier.

"We could send them away to boarding school," Gene said hopefully. He dipped his last fry into a kidney-shaped pool of catsup. He made a project out of it to avoid Amy's eyes.

"Wonderful," Amy said. "We'll send them to school in England and you and I will live in a villa on the Côte d'Azur and read French poetry and paint neo-cubist nudes. Jesus, Gene, grow *up*, will you?"

Gene and Amy were not bad people. They were beleaguered by debts they had foolishly allowed to accumulate until, at twenty-two percent interest, the debts took on an unearthly life of their own and became a fiscal Frankenstein monster that sought to destroy its creators. Gene and Amy were harassed daily by the thousand large and small demands of an underfunded, barely marginal, middle-class life-style. Every night they were afflicted by televised world events whose increasingly inventive perversities left them confused, angry, and spiritually at sea. The children, typically, were whiny ingrates who rarely rewarded their parents with a hint of promise, academic or otherwise. "You are a slob, just like your father," Amy once said to Buddy, in a fit of rage. Jill, on the other hand, filled Amy with silent dread. Her daughter was a miniature of herself, a brooding waxen doll. Sometimes she would catch Jill studying her with eyes that were too knowledgeable. Those dark eyes always seemed judgmental and full of sad reproach. She felt accused of some nameless crime by those eyes and was moved, frequently, to defend herself to her own daughter. It didn't make sense, but there it was, the heavy load of guilt. Amy once screamed, "I don't *deserve* this! I haven't done anything to you!" but knew, instinctively, it sounded not only crazy but *false*.

"All right," Gene said at last. "We'll do it." He felt old and heavy. He was prematurely gray and the smile lines around his eyes and mouth had hardened into permanent fissures that gave him the appearance of constant flinching. He was surprised daily by this face of his in the shaving mirror. He was only forty but he looked sixty. And yet he felt no different than he did when he was twenty. The mental picture he carried of himself was of a dark-haired, smooth-skinned boy with a good-natured smile. How had this happened? The last french fry he'd eaten had lodged itself in his chest, under his breastbone, where it scratched at him like a greasy, long-nailed finger. "We'll do it tomorrow," he said. "First thing after breakfast."

Amy got up and kissed him. "I'm so relieved, darling," she said.

Which means . . . Gene remarked hopefully to himself, new sweat beads glazing his lip . . .

"I'm in the moo-ood," Amy crooned, completing his thought.

They went up to bed. Amy was happy now. Soon, she felt, her problems would be solved. Soon, their priorities would be reordered and they would be able to concentrate on getting out of debt. Amy was only thirty-three years old and had seen enough of empty cupboards and overdrawn checking accounts and her daughter's accusing eyes. She wanted a secure, predictable life. She wanted to devote most of her time to income management, the search for safe investments, and to the establishment of a first-rate Individual Retirement Account. And she wanted to do this without *guilt*, or any other distraction.

Amy undressed slowly in the dim bedroom, revealing in tantalizing increments her still lovely body to her eager husband. Gene was already in bed, the chalk of liquid Maalox caking his lips. "Gortex straps," he suggested, hoarse with emotion.

"All right," Amy agreed. "Since you've decided to face reality like a grown-up, for once."

I turned my back on them at this point and left them to their constrained pleasures. I went to see the children. I danced my way down the creaky hall to their room. Left foot over right, hop and skip, right foot over left, turn and turn. Among other things, I am a dancer.

The children, never quite as stupid or indifferent as their parents believe, had heard it all. They were frightened, but not especially surprised.

"What will we *do*?" Jill asked her brother, Buddy.

"Play it dumb, like always," Buddy said.

Jill was nine and Buddy was going on twelve. They were beautiful children, blond as late summer wheat. They were tucked in their beds, the girl on one side of the room, the boy on the other. I kissed the girl and then the boy. The pages of the boy's comic book were riffled, as if by wind. I turned in slow, elegant circles between their sweet beds, but they saw only the shadows of their dreams.

The next day was Sunday. The family set out for the woods ostensibly to gather firewood for the coming fall. The children rode in the back of the pickup truck along with the chain saws and gas cans. It was a beautiful morning, cool and clear.

After Gene had turned off the main highway and had entered a narrow dirt road that led to the wooded foothills, Amy said, "Once we get into the trees, get off the road."

Gene slipped the Toyota into four-wheel drive, anticipating a rough climb. He leaned his head out the window and yelled back to the kids. "Hang on tight," he said. "Don't try to stand up or anything."

The engine labored as the truck struggled against the steep, loamy ground of the forest. "Keep switching back and forth," Amy said. "I want them to lose all sense of direction."

They traveled this way for nearly an hour. Gene, holding the wheel so tightly his hands were cramped and white, was sweating profusely. He was relieved when he found a dry creek bed that led out into a meadow. He accelerated through the wide field, which glowed almost unnaturally, like the core of a nuclear reactor, with wild flowers. He stopped in the middle of this exotic place and unscrewed the thermos. He took a long drink of whiskied coffee. "I'm lost," he said.

"Good," said Amy. "Keep driving."

On the other side of the meadow, the mountains began. Gene found an old logging road. It was very steep and he had to keep the Toyota in its lowest gear to manage the climb. Their ears popped and the air became noticeably cooler. The silver-gray stumps of ancient clear-cuts studded the steep slopes like rooted tables. Patches of snow between the great stumps looked like dropped linen. The air was purer here and the sky was so blue it seemed like the inside of an enameled egg.

They entered an area of standing-dead trees. "Good pickings," Gene said, stopping the truck and setting the brake.

"Keep going," Amy said. "We didn't come all the way up here for firewood, damn it."

Gene sighed and restarted the engine. They drove for another hour, passing more groves of dead trees, slash piles, and old, abandoned logs that sawyers had left behind for unknown reasons. The sun was low and smoky in the sky. The children, cold and hungry, were whining and tapping on the rear window of the truck cab. "We're almost there!" Amy yelled through the glass.

Gene looked at his wife. There was something in her face he had never noticed before but would always see from this day on. If he had to name it he would call it "grim determination," but even this description seemed to fall short. Amy was an attractive woman, but the set of the jaw and the cast of her eyes undercut her beauty. It was as if another Amy, the "real" Amy Underhill, had surfaced at last. Gene felt a sinking sensation in his abdomen, which he misconstrued as excitement.

When they were at an altitude where only stunted dwarf trees grew, they stopped and got out of the truck. There were a few beetle-killed trees, none of them more than twelve feet tall, on the upslope side of the truck. Gene went after these with the smaller of his saws. Amy took the children for a walk to gather berries. She herded them across screes of unstable shale, through thick, angry patches of scrub pine, across snowfields, and, finally, to a sheltered area where an abundance of huckleberry bushes grew. She gave the children a large plastic bag each. "Fill them with berries," she said, "while daddy cuts a load of wood. Then we'll go into town and eat at McDonald's. You'll have a real appetite by then."

She walked swiftly back to the truck, which was half loaded with firewood. "Shut off that saw and let's go!" she yelled at Gene, who was about to fell another dwarf tree.

Gene switched off his saw. "Hey, no sense in going back with half a load," he said, grinning sheepishly. She still had that look on her face, the look that made him believe no one ever knows the person they live with, and that nothing in the world is constant.

"Don't play for time. It won't work. We're going through with this, Gene."

"Whatever," Gene said, realizing that he could not match her resolve. He started the truck, hoping the children would not hear it, then hoping they would. "We are pretty darned evil," he said, mostly to himself.

"Uh-huh," Amy answered. "We're real novelties."

"But people just do not abandon their kids in the mountains!"

Amy didn't respond to this outburst. How could she respond to a silly remark that represented, so unconditionally, the generic pudding that served as her husband's brain?

I left them just as Gene was about to notice that Amy had changed again, and not just in her expression. She seemed *physically* different now.

The bridge of her nose, for example, was beaky and shinier than before, her lips thinner, the angular jut of her jaw more acute, her tall forehead striated with astonishing areas of depleted pigments. He would tell himself (what choice did he have?) that these were only shades of difference that he might have noticed earlier had he been more attentive—people do change, after all—but this threadbare argument would be shredded before the honest rage of his nightmares.

I soared into the sky on my glossy black wings and sailed toward the children. They hadn't heard the truck start and were still picking berries. I watched them from a majestic altitude, enjoying the thermals, the heckling squadrons of starlings, and the unmatched beauty of the northern forests.

By the time their plastic bags were nearly filled with the dark red berries, the sun had slipped below the horizon. The cold mountain air crept out of the shadows, where it had survived the day, to reclaim the evening and coming night. "We'd better head back to the truck," Buddy said, looking up into the deepening sky, where the brightest stars were already twinkling.

But the long shadows the mountain put down obscured the trail. When they arrived at the steep scree of shale it was too dark to find the path that crossed it. And as Buddy stepped out onto the precarious slope of loose rock, he started a small landslide. The lonely echo of clattering rocks made Jill whimper. Buddy scrambled back to safety.

"What are we going to *do?*" Jill cried.

Now an ambassadorial bear with cubs, I ambled out of some huckleberry bushes behind the children, my long, red mouth dripping with my favorite fruit. My two cubs rollicked alongside.

"Oh no!" Jill cried. "It's a bear!"

"Don't move," Buddy said. "They can't see very well. Maybe she hasn't noticed us."

"Don't be afraid, children," I said, sweetly as my crude vocal cords would allow. I stopped directly in front of them and rolled on my back. My playful cubs pounced on me and bit my furry breasts. I slapped them away and growled, startled somewhat by the aggression of the little beasties, then gathered them up in my arms and we rolled together through thick spears of bear grass, chuffing and moaning with bear-family pleasure.

The boy hugged his little sister protectively. In the dying light their pale faces glowed supernaturally. Bears can see these auras; most humans cannot. "Follow me, children," I said. I turned from them and ambled away, downslope, into the thicket below.

It was almost dark by the time they arrived at my house. I vanished into my own shadow and watched them from several vantage points at once. What fine, holy animals they were!

"What is that?" the girl asked her brother.

"A house," he said. "A funny-looking little old house."

They came closer, close enough to reach out and touch the delicious walls. "I think it's made out of food," the boy said, licking his sticky fingers.

"Cake!" shrieked the girl. "It's a cake house!"

They pushed open the hard marzipan door and entered. I was seated at the table in a more customary form. "Good evening, little ones," I said, my ancient voice scratchy and dry.

The girl screamed and the boy picked up a piece of firewood, which he held in both hands as a weapon.

"There's nothing to be afraid of, children," I said, smiling.

"It's a witch!" cried the girl. "A horrible old witch with dead gray teeth!"

"Let's go," the boy said, pulling his transfixed sister toward the door.

"You must stay at least for supper," I said.

Because they were very hungry by now, they approached the table but took seats at the opposite end. I smiled at their caution. "Too much caution can become a bad habit, my dears," I said, though they could not understand the significance of my words. I changed the subject. "Let's play a game, children."

"First we eat," said the boy. He was a hardheaded little rascal who appeared far brighter and more sure of himself than his slipshod, weak-willed father.

I set a good table of vension, broiled grayling, wild asparagus, goat's milk, sunflower bread with dandelion honey. They ate like little pigs. Their naïve unchecked appetite made my heart expand. Too soon they would be concerned with calorie counting, cholesterol content, and all the other drivel that makes the alimentary canal a quivering battleground of false causes.

When they finished this fine meal, they sighed in real contentment and gratitude. "You're welcome," I said, not in rebuke but in response to their little burps and the slack-jawed trance of happy satiation.

The girl became drowsy and fell asleep at the table. I carried her to a bedroom I had prepared in advance. When I rejoined the boy, he said, "Jill's had a hard couple of days, ma'am." His eyes held mine and did not blink. I liked him. He seemed to grow more mature by the minute. He would do well in the difficult world ahead.

"How about you?" I said. "Are you ready for a little game? You might win a nice prize."

"Sure," he said. His trust was edged with a steely-eyed wariness, but he was not one to play it safe, knowing instinctively that the only real way to lose was to not play at all.

"Then come with me. I'll show you something you won't forget."

I took him out to my barn. "Where are the animals?" he asked. I held up my stick and pointed upward. "Hey, there's no *roof* on this barn. How come?"

"To let the starlight in," I said. I touched his shoulder with my stick. He jumped straight up as if I'd given him an electric shock.

"What's that music?" he asked.

"Stars," I said. "They sing on long wires of light. Listen." What the boy heard was this:

> only the child
> can see the hand
> that made the wild
> mysterious land

I touched his other shoulder with my stick and he jumped again. When he came down he landed on his hands and knees. "Enjoy yourself," I said. "I'll be back for you later."

The boy had jumped the line that separates human folly from the natural order, and he was at that moment running through the woods on all fours with a pack of wolves. He ran and ran, chasing the hart, feeling the joy of speed and strength, the comfort of the tribe and the unchecked lust of the hunt. When he grew tired he returned to his slumber, then woke to the music of the stars, which he would forget only at his peril.

The next morning the girl demanded to know what I'd done with her brother.

"He's been playing a game," I said.

"You lie," she said, stern as her mother.

I gave her a witchy smile, sinister and cunning. "Help me clean this house, you snot," I said.

My profound ugliness intimidated her. She picked up a broom. Then, as was customary, I made what all the children see as my fatal mistake. I bent over next to the open door of my oven, pretending to scour a spot of grease from the floor, and waited for the blow. She delivered it on schedule. The broom whacked me across my bony old buttocks and I obliged her by falling headfirst into the oven. For effect, I let loose a blood-chilling scream of vile curses that antedate the development of speech organs in the so-called *Homo sapiens*. She slammed the iron door shut and wedged her broom handle against it so that it could not be opened. Then she turned the gas up high. I heard the pilot light ignite the ring of gas and searing heat blew up into my face.

The boy entered the house then. He was still groggy from his hard sleep and was trying to adjust the vagrant grammar of his dreams to the tight parsings of authorized reality. When he understood what his sister had done, he became upset. "She didn't mean us any harm, Jill," he said.

"Yes, she did!" Jill cried out, wounded by Buddy's ingratitude. She had saved them, hadn't she, from the witch's evil schemes?

Buddy noticed the Polaroids I had taken of them while they slept. I'd tacked them up on the wall. He went to the pictures and stared at the angelic towheads, who resembled their parents only superficially. "See," he said, "she liked us well enough to take our pictures, Jill."

"What's that *smell*?" Jill asked, her eyes widening in delight.

The house was filling with a fragrance that was so sweet, so tempting, that their mouths began to water instantly. They forgot the Polaroids, forgot their argument, and could think of nothing else except the wonderful aroma and where it might be coming from. It was coming from the oven, of course, and as if to underscore this fact, the buzzing of the timer rattled the air.

The boy went to the oven and peeked in. Inside, perfectly baked, was an angel food cake. (*C'est moi.*) The boy took it out, using pot holders, and set it on the table.

"Maybe I was only dreaming about a witch," the children said in unison.

Only dreaming or, worse, *It was only a bad dream* are the formulas that have exiled me from the world for several hundred years. Children would have those scoffing catchphrases stenciled into their brains and the useful truth of their dreams would be dismissed time and again until the children grew into gray, dreamless entities of no consequence who would commit blunder after blunder on their murderously banal trip to the grave.

I suppose the story must end there, though the writer is pressing for one of his patented, neatly delivered, full-circle endings. For instance, he would like to see Buddy and Jill, older and honed to an edge by the harsh world, make their way home and confront their parents. Buddy would have a Ruger .357 magnum in his belt and Jill's purse would be stocked with street drugs. (The writer has other murky ideas, generated by his need for what he thinks of as *neatness*. He calls these blind spots "satisfying endings." My motto is: Never trust an anal narcissist. The flattering mirror he cavorts in front of shows a geometrically precise world, tied up neat as a Christmas package.) The writer would like to tell you something about me, as an object of (in this case) blame. But he hasn't understood yet the extent of my influence, the depth of my interest, or how he is my last refuge in a world that has excluded me. He is one of you, after all, no better and no worse. For example, he would like to know where I am *now*, when he needs me most. He doesn't realize that I'm always here, in his word processor, among the binary digits of the software, in the wiring and microchips, in the copper and silicon atoms, down among the leptons and quarks and gluons, and further, where time and space no longer exist, in the null of nulls, riding the crest of wave after wave of pulsing energy, a cosmic surfer, everywhere and nowhere, inside and outside, locus of a geometry of tucks and puckers. And I am in the stymied axons and dendrites of the writer's poor brain, break-dancing on the cerebral dunes as he rises from his desk and goes out to the kitchen for his twelfth cup of coffee, hoping for the final rush of syllables that chase and corner all the meanings of the story and truss them up with granny knots of inevitability. But there are large densities in the dross of his being, crazy opacities, flashes of perfect nonsense. He tries so hard, but he never says exactly what he means. (Though he means everything he says.) He is my puppet, but, alas, he is on very loose strings.

Just now, he's in his backyard sipping tequila from a flask, refusing to let the story go. He has climbed up to the top branches of his willow tree. It is a windy summer's night, and the stars are blowing through the whipping leaves like hissing, incandescent moths. "If I end it there," he complains to me, "no one will get the point!"

Let's leave him up the tree. He's not quite bright enough to trust you. Also, if we allowed him to design an ending and bandage it to the story, who's to say he wouldn't produce a monster? No. It's *your* story, reader, and you are always in the middle of it.

JOHN M. FORD

Winter Solstice, Camelot Station

John M. Ford is a successful writer in several genres, but he occasionally strays back into the fantasy field with a short story or poem; his stories in the *Liavek* anthology series (edited by Will Shetterly and Emma Bull) are particularly recommended.

Each year in late December, Ford sends out a poem to friends to herald the coming new year. This particular poem found its way to publication in the Arthurian anthology *Invitation to Camelot*. And then it found its way here.

—T. W.

WINTER SOLSTICE, CAMELOT STATION

John M. Ford

Camelot is served
By a sixteen-track stub terminal done in High Gothick Style,
The tracks covered by a single great barrel-vaulted glass roof framed
upon iron,
At once looking back to the Romans and ahead to the Brunels.
Beneath its rotunda, just to the left of the ticket windows,
Is a mosaic floor depicting the Round Table
(Where all knights, regardless of their station of origin
Or class of accommodation, are equal),
And around it murals of knightly deed's in action
(Slaying dragons, righting wrongs, rescuing maidens tied to the
tracks).
It is the only terminal, other than Gare d'Avalon in París,
To be hung with original tapestries,
And its lavatories rival those at Great Gate of Kiev Central.
During a peak season such as this, some eighty trains a day pass
through,
Five times the frequency at the old Londinium Terminus,
Ten times the number the Druid towermen knew.
(The Official Court Christmas Card this year displays
A crisp black-and-white Charles Clegg photograph from the King's
own collection.
Showing a woad-blued hogger at the throttle of "Old XCVII,"
The Fast Mail overnight to Eboracum. Those were the days.)
The first of a line of wagons have arrived,
Spilling footmen and pages in Court livery,
And old thick Kay, stepping down from his Range Rover,
Tricked out in a bush coat from Swaine, Adeney, Brigg,
Leaning on his shooting stick as he marshalls his company,
Instructing the youngest how to behave in the station,

To help mature women that they may encounter,
Report pickpockets, gather up litter,
And of course no true Knight of the Table Round (even in training)
Would do a station porter out of Christmas tips.
He checks his list of arrival times, then his watch
(A 'moon-phase Breguet, gift from Merlin):
The seneschal is a practical man, who knows trains do run late,
And a stolid one, who sees no reason to be glad about it.
He dispatches pages to posts at the tracks,
Doling out pennies for platform tickets,
Then walks past the station buffet with a dyspeptic snort,
Goes into the bar, checks the time again, orders a pint.
The patrons half turn—it's the fella from Camelot, innit?
And Kay chuckles soft to himself, and the Court buys a round.
He's barely halfway when a page tumbles in,
Seems the knights are arriving, on time after all,
So he tips the glass back (people stare as he guzzles),
Then plonks it down hard with five quid for the barman,
And strides for the doorway (half Falstaff, half Hotspur)
To summon his liveried army of lads.
Bors arrives behind steam, riding the cab of a heavy Mikado.
He shakes the driver's hand, swings down from the footplate,
And is like a locomotive himself, his breath clouding white,
Dark oil sheen on his black iron mail,
Sword on his hip swinging like siderods at speed.
He stamps back to the baggage car, slams mailed fist on steel door
With a clang like jousters colliding.
The handler opens up and goes to rouse another knight.
Old Pellinore has been dozing with his back against a crate,
A cubical chain-bound thing with FRAGILE tags and air holes,
BEAST says the label, QUESTING, 1 the bill of lading.
The porters look doubtful but ease the thing down.
It grumbles. It shifts. Someone shouts, and they drop it.
It cracks like an egg. There is nothing within.
Elayne embraces Bors on the platform, a pelican on a rock,
Silently they watch as Pelly shifts the splinters,
Supposing aloud that Gutman and Cairo have swindled him.

A high-drivered engine in Northern Lines green
Draws in with a string of side-corridor coaches,
All honey-toned wood with stained glass on their windows.
Gareth steps down from a compartment, then Gaheris and Agravaine,

All warmly tucked up in Orkney sweaters;
Gawaine comes after in Shetland tweed.
Their Gladstones and steamers are neatly arranged,
With never a worry—their Mum does the packing.
A redcap brings forth a curious bundle, a rude shape in red paper—
The boys did that themselves, you see, and how *does* one wrap a
unicorn's head?
They bustle down the platform, past a chap all in green.
He hasn't the look of a trainman, but only Gawaine turns to look at
his eyes,
And sees written there *Sir, I shall speak with you later.*

Over on the first track, surrounded by reporters,
All glossy dark iron and brass-bound mystery,
The Direct-Orient Express, ferried in from Calais and Points East.
Palomides appears. Smelling of patchouli and Russian leather,
Dripping Soubranie ash on his astrakhan collar,
Worry darkening his dark face, though his damascene armor shows no
tarnish,
He pushes past the press like a broad-hulled icebreaker.
Flashbulbs pop. Heads turn. There's a woman in Chanel black,
A glint of diamonds, liquid movements, liquid eyes.
The newshawks converge, but suddenly there appears
A sharp young man in a crisp blue suit
From the Compagnie Internationale des Wagons-Lits,
That elegant, comfortable, decorous, close-mouthed firm;
He's good at his job, and they get not so much as a snapshot.
Tomorrow's editions will ask who she was, and whom with . . .

Now here's a silver train, stainless steel, Vista-Domed,
White-lighted grails on the engine (running no extra sections)
The Logres Limited, extra fare, extra fine,
(Stops on signal at Carbonek to receive passengers only).
She glides to a Timken-borne halt (even her grease is clean),
Galahad already on the steps, flashing that winning smile,
Breeze mussing his golden hair, but not his Armani tailoring,
Just the sort of man you'd want finding your chalice.
He signs an autograph, he strikes a pose.
Someone says, loudly, "Gal! Who serves the Grail?"
He looks—no one he knows—and there's a silence,
A space in which he shifts like sun on water;
Look quick and you may see a different knight,

A knight who knows that meanings can be lies,
That things are done not knowing why they're done,
That bearings fail, and stainless steel corrodes.
A whistle blows. Snow shifts on the glass shed roof. That knight is gone.
This one remaining tosses his briefcase to one of Kay's pages,
And, golden, silken, careless, exits left.

Behind the carsheds, on the business-car track, alongside the private varnish
Of dukes and smallholders, Persian potentates and Cathay princes
(James J. Hill is here, invited to bid on a tunnel through the Pennines),
Waits a sleek car in royal blue, ex-B&O, its trucks and fittings chromed,
A black-gloved hand gripping its silver platform rail;
Mordred and his car are both upholstered in blue velvet and black leather.
He prefers to fly, but the weather was against it.
His DC-9, with its video system and Quotron and waterbed, sits grounded at Gatwick.
The premature lines in his face are a map of a hostile country,
The redness in his eyes a reminder that hollyberries are poison.
He goes inside to put on a look acceptable for Christmas Court;
As he slams the door it rattles like strafing jets.

Outside the Station proper, in the snow,
On a through track that's used for milk and mail,
A wheezing saddle-tanker stops for breath;
A way-freight mixed, eight freight cars and caboose,
Two great ugly men on the back platform, talking with a third on the ballast.
One, the conductor, parcels out the last of the coffee;
They drink. A joke about grails. They laugh.
When it's gone, the trainman pretends to kick the big hobo off,
But the farewell hug spoils the act.
Now two men stand on the dirty snow,
The conductor waves a lantern and the train grinds on.
The ugly men start walking, the new arrival behind,
Singing "Wenceslas' " off-key till the other says stop.
There are two horses waiting for them. Rather plain horses,
Considering. The men mount up.

By the roundhouse they pause,
And look at the locos, the water, the sand, and the coal,
They look for a long time at the turntable,
Until the one who is King says "It all seemed so simple,
once,"
And the best knight in the world says "It is. We make it hard."
They ride on, toward Camelot by the service road.

The sun is winter-low. Kay's caravan is rolling.
He may not run a railroad, but he runs a tight ship;
By the time they unload in the Camelot courtyard,
The wassail will be hot and the goose will be crackling,
Banners snapping from the towers, fir logs on the fire,
drawbridge down,
And all that sackbut and psaltery stuff.
Blanchefleur is taking the children caroling tonight,
Percivale will lose to Merlin at chess,
The young knights will dally and the damsels dally back,
The old knights will play poker at a smaller Table Round.
And at the great glass station, motion goes on,
The extras, the milk trains, the varnish, the limiteds,
The *Pindar of Wakefield*, the *Lady of the Lake*,
The *Broceliande Local*, the *Fast Flying Briton*,
The nerves of the kingdom, the lines of exchange,
Running to schedule as the world ought,
Ticking like a hot-fired hand-stoked heart,
The metal expression of the breaking of boundaries,
The boilers that turn raw fire into power,
The driving rods that put the power to use,
The turning wheels that make all places equal,
The knowledge that the train may stop but the line goes on;
The train may stop
But the line goes on.

GENE WOLFE

The Boy Who Hooked the Sun

This deceptively simple little fable seems like it ought not to have been written by Gene Wolfe at all, but merely passed down to him by that other master fantasist: Anonymous.

—T. W.

THE BOY WHO HOOKED THE SUN

Gene Wolfe

On the eighth day a boy cast his line into the sea. The Sun of the eighth day was just rising, making a road of gold that ran from its own broad, blank face all the way to the wild coastline of Atlantis, where the boy sat upon a jutting emerald; the Sun was much younger then and not nearly so wise to the ways of men as it is now. It took the bait.

The boy jerked his pole to set the hook, and grinned, and spat into the sea while he let the line run out. He was not such a boy as you or I have ever seen, for there was a touch of emerald in his hair, and there were flakes of sun-gold in his eyes. His skin was sun-browned, and his fingernails were small and short and a little dirty; so he was just such a boy as lives down the street from us both. Years ago the boy's father had sailed away to trade the shining stones of Atlantis for the wine and ram skins of the wild barbarians of Hellas, leaving the boy and his mother very poor.

All day the Sun thrashed and rolled and leaped about. Sometimes it sounded, plunging all the Earth into night, and sometimes it leaped high into the sky, throwing up sprays of stars. Sometimes it feigned to be dead, and sometimes it tried to wrap his line around the moon to break it. And the boy let it tire itself, sometimes reeling in and sometimes letting out more line; but through it all he kept a tight grip on the pole.

The richest man in the village, the money-lender, who owned the house where the boy and his mother lived, came to him, saying, "You must cut your line, boy, and let the Sun go. When it runs out, it brings winter and withers all the blossoms in my orchard. When you reel it in, it brings droughty August to dry all the canals that water my barley fields. Cut your line!"

But the boy only laughed at him and pelted him with the shining stones of Atlantis, and at last the richest man in the village went away.

Then the strongest man in the village, ths smith, who could meet the charge of a wild ox and wrestle it to the ground, came to the boy, saying, "Cut your line, boy, or I'll break your neck."

But the boy only laughed at him and pelted him with the shining stones of Atlantis, and when the strongest man in the village seized him by the neck, he seized the strongest man in return and threw him into the sea, for the power of the Sun had run down the boy's line and entered into him.

Then the cleverest man in the village, the mayor, who could charm a rabbit into his kitchen—and many a terrified rabbit, and many a pheasant and partridge too, had fluttered and trembled there, when the door shut behind it and it saw the knives—came to the boy saying, "Cut your line, my boy, and come with me! Henceforth, you and I are to rule in Atlantis. I've been conferring with the mayors of all the other villages; we have decided to form an empire, and you—none other!—are to be our king."

But the boy only laughed at him and pelted him with the shining stones of Atlantis, saying, "Oh, really? A king. Who is to be emperor?" And after the cleverest man in the village had talked a great deal more, he went away.

Then the magic woman from the hills, the sorceress, who knew every future save her own, came to the boy, saying, "Little boy, you must cut your line. Sabaoth sweats and trembles in his shrine and will no longer accept my offerings; the feet of Sith, called by the ignorant Kronos, son of Uranus, have broken; and the magic bird Tchataka has flown. The stars riot in the heavens, so that at one moment humankind is to rule them all, and at the next is to perish. Cut your line!"

But the boy only laughed at her and pelted her with the shining stones of Atlantis, with agates and alexandrites, moonstones and onyxes, rubies, sardonyxes, and sapphires; and at last the magic woman from the hills went away muttering.

Then the most foolish man in the village, the idiot, who sang songs without words to the brooks and boasted of bedding the white birch on the hill, came to the boy and tried to say how frightened he was to see the Sun fighting his line in the sky, though he could not find the words.

But the boy only smiled and let him touch the pole and feel the strength of the Sun, and after a time he too went away.

And at last the boy's mother came, saying, "Remember all the fine stories I have told you through the years? Never have I told you the finest one of all. Come to the little house the richest man in the village has given back to us. Put on your crown and tell your general to stand guard; take up the magic feather of the bird Tchataka, who opens its mouth to the sky and drinks wisdom with the dew. Then we shall dip the feather in the blood of a wild ox and write that story on white birch bark, you and I."

The boy asked, "What is that story, Mother?"

And his mother answered, "It is called "The Boy Who Hooked the Sun." Now cut your line and promise me you will never fish for the Sun again, so long as we both shall live."

Aha, thought the boy, as he got out his little knife. *I love my mother, who is more beautiful that the white birch tree on the hill and always kind. But do not all the souls wear away at last as they circle on the Wheel? Then the time must come when I live and she does not; and when that time comes, surely I will bait my hook again with the shining stones of Uranus, and we shall rule the stars. Or not.*

And so it is that the Sun swims far from Earth sometimes, thinking of its sore mouth; and we have winter. But now, when the days are very short and we see the boy's line stretched across the sky and powdered with hoarfrost, the Sun recalls Earth and her clever and foolish men and kind and magical women, and then it returns to us.

Or perhaps it is only—as some say—that it remembers the taste of the bait.

JOAN AIKEN

Clem's Dream

Joan Aiken is a celebrated British author whose work runs from adult mystery novels to children's picture books. She is the author of more than three dozen books for children, including *The Wolves of Willoughby Chase, The Whispering Mountain, Nightfall*, and a recent picture book (with artist Alan Lee) *The Moon's Revenge*. She has won the Lewis Carroll Award, the Carnegie Medal, the Guardian Award for Children's Fiction, and the Edgar Allan Poe Award.

"Clem's Dream" is an elegantly simple original fairy tale, luminous and perfect as the pearl in Clem's story. It comes from the pages of Aiken's most recent collection *The Last Slice of Rainbow* (nicely illustrated by Alix Berenzy).

Aiken currently divides her time between homes in Sussex, England, and New York City.

—T. W.

CLEM'S DREAM

Joan Aiken

Clem woke up in his sunny bedroom and cried out, "Oh, I have lost my dream! And it was such a beautiful dream! It sang, and shouted, and glittered, and sparkled—and I've lost it! Somebody pulled it away, out of reach, just as I woke up!"

He looked around—at his bed, his toys, his chair, his open window with the trees outside.

"Somebody must have come in through the window, and they've stolen my dream!"

He asked the Slipper Fairy, "Did you see who stole my dream?"

But the Slipper Fairy had been fast asleep, curled up in his slipper with her head in the toe. She had seen nobody.

He asked the Toothbrush Fairy, "Did you see who stole my dream?"

But the Toothbrush Fairy had been standing on one leg, looking at herself in the bathroom mirror. She had seen nothing.

Clem asked the Bathmat Fairy. He asked the Soap Fairy. He asked the Curtain Fairy. He asked the Clock Fairy.

None of them had seen the person who had stolen his dream.

He asked the Water Fairy, "Did you see the person who stole my dream?"

"Look under your pillow, willow, willow, willow!" sang the Water Fairy. "Open your own mouth and look in, in, in, in! Then, then you'll know, ho, ho, ho, ho!"

Clem looked under his pillow. He found a silver coin.

He climbed on a chair and looked in the glass, opening his mouth as wide as it would go.

He saw a hole, where a tooth used to be.

"The Tooth Fairy must have come while I was asleep. She took my tooth, and paid for it with a silver coin. She must have taken my dream, too. But she had no right to do that."

At breakfast, Clem asked, "How can I get my dream back from the Tooth Fairy?"

The Milk Fairy said, "She lives far, far away, on Moon Island, which is the other side of everywhere."

The Bread Fairy said, "She lives in a castle made of teeth, at the top of a high cliff."

The Apple Fairy said, "You will have to take her a present. Something round and white. Otherwise she will never give back your dream."

Clem went into the garden. He said, "How can I find my way to Moon Island, on the other side of everywhere? And what present can I take the Tooth Fairy?"

"Go up to the top of the hill, the hill, the hill, the hill," sang the Grass Fairy, "and put your arms around the stone, the stone, the stone that stands there. If your fingers can touch each other, around the other side, then the stone will grant your wish."

So Clem ran up to the top of the green, grassy hill.

There stood an old gray stone, tall as a Christmas tree. Clem tried to put his arms around it. But his arms would not quite reach; his fingers would not quite touch.

"You need to grow, to grow, to grow, to grow," sang the Grass Fairy. "Ask my sisters to help you, help you, help you, help you."

So Clem ran back to the house and called for help. The Bread Fairy, the Water Fairy, the Milk Fairy, and the Apple Fairy all came to the top of the hill and helped him. They pulled him longways, they pulled him sideways. By and by, when they had pulled and pulled and pulled, he was able to make his fingers meet around the other side of the old gray stone.

"Now you may have your wish," said the Stone Fairy.

"I wish for a boat," said Clem, "to take me to the Tooth Fairy's castle on Moon Island, on the other side of everywhere."

A laurel leaf fell into the brook, and grew till it was big as a boat. Clem stepped into it.

"Away you go, you go, you go, you go," sang the Water Fairy, and the boat floated away with Clem, down the brook, along the river, and into the wide, wide sea.

The sea is all made of dreams. Looking down into the deep water, Clem could see many, many dreams. They gleamed and shifted under his boat like leaves made of glass—gold, green, black, and silver. But nowhere could Clem see his own dream, nowhere in all the wide sea.

The boat traveled on, day after day, night after night.

In the distance, Clem saw many monsters. There was the Spinach Monster, all greeny-black, the Shoelace Monster, all tangly, the Stair Monster, all cornery, the Seaweed Monster, all crackly, and the Sponge Monster, all soggy.

But the Water Fairy tossed handfuls of water at them, and they did not dare come too near.

At last the boat came to Moon Island, on the other side of everywhere. Moon Island is round as a wheel. Its rocky beaches are covered with oysters, and black stones as big as apples. Up above are high white cliffs. And on top of the highest cliff of all stands the Tooth Fairy's castle, which is all made out of teeth.

"How shall I ever manage to climb up that cliff?" said Clem. "And what present can I take the Tooth Fairy so that she will give me back my dream?"

"Sing a song to the oysters on the beach," the Water Fairy told him. "They are very fond of songs."

So Clem sang:

> "Night sky
> Drifting by,
> How can I climb the rock so high?
> Moon beam,
> Star gleam,
> Where shall I find my stolen dream?"

All the oysters on the beach sighed with pleasure, and opened their shells to listen to Clem's song.

The King of the Oysters said, "Stoop down, Clem, feel with your finger inside my shell, and you will find a pearl. Take it to the Tooth Fairy, and perhaps she will give you back your dream."

Clem stooped and gently poked his finger inside the big oyster shell. There he found a pearl as big as a plum. It just fitted in the palm of his hand. He also picked up one of the round black stones off the beach.

"Thank you!" he said to the King of the Oysters. "That was kind of you. I will take this beautiful pearl to the Tooth Fairy, and perhaps she will give me back my dream. But how shall I ever climb up this high cliff?"

"Sing your song again, again, again," sang the Water Fairy. "And perhaps somebody else will help you."

So Clem sang:

> "Night, sleep,
> Ocean deep,
> How shall I climb the cliff so steep?
> Rain, mist,
> Snow, frost,
> How shall I find my dream that's lost?"

Then snowflakes came pattering down out of the sky and built Clem a staircase of white steps that led, back and forth, back and forth, crisscross, all the way up the high cliff.

And so Clem was able to climb up, step by step, step by step, until he came to the very top, where the Tooth Fairy's castle was perched.

The door was made of driftwood, white as paper.

Clem knocked on the door with his black stone. When he shook the stone, it rattled, as if it held loose teeth inside it.

Clem knocked once. He knocked twice. He knocked three times.

"Who is banging on my door?" cried an angry voice.

"It's me, Clem! I have come to ask for my dream!"

Slowly the door opened, and the Tooth Fairy looked out.

The Tooth Fairy is the oldest fairy in the world. Before the last dragon turned to stone, she was building her castle, and she will be building it when the seeds from the last thistle fly off into space. Her eyes are like balls of snow, and her hands are like bunches of thorns. Her feet are like roots. Her teeth are like icicles.

"Who are you?" said the Tooth Fairy. "How dare you come knocking at my door? I never give back a tooth. Never!"

"I'm Clem. And I don't want my tooth back. I want my dream back!"

The Tooth Fairy gave Clem a crafty look.

"How can you be certain that I have your dream?"

"I'm certain," said Clem.

"And if I have it, here in my castle, how can you find it?"

"I'll know it when I see it," said Clem.

"Oh, very well. You may come in and look for it. But you may stay only seven minutes."

So Clem went into the Tooth Fairy's castle—along wide halls and into huge rooms.

The fairy shut the door behind him, and pulled the bolt, which was made from a serpent's tooth.

Clem wandered all over the castle—up winding stairways, around corners, through galleries, up onto the tops of towers, out on balconies, down into cellars, under arches, across courtyards.

Everything was white, and there was not a single sound to be heard. Not a mouse, not a bird.

He began to fear that he would never find his dream.

"You have had six minutes!" called the Tooth Fairy.

Her voice rang like a bell in the hollow castle.

But then, just after that, Clem heard the tiniest tinkle, like water dripping into a pool.

"Look up," whispered the Water Fairy. "Look up, up, up, up!"

Clem looked up, into a round, empty tower. And high, high, high, high, far, far up, he saw something flutter—something that gleamed, and twinkled, and shone, and sparkled.

"It's my dream!" shouted Clem joyfully. "Oh, oh, oh, it's my beautiful, beautiful dream!"

At the sound of his voice, the dream came floating and fluttering down from the high cranny where the Tooth Fairy had hidden it; like a falling leaf it came floating and fluttering down, and then wrapped itself lovingly all around Clem.

"This is my own dream," he told the Tooth Fairy. "And here is a pearl, which I brought for you. Now I shall take my dream home."

At the sight of Clem joyfully hugging his dream, the Tooth Fairy became so sad that she began to melt. She grew smaller, like a lump of ice in the sun.

"Don't, don't, don't take your dream away, Clem! Please, please leave it with me!" she begged. "It is the only beautiful thing I have, in all this silent whiteness. It is the most beautiful thing I have ever seen. If you leave it with me I will give you a hundred years!"

"I don't want a hundred years," said Clem. "I would rather have my dream."

"I will give you a carriage, to travel faster than the sun!"

"I would rather have my dream."

"I will give you a bonfire that you can carry in your pocket."

"I would rather have my dream."

"I will give you a ray of light that can cut through stone."

"I would rather have my dream."

"I will give you a garden that grows upside down and backward."

"I would rather have my dream."

"I will give you a word that will last forever."

"I would rather have my dream."

When the Tooth Fairy saw that Clem really meant to take his dream away, she grew sadder still.

"Very well," she said at last. "Give me the pearl, then."

She sighed, such a long deep sigh that the whole castle trembled. Then she pulled back the bolt made from a serpent's tooth, and opened the door. Clem walked out of the castle.

When he turned to wave good-bye to the Tooth Fairy, she was sitting huddled up on a tooth. She looked so old and small and withered and pitiful that he began to feel sorry for her. He stood thinking.

"Listen!" he called after a minute or two. "Would you like to *borrow* my dream? Suppose you keep it until the next time you come to take one of my teeth. How about that?"

"Yes! *Yes*! YES!"

Her white eyes suddenly shone like lamps.

So Clem gently let go of his dream and it fluttered away, back into the Tooth Fairy's castle.

"Good-bye, Dream—for a little while!" he called. "I'll see you next Tooth Day."

"Wait!" called the Tooth Fairy. "Since you have been so kind, Clem, I'll give you back your pearl."

"No, no, keep it, keep it! Why would I want a pearl? Put it into the wall of your castle."

Clem ran down the stair that had built itself of snow. On the stony beach down below, his boat was waiting for him. He jumped into it, and it raced back over the sea, over the floating dreams, red, black, silver, and green like leaves.

But Clem looked behind him and saw his own dream waving and fluttering like a flag from the tower of the Tooth Fairy's castle, and the pearl shining like a round eye in the wall.

"It won't be many months before she comes with the dream," thought Clem, and he poked with his finger in the gap between his teeth, where already he could feel a new tooth beginning to grow.

When he arrived home, the Bread Fairy, the Milk Fairy, and the Apple Fairy were there to welcome him.

"I have lent my dream to the Tooth Fairy," he told them. "But it won't be many months before she brings it back."

And he ran upstairs, washed his face, brushed his teeth, and jumped into bed.

He took with him the round black stone, which rattled gently when he shook it.

"The Tooth Fairy will look after my dream," he told the Slipper Fairy and the Clock Fairy. "She has it safe." Then he fell asleep.

When Clem was fast asleep, still holding the black stone, which rattled gently to itself, all the fairies came to look at him.

"He doesn't know," said the Water Fairy. "He doesn't know that he has brought away the most precious thing of all, all, all, all, all."

"If he ever learns how to open up that stone," said the Bread Fairy, "he will be more powerful than any of us."

"He will be able to grow apple trees on the moon," said the Apple Fairy.

"Or grass on Mars," said the Grass Fairy.

"Or make tick-tock Time turn backward," ticked the Clock Fairy.

"Well, let us hope that he uses it sensibly, sensibly, sensibly," said the Soap Fairy softly.

"Let us hope so," said the Curtain Fairy.

"Let us hope so," said the Bathmat Fairy.

But Clem slept on, smiling, holding the black stone tightly in his hand. And, by and by, he began to dream again.

LEWIS SHINER

Love in Vain

Lewis Shiner has been around for about ten years now, one of the new breed of Texas writers who aren't necessarily macho but can be punk when they want to be. His work is sometimes filled with the warm glow of nostalgia, other times fueled by anger at the way things are. His first novel, *Frontera*, was a Hugo Award finalist and his second, *Deserted Cities of the Heart*, is a Nebula Award finalist. Neither book prepares one for a story like "Love in Vain."

Here's a story that's at once frightening and yet somehow winsome, a tale both sentimental and brutally harsh in its attitudes toward relationships between the sexes. In the end, it's more ammunition in the battle of the sexes, but this time there's a serial killer who is at once a catalyst and an enigmatic, almost magical realist figure. Serial killers seem to be proliferating in epidemic proportions in modern times. They always kill strangers and seem impervious to analysis— which is one of their most terrifying aspects. That, plus the personal charm many of them possess, and the possibility they make us aware of: that we all carry the seeds of their inexplicable violence inside us.

—E. D.

LOVE IN VAIN

Lewis Shiner

For James Ellroy

I remember the room: whitewashed walls, no windows, a map of the U.S. on my left as I came in. There must have been a hundred pins with little colored heads stuck along the interstates. By the other door was a wooden table, the top full of scratches and coffee rings. Charlie was already sitting on the far side of it.

They called it Charlie's "office" and a Texas Ranger named Gonzales had brought me back there to meet him. "Charlie?" Gonzales said. "This here's Dave McKenna, from the D.A. up in Dallas?"

"Morning," Charlie said. I could see details, but they didn't seem to add up to anything. His left eye, the glass one, drooped a little, and his teeth were brown and ragged. He had on jeans and a plaid short-sleeved shirt and he was shaved clean. His hair was damp and combed straight back. His sideburns had gray in them and came to the bottom of his ears.

I had some files and a notebook in my right hand so I wouldn't have to shake with him. He didn't offer. "You looking to close you up some cases?" he said.

I had to clear my throat. "Well, we thought we might give it a try." I sat down in the other chair.

He nodded and looked at Gonzales. "Ernie? You don't suppose I could have a little more coffee?"

Gonzales had been leaning against the wall by the map, but he straightened right up and said, "Sure thing, Charlie." He brought in a full pot of coffee from the other room and set it on the table. Charlie had a styrofoam cup that looked like it could hold about a quart. He filled it up and then added three packets of sugar and some powdered cream substitute.

"How about you?" Charlie said.

"No," I said. "Thanks."

"You don't need to be nervous," Charlie said. His breath smelled of coffee and cigarettes. When he wasn't talking, his mouth relaxed into an easy smile. You didn't have to see anything menacing in it. It was the kind of smile you could see from any highway in Texas, looking out at you from a porch or behind a gas pump, waiting for you to drive on through.

I took out a little pocket-sized cassette recorder. "Would it be okay if I taped this?"

"Sure, go ahead."

I pushed the little orange button on top. "March 27, Williamson County Jail. Present are Sergeant Ernesto Gonzales and Charles Dean Harris."

"Charlie," he said.

"Pardon?"

"Nobody ever calls me Charles."

"Right," I said. "Okay."

"I guess maybe my mother did sometimes. Always sounded wrong somehow." He tilted his chair back against the wall. "You don't suppose you could back that up and do it over?"

"Yeah, okay, fine." I rewound the tape and went through the introduction again. This time I called him Charlie. Twenty-five years ago he'd stabbed his mother to death. She'd been his first.

It had taken me three hours to drive from Dallas to the Williamson County Jail in Georgetown, a straight shot down Interstate 35. I'd left a little before eight that morning. Alice was already at work and I had to get Jeffrey off to school. The hardest part was getting him away from the television.

He was watching MTV. They were playing the Heart video where the blonde guitar player wears the low-cut golden prom dress. Every time she moved, her magnificent breasts seemed to hesitate before they went along, like they were proud, willful animals, just barely under her control.

I turned the TV off and swung Jeffrey around a couple of times and sent him out for the bus. I got together the files I needed and went into the bedroom to make the bed. The covers were turned back on both sides, but the middle was undisturbed. Alice and I hadn't made love in six weeks. And counting.

I walked through the house, picking up Jeffrey's Masters of the Universe toys. I saw that Alice had loaded up the mantel again with framed pictures of her brothers and parents and the dog she'd had as a little girl. For a second it seemed like the entire house was buried in all this crap that had nothing to do with me—dolls and vases and doilies and candles and baskets on every inch of every flat surface she could reach. You couldn't walk from one end of a room to the other without running into a Victorian chair or secretary or umbrella stand, couldn't see the floors for the flowered rugs.

I locked up and got in the car and took the LBJ loop all the way around town. The idea was to avoid traffic. I was kidding myself. Driving in Dallas is a kind of contest; if somebody manages to pull in front of you he's clearly got a bigger dick than you do. Rather than let this happen it's better that one of you die.

I was in traffic the whole way down, through a hundred and seventy miles of Charlie Dean Harris country: flat, desolate grasslands with an occasional bridge or culvert where you could dump a body. Charlie had wandered and murdered all over the South, but once he found I-35 he was home to stay.

I opened one of the folders and rested it against the edge of the table so Charlie wouldn't see my hand shaking. "I've got a case here from 1974. A Dallas girl on her way home from Austin for spring break. Her name was Carol, uh, Fairchild. Black hair, blue eyes. Eighteen years old."

Charlie was nodding. "She had braces on her teeth. Would have been real pretty without 'em."

I looked at the sheet of paper in the folder. Braces, it said. The plain white walls seemed to wobble a little. "Then you remember her."

"Yessir, I suppose I do. I killed her." He smiled. It looked like a reflex, something he didn't even know he was doing. "I killed her to have sex with her."

"Can you remember anything else?"

He shrugged. "It was just to have sex, that's all. I remember when she got in the car. She was wearing a T-shirt, one of them man's T-shirts, with the straps and all." He dropped the chair back down and put his elbows on the table. "You could see her titties," he said, explaining.

I wanted to pull away but I didn't. "Where was this?"

He thought for a minute. "Between here and Round Rock, right there off the Interstate."

I looked down at my folder again. Last seen wearing navy tank top, blue jeans. "What color was the T-shirt?"

"Red," he said. "She would have been strangled. With a piece of electrical wire I had there in the car. I had supposed she was a prostitute, dressed the way she was and all. I asked her to have sex and she said she would, so I got off the highway and then she didn't want to. So I killed her and I had sex with her."

Nobody said anything for what must have been at least a minute. I could hear a little scratching noise as the tape moved inside the recorder. Charlie was looking straight at me with his good eye. "I wasn't satisfied," he said.

"What?"

"I wasn't satisfied. I had sex with her but I wasn't satisfied."

"Listen, you don't have to tell me . . ."

"I got to tell it all," he said.

"I don't want to hear it," I said. My voice came out too high, too loud. But Charlie kept staring at me.

"It don't matter," he said. "I still got to tell it. I got to tell it all. I can't live with the terrible things I did. Jesus says that if I tell everything I can be with Betsy when this is all over." Betsy was his common-law wife. He'd killed her, too, after living with her since she was nine. The words sounded like he'd been practicing them, over and over.

"I'll take you to her if you want," he said.

"Betsy . . . ?"

"No, your girl there. Carol Fairchild. I'll take you where I buried her." He wasn't smiling anymore. He had the sad, earnest look of a laundromat bum telling you how he'd lost his oil fortune up in Oklahoma.

I looked at Gonzales. "We can set it up for you if you want," he said. "Sheriff'll have to okay it and all, but we could prob'ly do it first thing tomorrow."

"Okay," I said. "That'd be good."

Charlie nodded, drank some coffee, lit a cigarette. "Well, fine," he said. "You want to try another?"

"No," I said. "Not just yet."

"Whatever," Charlie said. "You just let me know."

Later, walking me out, Gonzales said, "Don't let Charlie get to you. He wants people to like him, you know? So he figures out what you want him to be, and he tries to be that for you."

I knew he was trying to cheer me up. I thanked him and told him I'd be back in the morning.

I called Alice from Jack's office in Austin, thirty miles farther down I-35. "It's me," I said.

"Oh," she said. She sounded tired. "How's it going?"

I didn't know what to tell her. "Fine," I said. "I need to stay over another day or so."

"Okay," she said.

"Are you okay?"

"Fine," she said.

"Jeffrey?"

"He's fine."

I watched thirty seconds tick by on Jack's wall clock. "Anything else?" she said.

"I guess not." My eyes stung and I reflexively shaded them with my free hand. "I'll be at Jack's if you need me."

"Okay," she said. I waited a while longer and then put the phone back on the hook.

Jack was just coming out of his office. "Oh-oh," he said.

It took a couple of breaths to get my throat to unclench. "Yeah," I said.

"Bad?"

"Bad as it could be, I guess. It's over, probably. I mean, I think it's over, but how do you know?"

"You don't," Jack said. His secretary, a good-looking Chicana named Liz, typed away on her word processor and tried to act like she wasn't having to listen to us. "You just after a while get fed up and you say fuck it. You want to get a burger or what?"

Jack and I went to U.T. law school together. He was losing his hair and putting on weight but he wouldn't do anything about it. Jogging was for assholes. He would rather die fat and keep his self-respect.

He'd been divorced two years now and was always glad to fold out the couch for me. It had been a while. After Jeffrey was born, Alice and I had somehow lost touch with all our friends, given up everything except work and TV. "I've missed this," I said.

"Missed what?"

"Friends," I said. We were in a big prairie-style house north of campus that had been fixed up with a kitchen and bar and hanging plants. I was full, but still working on the last of the batter-dipped french fries.

"Not my fault, you prick. You're the one dropped down to Christmas cards."

"Yeah, well . . ."

"Forget it. How'd it go with Charlie Dean?"

"Unbelievable," I said. "I mean, really. He confessed to everything. Had details. Even had a couple wrong, enough to look good. But the major stuff was right on."

"So that's great. Isn't it?"

"It was a setup. The name I gave him was a fake. No such person, no such case."

"I don't get it."

"Jack, the son of a bitch has confessed to something like three thousand murders. It ain't possible. So they wanted to catch him lying."

"With his pants down, so to speak."

"Same old Jack."

"You said he had details."

"That's the creepy part. He knew she was supposed to have braces. I had it in the phony-case file, but he brought it up before I could say anything about it."

"Lucky guess."

"No. It was too creepy. And there's all this shit he keeps telling you. Things you wish you'd never heard, you know what I mean?"

"I know exactly what you mean," Jack said. "When I was in junior high I saw a bum go in the men's room at the bus station with a loaf of bread. I told this friend of mine about it and he says the bum was going in there to wipe all the dried piss off the toilets with the bread and then eat it. For the protein. Said it happens all the time."

"Jesus *Christ*, Jack."

"See? I know what you're talking about. There's things you don't want in your head. Once they get in there, you're not the same anymore. I can't eat white bread to this day. Twenty years, and I still can't touch it."

"You asshole." I pushed my plate away and finished my Corona. "Christ, now the beer tastes like piss."

Jack pointed his index finger at me. "You will never be the same," he said.

You could never tell how much Jack had been drinking. He said it was because he didn't let on when he was sober. I always thought it was because there was something in him that was meaner than the booze and together they left him just about even.

It was a lot of beers later that Jack said, "What was the name of that bimbo in high school you used to talk about? Your first great love or some shit? Except she never put out for you?"

"Kristi," I said. "Kristi Spector."

"Right!" Jack got up and started walking around the apartment. It wasn't too long of a walk. "A name like that, how could I forget? I got her off a soliciting rap two months ago."

"Soliciting?"

"There's a law in Texas against selling your pussy. Maybe you didn't know that."

"Kristi Spector, my God. Tell me about it."

"She's a stripper, son. Works over at the Yellow Rose. This guy figured if she'd show her tits in public he could have the rest in his car. She didn't, he called the pigs. Said she made lewd advances. Crock of shit, got thrown out of court."

"How's she look?"

"Not too goddamn bad. I wouldn't have minded taking my fee in trade, but she didn't seem to get the hint." He stopped. "I got a better idea. Let's go have a look for ourselves."

"Oh, no," I said.

"Oh, yes. She remembers you, man. She says you were "sweet." Come on, get up. We're going to go look at some tits."

The place was bigger inside than I expected, the ceilings higher. There were two stages and a runway behind the second one. There were stools right up by the stages for the guys that wanted to stick dollar bills in the dancers' G-strings and four-top tables everywhere else.

I should have felt guilty but I wasn't thinking about Alice at all. The issue here was sex, and Alice had written herself out of that part of my life. Instead I was thinking about the last time I'd seen Kristi.

It was senior year in high school. The director of the drama club, who was from New York, had invited some of us to a "wild" party. It was the first time I'd seen men in dresses. I'd locked myself in the bathroom with Kristi to help her take her bra off. I hadn't seen her in six months. She'd just had an abortion; the father could have been one of a couple of guys. Not me. She didn't want to spoil what we had. It was starting to look to me like there wasn't much left to spoil. That had been eighteen years ago.

The D.J. played something by Pat Benatar. The music was loud enough to give you a kind of mental privacy. You didn't really have to pay attention to anything but the dancers. At the moment it seemed like just the thing. It had been an ugly day and there was something in me that was comforted by the sight of young, good-looking women with their clothes off.

"College town," Jack said, leaning toward me so I could hear him. "Lots of local talent."

A tall blonde on the north stage unbuttoned her long-sleeved white shirt and let it hang open. Her breasts were smooth and firm and pale. Like the others, she had something on the point of her nipples that made a small, golden flash every time one caught the light.

"See anybody you know?"

"Give me a break," I shouted over the music. "You saw her a couple months ago. It's been almost twenty years for me. I may not even recognize her." A waitress came by, wearing black leather jeans and a red tank top. For a second I could hear Charlie's voice telling me about her titties. I rubbed the sides of my head and the voice went away. We ordered beers, but when they came my stomach was wrapped around itself and I had to let mine sit.

"It's got to be weird to do this for a living," I said in Jack's ear.

"Bullshit," Jack said. "You think they're not getting off on it?"

He pointed to the south stage. A brunette in high heels had let an overweight man in sideburns and a western shirt tuck a dollar into the side of her bikini bottoms. He talked earnestly to her with just the start of an embarrassed smile. She had to keep leaning closer to hear him. Finally she nodded and turned around. She bent over and grabbed her ankles. His face was about the height of the backs of her knees. She was smiling like she'd just seen somebody else's baby do something cute. After a few seconds she stood up again and the man went back to his table.

"What was that about?" I asked Jack.

"Power, man," he said. "God, I love women. I just love 'em."

"Your problem is you don't know the difference between love and sex."

"Yeah? What is it? Come on, I want to know." The music was too loud to argue with him. I shook my head. "See? You don't know either."

The brunette pushed her hair back with both hands, chin up, fingers spread wide, and it reminded me of Kristi. The theatricality of it. She'd played one of Tennessee Williams's affected Southern bitches once and it had been almost too painful to watch. Almost.

"Come on," I said, grabbing Jack's sleeve. "It's been swell, but let's get out of here. I don't need to see her. I'm better off with the fantasy."

Jack didn't say anything. He just pointed with his chin to the stage behind me.

She had on a leopard skin leotard. She had been a dark blonde in high school but now her hair was brown and short. She'd put on a little weight, not much. She stretched in front of the mirrored wall and the D.J. played the Pretenders.

I felt this weird, possessive kind of pride, watching her. That and lust. I'd been married for eight years and the worst thing I'd ever done was kiss an old girlfriend on New Year's Eve and stare longingly at the pictures in *Playboy*. But this was real, this was happening.

The song finished and another one started and she pulled one strap down on the leotard. I remembered the first time I'd seen her breasts. I was fifteen. I'd joined a youth club at the Unitarian Church because she went there Sunday afternoons. Sometimes we would skip the program and sneak off into the deserted Sunday school classrooms and there, in the twilight, surrounded by crayon drawings on manila paper, she would stretch out on the linoleum and let me lie on top of her and feel the maddening pressure of her pelvis and smell the faint, clinically erotic odor of peroxide in her hair.

She showed me her breasts on the golf course next door. We had jumped the fence and we lay in a sand trap so no one would see us. There was a little light from the street, but not enough for real color. It was like a black-and-white movie when I played it back in my mind.

They were fuller now, hung a little lower and flatter, but I remembered the small, pale nipples. She pulled the other strap down, turned her back, rotating her hips as she stripped down to a red G-string. Somebody held a dollar out to her. I wanted to go over there and tell him that I knew her.

Jack kept poking me in the ribs. "Well? Well?"

"Be cool," I said. I had been watching the traffic pattern and I knew that after the song she would take a break and then get up on the other stage. It took a long time, but I wasn't tense about it. I'm just going to say hi, I thought. And that's it.

The song was over and she walked down the stairs at the end of the stage, throwing the leotard around her shoulders. I got up, having a little trouble with the chair, and walked over to her.

"Kristi," I said. "It's Dave McKenna."

"Oh, my *God*!" She was in my arms. Her skin was hot from the lights and I could smell her deodorant. I was suddenly dizzy, aware of every square inch where our bodies were touching. "Do you still hate me?" she said, pulling away.

"What?" There was so much I'd forgotten. The twang in her voice. The milk chocolate color of her eyes. The beauty mark over her right cheekbone. The flirtatious look up through the lashes that now had a desperate edge to it.

"The last time I saw you you called me a bitch. It was after that party at your teacher's house."

"No, I . . . believe me, it wasn't like . . ."

"Listen, I'm on again," she said. "Where are you?"

"We're right over there."

"Oh, Christ, you didn't bring your wife with you? I heard you were married."

"No, it's . . ."

"I got to run, sugar, wait for me."

I went back to the table.

"You rascal," Jack said. "Why didn't you just slip it to her on the spot?"

"Shut up, Jack, will you?"

"Ooooh, touchy."

I watched her dance. She was no movie star. Her face was a little hard and even the heavy makeup didn't hide all the lines. But none of that mattered. What mattered was the way she moved, the kind of puckered smile that said yes, I want it too.

She sat down with us when she was finished. She seemed to be all hands, touching me on the arm, biting on a fingernail, gesturing in front of her face.

She was dancing three times a week, which was all they would schedule her for anymore. The money was good and she didn't mind the work, especially here where it wasn't too rowdy. Jack raised his eyebrows at me to say, see? She got by with some modeling and some "scuffling," which I assumed meant turning tricks. Her mother was still in Dallas and had sent Kristi clippings the couple of times I got my name in the paper.

"She always liked me," I said.

"She liked you the best of all of them. You were a gentleman."

"Maybe too much of one."

"It was why I loved you." She was wearing the leotard again but she might as well have been naked. I was beginning to be afraid of her so I reminded myself that nothing had happened yet, nothing *had* to happen, that I wasn't committed to anything. I pushed my beer over to her and she drank about half of it. "It gets hot up there," she said. "You wouldn't believe. Sometimes you think you're going to pass out, but you got to keep smiling."

"Are you married?" I asked her. "Were you ever?"

"Once. It lasted two whole months. The shitheel knocked me up and then split."

"What happened?"

"I kept the kid. He's four now."

"What's his name?"

"Stoney. He's a cute little bastard. I got a neighbor watches him when I'm out, and I do the same for hers. He keeps me going sometimes." She drank the rest of the beer. "What about you?"

"I got a little boy too. Jeffrey. He's seven."

"Just the one?"

"I don't think the marriage could handle more than one kid," I said.

"It's an old story," Jack said. "If your wife put you through law school, the marriage breaks up. It just took Dave a little longer than most."

"You're getting divorced?" she asked.

"I don't know. Maybe." She nodded. I guess she didn't need to ask for details. Marriages come apart every day.

"I'm on again in a little," she said. "Will you still be here when I get back?" She did what she could to make it sound casual.

"I got an early day tomorrow," I said.

"Sure. It was good to see you. Real good."

The easiest thing seemed to be to get out a pen and an old business card. "Give me your phone number. Maybe I can get loose another night."

She took the pen but she kept looking at me. "Sure," she said.

"You're an idiot," Jack said. "Why didn't you go home with her?"

I watched the streetlights. My jacket smelled like cigarettes and my head had started to hurt.

"That gorgeous piece of ass says to you, 'Ecstasy?' and Dave says, 'No thanks.' What the hell's the matter with you? Alice makes you leave your dick in the safe-deposit box?"

"Jack," I said, "will you shut the fuck up?" The card with her number on it was in the inside pocket of the jacket. I could feel it there, like a cool fingernail against my flesh.

Jack went back to his room to crash a little after midnight. I couldn't sleep. I put on the headphones and listened to Robert Johnson, "King of the Delta Blues Singers." There was something about his voice. He had this deadpan tone that sat down and told you what was wrong like it was no big deal. Then the voice would crack and you could tell it was a hell of a lot worse than he was letting on.

They said the devil himself had tuned Johnson's guitar. He died in 1938, poisoned by a jealous husband. He'd made his first recordings in a hotel room in San Antonio, just another seventy miles on down I-35.

Charlie and Gonzales and I took my car out to what Gonzales called the "site." The sheriff and a deputy were in a brown county station wagon behind us. Charlie sat on the passenger side and Gonzales was in the back. Charlie could have opened the door at a stoplight and been gone. He wasn't even in handcuffs. Nobody said anything about it.

We got on I-35 and Charlie said, "Go on south to the second exit after the caves." The Inner Space Caverns were just south of Georgetown, basically a single long, unspectacular tunnel that ran for miles under the highway. "I killed a girl there once. When they turned off the lights."

I nodded but I didn't say anything. That morning, before I went in to the "office," Gonzales had told me that it made Charlie angry if you let on that you didn't believe him. I was tired, and hung over from watching Jack drink, and I didn't really give a damn about Charlie's feelings.

I got off at the exit and followed the access road for a while. Charlie had his eyes closed and seemed to be thinking hard.

"Having trouble?" I asked him.

"Nah," he said. "Just didn't want to take you to the wrong one." I looked at him and he started laughing. It was a joke. Gonzales chuckled in the back seat and there was this cheerful kind of feeling in the car that made me want to pull over and run away.

"Nosir," Charlie said, "I sure don't suppose I'd want to do that." He grinned at me and he knew what I was thinking, he could see the horror right there on my face. He just kept smiling. Come on, I could hear him saying. Loosen up. Be one of the guys.

I wiped the sweat from my hands onto my pant legs. Finally he said, "There's a dirt road a ways ahead. Turn off on it. It'll go over a hill and then across a cattle grating. After the grating is a stand of trees off to the left. You'll want to park up under 'em."

How can he be doing this? I thought. He's got to know there's nothing there. Or does he? When we don't turn anything up, what's he going to do? Are they going to wish they'd cuffed him after all? The sheriff knew what I was up to, but none of the others did. Would Gonzales turn on me for betraying Charlie?

The road did just what Charlie said it would. We parked the cars under the trees and the deputy and I got shovels out of the sheriff's trunk. The trees were oaks and their leaves were tiny and very pale green.

"It would be over here," Charlie said. He stood on a patch of low ground, covered with clumps of Johnson grass. "Not too deep."

He was right. She was only about six or eight inches down. The deputy had a body bag and he tried to move her into it, but she kept coming apart. There wasn't much left but a skeleton and a few rags.

And the braces. Still shining, clinging to the teeth of the skull like a metal smile.

On the way back to Georgetown we passed a woman on the side of the road. She was staring into the hood of her car. She looked like she was about to cry. Charlie turned all the way around in his seat to watch her as we drove by.

"There's just victims ever'where," Charlie said. There was a sadness in his voice I didn't believe. "The highway's full of 'em. Kids, hitchhikers, waitresses . . . You ever pick one up?"

"No," I said, but it wasn't true. It was in Dallas, I was home for spring break. It was the end of the sixties. She had on a green dress. Nothing happened. But she had smiled at me and put one arm up on the back of the seat. I was on the way to my girlfriend's house and I let her off a few blocks away. And that night, when I was inside her, I imagined my girlfriend with the hitchhiker's face, with her blonde hair and freckles, her slightly coarse features, the dots of sweat on her upper lip.

"But you thought about it," Charlie said. "Didn't you?"

"Listen," I said. "I got a job to do. I just want to do it and get out of here, okay?"

"I know what you're saying," Charlie said. "Jesus forgives me, but I can't ask that of nobody else. I was just trying to get along, that's all. That's all any of us is ever trying to do."

I called Dallas collect from the sheriff's phone. He gave me a private room where I could shout if I had to. The switchboard put me through to Ricky Slatkin, the head of my department.

"Dave, will you for Chrissake calm down. It's a coincidence. That's all. Forensics will figure out who this girl is and we'll put another 70 or 80 years on Charlie's sentence. Maybe give him another death penalty. What the hell, right? Meanwhile we'll give him another ringer."

"You give him one. I want out of this. I am fucking terrified."

"I, uh, understand you're under some stress at home these days."

"I am not at home. I'm in Georgetown, in the Williamson County Jail, and I am under some fucking stress right here. Don't you understand? He *thought* this dead girl into existence."

"What, Charlie Dean Harris is God now, is that it? Come on, Dave. Go out and have a few beers and by tomorrow it'll all make sense to you."

"He's evil, Jack," I said. We were back at his place after a pizza at Conan's. Jack had ordered a pitcher of beer and drunk it all himself. "I didn't use to believe in it, but that was before I met Charlie."

He had a women's basketball game on TV, the sound turned down to a low hum. "That's horseshit," he said. His voice was too loud. "Horseshit, Christian horseshit. They want you to believe that Evil has got a capital *E* and it's sitting over there in the corner, see it? Horseshit. Evil isn't a thing. It's something that's *not* there. It's an absence. The lack of the thing that stops you from doing whatever you damn well please."

He chugged half a beer. "Your pal Charlie ain't evil. He's just dam-
aged goods. He's just like you or me but something died in him. You
know what I'm talking about. You've felt it. First it goes to sleep and
then it dies. You know when you stand up in court and try to get
a rapist off when you know he did it. You tell yourself that it's part
of the game, you try to give the asshole the benefit of the doubt, hell,
somebody's got to do it, right? You try to believe the girl is just some
slut that changed her mind, but you can smell it. Something inside
you starting to rot."

He finished the beer and threw it at a paper sack in the corner. It hit
another bottle inside the sack and shattered. "Then you go home and
your wife's got a goddamn headache or her period or she's asleep in front
of the TV or she's not in the goddamn mood and you just want to beat
the . . ." His right fist was clenched up so tight the knuckles were a
shiny yellow. His eyes looked like open sores. He got up for another
beer and he was in the kitchen for a long time.

When he came back I said, "I'm going out." I said it without giving
myself a chance to think about it.

"Kristi," Jack said. He had a fresh beer and was all right again.

"Yeah."

"You bastard! Can I smell your fingers when you get back?"

"Fuck you, Jack."

"Oh no, save it for her. She's going to use you up, you lucky bastard."

I called her from a pay phone and she gave me directions. She was at
the Royal Palms Trailer Park, near Bergstrom Air Force Base on the
south end of town. It wasn't hard to find. They even had a few palm
trees. There were rural-type galvanized mailboxes on posts by the gravel
driveways. I found the one that said Spector and parked behind a white
Dodge with six-figure mileage.

The temperature was in the sixties but I was shaking. My shoulders
kept trying to crawl up around my neck. I got out of the car. I couldn't
feel my feet. Asshole, I told myself. I don't want to hear about your
personal problems. You better enjoy this or I'll kill you.

I knocked on the door and it made a kind of mute rattling sound.
Kristi opened it. She was wearing a plaid bathrobe, so old I couldn't tell
what the colors used to be. She stood back to let me in and said, "I
didn't think you'd call."

"But I did," I said. The trailer was tiny—a living room with a green
sofa and a 19-inch color TV, a kitchen the size of a short hall, a single
bedroom behind it, the door open, the bed unmade. A blond-haired boy
was asleep on the sofa, wrapped in an army blanket. The shelf above him

was full of plays—Albee, Ionesco, Tennessee Williams. The walls were covered with photographs in dime-store frames.

A couple of them were from the drama club; one even had me in it. I was sixteen and looked maybe nine. My hair was too long in front, my chest was sucked in, and I had a stupid smirk on my face. I was looking at Kristi. Who would want to look at anything else? She had on cutoffs that had frayed up past the crease of her thighs. Her shirt was unbuttoned and tied under her breasts. Her head was back and she was laughing. I'd always been able to make her laugh.

"You want a drink?" she whispered.

"No," I said. I turned to look at her. We weren't either of us laughing now. I reached for her and she glanced over at the boy and shook her head. She grabbed the cuff of my shirt and pulled me gently back toward the bedroom.

It smelled of perfume and hand lotion and a little of mildew. The only light trickled in through heavy, old-fashioned venetian blinds. She untied the bathrobe and let it fall. I kissed her and her arms went around my neck. I touched her shoulder blades and her hair and her buttocks and then I got out of my clothes and left them in a pile on the floor. She ran on tiptoes back to the front of the trailer and locked and chained the door. Then she came back and shut the bedroom door and lay down on the bed.

I lay down next to her. The smell and feel of her was wonderful, and at the same time it was not quite real. There were too many unfamiliar things and it was hard to connect to the rest of my life.

Then I was on my knees between her legs, gently touching her. Her arms were spread out beside her, tangled in the sheets, her hips moving with pleasure. Only once, in high school, had she let me touch her there, in the back seat of a friend's car, her skirt up around her hips, panties to her knees, and before I had recovered from the wonder of it she had pulled away.

But that was eighteen years ago and this was now. There had been a lot of men touching her since then, maybe hundreds. But that was all right. I lay on top of her and she guided me inside. She tried to say something, maybe it was only my name, but I put my mouth over hers to shut her up. I put both my arms around her and closed my eyes and let the heat and pleasure run up through me.

When I finished and we rolled apart she lay on top of me, pinning me to the bed. "That was real sweet," she said.

I kissed her and hugged her because I couldn't say what I was thinking. I was thinking about Charlie, remembering the earnest look on his face when he said, "It was just to have sex, that's all."

*   *   *

She was wide awake and I was exhausted. She complained about the state cutting back on aid to single parents. She told me about the tiny pieces of tape she had to wear on the ends of her nipples when she danced, a weird Health Department regulation. I remembered the tiny golden flashes and fell asleep to the memory of her dancing.

Screaming woke me up. Kristi was already out of bed and headed for the living room. "It's just Stoney," she said, and I lay back down.

I woke up again a little before dawn. There was an arm around my waist but it seemed much too small. I rolled over and saw that the little boy had crawled into bed between us.

I got up without moving him and went to the bathroom. There was no water in the toilet; when I pushed the handle a trap opened in the bottom of the bowl and a fine spray washed the sides. I got dressed, trying not to bump into anything. Kristi was asleep on the side of the bed closest to the door, her mouth open a little. Stoney had burrowed into the middle of her back.

I was going to turn around and go when a voyeuristic impulse made me open the drawer of her nightstand. Or maybe I subconsciously knew what I'd find. There was a Beeline book called *Molly's Sexual Follies*, a tube of KY, a box of Ramses lubricated condoms, a few used Kleenex. An emery board, a finger puppet, one hoop earring. A short-barreled Colt .32 revolver.

I got to the jail at nine in the morning. The woman at the visitor's window recognized me and buzzed me back. Gonzales was at his desk. He looked up when I walked in and said, "I didn't know you was coming in today."

"I just had a couple of quick questions for Charlie," I said. "Only take a second."

"Did you want to use the office . . . ?"

"No, no point. If I could just talk to him in his cell for a couple of minutes, that would be great."

Gonzales got the keys. Charlie had a cell to himself, five by ten feet, white-painted bars on the long wall facing the corridor. There were Bibles and religious tracts on his cot, a few paintings hanging on the wall. "Maybe you can get Charlie to show you his pictures," Gonzales said. A stool in the corner had brushes and tubes of paint on the top.

"You painted these?" I asked Charlie. My voice sounded fairly normal, all things considered.

"Yessir, I did."

"They're pretty good." They were landscapes with trees and horses, but no people.

"Thank you kindly."

"You can just call for me when you're ready," Gonzales said. He went out and locked the door.

"I thought you'd be back," Charlie said. "Was there something else you wanted to ask me?" He sat on the edge of the cot, forearms on his knees.

I didn't say anything. I took the Colt out of the waistband of my pants and pointed it at him. I'd already looked it over on the drive up and there were bullets in all six cylinders. My hand was shaking so I steadied it with my left and fired all six rounds into his head and chest.

I hadn't noticed all the background noises until they stopped, the typewriters and the birds and somebody singing upstairs. Charlie stood up and walked over to where I was standing. The revolver clicked on an empty shell.

"You can't get rid of me that easy," Charlie said with his droopy-eyed smile. "I been around too long. I was Spring-heeled Jack and Richard Speck. I was Ted Bundy and that fella up to Seattle they never caught." The door banged open at the end of the hall. "You can't never get rid of me because I'm *inside* you."

I dropped the gun and locked my hands behind my head. Gonzales stuck his head around the corner. He was squinting. He had his gun out and he looked terrified. Charlie and I stared back at him calmly.

"It's okay, Ernie," Charlie said. "No harm done. Mr. McKenna was just having him a little joke."

Charlie told Gonzales the gun was loaded with blanks. They had to believe him because there weren't any bullet holes in the cell. I told them I'd bought the gun off a defendant years ago, that I'd had it in the car.

They called Dallas and Ricky asked to talk to me. "There's going to be an inquest," he said. "No way around it."

"Sure there is," I said. "I quit. I'll send it to you in writing. I'll put it in the mail today. Express."

"You need some help, Dave. You understand what I'm saying to you here? *Professional* help. Think about it. Just tell me you'll think about it."

Gonzales was scared and angry and wanted me charged with smuggling weapons into the jail. The sheriff knew it wasn't worth the headlines and by suppertime I was out.

Jack had already heard about it through some kind of legal grapevine. He thought it was funny. We skipped dinner and went down to the bars on Sixth Street. I couldn't drink anything. I was afraid of going numb, or letting down my guard. But Jack made up for me. As usual.

"Kristi called me today," Jack said. "I told her I didn't know but what you might be going back to Dallas today. Just a kind of feeling I had."

"I'm not going back," I said. "But it was the right thing to tell her."

"Not what it was cracked up to be, huh?"

"Oh yeah," I said. "That and much, much more."

For once he let it go. "You mean you're not going back tonight or not going back period?"

"Period," I said. "My job's gone, I pissed that away this morning. I'll get something down here. I don't care what. I'll pump gas. I'll fucking wait tables. You can draw up the divorce papers and I'll sign them."

"Just like that?"

"Just like that."

"What's Alice going to say?"

"I don't know if she'll even notice. She can have the goddamn house and her car and the savings. All of it. All I want is some time with Jeffrey. As much as I can get. Every week if I can."

"Good luck."

"I've got to have it. I don't want him growing up screwed up like the rest of us. I've got stuff I've got to tell him. He's going to need help. All of us are. Jack, goddamn it, are you listening to me?"

He wasn't. He was staring at the Heart video on the bar's big-screen TV, at the blonde guitarist. "Look at that," Jack said. "Sweet suffering Jesus. Couldn't you just fuck that to death?"

BRUCE BOSTON

In the Darkened Hours

Bruce Boston has written a number of poems and stories that feature rich imagery and a clarity of expression. His dark fantasies are neither offensive nor explosive, yet they hold their own substantial power: the power of precise language to contain and define the darkness in the human soul.

The poem that follows is a simple yet elegant illustration of that power, a visionary dark fantasy about memory and dreams.

—E. D.

IN THE DARKENED HOURS

Bruce Boston

So you are lost again
beneath the turning hub
of the fire flecked sky
and you call it a dream
as you wander the labyrinth
of streets and causeways,
past the shadow barges,
over the ice cloaked river,
down the rugged gullies
where you left behind
the satchels which hold
the weapons and the maps.

So you are lost again
where the night prevails
and you call it a dream
in the oldest city of all,
where the lighted towers
rise and fall like spokes
against the churning sky,
where the voices wail,
where you are engaged
in senseless conversation
with a host of familiar
strangers whose directions
lead you further astray.

So you must travel alone
without weapons or maps
to the house of your father,
past the wrought iron fences,

past the shores and lakes
of the naked arboretum,
past the fallen hillsides
and the deserted air field
where the burning engines
of destruction have fed.
So you climb the stairs
and discover the rooms
of your childhood have
blurred and shifted
like a moldering text,
door frames twisted
at elusive angles,
windows collapsed,
unbounded hallways
and shredded chambers
lifting off into space.

So you are lost again
in the night of the city.
So you must travel alone
to a house drawn from
your flesh and bones.
So you must do this
as the landscape changes.
So you must descend
the rugged gullies
while you forge
the faces of dead lovers.
So you must reassemble
the broken statuary
in your mother's garden
and leave your father's
books upon their shelves.
So you must speak with
the familiar strangers
who know your name.
So you must recite
from the annals
of your stillborn brother,
maniacal and devoted,

who takes your wrist
upon the stairs.

So you call it a dream:
this house you inhabit,
this city you traverse
with blind expectancy,
these faces you fashion
from the imperfect cloth
of memory transfigured,
these visions you conjure
in the darkened hours
with haunting replication.

RU EMERSON

A Golden Net for Silver Fishes

Ru Emerson's first novel was titled *The Princess of Flames* and was published to critical acclaim in 1984. Since then she has published *To the Haunted Mountains* and *In the Caves of Exile*. Her short fiction publications include a lovely story for young readers called "The Werewolf's Gift" in the anthology *Werewolves* (edited by Jane Yolen and Martin H. Greenberg) and a novella in the collection *Spell Singers* (edited by Alan Bard Newcomer.)

"A Golden Net for Silver Fishes" is a gentle story of fantasy that reads like an old folktale half-remembered, although it is newly sprung from the author's pen.

Emerson lives on a mountainside in the wilds of Oregon. This story comes from the pages of *Argos*, a magazine published in the Pacific Northwest.

—T. W.

A GOLDEN NET FOR SILVER FISHES

Ru Emerson

It was silent in the Old Wood, silent and dark. Beyond the thickness of trees, away from their heavy black shadow, the full moon glittered on the meadow, shone pale and blue on the roofs and fences of the village beyond it. The tiny farm town was likewise silent, windows dark, only the shift of cattle and goats locked in their sheds or the fretful cry of a baby to give away it was neither deserted nor a blue-white illusion. An owl's soft call teased at the edge of hearing, was blotted out by the incautious rustling of some frightened animal haring through a drift of leaves.

Leaves without number spread thickly from tree to tree: smooth oak-leaves piled upon the sharp-edged aspen and hawthorne, those mingling with cottony fluff and cottonwood leaves. Brown, sere leaves were a deep, crackly layer beneath the green and yellow ones downed by the storms of a week before. Fat maple leaves buried brambles, so that only the newest growth pushed through them.

The young vixen slid free of her den, a low sound deep in her throat warning the two kits to stay well within the hole until she called them. She worked forward through the tangle of thorn-brush, ears moving rapidly to catch the least sound. She'd know if the great owls were abroad; if one of the badgers was in a foul mood; if one of the bears had come down from the ledges deeper in the woods. On such a night, only they posed an immediate threat to her young; men slept in the houses, out across the shining meadow, their bows tucked behind heavy doors.

She reached the end of the bushes that protected her den, turned to growl another warning as a scrabbling behind caught her attention. Two enormous red ears popped back down out of sight. *Babies. Children. No caution to them. No sense. They'll learn.*

Her own ears pricked as a rustling of a different kind took them. Something walking through the great leaf-drifts without regard to what noise it made, wading through them with long, slow steps that produced a whispery swoosh. She edged back a body length, cast a brief glance toward her burrow, saw it empty and turned back to the clearing.

It was not a true clearing, the ground beyond the tangle where she crouched. There was a little space between the trees there, though; no brush underfoot snagged at feet or tore fur or clothing; even a tall creature could walk there. What came walking there came on two feet: human.

The vixen lay flat, scarcely breathing, but she sensed no immediate danger from this thing. It bore no weapons like men who hunted here now and again. Instead it held two odd things: in one hand, a slender, gleaming trident, with three spade-like points. In the other hand, slung across the back, was a shimmering net that glittered even in this dark place, shining with its own light and revealing the creature carrying it.

Female, by the look and smell of it. A female human in the woods alone, and at night! Truly human, she was, too: she had neither the look nor the odor of witch.

She wore a plain, dark gown that covered the upper part of her arms but bared her legs and feet, for she'd caught the stuff of the skirt up through a wide, practical girdle. Dark hair fell wild across her shoulders. She glanced around nervously—*and so should she be, to come alone to such a place*, the fox thought indignantly—and swung the bag to the ground.

A heavy, load, whatever it was: awkward and nearly as much as she could carry. She bent over it, breathing deeply, her eyes closed. Sweat beaded her forehead, caught bits of dark hair and pasted them to her cheeks and brow. The fox edged forward slightly, unable to decide what the bag was, what it contained. Magic: of course it was magic. None of the woman's magic, though. And it drew her, excited her curiosity. What was it that cast its own light and what was within it to shift and shimmer so?

Magic. Not clean magic either, and she could see, all of a sudden, something of the bag and its contents. Gold mesh gave its own yellow light, casting netshaped diamond shadows across the dead, brown leaves on which it rested. Within that golden mesh, something silver and shimmering-swift moved, first one way, then the other, across the net bag, back again. "By'r mother," the vixen whispered, and slipped her nose under a paw to hold it from trembling. Fish swam there, small, silvery fish darted back and forth, swimming in water no net could hold.

As she watched, the woman straightened, clutched the bag and pulled it open, cautiously, holding the edge high, twisting a golden thread firmly around her hand. With the trident, she ruffled through the dead leaves piled deep around the bag, transferred a tall and delicately balanced stack of them to the bag. They drifted loose, became lustrous, shining —alive. Slender, silvery fishes swam down and away to join the others.

As she worked, the woman sang in a low voice. The fox couldn't make out the words. But she knew sorrow when she heard it, and the curiosity was suddenly more than she could bear.

She warned her kits to stay deep in the den, out of sight, while she herself slid under the last of the bramble and into the open.

"Why do you sing, woman?"

"Oh!" In her surprise, the woman nearly lost hold of the bag, and one or two small fish slopped over the edge. They slid down the mesh part way, lost their sheen and floated, dead leaves again, to the forest floor. "Who speaks?"

"Only I, Veda. Why do you take the leaves?"

"Because I must—ah, I see you now. Good greetings, Red Lady Veda. I am Brynwyn."

"Good greetings to you, sorrowful Lady Brynwyn." Veda sat back on her haunches, her gaze divided between dark woman and radiant bag. "Why do you take the leaves? They shelter and protect those too small to dare the open forest. Is your need greater than theirs?" Silence. "Or your sorrow?"

"My sorrow is such that I would take the living leaves from the branches, if it would give me back my child." Brynwyn stared at the golden bag and its swimming mass as though seeing through it.

"Many lose children," Veda replied. Her own gaze kept returning to the shining bundle; she tore it away. Magic, not a clean kind. Such magic could bind, and her kits still needed her. "It is the way of things. We get others." The woman's loss smote at her; she had lost kits, once. She'd got others. But the pain of it—

"I'm sorry. It's not the same for me. She is—Edda is—" The woman swallowed, turned away.

"When did she die?"

"She's prisoner." Brynwyn ran a hand under her nose and sniffed loudly, rubbed her eyes hard. Her voice quavered. "And to win her free, I must fill the pool yonder with fishes."

"Ah." Suddenly it made sense, of a kind. *That* pool. Well, it was not really her business, Veda thought, she had matters of her own to tend, and the nixie Dri was no one to cross. As this human had learned. "Grant you luck in your quest, then, Lady Brynwyn."

"Thank you." The woman was bending over her bag again before the fox was out of sight. Veda took her kits out the back way. The woman's unhappy song followed them into the distance.

Brynwyn cleaned that pile of leaves to the base of the tree and all around it, and the bag was almost unbearably heavy when she swung it back onto her shoulder. Not too heavy to carry, however. The more fishes she brought to Dri's lake, the sooner the task would be done and the sooner Edda might again be hers.

Fool, she whispered to herself, as she staggered through the dark trees. The bag was damp against her back. Fool, on all counts. To have cared for Brienen enough to wed him when the sign of the wasting illness was already on him. Fool, more, to have settled all the love that had been Brienen's on their only child. But Edda was the image of Brienen, and without her life would have been dull and grey indeed after Brienen died.

Fool again, to let the child play away from her, knowing Edda had Brienen's curiosity, knowing the woods could be so unsafe. And so Dri had taken her, and when a terrified Brywyn had come looking for the child, Dri made the bargain: fish to fill her pond in exchange for the child.

But Dri ate so many of them every day, and the pool filled so slowly. *I'll have cleared the woods of fallen leaves, all of them, before she is satisfied.*

"Edda," she whispered, and a tear slipped down her face to mingle with the silvery fishes. She swallowed, pulled open a corner of the net and began to fill it.

The second pile of leaves was not as large as the first; but it would do to finish filling the net for this night. Behind her, for a distance of a barn length, the ground was bare. Dri would scold, but there was no help for it, she was too worn to carry more and the need to see the child was an unbearable pain.

"Lady?" A burring voice near her foot slid into her thoughts, bringing her back to the moment. "Lady Brynwyn?"

"Who—is it you, by my foot?" Brynwyn crouched down, one hand out-flung to keep the bag from tipping and spilling its precious, hard-sought cargo. It swayed gently with the motion of the fishes as they swam to one side, shifted, swam back. A bird no longer than her hand hopped onto her foot and then onto her free hand. She brought it nearer her face.

It stepped onto the side of her hand, gazed at her directly. It was a nightjar: small, mottled brown, hard to see even in the daylight, well-nigh invisible here and now. Small whiskers framed the blunt beak. "I heard you speaking with Veda," he said in his soft burring voice. "I am Crooh," the R rolled generously, "and I must ask you to open the nixie's enchanted net, for my family went in with your last handful of leaves."

"Oh, no!" Brynwyn whispered aghast. The bag trembled as she pulled the opening wide, and more fish sloshed over the edge to become leaves once again halfway to the ground. Crooh flew from her hand to catch the far strings in his beak as she thrust her hand into the net: his strength wasn't enough to keep the bag from tilting but the string loosened no further. Brynwyn's arm came out wet to the elbow, a motley collection of twigs, leaves and wet birds in her hand. Crooh's mate shook indignantly, splattering them all; the chicks made unhappy little sounds. Brynwyn deposited them on the ground, brought out leaves to surround and hide them. She drew the strings snug, and Crooh fluttered anxiously down.

Brynwyn knelt. "My apologies, brown lady."

"Huh." But Crooh murmured against her ear and she subsided on her pile of now dry leaves. The chicks crept under her wings and grew silent.

"And to you, Crooh."

"You undid the fault, do not fret it." He studied her. "You are the woman whose child the nixie holds." He didn't really need to ask. As a night flyer, he saw more of Dri than the day beasts did, knew more of her intentions than he cared to. More than even the owls did, since he was smaller and less visible—even to nixie-eyes. "She'll not let the child go," Crooh added gently. "You know that."

Brynwyn dropped heavily to the ground, one hand automatically steadying the net, and drew her knees up to her chin. "I . . . sometimes I fear it." She sighed miserably. "But she swore an oath, Dri did, that Edda would again be mine when the pond was filled with fishes."

"And how well have you done, filling that pond?" Crooh prompted quietly.

Brynwyn sighed again, let her eyes close. "She eats four parts of those I bring. I'll be worn into my grave before it's filled." Her gaze dropped to the pile of twigs, nightjar and birdlings. "I'm sorry for this, Crooh, but I have no choice. Dri may yet give me my child back. And it is the only way I can see her, my Edda, even though she isn't aware of me."

"No. Dri keeps her asleep, in a coracle woven of moonstuff."

Brynwyn's head came up and she stared at him. "How did you know that?"

"I've seen. When you pour out the fishes, the water in the pond rises with the weight of them, and the coracle sinks out of sight, beneath the water." The nightjar gazed at her, and there was sympathy in the brown eyes. "You cannot fill Dri's pond, by yourself and unaided. She's greedy, you cannot fetch faster than she can eat." Silence. "It would take all the fallen leaves from one side of these woods to the other; it would take those still on the trees, those not yet budded, years of them and more years still. Are you so patient? Or so strong?"

"If I must be." Brynwyn's chin was set but her shoulders drooped.

"If you can be," the bird corrected her softly. "And if you do what she wants, and if somehow you should fill her pond with fishes, when the last bagful goes in, the water will overflow the coracle and the banks. The pond will become a vast lake with the tall, dead trees that were this forest in its depths. It will drown all creatures foolish enough to remain near it—*and* the woman who fed it. The child will by then be of an age to take up the net."

"No." It was barely a whisper, a sound Crooh sensed more than heard. The bag of fishes swayed and sloshed; Brynwyn grabbed at it and held it firm, but her hand trembled.

"That is the nixie's intention. But there is a way to thwart her. If the coracle could be borne away, the leaves scattered, the net shredded, all at once—

Brynwyn let her head fall forward onto her knees. Crooh flew up to her shoulder and perched near her ear, casting a warning glance down to his wife, who was still muttering in her damp nest. She glared back up at him but quieted once again.

"If I tried that, Crooh, and failed, she'd take Edda forever, and kill me then and there."

"You've lost already; the nixie has the bargain fully balanced to her side. Your death waits for you, a handful of years hence. The child will have long years and hard, serving Dri before she too grows old and dies. Death for her and for you, now, instead: is that more a failure than your loss, and the child's, if you fill the pool?"

A pause. Brynwyn shook her head; her eyes were desperate. "I . . . I can't touch Dri's coracle, no one can. It's moonstuff, you can't hold that! It's like clutching at air, like building a box of water!"

"And those," Crooh said gently, a bob of his head indicating the net, "are dead leaves caught in a bag woven of rushes." Silence again. An owl hooted not far away and something bounded across the clearing, seeking the shelter of a thorn bush. "You can touch moonlight. The same as the leaves you push into that net shift against your back and leave your gown wet. You have only to see it, or to feel it, to know it." Brynwyn shook her head in silent disbelief. The spirit was gone from her once again; she scrubbed at her eyes with the back of her free hand. "Fear and grief blind you, woman, you cannot think it through in such a state. Take your net full of fishes, go see your child."

Brynwyn struggled to her feet. "You are that much right. I cannot think. I am tired and worn, and I see no way to do what you say."

"If there was a way," the bird urged. "If there was, would you spill the leaves?"

"I—if Edda—I don't know." She shook her head. "I'm sorry, Crooh. I don't know."

"Go. Look upon your child. Be ready." Crooh fluttered from her shoulder and vanished in the dark between the trees. Brynwyn stared after him, too exhausted to attempt to puzzle his meaning, too miserable to dare hope. The shifting bag was a weight against her leg, and the net rubbed her bare skin.

Middle night. Brynwyn staggered past the last trees, through the low willow brush that edged the stream, turned and followed it a distance. The meadow was ghostly, the grasses thick and soaked with dew; young frogs peeped and chirked at a distance, falling silent as she passed. The stream vanished in a bog; she turned away from it, bore right and climbed a low hill. A mirror of a pond, a circular mere, lay below her.

Brush and hedge-roses edged its north side, wild iris dipped into the water to her right; a few cattails clustered against the near bank. She stopped when her bare toes squelched into mud and water washed against her ankles. She stepped back onto firm ground, slung the bag from her shoulders. Waited.

"You are late. Do you not miss the child as much as you did?" The sibilant voice tickled her ears and the loose hair against her neck. Dri appeared as she always did, without warning, appearing to stand among the cattails and no higher than they, her skin and clothing shifting like the water behind her. Tonight she'd been gathering roses, and had twined them in her hair, in a band around her wrist.

Brynwyn kept her silence. It never did any good to argue with the creature, or to apologize, and she'd long since given over doing either. If she'd mentioned rescuing Crooh's mate and young, the nixie would have railed at her for it. "That is a fine bag you have for me—is it full? Well, full enough, I suppose, for now." Dri faded, vanished briefly, appeared suddenly mid-pond, and with a tinkling laugh dove beneath the water.

In her place, a shining skeleton of a round-boat slowly rose until it floated motionless on the still surface. Within the half circle of moonlight coracle, a sleeping child lay on her side, one small brown hand tucked under a flushed cheek. She vanished in a haze of tears. Brynwyn wiped them away and gazed hungrily at her child.

So near! Seven steps, straight distance, would have brought them together! But as soon as she entered the pond, the coracle would sink. As it would when she poured the contents of the net into the water.

"You have looked long enough. Now." Dri's resonant whisper filled her head, coming from everywhere and nowhere. "Not yet," Brynwyn begged, but her only answer was the demanding "Now." She turned, knelt by the bag, fumbled with the knot, spending as much time as she dared, her eyes all the while on the coracle. "Now!" Dri's shout made her ears ring. She dragged the bag to the water's edge and with one last anguished look at her sleeping child, loosed the ties.

Fishes and water began to pour in a sparkling stream from the net; the pool rose, lapped at her toes. The coracle began to sink. *"Now!"* There was a sudden anxiety in the nixie's order, and a growing sense of *something* in the air. The frogs were silenced, a wind bent the iris and rustled the dry cattails. Brynwyn snatched up the cords to halt the spill and spun around, her free hand raised in defense against whatever was there.

Birds, and more birds. An enormous shadow like a solid, single thing followed them across the meadow. Owls were there: the great horned, elf owls, the rare whites. Nighthawks. Nightjars by the hundred, or so it seemed to Brynwyn, who stood and stared up into the black masses of them.

Behind her the nixie shrieked in rage, but too late: the birds swept low, seized moonlight crossbeams and bore the coracle away. The bag fell from Brynwyn's hand; with sudden determination she caught it up, dragged it away from the pond and tore it open. A handful of fishes spilled from it, a cupful of water sloshed to dry ground. *Dry ground.* There was no more mud here, no water. The nixie's pool was shrinking.

Leaves swirled high in a whirlwind gust, blew across the meadow and vanished into the night. The net went up with the last of them, turned end for end, sailed across the pond and snagged on the rose bushes. Brynwyn ran after it.

Her sleeves ripped on thorns and blood trailed down her forearm as she fumbled for the long strings. She tugged: once, twice. The third time the ties came away in her hand. She stared at them: they were already unraveling on her palm. "Dry grass," she muttered. Brown, sere grass unwound itself and lay in shreds on the dwindling water.

She tore at the net. A pile of rushes lay at her feet; she caught them up in scratched and bleeding fingers, threw them into the wind and fled.

The pond was the size of a well and still shrinking; she could have leaped over it. There was no sign of Dri.

The wind blew a final gust, wailed across the grass, dragged Brynwyn's hair back from her face and cooled her cheeks. It fell to nothing then, gone as suddenly as it came. The meadow was silent, so silent she could hear the soft voices of nightjars, just over the hill. And among them, no louder than they, the call of a small child waking from a long nap.

JIM AIKIN

Dancing Among Ghosts

Jim Aikin has published one well-received novel, *Walk the Moons Road*, and numerous works of short fiction. A composer, he is the Associate Editor of *Keyboard* magazine. He lives in northern California, juggling three careers.

"Dancing Among Ghosts" is a splendid tale of contemporary fantasy and has my vote for the best story of the year. Like the artist in his story, Aikin paints a dark yet highly detailed scene, peopled with vivid characters, to draw you from your own world into his.

—T. W.

DANCING AMONG GHOSTS

Jim Aikin

The Almond Sauce wasn't thickening properly under the chicken, only scorching around the sides of the pan, and of course she had discovered halfway through mixing the special salad dressing that she was completely out of tarragon, and Tony was being no help whatever, which was definitely a disappointment—but then, he came from an old-fashioned family, so Carla guessed she had to make allowances. When she asked him to run down to the store for the tarragon and a couple of other things, he had wandered out of the room without actually saying no, and now he was sitting in the living room, banging out the same seven and a half bars of some fifties rock song over and over on the piano, which belatedly she realized she ought to have had tuned, just in case Guy or Dory played, or asked her to play. Tony was making the same thick-fingered mistakes every time, losing the beat, and starting again, all the while moaning tunelessly but emphatically, like a walrus flopping around on the floor of a shower stall. Carla wiped her hands on the brand-new apron, reached for the lid of the electric skillet to sniff the zucchini—and jerked her hand back, burned. The lid fell, slid, and bounced clattering to the floor. She sucked vigorously on her finger. "Damn!"

The piano and the walrus noises stopped. Tony appeared in the doorway, appraised the situation swiftly, and put on a grin that was more amused than solicitous. He leaned against the doorjamb and folded his arms. "Everything under control?"

She grabbed a dish towel and bent to retrieve the lid, which went under the faucet for a quick rinse. "I didn't know you played the piano."

"We had one for a couple of years when I was a kid." If he noticed her sharp tone, he ignored it. Which was one of the things she liked most about him—not only handsome, with his dark curly hair and square jaw, but willing to put up with her when she wasn't at her best. "My brother was the one that got the lessons. Lot of good it ever did him. You burn yourself?"

"A little."

He took her hand gently, examined and then kissed the red place, and murmured "*Cara mia.*"

Which was really very nice, she reflected. It almost made up for not getting the tarragon.

"What time did they say they'd be here?"

Carla glanced at the clock. "Seven. It's only twenty past. Why don't you set the table?"

As he was looking around in vague discomfort at the shuttered mystery of the cabinets, the downstairs buzzer buzzed. Normally she would call down to find out who it was, even when she was expecting guests. But with Tony here, she felt safe enough to be reckless. She thumbed the black button, held it down for a couple of seconds, and went back to the kitchen. The cabinets and drawers were still firmly closed, but in the other room the stereo came unobtrusively to life with the first notes of the new Pat Metheny album. She throttled her annoyance. He is trying to be a good host, she chided herself. It's just like a bachelor. He's not domesticated yet. Or maybe all men were like that. What did she know about home life, with her background? She turned everything on the stove down low, so it would keep for a few minutes, and hung her apron over the back of a chair.

When the doorbell rang, she sprang down the hall like a colt, but forced herself to pause in the entry to take a deep breath and survey herself swiftly in the mirror. Makeup in good order. (And the rest of her, much as usual—the straw-colored eyes set wide apart, nose a bit too large, generous mouth, hair cut fashionably short and streaked a lighter blonde than the roots.) A sudden stab of insecurity: she should definitely have worn something more conservative than the tight gray leather jeans and bright turquoise sweater. The Rossiters were nearly old enough to be her parents, but she had persuaded herself that a dress would look too obsequious, that they would feel more at home if they thought she felt at home. Now it was obviously the wrong outfit. Too late to do anything. She squared her shoulders, smiled, and opened the door.

The solitary figure outside, huddled inside a large dark coat and clutching a rectangle of cardboard under one arm, was not Guy and Dory Rossiter. Carla blinked stupidly. A single luminescent green eye peered back at her, set deep in a putty-colored face; the other eye was hidden behind a shock of unwashed black hair. "Joelle. I was expecting somebody else." She realized how awful that sounded. "I mean, gee, it's good to see you. It's been—how long has it been? Weeks. Hi. Come on in."

"I can't stay. I came to drop this off." Joelle Cogburn lifted the cardboard rectangle a few inches, let it fall back to her side.

"You've got to come in, at least for a minute. I never see you anymore. You're always hiding in your studio." Awkward seconds passed; Joelle made no move to enter. Carla realized she was still blocking the doorway. She stepped aside. "You're looking good." A transparent lie. Joelle looked dreadful. Maybe it was that horrible coat. The fabric was clumped and threadbare, and it was several sizes too large for Joelle's emaciated frame. If she had bought it in one of the secondhand shops where she got most of her clothes, it probably smelled, too, sour and musty. "Let me take your coat."

"I can't stay, really." Joelle's gaze slid uneasily. "You're expecting company. Anyhow, I'm in the middle of something. I have to get back." But she allowed Carla to herd her into the living room.

"You know Tony, don't you? You mean you two haven't met yet? Oh, I don't believe it. Well, I must have told you about him. He's—"

"I don't—," Joelle began.

"Tony, this is my friend Joelle. Joelle's the painter. We went to college together. I told you about when we went to Paris, didn't I? Joelle is the one I went with. Now Joelle, be nice to Tony. He's special."

If Tony was nonplussed by the coat, he gave no sign. He extended his hand with perfect seriousness. "It's a pleasure." Joelle tried to raise her right arm, noticed that it was occupied holding the cardboard rectangle, started to maneuver the rectangle, which was covered with stiff, crinkling brown paper, around to her other side, changed her mind, grunted, turned her back to Tony in order to set the rectangle with great care on the coffee table, and then, instead of turning back at once, proceeded to shrug, in a series of bony contortions, out of the coat, which Carla snagged before it could touch the floor, and picked the rectangle up again and tucked it after a moment of deliberation under her left arm, before extending her right. During this entire performance, poor Tony stood with his hand out, smiling the indulgent smile of a man who is used to dealing with wayward children and has nothing better to do. Having permitted him a quick, nervous handshake, she trapped the rectangle against her body again with her left arm and right hand both, as though afraid a gust of wind might tear it from her.

Now where to put the coat, Carla wondered, gazing around in muted alarm. Not on the couch. There might be fleas. Even roaches. At the very least, spots of wet paint. Not in the hall closet; the Rossiters might be here at any moment, and it would be awkward trying to warn Tony not to hang theirs next to it. And certainly not in the kitchen, not with dinner on. At last she bore it away into the bedroom, where it collapsed reluctantly in a corner on the floor, like a mangy bearskin whose bear has gone on to better things.

How could she explain Joelle to Tony? She certainly didn't want him to get the impression that, well, not bums—Joelle wasn't a bag lady or anything—but people who didn't take proper care of themselves, were constantly dropping in on her. That wasn't Tony's style at all. Carla rooted in the top drawer of the bureau and found, beneath the hairpins and eyeliner, the snapshot taken the week before she and Joelle left for Paris. They had gone off after graduation to study art and music and drink red wine with earnest young Marxists in the cafés on the Left Bank; Carla's Marxist, she remembered, ate quantities of garlic, and Joelle's stole her passport. The whole fiasco lasted less than two months. They had been in the hostel only three days when Carla picked up a newspaper and learned that Nadia Boulanger had died, which made confetti of the elaborate schemes Carla had concocted for getting introduced to her so she could show her the score of the *Nocturne for Orchestra*. Then Joelle's psoriasis flared up, and Carla got a bladder infection, and in the end they were both miserably seasick all the way home. But the girls in the photo didn't know that yet. One blonde and one dark, they were as alike as sisters, arms draped across each other's shoulders, grinning at the camera. Neither of them, when Carla looked closer, looked like anybody she knew. Or like anybody Tony would especially want to know. Feeling obscurely sad, she pitched the picture back into the drawer.

Back in the living room, Tony was saying, "Actually, if anything, sales is *more* creative than the so-called creative end of the business. What the artist produces is just a lump of coal. My job is turning coal into diamonds." He fingered a cuff link.

Joelle, in a paint-spattered sweatshirt and baggy trousers, was standing with one fist parked on her bony hip, head cocked sideways. Carla knew the pose. Expecting to see the disgusted sneer that would mean Joelle had decided Tony was a jerk, she stepped to Tony's side to protect him from Joelle's scorn, but then she saw that Joelle was barely listening. The iridescent green eyes were staring vacantly at some inner vista.

Carla leaned against Tony and walked her fingernails affectionately up his back. "Actually," she told Joelle, "it's a real coincidence, your dropping by tonight. The people that are coming, Guy Rossiter and his wife, Guy is in charge of the D'Arle account. He's the one who has to approve your work. If he likes it, he might even commission a whole series."

"I don't know if this is such a good idea," Joelle said. "I mean, I need the money. I don't want to sound ungrateful. But it didn't come out right. It kept getting away from me."

The downstairs buzzer buzzed. "That'll be them," Carla said. "Could you get it, hon?" To Joelle: "You did it the way I explained, didn't you? The woman rushing down the long hall?"

"That part's all right. But I wasn't sure where she was going, or why. I got confused."

"Joelle, you're beating yourself up again. We've had this conversation before."

"Yes, Mommy." Joelle wouldn't meet Carla's eyes. She stood staring down at the piano.

"I'm not your mommy, but somebody's got to talk some sense into you. You're incredibly talented; you know that. But you always assume the worst. You assume people are going to despise your work for no reason. It's like you're walking around with a big sign on that says, 'Reject me, I'm no good.' Is it any wonder people reject you? You don't give them a chance to do anything else. Honestly, how are you ever going to be successful if you let your feelings get in the way?"

Joelle looked up. For a moment something golden danced in her eyes, so like reflected flame that Carla thought, Oh, Tony lit a fire in the fireplace, how nice—and actually turned to admire the burning logs before she remembered that the apartment didn't have a fireplace. But all Joelle said was, "You're going to be mad at me."

"Don't be an idiot. I *will* get mad if you don't start acting more confident."

But Joelle wouldn't budge. "I *am* confident. I'm absolutely sure you're going to be mad at me."

The doorbell rang. Carla touched Joelle's arm and said in a lower voice, "Are you doing okay? You don't look well."

"I'm okay," Joelle blurted hoarsely. "I'm a little behind on the rent, is all."

"I thought Richard was helping with the rent."

Joelle's mouth went wooden. "I don't want to talk about Richard."

"I don't want to pry, but—are you eating? Have you got enough money for food?"

Joelle sank down on the edge of the couch and rubbed her knuckles stiffly. "I'm doing okay. I don't need much."

Into the living room sailed Guy and Dory Rossiter, plump and glittering, moving like sleek ships in a calm sea. Carla performed introductions. "Joelle didn't even know you were going to be here tonight," she finished. "She just came by to drop off her proposal for the d'Arle account, and I insisted that she at least stay long enough to meet you."

"Perhaps she should stay for dinner," Guy murmured agreeably, "so we can get better acquainted."

Which put Carla in an impossible bind. Joelle certainly needed a good meal, to say nothing of the value of getting her name and face firmly planted in Guy's notorious slippery mind. As simple a thing as an evening of sociable conversation might do her a world of good. And sending her off into the cold would be unthinkably cruel. On the other hand, she certainly wasn't dressed for dinner, and her abrasive turbulence could easily turn the party into a disaster. The occasion was important to Carla: not only her first evening of domestic entertaining with Tony as a couple, but her first chance to socialize with one of the agency vice presidents on something like an equal footing. Joelle would have been an intrusion, a disruption, even if she hadn't looked so disreputable.

All this flashed by in an instant. Carla smiled. "I don't see why not." If Guy was going to issue the invitation, though, at least let him make an informed decision. Carla gestured at the coffee table. "She was just going to show us the art she did for the layout." They all looked at the brown rectangle. "Well, go ahead," Carla said to Joelle. "Pick it up."

"I don't think this is such a good idea," Joelle said miserably. "Maybe I should just go."

Carla was getting irritated. Here she was trying to do Joelle a favor, and Joelle was too obtuse even to cooperate. Not only that, but what would Guy think the next time Carla brought him a freelancer, if this one never even got out of the starting gate? "Joelle's always shy about having people see a new painting," Carla explained. Which was true, as far as it went. "She has a big bed sheet rigged up in her studio, like a stage curtain on a curtain rod over the easel, so when you visit, you can't see what she's working on unless it's finished."

"I can feel it afterward," Joelle said in a sepulchral monotone. "Even if they don't say anything. Their eyes leave smears, and I can't get them out." If the sheet was raised when you came into the studio, Carla knew, it meant the painting was finished. You could look at it all you wanted, and say whatever you liked. Joelle accepted praise and criticism alike with a bored expression, nodding abstractedly, often changing the subject without acknowledging the comment. Once a painting was done, it was a child abandoned by its mother, Joelle seemed to want nothing further to do with it. Yet here she was, fingering a corner of the brown paper and nibbling at her lip. Carla had never seen her display this kind of diffidence.

"My dear," Dory Rossiter gushed, "artists are always so sensitive. I adore art. You must show us what you've done. You must."

"Well, I guess so." Joelle held the cardboard out crookedly in front of her. "But don't say I didn't warn you." The paper crackled as she lifted it.

They pressed forward. Standing on tiptoe so she could peer around Tony's shoulder without falling sideways over the coffee table, Carla was at the wrong angle to see details. At first glance, the gouache looked to be exactly what she had told Joelle the d'Arle perfume campaign called for—a young woman from the pages of a Gothic romance novel, fleeing (from some unnamed terror? toward the muscular arms of a young cavalry lieutenant?) down an endless hallway of brooding arches, her full skirt trailing behind her on the flagstone floor. The rich browns and floral highlights were perfect. Carla felt a moment of relief. Joelle had captured just the right mood to sell a perfume that, while not expensive, was meant to seem exclusive.

Dory Rossiter gasped, and Tony made a strangled sound. Carla wedged herself between Tony and Guy for a better look, and her warm glow drained into cold shock. The central figure in the painting, while wearing the right costume, fell somewhat short of a proper Gothic heroine's physical perfection. Her arms were slim, yes, and gracefully extended in poetic agitation. Her snow-white breast all but visibly heaved. Her face, however, was not lovely, not delicate, not alluring. The face was a bestial distortion, the jaw jutting forward to reveal vulpine lower teeth, the thick-boned hairy brow plainly modeled on a gorilla's. And from the walls around the woman, an elaborate frieze of imps and gargoyles leered menacingly down, demonic eyes glowing coal-red, their naked limbs obscenely intertwined.

Guy cleared his throat delicately. "It's really quite remarkable," he said. "I don't know that I've ever seen anything quite like it." He leaned forward to examine the brushwork. "Technically superb, of course. . . ."

Tony came to the rescue. "Guy, could I get you a drink? Dory, anything for you?"

Carla took Joelle's elbow. "If you'll excuse us for a minute?" She propelled Joelle in the direction of the bedroom. Over her shoulder she called, "Fix me a highball, would you?"

Joelle's green eyes glistened with tears. "How could you?" Carla stormed.

"I tried to warn you," Joelle said. "But you wouldn't listen."

"Cover it up, for God's sake. I don't want to look at it. Was this supposed to be some kind of sick joke, or did you seriously expect—*agh*."

Joelle's hands were trembling as she fumbled at the paper. "I did the best I could. I didn't want to, but I thought maybe somehow. . . . I knew you'd be mad. I knew I shouldn't have wasted the time on it." Her body twisted crooked, like a puppet whose strings are tangled.

"Well, for once you were absolutely right." But Carla's anger drained away suddenly, exposing the rocky bed of shame beneath it. "Oh shit, Jo, I'm sorry. Never mind. It's all my fault. I never should have—"

"You were only trying to help. It's my fault. I'm just no good. I shouldn't be allowed to live."

"Come on, honey, don't talk like that. It scares me when you talk like that." Carla rubbed Joelle's shoulder lightly, tentatively, wanting to embrace her and afraid she would spring away like a startled fawn. Joelle rocked woodenly, staring at the rug. "How are you and Richard getting along?" Carla asked, knowing it was the wrong thing to ask but able to think of nothing else.

"I told him to take his mud pies and clear out."

"Oh no. I'm so sorry." Richard, Carla recalled vaguely, sculpted in clay, great brooding lumps stuck with broken dowels and scraps of burlap.

"Don't be. He called me an illustrator."

"Because you were working on this?"

"Before that. Why do I have to get stuck with these creeps? Why?"

"Peter wasn't so bad."

"Peter was a faggot."

"Well, I suppose that did have some drawbacks. Joelle, I wish you'd at least think about getting some kind of job. I heard they're hiring at Bloomingdale's for Christmas."

"You know what they do to you at Bloomingdale's?" Joelle's voice rose hysterically. "They make this nice, neat cut around the top of your head, and they lift a section of the skull off—" She mimed the action. "—and they make you sit under a big conveyor belt in the basement while they stuff you full of bits and pieces of *dead toys*." The last two words shook with an acid mixture of laughter and dread.

"Joelle, are you feeling all right? You don't look well."

"They're all walking on glass."

"Well, all right. I guess maybe that's not such a good idea." Carla reached for her purse and brought out the checkbook and a pen. "How much do you need?"

"It's five hundred a month for that place. Do you believe that? Five hundred a month, and no heat. I called the landlord. I had to go down to the pay phone at the Laundromat."

"What's his name?"

"Weintraub. Morris Weintraub."

Carla hesitated, looked again at Joelle, licked her upper lip, and inked a check to Morris Weintraub for a thousand dollars. It would put a big dent in her savings, but she felt terribly guilty about the mess with Guy. It was all her fault, for not being more sensitive to what Joelle was trying to tell her. And besides, she didn't want Joelle to end up on the street, especially in this weather. "Give him this. And tell him to turn the heat back on."

Joelle stared at the check stupidly. "You don't have to do this," she asserted. "I don't need charity. I'll get by."

"It's a loan. And here—here's fifty dollars for groceries. I want you to be strong enough to take your stuff around to some more galleries. I just know somebody's going to love it before long. I can feel it. All you have to sell is one painting, and you can pay me back."

Joelle crushed the check shoving it into her pants pocket. "You should come by," she said. "As soon as I'm done with the new one, you have to come see it. I think maybe it's the best thing I've ever done."

"One of your ice palaces?" For the past year, Joelle had been doing interiors of oddly angled buildings—in the blue depths of whose transparent walls, weirdly refracted faces could sometimes be glimpsed, elongated like rubber masks and crying out in pain.

"No. You'll like this one. It's got music."

"Music in a painting?"

"At first I thought everybody could hear it. Dum-dah dum dum dum dum." Joelle's hand twitched in a spastic parody of an orchestra conductor. "It got so loud I couldn't sleep, and underneath it there were voices, a bunch of conversations all going at once. I though they were having a party downstairs, and I went down and screamed at them, but then I saw there wasn't any party. That's when I knew I had to paint it."

Auditory hallucinations. Great. "Joelle, I really think maybe you ought to see a doctor. I can find out—"

"There's nothing wrong with me," Joelle snapped. "I'm fine. You're just jealous. You're trying to confuse me into thinking I'm one of your ghosts."

"Ghosts?" Carla was drifting into the headache she usually got sooner or later trying to follow the twists and turnings of Joelle's private labyrinth.

"I have to be getting back." Joelle picked up the horrid coat. "They need me."

"What's this about ghosts?"

"The painting," Joelle explained, exasperated. "Only, see, they're my ghosts." She smiled thinly. "It makes all the difference."

"I still don't understand."

"You used to." After a queer, crooked, piercing look at Carla from under the lank lock of greasy hair, she said again, "You used to know." She squirmed into the coat, and shrank a little within its dark folds. "But you forgot."

2

A week after their first dinner party, they had their first argument. Tony wanted her to fly down to Fort Lauderdale for Christmas. For some reason that she couldn't quite put her finger on, Carla was desperate not to go.

"You don't like flying," Tony suggested.

"No, it's not that. I like flying. It's just—oh, I don't know." She didn't want to refuse point-blank, for fear he'd think she was rejecting him. If he thought that, he might start to lose interest in her. So she stalled, hoping he'd take the hint.

But he kept after her. "You'll have a great time, I promise. The weather is fantastic. Not like this crap." He gestured through the windshield at the lowering sky. Swirling down between the tall buildings, snowflakes were beginning to settle like a crust of powdered sugar on the rutted slush.

"I like New York at Christmas. All the Santas, and the lights. It wouldn't be the same in Florida. Why can't we stay here and have our own little tree and everything?"

"Mama is pestering me to meet you. And hey, I want to show you off. Anything wrong with that?" Tony flipped the Porsche into the left lane, accelerated around a truck, and plunged through a yellow light. "My brothers will be there with their wives, and they will *die* of jealousy. You're gorgeous. You'll be the star of the show."

"Well, it would be nice to get away from the cold for a few days."

"Right. They'll warm you right up. Real Italian hospitality. Make you feel like a member of the family."

A lump of cold grease congealed in Carla's throat. "I can't. I just can't." That's what it was—family. After five foster homes in nine years, and the convent school in between, she didn't know how to act around a real family.

"Have you got too much to do at the office? Because I'll talk to Guy."

"It's not the office."

"Mama's got the guest room all fixed up for you, and—"

"Whoa. Whoa. The guest room?" Carla covered her eyes with her hand, laughing but not really laughing. "Let's see if I've got this straight. They're going to treat me like a member of the family, but you sleep in your room, and I sleep in the guest room?"

"Mama's old-fashioned. You have to understand."

"Unh-unh. No, thanks. I spent too many years in guest rooms when I was a kid. If you're not honest enough to admit to her that we're sleeping together, and if she can't accept that, then it's not even worth discussing."

Tony's face darkened. "She's my mother."

"And how old are you, thirteen?"

"What's that supposed to mean? I live my own life. But she's entitled to respect."

"So am I, buster." She was surprised to hear her voice shake. Thirteen: that was the year she lived with the Martins in Cincinnati, Mr. Martin with his big red face always drinking beer at the kitchen table, and Mrs. Martin who never stopped sniffling and wiping her nose and whining about what a burden Carla was. She had prayed for the Martins to send her away, but when they did, she was surprised to find that it hurt just as much as the other times.

"It's only for a couple of days. What are you making such a big deal about?"

"If you don't know. . . ."

"I don't. Honestly, I don't. I'm *not* sure I *care*." They rode for several blocks in a silence punctuated by the thumps and whines of Tony's savage jerks on the gearshift. By the time he found a parking place, Carla was feeling thoroughly wretched. Wasn't this what she had always wanted —to be part of a family? What right did she have to march in and impose her own rules on them? You're simply not being sensible, she told herself sternly. What's so bad about a few days in Florida? You'll have to meet them sooner or later. Either that, or break it off with Tony. Which would be idiotic. Where are you going to find another guy with his kind of prospects? And if you do find another guy, and he falls for you, guess what? He'll want to take you home to meet his family.

Still scowling, Tony opened the door for her, and she stepped out into the biting wind. Well, all right. She'd go. She'd force herself. And probably end up having a wonderful time. But it wouldn't do to give in too quickly. It set a precedent. Let him stew for a few minutes.

The elevator, not plush but reasonably modern, whisked them up five flights. Tony took off his gloves, folded them, and put them in his coat pocket, still staring straight ahead. The door he knocked on was opened after a minute by a faintly shaggy young man in a rumpled shirt, who nodded and said, "Mr. Da Costa. Come on in. We've just got the basic tracks laid down."

The flat was larger than Carla's, but had far less free floor space. The living room was crammed with gear—a tall rack studded with winking lights and twitching needles, a tape deck with fat spools, and several keyboards on a tiered stand. She stopped just inside the door, awestruck as always by the mysterious alchemical apparatus of contemporary music. She had once shepherded a piece of hers through the recording process, but that was with a two-track Sony on a table at the back of the recital hall, and a pair of mikes stuck up in front of the faculty string quartet. This setup was in another galaxy.

Two electric guitar players, one with a six-string and one with a bass, coolly eyed the newcomers. The shaggy young man didn't introduce them. "Let me play you what we've got," he said. "See what you think." He tapped one button, and the tape whizzed, braked, reversed itself, and rolled forward. The speakers had no grill cloths, and the black cones pulsed and trembled with every beat.

The track was only sixty seconds long. When it had wrapped itself in a fast fade-out, Tony said, "What the hell was that crap? I thought you were doing the Cato jeans spot today."

The young man blushed. "Uh, that was the Cato jingle, Mr. Da Costa." Of course. Carla recognized the tune now, though she hadn't while it was playing. The arranger had built a haunting series of jazz chord substitutions on the hackneyed tune and poured them out like a layer of honey on a submerged girderwork of weirdly accented percussion, which boomed and echoed like distant cannon fire. "It's slow motion, is all, just like you wanted."

"I know what the Cato jingle sounds like," Tony stated. "That was not the Cato jingle. You think I don't know the Cato jingle when I hear it?"

"Uh, Tony. . . ."

"Not now, Carla. Look, Stu—"

"Steve," the young man corrected. "If you'll just let me explain, Mr. Da Costa. We were trying to do something a little creative here. Just listen to it once more before you make up your mind; that's all I ask. Let me explain the concept."

"You're not getting paid to be creative," Tony snapped. "You're not getting paid to have fucking concepts. Let the people be creative who know what the public wants. Okay?"

Steve rolled his eyes and squared his shoulders. "Sure, Mr. Da Costa. Anything you say."

"Because you won't last long in this business pulling stunts like that. Now let's get this thing turned around. I've got a deadline." Tony turned to the guitar players. "You boys know the Cato jeans jingle, right?"

The guitar players, both of whom were black, exchanged glances. "Yeah, we know it," one of them admitted.

"Well, play it. Play it slow. Dah, dah da-dah, dah." Tony's arm pumped up and down as he snapped his fingers. The musicians fell raggedly into line with him. "That's it. Keep it simple." Tony turned to Steve. "Well, what are you waiting for? Roll the tape."

"It'll be a lot easier if we program the drum machine first, Mr. Da Costa. We'll get a tighter groove."

"Drum machine? What the hell are you talking about?" Tony looked around, apparently noticing for the first time that there was no drummer in the little room, only an empty trap set huddled in one corner. "Where's the drummer?"

Steve patted a black box studded with big square buttons. "In here, Mr. Da Costa."

"Why didn't you hire a drummer? Or did he just not show up?"

"It's cheaper this way," Steve explained with weary patience. "Plus, it sounds better. Just give me a minute to program it, okay?"

Embarrassed that Tony was behaving so badly, and guiltily aware that it was her fault, Carla did her best to wander away, which was difficult in the confines of the little room. She leaned forward to examine one of the keyboards. The knobs and buttons and sliders on the panel were thoroughly intimidating, but she twiddled a bit at random, just to see what it felt like. At least the black-and-white part looked familiar. She poked a key—and the big speakers erupted in a cacophony of breaking glass. She jerked her hand back. But rather than shutting off, the crashing echoed on and on in a tangled, lurching roar. Both Tony and Steve turned to glare at her. Cheeks burning, she smiled meekly and sidled out the door. She wanted very much to stay and learn more about how the studio worked. One of the reasons she had been so excited about getting the job at the agency, a year and a half ago now, was that she wanted someday to get into music production. Well, today wasn't going to be the day.

The runner in the hall was badly frayed, and the kitchen showed few signs of domesticity, though the stove had evidently been cooked on a great deal. The table was littered with electronic components, tools, and bits of wire and solder, in the midst of which, like a plastic temple erected in the jungle, a small computer stood glowing. She sat. She wondered whether she might be disturbing some delicate process of assembly or repair by setting her purse and gloves in the midst of the clutter, but it didn't look like it. As nearly as she could tell without being a technician, there didn't seem to be any project actually in progress; it looked more as if bits and pieces of the insides of things had simply collected here, items that might once have had a function but now had none.

The computer, on the other hand, looked coolly functional. On the screen a video game was going through its demonstration loop. The game was called *The Amazing Snake*. In the demo the snake crawled out of its hole at the bottom of the screen and tried to wriggle up through the maze to the top. Blue daggers fell, and the snake twisted sinuously as it dodged them. A pair of red lips with white teeth came chomping toward it, and it had to dodge those, too. It ate a golden apple, and the daggers and the teeth froze for a moment. But always the snake got hit by one of the daggers before it got to the top. With a sad little noise, it would curl up into a ball and shrivel—only to appear a moment later at the bottom of the screen, idiotically cheerful and determined.

Usually Carla had no use for video games, but for some reason this one captivated her. After watching five or six repetitions, she drew the keyboard to her and started punching keys at random. In a minute she got the game to start, but she had no idea how to control the snake. It lay writhing cutely at the bottom of the screen until one of the daggers impaled it. She got three snakes, and the same thing happened to all of them. After the third snake, the screen flashed "GAME OVER" and went back into the demo loop.

In another minute she had figured out how to manipulate the snake with the cursor keys, but it was still getting killed every time. She hunched forward over the keyboard and started a new game. There was a pattern in the way the daggers came down the screen, if only she could figure out what it was. Scraps of music floated in from the other room, woven around a wordless rise and fall of voices. After a while the two guitar players ambled in. Carla didn't even look up at them. One drew himself a glass of water from the tap, shook his head, and said, "Man, what a way to make a living." His friend said, "You got that right." After a minute they ambled out again. The keyboard chords from the other room broke off, leaving only naked drum hits, which went on and on in an irregular pattern. "I'm getting it," she heard Tony exclaim. "I'm getting it!" Carla was getting it, too. Throwing her body from side to side in useless sympathetic exertion, she nearly succeeded in steering the snake to the top, but the spastic drumming broke her concentration, and the snake died again. And again. And yet again.

"That's a blind alley. You've got to start off to the right, wait 'til the first barrage falls past, and dodge back to the left."

She looked up. Steve was standing beside her, looking more harried and disheveled than he had half an hour before. She hadn't heard him come in. "I'm no good at these things," she apologized.

"It's nothing, once you get the hang of it. My high score is over a hundred thousand." Carla's best score so far was 160. "The better you get, the faster things come at you. Play it for an hour or so, and when you stop, you'll keep seeing the daggers raining down and the snake twisting away from the teeth. It does something to your brain." In the other room the bass guitar rumbled into life again, marching through a sludgy version of the Cato jingle. Steve shook his head sadly. "Can you beat the stones on that guy?"

"Mr. Da Costa and I," she said coldly, "are engaged to be married." It was a pointless lie. She wondered why she had said it.

"Sorry, I don't seem to be doing anything right today."

She wanted to say, *The way you were doing the jingle, before Tony butted in, that was right. That was wonderful.* She wanted to say, *I wish I knew what those chords were.* But this was Tony's account, and she didn't want to cause any more friction.

"Basically, it doesn't matter," he went on. "I'll do what I gotta do. If you want to be a success in this business, you just have to keep on pluggin'."

She nodded. "That's exactly right. I wish you could talk to a friend of mine about that. She's a painter, and—oh my God."

"Something wrong?"

"Excuse me." Carla jumped up, rattling all the junk on the table. She grabbed her purse and plunged down the hall. "Tony! Tony!"

Tony, his tie loosened, was frowning in perplexity at the drum machine. "It's not working right," he declared. "Why won't it—"

"Tony, we've got to go."

"It's the auto-correct, Mr. Da Costa," the bass player explained. "If you don't hit the beat—"

"Tony, listen to me. You're not listening to me."

"Darling, I'm right in the middle—"

"I know. I'm sorry. I just remembered. I was supposed to meet Joelle for lunch, and I forgot all about it."

"So what? Phone her. What's the big—"

"She doesn't have a phone. We have to drive down there."

"Carla, darling." He put a hand on her shoulder. "Believe it or not, this is not the first broken lunch date in the history of New York City. If you'd like, we can swing by after we're finished here."

"Tony, the lunch date was *yesterday*. Why don't I take the car and come back for you? Or you can take a cab and meet me somewhere."

"I don't want you going down into that neighborhood by yourself. It'll be dark in ten minutes."

"Tony, I will go to Lauderdale with you. I will sleep in the guest room. I will even kiss your mother on the cheek. Only *please*, let's go down there right now. I'm worried about Joelle. She's not well."

Tony seemed to be about to say something, but he checked himself.

"All right. You can finish up by yourself, Stan. You know what I want. Have a cassette on my desk in the morning."

"I'll have to work all night." Steve rumpled his hair. "But okay. You'll have it."

As they waited for the elevator, Tony jerked his gloves on one stiff finger at a time. "Do you believe the arrogance of that kid? Thinking he could get away with a stunt like that. Slipping his own music in instead of the jingle. I think I'll turn the cassette down, no matter how good it is."

"He seems pretty talented," Carla ventured.

"Talented kids are a dime a dozen. Trouble is, when they're too talented, they're impossible to work with. They get temperamental. Look at your friend Joelle. She's talented. She's also a mess. I don't know why you bother with her."

"Sometimes I wonder myself. You never knew the old Joelle. She had a lot of emotional problems, but she was fun. We had some great times together. Now she's—I don't know. I feel like I hardly know her. When she called me Monday, she was barely coherent. Maybe that's why I blocked it out. She kept rambling on about her new painting. Said she'd just finished it. There was something about it that bothered her, but I couldn't make head or tail of what it might be. She'd start to give me a straight answer, and then she'd go off on another tangent. Maybe 'bothered' is the wrong word. She sounded excited, but confused. And scared. And defiant." Night had fallen on the city while they were indoors. A bus rolled by, the passengers immobile profiles framed in trapezoids of light. "She kept saying, 'They're calling me.' "

"I thought you said she didn't have a phone."

"She said, 'They need me to make the steps come out right.' That's what it was. 'They need me to make the steps come out right.' "

"The steps." Tony sounded bored.

"It was something about dancing. Dancing and ghosts. It didn't make any sense. But it gave me chills."

"She's a wacko. You'd be a lot better off if you got her out of your life for good."

"She needs me. She doesn't have any family." Either. "I'm all she has."

"That's not your problem," Tony said. "Speaking of family, though, I just wanted you to know that I didn't appreciate being manipulated back there. I don't want you coming to Florida to do me a favor, in exchange for another favor. I want you to come because you want to come, because it means something to you." He unlocked the car door on the passenger side, but held it open only a few inches, so that she couldn't slide in without facing him.

"Okay," she said. "I'd already decided I was coming. I just hadn't told you yet. You're right. I should never have tried to use it against you. Sometimes I just don't think."

Joelle's studio was on the top floor of a dilapidated walk-up on the edge of the Village. The door of the building was ajar. Tony maneuvered the car expertly into a tiny parking spot half a block down, and dragged a garbage can away from the curb so Carla could get out. She had left her gloves lying beside *The Amazing Snake*, and the metal edge of the car door was a knife of ice cutting across her fingers.

Even the cold couldn't rinse the smells of cabbage, cheap wine, and unwashed humanity from the hallway. Up three creaking flights, Tony stood scowling at the unsavory darkness while Carla stunned her knuckles pounding on the door. It was scarred and stained; the pale outline of a 6 was still visible at the center of the upper panel, punctuated by three rust-streaked wounds where nails had held the numeral in place. A TV set blaring faintly from the floor below was the only response. After a minute she pounded again, and called Joelle's name.

"She's gone out," Tony said.

Carla rattled the doorknob. "Maybe. I've got a bad feeling about this. Maybe we ought to get the super to let us in. Once, when we were in college, she—" Carla pressed her lips together, unwilling to go on.

"She what? Went out for a walk?"

"Go find the super, please, Tony? I'll wait here."

Their sophomore year, Joelle had swung precipitously between outbursts of hysterical good humor and spells of sullen withdrawal. For days at a time, she sat on her bed, hair uncombed, responding to overtures with vague grunts, or by averting her face, or not at all. Coaxing did no good, but periodically some internal balance would tilt the other way. She would rouse herself, dress, and plunge into life with feverish determination, running everywhere rather than walking, fidgeting uncontrollably when she tried to sit still, chattering interminably about whatever lanced across her mind. Her laugh was like breaking glass.

It was Carla who rode beside her in the ambulance, and sat in the waiting room while they pumped the pills out of her stomach. That one had been hushed up, but the next year it was a razor blade, and they kept Joelle a week for observation. Cooped up in a tiny room in a youth hostel while the Paris skies dumped rain, Carla was finally irritated enough, by her own urinary distress and by Joelle's obtuse defiance and self-pity, to bring the incident up. "You know what you are?" she demanded. "You're just selfish. You don't give a damn about anybody or anything. You remember that time you made such a mess out of killing yourself? It was me that cleaned up the bathroom—me on my hands and knees wiping up your damn blood! Did I get any thanks? Did you even bother to ask who took care of your mess?"

The rain drummed on the roof. "What did you use?" Joelle asked after a while.

"What do you mean, what did I use? A towel."

"What did you do with it? Did you keep it?"

"Please. I threw it away."

"You ought to have kept it," Joelle said. "I wish you'd kept it."

Tony's head appeared in the stairwell. "No luck," he announced.

By standing down there and looking up at her, Carla could see, he was trying to will her to give up and come down. She turned back to the door and surveyed it dubiously. "Maybe we ought to pick the lock," she said. "She might be hurt."

With a little sigh, he trudged the rest of the way up the stairs and put a heavy arm around her shoulders. "You're letting your imagination run away with you," he said. "She's probably downstairs watching TV with the neighbors."

"Do you know how to pick locks?"

"No, and I'm not—"

"Neither do I. Let's break it down."

"Darling, that's against the law. Would you please try to be a little bit rational here? This is not *Cagney & Lacey*."

"Break it down, Tony. If you don't, I will." Tony raised an eyebrow condescendingly. She set her jaw. "I will. Watch me."

He shrugged. "Okay. First rule of television detective work: Never break down a door until you checked to make sure it's locked. Saves a lot of trouble." He jiggled the doorknob, but it failed to turn. He shoved experimentally, and the latch and hinges rattled loosely. Placing both palms flat against the panel, he tried lifting sideways to pull the latch clear of the strike plate, but this did no good either. He rubbed his jaw for a second, and then stood back a pace and drove his foot squarely into the door just beside the knob. At the second kick the flimsy wood splintered and tore. By pushing the ragged tear open with both gloved hands, he was able to force it wide enough to reach through and twist the dead bolt. "Nice security," he commented. Downstairs the TV was still blaring; if the other tenants had heard the noise, they chose not to investigate.

The apartment was as cold as the landing. To the left a bare bulb glowed in the kitchen ceiling. The refrigerator was standing open, nothing inside but a blue-and-white milk carton. Pans and plates were piled in the sink, and the spigot dripped a measured *plonk, plonk, plonk*. To the right the studio was deep in shadow, a streetlight throwing the shapes of windows faintly on the ceiling. "Joelle? Joelle?"

3

They found her sprawled on one side on the bathroom floor. Her face was mottled blue and gray. The eyes and mouth were open, and a crust of foam had dried on the lips. She was naked below the waist, and the bones of her knees and ankles stood out like chalk, as if they were already trying to force their way through the skin. The medicine cabinet was standing open, and empty pill containers lay scattered across the floor. Carla swayed against the wall, turned her head away, gripped the edge of the sink to keep from falling. "C—" She tried again; this time she got it out: "Call an ambulance."

Tony knelt and pressed a thumb in the notch below Joelle's ear. Carla couldn't look at the face. There was dried paint in the crevices around Joelle's gnawed fingernails. Tony shook his head slowly. "She's been dead for hours."

"Shit. *Shit*." Carla slammed her open hand against the wall. It stung.

"I'll call the cops." Tony stood up slowly and moved past her toward the stairs. She stood leaning against the bathroom door for a while longer, not looking at the cold, stiff, naked thing lying contorted on the floor. "I'm sorry, honey," she said softly. "I tried. I tried to tell you, but you never did listen." After a while she pushed herself upright and walked unsteadily away. The kitchen was uninviting. She turned and went into the studio.

She had to grope for the light switch. At the heavy snap a white glare flooded the room. Joelle's last painting stood braced between the twin pillars of the easel, which stretched from floor to ceiling. Twelve feet long and six feet high, the canvas leaped with color, swirled and sparkled with grand sweeps of glittering detail. Tears, wrenched free by the painting's beauty, flooded Carla's eyes, smearing the image into thick cobwebs of light. Gasping and sniffling, she pulled out a handkerchief.

When she could see again, she found that the painting was of the interior of a ballroom, a magnificent high-ceilinged chamber in some palace of a century gone by, bejeweled with mirrors and chandeliers. Joelle had never been seduced into impressionism or abstraction; her subject matter was as anachronistic as her craft was meticulous. A masked ball was in progress in the ballroom: across the broad floor nearly a hundred figures were poised in the patterns of a complex and courtly dance. On a balcony between marble pillars, musicians were playing.

Carla stepped closer, fascinated. There were several sorts of people in the painting. What caught her eye first were the silhouettes. Six or seven figures, scattered here and there, were nothing but black cutouts, oddly jarring against the riot of three-dimensional color that flowed around them. Curtsying to her partner, a silhouette of a lady whose hair was piled in high curls, her mouth open in gay laughter behind a fan. In the midst of a group against the wall, a silhouette of a gentleman taking a pinch of snuff.

Most of the dancers were unreal in a different way. They were ecto-plasmic, tenuous, only half visible. Though their features were discernible in the pastel light with which they glowed, the room behind them could be glimpsed through them. Some of the ghosts were wearing elaborate masks—boars' heads, tragicomic painted faces of stiff plaster, confections of feathers and lace. A few of them, while nonetheless aristocratic, were entirely naked.

Among the silhouettes and ghosts were ten or twelve fully rendered, solid people. A little girl in adult finery standing in a doorway, her mouth half open in surprise or delight, her mother's translucent hand resting on her shoulder. One of the musicians, his eyes closed, cheeks ruddy, head thrown back as he sawed contentedly on a viol. A jolly gentleman with a long wig of tight ringlets, whose portly stomach was threatening to burst his trousers. A young woman in a cat mask, who was lifting her skirt as she turned so that her petticoats and an ankle flashed. They were as real as the walls around them, but though they danced among and conversed with and laid their hands upon the hands of ghosts, they gave no sign that they knew, or cared.

The painting quite literally took Carla's breath away; for long seconds she breathed shallowly through her mouth, afraid the slightest turbulence would sweep the magical vitality of the canvas into a meaningless jumble, like a living animal made of dead leaves. She was unsure at first why it had such a striking effect. Not simply because its vibrancy contrasted so forcibly with the cold, still body on the bathroom floor. Nor simply that it was the last work that would flow from Joelle's fevered brush. Not even the extraordinary ballroom scene itself. At last, Carla thought she understood: of Joelle's perpetual torment, the angst that had driven her for as long as Carla had known her, the painting bore not a trace. Even with the ominous silhouette figures, even with the sense of barely con-tained chaos, it was a testament of joy.

Or was there more to it than that? Something maddeningly elusive, and terribly important. But what? Carla's eyes darted into the painting, drinking up clues: the folds of a satin skirt, the polished buckles on a gentleman's shoes, the shifting scintillation of the chandeliers. A ghostly oboist's cheeks huffed as he tootled. The opaque viol player's arm was raised to push the bow across the strings, and the knuckles of his other hand stood out, tense but graceful, at the instrument's neck. Carla felt she could almost hear the seductive throbbing of that viol. She stepped closer. Now the painting was all she could see. It wrapped itself around her, the grand sweep of the dance cascading toward her and away. The ballroom was a bottomless sea of faces, hands, ribbons fluttering, sparkling tiaras—and her head whirled, she was falling into the sky, the translucent dancers swathed in pulsing light, smiling at one another, at her, unfolding web of turning, stepping, a nod, a hesitation, the oboe's careless tune skipping across a low river of conversation, the mingled scents of perspiration and perfume.

A hand tugged at her hand, and she curtsied to the gentleman in a powdered wig who stood bowing before her. He offered his arm, she took it, and they promenaded down the room. Her petticoats rustled. Three paces and a dip to the left, three more and a dip to the right. Her feet knew the steps. (Petticoats?) Now sweep forward, now back. She smiled at her escort, whose eyes twinkled. Something odd was going on, but she was too busy dancing to think what it might be. Weren't these people supposed to be transparent? But what an odd thought! Why should she think that? Their flesh was as solid as hers.

A face flashed past, pale, hauntingly familiar, iridescent green eyes and gaunt cheeks under severe center-parted black hair. Carla stumbled. Suddenly her legs were heavy and stupid. She frowned at her feet, invisible in their soft slippers beneath the layers of flaring skirt. Concentrate. If you spoil the dance, the ladies will whisper behind their fans. You won't be invited back. Twice more she glimpsed the dark-haired woman, now across the room, now swept down the line as the harpsichord trilled out a march. There was some reason, Carla felt, why she ought to know the other woman, something urgent she must say to her. But it was difficult to think about anything while keeping step.

The intricacies of the dance seemed interminable. Twirl to the left, a kick, and place her hand atop the next gentleman's. But at last the musicians wove a final ornate phrase into a stirring cadence. She curtsied again to her partner. He murmured some pleasantry, but she wasn't listening. She felt thoroughly confused, and somewhat frightened. Where was she? How had she come here? Did she know these people? It all seemed so natural, and yet—

"Does milady feel faint?" her partner inquired solicitously. "Perhaps a breath of air—"

"No, I'll be fine." She gazed distractedly from side to side, desperate for some clue. There! The black-haired woman, who was just now turning away, as if she might have been looking in this direction. Carla forged a path among the couples milling on the parquet floor, but the black-haired woman, after a swift frightened glance, slipped out a door.

Carla pressed forward. What am I doing? she asked herself. Am I insane? Why am I following this person? Who is she? Who am I, for that matter? Do I have a name? She faltered, uncertain, at the door. Was this the right door? A long hallway stretched out before her, rows of heavy pillars flanking dim arches. Was that the black-haired woman rushing away from her down the hall? Or only a shadow, a gust of wind that set the candles flickering?

A footman in livery materialized before her, bearing a silver tray laden with a crystal decanter and several goblets. "Wine, milady?" The wine lay as motionless in the heart of the decanter as an enormous ruby.

"Did you just see a woman come this way?"

"The wine is of an excellent vintage." The footman proffered the tray. Around its rim, their tails in one another's mouths, undulated a design of embossed snakes.

She tore her eyes away from the snakes. "Why don't you answer me? Did a woman come this way? Did you see where she went?"

"Milady seems troubled—if she will forgive my saying so. The wine, she will find, is an excellent antidote. Those who drink of it forget all care."

Impatient, Carla brushed the man aside and plunged down the hall. It was longer than she expected—quite long, in fact—and she felt sure she was being watched; but when she turned to look back, the men and women laughing and drinking in the grand ballroom were paying no attention to her. The festive scene beckoned, and in her breast a flame leaped in answer to those in the chandeliers. But she was determined not to be deflected. She set her jaw and hurried on.

Ahead, on the left, a door set with beveled panes of glass stood just slightly ajar. Beyond the door was darkness. After taking a deep breath, which failed to quell the tripping of her heart, she opened the door and stepped through.

Night. Jasmine. A dove calling. Soft moonlight, and overhead ten thousand stars. The black-haired woman had stopped by a low stone balustrade. Beyond her stretched dark lawn smudged with pale statues, and shrouded in shadow the curving hedges of a formal garden.

"Joelle!"

The black-haired woman turned slowly to face her, head held high, porcelain neck as slender as a swan's above bare shoulders. For a moment, Carla thought she must be mistaken. She remembered Joelle now, and knew that Joelle had never had this calm grace. "Begging madame's pardon, but it seems she has confused me with somebody else." The green eyes flashed.

"Joelle, it's me! At least I think—this is all crazy. Where are we? What is this place?"

Terror flickered across Joelle's face, and was gone so quickly Carla wasn't sure she had seen it. "Are you enjoying the party? You haven't drunk the wine yet, have you? You must have some wine at once."

"I don't want any wine. I want you to tell me what's going on. I was in your studio. We'd just found—" No, she couldn't say that. "It was cold and dark. And then I heard the music—and the next thing I knew, I was here."

"A place that was dark," Joelle said quietly. "And cold. Perhaps I could remember being in such a place, if I had not drunk the wine. It is of no importance. Now I am here, and now you are here, and soon the dance will begin again."

Carla looked out across the dark formal garden. The statues weren't at all where she remembered seeing them only moments before. They had shifted somehow, like congealed smoke.

"I find it peaceful here," Joelle said.

Carla shivered. "I don't like it at all." Or was that true? Her body felt buoyant, tingling, electric. But everything she saw, or heard, or touched, was almost frighteningly strange. "I don't want to be here," she insisted. "I want to be back in—that other place. You brought me here. You may not know it, but you did. You've got to tell me how to get back there."

"Well, there is one thing you might try." Joelle's cool facade melted into an impish smile. "Click your heels together three times," she said with a twinkle, "and say, 'There's no place like New York.' "

"Aha! You admit it!"

Joelle only smiled seraphically, and spread her hands and cocked her head in a graceful shrug.

Carla looked at her friend appraisingly. "So you haven't drunk the wine, either."

"How much fun would it be if I didn't know the difference? But I don't have to think about the other place if I don't want to. Your being here reminds me. You have to go away. You don't belong here."

"Neither do you. This place isn't *real*. You created it somehow."

Joelle laughed, a humorless bark. "You don't know how wrong you are. The other place—that was the place that wasn't real. All the nasty things clawing at me, getting their slime all over me. You kept dragging me back, but this time I was too smart for you. I fixed it so you can't ever make me go back."

"And you think you can just stay here. Forever."

Joelle nodded vigorously. "Why shouldn't I? That's the kind of place this is. All the patterns fit. The colors match. The movement is perfectly contained. Do you have any idea how nice that feels? After all those years, I finally got it right."

"It sounds lovely," Carla admitted.

"There's just one thing. You don't belong. I could feel it when you got here. The steps started being wrong. You've got to go back now."

"I don't want to leave you here. We'll never see each other again."

Joelle shrugged. "Maybe I'll think about you once in a while."

"I'm supposed to say that about you. You make it sound as if I'm the one that's dead."

Joelle said nothing.

"It is nice here." The scent of the night flowers was as thick as syrup. Carla's body was made of bubbles; it was made of cloud. "Could I—do you suppose I could stay for just a little while?"

"I told you. This isn't your place. You make the steps come out wrong."

"Just one more dance. Joelle, please!"

"That's not my name now. My name is Lucy." Within the palace a fanfare flourished. "You have to make your own place."

"What do you mean? How?"

"That's what you have to find out. It's hard."

"It's impossible. I don't even know where to start."

"Or—there might be another way." Joelle considered for a moment. "Yes. If you got here once, there's a way you could come back. You have to figure out a way to make the steps come out right."

"The steps. You're talking in riddles, Joelle."

"Either you know, or you don't know. I don't think you know. I think your coming here was an accident. I sucked you in after me, like a tornado." Joelle pointed at Carla's feet. "See? You're walking on glass."

Carla looked down. On all sides the broad paving stones were solid blocks. But the one directly beneath her was transparent, and through it she could see a nether sky thick with stars. Not a reflection, either. When she lifted her skirts to look, no upside-down Carla peered back at her. Suddenly dizzy, she staggered backward and sank down on a bench.

The fanfare sounded again. "The next dance is starting," Joelle said. "They need me. Good-bye." Framed by the light that spilled through the prismatic panes of the door, she raised her fan and spread it before her face, then turned and swept back into the place.

Carla shivered, and hugged herself. I won't let her turn me away like that, she vowed. I have as much right to be here as she does. I'll stay for another dance, at least. And I won't drink the wine, either. But she felt too weak to stand. Something tugged at her deep within, something that slid like heavy oil. She closed her eyes.

Loud masculine footsteps came clumping toward her. "They asked us to wait. Said they'd be here in a few minutes."

She opened her eyes, and started in alarm. She was back in the studio, sitting on a bare wood chair, wearing not a gown but her heavy alpaca coat. Tony was standing over her. "Are you okay?"

"I—I'm not sure. I felt—peculiar for a minute. Faint. I felt faint. That must have been what it was."

"You want a glass of water or something?"

"I'll be all right." The painting was jarringly active in the bleak room, like a greenhouse seen in a fever. She stood up and moved toward it. Her legs were wobbly. "Tony? Talk to me. Say something."

His voice behind her. "What do you want me to say?"

"Anything." Throw me a rope. Pull me in. With his presence like a rock behind her, she could look at the dancers, feel the ache in the bones of her fingers yearning to reach out to them, and still jam her hands deeper into her coat pockets and hear the traffic noises outside.

"So those are the ghosts, hunh? I think it's a miracle she could paint at all, living in a dump like this. I would have killed myself years ago."

"You don't get the impression that it's—almost *moving* or anything, do you?" Distantly, she could still hear the throbbing of the viol. She scanned the crowd for the black-haired woman with the slim neck and bare shoulders, but didn't see her.

"Moving? You mean like an optical illusion? Like one of those things where you put red against green, and every time you move your eyes, it jumps?"

"Something like that." Suddenly she was worried that Tony *would* see the painting move, that he would be drawn into it as she had been. Or that somebody else might come along and disturb Joelle's perfect world. "I want it," she said decisively.

"What?"

"I want to take it with us."

"Why, for God's sake? It's too big for your apartment."

"It's not. I know exactly how to work it. I'll rearrange the living room. I'll put the bookcase in the bedroom, and the piano—"

He put his hands on her shoulders. "Slow down. You're babbling.

They'll have to seal the place up. We don't even know that her death was an accident."

She's not dead, Carla wanted to say. I spoke with her. Sensibly, she said nothing aloud.

"I suppose you could arrange to get your hands on it in a couple of weeks," Tony conceded, "if you haven't—" He glanced at the painting and shuddered. "—come to your senses by then. Who's her next of kin? Do you know if she left a will?"

"Oh." Carla had forgotten that real life could be so complicated. "I think she has a cousin out in Ohio someplace. But if she'd ever made out a will, I'm fairly sure she would have told me."

"In that case, forget it. If the probate court doesn't just lose her stuff, which they do once in a while with indigents, you'll be lucky to get it by next summer. *And* they'll bill you for storage. Not just on the one painting, on all of 'em." He gestured at the shadowy rack in the corner, where huge rectangles jostled. "*And* somebody will have punched a hole in the canvas by then, or else there'll be water damage. Better forget the whole thing."

"No. I can't. She wanted me to have this one, Tony. I can feel it." Maybe I can even find a way to make the steps come out right. Whatever that means. No, don't be crazy. In the first place, you don't want to go back there. Who knows what it's really like? It could turn into a nightmare. And in the second place, even if you did want to go back, you couldn't, because there's no place to go back to. It wasn't real. Whatever just happened, it wasn't real. This is real. I'm trying to protect Joelle, that's all. Wherever she is now. No, even that's crazy. All it is is, I want something to remember her by. "Look—the police aren't here yet. Why don't we just take it outside now, and kind of put it someplace—"

"Like on the sidewalk."

"Or in somebody's apartment. *Please*, Tony, say you'll help."

He curled his lip in amusement. "You've really got a thing all of a sudden about this painting, don't you?"

"So I'm being silly. Humor me."

"You're not being silly. I like you when you're being silly. Right now you're being completely unreasonable."

"All right," she snapped. "Be that way." Stepping up beside the easel, she lifted one side of the painting. It was heavier than she expected. Tony watched, arms folded. After glaring at him, she moved in behind the canvas and tried to find a way to grip it. Joelle must have been able to manage somehow. Grab the top stretcher bar like this, and then the crossbar. . . . She thought she had it, but then the other corner dropped free of the easel, and she swayed dangerously. "Tony, help me!"

"I'm having more fun watching!"

"If you don't help me, you can forget about Fort Lauderdale."

"I told you before, no wheeling and dealing. I don't like it."

"Okay, Okay. I'm sorry. I'll go to Fort Lauderdale whether you help me or not. Now, would you please help me?"

She heard knuckles on a door, and new footsteps. A man's voice said, "You the guy that called?"

"That's right, officer. The body is—"

"Hey, that's a new one. A painting that walks. You, lady." The cop peered around the edge of the canvas. Carla felt herself blushing. "You plannin' to go somewhere?"

"No," she said, feeling like a complete idiot. "It was crooked. I was trying to straighten it."

"Sure. Look, I gotta go look at a stiff, and then radio in for Homicide. You be here when I get back. Don't go runnin' off, okay?"

"Don't talk about her that way." The tears were starting again. "She was my friend."

"Whatever. You just stay put." The square face and the mustache went away. Carla stood helpless, the painting gripped in both hands. Her arms and shoulders were starting to hurt, and she was crying again. She needed to wipe her eyes and blow her nose, but she couldn't get into her purse for a handkerchief. "Tony!" she wailed.

When he didn't come, she lowered the painting carefully to the floor, sidled out from behind it, and leaned it back against the easel. The vivid rectangle of blues and greens and yellows radiated into the streaked and shadowed browns and grays of the room, perfection surrounded by filth. The cop's walkie-talkie coughed a few times. Carla shivered. She didn't want to see what they were doing to Joelle, but it seemed disloyal to Joelle to wait here, so after a while she crept softly down the hall.

Tony and the cop were both standing, pressed close together in the narrow bathroom. Their backs were to the door. Tony was saying something. The cop nodded. Tony turned and came down the hall toward her and took her arm. "Come on. Let's go."

"Don't we have to give a statement or something?"

"Yeah. Officially, we never left the apartment. We're just going to take the damn painting down to the second-floor landing and stash it behind the stairs for a while. And if you're real nice and say, 'Yes, officer,' and 'No, officer,' maybe he'll let me keep it company while you're talking to the coroner, so the neighbors won't get any ideas about taking it down to the pawnshop."

Relieved and excited, but confused, she helped him lift the painting.

They moved awkwardly toward the stairs. "What happened? I thought you said—"

"Yeah. I gave him a hundred bucks." Tony paused to get a better grip on the stretcher bar. "You owe me."

4

But what with the rush of Christmas shopping, and packing to fly down to Lauderdale, and unpacking when she got back, and then in January her promotion, which meant she suddenly had hours of work to bring home every night, and then the preparations for the wedding, which Tony wanted to have in April because his parents had already scheduled their Mediterranean vacation for June, she never did quite get around to hanging the painting. At first she had it leaning against the couch, but then there was nowhere to sit except the piano bench. After a couple of weeks, she wrestled it onto one end and leaned it against the bookcase. Now at least she could sit on the couch, but the painting, being too long to stand vertically in a room with a normal ceiling, protruded into the center of the living room like a garage door that would neither open nor close, forcing her to detour around it twenty times a day. No matter where it was, it unbalanced the room drastically. Sometimes the couch and the piano seemed to be in danger of sliding down into it, as if they were leftover vegetables and it the drain in the kitchen sink, and at other times it was obviously much higher than the rest of the room, so that the furniture looked as if it had tumbled out like dice from a cup. "Why don't you just put the damn thing in storage?" Tony wanted to know. "I'm going to hang it," she insisted. "Next week for sure." She wasn't about to admit that she had been foolish to insist on bringing it home. Three miles with the two of them leaning out the windows of the taxi in the cold wind! (And when they went back to pick up the Porsche, of course three of the hubcaps had been stolen.) More important, she felt that she owed something to Joelle. Keeping her last painting on display in the living room, where any visitor could see what genius the world had scorned, was certainly a small enough gesture. All the same, she found day by day that she was less fascinated by the ballroom and the dancers, and more apprehensive every time she looked at them. They seemed a little less threatening now that she had to turn her head sideways to make them out, but not much.

At night, lying awake in the dark, alone or with Tony snoring beside her, she was sure she could hear the low throbbing of the ghostly viol in the other room. Some nights it was so soft she could mistake it for her own heartbeat; but if she listened closely, it seemed to get louder, to the point where she could make out the bass line of a whole movement, complete with sequences, repeats, and the modulation to the dominant. It was only her imagination, of course. The painting was an ordinary painting, no more, a thing of canvas and pigment. However evocative they might be, paintings did *not* make music. Thinking that they could was pure idiocy. One night, feeling enormously embarrassed, she set a cassette recorder out on the nightstand and turned it on when the music started. But when she played the tape back the next morning, there was nothing on it but hiss. Somehow, this was less than reassuring. Now *she* was the one who was hearing things. Could Joelle's mental instability have been contagious? No, that was ridiculous. Obviously the whole episode had been a hallucination brought on by shock. Incredibly detailed, yes, but her own unconscious had supplied whatever details the painting itself hadn't provided. Dwelling on such a bizarre and meaningless incident was morbid, morbid, morbid. Thinking she heard the viol at night had to be some weird kind of displaced grief. Undoubtedly she ought to see a shrink, deal with the feelings, get it over and done with. To think she had seriously considered, even for a moment, something as lunatic as trying to make the steps come out right! Whatever that might mean. The idea that anything out of the ordinary might actually have happened wasn't even worth considering. This was New York, after all. This was the 1980s. Dead women simply did not go around sucking their friends into paintings.

Now that she was a junior account executive rather than a mere administrative assistant, Guy Rossiter put her in charge of an actual account. It was a very small account, but she knew she had to handle it exactly right. This was the opportunity she had been working toward ever since college—real responsibility, and the stability and respect that went with it. The client, a Mr. Edwin Abernathy, was short and fat and quite bald, and when he got angry, which he did at every opportunity, his voice would squeak and his upper lip would sweat. He was in persian rugs. The rugs were ridiculously expensive ("A Hakim says you've arrived"), and Mr. Abernathy expected Carla to help him sell an improbable number of them. He made disparaging remarks about the art department's roughs, he whined about the color reproduction when he saw the proofs, and he flatly refused to believe how much a two-thirds vertical cost in *The New Yorker*. He ordered her to get him a discount. "Yes, Mr. Abernathy," she found herself saying. "Certainly, Mr. Abernathy. I agree completely, Mr. Abernathy. We'll look into it, Mr. Abernathy." When she hung up the phone, she felt as if an army had marched over her. She stared at nothing, trembling slightly.

The viol's tune snaked across her mind, clearer than ever. G major, of course. A dotted rhythm. What would the melody be, above a bass line like that? She scrabbled in a desk drawer, looking for music paper. She thought she remembered dropping some in there one day when she was making room in her briefcase for a stack of media abstracts, but it was gone now. A notepad, then. She drew quick, wobbly staves: ¾ time. A pickup. Continuo?

She listened for the tune, but it was gone. Something like this, though. She sketched four bars, frowned at them, erased one note and then another, scribbled furiously. The second and third versions of the line looked no more correct than the first. She wadded the sheet of paper up and pitched it at the wastebasket. It bounced onto the carpet. She drew more staves, carefully this time, and tried again Maybe it wasn't ¾. Maybe it wasn't a saraband. Maybe it was an allemande. Must be. Sarabands never had pickups. Or did they? She couldn't remember. Or maybe there was more than one movement. That would explain the confusion. Allemande, saraband, courante, minuet, gigue. Some kind of motivic cell to tie them all together. Up a third and back down by seconds, then up a fifth and back down. That would invert nicely starting on either the third or the fifth, or even on the seventh over the dominant. . . .

She stopped, realizing what she was doing. This was ridiculous. Sitting in an office in midtown Manhattan, roughing out a Baroque dance suite—a twelve-tone row, perhaps, or some minimalist phase patterns with hocketing—that you could take seriously. Even so, this would be the wrong time and place for it. She tore the second piece of paper out of the pad, retrieved the first and carefully smoothed it, placed one atop the other, and tore them both into tiny squares. As she was dumping the little yellow scraps firmly into the wastebasket, Tony came in. He nodded approvingly. "Getting rid of the evidence. Always a good idea. Mind if I take a look?" Bending over, he retrieved a ragged sheaf.

"It's nothing," she told him. "Nothing at all."

In the big mirror in the upstairs lobby, on her way out for lunch, out of the corner of her eye, she thought for a moment that she saw a gentleman in periwig and knee breeches, taking a pinch of snuff.

She whirled and stared. There was nobody, only an old black man in coveralls pushing a broom.

She dismissed the idea that she was being haunted, but she admitted that she was obsessed, and she didn't like being obsessed. Her unconscious, she decided, had turned traitor. It was throwing out ballroom imagery at random because the stuff never had a chance to drain away; every time she walked past the painting, it gave her a fresh refill. That evening she tried to drape a sheet over it, but none of her sheets was big enough. Even when she safety-pinned two of them together, a band of color leaked out. All right, then. Let Tony make fun of her. She had had enough. After a quick trip downstairs to make sure there was room in the basement, because she knew she'd never be able to get the painting back *up* the stairs by herself, she dragged it out and down three flights —bump, bump, slide, bump, turn, slide, bump, bump. Halfway through the basement door, breathing hard, she thought she felt a hand touch her hand. She dropped the painting and shrank back with a stifled cry. But the touch—and of course it couldn't actually have been a touch— was not repeated. Under a single forty-watt bulb, the ballroom scene was less imposing than it had been upstairs. It glittered dimly, rippling with hypnotic allure, but failed to enfold her. Gathering her courage, she wrestled the canvas into a leaning position against the handlebar of a rusty one-wheeled bicycle. She got thoroughly dusty clearing a space against one wall, and when she finally got the painting maneuvered into place and discovered how obscenely exotic the ballroom looked surrounded by shipping trunks and old end tables, she was too exhausted to drag it out again and turn it around to face the wall. Instead, she went back upstairs for the sheets and safety pins. Having installed the makeshift shroud, she dusted her hands off firmly, locked the basement, and went upstairs without looking back.

For a week or so, she rose early, plunged into her work at the agency with deliberate enthusiasm, and came home at night dead tired, to fall into a dreamless sleep. The night came, however, when she awakened to hear scraps of music whispering under the bedroom door. Scalp prickling even as she damned herself for her own foolishness, she unplugged a lamp and tiptoed out brandishing it, expecting, as in a bad *Twilight Zone* episode, to see that the painting had magically returned to haunt the apartment. It hadn't, of course. But she felt too fidgety to go back to bed. Instead, she sat down and tried to pick out the gavotte (was it a gavotte?) on the piano. Something like that, yes. She hopped up and dug the score paper out of the piano bench. Now a pencil. In the kitchen. She jotted down a phrase, crossed it out, sketched another, added an alto line, chewing the pencil and jerkily conducting the air the way she had in college. Do you suppose this would be easier, she chided herself, if you did a little composing once in a while? But that was ridiculous; whatever she would be composing, if she were composing, it certainly wouldn't be gavottes. After an hour or so, she had the sensation that she was actually getting somewhere, that at least the first phrase of a binary-form gavotte was down on paper and that it did resemble closely the piece the viol had actually been playing. Eyelids grainy, she dragged herself back to bed. But in the morning she could barely tell which notes were on lines and which on spaces. Some of the bars clearly had too many beats, or too few. Disgusted with herself, she tossed the scribbled sheets in the garbage.

The next afternoon, Guy Rossiter called her into his office. Mr. Abernathy was there, pacing up and down in an eddying cloud of cheap cigar smoke. "Ah, Carla," Guy said smoothly. "I'm afraid we've got something of a problem. Mr. Abernathy has just received his bill."

"It's outrageous," Abernathy interjected.

Carla said, "I checked the bill myself, Mr. Rossiter."

"It's about this item here." Guy pushed the bill toward her on the desk and tapped it with a manicured nail. "The *New Yorker* insertion. Mr. Abernathy tells me that you promised him there would be a 15 percent discount."

"I promised him I'd look into it, and I did. There was no basis for a discount, not unless we went to a ten-time rate, and that would have been only 5 percent. My understanding was that Mr. Abernathy wanted only the single insertion, so we had to pay full price."

"That's not what you told me," Abernathy squeaked. "You told me there'd be a discount. This is totally unacceptable."

"It is only a verbal agreement by a junior employee," Guy said, looking faintly embarrassed, "but of course we'll be happy to honor it. Carla, please prepare Mr. Abernathy a new bill that reflects the discount."

She opened her mouth to protest—and stopped. Where Guy's hand hovered above the desk, she could see his glasses, and the edge of the blotter, quite distinctly *through* the hand. And the back of the chair through his chest. Head spinning, she turned to Abernathy and reached for his arm to steady herself, but he was shimmering slightly as well, not really transparent but not fully opaque, either. She stifled a gasp. She had a wild impulse to turn and run, but a sensible scrap of her mind hauled her back. This was her first account after a big promotion. She *had* to keep herself under control, no matter what. With a supreme effort of will, she stared straight at Guy until he stopped being gauzy and solidified once more. "Of course," she said evenly. She turned to Mr. Abernathy. "I'm really very sorry about the misunderstanding," she informed him. "I'll take care of it right away."

"That's more like it." Abernathy stuck his cigar into his face and turned to stare out the window.

"Will that be all, Mr. Rossiter?"

"For now, yes. I'll want to talk to you a little later."

As she shut the door very quietly behind her, she was fighting her legs, which wanted to twitch and buckle. Nothing had happened, nothing at all. It was just the cigar smoke drifting in odd patterns, irritating her eyes. Once she had gotten a drink from the drinking fountain and started to calm down, she could see that Guy must know she would never have promised a discount. But in the interest of keeping the account, he was perfectly willing to shame her in front of a client. Later he would be fatherly, maybe even apologize. And she'd tell him, she knew, that it was all right, that it wasn't important, that he'd done the right thing. It *was* the right thing, too. Keeping the account happy was worth a few dollars. Abernathy would be good for ten times as much business if he thought he'd put one over on them. Or maybe he actually had misunderstood. Either way, it was silly of her to get mad. Silly and dangerous. She'd have to remember to keep a tighter rein in future.

The week before the wedding, Tony had to fly down to New Orleans unexpectedly to supervise a TV spot that was being shot on location, so Carla was left to close up her apartment by herself. He already had furniture, of course, and dinnerware, and sheets and towels. She sorted her possessions into one stack to keep and another stack for Goodwill. But things kept bouncing from stack to stack. If she kept everything that had sentimental value, Tony's flat—their flat—would be jammed with useless junk. It was a struggle deciding what simply had to go, no matter how she might feel about it, and what she was actually justified in keeping. Tony, being more sensible about such things, would have been a big help, but Tony was in New Orleans. There were the cartons of books she'd kept from college, for instance—ethics, comparative religions, Greek tragedies. Why keep carting it all around? And the bust of Mozart that the Sisters had given her when she got the scholarship. It was too large, and not in very good taste, but the piano would look lonely without it. She wasn't even sure how Tony felt about the piano, if it came to that. It was only an old Ivers & Pond spinet, with deep scuff marks on the legs, a spongy action, and a muffled, nasal tone. On their combined salaries, they'd be able to afford a really nice baby grand. Maybe she ought to have it hauled away. On the other hand, getting Tony to agree to buy a good piano might be easier if she had a bad piano around for him to be embarrassed by. She dithered.

At last, knowing that Tony would be back in a day or two, and that he wouldn't be pleased to see that she was still entangled in the packing process, she talked Honey Maxwell into coming over on Saturday on the pretext of needing help wrapping dishes. Honey was from Tennessee, and had drifted into the secretarial pool at the agency after an unsuccessful modeling career. She had long legs and flawless skin and curly hair the color of her name. During the first weeks when she was going out with Tony, Carla had worried that he was casting an eye too often and too appreciatively in Honey's direction, stopping by Honey's desk on too many transparent pretexts. But Honey drew her aside and drawled, "Don't worry, sugar, I never touch another woman's man. My mama tried it once, and the other woman shot her." Since then, Carla and Honey had gotten along fine.

Honey arrived in jeans and a work shirt tied at the midriff, and stood, fists on hips, surveying the wreckage of the living room. "How much rent do you pay on this place? It's cozy. Have you given notice yet? Me and a girlfriend could get along in here just fine. Little lace curtains and things."

"Oh, that reminds me. Look at this." Carla dug in a box and carefully unwrapped the tissue from around a pair of dolls in period costume that she had picked up in Paris.

"Well, aren't they cute? Look at that."

"This one's ear broke off," Carla confessed, "but I glued it back on."

"You can hardly see the crack. They are darlin'."

"Do you want them? I can't keep everything, but I just hate to throw them away."

"Why, sure, I guess. What else you got in there?"

So they spent an hour on the floor, drinking coffee and delving into cartons and oohing and ahhing over this and that. Every item reminded Carla of some story from her past. She talked about growing up and college and her job and Tony and Tony's parents and how they were flying up for the wedding even though it was to be a small civil ceremony.

"You gonna have anybody stand up for you?" Honey wanted to know.

"No." Carla stared into her coffee. "I had a friend in college that for years I thought would just naturally be my maid of honor, but we kind of drifted apart. She died just a couple of months ago."

"That is so sad."

"She killed herself. I miss her. I didn't always treat her as well as I should. But she made it hard. She was—crazy, basically."

"I had a cousin once went crazy," Honey said, nodding soberly. "They had to lock him up. Said he was a menace. He was, too. Slashed ever so many tires one time before they caught up with him, and killed a dog. . . ."

"Joelle wasn't a menace, except to herself. She just never could quite figure out how to live in the real world, you know?"

"Elmer was like that. He *definitely* was not livin' in the real world. Some of the things he said he saw—aliens from space and who knows what-all. Mama made us all go down visit him one time, in the nuthouse, and the way he carried on! Said the whole place was on fire, I remember that. An' I was the Blessed Virgin Mary, he said—not that we was R.C., you understand, just his mind worked that way—and I hadn't been a virgin for a good two years, only I didn't dare set him straight, not with Mama standin' there." She laughed merrily. "Good old Elmer. I hadn't thought about him in I don't know how long."

"Thanks. I needed to hear you say that. I think I was starting to build Joelle up into more than she was, because of the way she died. I got to thinking—you know, that she was in touch with some weird power, some mystical force. But she wasn't. She was just a poor, scared, confused woman. I mean, her paintings were great, they were wonderful, but there was never anything more to it than that."

"I don't follow you, sugar. What more would there have been?"

Carla laughed uneasily. "Well—promise you won't tell anybody at work. I would die if it got back to Tony."

"My lips are sealed."

"I'm glad this came up. I guess I needed to tell somebody. What happened was, I had this sort of psychic experience, the night Joelle died. She had just finished a painting the day before, and I—how can I put this? I thought I saw her in the painting. It was incredibly vivid. I mean, she spoke to me. In the painting. After she died."

Honey's shoulders bunched in a shiver. "You're givin' me the willies, girl."

"I know. It gives me the willies, too. I try not to think about it. But I don't believe in ghosts. It was shock, that's all. We'd just found her, on the bathroom floor, and I was in a state of shock. I kind of blacked out for a minute. Come on." Carla scambled to her feet. "I'll show you."

"Show me what?"

"The painting. Bring your coffee. It's downstairs."

Honey unfolded her legs and stood up. "Do I want to see this?"

"Sure. It won't hurt you. It's just a big painting. It's a ballroom scene. There are like a hundred people in this big ballroom, and they're dancing a gavotte or something. It's right out of the eighteenth century."

"You mean with the petticoats and all?"

"And the wigs and brass buckles." Carla snapped back the dead bolt and led the way down the hall. "I haven't figured out yet what I'm going to do with it when I move. Maybe give it to Goodwill."

"I don't know if they take paintings, sugar."

"No, I guess not. What we ought to do, we ought to just haul it out to the dumpster right now. Unless you want it. Hanging onto it is like hanging onto Joelle. It'd be healthier to get the whole thing behind me."

"Well, let me take a look at it first. It doesn't sound like my style, but you never know."

Carla unlocked the basement door and groped for the light switch. The bulb flared. A rat, or something that sounded like a rat, skittered away into a corner. She led the way across the cold and musty room. Honey, looking dubious, picked her way gingerly among the cartons and broken things.

The painting was still draped with the pinned sheets, which had sagged in uneven folds. Standing at one end of the canvas, Carla flipped the sheets up and back. Dust billowed, and Honey sneezed and waved it away from her face. "She really was quite a painter," Carla said. "What do you think?"

Honey's brows pinched. "I don't get it," she said. "You said there was a bunch of people dancin'?"

Carla stepped back to look at the painting. And cried aloud in dismay. A chill struck at her core and rushed outward, as if her blood were being sucked away into some icy underground reservoir.

The ballroom—and clearly it was the same ballroom—was shrouded now in night. Blue moonlight pooled beneath an open window. A single candle was guttering in its holder by one of the music stands on the balcony; at the edge of its fading glow, a yellow sheet of parchment, tattered and dog-eared, lay forgotten where it had fluttered to the floor.

Of the dancers, the musicians, the servants, of the ghosts and silhouettes and all the rest, not a trace remained.

"You s'pose she used some kind of disappearin' ink? Or is this just a different painting?"

Carla shook her head. "It's the same painting." The heaviness in her heart was as thick as the day she found Joelle lying dead. But this time it was a part of herself she had lost. Half blinded by tears, she stepped toward the painting and reached out to pick up the sheet of parchment. But her fingers bumped the surface of the canvas. She grasped at the air again, knowing it was futile, feeling the emptiness where the fingers met the thumb.

"Brrr," Honey said. "It's chilly in here."

"Let's go upstairs." Carla stepped back—and her foot hit something that clattered and clanked. A tray and a bottle. The tray was badly dented, and cheap tarnished metal showed through the ragged gaps where the paint had flecked off. The bottle was dark green and had a plain cork. It had fallen on its side when she kicked it. She picked it up and turned it around. There was no label, only smudged dust. By its heft and gurgle, it was nearly full; and by its dark opacity, the wine was red. "Where did this come from?"

"It was there all the time, sugar. At least, I guess it was. I didn't notice. You musta stepped right around it. If it'd been a snake, it woulda bit you."

Snakes. Of course. Carla knelt and examined the tray. In the patches of paint that still clung to the scratched metal, she could just make out a crude design of snakes with other snakes' tails in their mouths.

She tossed the tray aside and stood up. "Let's go upstairs," she said with forced enthusiasm. "You want a glass of wine?"

Honey looked at the bottle doubtfully. "My Mama taught me never to drink liquor from a bottle that didn't have a label on it."

"Well, then maybe I'll drink it myself." Carla switched off the light and pulled the basement door shut. "Or maybe I won't." Which would be better, she wondered as she followed Honey up the stairs. To know, always, what you had missed in life? Or not to know?

HONORABLE MENTIONS

1988

Julio Buck Abrera, "Salvage," *Interzone #24*.

Thomas Adcock, "The Dark Maze," *Ellery Queen Mystery Magazine*, February.

Joan Aiken, "The Tree Who Loved a Girl," *The Last Slice of Rainbow*.

——, "The Voice in the Shell," *The Last Slice of Rainbow*.

Scott Baker, "The Sins of the Fathers," *Ripper!*

J. G. Ballard, "Running Wild," *A Hutchinson Novella*.

Clive Barker, "Coming to Grief," *Prime Evil*.

John Bart, "King Bran," (poem) *Way Down and Others*.

Charles Beaumont, "The Carnival," *Charles Beaumont: Selected Stories*.

——, "The Man with a Crooked Nose," *Charles Beaumont: Selected Stories*.

Susan Beetlestone, "Face Lift," *Interzone #26*.

Nancy Varian Berberick, "Ransom Cowl Walks the Road," *Women of Darkness*.

Bruce Bethke, "The Skanky Soul of Jimmy Twist," *Amazing*, May.

Michael Blumlein, "The Domino Master," *OMNI*, June.

——, "The Promise of Warmth," *Twilight Zone*, August.

Bruce Boston, "Mammy and the Bright Flies," *Skin Trades*.

Scott Bradfield, "Dream of the Wolf," *OMNI*, July.

Steven Brust, Gregory Frost, and Megan Lindholm, "An Act of Love," *Spells of Binding*.

Edward Bryant, "Chrysalis," *Tropical Chills*.

——, "Skin and Blood," OMNI, April.

——, "While She Was Out," *Pulphouse #1*.

Ronald Burnight, "The Dorset Street Vampire," *2 A.M.*, Winter.

Pat Cadigan, "The Edge," *Ripper!*

——, "Heal," *OMNI*, April.

——, "My Brother's Keeper," *IASFM*, January.

Jack Cady, "By Reason of Darkness," *Prime Evil*.

Orson Scott Card, "Dowser," *IASFM*, December.

Lin Carter, "Perchance to Dream," *Crypt of Cthulhu #56*.

Graham Charnock, "She Shall Have Music," *Other Edens II*.

Randolph Cirilo, "Faith of our Fathers," *Pulphouse #1*.

Sarah Clemons, "A Good Night's Work," *Ripper!*

Rick Cook, "Revised Standard Virgin," *Swords and Sorceresses*.

Bruce Coville, "Homeward Bound," *The Unicorn Treasury*.
Bill Crenshaw, "Flicks," *Alfred Hitchcock's Mystery Magazine*, August.
Kara Dalkey, "Portrait of Vengeance," *Spells of Binding*.
Charles de Lint, "Scars," *The Horror Show*, Spring.
——, "The Drowned Man's Reel," (Chapbook).
——, "That Explains Poland," *Pulphouse #2*.
Rick DeMarinis, "The Handgun," *The Coming Triumph of the Free World*.
Thomas M. Disch, "The Brave Little Toaster Goes to Mars" (picture story book)
——, "The Silver Pillow," A Tale of Witchcraft, (Chapbook).
Buzz Dixon, "The Angry Dead," *Eldritch Tales #17*.
Colleen Drippe, "Alice Fay," *Tales of the Unanticipated #3*, Winter/Spring.
Harlan Ellison, "The Avenger of Death," *OMNI*, January.
——, "Eidolons," *F & SF*, July.
——, "She's a Young Thing and Cannot Leave Her Mother," *Pulphouse #1*.
Ru Emerson, "The Werewolf's Gift," *Werewolves*.
Carol Emshwiller, "Fledged," *OMNI*, December.
Elizabeth Engstrom, "Fogarty and Fogarty," *F & SF*, April.
Dennis Etchison, "The Blood Kiss," *The Blood Kiss*.
——, "Call 666," *The Blood Kiss*.
Joe Clifford Faust, "The Right Tools for the Job," *Grue #8*.
Jules Faye, "The Cafe of the Beautiful Assassins," *Fantasy Macabre #10*.
Stringfellow Forbes, "Pastries," *Ellery Queen Mystery Magazine*, January.
John M. Ford, "Riding the Hammer," *Spells of Binding*.
Christopher Fowler, "Perry in Seraglio," *City Jitters*.
——, "Vanishing Acts," *City Jitters*.
Robert Frazier, "Things that He Cannot Name are Lost," *Twilight Zone*, April.
Esther M. Friesner, "A Winter's Night," *Werewolves*.
Gregory Frost, "Lizaveta," *IASFM*, Mid-December.
——, "The Vow that Binds," *Invitation to Camelot*.
Peter T. Garrett, "Our Lady of Springtime," *Interzone #25*.
Ray Garton, "Monsters," *Night Visions VI*.
Benjamin T. Gibson, "Night-Glo," *The Horror Show*, Winter.
Ann Goldsmith, "No One is the Same Again," (poem) *Quarterly* Fall.
Stefan Grabinski, "Szamota's Mistress (Pages from an uncovered diary)," translated
    by Miroslav Lipinski, *The Grabinski Reader*.
Charles L. Grant, "City Boy," *F & SF*, October.
——, "Last Night, in the Kitchen," *Twilight Zone*, June.
——, "My Shadow in the Fog," *Ripper!*
——, "Now and Again in Summer," *Fantasy Tales*, Fall.
Geary Gravel, "Old Toad," *Tales from the Witch World, Book 2*.
Colin Greenland, "The Wish," *Other Edens II*.
Karen Haber, "Samba Sentado," *Women of Darkness*.
Melissa Mia Hall, "The Unloved," *Women of Darkness*.
Elizabeth Hand, "Prince of Flowers," *Twilight Zone*, February.
Rory Harper, "Triage," *F & SF*, February.

M. John Harrison, "The Gift," *Other Edens II*.

Brian Hodge, "Red Zone," *The Horror Show*, Winter.

Nina Kiriki Hoffman, "Works of Art," *Pulphouse #1*.

Robert Holdstock, "Time of the Tree," *Gaslights and Ghosts (World Fantasy Convention program book)*.

Jeannette M. Hopper, "Fine Chocolates," *Fourteen Vicious Valentines*.

——, "Two From the Dragon," *Not One of Us #4*.

——, "We Lose it, Somehow," *Pulphouse #1*.

C. Bruce Hunter, "The Farmer and the Travelling Salesman's Daughter," *Fantasy Tales*, Fall.

Alexander Jablokov, "Deathbinder," *IASFM*, February.

Philip Sidney Jennings, "Sleeping Beauty," *South-East Arts Review*.

Roger Johnson, "The Melodrama," *Ghosts and Scholars 10*.

Diana Wynne Jones, "The Green Stone," *Gaslights and Ghosts (World Fantasy Convention program book)*.

Kathleen Jurgens, "Dreamlover," *Deathrealm #6*.

David Kaufman, "Goodbye to Minister Jacobs," *Alfred Hitchcock's Mystery Magazine*, December.

Yasumari Kawabata, "Immortality," translated by Lane Dunlop and J. Martin Holman, *Palm-of-the Hand Stories*.

——, "The White Horse," translated by Lane Dunlop and J. Martin Holman, *Palm-of-the-Hand* Stories.

Garry Kilworth, "Beyond Byzantium," *Gaslights and Ghosts (World Fantasy Convention program book)*.

——, "The Looking Glass Man," *OMNI*, March.

Katharine Eliska Kimbriel, "Night Calls," *Werewolves*.

Stephen King, "Dolan's Cadillac," (Chapbook) *Lord John*.

——, "The Reploids," *Night Visions V*.

Roberta Lannes, "Auntie," *Lord John Ten*.

Tanith Lee, "Foolish, Clever, Wicked and Kind," *Arabesques*.

Ursula K. Le Guin, "Catwings," (picture story book).

Thomas Ligotti, "In the Shadow of Another World," *Dagon #21*, March-May.

——, "The Spectacles in the Drawer," *Tales of Lovecraftian Horror #2*.

Megan Lindholm, "The Unicorn in the Maze," *The Unicorn Treasury*.

Bentley Little, "Skin," *The Horror Show*, Winter.

Frederico Garcia Lorca, "The Dance to the Moon in Santiago," (poem) translated by Carlos Bauer *Ode to Walt Whitman and other Poems*.

Brian Lumley, "The Sun, the Sea, and the Silent Scream," *F & SF*, March.

Ian McDonald, "King of Morning, Queen of Day," *F & SF*, February.

Michael McDowell, "Halloween Candy," *Tales from the Darkside*.

——, "Inside the Closet," *Tales from the Darkside*.

Patrick McGrath, "The Angel," *Blood and Water and Other Tales*.

Sara Maitland, "Angel Maker," *A Book of Spells*.

Sue Marra, "The Internationally Known Madame Defarges," (poem), *Not One of Us #4*.

George R. R. Martin, "The Skin Trade," *Night Visions V.*

Valerie Martin, "Death Goes to a Party," *The Consolation of Nature.*

Charles Marvin, "Brontosaurus," *The Little Magazine*, Volume 15 #3/4.

Lisa Mason, "Guardian," *IASFM*, October.

Elizabeth Massie, "Hooked on Buzzer," *Women of Darkness.*

Richard Christian Matheson, "Sirens," *Silver Scream.*

William Mayne, "Boy to Island," *All the King's Men.*

Victor W. Milan, "Puppets," *Wild Cards IV: Aces Abroad.*

John Miller, "Beasts of Burden," *Wild Cards IV: Aces Abroad.*

John Morressy, "Mirror, Mirror, Off the Wall," *F & SF*, August.

A. R. Morlan, "Night Skirt," *The Horror Show*, Winter '87.

David Morrell, "Orange is for Anguish, Blue for Insanity," *Prime Evil.*

James Morrow, "Diary of a Mad Diety," *Synergy Volume II.*

Sharan Newman, "The Palace by Moonlight," *Invitation to Camelot.*

Carol Orlock, "Nobody Lives There Now, Nothing Happens," *Women of Darkness.*

Jeffrey Osier, "Why I Dropped Out of Art School," *Deathrealm* #7, Fall/Winter.

Barbara Owens, "Sliding," *Twilight Zone*, August.

D. P. Pavlovec, "From Out of my Heart," *2 A.M.* Summer.

Terry Pratchett, "Sphinx," *Gaslights and Ghosts (World Fantasy Convention program book).*

Tim Powers, "Nightmoves," *Twilight Zone*, April.

Carol Reid, "Builders of Coffins," *Fantasy Macabre* #10.

Leonard Wallace Robinson, "Charlotte Waiting Before Dying," (poem) *The Atlantic Monthly*, February.

Spider Robinson, "The Paranoid," Pulphouse #2.

John B. Rosenman, "Diana in the Rain," *Not One of Us* #3.

——, "Rock of Ages," *Cemetary Dance* #1, December.

Archie N. Roy, "The Visit," *Fantasy Macabre* #11.

Alan Ryan, "The Lovely and Talented Maxine Kane," *The Bones Wizard.*

David J. Schow, "The Falling Man," *Twilight Zone*, August.

Barbara Selfridge, "This Close to the Edge," *Unholy Alliances: New Fiction by Women.*

Bob Shaw, "Dark Night in Toyland," *Interzone* #26.

Charles Sheffield, "The Courts of Xanadu," *IASFM*, April.

Lucius Shepard, "Jack's Decline," *Ripper!*

——, "The Scalehunter's Beautiful Daughter," *IASFM*, September.

——, "The Way it Sometimes Happens," *IASFM*, December.

——, "A Wooden Tiger," *F & SF*, October.

John Shirley, "The Rubber Smile," *Fly in my Eye* #2.

——, "Six Kinds of Darkness," *High Times*, March.

Susan M. Shwartz, "The Wolf's Flock," *Werewolves.*

Dan Simmons, "Metastasis," *Night Visions V.*

——, "Iverson's Pits," *Night Visions V.*

Isaac Baschevis Singer, "The Jew from Babylon," *The Death of Methuselah and Other Stories.*

John Skipp and Craig Spector, "Not with a Whimper," *Twilight Zone*, February.

Sherwood Smith, "Monster Mash," *Werewolves*.

Martha Soukup, "Having Keith," *IASFM*, June.

Brian Stableford, "The Man Who Loved the Vampire Lady," *F & SF*, August.

——, "The Growth of the House of Usher," *Interzone #24*.

David Starkey, "About Half," *Fantasy Macabre #10*.

Peter Straub, "The Juniper Tree," *Prime Evil*.

Brad Strickland, "What Dreams May Come," *F & SF*, December.

John Strickland, "Terrorstorm," *The Horror Show*.

Somtow Sucharitkul, "The Madonna of the Wolves," *IASFM*, November.

Tim Sullivan, "Knucklebones," *Ripper!*

D. W. Taylor, "Lessons in Wildlife," *Noctulpa #3*.

Melanie Tem, "Chameleon," *IASFM*, March.

——, "Aspen Graffiti," *Women of Darkness*.

Steve Rasnic Tem, "Among the Old," *Pulphouse #1*.

——, "Grim Monkeys," *Tropical Chills*.

——, "The Lie," *2 A.M.*, Winter.

Sheri S. Tepper, "The Gardener," *Night Visions VI*.

Gay Parrington Terry, "Grasping the Bird's Tale," *Twilight Zone*, April.

Kurt Tidmore, "The Equilibrist," *Soho Square*.

Robert Twohy, "Snapshots," *Ellery Queen Mystery Magazine*, January.

E. J. Wagner, "Bright Scissors, Sharp as Pain," *Ellery Queen Mystery Magazine*, September.

Howard Waldrop, "Wild, Wild Horses," *OMNI*, June.

Ian Watson, "The Mole Field," *F & FS*, December.

——, "The Resurrection Man," *Other Edens II*.

Susan M. Watkins, "Mole," *The Horror Show*, Fall.

Ron Weighell, "Againbite," *Ghosts and Scholars 10*.

Lori Ann White, "All I Want for Christmas Is My Two Front Teeth," *Pulphouse #1*.

Cherry Wilder, "The House on Cemetary Street," *IASFM*, Mid-December.

Chet Williamson, "The Music of the Dark Time," *Twilight Zone*, June.

F. Paul Wilson, "Cuts," *Silver Scream*.

——, "Feelings," *Night Visions VI*.

T. M. Wright, "His Mother's Eyes," *Twilight Zone*, June.

William F. Wu, "On a Phantom Tide," *Pulphouse #1*.

——, "Wild Garlic," *Eldritch Tales #15*.

Thomas Wylde, "The Cage of Pain," *IASFM*, March.

Jane Yolen, "The Quiet Monk," *IASFM*, March.

Ree Young, "One Night Stand," (poem), *Noctulpa # 3*.

ABOUT THE EDITORS

Ellen Datlow is the fiction editor of *OMNI* magazine, and has edited several anthologies, including *The Books of OMNI Science Fiction* (Zebra) and *Blood Is Not Enough* (William Morrow/Ace Books), as well as a forthcoming collection of stories about alien sex, from E. P. Dutton. She has published a number of award-winning stories by outstanding authors during her tenure at *OMNI*. She lives in Manhattan.

Terri Windling was for many years the fantasy editor at Ace Books. Now she is concentrating on her own art and fiction at The Endicott Studio in Boston, but she keeps an editorial hand in as a Consulting Editor for fantasy at Tor Books. She has edited many fantasy anthologies, including the World Fantasy Award–winning *Elsewhere* collections. She edits the Adult Fairy Tales series of novels and co-illustrated a children's fantasy book with Sheila Berry. She lives in Boston on Beacon Hill, and commutes regularly to New York City.

ABOUT THE ARTIST

Thomas Canty is one of the most distinguished fantasy artists on the scene today. Winner of the World Fantasy Award for Best Artist, he has painted many jackets and covers for books, and is a noted book designer. He and his wife live in Braintree, Massachusetts.

ABOUT THE PACKAGER

James Frenkel is the publisher of Bluejay Books, which was a major publisher of science fiction and fantasy from 1983 to 1986. Since then he has been a consulting editor for Tor Books and a packager. Editor of Dell's science fiction in the late 1970s, he has published some of the finest new science fiction and fantasy authors, including Greg Bear, Orson Scott Card, Judith Tarr, John Varley, and Joan D. Vinge. He lives in Chappaqua, New York.